<=== BOOK ONE ===>
THE WILDHEART SERIES

BOUND BY BLOOD AND FATE

GABRIELLA WILDER

Gabriella
WILDER
FANTASY &
ROMANCE AUTHOR

Contents

Dedication — v

Epigraph — vi

Bound By Blood And Fate — vii

Author's Note — viii

Map Of Luminara — ix

Pronunciation Guide — x

Prologue — 1

1. The Call Beyond The Village — 5

2. Family Ties — 11

3. Tales From The Past — 25

4. Of Legends And Lies — 41

5. Whispers Of The Forbidden River — 54

6. Beyond The Edge — 60

7. Threads Of Destiny — 74

8. To Trust Or Betray — 84

9. Beyond The Boundary — 95

10. Where Shadows Gather — 106

11. The First Cut — 116

12. Lessons In Steel — 121

13. A World Turned Inside Out — 130

14. The Edge Of Loyalty — 141

15. Unraveling — 152

16. A Test Of Faith — 169

17. Wild Lies, Wilder Truths — 184

18. Lessons In Shadow — 194

19. Friends Of The Forest — 213

20. One Step From Falling 223

21. Cloaked In Shadows 234

22. Weapons Of Choice 250

23. Echoes Of Forgotten Truths 261

24. Bound By Secrets 274

25. Eyes In The Dark 285

26. A Lesson In Survival 306

27. A Birthday Like No Other 315

28. Something Like A Warning 323

29. Allies Or Enemies 340

30. Ties That Bind, Ties That Break 357

31. The Hardest Goodbyes 369

32. Into The Unknown 383

33. Claws In The Dark 397

34. Borrowed Time 417

35. Truth And Treason 427

36. Rise Or Fall 437

37. Reflections In The Water 448

38. When Legends Fall 465

39. Footsteps In The Dark 481

40. An Unwanted Gift 494

41. Wings Of Freedom 507

42. The Veil Of Silence 516

43. Roots Of Rebellion 531

44. The Other Side Of Loyalty 545

45. To Strike Or To Surrender 562

46. Bound By Chains And Hidden Truths 576

Acknowledgments 586

About the Author 588

For the wild hearts, the ones who hear
the call of fate and answer it—even
when it leads into the dark.

For the little girls who were told their
dreams were too big—dream bigger,
and don't stop reaching.

And for those who feel they're destined for
something greater but fear the unknown:
Trust in yourself.
You may never feel fully prepared, but start
anyways; that is when the magic begins.

"Perhaps some paths are meant to be walked alone,
as we learn the strength we carry within ourselves."

-Unknown

Bound By Blood And Fate

Bound By Blood And Fate is Book One in the Wildheart Series.

"*Some truths are buried too deep to stay hidden forever.*"

Raine Roghnaithe has always known two things—she was never meant to live and die in her small village, and turning eighteen means she can finally break free from the expectations that have bound her since birth. Her birthday should be a simple milestone, celebrated with family and far too much cake. Instead, it becomes the first step into a world she was never meant to see.

Beyond the wall of trees she's always known lies a realm woven with shadows and secrets, where betrayal cuts deep and every promise demands a price. Hunted by forces she can't yet understand, Raine must decide who to become—the obedient daughter her village raised, or the warrior she has always longed to be.

In a world where loyalty is fleeting and family ties are tangled in lies, survival will demand more than strength. It will demand sacrifice. And when the choice comes, she'll have to ask herself—

What would you do to protect the ones you love?

Now, she carries the answer like a blade in her hand.

Anything.

A Note to Readers:

While this story is one of courage, connection, and resilience, it also contains moments that may be difficult for some readers. Within these pages, you will find depictions of death, child loss (not involving the main character), and scenes of battle that include blood and injury. Please keep this in mind when reading and prioritize your well-being by stepping away if you need to.

Author's Note

This story began the way most of my stories do—as a single spark in the quiet. A burning question that refused to leave me alone.

What would you sacrifice to protect the ones you love?'

Raine's journey came to life piece by piece—shaped by old myths, bonfire stories, and the promise of ruin lurking just beyond the border.

I wanted to create a world where beauty and danger coexist, where loyalty is tested, and where the line between fate and free will is never quite clear. For me, this isn't just another fantasy world; it's where real life and magic meet. It's a place built on resilience and choice, and I hope it becomes as unforgettable to readers as it's been to me.

Bound by Blood and Fate is the first step into that world. It lays the foundation of Luminara and introduces only a handful of the characters whose paths will twist and tangle throughout the series. You'll meet immortals who have lived lifetimes steeped in secrets, humans who are braver than they realize, and a girl whose fire runs deeper than she knows. There will be betrayals. There will be moments that try and break her. And there will be moments where she learns that strength isn't about being unshakable—it's about rising, even when you don't know where you're headed.

This is only the beginning. The road ahead is dangerous, tangled with truths that will challenge everything Raine believes, not just about the world she's in, but about herself.

If you take anything from this book, let it be this: you are more than the cage you were born into, more than the chains you've carried, and more than the mistakes you've made. Life is about a series of choices, and you just have to keep going—one step, one breath, one choice at a time.

Welcome to the Wildheart Series.

I'm so glad you're here.

Gabriella Wilder

LUMINARA
Dearmadra Mountains
Rioga
Ceannairi
Immorro
Dermaine
Rioga City
"The Main City"
The Forbidden River
Frenhill
Laochra
The Witral Woods
N
W
E
S

Pronunciation Guide

Places:
Luminara - Loom-in-are-ah
Laochra- Low-craw
Rioga- Ree-Oh-gah
Dermaine- Der-main
Immorro - Imm-or-O
Ceannairí- See-in-air-E
Dearmadta- Deer-mah-tha

People:
Raine Roghnaithe- Rain Row-nay
Baren - Bare-on
Wren- Ren
Leighna - Lay-na
Inina- In-E-na
Silas- Sigh-las
Edric- Ed-rick
Lugh- Loo
Manakel - Man-a-kel
Aeron - Air-on

Micaiah- Mah-k-eye-ah
King Saoine- Sao-win
Queen Sarda- Sar-da
Queen Deardra - Dear-draw
King Callix - Cal-ix
Queen Verena- Ver-E-na

<u>*People:*</u>

Dela - Day-la
Fern - Fern
Alfreda- Al-fray-da
Caden- Cay-den
Kaia- K-eye-ah
Meriol- Merry-ol
Corvina- Core-VEE-nah
Arella- Ah-rella
Carmenta - Car-men-ta
Elea- Elle-E-ahh
Roan - Rown

<u>*Other:*</u>

Sciathain- Sigh-ahh-than
Dryad- Dry-add
Osiris- Oh-sigh-riz
Barolf- Bar-ol-f
Oilliphéist- All-if-heis-shh-t
Abhartach- A-bar-tack

Amadán- Oma-daw
Banrion- Ban-REE-on
Deartháir- Jar-her

Prologue

A hero's journey never begins with the truth—sometimes it starts with a lie.

I should've known the moment I crossed that line, there was no going back. But anyone who knows me would tell you I don't back down easily. That if you prepare accordingly, fight hard enough, and ask the right questions, you'll find the answers. That knowledge is power, and with the truth on your side, you can control your own fate.

Turns out, I was wrong.

It was either destiny or sheer stupidity that led me here—trapped in the bowels of a dungeon, swallowed whole by the kind of darkness that seeps beneath your skin and takes root. My back pressed against the cold, unyielding stone, the damp clinging to my clothes like a second skin, heavy with filth and failure. The air thick with rot and something else, something older, more insidious, like the bones of the forgotten whispering their grievances into the void.

Chains biting into my wrists, their cruel metal warmed only by the bruises blooming beneath them, a stark contrast to the chill leaching into my veins. Shadows stretching long in the wavering torchlight, flickering like dying embers, their forms shifting, twisting, watching. I swear they whisper, their voices slithering through the silence, curling around me like a noose, tightening with every breath. They mock me, a chorus of unseen specters murmuring of failure, of choices that led me here, of the inevitability of what comes next.

And for the first time in my life, I have no answers.

As the last remnants of daylight bleed through the fractured stone walls, marred like the certainty I once carried, the weight of solitude presses in. The darkness is no longer just around me; it's inside me, stretching its fingers through the cracks of my resolve.

I don't know how long I will last in this wretched place.

Or if I even want to.

A sound stirs in the darkness—soft, curling at the edges of the silence like breath against my ear.

Raine.

It's barely more than a whisper, but it slithers through the still air, wrapping around me with a quiet mockery, pressing against the fragile space between sanity and fear.

I squeeze my eyes shut, exhaling sharply. The mind plays tricks when it's desperate for answers, for hope, for anything but this. But no matter how many times I try to shake it, the truth remains.

I am here.

I am trapped.

I am not where I'm meant to be.

And whether the voices are real or simply a cruel trick of my own unraveling thoughts, they are right about one thing.

My name *is* Raine Roghnaithe, but my family calls me Wildheart, a fitting title for someone who never walks away from a challenge. But sitting here now, another word feels far more appropriate.

Naive.

I used to believe I knew the difference between right and wrong. Between truth and lies. Between friend and foe. But somewhere along the way, those lines bled into one another, blurred beyond recognition, until I could no longer tell the difference between a lifeline and a snare.

I don't know who to trust.

I don't know what to believe.

And everything I thought I *did know* was a lie.

It's funny, really. I always imagined my story beginning with 'Once upon a time,' like the great legends I grew up hearing. That I would embark on some grand adventure, face impossible odds, and live to tell the tale of my hero's journey.

But this?

This feels less like a story and more like a warning.

And I don't know what's worse—the fact that I was captured before I even had the chance to fight, or the nagging suspicion that maybe… *maybe* I walked straight into it. That the freedom I spent my life craving came with a cost I never stopped to consider.

But I'm getting ahead of myself.

To understand how I ended up here—why this is the *exact opposite* of the path I was meant to take—we have to start at the beginning.

Just over a week ago, to be exact. When I was still the girl who thought she had it all figured out. When my biggest concern was turning eighteen and disappointing my parents. When I didn't expect to be confronted with a truth so sharp it carved its way through everything I thought I knew, leaving me here sitting on the cold, jagged stone, as if the very foundation of my world had splintered beneath me.

But alas, here I am.

Dramatic? Maybe. But so is the undeniable fact that, whether I like it or not, my fate has already been decided. Even if I have no idea what it looks like. Which, for someone who prides herself on questioning everything, the not-knowing is a humiliating blow to my reputation as a know-it-all.

But hey, if I make it out of this alive, then I'll have plenty to say.

And if not?

Well, I suppose this could double as my memoir.

So, let's rewind. Because somewhere, buried in the wreckage of the last seven days, there was a moment—a single, stupid choice I made—that led me straight into this mess.

And to understand how I got here…We have to start there.

1. The Call Beyond The Village

The bowstring snapped against my fingertips as I released the arrow, its sharp twang echoing in the quiet morning air. But as usual, it was another miss. The thud of the arrow hitting the earth far from the target sounded almost like a mockery. I exhaled sharply, no longer surprised or frustrated. It was always the same result, no matter how much I prepared, or how many hours I spent out here, alone, the shadow of the woods and my failure always loomed. My aim was always just a little off, a little too slow, a little too weak. And even if I did manage to hit my mark one day, I knew it wouldn't matter. These abilities—this weapon, these skills—I would never be allowed to wield them in front of anyone but myself.

The weight of disappointment settled into my chest, like a stone pressing down on my heart. I stood still for a moment, just listening to the sound of my heartbeat, the only rhythm I could rely on anymore. My gaze drifted back to the target, where the arrow had fallen short, now buried deep in the dry earth. My hand curled around another one, the smooth wood cold against my skin. The weight of it in my hand felt heavy, not just because of its physical weight, but because of the anger simmering beneath my ribs. Anger at the injustice of it all.

I nocked the arrow and drew the string back, my teeth gritted, my breath sharp in the cold air. The bow creaked under the strain, the muscles in my arms burning, not from the effort, but from the sting of frustration and the years of pent-up rage.

In the territory of Rioga, the law said I was never meant to do this. A girl's hands were meant for kneading bread, not gripping a weapon. Her body made for bearing children, not holding ground. Her voice for pleasantries, not for commands or war cries. I was meant to live in the hush of shadowed rooms, in the clatter of kitchenware, in the soft, repetitive rhythm of sewing needles.

According to our laws, what I was doing was illegal. I wasn't allowed to wield a weapon, fight, or protect myself. Girls were meant to be gentle. Quiet. Submissive. Contained.

But I was none of those things.

The string bit into my fingers as I held the draw, shoulders locked, chest tight. This was the one place I felt like I belonged, not in classrooms, or kitchens, or behind a needle, but here, where strength came from muscle and will, where I could aim at something and watch the world narrow into a single target.

I exhaled and released.

The arrow flew, wavered, and buried itself in the dirt far from where I'd aimed. The sound echoed louder than it should have, a taunting reminder that I was still not good enough. A dull thud of failure.

I growled under my breath, the sound scraping across my nerves as frustration rose hot in my chest. I had to bite back the urge to hurl the bow into the trees, hear it crack, feel something besides my resolve breaking. But these were Wren's arrows, and I couldn't risk losing them, or the trust he'd placed in me.

For eight years, this clearing had been my only sanctuary. A strip of earth and air where I could exist outside the cage I'd been born into. Hidden from prying eyes, it was the only place I could be who I was meant to be. Where no one could judge me for wanting something more, or tell me that it was wrong to dream of a life of adventure outside of Laochra. This clearing was the only spot I was free to do something that gave me a sense of peace and purpose, even if I could never share it with anyone.

My brother Wren had taught me here. Showed me how to hold a bow, how to move with a blade, and how to fight back to protect myself. But if anyone found out I'd been training, it wouldn't be me who paid for it. It would be him. Wren's position as a trainer would be stripped. His reputation would be ruined, and my family would be branded as outcasts for allowing my behavior. So I was careful. *Very careful.*

I couldn't let that happen, to *him*, to *them*. Not for an unrealistic dream. Not for a selfish desire. Still, it didn't stop the resentment that bubbled up inside of me when I thought about how unfair the laws were simply because of my gender, something I had no control over.

I tightened my grip on the bow, knuckles pale, jaw locked against the weight of everything I couldn't say.

It wasn't fair. I wasn't like the other girls.

While they dreamed of marriage, of settling down, of filling their homes with children, I longed for something else. Something greater. I longed for open skies, adventure, and roads that led somewhere far from the stifling walls of Laochra. Of battles worth fighting, of freedom, and a life I'd chosen for myself, one where I wasn't bound by expectations.

In the early mornings, before anyone else in the village woke, I would sneak out. I'd run barefoot through the fields, chasing the wild animals that darted through the grass, listening to the sound of the world coming alive. I'd sit in the barns with the chickens, scratching behind their feathers and watching the sheep roam free. And I'd slip into the village streets when no one was awake, just to see the quiet of the empty lanes, to pretend for a moment that the world was mine.

It didn't matter if people called me reckless. It didn't matter if they thought I was strange. *I* didn't care. Because I'd rather be filthy and free than caged in a house, bound by a life that catered to the mundane, and if *that* made me an outsider, so be it. It was better than fitting into their suffocating world. At least, out here, I could breathe.

Despite the mockery I faced in my classes and around the village, home was my safe haven. The laughter and love of my parents, the protection of my older brothers, Baren and Wren, and the wisdom and warmth of my grandmother, Leighna—home was the only place I felt like I belonged. In this small, quiet corner of the world, I didn't need anyone else to understand me. But outside our home, things were never quite as simple. The more I longed for something more, the more suffocated I felt. The world around me had its rules, its expectations, and I knew deep down I was destined for something greater. But I *also* knew the world would never accept me for who I truly was; someone with ambitions that reached beyond the life mapped out for me.

I shifted my focus back to my grandmother, her hands covered in dirt as she planted chervil, sage, and rosemary with a reverence I couldn't quite explain. She was so focused, so absorbed in the earth, in her garden, that the world around her seemed to fade away. I smiled softly, a rush of warmth spreading through me. My love for nature, the deep connection to the land—it had come from her. It was something we shared. Her hum, low and gentle, carried on the autumn breeze, blending with the soft rustling of the trees as she worked.

She was lost in her own world, completely unaware of my repeated failures with the bow. Another arrow gone astray, another miss. I muttered under my breath, frustrated, but her presence grounded me in a way nothing else could. She was in her element, and for a fleeting moment, I almost envied the peace she found in the soil, in the rhythm of her gardening. I longed for that tranquility, but the fire inside me burned too brightly, keeping me restless.

I cursed softly again as I retrieved another arrow from my quiver, trying to force calm into my hands. It was pointless to let my frustration get the better of me, not with my grandmother so close. I didn't want her to see, to offer me one of her famous "stress-free tonics" or suggest I take a break. As much as I adored her, sometimes it felt like no one truly understood the fire that smoldered within me. No one saw the endless yearning for more, the desire to break free from the life that was already mapped out for me, a life of gentleness and submission.

How could they? They'd never been in my shoes, never felt the weight of the expectations pressing down on me, the suffocating desire to live outside of the box they'd built around me.

I pivoted on my heel, the sound of dry leaves crunching beneath my boots, the scent of autumn thick in the air. The change in season was undeniable—crisp, biting winds began to stir, even though it was only mid-September. My breath was visible now, the mornings colder, the days shorter. Autumn was creeping in, and with it came the looming reminder that my eighteenth birthday was one week away.

I took a deep breath, the weight of my future settling heavily on my chest. No longer could I be content with the role of dutiful daughter, with the gentle path planned for me. I wanted more. I longed for adventure, for freedom, for a life that wasn't tethered by the expectations of this small village or the world beyond it.

But how could I even begin to break free?

I'd spent my entire life living in the shadow of Baren and Wren, both perfect in every way, their futures so clear and bright. How could I ever live up to the standards set for me when I didn't even know if I had the courage to stand up for myself and leave?

I gripped the bow tighter, my heart thumping against my ribs as I set another arrow in place. Years of training—years of secret lessons with Wren—felt like they were slipping through my fingers. It was always the same. I'd never be able to use this skill, not in public, not in the way I wanted.

I released the arrow, and it sailed through the air—again, it missed. The familiar frustration settled in, but there was something new beneath it now, something sharper, more urgent. Time was running out, and I wasn't ready. I wasn't ready to live the life expected of me as I turned of age, and I feared I never would be.

I had never even stepped outside of my village, so I didn't know how to be anything else, or how to break free.

2. Family Ties

From the moment I took my first breath, Laochra had been my home. A small, secluded village nestled in the untamed wilderness of Luminara, just beyond the bustling city of Rioga. Generations of families had established their roots here, either inheriting their ancestral homes or building cozy cottages on the same property, sharing the land with their relatives. It wasn't uncommon for parents to pass down the land itself, with children adding their own small homes nearby, creating close-knit clusters of family dwellings.

Being one of the smallest and most isolated villages in the region, there wasn't much to attract outsiders to Laochra. There were no bustling markets to draw traders, no skilled artisans to craft treasures, not even a school where our children could learn. The nearest blacksmith lived miles away, and the luxuries we couldn't produce ourselves had to all be fetched from Rioga or towns just outside the city. For most, it wasn't a place you'd *choose* to settle; it was a place where people stayed because it was all they'd ever known.

In Laochra, everyone knew everyone. It was the kind of place where the same faces greeted you every morning, where change was as rare as outsiders.

If we were known for anything, it was our proximity to the Forbidden River. Not exactly something to boast about. The river was as much a curse as it was a curiosity. Tales of dark magic, strange creatures, and chilling whispers shrouded it in a veil of mystery. Its murky depths were the heart of countless stories told to frighten children into obedience, the backdrop of whispered warnings among the older villagers. No one dared approach it—not since the river's dark legend was sealed in blood and tragedy.

And yet, despite the river's sinister reputation, Laochra thrived in the shadow of both the river and the woods surrounding it. Towering trees embraced the village like a watchful sentinel, their dense canopy stretching endlessly along our border. The woods weren't welcoming; they were ancient and primal, a wilderness no one dared venture into. It had been almost a century since anyone had dared to step beyond its outer edge, and even now, its presence carried an unspoken weight.

As the saying goes in Laochra: a village is only as strong as its people, and being such a small community, we had no choice but to rely on one another for survival. Everyone's name, story, and family matters were common knowledge. Even the smallest of actions did not go unnoticed; sneezing in your own home could result in your neighbor showing up with herbal remedies within hours. (*Probably made by my grandmother.*) And while some may find this level of closeness cozy and comforting, as the *'curious girl who asked too many questions,'* I often felt suffocated by the constant scrutiny.

The gossip that circulated was rarely scandalous, but rather prying eyes watching my every move, hoping for a slip-up. In a village where everyone knew everything about each other, keeping secrets was nearly impossible. That's why I always took precautions when training in my backyard. It was *one* secret I intended to keep hidden from the ever-watchful eyes of my nosy neighbors.

Laochra wasn't perfect, but it was ours. Every corner, every cracked stone on the paths winding between the cottages, carried the weight of history. For better or worse, it shaped who I was and proved I wanted a life beyond this quiet, simple one tucked away from the chaos of the world beyond. Or so I thought.

I crouched down to retrieve the three arrows that had narrowly missed their target on my well-worn practice board, brushing away bits of loose dirt that clung to them. One arrow caught my eye—a bent head that rendered it useless. My fingers traced the warped metal, feeling the jagged indentation where it must have hit something hard.

While examining the other two arrows, I took in the familiar surroundings of my backyard. My grandmother's overflowing garden beds bordered the space, a wild, chaotic beauty of fragrant herbs and vibrant wildflowers that she lovingly planted each year. The air was rich with the mingling scents of lavender and thyme, grounding me in the here and now. In the center of the yard lay the large clearing where Wren and I had spent countless weekends. The memories rushed back—him teasing me when I missed a target, our laughter during makeshift picnics, and the warm summer sun that once felt endless. Those were some of my favorite days.

Nearby stood the glass-paneled greenhouse, sunlight glinting off its panes. Inside, rows of drying herbs hung in neat bundles, and tiny green shoots peeked from soil-filled trays. My grandmother was always preparing, always thinking of the seasons ahead, and at the start of fall, she always started her winter herbs. Beside the greenhouse, a wood-paneled shed sat sturdy and practical, its interior packed with tools, targets, and supplies. Just past both buildings, the fire pit my dad had built was a small monument to simpler times, surrounded by smooth stones and a weathered picnic table. It was where we'd gathered for cookouts and storytelling, passing down stories that felt as old as the village itself.

This backyard was more than just a space; it was my sanctuary, a tapestry of memories woven together by laughter, love, and a sense of safety. But even as a child, that safety had never felt absolute. Beyond the edges of our land loomed the Witrial Woods, its towering evergreens a constant, foreboding presence.

The trees had always been there, silent and unyielding, a barrier between the known and the unknown. As a child, I used to imagine what secrets it held—monsters, immortal beings, treasures hidden beneath its thick canopy. My imagination had run wild, fueled by the whispered stories passed down by the village elders. But, as I grew older, the forest became something else entirely. I started to wonder if the danger wasn't out there in its depths but here within our village, within the smallness of our lives and the way we clung to stories that kept us from questioning, from exploring, from evolving.

Lost in thought, I turned toward the dense evergreens, their shadows stretching like fingers over the ground. That's when I heard it—a faint humming, soft and melodic, threading through the still air. I froze, my heart quickening as the sound washed over me. It wasn't a song I recognized, but there was something achingly familiar about it. Sweet, haunting, and impossibly distant, it tugged at something deep inside me, stirring emotions I couldn't place.

Curiosity bloomed, taking root before I could stop it. The urge to find the source of the sound clawed at me, pulling me toward the forest's edge. What was it? *Who* was it? And why did it feel as if I already knew the answer, as if the humming was calling to a part of me I didn't yet understand?

I stared into the thick barrier of trees, my breath hitching as I wrestled with the temptation to cross the invisible line between safety and uncertainty.

"Raine, honey, are you coming in to wash up before dinner?" My grandmother's voice echoed through the garden, breaking my concentration. I whirled around, using the target board to steady myself as a wave of dizziness washed over me. There she was, standing at the back door, her apron still covered in dirt, her eyes crinkled with a warm smile as she waited expectantly for my answer. The scent of freshly dug earth and blooming flowers wafted towards me, mingling with the delicious aroma of dinner cooking inside. My stomach growled loudly, reminding me that I hadn't eaten much besides an apple today, and the thought of dinner made my mouth water.

I nodded and began folding the legs of the target board before walking towards the shed. A gnawing hunger pulsed in my stomach, but it was accompanied by a strange feeling I couldn't quite place. Ignoring it for now, I looked back at the woods one more time, noting that all traces of the humming and alluring melody were gone.

The scent of unfamiliar spices and rich game meats filled our home, which meant my father had returned from his journey. His trips were always a source of excitement, especially when he brought back exotic vegetables and meats not commonly found in Laochra. Most farmers in our community relied on raising chickens and sheep for sustenance, so the chance to taste new and different types of meat was always a treat.

As the sun dipped below the horizon, painting the sky in hues of gold and crimson, I could feel the familiar energy buzzing in the air.

It was bonfire night, the heartbeat of our little village, a cherished tradition that brought everyone together from April to October. No matter the chaos of the week, this one night was sacred—a time for stories, food, community, and the warmth of a fire that seemed to breathe life into all of us.

Every Saturday night, the entire village gathered around a roaring fire, with the elders sitting at the forefront.

As a child, I had hung on their every word, my young mind spinning wild images of heroes and monsters, Kings and Queens, of brave sacrifices and unimaginable magic. Even now, the pull of their stories was undeniable. Their voices would rise above the crackle of the fire, sharing tales of ancient treaties, immortal rebels, and bloodshed, while weaving together threads of history and myth until it was impossible to tell where one ended and the other began.

But the stories weren't the only thing I looked forward to. My stomach grumbled at the thought of roasting bread over the open flames, a tradition that hadn't lost its charm even as I grew older. The memory of the bread's crispy, golden crust and the sweet, sticky pull of melted chocolate or cheese made my mouth water. There was nothing like the salty, buttery flavor of the bread mixing with the richness of the chocolate. It was my favorite combination—simple, indulgent, and perfect.

In Laochra, luxuries like these were rare and only indulged in when local merchants returned home on weekends. Salt was especially scarce, as there were no mines on our side of the border, making it a prized commodity among the community.

But the highlight of every bonfire night was always the stories told by the elders. Their words were like the flames themselves—warm, mesmerizing, and impossible to look away from. Every retelling was the same: the legend of how the three kings of Luminara had divided their lands and forged a treaty for the benefit of their people. The story warned of the dangers that lay beyond the borders of our village—the creation of the forbidden river and the dark woods where immortals were said to reside. Immortals, *according to the elders*, were cunning and malevolent creatures, incapable of goodness or trust.

As children, we accepted these tales as undeniable truths. But as I grew older, the cracks in the narrative became harder to ignore. The more I listened, the more I questioned.

When was the last time anyone had even seen one of these immortals?

Why did the stories always hinge on the same vague warnings?

By the time I was twelve, my constant interruptions and questions had earned me wary glances from the elders. They didn't appreciate my habit of poking holes in their neatly woven tales, but deep down, I couldn't help but challenge the supposed truth behind the legends and the existence of immortal beings in our midst.

One bonfire night in particular stood out vividly in my memory. The air was still, the kind of quiet that makes every rustle of leaves or crackle of firewood seem louder than it should. The flames flickered high, casting long shadows across the gathered faces. I sat cross-legged on a soft woven blanket near the front, close enough to feel the fire's heat against my skin. My heart thudded with anticipation, not for the story itself—I had heard it dozens of times before—but for the questions brewing in my mind.

Soren, the elder reciting the story that week, began speaking, his voice carrying a practiced rhythm, his words weaving a tapestry of ancient kings, fragile peace, and the looming threat of immortals. I listened, absorbing every detail, but the questions in my mind grew louder with every sentence.

Finally, I couldn't hold back. I raised my hand, cutting through his words mid-sentence. The crackle of the fire filled the sudden silence as every head turned to look at me.

"But wait," I said, trying to keep my voice steady despite the nervous energy building inside me. *"If the immortals really wanted to cross the border, wouldn't they have found a way around the river by now?"*

My question lingered in the air, heavy and uninvited. For a moment, the only sound was the soft popping of the firewood. Soren paused, his mouth slightly open, caught off guard. I could feel the weight of the villagers' stares, some curious, others annoyed.

He straightened, shifting his feet, his expression tight. *"The river was created specifically to stop them,"* he said, his tone measured but firm. *"Its magic is absolute. No immortal can ever cross it."*

"But how do we know that for sure?" I pressed, leaning forward slightly. *"Has anyone actually seen an immortal try? And if they're so dangerous and powerful, why haven't they found another way to reach us?"*

A ripple of murmurs spread through the crowd, and I caught the frown of another elder seated nearby. My grandmother, sitting a few rows back, cleared her throat softly, a subtle warning.

Soren's eyes narrowed. *"Child,"* he said, his voice sharp now, *"it is not our place to question the will of the gods or the truths passed down to us by our*

King. The legends exist to protect us and to ensure our survival, which they have for the past century. Do not let your curiosity lead you down a dangerous path."

I sat back, heat rising to my cheeks—not from the fire, but from the tension crackling in the air. I lowered my gaze, but my thoughts raced on, defiant. I wasn't *trying* to challenge the gods or dismiss the elders' wisdom. I just wanted to understand.

That night, as the stories continued and the fire burned low, I stayed quiet, but my mind refused to settle. If the elders were wrong, if the immortals were more than just villains in their tales, what did that mean for us? And *why* did the mere act of asking questions feel just as forbidden as the river?

Each week, I noticed inconsistencies in the story, even though they claimed it had been recited the same way for generations. At first, they'd indulge me with patient smiles, offering half-hearted explanations to my questions. But their patience wore thin, and it wasn't long before my interruptions earned me sharp glares and exasperated sighs. These days, they wouldn't even look at me when I raised my hand during storytelling time, as if ignoring me would make me stop asking questions. It never did.

To me, our history felt like a game of broken telephone, each retelling twisting the narrative slightly, muddying the truth just enough to raise suspicion. Despite their warnings about the immortals and their *so-called* evil nature, I couldn't shake the feeling that the elders were leaving something out—something important.

"There goes Raine's brain," Wren said with a smirk, his voice dripping with mockery as he shoved another piece of bread into his mouth. "No doubt thinking about all the ways she can challenge Micaiah during tonight's story."

Our grandmother gave him a sharp look. "Wren, enough," she chastised, shushing him with a wave of her hand, but I could see the ghost of a smile tugging at her lips.

I stuck out my tongue at him in defiance. "At least *I* think about the stories," I shot back, "instead of sneaking off halfway through to head to the barn with—"

Wren's foot connected with my shin under the table, cutting me off mid-sentence. I cursed, glaring at him as he leaned back in his chair, arms crossed, giving me a warning look.

From the corner of my eye, I saw my dad stifle a laugh, his shoulders shaking as he covered his mouth. My mom rolled her eyes, *clearly* unimpressed with our antics.

"You're just mad because I'm right," I said, puckering my lips and making exaggerated kissing motions at Wren.

He scowled, "You're lucky I didn't aim higher," he muttered under his breath, but the corner of his mouth twitched in an almost smile.

Everyone in the village knew why teenagers always left the bonfire early to *"help clean the barn,"* but it wasn't exactly endorsed or a topic of polite conversation.

From across the table, I caught my dad whispering something to my mom, a mischievous grin spreading across his face. She shook her head, trying to hide her own smile.

Despite our bickering, these Saturday and Sunday meals were some of my favorite moments, especially now that we were all adults. The small round kitchen table, scarred from years of use, held more memories than I could count. Family arguments, quiet mornings, laughter so loud it made the windows rattle—it had all happened here.

The warm light from the old chandelier above cast a soft glow on our faces, making the moment feel timeless. As my grandmother passed a plate of roasted vegetables across the table, her hand brushed mine, and I couldn't help but feel a pang of gratitude.

"Try not to get yourself kicked out of the story circle again tonight," my mom teased lightly, pulling me back to the present.

I grinned, already anticipating the elder's exasperated expression when I inevitably interrupted him again. "No promises."

Suddenly, the sound of Baren's chair scraping against the wooden floorboards jolted me out of my thoughts. He had been uncharacteristically quiet all evening, and it left me wondering what was on his mind. He muttered something about changing upstairs before disappearing down the hall, leaving me with more questions than answers.

Before I had the chance to follow up, my mom gave me a knowing look and started gathering the plates. Taking the hint, I grabbed the glasses and followed her into the kitchen, the clinking of dishes breaking the quiet hum of the evening. We worked in a rhythm that spoke of years of practice, her rinsing and me stacking plates, though she never let me forget I wasn't much help growing up.

"Go on now, Raine," she said, swatting my arm with a dish towel when I lingered too long. "Or you're going to be late for the bonfire. *Again.*"

I rolled my eyes with a laugh, taking her playful shove as permission to leave. It wasn't like I'd argue—I had a knack for avoiding dish duty, a fact that thankfully amused her more than it annoyed her.

"Thanks, Mom," I called, darting out of the kitchen and towards the stairs. My hurried steps echoed through the old house, and in my rush, I nearly tripped over my own feet at the first step. Catching myself, I slowed down, a sheepish grin spreading across my face even though no one had seen it.

As I climbed, a wave of nostalgia hit me. Every creak of the stairs felt like an echo of my childhood, when Wren and I would race to our rooms, or when I'd sit halfway up, eavesdropping on the adults below. The walls were lined with faded photographs and handmade quilts, each one telling a story of our family's history.

I reached out and trailed my fingers along the banister, the wood worn smooth from years of hands brushing over it. This house held so many memories—some joyful, others bittersweet. It had been the backdrop of countless moments in my life, and walking through it always felt like stepping back in time.

Distracted, as usual, I paused at the top of the stairs, my mind wandering to the stories of the elders, the hum of the bonfire, and the mysterious stillness in Baren's mood tonight.

I was always late, not just because I couldn't keep track of time, but because I couldn't help daydreaming, letting my thoughts drift like leaves on a breeze. Shaking my head to clear it, I pushed myself forward. I needed to get ready before Mom changed her mind and called me back downstairs. If I showed up late, Wren would never let me hear the end of it, and I'd already given him plenty of ammunition for teasing tonight.

I pushed open the door to my room, and the familiar, calming scent of lavender drifted towards me. It was the kind of scent that clung to everything my grandmother touched—her clothes, her hands, even the leather of her journal. She was already there as if she'd been waiting for me. She stood by the doorway, her presence commanding without trying, adjusting the drape of her deep blue shawl over one shoulder. Her golden necklaces caught the soft glow of the fading sunlight, each piece glinting like it held its own story.

Her eyes, those sharp, captivating blue-green orbs, met mine with their usual mix of warmth and knowing. They always seemed to glow, the kind of color so vivid and unique it felt like Mother Nature herself had painted them.

Her hair, though, was its own masterpiece. A blend of soft blonde, white, and streaks of silvery gray that seemed to shimmer with every movement, like moonlight caught in the branches of a tree. Today, it was loosely braided, though several wavy strands had slipped free and framed her face in an almost artful chaos. Some days, she let it flow wild and untamed, mirroring her free spirit. But the braid, though simple, gave her an air of quiet authority—a reminder of her role not just as my grandmother, but as the heart of this family.

She was dressed in her usual earthy tones, her long, flowing dress swaying slightly as she shifted her weight. The deep blue shawl draped over her shoulders brought out the cool hues of her eyes. Even in her simplest attire, she looked like she belonged in a portrait, painted by someone who couldn't decide whether they were in awe of her presence or her grace.

But it wasn't her elegance that struck me most—it was her hands. Hands that looked soft at a distance but, up close, told a different story. Strong, weathered hands, capable of coaxing life from the soil or healing with the lightest touch. Hands that had planted every herb in her garden and worked tirelessly to keep our family steady, no matter what storms came our way. They rested lightly on the door frame, her fingers tapping gently as if to remind me that time was ticking.

I sat down at our shared vanity, but my eyes kept circling back to her. She was a contradiction in every sense—gentle yet unyielding, earthy yet otherworldly, practical yet steeped in mystery. Watching her, I couldn't help but feel a pang of awe, the same way I did when I was a child.

She caught me staring and tilted her head slightly, her lips curving into a small, knowing smile. "I'll see you there soon, my Wildheart," she said softly, her voice as soothing as the lavender that clung to the air around her.

I let out a quiet laugh at the nickname. *Wildheart*. She'd called me that for as long as I could remember, claiming it suited me perfectly. She said I was just like her when she was younger—curious, stubborn, and constantly testing boundaries.

Before I could think of a clever response, she turned back to the door but paused with a mischievous glint in her eye. "Oh, and try not to give Micaiah a hard time tonight. He already asked me if I could make you stay home." Her tone was amused, but the warning was clear.

I rolled my eyes, about to protest, but she didn't wait for my response. She pulled the door closed behind her, muttering to herself just loud enough for me to hear, "As if anyone could ever *make* that girl do anything, let alone tell her not to."

A grin spread across my face as her footsteps faded down the hall. If Micaiah thought I was going to sit quietly through another round of his embellished stories, he clearly hadn't learned anything about me by now.

My grandmother knew me better than anyone else. Despite the decades between us, she wasn't just family; she was my closest friend and confidant. Sharing a room with her might have seemed strange to some, but to me, it felt natural. She was the one person who let me be entirely myself, never judging, only guiding me with her quiet wisdom and unwavering love.

After she left, I took a moment to let the silence settle around me, basking in the lingering warmth of her presence. Her graceful strength never failed to amaze me. It was a quiet kind of power, the kind that didn't need to announce itself but was felt all the same.

For a brief moment, I stood still, appreciating the comfort of this room, this house, and the life we'd built here together. But reality quickly caught up to me when the sound of the front door slamming shut echoed through the house.

My heart leapt in panic as I realized how late I was running. "Dammit," I muttered under my breath, scrambling to get myself together.

I rifled through my wardrobe, tossing clothes over my shoulder in search of something decent to wear. In my rush, my elbow knocked into a small wooden box on the top shelf, sending it tumbling to the floor. Its lid popped open, spilling tiny jars filled with seeds and dried herbs onto the floorboards. They glinted faintly in the fading sunlight, unfamiliar but oddly intriguing. I crouched down, tempted to inspect them, but there wasn't time. My curiosity would have to wait.

Kicking the box under the bed, I reached for my boar bristle brush and settled in front of the vanity. Its smooth, worn handle fit perfectly in my hand, a comforting weight I'd held countless times before. As I dragged the bristles through my long hair, I felt the soothing scrape against my scalp. The sensation grounded me, easing the tension after a long and trying day.

My hair, chestnut brown, wild and thick, spilled down past my shoulders in unruly waves that refused to be tamed. Each strand felt like it carried a memory—running through the streets, training with Wren, or sitting under the sun for hours, lost in thought. I swept it over one shoulder, my fingers weaving it into a fishtail braid. It wasn't as neat as the ones my grandmother used to do when I was a child, but it would suffice. I tied the end with a small emerald ribbon, the same one she had gifted me years ago. It was more than an accessory—it was hers when she was younger and a piece of her I carried everywhere, a reminder that no matter where I went, I was never alone.

I stood and glanced at my reflection in the mirror. The person staring back at me wasn't a little girl anymore. My legs were strong, toned from years of sprinting through the village and training with Wren. My arms, though slim, carried the strength of someone who could wield a bow and daggers with precision. My waist remained lean, though my love of chocolate had added a softness to my hips that I secretly didn't mind.

The sun had left its mark on my skin, scattering freckles across my cheeks and nose like a constellation. A rosy flush warmed my sun-kissed complexion, highlighting my rounded nose and full lips. I wasn't the kind of beautiful that stopped people in their tracks, but that had never mattered to me.

It was my eyes that stood out the most. A gift from the women who came before me, they shifted from green to blue depending on the light, their depths carrying the stories and strength of my lineage. When I looked into them, I saw my grandmother's wisdom, my mother's quiet resilience, and a flicker of my own determination. They were my favorite feature, a constant reminder that I came from a line of women who had faced the world's challenges head-on and endured.

I straightened my braid, grabbed my boots, and made for the door. Tonight wasn't just another bonfire night—it was another chance to carve out my place in the legacy of those who came before me. And as always, I planned to do it on my terms.

3. Tales From The Past

My heart pounded in my chest as I sprinted out of my small wooden house, desperate to make it on time. The golden light of the setting sun cast long shadows across the village as the narrow street stretched before me, flanked by modest wood-paneled houses on one side and flourishing farms on the other. The smell of fresh earth and hay lingered in the air, mingling with the faint scent of wood smoke from chimneys that curled into the night sky. It was a peaceful, tranquil evening, but not for me. Not tonight. I was late.

The usual bustle of the village had dwindled, the air heavy with the promise of evening. The streets, usually teeming with people, were eerily empty. Most of the villagers had already gathered in the center square for the bonfire. I could already hear it—the crackle of the fire in the distance, the hum of laughter, the chatter of friends and neighbors. I pushed myself harder, my feet pounding against the well-worn path, feeling the urgency in each step.

I passed the old farm with its sheep and chickens, now quiet, the animals already tucked away for the night. The sound of their usual clamor was replaced by the occasional chirp of a cricket and the soft rustle of the wind moving through the tall grass.

As I neared the end of the street, my breath coming in quick bursts, I looked back towards my house. The village was small—too small to be anything but a tight-knit community—and as such, there were no official street names. With only 36 dwellings and three roads, everyone knew one another, and each person's life was intertwined with the next. My family's house was at the very end of the third street, nestled just before the edge of the forest—a place that had been both a blessing and a curse over the years, offering us both privacy and isolation in equal measure.

My house, though small, was the perfect home, filled with the warmth of those who had come before me. It held the legacy of generations within its walls—wooden beams that had been hand-carved, the mortar and stone that had endured for over a hundred years. The original structure had been built by my great-great-grandparents, their hands and hearts woven into the very bones of the house. Over time, my grandparents and parents had made small updates, like adding a second story before Baren was born, but our home remained simple and unassuming.

Despite its size, we somehow managed to fit six people under our roof— quite a feat, considering there wasn't much space. The house, with its low beams and worn wooden floors, felt cramped but cozy.

My parents worked tirelessly—my mother, an instructor, spent her days teaching the village's children and passing down what knowledge she had to others. My father, a traveling merchant, would leave for days at a time, and even my grandmother contributed by selling her homemade herbs and tinctures that she lovingly crafted in the small garden behind our house.

The village didn't have a formal school, but that didn't stop the women in town from banding together to create their own education program. The women would rotate, teaching classes throughout the day, each taking on different age groups. It was far from a formal structure, but it worked and was all we knew. We learned to read, to write, to think for ourselves— all thanks to those tireless mothers and grandmothers who refused to let the world outside dictate our future.

We were fortunate. In a rare way, we didn't struggle with backbreaking labor, didn't fight to survive. We were content, blessed by the land and the pact that had been forged years ago—the treaty, signed by King Saoine of Rioga. That treaty, which promised provisions and protection in exchange for loyalty, had been upheld by each new king, a symbol of trust between ruler and citizens. For a century, the peace had reigned, and in this village, it had become more than just an agreement; it had become a way of life.

Still, despite the comfort of our simple life, I could feel something stirring beneath the surface. There was a tension, a yearning in me that felt out of place in a village so content with its peace. My heart raced, my thoughts turning to the future that loomed closer with every passing step. The quiet life of my ancestors wasn't enough anymore. Not for me.

As I raced toward the sound of the bonfire, my house became a brief blur in my peripheral vision, the newer two-story homes I passed standing tall against the backdrop of the fading light, their windows glowing warmly from within. Their facades were well-kept, with fresh paint that contrasted against the weathered, more humble homes that dotted the village. Most of the original structures dated back over one hundred years, simple yet sturdy homes that had been passed down through generations, and most people didn't require much more.

I finally reached the village square, panting as I pulled a wooden stool closer to the crackling fire. The warmth of the flames felt comforting, almost soothing, but the anticipation in the air kept my heart racing. As I settled into the chair, I could feel the weight of the crowd's curious eyes on me, their eyes following my every move. The murmurs rose, swirling around the fire, as we all waited for the story to start.

Micaiah, the elder in charge of tonight's storytelling, shot me a stern look from across the fire. His gaze was sharp, yet his face was calm, as if he'd expected me to show up late and could finally start. He held up a hand, silencing the crowd with a single motion. The murmurs hushed almost immediately, the air thick with anticipation as if the night itself had drawn a deep breath.

I fidgeted in my seat, my palms clammy despite the heat from the fire, feeling the weight of every pair of eyes still on me. The flames flickered and danced, their light casting strange, flickering shadows on their faces, each one waiting for the first word, the first line of the story that would transport us all for the evening.

"*Long ago,*" Micaiah's voice rumbled, low and dramatic, drawing every ear in the circle to him. He was a master of tension, making each word hang in the air, thick and heavy. "*Dermaine and Rioga were allies, their lands united by open borders and trade. But that was before the immortals came.*" He paused, his eyes sweeping over the crowd, taking in every face as if he could hear their hearts beat in unison with his words. "*Before the bloodshed.*"

I shifted uncomfortably, rolling my shoulders as I leaned forward slightly. Micaiah had that effect on people—his voice would stir up a storm of tension in the air, and even I couldn't escape the weight of it. I resisted the urge to mutter something under my breath. His flair for the dramatic was so predictable. I already knew how he was going to spin this—building up to the part where the immortals came in, blood-stained and slaughtering humans. Classic Micaiah.

He continued, his voice thickening with every word, making sure the suspense clung to each syllable. "*Back when the world was united, all three territories in Luminara were in allegiance with one another. The borders were wide open, allowing both humans and immortals to roam free in peace and unity.*"

The fire crackled beside me, sending sparks into the air, the heat from the flames briefly warming my face as the evening chill settled in. "*But two hundred years ago, people began to vanish—ordinary folk, gone without a trace. Others weren't so lucky. They were found torn apart along the outskirts of Dermaine, their bodies mangled beyond recognition, as if something wild had feasted on them. No mortal blade could've done what was found of their remains. No human rage could've carved that deep. And so the whispers began... of immortals with blood on their teeth and no soul left behind their eyes. They were starving, savage, and soulless."*

A shudder ran through the crowd, especially from the younger children hearing this story for the first time. I could see their wide eyes, their fear hanging in the air like the smoke from the fire. The thought of immortals—beings who could easily slip into our world and vanish just as quickly—was terrifying, and I couldn't blame them for being afraid. The danger of it all was enough to make anyone's blood run cold. Even I had to admit it was a chilling thought, though I refused to show it.

The fire crackled, filling the silence that followed. Maybe it was just a story. An old man's hatred dressed in legend that had been passed down for generations. But still… something in the way he said soulless made my chest tighten. Like a truth hidden inside a lie. Like a warning that didn't care if I believed it, because no one would ever know the full truth.

Micaiah stood in front of the bonfire, his dramatic purple cloak billowing slightly in the breeze as if even the wind wanted to participate in his performance. The gold embroidery along the edges gleamed in the firelight, matching the flair with which he gestured as he spoke. His beard, thick and streaked with gray, puffed up with every word like it carried the weight of a thousand lifetimes, and his deep, gravelly voice rolled through the crowd, overly theatrical with every twist and turn of the tale.

I sighed, trying not to roll my eyes. He always made everything sound like the end of the world—each word, each pause deliberately drawn out for effect. His steel-gray eyes darted across the gathered villagers, seeking reactions like a performer gauging his audience, and when someone leaned forward just slightly, he'd pounce, turning up the drama even more.

His hair, combed back but slightly unruly at the edges, added to the exaggerated image, as though he were some ancient prophet instead of a man who spent most of his time overseeing fields and scolding children for stealing apples. It wasn't that I didn't respect him—he was an elder, after all—but his flair for the theatrical made it hard to take him seriously.

I crossed my arms, resisting the urge to point out the way he leaned into the firelight for effect, his voice lowering to a conspiratorial tone like he was about to share a secret no one in the village had heard a hundred times before. This wasn't storytelling—it was a performance, and Micaiah loved his stage.

His voice dropped again, just the right amount of quiet before he delivered the next piece of the story. *"There were rumors about a band of rebels in Immorro—immortals who were hungry for more than what their cursed lands could offer. They wanted our territory, our city, our resources, our people. And so, the three great kings of old—Rioga, Dermaine, and even Immorro itself—met under shadowed skies to draw the line. A border treaty carved in fear and blood, one that would keep the immortals locked behind it. Or so they thought."*

The wind picked up, rustling the leaves in the trees, the sound adding an eerie undertone to Micaiah's words. *"The treaty didn't stop humans from crossing into Immorro. But anyone who stepped over that border did so by choice, and they knew it might be their last."* His voice took on a dark edge, the wind seeming to whisper along with him. *"Just beyond the line, the land had been infiltrated by the rebels. Immortals twisted by hatred, thirsting for blood and vengeance after being cast out. And they made sure any human foolish enough to cross paid the price for sentencing them to centuries of separation."*

I could feel my pulse quicken, the vivid imagery of immortals lurking in the shadows behind that line, their bloodlust and revenge waiting to spill over. Micaiah's voice boomed again, echoing through the clearing, his words ringing in the night. His dramatic pauses had grown longer, each one a beat that made the crowd lean in closer as if the very earth was holding its breath. The fire crackled louder, snapping as the tension mounted.

"What began as a fragile idea, a desperate attempt at peace, soon became law." Micaiah continued, his focus turning inward for a moment like he could see it all playing out in front of him. *"The treaty was signed, the borders drawn, and with it, all three territories were split for good. Immortals, who once walked among us, were forced back into the shadows of Immorro, a land sealed off by fear, distrust, and the blood that had already been spilled."*

He paused, letting the weight of his words hang in the air. *"Their stories of hunger, vengeance, and the wrath of the old blood didn't fade. They became warnings. Whispers passed down to remind us what happens when you trust something that cannot die."*

I bit my lip, fighting the urge to roll my eyes. I knew the history, knew it by heart. It had been passed down for generations, these stories of our past. But how long could they keep recycling the same old legends? It had been over a century since any immortal had been seen in Rioga, and still, we sat here, week after week, listening to the same fearful tales. The fear that history might repeat itself, that an immortal might emerge from the depths of the forest, sounded impossible. Yet, here we were, still living under the shadow of it all, haunted by old stories of blood and vengeance.

Micaiah continued, dragging me back into the present. *"The border stood for over a century keeping our people and all of Rioga safe; however, one hundred years ago,"* he began, his voice low and deliberate, *"The Royal family of Immorro requested a meeting to finally remove the border."* He paused for dramatic effect, his eyes lingering on the younger faces in the circle. *"The rebellion had already begun. Immortals were rising up, not just against the monarchy, but against the very borders that confined them. They believed the treaty was a betrayal. That their own king had chained them to a dying land. And they were willing to do whatever it took to reclaim their freedom—no matter the cost."*

He leaned forward, voice low, but his expression thundered with certainty. *"They were thirsty for vengeance. For blood. For what they believed was rightfully theirs. The rebels were no peacekeepers. They were predators in waiting."*

The fire crackled sharply as if punctuating his words, casting flickering shadows that danced over the faces of those gathered. A faint breeze rustled the trees behind us, the sound like whispers in the dark. Micaiah's voice rose and fell, painting vivid images of the immortals' rebellion and their insatiable thirst for blood and power.

"They felt entitled," he said, his voice sharpening like a blade, *"to roam freely across all of Luminara without consequence. As if the world was theirs to claim."*

He paused, letting the words settle, before continuing with a scowl that crept across his face. *"Back then, when the lands were still united, we had everything. Abundant trade. Open borders. Access to the springs, the forests, and the sea. There was no limit to what we could grow, craft, or share. But when the immortals turned, when they wanted more, when they demanded it all, those luxuries vanished with them."*

I shifted on my stool, trying to ignore the ache in my back. Micaiah was laying it on thick tonight, his voice dripping with urgency and melodrama. He had a way of twisting history into a story that felt like it was clawing its way out of the past to haunt us in the present.

I stole a glance around the circle. Some of the younger children were wide-eyed, their mouths slightly open, no doubt imagining immortal rebels lurking in the shadows, waiting to pounce if they stepped out of line. Even some of the adults leaned forward, as if Micaiah's tale was new to them. I couldn't help but sigh internally. Surely not every immortal was a bloodthirsty monster. But in this village, those were the only ones we heard about.

Micaiah's voice softened, drawing everyone closer. *"The rebellion terrified the Immorro Royal family,"* he said, each word laced with warning. *"So they did what frightened rulers always do, they tried to bargain. They believed that by removing the border treaty, they would calm their people and quell the unrest."*

He leaned forward then, voice dropping into a hushed, conspiratorial whisper. *"But in a land ruled by three territories and three kings, they couldn't do it alone. They needed at least one mortal crown to stand with them. One voice strong enough to shift the balance."*

The fire cracked, and a few people in the circle shifted. *"They went first to Dermaine,"* he continued, *"their closest and most vulnerable neighbor. The King and Queen were swayed, ensnared, some say, by immortal persuasion. Their minds twisted, intentions blurred, but they agreed to revoke the treaty and form an alliance with Immorro."*

I rolled my eyes discreetly, though the tension in the air was palpable. No one else moved. Not even the fire dared interrupt him now.

"When King Saoine of Rioga found out," Micaiah said, his voice regaining its weight, *"he knew what was coming. He'd heard the stories, tales passed down by his father and his grandfather before that. Warnings of what the immortals did the last time they crossed our borders. Of what they'd do again if given the chance."*

The firelight glinted off Micaiah's face, making his expression seem almost otherworldly. Like the story itself was shaping him as he spoke.

"King Saoine remembered the tales of an immortal witch who had cursed his bloodline... of lives lost, kingdoms burned, and the chaos that followed. All of it, born from the immortals' selfish hunger and their utter disregard for human life." He let the words hang, heavy and final, letting the fire crackle through the silence before continuing.

"For generations, Rioga had paid the price of their existence. Bloodshed. Fear. Loss that never fully healed. And King Saoine swore he would not let his people suffer that fate again."

"So, out of necessity—out of duty to his kingdom—he summoned every soldier under his command to the border, vowing to protect the territory at all costs. Hundreds answered. Brave men who showed up, not for glory, but for their families. Their homes. Their way of life. But it wasn't enough."

Gasps and murmurs spread through the crowd, as predictable as the fire's crackle. I resisted the urge to groan aloud. The dramatic pauses, the feigned shock from the audience—it was all so rehearsed, so painfully predictable.

Micaiah's gaze swept the circle, voice growing heavier. He exhaled like the weight of the past still lived in his lungs. *"Our human weapons were no match for immortal vengeance. They came without mercy, shadows through stone. And they slaughtered them all."*

The fire flared for a moment like it was reacting to Micaiah's words, too. I could hear faint gasps from the children, their fear a tangible thing in the cool night air.

"One by one, the King watched his army fall, every friend, every commander, every man who stood for him, cut down by creatures who felt nothing but hunger for the pain they believed we owed them."

My stomach tightened, not from fear, but from frustration. Maybe parts of Micaiah's tale were true. But the way he told it turned every immortal into a villain. As if cruelty was carved into their bones.

Truth, as I understood it, was rarely so sharpened and singular. It wasn't all or nothing. Good or evil. And blanket statements like his were dangerous, like saying all humans were noble, when I knew damn well they weren't.

"The immortals showed no mercy," Micaiah concluded, his voice thick with sorrow. *"They tortured and butchered everyone who dared to fight for our land and our people. Every soul lost that day died protecting the very earth we call home."* He let the hard truth settle. Then added, quieter, *"Everyone... except the King."*

The silence that followed was deafening, broken only by the occasional crackle of the fire. I clenched my jaw, forcing myself to stay quiet, though my thoughts churned. Shadows danced from the towering trees, their branches twisting like skeletal hands in the dim light. The forest seemed to press in around us, amplifying the weight of his words.

"Callix, the King of Immorro," Micaiah said, his tone heavy with foreboding, *"stepped forward amidst the chaos. And with a single motion, just one raised hand, he brought the rebels to a halt and spared King Saoine's life."*

He paused dramatically, letting his words settle like an oppressive fog, curling thick and silent around the fire. *"But not without a cost,"* he added, his eyes gleaming in the flickering firelight. *"Callix demanded a favor in return, a debt the King would one day be forced to repay."*

He let that hang, like smoke waiting to be inhaled. A faint shiver ran down my spine, though whether it was from Micaiah's words or the chill creeping in from the forest, I couldn't say. The fire seemed dimmer now, its warmth insufficient against the growing weight in the air.

"Some say the Immortal King acted out of mercy," he continued, his voice barely above a whisper. *"Others whisper it was part of a deeper scheme. A way to keep Rioga bound. Leashed. And indebted."*

Looking around the circle, his voice turned colder. *"No one knows what truly motivated Callix that day. But a favor like that is never granted for free."*

I leaned back, resisting the urge to roll my eyes. Micaiah's storytelling was good, I'd give him that, but it always followed the same overdone pattern. He had the younger kids hooked, their wide eyes fixed on him as though he were conjuring the events himself. Meanwhile, I noticed my grandmother watching from her seat behind him, a faint, knowing smile tugging at her lips. She caught my expression and raised a brow. I'd seen the look many times before; it was expectant yet patient, like she was daring me to interrupt. I stayed silent, though not wanting to interrupt just yet. Micaiah might've been skipping some of the finer details, but the part about Callix's favor always intrigued me. What would an immortal King even want from someone with no power? But before I could dwell on it, the story continued.

"In the aftermath of the battle, King Saoine returned to Rioga with his life intact but his spirit broken. The slaughter of his men weighed heavily on him, and thoughts of revenge consumed him. Yet, despite the rage burning in his heart, there was no escaping the favor he owed Callix—a debt that loomed over him like a curse."

The fire popped loudly, making one of the younger children jump. I smirked but quickly masked it as Micaiah turned to glance at the circle, his focus lingering on the little ones for effect.

He drew in a long breath, his voice lowering again. *"But fate had other plans for our King. At the time, his beloved wife, Queen Sarda, was pregnant with their second child. Complications arose, and it became clear that the birth might claim both the Queen and their unborn child if they didn't act fast."*

The murmurs of the crowd quieted as the tension thickened. The shadows cast by the firelight seemed to shift, elongating and flickering ominously. I glanced at the sky, now ink-black and starless, a perfect backdrop for Micaiah's grim tale.

"King Saoine," Micaiah said, his voice heavy with drama, *"paced the grand halls of the castle, his mind racing with regrets. The royal healer had warned him that the child was not yet ready to be born, but time wasn't on their side. The Queen's condition worsened by the hour, and it seemed certain neither of them would survive much longer."*

Micaiah paused, a log in the fire shifted, sending a cascade of sparks upward as he sipped from his canteen. The flickering light caught as he lifted it to his lips, and I instinctively knew it was filled with whiskey, not water. I'd been close enough to smell it on him in the past when asking questions, and knew it was his drink of choice. I smirked, glancing at my grandmother again. Her smile widened in silent acknowledgment, letting Micaiah continue his dramatic version uninterrupted.

"The King was certain this was no natural complication. He believed it to be his family's curse—a wicked spell cast generations ago by an immortal witch determined to end the Rioga bloodline."

He swirled his tunic dramatically, mimicking a magician conjuring dark spells. A few of the younger kids shrieked, and some of the older ones began to shuffle toward the barn, eager to escape this part of the story. I stayed seated, suppressing a chill of my own. This part always struck a nerve and was the hardest to sit through.

Micaiah leaned forward, his voice dropping to a near whisper. *"This witch,"* he said, his words laced with venom, *"fell in love with a Riogan prince. A second son. He swore his heart to her, promised her forever. But fate had other plans."*

He let the fire crackle for a moment before continuing.

"His elder brother, the one destined for the throne, died suddenly. And with that, the crown passed to the second son. Duty replaced love. And without hesitation, he cast the witch aside. Broke her heart. Broke their bond and chose a noblewoman to marry instead, naming her his queen."

He paused, letting the weight of the betrayal sink in.

"The witch's love turned into fury. Her heartbreak, into vengeance. And so she cursed the Rioga bloodline."

His voice rose, mimicking her long-forgotten words. *"'You may rule these lands now,' she told him, 'but your line will end in ruin. You will never know the comfort of legacy. No king born of your name will have more than one heir. And when that heir falls...so too shall your kingdom.'"*

The fire crackled again, louder this time, as though it, too, felt the tension of the tale. I couldn't help but scoff softly. If this witch was so powerful, why in all these years had she not tried to break the wards keeping immortals out of our lands? It was a question I'd asked myself countless times, one that no elder seemed eager to answer.

Micaiah's voice took on a hushed, almost reverent tone as he delivered the next part. *"Every Rioga King since has borne only one son, the curse clinging to their bloodline like a shroud. No king dared challenge it. No queen dared hope for more."*

He glanced around the fire, letting the silence settle. A ripple moved through the circle, and Micaiah's stare sharpened. *"So when King Saoine's beloved wife, Queen Sarda, discovered she carried a second child, the King prayed desperately that the curse was nothing more than a legend. But deep down, he knew this was another battle they might not win."*

He paused, eyes flickering in the firelight.

"From the moment they could walk, each Riogan prince was bound to the palace. They trained, studied, and were kept behind stone walls until it was their time to rule. Fear ruled the halls. Not just fear of their immortal enemies... but of fate. Because if a prince died, so did their entire family line."

His voice softened now, weighted with grief. *"When the Queen fell ill, the King, grief-stricken and desperate, turned to the gods. He fell to his knees in the great hall, crown cast aside, pride forgotten, and begged for mercy. He offered everything, his title, his fortune, his very soul, if only they would save her. If only they would spare the child she carried."*

A chill crept up my arms, and I pulled my cloak tighter. The fire's warmth seemed to falter as Micaiah's words continued. *"And then,"* he breathed, his voice barely more than a whisper, *"as if the gods had heard his plea, a servant entered the hall, her arms laden with blood-stained towels."*

He paused, the fire popping like punctuation. *"She hesitated...her voice trembling as she spoke of a legend she'd heard as a child. One of immortal healers, gifted beings, said to pull souls back from the edge of death."*

He let the weight of it settle before continuing, his voice swelling with urgency. *"Clinging to that fragile glimmer of hope, the King sent word to his three most trusted generals; men who had remained behind to guard the Queen and their firstborn son while battle raged along the border. He gave them one order: make the two-day journey through Dermaine into Immorro and beg Callix, the Immortal King, to send his finest healer."*

I scoffed under my breath. The arrogance of King Saoine never failed to astound me. Turning to someone he despised, someone he'd called a monster and believed was soulless, all because he was desperate.

My hand shot up before I could think better of it. "How do we even know this is true?" I asked, cutting through Micaiah's narrative. "Why would the King request help from someone he considered evil?"

Micaiah ignored me entirely, which was irritating but not surprising, and people glared, obviously irritated by my interruption, and he continued as if I hadn't spoken at all. *"Callix, whose army now patrolled the borders to prevent further bloodshed, received word of the King's plea before the generals had even arrived."* Micaiah's voice lowered, reverent again, as if even the forest had stopped to listen.

"There were whispers in the trees, old magic stirring, and knowing he would've done the same for his own wife, Callix prepared."

"He assembled his finest healer, cloaked in midnight blue, and a procession of royal guards to escort her safely to the edge of Immorro. They met the generals at the border, no blood drawn, no blades raised."

A few heads nodded solemnly, as if that peace alone was a miracle.

"But by the time the healer reached Rioga," Micaiah said, voice thickening with sorrow, *"Queen Sarda was slipping. Her skin pale, lips grey, her breath shallow as shadows. The room reeked of iron. The sheets stained crimson. The air... heavy with death."*

He paused, letting the image settle like smoke in the lungs.

"The healer took one look at the Queen and knew there was little time left. Perhaps none at all."

His voice dipped again, quieter now, aching.

"But the King... oh, the King. He knelt beside her, tears streaming freely, his crown forgotten on the stone floor. He clutched her hands like they were the last tether to his soul and begged the healer to use every ounce of magic she possessed to save his wife. He told her life without Sarda was no life at all. That he would give anything and everything. If only she would stay."

I blinked, my thoughts drifting. What would it be like to love someone so fiercely, so deeply, that you couldn't imagine life without them? I'd heard stories of my grandparents' love and seen glimpses of it in my parents' devotion to each other, but it felt like something out of reach, like trying to grasp a star in the sky.

"The healer agreed to try," Micaiah said, his voice dipping into something colder, darker, *"but the moment she laid her hands upon the Queen, she felt it."*

A hush fell over the fire.

"A presence, ancient and suffocating, wrapped itself around the Queen like a shroud. It wasn't an illness. It wasn't fate. It was the witch's curse."

His words struck like a cold wind.

"It was ancient and unbreakable. Woven into the very blood of the Riogan line. No spell could unmake it. No power could chase it out. Because it didn't just want the Queen's life." Micaiah's voice turned grim. *"It wanted vengeance. And it came, as always, at the hand of an immortal."*

The air seemed to grow colder, the forest pressing closer, the fire's light dimming. I pulled my cloak tighter, suddenly uneasy.

"At the foot of the bed, the King stood trembling, fists buried in the crimson sheets. The healer stepped back, silent... and that silence said more than any truth could bear."

"And the King," Micaiah drew a breath. *"he fell to his knees, shattered. His wife's lifeless body a cruel echo of every warning he'd ever ignored. Of every story passed down through blood and grief. A reminder of the curse that had plagued his family for generations and still remains today."*

The fire hissed, the sound cutting through the silence that followed. My chest tightened, an inexplicable sadness blooming there. Despite my doubts, despite my frustrations with this story, something about it resonated. Perhaps it was the raw desperation, the unrelenting cruelty of fate. Or maybe… it was the creeping suspicion that, buried in the legend, there was truth.

4. Of Legends And Lies

I sprinted after Wren, my feet pounding the uneven ground, the crisp night air slicing through my lungs with each gasping breath. My heart was a drumbeat of urgency as the barn loomed closer, its weathered wood glowing faintly in the warm light spilling out through the slats. Every instinct screamed for me to turn back—this place reeked of memories I wanted to forget—but I forced my legs to keep moving. I had no choice. He had to hear what I'd overheard while in line for bread.

I skidded to a halt just before the infamous kissing barn came fully into view. Wren stood outside, his broad figure silhouetted against the golden glow from inside. The faint strains of laughter and music spilled out, carried on the cool breeze, a stark contrast to the storm brewing in my chest. My pulse quickened, nerves tangling in my stomach, but against my better judgment, I cupped my hands around my mouth and called his name.

"Wren!"

My voice wavered, but it was loud enough to cut through the barn's hum. He turned, his sharp features catching the light, and frowned in my direction. A group of girls stood near him, giggling and vying for his attention. He said something to them—I couldn't hear what—and started toward me, the curiosity in his expression softening some of my panic.

"Ray, what's wrong?" he asked, his tone calm, almost amused, as though nothing in the world could possibly rattle him.

I didn't bother with pleasantries. "Wren, you won't believe what I just overheard!" The words tumbled out before I could stop them, fast and frantic.

He raised a brow, his deep blue eyes flickering with impatience. "I'm guessing something so important that it couldn't wait?" he chuckled, no doubt making fun of the way I always got excited over the smallest details.

I rolled my eyes in response. "No, it can't." I stepped closer, lowering my voice as though the barn itself might overhear. "Micaiah was talking about the King's dungeon," I said, each word charged with urgency. "He said the healer who killed Queen Sarda isn't just a legend. She's real, Wren. A real immortal. And she's been locked up in the castle this whole time."

I searched his face for a reaction—shock, disbelief, anything—but all I got was an exaggerated roll of his eyes.

"Raine," he said, his voice dripping with skepticism, "it's just an old wives' tale. Every village has them. He's just bored and probably trying to get attention."

"This isn't like the other stories," I protested, frustration bubbling to the surface. "You didn't hear the way he said it. There was something… different about this one. He sounded certain."

My stomach sank at his dismissal as he shrugged, crossing his arms and leaning casually against the barn's outer wall. "You do realize we're one of the only villages in Rioga still repeating this story, right? It's a relic at this point, and who even knows what's true and what's not anymore."

"But—"

"And," he interrupted, holding up a hand, "I've been near the castle plenty of times, and I've never heard anything like this from anyone there. If it were true, don't you think it would've spread by now?"

I hesitated, his calm logic chipping away at my urgency. "Maybe, but—"

"Micaiah hasn't even left Laochra in years, Ray. If it were true, why would he wait so long to 'share' this part of the story?"

His tone was so matter-of-fact, so dismissive, that it stung. I felt the weight of my earlier excitement slip through my fingers like sand. He was probably right—Micaiah did have a flair for the dramatic, and he loved nothing more than an audience. Still, a stubborn flicker of hope remained, refusing to be snuffed out completely.

"I don't know," I murmured, more to myself than to Wren. "It just… felt real."

Wren sighed and placed a hand on my shoulder, his expression softening. "Look, Ray, I know you've got a big imagination, and that's admirable. But you can't believe everything Micaiah says. Trust me, it's just another story to create a dramatic backdrop for his retelling."

I nodded, though the uncertainty still churned in my chest. As Wren turned back toward the barn, the laughter and music pulling him in again, I stayed rooted in place, staring at the ground. Just another story.

But what if it wasn't? I couldn't shake the feeling that I'd stumbled onto something far more important than either of us realized, but I just solemnly nodded, hoping he just didn't understand the significance yet.

Wren ruffled my hair in that infuriatingly familiar way, the gesture tugging at memories of a simpler time when we were just kids running barefoot through the fields. "You better hurry back," he said, grinning. "Don't want to miss out on the bread and chocolate. Rumor has it, there are two kinds of cocoa tonight."

He turned toward the barn without waiting for my reply, the glow from within drawing him like a moth to a flame—and probably to the girls waiting for him there. I watched him go, biting back the retort on the tip of my tongue. Rumors. That's all anyone cared about. Baseless whispers and half-truths that drifted through the village like smoke, thick enough to obscure reality but never solid enough to grasp. At least this one wasn't about me.

But I didn't want more rumors. I wanted answers.

Turning toward the path back to the fire, my thoughts churned. The healer. Knowing there might be more to her story, her ending changed everything. She wasn't just some shadowy figure in an old legend anymore. The way Micaiah told it—whether he meant to or not—made her feel real, tangible. I never saw her as an evil immortal, but someone who had been wronged, someone trapped in the middle of a much larger truth.

If she were real, someone had to know more. Maybe more than one person. And if that was the case, then this wasn't just a village story to create drama; it was a mystery waiting to be unraveled.

When I reached the fire, its warm glow welcoming me back, my grandmother handed me a piece of salty bread wrapped in cloth, its edges slightly crisped from the heat. The smell of melted chocolate hit me instantly, making my mouth water.

"Thought you might want this," she said with a knowing smile.

"Thanks," I murmured, taking the bread. As Wren had predicted, the rest were long gone, and if it weren't for her, I would have missed out. I bit into the soft bread, the rich, gooey chocolate filling melting onto my tongue, its warmth spreading through me like comfort incarnate.

But even the sweetness couldn't distract me for long. My mind kept pulling me back to Wren's dismissive shrug, to the knowing gleam in Micaiah's eyes as he spun his tale by the fire, and what I overheard him sharing in secret afterwards.

What if there was truth to it? What if the healer wasn't just a character in a story about heartbreak and tragedy? What if there were beings with gifts so powerful they could heal others, and we were being kept in the dark out of fear?

I glanced at the firelight flickering against my grandmother's face. Her expression was calm, serene even, as she folded the cloths that had once wrapped the bread before the fire. Her hands moved with practiced ease, but I couldn't stop wondering—how much did she know?

She was an elder and had answered more of my questions than anyone else ever dared. But that didn't mean she'd told me everything.

There were still gaps. Still pieces missing. And I could feel it; not in anything said, but in what wasn't. In what was carefully left out. Because silence could lie just as easily as words, and knowing more than you admit was still a kind of untruth. I wondered then what else they knew, and what truths had been buried beneath the weight of tradition, fear, or loyalty.

I took another bite, but the taste didn't register. The mystery of the healer, the woman who had *supposedly* killed the Queen, who had been imprisoned for generations, had taken root in my thoughts, refusing to be ignored. Whether Wren cared or not, I would find out what became of her because I didn't want to believe that was where her story ended. It was too convenient, too easy, considering everything we'd learned about immortals was centered on their inability to die.

Jostling me out of my thoughts, Micaiah began, his voice carrying over the crackle of the fire. The flames flickered wildly, their glow painting his face with shadows that made him look more dramatic, if that was even possible.

"The King's heartbreak broke him." He let the words hang for a beat. *"Stricken with grief, he looked at the healer, not as the woman who tried to save his wife, but as the one who had failed her."*

His tone darkened, the flames flickering lower as if the story itself dimmed the night. *"His voice cracked as he screamed, 'Treason!' A single word, choked by sorrow. His hand trembled as he pointed at her, desperate for someone to blame."*

"She was the finest healer Callix had, and still... the Queen died beneath her touch." Micaiah's voice dropped to a chilling whisper. *"The guards moved without hesitation. They seized the healer, dragged her from the Queen's chamber, and threw her into the dungeons, chained to the cold, damp stone, left alone in silence and darkness while the King mourned above."*

He looked into the fire now, his tone quiet but unwavering. The imagery wrapped around me, and I could almost hear the metallic clang of chains and the echo of desperate pleas within the dungeon's shadowy depths.

"From that day forward, King Saoine vowed to rid Rioga of immortals and their magic, every trace, every whisper. To him, they were the rot beneath the

roots of peace, the reason death and darkness haunted his kingdom. And he would purge them all to protect what remained."

I barely heard the rest. My thoughts spun wildly, unable to shake the unease coiling in my stomach. Micaiah's words clung to me like cobwebs, sticky and inescapable. How much of this tale was fact? And what other truths were hidden behind the curtain of legends we were spoon-fed and forced to believe?

I felt her stare before I saw it. Turning toward the fire, I found my grandmother's eyes across the flickering light, steady, unreadable at first, but slowly softening into something that looked like concern. The kind that didn't need words to make itself known.

There was always a thread between us, thin but unbreakable. A quiet bond that ran deeper than blood, tethering our thoughts and emotions in ways neither of us ever had to explain. She didn't speak, but her worry pressed against me all the same. Heavy. Familiar. Unspoken, but loud.

Her knowing eyes reminded me of simpler days, of being eight years old and breathlessly excited to befriend Evanora and Asteria. They were cousins and close friends long before I joined their circle, but they welcomed me in. And for a time, I felt like I finally belonged somewhere that wasn't just within my own walls.

For months, we were constant, sharing secrets, laughter, and our dreams for the future. I had never had a best friend, outside of Wren and my grandmother, and they were starting to feel like they could be, too. But time has a way of showing you who was walking beside you and who was simply passing through.

As years stretched on, so did our interests, and they drifted, leaning into the village's quiet expectations. They were content focusing on embroidery, homemaking, and futures shaped like everyone else's. I was not.

I didn't fit their mold. And when I stopped pretending I wanted to, they stopped pretending I belonged. I never resented their choices. I understood them, but the sting of being left behind doesn't disappear just because you see it coming.

After that, trusting people outside my family felt like setting myself up for failure. So I learned to keep my distance.

The realization hit me then, sudden and sharp, I was the only one my age still sitting by the fire. The others were likely at the barn with Wren, laughing, dancing, living as if stories like this one didn't hang heavy in the air. The thought gnawed at me, but I pushed it aside. I didn't belong with them, not anymore. And maybe I never had.

My grandmother's worried and questioning stare caught me again, pulling me from my thoughts. This time, her lips curved into a small, reassuring smile. The warmth of her presence settled over me like a blanket, softening the edges of my unease. She didn't need to ask if I was okay; her unspoken question was clear in the way her eyes searched mine.

I forced a smile, offering her the answer I knew she wanted. "I'm fine," I mouthed, even though it wasn't entirely true. The weight of the healer's outcome sat heavily on my chest, a puzzle with missing pieces that begged to be solved.

She nodded, seemingly satisfied, and returned her attention to the fire. But I couldn't let it go. My thoughts churned as Micaiah's voice rose again, pulling us deeper into the King's grief.

"The King couldn't bear the silence of his once-bustling castle," he continued, his voice now tinged with sorrow. *"Every corridor echoed with what was missing—his wife's laughter, her presence, her love."*

He paused, letting the fire crackle beneath his words.

"Even looking at his son became a torment. The boy's green eyes and sandy-blonde hair mirrored the Queen too perfectly. It was as if grief had been carved into his features, a living reminder of what he had failed to protect."

Micaiah fell silent for a breath, and I leaned forward without meaning to—drawn in, despite the tight knot forming in my chest.

"The King was plagued with indecision. Grief clouded reason, and the weight of loss made every choice feel impossible. But he knew one thing: he couldn't let more death creep into Rioga."

Micaiah's voice gained weight now, laced with belief passed down through generations. *"He knew he had to act. That doing nothing was its own kind of failure. To him, every thread of tragedy, the curse, the Queen's death, the blood spilled at the border, led back to the same origin: the immortals."*

He leaned forward, firelight sharpening his expression into something grim. *"The King believed immortality was a curse masquerading as power. A life without death would become dangerous and reckless. Untethered. Without the end to anchor them, the immortals had no restraint. He feared what they could become over time, if what they already were was so evil."*

Micaiah's tone turned solemn again, final.

"He understood Rioga would not know peace until the last immortal was gone from its lands, and vowed to do whatever it took to make that possible."

Some of the adults clapped at this, their enthusiasm grating against my nerves. It was as though they believed every bit of peace we'd known for the last century was owed solely to the King's brilliance, not the impenetrable barrier that now made it impossible for an immortal to infiltrate. I couldn't help but feel a pang of frustration at their blind reverence. Yes, he'd endured tragedy, and yes, he'd acted to protect his people—but did that mean he deserved unwavering praise?

"Determined to safeguard his city, he traveled to each neighboring village with his generals, recruiting more men to fight in his army," Micaiah continued, his voice carrying over the crackle of the fire. The shadows danced along his face, his tone imbued with reverence as he described the King's mission. *"He offered them generous wages and future provisions in exchange for their loyalty. And once he had enough soldiers armed and willing to fight, he sought an audience with Dermaine's King and Queen to discuss reinstating the border between both human territories and Immorro."*

I shifted on the log, my mind snagging on the glaring omissions in his story. A conveniently forgotten truth hovered at the edge of my thoughts, something my grandmother had shared with me in private to ease my constant questions.

When the King first sought soldiers to fight for Rioga, women had also volunteered to join the ranks, eager to defend their homes and families as well. At first, being desperate for numbers, they welcomed them into the fold, but the arrangement didn't last long. Some of the men, outraged that their wives were spending more time wielding swords than tending to domestic duties, began to rebel. The King, eager to appease the men and secure their loyalty and allegiance, banned all women from training or serving in his army.

I clenched my fists at the memory of my grandmother's words, the injustice sparking a familiar flame inside me. It wasn't just unfair—it was insulting. Especially since, as Wren liked to remind me, I was more skilled than half the boys who trained with him.

"The King trained and stationed his newly formed army at our borders," Micaiah continued, oblivious to my thoughts. *"He knew the treaty might be abolished and wanted his soldiers ready to defend against any retaliation from Immorro and their band of rebels."*

I wondered if he even knew the full story, or if he cared that he was missing a ton of facts. But I doubted it. His version was always seamless, a polished retelling meant to inspire awe, not questions, something I could picture him rehearsing hundreds of times just to perfect his timing and dramatic pauses. As if on cue, he continued.

"The soldiers stood guard as the King made his way to the castle in Dermaine. The memory of his previous army, slaughtered at the hands of immortals, weighed heavily on him as he journeyed those same hills. But it fueled his resolve, driving him to seek a solution in keeping the border intact no matter the cost."

Micaiah paused, lifting his canteen for a sip. The firelight reflected the tension in his features, his hesitation hinting at the gravity of what came next.

"Initially, when presenting his request, the King of Dermaine refused," he said after a moment, lowering the canteen. *"He feared breaking his alliance with Callix, knowing it could provoke the immortal King's wrath. But Queen Deardra saw something in our King that moved her. Perhaps it was his grief— the pain of losing his wife, his unborn child, and his army—or perhaps it was his desperation. Either way, she proposed an alternative. She suggested severing Dermaine's alliance with Rioga instead, and establishing a permanent border*

that no one, neither immortal nor mortal, could cross."

A ripple of murmurs spread through the crowd, as it always did at this part of the tale.

"Our King, puzzled by her suggestion and newfound allegiance with Immorro, wondered how and if such a border could even be created. What would it take? How long would it last? But in the end, his desire for his son's safety and the security of his people outweighed his doubts. He blindly agreed, not fully understanding the gravity of his decision."

I leaned forward slightly, the crackle of the fire filling the silence as Micaiah paused again to take a drink. His fingers tightened around the canteen, a subtle sign of nerves that made me wonder if he knew more than he was letting on.

So far, he'd mostly stuck to the familiar script. Every detail fit seamlessly into the story we'd all heard a dozen times before. Yet I couldn't shake the feeling that he was holding something back.

I let the tension simmer, watching him closely as he prepared to continue. Part of me hoped for a slip, a crack in his polished retelling that might reveal the truth hidden beneath. But for now, I stayed silent, listening with sharper ears than ever.

The flames crackled softly, the warmth licking at my face as I stared into the heart of the bonfire, letting the embers dance before my eyes. Around me, the circle of villagers sat in hushed anticipation as Micaiah's voice carried through the night. *"Queen Deardra's lips curved into a faint smile as she raised her hands,"* Micaiah began, his tone deepening with the weight of her presence. *"In a voice filled with quiet power, she simply said, 'It is done.'"*

The firelight danced across his face, his expression serious as he recounted the Queen's moment of triumph. I could almost see her in my mind—a figure of quiet authority, the tension in the room thickening with her words.

"The King and his generals exchanged uneasy glances," Micaiah continued, his voice dropping low, drawing us closer to the story. *"They wondered how a physical border could withstand immortals with unknown strength and*

power. But before he could ask, Queen Deardra raised her hands again toward the sky. The air grew dense, and the ground beneath their feet trembled as though the earth itself stirred awake."

The flames hissed as a log split, sending a shower of sparks into the air. I shivered, though it wasn't from the cold.

"From the castle windows, they watched as the earth tore apart in the distance," Micaiah said, his hands gesturing as though he could summon the scene himself. *"Water surged forth, roaring with unnatural force, its surface glowing faintly with an unearthly light that matched the Queen's aura. The river rushed across the land, carving a deadly path that no one, not even an immortal, could cross unscathed."*

I glanced around the circle, noting the mesmerized expressions of those listening. The story always held them captive, even those who had heard it a dozen times before. I didn't blame them. This part of the legend—this moment when Queen Deardra revealed her unimaginable power—was my favorite part. It showed that, for once, the Queen was the most powerful presence in the room, proving that a woman didn't need to bow to the expectations of men. I envied the assurance and strength it must have taken for Queen Deardra to defy not only her husband, the King, but her kingdom as well, all to protect lives she had no claim over.

"A chill ran down the King's spine as the realization hit him," Micaiah continued, his voice steady but tinged with something darker, *"The Queen hadn't just created the river; she had summoned it, bending earth and water to her will. Turning back to them, her gaze was sharp as steel, and in that moment, the King no longer saw her as his neighbor and ally. No, she was something far more dangerous."*

Micaiah paused, letting the tension settle before leaning forward, his voice dropping to a near-whisper. *"Stunned and confused, the King asked how it was even possible. But the Queen's reply was colder than the river she had just summoned. She let him in on a little secret; she was not only Dermaine's Queen, but Callix's eldest daughter and a Princess of Immorro."*

The fire popped sharply, and I jumped slightly, my heart racing. The reveal always struck me, no matter how many times I'd heard it. The betrayal, the weight of her lineage, the way it shattered the King's perception of safety—all of it felt raw and unsettling.

"*Queen Deardra, unaffected by our King's shock and horror, informed him that the river now ran along the entire edge of Rioga's lands, its magic deadly to any being who dared to cross,*" Micaiah said, his eyes scanning the crowd. "*She spoke vaguely of creatures that would patrol its depths, hidden but everwatchful, ready to strike down any who tested its waters. No human, magical, or immortal being could cross over or through the river without being stripped of their powers and suffering the most excruciating death.*"

He paused slightly, catching his breath before continuing. "*The Queen didn't explain how the magic worked, but assured the King it would hold. Reminding him that the threat of death was enough to keep immortals at bay.*"

I swallowed hard, the image of the glowing river he described vivid in my mind. Micaiah's descriptions of the whispers, the strange ripples on the surface, and the unseen forces lurking below were enough to make my skin prickle.

He straightened, his voice taking on a tone of finality. "*The King thanked her, grateful and eager to leave the castle and its magic behind. With his generals beside him, he boarded the enchanted boat she had crafted, one that could cross the river only once, never to return.*"

Micaiah's gaze swept the fire circle, and the flames seemed to rise in kind. "*They journeyed in silence, watching the shadows of Dermaine fade behind them, until at last, they stepped onto Riogan soil once more. The King looked upon the untouched land, breathed in its stillness, and declared it 'blessed and fit for a hero.'*"

He paused, the firelight catching the pride in his voice. "*And so, Laochra was born.*"

I didn't believe for a second that the King had said something so poetic, or was the one to name our little village, but I kept my mouth shut, letting Micaiah finish. His eyes lingered on mine for a moment, as though he expected a comment or challenge, but when I remained silent, he nodded slightly and continued with a glimmer of triumph.

"*Even now, the river glows faintly, deep within the Witrial Woods,*" He said, his voice quieter now, almost reverent. He glanced toward the towering trees that lined the edge of our village, as if the woods themselves were listening. A silent reminder. Always there. Always watching.

"They say that hidden between the trees, the river's waters still hum with magic, alive, pulsing, waiting." He let the words stretch. *"Some claim creatures linger below the surface... hungry, patient, and still biding their time for anyone foolish enough to test the old stories."*

The fire popped, and a few younger listeners shifted nervously.

"But the waters have remained still for a century. Barren. Untouched. No immortal has dared to cross since."

Micaiah's voice dropped further, almost to a whisper. *"And yet, on the stillest nights, if you listen closely, some say you can hear them echoing off the river banks. Faint whispers in the dark, whether from the condemned or the magic itself, no one knows."*

He straightened slightly, the firelight flaring against his profile like punctuation. *"But one truth remains: the river still protects us. Its magic is old and remains a mystery, but it does not forget why it was created and who it was meant to keep out."*

I stared into the fire, my thoughts swirling. The river, the whispers, the deadly magic—it all felt so distant yet so close, like the shadows beyond the trees. I wondered, not for the first time, if the river was truly as impenetrable as the story claimed. And what would happen if an immortal ever found a way to cross it?

The thought sent a shiver down my spine. That was one question, no matter how curious, I didn't dare share aloud.

5. Whispers Of The Forbidden River

The fire crackled low as Micaiah brought his story to its dramatic conclusion. His voice, rich with authority, rang out against the stillness of the night before delivering the final warning.

"But the danger doesn't lie in the river alone," he said, his voice low and deliberate. *"The forest that guards it, the Witrial Woods, holds magic of its own. It seeps through the bark, coils around the roots, and listens to every footstep."*

The familiar warning hung in the air, its weight palpable. Around the fire, the younger children huddled closer, their wide eyes reflecting the flickering flames. Most of the villagers took the cautionary tale as gospel, their fear so deeply ingrained that even the mere mention of the river sent a shiver through the crowd.

But tonight, Micaiah added something extra as he leaned in, his tone dropping into a conspiratorial whisper as he addressed the children sitting cross-legged at the front.

"If there's one lesson to carry from this tale," he said, eyes scanning the circle, *"it's this: stay out of the Witrial Woods. The forest is not your friend. It remembers the blood that was spilled. And it will lure you to the river, not as a*

traveler..."

He paused, his voice barely above a whisper. *"...but as a sacrifice."*

The fire flickered, shadows dancing like branches swaying in windless air. *"And remember,"* he added, his voice heavy with reverence, *"we only know the history of our village because of the brave King Saoine, who risked his own life, and saved this land."*

From the back of the gathering, a booming voice interrupted, *"Obedience to Rioga and all the Kings before!"* The shout echoed through the clearing, breaking the tension. It was Farkas, as usual, his obsession with royal allegiance unmistakable.

I rolled my eyes, biting back a comment. Farkas' unwavering loyalty grated on my nerves, but I couldn't deny that I shared his fascination, though mine wasn't for the Kings themselves but for the fragments of truth buried within their stories. Still, I offered him a silent apology.

Micaiah barely acknowledged the interruption, straightening as he pressed on. *"Yes, our gracious King chronicled every detail of this tale and spread it across the villages. He warned of the immortals' cunning and the river's danger, urging all to guard their homes and hearts against deception. After all, Queen Deardra of Dermaine had done just that—hidden among her people, concealing her true nature."*

I crossed my arms, staring at the fire as his words washed over me. How much of this was the truth? And how much had been twisted, rewritten to suit the King's legacy? My mind raced with questions I'd never dare ask aloud, piecing together fragments of the story like a puzzle with missing pieces.

"—which is why it's important to stay until the end of the fire each week," Micaiah was saying, his voice pulling me back to the present, *"to remember why we can live peacefully and free from immortal terror. To honor the sacrifices made."*

The crowd erupted into applause, and Micaiah gave a theatrical bow. To them, his retelling was a stage performance, a ritual to reaffirm their safety and unity. To me, it was a reminder of how stories could shape—or obscure—reality. How could anyone truly know what lay within the river or the magic it held, if no one had dared to test it in nearly a century? How much of the familiar story was fact, and how much was just old fears, exaggerated over generations and used as a warning?

I lingered by the fire as the villagers dispersed, the sounds of footsteps fading into the night. The embers glowed faintly, casting long shadows across the clearing. A light tug on my arm broke my reverie, and I looked up to meet my grandmother's knowing gaze.

The crowd had vanished, leaving only the two of us.

We walked in silence down the path toward home, the cool night air heavy with the scent of pine and smoke. The faint rustling of leaves was the only sound while I wrestled with the endless questions burning in my mind. Finally, I couldn't hold back.

"Do you think the river actually has the power to kill an immortal?" I asked quietly. My voice barely rose above a whisper, as though the forest itself might be listening. "And why is it called the Forbidden River? Who even named it in the first place?"

My grandmother's arm slipped around my shoulders, pulling me close. Her presence was an anchor against the unease coiled in my chest. She glanced at me, a small smile playing on her lips, though her eyes held something deeper—an echo of old memories.

"I'm not too sure," she admitted, her voice soft but steady. "What I *do* know is that my parents told me the stories passed down to them. Warnings from the past, when villagers heard screams coming from the water's edge." She paused, her gaze distant. "So maybe there *is* some truth to it."

The weight of her words settled over me as we walked on, the shadows of the forest pressing closer with every step. If there was truth in the stories, how much had been lost to fear? And if there were screams, whose voices had been silenced by the river's cold embrace?

We walked the rest of the short distance in silence, the night heavy with unspoken words and unanswered thoughts. The dirt path crunched beneath our feet, the cool air swirling around us as shadows from the trees danced across the ground, shifting with the gentle sway of the branches.

My mind churned, replaying Micaiah's warnings and my grandmother's cautious words, all circling back to the river—the forbidden river.

No one knew how it came to bear that ominous name, but it felt as if the title had always existed, like a divine edict carved into the fabric of our world. A warning from the gods themselves, whispered down through generations, meant to keep us from wandering too close. The name alone held a power that sent chills down the spine—a silent promise of death to any who dared to test its waters.

The tales of what lay within the river's depths were vague, almost as if even the storytellers were too afraid to conjure the details. All we were told was that no one who had ventured into the water ever returned. The river's magic, or perhaps its monsters, was strong enough to kill an immortal, so thinking of what it would do to a human like me was beyond comprehension.

The Witrial Woods loomed ahead, its dark green canopy stretching high into the night, blotting out the stars. The forest was more than a barrier; it was a gateway, standing guard over whatever secrets the river held. The dense undergrowth and towering evergreens seemed alive, their twisted branches forming shapes that hinted at something watching, waiting.

Sometimes, when the wind picked up, it wasn't just the rustle of leaves I heard. There were whispers, faint but unmistakable, carried on the breeze like voices from another world. They seemed to call my name, luring me closer. I wasn't reckless enough to enter—at least, not yet—but the pull was undeniable and warnings could only hold me back for so long.

My grandmother's watchful eyes lingered on me longer than anyone else, especially when we passed the woods. She could see it in me—the restlessness, the yearning for more than the narrow boundaries of our village. Her worried glances were a silent reminder of the danger she saw in me. I promised myself I wasn't impulsive, but I couldn't ignore the voice in the back of my mind wondering how long I could resist, even just stepping in with one foot.

At night, I would sit by my bedroom window, staring at the forest. I could picture the once sparse line of saplings that had since grown into the dense wall of evergreens, their branches intertwining to form an almost impenetrable barrier. The way they swayed in the moonlight felt like an invitation, a dare. My heart would pound at the thought of stepping beyond them, of venturing into the unknown.

The elders spoke of the river in hushed tones, their faces creased with worry whenever it came up. The river was a forbidden topic, mentioned only in the safety of bonfire nights, under their watchful eyes. To them, the river was a terror, a living reminder of something long buried. But to me, it was more than a danger. It was a mystery. And mysteries, no matter how dangerous, always called to me. We weren't even allowed to talk about the river when the heat of summer made the idea of diving into its cool depths so tempting. I'd imagine the refreshing water, the coldness sinking into my skin, and for just a moment, it felt like I was tasting freedom. But of course, I was only left to dream.

My grandmother always made sure to remind us of the precariousness of the river, her voice heavy with the weight of years spent living in Laochra. She'd tell us stories—stories of deadly creatures lurking in the forest, their eyes glinting in the shadows, waiting for the unsuspecting traveler. Her eyes would narrow when they landed on me, always lingering just a moment too long, as if she knew, deep down, I would be the one to ignore her warnings. She was right, of course—because no matter how many times she spoke of the dangers, my curiosity only grew.

There was something about the river that called to me, something I couldn't quite explain. What if it was all an exaggerated story, and there was something beautiful waiting for me beyond those foreboding trees? And the fact that no one had ventured near it in so long only fueled my intrigue. What if there were secrets hidden in that forest, secrets no one had dared to uncover?

Despite everything I was told, I felt called to the forest. I had never even set foot inside, but the mere sight of it—the towering trees, the whispering wind—felt like an invitation. The forest was a living thing, its presence both comforting and unsettling. And the river, always just out of reach, felt like an unattainable promise.

No one, not even the immortals, dared challenge the power of the river. For a hundred years, it had been forbidden—untouchable. And yet, it called to me, an unrelenting whisper in the back of my mind. My grandmother's warnings lingered like shadows, her stories of the river's magic passed down through generations. She spoke of its mysteries, how no one truly knew what would happen if a human stepped into its waters. But the fear it inspired was enough to make even the boldest souls hesitate. Still, whenever I stood in my backyard, staring out at the towering trees that concealed the river from sight, I felt an ache deep in my chest, as though the river itself was pulling me toward it.

I couldn't stop myself—the thought of stepping into those dark woods, of crossing the boundary that had kept the village safe for generations, was intoxicating. What would it feel like to break the rules, to defy everything I'd been taught and uncover the secrets waiting on the other side? The forest wasn't just forbidden; it was a place of untold possibility. The evergreens, once towering obstacles, now felt like an invitation—one I knew I couldn't resist forever. One day, I would leave the safety of my backyard. One day, I would step into the trees and discover what the forest was truly hiding.

6. Beyond The Edge

With thoughts of immortal healers and shimmering rivers swirling in my mind, I slipped into a restless sleep. As always, the forest was there, waiting for me like an old friend cloaked in shadow. This dream wasn't new—it had haunted me in fragments since I was six, always familiar yet ever-changing. Even now, as the cool night air seemed to brush against my skin, I felt the dream's pull, its vivid grasp blurring the line between fantasy and reality.

In the dream, it was early morning. The air carried that crisp bite of autumn, the kind that hinted at colder days ahead but still smelled of lingering leaves and earth. My surroundings seemed sharper in this place, the colors more intense than reality. A peculiar orange-and-green leaf caught my eye as it tumbled gracefully across the dew-kissed grass, spinning in tight circles before stopping like it had been waiting for me.

I crouched down to take a closer look, marveling at how vibrant it was, the veins glowing faintly like threads of gold. When I glanced up, I saw no tree it could have fallen from, only the dense evergreens that lined the edge of the forest. The leaf moved again, this time with a deliberate sort of grace as if carried not by the wind but by an unseen hand. It danced across the ground, toward the shadowed entrance of the woods, beckoning me to follow.

In the real world, I had never stepped past the edge of the forest. My grandmother's warnings had always been enough to keep me at bay. But here, in this dream, there was no fear—only curiosity. The pull was undeniable, a silent promise that something extraordinary waited for me beyond the veil of trees. Without hesitation, I stepped forward, my bare feet sinking into the damp, cool soil.

The forest was alive in a way I couldn't explain. The leaves above whispered secrets as the wind stirred them, creating patterns of light and shadow that seemed to guide my path. The deeper I ventured, the more the world around me seemed to shift. The air grew thicker, humming with a strange, electric energy that I could feel against my skin.

Then I saw it—the blue shimmer of the river, teasing me from the distance. It was barely visible through the trees, but it called to me, just as it always did in these dreams. The light reflected off its surface like liquid diamonds, dazzling and otherworldly. I felt my chest tighten, not with fear but with longing.

As I moved closer, a sound began to weave through the stillness. It wasn't just the rustle of leaves or the distant cry of a bird; it was a melody—soft, haunting, and achingly familiar. It wrapped around me like my grandmother's lullabies, the ones she used to sing when I was small, her voice low and soothing. But this song carried something else—something sharper, more urgent, as though it wanted to be heard but feared being understood.

The closer I got to discovering the river, the louder the song became, until it felt like it was coming from inside me. My heart raced, and my hands tingled, as if they were reaching for something just out of sight. The shimmering water beckoned, the voices within it both warning me to stay away and urging me to step closer.

And then, as always, the dream blurred. The river's glow dimmed, and the song faded into silence. I woke with a start, the air in my room heavy and still. My heart pounded against my rib cage, the pull of the dream still clinging to me.

I lay there in the darkness, staring up at the ceiling, trying to catch my breath. The forest's call echoed in my mind. It always did. No matter how vivid the dream, it left behind more questions than answers, and tonight was no different.

What lay beyond those trees? What secrets did the river hold? And why did it feel like, someday, I'd be the one to uncover them?

I shifted restlessly, trying to fall back asleep, the dream growing more vivid, pulling me deeper into its grip as soon as I closed my eyes. I was back in the forest again, the same familiar trees towering above me. Their bark seemed to ripple, faces carved into the wood like ancient sentinels watching my every move. Their eyes, human-like and unblinking, followed me, their expressions impossible to decipher. Were they curious or cautious? Friendly or foreboding?

I stood frozen, their silent scrutiny rooting me to the spot. My breath hitched as I tried to convince myself they weren't real, but the weight of their gazes pressed down on me, heavy and undeniable. Then, just beyond the dense line of trees, a faint blue light flickered—soft, inviting, and impossibly beautiful.

The blue shimmer tugged at something deep within me; it sparkled like sunlight dancing on water, its glow so vibrant I ached to be closer. My feet moved before I could stop them, carrying me toward the light.

But just as I was about to reach the edge of the water, I felt it: my grandmother's grip. It wasn't physical, not in this dream, but her presence was as real as the soil beneath my feet. Her eyes burned into me, a silent fury heavy with disappointment.

I stopped in my tracks, torn between the pull of the river and the weight of her warning. Her voice echoed in my mind, sharp and unyielding: *'Even dreaming of the river could bring trouble. Don't go looking for things you don't understand.'* The dream began to unravel, her grip dragging me backward until the river's glow faded into darkness.

I stirred awake, her words still ringing in my head. I rolled over in my bed, trying to shake the heaviness in my chest, but the memory of the dream clung to me like a shadow.

Sometimes, the dream lasted longer, changing in small ways. The crisp autumn air might shift to the warmth of summer, or the leaf I followed would become a delicate flower drifting on the breeze. The melody would morph, too, the low and sweet voices replaced by my grandmother's raspy hum.

Yet, no matter how the dream changed, one thing remained constant: I was always my six-year-old self. Too eager, too curious, and always chasing the river I was never allowed to reach.

The first couple of times I had the dream, I woke up in a cold sweat, my heart pounding against my ribs. Sharing a room with my grandmother, she was always at my bedside the moment I bolted upright, her keen eyes fixed on me like she already knew what had stirred me and was flipping through the pages of my thoughts before I could turn them myself.

"Tell me everything," she would say, her voice soft but commanding. My grandmother had a way of sensing the energy and meaning of dreams like she was attuned to something deeper, something beyond the veil of ordinary understanding. If anyone could help me make sense of what I'd seen, it was her.

I recited every detail I could remember: the towering trees, the faces carved into the bark, the creatures with human-like eyes watching me, and, of course, the orange and green leaf. I told her how it drifted ahead of me, almost playful, leading me deeper into the woods, and how, no matter how far I ventured, I never reached the river. She always appeared, pulling me back just before I could glimpse its shimmering surface.

Her response was always the same. *"Dreams are reflections of our subconscious, Raine,"* she'd say, her voice steady but tinged with an edge of worry. *"They reveal our fears and desires, but they don't always reflect the truth."* She was convinced that my inability to see the river was a warning—a clear sign to stay away from it, both in my dreams and in real life.

But staying away was easier said than done.

Each time the dream returned, the pull of the leaf grew stronger, its colors more vibrant, its path more deliberate. It felt like I was being drawn toward something ancient, something hidden just beyond the edges of my understanding. The forest seemed alive in those dreams, its whispers and songs calling me closer. Yet, no matter how desperately I chased the truth, my grandmother would always appear, her presence yanking me back to safety.

Her insistence that the dream was a warning only increased my curiosity. It wasn't just a dream—it couldn't be. The way the leaf hovered in the air, its movements purposeful and teasing, haunted me for years. I couldn't shake the feeling that it was more than just a random fragment of my imagination.

"What does it mean?" I'd ask her again and again, desperate for answers.

"It means you're not ready," she'd reply, her tone final as if that was the end of the discussion. But her eyes would linger on mine a moment too long, and I could see it—the fear behind her sternness, the secrets she was so desperate to keep hidden. But what was I not ready for?

When the dream continued over the years and I shared it with her, I began noticing subtle shifts in her demeanor. At first, she would listen patiently, her face calm and reassuring, her words carefully chosen to comfort me. But one morning, as I recounted every detail—the strange leaf, the songs, the creatures in the trees—I caught something flicker across her face. Worry. It was there for only a moment before she replaced it with her usual soft smile. But that particular smile never quite reached her eyes.

In that fleeting moment, I knew she was lying to me. It wasn't a conscious thought but something deeper, an instinctual knowing that sank into my chest like a stone. My grandmother, the one person I trusted above all others, was keeping something from me. The realization felt like a betrayal—a quiet, insidious crack in the foundation of my unwavering trust in her.

After that, I stopped telling her when the dreams returned.

But even as I kept them to myself, I felt the weight of her silence growing heavier between us. It was a silence louder than any words she could have spoken, filled with unspoken truths I was too afraid to ask about. Sometimes, I'd catch her watching me when she thought I wasn't looking, her expression masked. Was it fear? Regret? Guilt? I couldn't tell. But whatever it was, it confirmed my suspicions: she knew more about the forest and the river than she was letting on.

Whenever we gardened together and I'd find my focus drawn toward the dense line of trees at the edge of our property, she would give me a look—a mix of disapproval and understanding. She always told me the same thing, "It's not safe, Raine. That's all you need to know."

And yet, I couldn't shake the feeling that her warnings weren't just about my safety. They were about something she was trying to hide.

As I grew older, the dream appeared less frequently, but when it did, it felt different—more vivid, more like a memory than a dream. The faces carved into the trees became sharper, their expressions almost alive. The creatures in the forest seemed to study me with more intent, their eyes glinting with recognition. And the river... it was still just out of reach, its blue shimmer teasing me from a distance.

Then, when I was fourteen, the dream shifted.

Instead of the usual silence when my grandmother pulled me out of the forest, she crouched down in front of me, her arms wrapping around me in a tight hug. I remember the warmth of her embrace, the way she whispered in my ear, *"Don't worry, Raine. You're safe. You're always safe with me."*

There was that word again. Safe.

Her voice was steady, but her grip on me was too firm, her tone too insistent, as though she were trying to convince herself as much as me. And then she said something new, something that sent a chill through me: *"Wildheart, I need you to promise me you won't go into the woods again. If you can do that, then this will stay our little secret."*

The first time I had that version of the dream, I woke up startled, my skin damp with sweat. It was so vivid, so detailed, that it felt like my mind had unlocked a hidden memory I didn't know existed. But I told myself it wasn't real. It couldn't be. I would have remembered, wouldn't I?

Still, the words stayed with me, echoing in the quiet corners of my thoughts. My grandmother was hiding something, and if it wasn't about the river or the forest, then it was about me.

I woke early this morning, my mind tangled with the weight of last night's story and the secret I overheard. Micaiah's words replayed in my head, every detail sticking like burrs I couldn't shake off. The healer, the Queen, the dungeon—what had really happened? If anyone could help me untangle the truth, it was my grandmother. She knew more about Rioga's history than anyone. But did I dare bring it up?

Our relationship had only recently returned to the familiar ease I cherished, and I didn't want to risk disrupting it by dredging up old curiosities—the kind that had always made her wary, afraid they'd lead me down paths better left untraveled.

I rolled out of bed, slipping into a pair of baggy pants and a loose sweater. The smell of dew drifted through my open window, and I knew she'd already be in the garden, rising with the sun as she always did. If I wanted to catch her alone, I had to act quickly; Sunday mornings were usually busy around here.

In the kitchen, I busied myself making tea, her favorite blend of lavender, rose, passionflower, and chamomile. It was an old trick of mine, one I hadn't used in years: calm the waters before wading in too deep. The kettle screamed, startling me from my thoughts. I poured the tea into two cups, filling them to the brim, and stepped outside.

The garden was alive with the smell of sage and rosemary, her hands already busy pulling stems from the overflowing beds. She didn't glance up, but I knew she'd sensed me.

"Good morning," she said, her voice calm and steady.

I approached with the tea, a peace offering of sorts. She took one look at the steaming cup and smirked, a knowing expression that said, You're up to something.

Without another word, she handed me a basket and gestured to the sage. "If you're going to hover, you might as well help."

I swallowed hard, realizing my attempt at subtlety had failed before I'd even started. Stress-relief tea? I may as well have been holding a sign saying, This is a trap.

Still, I played along, kneeling beside her and plucking the fragrant stems from the soil. For an hour, we worked side by side, the rhythmic sound of snipping and gathering filling the space between us. My tea cooled, untouched, while my nerves simmered. Every time I opened my mouth, the words died in my throat.

Finally, she broke the silence, glancing at me with a raised brow. "You've been quiet this morning. Something on your mind?"

I cursed my predictability. "So…" I began, my voice shaking despite my best efforts to keep it casual. "I've been thinking about last night. You know how the story mentions the healer not being able to save the Queen? And then her being taken to the dungeon?" The words tumbled out in a rush. "What happened to her after that? Did she escape? Did she die? Or get thrown into the river like Wren said? I just—"

"Raine, my curious child," she interrupted gently, setting down her shears. Her expression shifted with something I couldn't quite place— concern, maybe, or reluctance—before settling into calm neutrality. "No one knows what became of her because the King never thought to document her further. She was just a small part of the story, and the focus was always on how our world came to be."

And that was that. Her hands returned to the basket, plucking sage as if she hadn't just shattered my hope for answers, but then her hand lingered, and she softly added, "I like to imagine the King granted her mercy, that she fled before they created the river and headed back to her home. But truthfully, no one can say for sure. The King never mentioned that part in his story, so I fear her fate is lost to time."

Her answer was simple and practical. It should have been enough. But it wasn't.

I stayed quiet, pretending to accept her words, even as the ache of unanswered questions gnawed at me. She moved on to the next row, her voice soft as she began humming a sweet, familiar tune, the same one that echoed in my dreams.

I picked up my basket and followed her, forcing myself to focus on the earthy scent of the herbs and the warmth of the sun on my back. If she didn't know the truth, no one would. Chasing it would only drive me mad.

But as I worked, I couldn't shake the feeling that somewhere, someone knew more. And I wasn't sure I could let it go.

The rest of the day passed in quiet simplicity. We gathered for a hearty breakfast, as was our tradition when everyone was home and Dad and Baren discussed their upcoming three-day merchant trip. By mid-morning, they were gone, their laughter and heavy footfalls fading as they rode off toward the city. Wren had stationed himself out back, cleaning daggers and arrows with practiced ease, preparing for his own training classes tomorrow. Mom, ever the social butterfly, had left to visit a friend, experimenting with a new recipe she planned to teach this week.

A typical Sunday—everyone together briefly before scattering to their routines. And yet, I felt restless, out of place in the mundane. The quiet was too loud, the stillness too stifling.

With nothing pressing to do, I decided to walk through the village. The streets were lively with neighbors chatting, children playing, and the animals mulling around the fields. I nodded and smiled as I passed familiar faces, trying not to draw unnecessary attention, but my attention was elsewhere.

It wasn't long before my eyes drifted to the Witrial Woods in the distance. Standing at the edge of the woods in our backyard, I'd often swear the trees were breathing, their leaves rustling not with the wind, but with breath. The air around the forest always felt thicker, charged with an energy I couldn't explain, like a storm was about to break but never did. Sometimes, I could feel it tugging at me, a force that wrapped around my chest and pulled me closer, whispering promises of secrets hidden within.

One day, I was certain I'd heard music—soft and melodic, like a lullaby floating on the breeze. It was faint, almost indistinct, but it stopped me in my tracks. The tune was hauntingly familiar, echoing the muffled songs from my dreams. Against my better judgment, I'd ventured close to the edge of the woods to retrieve one of Wren's arrows and hear more. But as I neared the treeline, the music faded, leaving me with nothing but the sound of my own breathing and the steady rustle of the wind. But as I bent to pick up the arrow, I saw them—tiny, glowing figures flitting between the trees. Fairies. Or at least, that's what they looked like. I'd stood frozen, my heart pounding, as I watched their delicate wings shimmer in the dappled sunlight.

The memory sent a shiver down my spine. The trees themselves felt alive, their twisted, gnarled trunks resembling ancient hands reaching for the sky. Moss clung to the ground in thick, velvety layers, and the air was heavy with the scent of damp earth and decaying leaves. It was beautiful, yes, but also overwhelming, as though the forest were a being with a will of its own. The very ground alive and pulsing with forgotten magic.

Maybe it was all in my head. Maybe it was just my imagination, fueled by years of dreams that had blurred the lines between fantasy and reality. But deep down, I wasn't so sure.

The faces in the trees, the songs in the wind, the pull of the forest—they didn't feel like figments of a child's imagination anymore. They felt real, tangible, like pieces of a larger puzzle waiting to be uncovered.

What if everything I thought I knew was a lie?

The thought lingered, heavy in my mind, as I walked toward the heart of Laochra. The village square had been bustling with firelight and excitement last night, but was just an empty space connecting the roads today.

Back in July, I remember returning from the bonfire, the smell of smoke and chocolate still clinging to my hair. The night was unusually quiet, the kind of quiet that presses in on you. I was restless and not ready for sleep, so I walked out to the backyard, my favorite spot to unwind, and heard it—a faint noise, something like the soft rustling of wings. Curious, I looked up.

There it was, a massive bird, its wings cutting through the moonlight like blades. The bird was unlike anything I'd ever seen, its black feathers so dark they seemed to drink in the light around them. It circled gracefully, its wingspan stretching impossibly wide, casting a shadow over the edge of the woods. For a moment, I was entranced, rooted to the spot, staring at this strange, majestic creature.

I turned back, hoping to get my grandmother's attention, to come outside and point it out, but before I even reached the door, it was gone— vanished into the night as if it had never been there at all.

I told myself it was impossible, that birds don't just disappear, but the memory of its wings lingered in my mind. In the weeks that followed, I spotted it again, or at least I thought I did. Sometimes during my training, when the world felt quiet and still, I'd catch a glimpse of it in the distance. Other times, during my morning runs, I'd hear the faint beat of wings overhead, only to look up and find nothing there.

I began to think of it as my guardian bird and named it Onyx, for the way its feathers shone like polished stone in the faintest light. But it only ever appeared when I was alone, which made me question whether it was real at all. Maybe I was letting my imagination get the better of me, weaving stories to make the forest even more mysterious than it already was. Nevertheless, every time the bird appeared, I couldn't help feeling envious of its beauty, its freedom, and the ability to fly wherever it desired.

I sat in the backyard, letting the afternoon sun warm my face, a cup of tea in my hand, while watching my grandmother finish her harvest. The soft breeze carried the scents of rosemary and lavender, mingling with the earthy aroma of soil freshly turned. It was peaceful, a perfect day to let my mind wander. Her hands moved with practiced ease as she separated the sage leaves from their stems, humming softly under her breath, and I thought back to this morning when I asked her about the healer from the stories. She hadn't given me the answers I hoped for, but watching her now, I was reminded that she held her own quiet healing power.

She wasn't formally trained, but everyone in the village knew her as the one to turn to for remedies and tonics. Our garden wasn't just a source of food; it was her apothecary and medicine cabinet. There was something ethereal about the way she worked with plants, using every part for food or medicine, trading her knowledge and remedies for other goods the villagers offered.

As a child, I'd sit beside her, watching as she mixed herbs and flowers with an almost instinctual precision. She knew which plant eased headaches, which flower soothed burns, and which roots could help an aching stomach. She'd once told me it was knowledge passed down from her mother, who had learned from a healer herself.

And now, I couldn't help but wonder—was there a connection between that healer and the one in the stories? The thought sent a spark of curiosity racing through me. What if the knowledge my grandmother carried was more than just practical wisdom? What if it was a link to the past, to a lineage that stretched back to the days of the cursed river and the Queen's betrayal?

I looked toward the trees, the edge of the woods blurred by the heat of the afternoon sun, and felt the familiar pull in my chest. The river, the bird, the immortal healer—they were all connected somehow. I just didn't know how or why. But I was determined to find out.

My fingers brushed the edges of a rosemary sprig I'd plucked from my tea, its fragrance lingering on my fingertips. I smiled faintly, the scent bringing back memories of childhood, when I was my grandmother's constant shadow. Wherever she went, I followed, her small apprentice in the garden, the kitchen, and even the market. I much preferred her company to that of the other girls in the village. There were only five near my age, and they seemed to thrive on gossip and stolen glances at the boys training in the fields.

Those same boys—loud, brash, and laser-focused on preparing for a war we all knew would never come—had no time for someone like me, and honestly, I didn't care much for their attention. The girls teased me for my disinterest and called me odd for spending more time with herbs than with people, but I stopped trying to fit in with them long ago. They didn't understand me, and I didn't have the patience to try and explain myself.

I sighed softly, my eyes shifting to my grandmother as she moved to the next bed of herbs, her hands deftly plucking leaves and stems. My brothers, Baren and Wren, had always seemed to lead far more exciting lives—training with weapons, learning survival skills, venturing out of the village in ways I could only dream of. I envied them.

Sometimes, I even wished I'd been born a boy. Not because I hated being a girl, but because it felt like the world would have opened up to me in a way it never would now. I shook off the thought, trying to ground myself in the moment, but the ache of what I would never have always lingered.

I wanted more. More than the quiet, predictable days of village life, more than a life measured by the herbs in our garden and the passing seasons. I wanted to see the world, to uncover its mysteries, to know what lay beyond the trees that had stood watch over my childhood like ancient sentinels. But every time I thought about stepping over that boundary, I felt the weight of the warnings pulling me back. Yet, even with her words ringing in my ears, the pull of the unknown was always a little stronger.

Now that the afternoon sun had started to dip, Wren was out back with us, his practiced movements fluid and sharp as he worked through a ridge-hand strike. He'd been talking nonstop about shadowing his trainer tomorrow, excited by the prospect of teaching one day. While I watched him, my fingers tightened around the cup in my hands. I wanted it too.

When I was eight, I'd begged to train alongside my brothers. We wrestled on weekends, tumbling through the grass, and I even won some of the time—enough to think I had a chance at being a soldier. I'd been so excited, imagining myself wielding a blade, learning to fight, and becoming something stronger.

But when I told my father, he'd only smiled and said, "Training isn't the place for a little girl. There's blood and bruising, injuries you don't need to see or endure. It's better this way, my little Wildheart."

That night, I'd cried myself to sleep, my heart heavy with disappointment. I finally found something that excited me, something I felt I could be good at, and I wasn't even allowed to try. I'd never felt more out of place, more unsure of where I belonged.

As Wren moved through his strikes, his expression focused, I felt that old ache creeping back in. I didn't fit in with the other girls. I didn't belong among the boys. And sometimes, I wondered if I belonged anywhere at all.

7. Threads Of Destiny

The morning air was sharper than I expected, the kind of chill that bit straight through my clothes and set my nerves on edge. I stood at the forest's edge, staring into the shadows between the trees, where the golden leaves of early autumn swayed in the wind like they were trying to tell me something. The pull in my gut was as strong as it had ever been, maybe stronger, and for a moment, it felt like the forest was breathing—alive and aware.

It had been years since I stood this close, and yet, nothing about it had changed. The same whispering wind, the same quiet chattering of birds somewhere deep within. It was the same dream I'd had since I was a child: the forest calling to me, offering a glimpse of something extraordinary just beyond reach. But today, this wasn't a dream, and I wasn't six years old anymore.

I closed my eyes, trying to steady my breath, but the memories rushed back anyway, vivid and overwhelming. I could see myself as a child, tiny hands reaching for a glowing leaf I swore wasn't real. Back then, I was desperate to follow that pull, to step over the invisible boundary that separated the village from the woods. But my grandmother's voice would always cut through the haze of my curiosity, sharp and clear.

"Don't go too far, Raine. The forest... it's not what it seems."

I could still hear her now, the words like an echo that wouldn't leave me. But this time, she wasn't here to stop me. Neither was Wren, off in the city training, nor my father, too far away to notice the boundaries I was testing. I was alone, free to make my own choice.

A twig cracked under my foot, snapping me back to the present. I looked down at the damp earth where my boot had sunk slightly, the rich soil clinging to the edges. My heart pounded, though I wasn't sure if it was from the sound or the realization of how close I was to stepping over the line.

I shouldn't be here.

But I couldn't ignore the pull any longer. It was stronger than fear, stronger than reason, stronger than every warning my grandmother had ever given me.

I remembered my father re-telling my grandfather's stories, the way his voice softened when he talked about the lands beyond the river, where people lived in houses carved from stone and gardens were overflowing with flowers as if magic itself had grown them. As a child, I'd imagined myself there, walking through those villages, marveling at wonders I'd only heard about in whispered tales.

"One day, you'll see them for yourself," he'd said, ruffling my hair with a grin. "If you're lucky, you'll see things I've only dreamed of."

But my grandfather's stories felt like fragments of a world I'd never know. Standing here, so close to the forest, I wondered if I'd ever escape this village. Was I destined to live my life within these walls, bound by duty and tradition, or was there something waiting for me out there, just beyond the trees?

The forest felt alive, its shadows shifting as though they were watching me, waiting for me to decide. My grandmother's voice echoed in my mind again, a ghostly reminder.

"Don't go too far..."

I took another step, my foot sinking deeper into the soft earth. The air here was heavier, charged with something I couldn't name. It stood silent, its shadows stretching like an invitation, and I let my thoughts wander, tethered to the line between what was and what could be. What if the forest wasn't just calling to me but offering me exactly what I needed? Something the village could never give—a chance to break free of the expectations that felt like shackles tightening around me with every passing year.

I hesitated, caught between the familiar safety of the village and the unknown that loomed ahead. The wind picked up, rustling the trees, and for a moment, it almost sounded like a voice, low and inviting.

I wasn't sure if it was bravery or recklessness, but I knew one thing: I couldn't stand at the edge forever.

I had always wanted more. The other girls in Laochra dreamed of courtship, of being the center of the home, of a future that revolved around familial duties and children. They saw it as the pinnacle of their lives, something to strive for. But for me, it felt like stepping into a cage. The thought of spending the rest of my days embroidering, pouring tea, or making bread, and attending festivals just to impress a future husband made my skin itch. Every time I sat through one of those etiquette lessons, forced to smile and nod while the elder droned on about proper posture and delicate manners, I wanted to scream. It wasn't that I didn't appreciate the life my village offered, but it felt too small for me.

Even now, I could picture the girls I'd grown up with in five years' time—married with children tumbling at their feet, their cottages full of warmth and laughter. A life stitched neatly within the borders of Laochra. And maybe that could have been my future too, if I'd wanted it.

But the thought of bowing to the rhythm of village life made my chest tighten. Courting, marriage, a household to tend—it felt like suffocating punishment disguised as tradition, the kind everyone blindly accepted without asking for more.

While the other girls whispered about potential suitors and spun fantasies of who might ask them to dance at the next fire festival, I dreamed of something else entirely. Streets lined with shops displaying spices and foods I couldn't name, the air alive with scents I'd never smelled before. Market stalls bursting with colors I'd never seen, filled with voices and music drifting through the crowd, where strangers traded not just handmade goods but stories.

My father's tales painted those places into my mind, cities that pulsed with life, where peace once wove humans and immortals together, where freedom was more than a rumor. He might have never been outside of Rioga's borders, but he'd heard stories about how different Luminara once was. How merchants would roam all three territories freely, and I knew he longed for that freedom, too, even if he never said it aloud. I also knew that longing was the spark that lit the fire in me, where my restlessness was born.

He always returned from his journeys with fragments of the world beyond Laochra, as though he knew I needed proof it was real. Fabric dyed in impossible hues. A herb so sharp its scent clung to my skin for days. Chocolate so rich that it melted like sin on my tongue. I hoarded them like treasures, each one a reminder that something greater waited beyond these narrow streets and familiar faces.

And then there was Wren. Reckless, sharp-tongued, forever laughing off rules he broke simply by existing. Sure, he loved to joke about kissing, and maybe he liked the thrill of attention from girls, but I knew he didn't want to settle down here either. He had dreams bigger than Laochra, too, dreams of Rioga City and a place in the King's guard. It stung knowing he could chase that freedom, while for me it remained only a dream.

But Wren understood me in a way no one else did. He recognized the same hunger in me. While Baren treated me like glass, something fragile that needed protection, Wren saw me for what I was: restless, unyielding, unwilling to accept the role carved for me. Our secret training sessions were never just about blades, bows, or sparring; it was an act of rebellion. A way to steal back a piece of the freedom we both craved. Out in the clearing, under an open sky, sparring with my brother, I felt closer to the girl I wanted to be. Someone stronger. Braver. Someone more than what was expected of me. And every time he let me win, *because I knew he did*, I tasted a life just beyond my reach.

The Witrial Woods loomed ahead, its silence filled with a tapestry of shadows threaded with promise. What if stepping beyond the border was exactly what I needed to be free? Maybe the woods were the doorway I'd been waiting for. A beginning, not an end. I drew in a breath, the cool air biting my lungs as I let it steady me. My eighteenth birthday was approaching, and with it the chance to finally decide who I was meant to be. I didn't know what my future looked like or what awaited me, only that it wasn't in Laochra. And I wondered, *not for the first time*, if my need to escape was strong enough to pull me across that line of trees.

My family had always been the one constant, the anchor that steadied me, and the reason I hesitated whenever I imagined leaving Laochra behind. We were close, clinging to time together even as we grew older and our paths began to drift. I pitied my parents in a way, though. All three of their children had resisted the traditions that marked adulthood—courting, marriage, settling down. Not because of anything lacking at home. If anything, it was the opposite.

My parents' love was the kind most people spent their lives searching for. We saw it in the way my father's hand always found my mother's when he returned from his travels, in the way her face lit at the sound of his voice, in how his shoulders unburdened the moment their eyes met. Their love was steady, luminous, undeniable. But instead of filling me with dreams of finding the same, it left me questioning. If such rare devotion existed here within our walls, what else might exist beyond them? What wonders, or truths, waited in the world outside?

Baren, my oldest brother, never understood my need to rebel. He had always been fiercely protective of me, but as we grew older, it hardened into something that felt less like comfort and more like confinement. He believed my place was in Laochra, accepting the life every girl was expected to lead—preparing for marriage and motherhood, learning homemaking skills, and remaining safe within the village walls. I knew he thought he was doing what he should by looking out for me, but his refusal to see anything beyond tradition only made me feel smaller. And the more he pushed about what I *should* want, the more I rebelled, wanting to prove him wrong.

At first, I fought him openly, arguing, demanding to be included in things he believed weren't meant for girls. But my defiance only confirmed his belief that I was immature and still a child in his eyes. So rebellion took on another shape. Training became more than defiance—it became a way to prove I was strong and capable. Each bruise, every small victory, carved a space where I could exist on my own terms. A place where I didn't have to fit neatly into the mold laid out for me.

Baren's disapproval didn't discourage me. If anything, it drove me forward, becoming more determined to prove him wrong.

But I could never explain it properly—not to him, not to my mother, not even to Wren. It wasn't that I *hated* Laochra or the life my family had built here. I cherished the safety, the love, the closeness of home. What I couldn't bear was the inevitability, the way every passing day drew me closer to a future I didn't want. The weight of expectations pressed down on me, heavy and suffocating, like invisible chains tightening as my eighteenth birthday crept closer.

Soon, I would finish my lessons and would be expected to choose. Would I focus on courtship, homemaking, and honing the skills that would make me a great wife and mother in the future, or get a respectable job? A job was ideal, but the type of work that stirred something in me, that made my heart race, was all beyond Laochra's walls. Existing in places I'd never seen, the same cities my father spoke of with wonder, places alive with stories, color, and change.

And yet, dreaming of leaving was easier than stepping into the unknown. As much as I longed for a future beyond this village, the thought of walking through the woods, of navigating unfamiliar places alone, terrified me. I wasn't ready. *Not yet.*

So I was stuck, lingering in the in-between, caught between the safety I knew and the possibility I ached for. Each day felt like standing on the edge of a cliff, staring at the world below, knowing I could leap but unsure if I was brave enough to spread my wings.

When I was younger, I'd sit cross-legged by the hearth, clinging to every word of my father's stories. He spoke of cities that glittered long after nightfall, markets bursting with color and sound, mountains that cut the sky in the distance, and air that smelled of salt and freedom. Each tale painted a picture of a world much wider than our three quiet streets, and I'd hug my knees, aching for the day I might see it all for myself.

For a long time, I dreamed I'd follow in his steps, take over the merchant trade, and never live the same day twice. It seemed so natural—to explore, to barter, to let life unfold with the unexpected. But tradition didn't bend for dreams. The trade had been passed to him from my mother's father, Edric, who had taught my father everything he knew since he had no sons of his own. So, when it came to inheritance, the path was clear: it would pass to a son, even one who wasn't blood related, but not a daughter.

My father always said the journeys were exhausting, but worth it—the time away made home sweeter. I envied him that balance, the way he could taste the world and still return to love waiting at the door. I used to watch my mother's face brighten the moment she spotted his carriage in the distance, joy so radiant it filled the house before he even stepped inside. Their love was almost magical in its simplicity, but it never stirred in me the desire to chase a romance of my own. If anything, it proved that love could wait—adventure couldn't.

Most girls in Laochra never questioned the life set out for them: mornings filled with chores, afternoon lessons in homemaking, etiquette, and any other skill that would appeal to prospective suitors. By eighteen, they'd be ready to court with the intention of marriage and starting a family, their paths already stitched neat and small. They were content with that, but I never was.

Our schedules were pretty structured growing up with reading, writing, and history, but at the age of fifteen, the curriculum changed. Gone were lessons on basic skills and knowledge, and our learning became a reflection of the lives we were expected to lead. The girls' classes focused on homemaking and other skills that would prepare us to be good wives and mothers.

We got to choose which topics to pursue, creating a path tailored to our strengths and future roles. Some leaned into weaving, sewing, or managing a household budget. Others explored cooking, gardening, or childcare. But nothing appealed to me.

I wanted more than the routine that governed our lives. I wanted more than the neatly sewn hems and the perfectly baked pies. I wanted the thrill of walking through a new city, the wind from a distant shore in my hair, the chance to make my own choices.

The boys were different. By fifteen, they started focusing on whether they wanted to learn a trade skill or train for a position in the King's army. My brothers envied the ease with which my classes turned. To them, my life was enviable—free of bruises, sore muscles, long hours in training, and the heavy expectations of becoming soldiers and providers.

Wren had always known he wanted to be a trainer; he spoke of it with certainty that made my chest ache. Whether for the army or smaller village groups, it didn't matter to him; he just wanted to teach and lead.

When I was ten, I begged Baren to let me train with him. He laughed it off, patronizing, saying it wasn't for girls. But Wren surprised me. When Baren was around, he'd shake his head with a small smile and say I wouldn't enjoy the strict routines they had to follow, or that there was no need to learn when there would never be a threat in Laochra to defend against. But one afternoon when Baren was away, he tossed a wooden sword at my feet, mischief lighting his eyes as he took in my dirt-stained knees and hands. "Come on, Wildheart. Let's see what you've got."

And then we continued our lessons in secret over the years, the days spent learning how to defend myself becoming my lifeline. Wren never treated me like I was fragile, though I knew he held back to keep me from getting hurt. He made it seem like he was the one benefiting, using me to sharpen his skills, but I knew better. He wanted me to feel strong, capable, and included. And when Baren found out and scolded him for indulging my fantasies and encouraging my restlessness, Wren always had the perfect excuse. "She's good practice for me to train," he'd say with a casual shrug.

I knew it wasn't entirely true, but I appreciated it anyway. Wren indulged me because he believed in me, even if he didn't understand why I was so adamant about learning how to fight.

So I built a double life. By day, I learned the skills my mother and grandmother passed down, focusing on gardening, cooking, and the things expected of me within the house. But in stolen hours, I trained. Early mornings in the yard, afternoons with makeshift weapons hidden among the tools in the shed.

It was the perfect arrangement. By staying home during the day, I avoided the prying eyes of villagers or other girls in their tailored classes. It also gave me the freedom to train at home in secret. To the villagers, I was simply a dutiful daughter learning the skills I'd need to one day run a household. But in my heart, I was someone else entirely—someone who refused to be small and stuck here.

Wren saw it, saw my drive, my devotion, my fierce determination, and thankfully never doubted me. His belief kept the fire inside me alive. With every sparring match, I felt the taste of freedom, sharp and intoxicating. For those fleeting hours, I wasn't just another girl in Laochra, bound by the rhythm of tradition. I was Raine—wild, relentless, and dreaming of a future as vast and untamed as the world my father's stories promised.

8. To Trust Or Betray

Waking up alone on a Tuesday morning wasn't unusual. It was almost comforting in its predictability. My grandmother was probably out tending to an elderly friend, her laughter and wisdom carrying over tea and cookies. Baren was with Dad, still trying to decide if the life of a merchant was what he wanted. They wouldn't be back until tomorrow evening. Wren had stayed in Rioga last night, claiming training had run late. Suspicious as it sounded, I couldn't help but marvel at the thought of him away from Laochra, seeing places I could only dream about. Mom was likely at Mara's house, her best friend for years, and my go-to guess whenever she was unaccounted for.

Barefoot, I padded down the stairs, the cold wood sending a little jolt through my toes. The morning air carried a sharp chill, a reminder that summer's warmth was starting to slip away. I made a cup of tea, wrapping my hands around the mug as the steam warmed my face. Heading back upstairs, I paused by the window. The scent of pine and damp soil drifted in through the screen, grounding me.

I closed my eyes, breathing deeply. The house was utterly still, wrapped in a kind of quiet that felt rare and precious. For a moment, I let myself sink into it, the quietness of today pulling me back to another morning—one so similar it felt as though time hadn't moved at all.

It had been exactly a year ago, a week before my seventeenth birthday. I remember it vividly. It was an early Saturday, the kind where the sun barely kissed the tops of the trees and the promise of fall was just beginning to show in the faintly golden edges of the leaves. The days were still warm, but the mornings carried a briskness that hinted at the change to come.

The house had been empty then too; everyone scattered for one reason or another. For the first time in what felt like ages, the silence wasn't oppressive—it was liberating. I'd grown used to waking at dawn to train on weekends, but without Wren's guidance, the urgency to rise with the sun had faded. Still, his voice echoed in my mind, as it often did: *"A soldier out of practice is as useless as one with no training at all."*

So I practiced—alone.

That morning, the house felt emptier than usual, too. Not even my grandmother was outside, at least not where I could see her. It was just me, and for once, I marveled in the solitude. It was a chance to claim the space as my own, to breathe without anyone else's expectations pressing in around me.

My training wasn't the same without Wren's steady encouragement or the occasional teasing that broke up the intensity. But I still felt the thrill of it. The weight of a dagger in my hand, the precise pull of a bowstring—it wasn't just practice. It was rebellion. It was power.

I remember stepping out onto the dew-damp grass, the air crisp against my skin. The dagger felt heavy in my grip at first, but as I moved through the drills Wren had taught me, it became an extension of myself. Each strike, each block, each step forward was a reminder of how far I'd come. These weren't skills I was supposed to have. Girls like me weren't meant to wield daggers or nock arrows. But I did, and every perfect strike felt like a quiet victory against the world that tried to box me in.

That morning, I wasn't just Raine, the girl from Laochra. I was something more—someone who could shape her own destiny. Alone in the stillness, with the rhythm of my movements and the steady thud of my heartbeat, I felt it. Freedom. That day, a year ago, had been the first time I truly felt it: the pull, the unshakable desire to break free from the life everyone else thought I was meant to live. I knew I wanted more. I just didn't know what *'more'* was yet.

My family had tried to understand; *tried being the keyword.*

When I sat them down after my birthday later that week, explaining that I wasn't planning to court at eighteen like the other girls, their reactions had been…mixed. Dad had nodded, more out of respect than approval, while Mom pursed her lips and asked, "Are you sure?" Baren had barely contained his disapproval, muttering something about "selfishness." Wren, of course, had smirked, his usual way of showing support without saying a word. They had known for years I wasn't like the other girls—I never hid it—but knowing and accepting were two different things.

The month before that dreadful conversation was the catalyst that helped solidify my reasoning that I was just built differently. It was after the annual bonfire, the kind of night when the stars shone so brightly you could almost forget how small our town was. Wren had invited me to the "after-party" at the old barn—a rare gesture that left me both anxious and excited. I'd never been to one of these gatherings before, but it felt like a rite of passage, a chance to be included in something bigger than myself.

When we arrived, the barn was alive with laughter and whispers. Boys and girls paired off, disappearing into corners or sneaking outside, and for the first time that night, unease crept over me. This wasn't my world. The excitement I'd felt earlier by being included was replaced by a hollow discomfort as I watched them giggle and flirt. I'd never cared about courting the way the other girls did. While they gossiped about who they'd marry, I spent my time training, dreaming of places beyond Laochra.

Then Henri came over.

He wasn't someone I knew well, though I'd seen him around town. Tall, broad-shouldered, sandy blonde hair, and an air of arrogance that seemed to precede him. He sauntered up with a smirk that set my teeth on edge, looking at me like I was a challenge he was eager to conquer. Something inside me snapped.

When he stepped closer, the words he said were lost in the roar of my pulse. He leaned forward, closing his eyes as his lips drifted towards mine, and without thinking, I drew back my fist and punched him square in the throat.

The barn went silent.

Henri stumbled, gasping for air, his eyes wide with shock and humiliation. The other boys stared, frozen in place, while the girls covered their mouths to stifle gasps. It was as if time itself paused, everyone waiting to see what would happen next.

I didn't wait. As Henri clutched his throat, I leaned in, smiling sweetly, and whispered, "I don't know what gave you the impression that I would ever want to kiss you, but I'll spell it out. I'd rather face the river's curse 100 times than ever kiss someone as revolting as you."

The insult landed harder than my punch. Rage flared in his eyes, and he lunged for me. But before he could reach me, Wren was there, grabbing the edge of his shirt and yanking him back.

Henri's momentum faltered, and in that split second, I kicked him in the gut. Hard.

He doubled over, and as Wren released him, he crumpled to the dirt floor with a loud thud that echoed through the barn. The silence turned into hushed murmurs. I could feel their eyes on me, wide with disbelief.

Still, I wasn't done. He needed to learn to ask before casually walking up to someone and expecting them to kiss you back. Calmly, I bent down, extending my hand to Henri as if offering to help him up. He hesitated, glaring at me with a mixture of fury and humiliation, but eventually reached out. Just as his fingers grazed mine, I pulled my hand back, kissed my index and middle fingers mockingly, and pressed them to his scowling lips.

His brow furrowed further, and his face turned beet red as the barn erupted into stunned laughter.

I spun on my heel, grinning, and left without looking back, Wren trailing silently behind me. We walked home in silence, his arm in mine, the night air cool against my flushed skin. Wren didn't say anything, but he didn't need to. His steady presence told me everything I needed to know: he was proud of me.

Now, over a year later, Henri's insults, calling me "crazy girl" or "spinster forever," were a distant memory. The boys in town avoided me, crossing the street if they saw me coming, but it didn't bother me. If anything, it amused me. I wasn't the one who'd left that barn with a bruised ego.

I wasn't even the girl they whispered about anymore. I was a woman who knew her strength. And while I still didn't know exactly where life would take me, I was certain of one thing: wherever I ended up, it wouldn't be as someone else's idea of who I should be.

Smiling to myself as I recalled that day in the barn, I glanced back out the window in my room. My grandmother was back in the garden, her weathered hands busy gathering herbs. She caught my eye and waved, a serene smile on her face. I waved back and turned toward the closet, my thoughts shifting to the day ahead. My eighteenth birthday was only a week away, and though everyone else seemed to think it was monumental, I didn't feel any different. Sure, I was one year older, but nothing extraordinary was waiting for me, just the vague expectation to figure out my life.

With a sigh, I rifled through my closet, searching for my training clothes. My thicker pants were predictably buried under a heap of crumpled sweaters. Yanking them free, I stumbled back, tripping over the pile and landing on the hard floor in an undignified heap. "Great start, Raine," I muttered, untangling myself.

As I sat there, brushing my hair out of my face, a flash of silver caught my eye. Frowning, I leaned forward to get a better look. There, resting on my grandmother's bed, was her journal.

My breath hitched.

I couldn't remember ever seeing her journal left out like this. She carried it everywhere, always tucked safely in her deep pockets or tucked under her arm. It wasn't just a book to her—it was an extension of herself, a piece of her soul she kept close. She was always jotting down new tonics, heartfelt words from my mom, or even tallying up my victories against Wren during our training sessions.

When I was younger, I'd begged to read it once, but she'd refused with a firm but kind smile. *"Some things are meant to be private, my dear. A journal is where the heart whispers its secrets. Promise me you won't peek without permission."* I had promised, and up until this moment, I'd never been tempted.

But now… it was right there.

The silver buckle gleamed in the soft light filtering through the window, and I swore, for just a moment, it shimmered unnaturally, like moonlight on water. My pulse quickened. That wasn't possible, was it? Shaking my head, I tried to dismiss the thought, but something about the journal felt off. It seemed to hum, a faint vibration that I might've imagined but couldn't ignore.

I stood slowly, my eyes darting to the window. My grandmother was still in the garden, her back to the house. Surely this was some kind of test. She liked to do that—leave a tempting distraction to see if I'd stay disciplined. Or maybe she'd just forgotten it.

The thought was almost laughable. My grandmother didn't forget things.

The pull of the journal grew stronger like it was calling to me with a reverent hum. But that was impossible, journals couldn't hum. My fingers itched to open it but I told myself to look away, to focus on something else, even as my curiosity gnawed at me. I always wondered how she had kept the same journal for decades without running out of space. What was so important that she kept it with her always?

Before I could second-guess myself, I crossed the room and reached for it. My hand hovered over the buckle, my heart pounding in my chest.

Just one look, I told myself. Just to see.

The buckle clicked open with a sound that seemed to echo in the quiet room. I winced, my gaze darting to the door. Nothing. Letting out a breath, I flipped open the cover, half-expecting to see her familiar handwriting scrawled across the pages.

But the first page was blank.

I frowned and turned to the next. And the next. Blank. Every single page was empty.

That didn't make sense. I'd watched her write in this journal almost every day. It was her ritual—early mornings with tea or late nights by the fire. So why were the pages empty?

My fingers traced the edges of the leather, lingering on the slash mark I knew so well. She'd told me the story of that mark a hundred times—how it was left by the blade of a thief during a fight with my grandfather at her side. This was her journal. There was no mistaking it.

The hum from within grew louder, sending a chill down my spine. It wasn't just my imagination. Something about this journal was alive, and it was responding to me, luring me in the same way the forest did.

Before I could process what was happening, the faint creak of the kitchen door broke the silence.

I froze.

Footsteps echoed through the house, soft but deliberate. My heart pounded as I fumbled to close the journal. The hum faded the instant the buckle clicked back into place, leaving me with only the sound of my ragged breathing.

The footsteps were on the stairs now.

I shoved the journal back onto her bed and turned to the scattered clothes on the floor, pretending to search for something as the door creaked open behind me. In a panic, grabbing the nearest thing my hand could find, a small hair clip off the floor, I blurted "Found it!" and held it up with a sheepish grin that even I didn't believe.

Her sharp eyes flicked to the bed, where the journal rested untouched—or so it appeared. She said nothing, only giving me a small, knowing smile.

"Breakfast is ready," she said after a pause. "Don't take too long." She moved with her usual unhurried grace, walking over to her bed to pick up the journal.

I held my breath, my pulse roaring in my ears as she clasped the journal tightly against her side and turned to leave. For a fleeting moment, I thought I was in the clear. Relief started to bloom in my chest.

But then she paused.

The door creaked open again, and she stepped back inside, her stare sharper this time, amusement dancing in her eyes. Without saying a word, she reached over to my side table, swiped a pen, and gave me a look that sent a chill down my spine.

It wasn't anger. It wasn't disappointment.

It was knowing.

She knew. Somehow, she always knew.

I sat rooted to the spot, unable to speak, unable to even move, as she gave me one last glance—a faint smirk playing on her lips—before she turned and left the room for good. The kitchen door creaked open and closed again moments later, signaling her return to the garden.

I finally exhaled fully, my chest heaving as the tension drained from my body. But the relief was fleeting, replaced almost instantly by a gnawing feeling deep in my gut.

This had been a test. A deliberate test. And I had failed.

I stared at the spot on the bed where the journal had been, my mind racing with questions I couldn't answer. The blank pages. The strange humming. The way the journal had to have been overflowing with decades of stories, yet it appeared completely ordinary from the outside.

What was she hiding? And why had the journal called to me like that, as if it wanted to be opened and discovered?

The thought unsettled me, but it also sparked something else—determination.

I wasn't a child anymore. Whatever secrets my grandmother had been keeping from me, whatever truths she thought I wasn't ready for, I would uncover them. I couldn't ignore the pull any longer, the sense that there was something bigger at play—something she'd hidden in plain sight for years.

I clenched my fists, my resolve hardening. And if she wasn't going to tell me, I'd find out for myself. Every secret. Every answer.

No more waiting. No more tiptoeing around mysteries.

It was time to uncover the truth.

I headed downstairs, determined to push all thoughts of the journal from my mind. But the moment I entered the kitchen, my resolve wavered. Sitting on the counter, waiting for me like a silent olive branch, was my favorite mug, filled with freshly brewed yerba mate. Steam curled gently from the surface, and next to it lay a spoon already dripping with honey.

A peace offering.

I hesitated, then picked up the mug, the warmth radiating into my palms. I stirred in the honey slowly, watching it dissolve into swirling amber ribbons. The motion mirrored the thoughts churning inside me— questions about the journal, the blank pages, and the secrets she'd been keeping.

This wasn't just about a journal anymore. It was about trust.

I raised the mug to my lips, the familiar earthy taste grounding me momentarily. My eyes drifted to the inscription on the side of the ceramic—Wildheart—and a faint smile tugged at my lips.

The nickname was a gift from my dad, one he'd christened me with when I was eight. I could still hear his booming voice, laughing as I darted through the grass, my hair tangled with leaves and my clothes streaked with mud.

"The world better watch out, we've got ourselves a Wildheart!" he'd shout, his tone half-teasing, half-proud.

I'd climb onto a kitchen chair, declaring myself undefeated in wrestling matches with Wren, my fists in the air like a champion boxer. Wren would egg me on, chanting, *"Wildheart! Wildheart!"* until we were all laughing too hard to continue.

Those were the days when everything felt simpler. Where mess was magic, dinners were loud, and questions, fueled by my endless curiosity, were encouraged. My grandmother's voice echoed in my mind, *"You've never met a question you don't like."*

But now, I wasn't sure if she would answer the ones I had. At least not with the truth I wanted to hear.

I glanced out the kitchen window, and there she was, sitting in the garden as though nothing had happened, her journal balanced on her lap as the pen moved across the pages in fluid strokes, her face calm and focused.

My chest tightened as I remembered the journal's empty pages. How was it blank, even though I've seen her writing in it just like now?

I gripped my mug a little harder, swallowing a bitter lump in my throat. It wasn't the tea. It was guilt.

With a deep breath, I opened the back door and stepped into the garden to join her. The fresh scent of sage filled the air, mingling with the faintly sweet aroma of tea. My grandmother didn't look up immediately, her pen still gliding across the page.

When she finally noticed me, she closed the journal with a slow, deliberate motion. The silver buckle clicked into place, and she slid it into her pocket with the same ease as tucking away a piece of herself.

Her eyes met mine, sharp and knowing.

Her smile was deceptively sweet, the kind of smile she'd taught me to use when I needed to mask my true intentions. It was a challenge, clear as day.

Game on.

I returned the smile, making mine just as pleasant, even though my pulse quickened. The tension between us was thick, a silent acknowledgment that neither of us was going to back down.

"Thank you for the tea," I said, forcing my voice to stay steady.

"Of course, honey. I know training days can be long," she replied, her tone as smooth as the tea I was sipping.

I nodded, keeping my expression neutral, but inside my thoughts raced. How much did she know? Had she seen through my earlier curiosity? Or was she baiting me, waiting for me to make my move?

The journal in her pocket seemed to hum again, a phantom echo of the strange pull it had on me. It was as though it knew I wasn't done.

And as I stood there, my tea growing lukewarm in my hands, one thing was clear: this was going to be harder than I thought. But I wasn't about to give up.

Wildhearts didn't quit.

9. Beyond The Boundary

I spent the day focusing on archery, knowing full well it was my weakest skill. It had become painfully clear since Wren upgraded me to the heavier battle arrows. When we first started training, he'd bring home his lighter practice arrows and training daggers. I was fast—*really fast* back then, landing shots with precision felt as effortless as breathing.

But that changed last month when Wren handed me the battle arrows, their weight solid and unyielding in my hands. The confidence I'd spent years building unraveled as I realized how much harder they were to aim, how much more strength they required.

I could still picture his grin that day, wide and encouraging as he placed the new arrows in my hands. "This is the real deal, Wildheart," he'd said with a wink, using the nickname he'd used since we were kids. I'd laughed it off at the time, accepting the challenge with more bravado than I felt. But now, a month later, I was still struggling.

By midday, I'd set up the target ring near the edge of the forest, where the thick trees offered shade and solitude. The air was cool, carrying the faint, earthy scent of fallen leaves and damp moss. It should've felt peaceful, but something about the forest unnerved me today. I could hear something, voices. Faint, almost imperceptible, but there. I paused, my heart quickening as I listened again. Impossible. No one ventured into the forest. No one with a sane mind, anyway.

I shook it off and tightened the last leg of the target, and glanced back at the house. My grandmother stood at the window, watching with that same cautious expression she always wore when I trained.

I gave her a quick, reassuring smile and muttered under my breath, "Come on, Raine. You're stronger than this." It was what Wren used to say whenever I doubted myself, his voice steady and sure even when I wasn't.

Taking a deep breath, I nocked one of the broadhead arrows and pulled the string back. The weight strained my arms, my muscles trembling as I struggled to steady my aim. I focused on the target, willing the arrow to fly true, and released.

It fell short. Again.

Frustration simmered under my skin as I retrieved the arrow and tried again—and again. For hours, I continued, each miss grinding away at my patience until I was fuming. My stubbornness ran deep. *You can do this, Ray,*" Wren's voice echoed in my mind again, but it wasn't just his voice; it was my Grandmother's too. Her eyes had silently followed me all day, full of quiet pride, reminding me that quitting wasn't in my blood. The arrows landed closer to the target with time, but none found the bullseye. I wasn't used to this—*to failing.*

My grandmother stepped outside just as I lined up my final arrow for this round. She called out, saying she'd be out front helping my mom bring in her market purchases. I nodded in response, not trusting my voice to sound steady.

This was it. My last shot for the day.

I squared my shoulders, took a deep breath, and aimed. My fingers released the arrow, and for a moment, everything felt right. The tension of the bowstring, the weight of the arrow—it all felt like it had aligned. But as it soared through the air, the arrow veered off course, flying over the target and into the forest.

I froze, watching it disappear into the dense shadows. The voices started again—soft, barely there, like whispers carried on the wind.

I shook my head, forcing myself to stay grounded. "It's just an arrow. In and out," I muttered, repeating it like a mantra. I could grab it quickly and be done.

But my feet hesitated at the edge of the trees.

The forest, usually a comforting presence, felt different today. The shadows seemed darker, deeper, like they were waiting for something, or someone. The whispers grew louder, more insistent, but the words were unclear, slipping away the moment I tried to make sense of them.

I stepped forward, the crunch of leaves beneath my boots unnervingly loud. My heartbeat quickened as I moved deeper into the trees. The air grew colder, carrying an almost electric charge that prickled at my skin.

"We've been waiting for you," the voices whispered.

I spun around, searching for the source, but there was nothing—just trees stretching endlessly in every direction.

"You've come back to us."

The words chilled me, even though I didn't understand them. They felt... personal. Like they were meant for me.

I pressed on, trying to block out the whispers. I told myself I had to find that arrow, had to retrieve it for Wren. He'd risked so much bringing them to me—his reputation, his position.

I thought back to the first time he'd "forgotten" his arrows here on purpose, gifting me precious extra time to train with them. I knew he probably got reprimanded for it every single time, but I couldn't express how much I appreciated it. These arrows were vital to his training— his trainers counted them religiously at the end of each week, and any missing arrows meant trouble. They didn't care about excuses; to them, a missing arrow was a mark of irresponsibility.

I couldn't let Wren carry that label because of me. I couldn't let my carelessness cost him everything.

The forest loomed darker as I pressed deeper, my boots crunching against fallen leaves and branches. I was more than twenty feet in now, scanning desperately, but the arrow was nowhere in sight. My breath quickened. This should have been easy—just grab it and go. So where was it?

I took a shaky step forward, then another, each footfall heavier than the last. The forest had always felt alive to me, but not like this. This was wrong. The trees didn't just seem tall—they loomed, twisting slightly, almost as if leaning toward me. The wild grass swayed, not with the breeze, but with an eerie rhythm I couldn't hear but felt deep in my chest.

"You've come back. Why did you wait all these years?"

The voice was clearer now, sharp and accusing, and I swore it was coming from every direction at once. My heart pounded, each beat louder than the last. I turned in a slow circle, searching for the source, but the forest only seemed to grow darker and more tangled around me.

"Who's there?" I demanded, though my voice barely rose above a whisper.

No answer. Just more movement—the grass, the branches overhead, all swaying, beckoning. The whispers grew louder, urgent now, blending in a chaotic chorus. My panic surged, clawing its way up my throat.

"This isn't real," I told myself, trying to keep my voice steady. "It's just my imagination…"

But even as I said it, I didn't believe it; something about this was unmistakably different, terrifyingly so. No amount of training, no lessons, had prepared me for this. The trees seemed to close in tighter with every step, their dark shapes twisting and leaning toward me as if conspiring to cut off any escape. I turned sharply, desperate to find a familiar landmark, but there was nothing. The house, the clearing, even the path I'd followed—all of it was gone, swallowed by the suffocating forest.

My heartbeat quickened, drowning out everything else—birds, the rustling leaves, even the whispers—but the erratic rhythm of the forest pulsed in time with it, as though mocking my fear.

I forced another step forward, my pulse roaring in my ears. Just find the arrow. Just get it and go. The words looped in my head, a desperate mantra to drown out the rising panic. But the whispers wouldn't let me go.

"Keep going," they urged, faint and haunting, but something was wrong. Everything about this moment felt wrong.

The tightness in my chest came first, subtle and creeping, like my lungs were suddenly too small for the air I needed. By the time I noticed, the panic had already taken hold. My breathing quickened, each shallow gasp doing nothing to steady me. The forest pressed in, the trees leaning closer, their branches curling downward like grasping hands.

I tried to move faster, to push past the gnawing fear, but the ground itself seemed alive, shifting and rippling beneath me. Every step was heavier than the last, the earth tugging at my boots, the air thick and choking.

"You shouldn't have come."

The voices sharpened, growing louder, and I spun around, searching desperately for their source. My hands trembled as I swept them over my ears, willing the whispers to stop, but they only grew louder.

"You're not welcome here."

"Foolish girl. Weak."

"You'll never survive."

My pulse raced, erratic and dizzying. I stumbled over an exposed root, catching myself just before I hit the ground. I looked up, blinking through the shadows, and froze. The voices surrounded me, overlapping until they were all I could hear.

"Save us."

"Free us."

"You're the only one who can."

My vision blurred, my mind spinning as the forest seemed to close in around me. The trees weren't just looming—they were alive, their branches stretching and curling toward me like claws. They snagged my sleeves and scraped my skin, pulling me deeper into their clutches.

"Stop," I whispered, my voice cracking. "Leave me alone."

But the whispers didn't stop. They only multiplied, high-pitched and cruel, weaving together into an eerie symphony. I turned in circles, frantic, but there was no one—only flashes of movement in the shadows.

Laughter. Faint, sharp, and mocking.

My breath hitched as tiny, winged shapes darted through the darkness. Fairies. Real and far more menacing than I'd ever imagined. Their cruel eyes watched me, glinting like shards of glass, their voices dripping with malice.

"You can't escape."

The ground shifted again, softening beneath me. I looked down and felt my stomach drop. My boots were sinking, swallowed by the earth. The soil rippled, dark and wet, clinging to me like tar. I pulled hard, desperate to free myself, but the more I struggled, the faster I sank.

"No. No, no, no!" My voice cracked as I clawed at the ground, my hands slipping uselessly through the thick, shifting mud.

The forest responded, branches curling tighter, their sharp tips grazing my arms, my face. It felt alive, hungry. My legs were trapped now, the cold earth creeping higher, dragging me down.

"You should've stayed away."

The whispers were everywhere, inside my head, beneath my skin. I couldn't shut them out. My breaths came in ragged gasps, my chest aching, my vision blurring. The mud was at my thighs now, its icy grip numbing my legs.

"Help!" I screamed, my voice hoarse and desperate, but it vanished into the darkness, swallowed whole by the forest.

I clawed at the branches, at the ground, at anything I could reach, but my hands were trembling, my strength failing. The earth surged higher, its cold touch climbing past my waist. My arms were pinned now, held fast by the forest's wooden fingers.

"Stop!" I sobbed, tears streaking down my face. "Please!"

The whispers only laughed, their cruel words swirling in the air around me.

"You're ours now. She tried warning you."

The ground tightened around my chest, pressing the air from my lungs.

I gasped, choking, but there was no air left to breathe. Darkness crept in at the edges of my vision, the world spinning, blurring.

I was sinking. Drowning. Consumed.

And then—there was nothing.

My mind felt like it was wading through sludge, heavy and slow, as I stared up at the dark sky. I blinked hard, trying to clear the fog clouding my thoughts, but nothing helped. I wasn't in the forest anymore. I was in my backyard, lying on the grass, the soft blades pressing against my skin. My limbs were trembling, weak, like I'd run for miles and collapsed here. The ground beneath me was firm, yet I could still feel the phantom grip of the forest pulling at my ankles, the mud sucking me under.

Shakily, I sat up, the world tilting slightly as I did. My fingers twitched against the damp grass, and that's when I noticed it—something smooth and hard clutched tightly in my hand. My breath hitched as I unfurled my fingers.

Wren's arrow.

I stared at it, my mind spinning. How? How was this possible? One moment, the forest was consuming me, the ground swallowing me whole, and now I was here, the arrow pressed into my palm like it had always been there.

My thoughts were sluggish, disjointed, fragments of the forest flashing through my mind like jagged shards of glass: the whispers, the branches reaching for me, the fairies' mocking laughter. And then... the shadow. That dark presence looming over me, the moment before everything had gone black.

I squeezed the arrow tightly, the wood biting into my palm. It should have been reassuring, but it wasn't enough to silence the chaos in my head. The forest had let me go—but why?

The sound of the back door slamming jolted me. I looked up sharply, my heart pounding all over again, as my grandmother rushed out, her face pale and stricken with fear.

"Raine!" she cried, her voice trembling as she hurried toward me. She dropped to her knees in the grass beside me, her hands gripping my shoulders. "What happened? Where were you?"

I opened my mouth to answer, to explain, but no words came. My throat burned, raw and dry, as if I'd been screaming for hours. I raised a shaking hand and pointed toward the woods, my fingers barely steady enough to hold the arrow.

Her gaze followed my gesture, her expression shifting in an instant. Her fear hardened into something colder, sharper, like she already knew. She helped me to my feet, her grip steady and unyielding even as my legs wobbled beneath me. She guided me to the garden bed, easing me down onto the edge as if she were afraid I might collapse again.

She stepped back, her eyes flicking toward the treeline. "Stay here," she said firmly.

No.

The word screamed in my mind, but when I tried to voice it, all that came out was a hoarse, broken whisper. I reached for her, gripping her sleeve with what little strength I had left, but she gently pulled away, her eyes fixed on the forest.

Panic surged anew, raw and overwhelming, as I watched her take a step toward the trees. My breath quickened, my chest tightening like a vice, and I pressed a hand to my sternum, trying to steady myself.

Don't go in there, I wanted to yell, but my voice was useless.

The dizziness returned, a wave of nausea crashing over me as I squeezed my eyes shut, desperate to block it all out. But the darkness behind my lids betrayed me. The memories were waiting there: the branches clawing at my arms, the fairies laughing, the ground consuming me, pulling me into its cold, suffocating depths.

I opened my eyes, forcing them to stay on her retreating form. She paused at the edge of the forest, one hand hovering near the trunk of a massive oak. I wanted to run to her, to grab her and pull her back, but my body refused to move. My legs felt like lead, and my lungs ached with every shallow, frantic breath.

"Gran," I finally croaked, the word barely audible, but she didn't turn around.

I could only watch as she stepped into the shadow of the trees and disappeared.

Through the blurry haze, I saw her standing at the edge of the woods, motionless, her back to me. A chill rippled through me as I noticed she wasn't alone.

I blinked, squinting to focus, my vision swimming from exhaustion and fear. A tall figure loomed beside her, half-concealed by the shadows of the trees. His outline was jagged, shifting like smoke, not fully solid. But there was something that felt wrong about him. Something impossible. My chest tightened. This couldn't be real; he couldn't be real. It had to be another trick, another hallucination.

Yet the longer I stared, the more real he became. His sheer size dwarfed her, his form commanding, as if the shadows themselves bent to his will, wrapping around him like a living thing. And then I saw them—wings. Or something like wings, unfurling behind him, curling like tendrils of black smoke. They rippled in the faint light, not feathers but something darker, fluid, and alive.

Men didn't have wings.

I swallowed hard, my heart hammering in my chest as I fought the wave of dizziness threatening to pull me under. I tried to move, to push myself off the garden bed and run to her, but the world tilted sharply, my body refusing to obey. My hands clawed at the grass as I struggled to hold myself upright.

"Gran!" I rasped, but my voice came out weak and broken, swallowed by the air between us.

My head spun as I tried to focus on the figure again. His features were still obscured, hidden by the forest's embrace, but the power radiating from him was suffocating. It wasn't just his height or the unnatural wings—it was the way the darkness clung to him like it was a part of him. Like he was part of it.

And my grandmother… she was calm.

She stood before him, her posture steady, unshaken, as though this was something she'd done a thousand times before. She wasn't afraid of him, wasn't afraid of the forest that had just tried to consume me. She was speaking to him, her lips moving in soft, deliberate words I couldn't hear.

Panic clawed at my chest, my pulse roaring in my ears. Why wasn't she scared? Why was she so close to the woods? To him?

The forest was darkening, shadows creeping outward as the sun dipped lower on the horizon. My instincts screamed for her to step away, to leave this impossible figure behind, but she stayed. Her hand lifted slightly, a gesture that looked almost…familiar, like she was greeting an old friend.

I tried to sit up straighter, to call out to her again, but my body wouldn't cooperate. My head throbbed, my vision blurring as I squinted at the figure. Was there anyone else with him? I scanned the treeline frantically, but my focus slipped, my strength faltering.

A wave of nausea hit me, and the next thing I knew, I was back on the grass. My body collapsed under the weight of exhaustion and fear. The arrow slipped from my hand, forgotten in the haze, and I stared up at the darkening sky, my breath shallow and ragged.

That night, sleep claimed me, but it was far from peaceful.

In my dreams, he was there. The shadowed figure with wings like smoke, towering above me. His presence was overwhelming, yet not entirely terrifying. His eyes—calm and steady, piercing through the darkness—felt almost… familiar. I couldn't place why, but the sense of knowing struck something deep inside me, pulling me closer to him.

The wings shifted, curling around him like a shield, not menacing but protective. He didn't speak, but his stare carried an unspoken message, one that chilled me as much as it comforted me. I couldn't tell if he was a savior or a predator, protector or destroyer. But I couldn't look away.

I felt drawn to him, even as unease tightened in my chest. And when

I woke, the memory of him lingered, etched into my mind like a scar I couldn't forget.

10. Where Shadows Gather

Waking up at dawn, I blinked furiously, my breath hitching as my heart raced. *Where was I?* My eyes darted around the room, taking in the soft glow of morning sunlight filtering through the curtains, the faint smell of sage and lavender wrapping around me like a warm embrace. My mattress was soft beneath me—a stark contrast to the cold, damp forest floor I remembered.

Home. I was home. I was safe.

I pressed my palms against the quilt, grounding myself, but the tension in my chest refused to ease. Yesterday's events pressed against my mind, jagged and unreal. It had to be a nightmare, didn't it? The forest, the man, the shadows—none of it made sense. Magical forests didn't exist.

And yet...

I didn't remember coming upstairs. Didn't remember changing into my sleep gown or collapsing into bed. But here I was, surrounded by the familiar, every detail screaming normalcy. The ache in my body, though—that was harder to explain away.

Rolling over, I winced as a sharp pain flared in my ribs. My muscles protested the movement, stiff and sore as if I'd run for miles or wrestled against something far stronger than me. I tried to dismiss it as a coincidence. Maybe I'd fallen or strained myself in the garden yesterday.

But no. Deep down, I knew better.

I shook my head, forcing the thoughts away. Dwelling on it wouldn't help—not now. I needed fresh air and clarity. And I needed answers. My grandmother knew something; she always did. The forest, the man, the shadows—they gnawed at the edges of my mind, demanding an explanation.

I glanced toward her side of the room, already knowing it would be empty. She was always up before dawn, tending to the herbs or preparing tinctures. Still, I checked. The emptiness only added to the unease clawing at my chest.

Dragging myself out of bed felt like wading through quicksand. Every step sent a dull ache rippling through me, but I pushed on, descending the stairs as quickly as my shaky legs allowed. The smell of tea and oats wafted through the air, mingling with the faint aroma of honey. My stomach growled, reminding me I hadn't eaten yesterday.

At the bottom of the stairs, my mom stood waiting. Her eyes locked onto me the moment I appeared, wide and full of worry.

"You should eat something," she said, her voice firm but gentle as she gestured toward the table.

I wanted to argue, to tell her I didn't have time for breakfast, but the look on her face stopped me. Resigned, I slid into the chair, letting her place a bowl of oats and a plate of fruit in front of me.

The moment the first piece of fruit touched my lips, the memories came rushing back with brutal clarity. The forest. The branches. The man cloaked in shadows, his presence overwhelming, his eyes piercing. My body stiffened, my mouth dry, and I felt sweat bead on my brow. I gripped the edge of the table, my mind spinning, desperate to ground myself. The forest had been real—I could feel it in my bones. There was no logical explanation for what had happened, no way to rationalize how *the trees* could reach out, or how I ended up clutching Wren's arrow like it was a lifeline. Magic like that didn't exist anymore—not since the days of the King, hundreds of years ago.

But my gut said otherwise.

I froze, the taste of the fruit turning sour in my mouth. My hand trembled as I set it down, gripping the edge of the table for stability. I shook my head, forcing the thoughts away before my panic could overwhelm me again. My mom's eyes lingered on me, concern etched into every line of her face, so I forced a smile. A fake one, but enough to convince her I was fine. I forced myself to chew, to eat enough to quiet her worries, though every bite felt mechanical, my mind elsewhere. When she finally stopped hovering, I stood, the chair scraping against the floor as I pushed it back.

"I'll be outside," I murmured, my voice hoarse and strained.

She hesitated but nodded, her worry still palpable as I stepped outside.

The morning air was unseasonably warm, the sun already high despite the early hour. I took a deep breath, the scent of earth and grass filling my lungs, calming me slightly. My feet carried me toward the garden beds, where my grandmother often worked.

But she wasn't there.

I scanned the yard, my eyes skimming over the treeline without fully focusing on it. I didn't want to see the forest, didn't want to think about it, but the memories lingered just beneath the surface, ready to drag me under.

Rounding the corner of the house, I froze.

There, standing just beyond the herb garden, was him.

My heart stuttered, the blood roaring in my ears as my breath caught in my throat. It was the man from the forest.

He stood tall and imposing, his silhouette shimmering faintly in the sunlight, as though the air itself bent around him. The shadows that had once seemed wild now clung to him with purpose, moving in a way that felt deliberate and controlled.

I searched for the wings but saw none—only the commanding figure of a man who seemed both utterly foreign and disturbingly familiar.

He didn't speak, didn't move, but his eyes found mine, steady and unnervingly calm. My body screamed at me to run, to turn away and forget I'd ever seen him. But I couldn't move.

The weight of his presence rooted me to the spot, my heart pounding so hard it felt like it might shatter.

This wasn't a dream.

He was real.

And he was waiting for me.

My first instinct was to scream—to yell loud enough for my mom to hear, for the neighbors to come running, even the ones I barely liked. But the sound lodged in my throat, refusing to come out. My heart hammered in my chest as my eyes darted around the yard, frantically searching for my grandmother. Where was she?

My head spun as fear clawed at me, wild and insistent. *He* has something to do with this. Every alarm bell in my body screamed at me to stay away, to retreat to the safety of my house. But I couldn't. Not without knowing where my grandmother was, or worse, what had happened to her.

She was always in the garden at this time. And before yesterday, I had never seen this man before.

Who was he?

How could I possibly know he wasn't here to hurt me—or my family? No decent person lurked in the shadows of the forbidden woods, let alone emerged uninvited into someone's backyard. And no decent man bent shadows to his will like they were living things, wrapping themselves around him with dark obedience.

The stories about the forest—about the dangers that lurked beyond the trees—suddenly felt much more real, as though every whispered warning was born from him.

My heart pounded harder, my breath shallow and uneven. But I couldn't look away.

I had to tilt my head back, *far back*, to meet his stare. He towered over me, at least a full foot taller, his broad shoulders and chest seeming to take up all the space in the room. Next to him, I felt impossibly small, like I might disappear entirely if he stepped just a little closer.

His skin, a sun-kissed bronze, gleamed faintly in the dim light, smooth yet highlighted by the faintest imperfections that only made him more striking. A shadow of stubble dusted his jaw and upper lip, the kind that wasn't quite deliberate but made him look effortlessly rugged. Every sharp plane and angle of his face seemed crafted by the gods to draw attention—his high cheekbones, the strong slope of his nose, and a jawline that could have been cut from stone.

But it was his eyes that unraveled me. Hazel, almost too vivid to be real, with flecks of molten gold that shimmered as if they had a light of their own. They pinned me in place, sharp and unyielding, and in their depths, I caught the faintest glimpse of something wild and ancient, like he was more than he appeared.

He shifted, the faint rustle of leather and fabric drawing my attention lower. His frame was massive, built like someone who had spent years carrying burdens far heavier than just his weight. I swallowed hard, feeling dwarfed by him, and as he leaned just slightly toward me, I caught the faintest scent of cedar and something darker—smoke, maybe.

And still, I couldn't stop gawking. Every detail—his full lips, the faint scar cutting across his left eyebrow, the way his thick, black hair curled slightly where it brushed the base of his neck—etched itself into my mind.

The seconds stretched into what felt like hours. My body trembled, my legs refusing to obey my mind's frantic commands to move—whether forward or back, I couldn't decide.

He arched an eyebrow, and a faint smirk tugged at the corner of his lips as if he could hear the erratic pace of my thoughts. I flushed, realizing too late I'd been staring openly.

"Are you done staring yet?" he asked, his voice smooth, warm, and laced with amusement. "I know I'm a lot to take in, but usually people try to be a bit more subtle in their gawking."

Heat exploded across my face, rushing to the tips of my ears. My cheeks burned, and I knew I was blushing furiously, probably the color of ripe strawberries. I blinked, forcing myself to look away, my throat tightening as I swallowed back the lump of embarrassment that threatened to choke me.

Great. Not only had he noticed, but he dared to call me out on it.

For a moment, I stood there, frozen, caught between mortification and the nagging pull of my unanswered questions. But then, somehow, I found the will to move. I forced one foot forward, then another, every step slow and deliberate.

My heart thundered in my chest, each beat loud and erratic as his golden eyes tracked my approach. The smirk on his lips faded, replaced by something unreadable.

I stopped just short of him, close enough to feel the subtle hum of energy that seemed to radiate from him but far enough to maintain some semblance of space.

He was good-looking—undeniably so. If even half the boys in this town had looked like him, I might have rethought my ideals about marriage, or at least snuck off to the barn for a kiss or two. That thought alone sent heat rushing to my cheeks, and before I could stop myself, my eyes darted to his lips. They were full and smooth, the exact shade of a ripe grapefruit, inviting and impossible to ignore.

The sharp sound of him clearing his throat snapped me out of my ridiculous trance, dissolving the inappropriate thoughts swirling in my head.

Focus, Raine.

There were far more important things to worry about—like who this man was and what he had done with my grandmother.

"Before you ask," he began, his voice smooth but edged with something guarded, "your grandmother is safe."

I narrowed my eyes at him, suspicion building. He couldn't possibly know what I was going to ask—or why I didn't trust a single word coming out of his too-perfect mouth.

"She went to a neighbor's house," he added, seemingly unbothered by my silence, "to source an herb she needed."

That was a laughable lie. No one in this village grew half the herbs we did. He might as well have told me she'd wandered off to the moon for supplies. My mind spun, cataloging every possible scenario of what could really be going on. Did he think I'd just take his word for it? My silence must have stretched too long because his head tilted slightly, those golden eyes studying me like I was some sort of puzzle he intended to solve.

The weight of his gaze sent a fresh wave of self-consciousness crashing over me. Had I even combed my hair this morning? Brushed my teeth? I cursed inwardly as I took in my appearance. I was still wearing my old sleep dress, which now clung to me in ways it hadn't before and barely reached my knees. My legs—pale, bare, and completely unprepared for company—were on full display, and of course, I wasn't wearing shoes. I could feel the embarrassment creeping up my spine, hot and suffocating, as I imagined how I must look through his eyes.

Meanwhile, he looked like he belonged at an extravagant royal event. Probably spent his days around women just as divine as him, effortlessly stunning people who seemed crafted by the gods themselves. And here I was. Ordinary human Raine, with uneven tan lines and flushed skin, standing barefoot in a slip that felt more like a punishment than clothing.

"Who are you?" The words tumbled out before I could stop them, sharper than intended.

The corner of his mouth lifted in a faint smirk like he'd expected the question. "Manakel," he said. "I am a Sciathain and was sent here to help you."

I snorted internally. He was a what? What the heck was a Sciathain, and what could he possibly be here to help me with? Undeterred by my confusion, he continued, "You must be R—"

"Wildheart," I interrupted, thrusting my hand between us. "My name is Wildheart."

His brow lifted slightly, a silence written across his features, but he took my hand anyway. His grip was firm, too warm, unnaturally so, as if he carried fire in his veins. "Hello, Wildheart," he said smoothly. "Nice to meet you in the light of day—when the forest isn't trying to kill you."

My breath hitched. What? My hand froze in his, my heart hammering in my chest as his next words fell like stones in the silence.

"You're welcome, by the way," he murmured, leaning in just enough for his breath to brush against my ear.

I jerked back as if burned, and he released my hand, turning on his heel as if the conversation were over.

Wait. What did he just say? The forest was trying to kill me? Did that mean… No, it couldn't have been real. But if it wasn't, how did he know? Why was he here? My mind reeled, the memory of being trapped, groped by vines, and swallowed by mud was now impossible to ignore.

He strode toward the target board propped up against the house like it was his to mess with. My pulse quickened at the familiarity he was exuding, and something felt off.

"Why are you touching my target?" I demanded, my voice sharper than intended.

He didn't even flinch, but for a brief second, I saw something flicker in his eyes, a flash of surprise, maybe, before he masked it with that perfect, infuriating composure. He wasn't used to being questioned. I wasn't used to letting people walk all over me, either.

He glanced at me, eyes flicking over with barely concealed boredom before returning his attention to the target, ignoring me completely. His nonchalance made my blood boil. I didn't care who he was—he wasn't going to act like he owned the place.

"Hey!" I snapped, taking a few quick steps toward him. "Why are you touching my target?"

He spared me a glance, that amused, insufferable spark still dancing in his golden eyes. "Why shouldn't I? It's not like *you're* using it."

That was it. My anger flared, rising like a wave that had no intention of crashing. "Because it's mine, and I was just about to," I said, planting myself firmly in front of him. "And unless you'd like me to start rummaging through your things uninvited, I suggest you step away."

He didn't even seem phased by my challenge. He just continued adjusting the target, pretending I wasn't there, as if I were some obstacle to be ignored. My hands tightened around the wooden board, unwilling to let it slip from my grasp. The wood was cold, grounding me, but I could feel the thin, gnawing anxiety in my stomach—he could easily take it from me, just like he could take anything else if he wanted. But I wasn't giving in. *Not yet.*

His eyes flicked up again, clearly searching for my bow and arrows. Like I was going to willingly hand over my weapons to a stranger. *Not a chance.*

"What?" I asked, raising an eyebrow, pretending I didn't know what he was looking for. He looked at me again, this time with more frustration, as if I were somehow being deliberately difficult.

He exhaled sharply, muttering under his breath as he tilted his head slightly, assessing me, his lips twitching and suppressing a grin. "If you won't tell me where you keep your ammo," he began, drawing it out, "then answer me this: Do you normally wield arrows dressed like that?" he snapped, gesturing to my sleep dress. "I mean, yesterday's outfit was far more appropriate for training. Unless, of course, you're planning to storm into the forest barefoot and half-naked for fun?"

The audacity. "Half-naked?" I repeated, incredulous. "Excuse me?"

His lips quirked up into a full smirk now, but something shifted in his expression—something dark, fleeting, and impossible to pin down. Was it pain? Or hunger? Whatever it was, it was gone as quickly as it appeared.

He stepped back, looking toward the forest as his tone shifted.

"Listen, *Wildheart*," he said, voice clipped. "There are things going on that you don't understand yet. Plans far bigger than you could even imagine. But you will, in time. For now, you need to focus more on training and *actually* hitting your target. What use is doing this if you're not doing it properly?"

I bristled. "What makes you think I'm not doing it properly? And how do you even know I'm not hitting my targets?"

His eyes met mine, steady and unrelenting. "Because I've been watching. And when you're alone, you're slacking."

The words hit harder than they should have. *Slacking?* Sure, I hadn't been as consistent lately—Wren's absence had thrown me off—but how would he know that? And why did my training even matter? It's not like I'd need those skills anytime soon. My chest tightened as I stared at him, every instinct screaming that he knew more than he was letting on.

Why in the world was this man even here? And why couldn't I shake the feeling that my world was about to change forever?

11. The First Cut

Against my better judgment, I stormed off without answering him. There was no way I was letting him have the last word. My footsteps were heavy with frustration as I made my way back to the house, his words ringing in my ears. Slacking? Half-Naked? Who was he to say that? He didn't know me, didn't know the hours I had put into training or the blisters and bruises I'd earned trying to keep up with Wren.

Still, a stubborn part of me felt a spark of determination ignite. If he thought I'd been slacking, fine. I'd prove him wrong.

I went straight to my room, yanking open the dresser and grabbing a pair of fitted training pants and a thin black sweater—practical, warm, and perfect for showing I meant business. As I stripped out of my sleep dress, a flash of my reflection caught my eye in the mirror.

I groaned. My hair was a disaster—tangled, matted, and there, stuck in one of the knots… was that a *leaf*? Of course, it was. I hadn't brushed it after waking up on the ground yesterday, rolling around like some feral animal. Another stubborn reminder of my humiliating escape from the forest. With a wince, I yanked a brush through my hair, each knot a painful tug that seemed to echo my embarrassment. This man, as infuriating as he was gorgeous, had literally carried me away like some helpless damsel in distress. The thought gnawed at me. And that infuriatingly smug expression when he said I was welcome, as if rescuing me had been a favor he'd been burdened with. The thought sent heat rushing to my cheeks, but I ignored it, focusing instead on braiding my hair with swift, angry fingers.

I tied the braid off with a gold ribbon, an impractical choice, but one that made me feel just a little more in control. This wasn't for him. It was for me. A reminder that I wasn't going to let some stranger rattle me, no matter how sharp his words or how deep his golden eyes seemed to see.

When I finally stepped back downstairs, the house was quiet, save for the soft creak of the kettle heating on the stove. My mother must have filled it before leaving, as she often did. I couldn't help but feel a small pang of gratitude for her thoughtfulness.

On a whim, I reached for two cups, filling them both with yerba mate. The earthy scent wafted upward, grounding me as I poured the hot water. My movements were automatic, my thoughts elsewhere, mostly on him.

The moment I stepped outside, I saw him. Still trying to figure out if this was real and why he was really here. Manakel sat by the garden bed, methodically retying the arrowheads with precision. They had started coming loose, and Wren had been so busy lately that I hadn't asked for his help. I hated to admit it, but I was grateful to be getting newly tied arrows. They always aimed better and hit the target more reliably. He looked oddly at ease, the tension from earlier nowhere to be seen. For a moment, I stood there, the cups warming my hands, watching him.

Against my better judgment, I walked over and placed a mug beside him before heading toward the shed to grab my bow.

He didn't look up immediately, his hands continuing their work, but when he finally noticed the cup, he paused. His gaze lingered on it, almost suspicious, as if it might contain poison.

"It's not poisoned," I said quickly, raising my hands in mock defense. "I swear. I just figured you might be thirsty. But if you don't like tea…" I trailed off, suddenly aware of how ridiculous I sounded.

When he still didn't move, I shifted awkwardly, gripping my bow tightly. "You don't have to drink it," I added, my voice softer now. "I just thought…"

"You thought?" His voice cut through my rambling, and when I glanced up, his golden eyes were fixed on me again. There was something about the way he looked at me—steady and intense, like he was searching for something he couldn't quite place.

I swallowed hard, suddenly feeling exposed, as though he could see through every layer I'd built to protect myself. After what felt like an eternity, he reached for the cup and brought it to his lips.

The sight of him holding the delicate mug in his large hands was almost comical, but when he took a sip and let out a low, approving hum, any amusement I felt was quickly replaced by something else—a warmth I didn't want to name.

"Yerba mate," he said, his voice softer now. "It's been a long time since I've tasted this."

I blinked, caught off guard by the unexpected appreciation in his tone. "Well," I managed, my voice faltering slightly, "I'm glad you like it."

He nodded, taking another sip, and for a brief moment, the tension between us seemed to ease. But just as quickly, the moment passed, and he set the cup down, his expression shifting back to that same veiled mask.

"Thank you," he said, his tone polite but distant, as if thanking me for tea was something he rarely did.

I nodded, clutching my bow tightly and turning toward the target. I had no idea what to make of him, but one thing was clear—I wasn't about to let him keep me off balance. Not if I wanted to show him how wrong he was.

Manakel handed me an arrow, his fingers brushing against mine as he did. A small smile tugged at the corners of his lips, softening the sharp edges of his otherwise stoic expression. It was a rare sight, that smile, fleeting and unexpected, like a glimpse of sunlight through storm clouds. He seemed like the kind of man who scowled more often than not, his features chiseled into an eternal mask of strength, danger, and indifference. Yet here he was, smiling.

I pretended not to notice, but inwardly, I clung to the image, storing it away like a precious secret. Seeing him like this—unguarded—felt like winning a battle I hadn't even known I was fighting. Whatever gods were watching, I silently thanked them that I'd seen this side of him and not the wrath that undoubtedly simmered beneath his surface.

I nodded in silent acknowledgment, gripping the arrow as I turned toward the familiar patch of worn grass. It was my usual spot, the hours of practice wearing the ground into a natural marker. My heart pounded in my chest, each beat a reminder of the weight of his focus on me. I moved into position, the bow familiar in my hands, the arrow settling against the string with practiced ease.

The world narrowed. It was just me and the target now. My breathing steadied, the chaos of the morning slipping away as I focused on the bullseye.

The first hint of his approach was the faint shift of air behind me, but I didn't register it until I felt the warmth of his fingers brush against my arm. I faltered, my pulse spiking as his hands adjusted my stance.

"Wider," he murmured, his deep voice low and steady, vibrating through me. His hands lingered for only a moment as he guided my legs into a better position, then retreated. Yet the warmth of his touch remained, seared into my skin as if it carried some residual power.

I swallowed hard, trying to regain my composure as he stepped back. His presence was inescapable, a heavy, watchful weight at my back. I knew his eyes were on me, analyzing and judging every movement I made. It was maddening.

Wren's advice came to mind, unbidden: Find a phrase or a mantra to center yourself. It'll help focus your energy, especially under pressure. At the time, I'd thought it was nonsense—how could words possibly help when chaos surrounded you? But now, with Manakel's intense gaze burning into me, I wished I had something to anchor myself.

I inhaled slowly, drawing the arrow back until the string was taut. The tension hummed between my fingers as I steadied my aim, locking my focus on the center of the target. I released the arrow, exhaling as it flew.

For a moment, everything felt perfect. The arrow sliced through the air, swift and sure. My heart leapt as I watched it soar straight toward the bullseye. This was it. I had done it.

But then, something shifted. The arrow faltered, the momentum bleeding away too soon. My stomach clenched as it dipped lower, skimming the bottom edge of the board before clattering to the ground with an unceremonious thud.

The thrill of success evaporated, leaving behind a cold pit of disappointment. My chest tightened as I lowered my bow, the sound of the arrow hitting the ground ringing in my ears. I didn't dare turn to look at Manakel, but I could feel his presence behind me, unyielding and all too aware of my failure.

I had wanted to impress him—to prove that I was capable, strong, worth his attention even if it pained me to admit it. Instead, I'd stumbled, and the sting of it settled deep. My cheeks burned as I resisted the urge to apologize, to offer some excuse for the poor shot.

But excuses wouldn't change the result. And I knew better than to expect sympathy from someone used to perfection.

12. Lessons In Steel

After a few more missed arrows, I felt utterly defeated. Normally, I'd grit my teeth, shake off the frustration, and push myself harder. Persistence had always been my thing—it was what separated me from others who gave up too soon. But today, something was different. Everything felt off. Maybe it was the looming presence of the man behind me, his watchful eyes cutting through my confidence. Or maybe it was the weight of knowing my eighteenth birthday was fast approaching and all the uncertainty it promised. And then there was the exhaustion. Yesterday's ordeal had left me drained in ways I hadn't fully realized until now. My limbs ached, my focus wavered, and the thought of mustering more strength to continue felt impossible. I drew in a shaky breath, determined not to let any of this show.

Before I could say anything, Manakel stepped closer. He held out my cup of tea, his large hand almost swallowing the delicate mug. I took it gratefully, offering him a soft smile as I wrapped my fingers around the warm ceramic.

For someone so intimidating, he had a grounding energy, his presence solid and unshakable. I wasn't sure if it was his size, his quiet confidence, or just the fact that he'd been there to pull me out of the forest when I needed help most. But whatever it was, I was glad he was here. The trees loomed in the distance, their shadows long and dark, a constant reminder of how close I'd come to something far worse yesterday. With him nearby, the fear seemed to shrink, fading into the background.

As I sipped the last of my tea, curiosity bubbled to the surface. For all the time we'd spent in silence, communicating through awkward glances and the occasional remark, I realized I didn't know anything about him beyond his name. And that wasn't enough.

Placing the mug down, I finally let my curiosity win. "So… why are you here again? I don't remember what you said earlier." I tried to sound casual, but the question hung in the air like a challenge.

He glanced at me, an amused glint in his golden eyes. "You don't remember because I never told you," he said, his lips curving into a smirk.

Caught, I laughed and raised my hands in surrender. "Alright, fair enough. But can you really blame me for being curious? A giant stranger saves me from the woods and then spends the whole day watching me miss targets. Don't you have better things to do?"

"So, you think I'm a giant, do you?" His voice dipped into a teasing tone, his focus flicking down to me. "Well, Wildheart, you haven't seen all of me yet to make that declaration."

The words hung in the air, their meaning sinking in a beat too late. My cheeks flamed instantly. Was he flirting? And worse—did I… like it?

"Wait," I shot back, rolling my eyes in an attempt to mask my embarrassment. "That's what you got out of everything I said? That you were a giant? Seriously?"

He just smiled again, a smug little tilt of his lips that made me want to punch him—or maybe kiss him. Not that I was counting, but that made what, six smiles today?

Definitely not counting.

"Well?" I pressed, crossing my arms. "Why don't you answer it now? Why are you here?"

His smirk faltered, his expression softening. For a moment, he seemed to weigh his answer carefully, as though deciding how much to reveal. "There's more going on in Luminara than you realize," he said finally, his voice low. "But for now, let me reassure you that I'm here to help you, not harm you."

Help? With what, exactly? His answer only left me with more questions, but something in his tone made me pause. Whatever he wasn't saying felt bigger than I was ready for, and I wasn't sure I wanted to press him—not yet.

Before I could retrieve the scattered arrows and try again, Manakel reached out, his hand brushing mine as he gently stopped me. "Maybe arrows aren't where we should be focusing today," he suggested, his voice calm but firm.

I opened my mouth to protest, but he cut me off. "I know you're capable," he said. "I'm just saying today isn't the day. Why don't you show me what you know about wielding daggers, instead?"

The word sent a spark of excitement through me. Daggers were my thing. I'd trained with them for years, honing my skills to the point that even Wren, who never handed out compliments, had admitted I was better than some of his seasoned trainees. If Manakel wanted to see me handle daggers, I was more than happy to oblige.

I hurried to the shed, grabbing two sleek, polished blades. As I turned back toward him, my mind raced with possibilities. I pictured myself pulling him in close, sliding the blade to his throat, and making him yield. A grin tugged at my lips. This was going to be fun.

Manakel stood in the same spot, watching me with that unshakable calm of his. Somehow, he looked like he belonged here, standing tall and confident against the backdrop of my backyard. I'd spent countless hours in this space, filled with memories of family and training with Wren, but Manakel's presence didn't feel out of place. If anything, it felt… right.

Sizing him up, I took note of how much bigger he was than Wren. I'd need to adjust my techniques; that was clear. Wren was quick and nimble, but Manakel was built like a mountain. As I approached, I held out one of the daggers, offering him a fair fight. He shook his head, his lips quirking into another infuriating smirk. "You keep it," he said. "You might need both to take me down. And I don't need any at all if I wanted to take a tiny threat like you down to the ground."

My cheeks flushed at his words, my earlier thoughts spiraling into dangerous territory. Now it was the two of us on the ground, me straddling his legs, pinning him, a dagger at his throat, teasing him until he yielded.

He must have noticed the flicker of something in my expression because he cleared his throat, the teasing glint in his eyes faltering. I blushed harder, trying to shake off whatever this strange energy between us was.

Was this what all the girls in town felt around boys? If so, I was starting to understand the appeal.

"How do you want me?" I called out, my question innocent, but as soon as the words left my mouth, I realized how they could be taken. The heat rushed to my neck, and my heart skipped a beat as I watched Manakel's eyes widen.

I stumbled over my words, desperately trying to backpedal. "I mean… is there a specific way you want to begin? A technique or something? Or… did you just want to go at it and see what happens?"

His expression flickered for a moment, and then he turned away as if needing a moment to collect himself. I could feel the heat creeping up my face and forced myself to look at the ground for a second, hoping he didn't notice how flustered I was.

When he finally spoke again, his voice was steady, though a faint glimmer of amusement still lingered in his eyes. "Why don't you start? I'll adapt based on your moves. I want to see how you'd handle a real threat."

That was something I could work with. I nodded, feeling the tension in my body ease as I palmed the daggers just as Wren had taught me. Keep your weapons hidden until the moment is right. I was fairly certain Manakel knew I had two daggers tucked away, but that didn't mean he knew where I was hiding them. I kept them at my waist, beneath my shirt, just out of view but ready to be drawn at a moment's notice.

I circled him slowly, watching his every move, every twitch of muscle. But he didn't move, didn't seem to flinch. His eyes stayed locked on mine—calm, measured, waiting for me.

The air between us felt thick with something unspoken, something more than just the usual sparring. My heart pounded in my chest as I realized this wasn't just training; this was something else.

I took a deep breath, cleared my mind of the noise, and made my move. I lunged forward, swift and fluid, like Wren had taught me. My first strike was aimed at his side, light and fast, just to see how he would react. But before the blade could even get close, he moved with blinding speed, sidestepping my strike like it was nothing. His hand brushed my arm, redirecting my momentum without breaking a sweat.

"Not bad," he murmured, his voice low and approving, but there was something in his tone that made my blood simmer. "But you'll need to be faster than that to catch me."

I smirked, my confidence flaring in response. He had no idea how fast I could move.

I shifted my weight, daggers glinting in my hands. I watched him closely, trying to get a read on his next move. He stood at ease, his body poised but relaxed, like a spring coiled just below the surface, waiting to snap. I feinted to the right, hoping to catch him off guard, but before I could make the move, I spun left, swiping one dagger at his side.

He was too fast. Too damn fast. Before I could complete my strike, he sidestepped again, his hand snapping out to grab my wrist in a grip that felt like iron, yet gentle enough not to crush my bones.

I tried to twist free, but he didn't budge. He released me with a lazy flick of his wrist, his gaze never leaving mine. There was a small, amused smile at the corners of his lips, like he already knew the outcome.

I wasn't going to give him the satisfaction of underestimating me. I re-positioned myself, shifting my weight, ready to go again.

This time, I aimed for his shoulder, moving quicker than before, focused on speed and precision. But Manakel wasn't impressed. In one smooth motion, he caught my wrist mid-swing, using my momentum against me. He turned, pulling me forward with an effortless motion that left me off balance. My first dagger clattered to the ground.

Undeterred, I spun in place, ready to strike with my other dagger. My body moved on instinct, but he was already one step ahead. Before I could react, he ducked beneath my blade and stepped inside my guard with terrifying speed.

His hand shot out, grabbing my remaining wrist, and in one swift motion, my second dagger slipped from my fingers. And I was disarmed. In seconds.

A surge of frustration hit me like a wave. But I didn't have time to dwell on it. Manakel's other hand moved fast, catching me by the waist and pulling me into him, too close, too suddenly. My breath caught in my throat. I could feel the warmth of his body, the strength in his arms that held me firm without hesitation.

I realized at that moment how outmatched I was. He had completely neutralized me, and I bet it wasn't even half of what he could do.

His breath brushed my ear, warm and steady, and his voice dropped to a soft command. "Yield."

I wanted to fight it. I wanted to keep going, to prove that I could get back on my feet and finish this. But in my gut, I knew it was pointless. He'd disarmed me, outmaneuvered me, and now he had me in his grip. There was no way I could win this.

My shoulders sagged, and I let out a frustrated breath. "Fine," I muttered, trying to make my voice sound more annoyed than defeated. "I yield."

The moment the words left my mouth, Manakel released me. His eyes were guarded, but there was something else flickering in them, something that made my pulse quicken. He gave me a slow nod—no smugness this time. There was only respect.

"You're good. Better with these for sure," he said, his voice quieter now, almost admiring. "But you still have a lot to learn."

I scowled, wiping the sweat from my forehead as I bent down to pick up my daggers, feeling the weight of my defeat. But despite the frustration gnawing at me, there was a small part of me that couldn't help but feel a flicker of pride.

"I'll get better," I promised, my voice more confident than I felt.

Manakel's smile was subtle, but it was there. "I'm counting on it, Wildheart."

I lost track of time, something I frequently did, but it wasn't until the sun began to dip lower in the sky that I realized how late it had actually gotten. My grandmother still wasn't back, and the worry that had been nagging at the back of my mind all day finally bloomed into something more substantial.

As much as Manakel had been a distraction, keeping me occupied with his quiet presence and sharp gaze, it was unlike my grandmother to be gone all day without at least telling me. My mom hadn't even come back yet, and I was left here alone with him. The silence between us had stretched for hours, and I tried to tell myself that it wasn't that bad. I didn't feel unsafe with Manakel. I'd known that the minute I saw him, but I still didn't *know* him. I didn't know why he was here or what he wanted with me.

The growing knot in my stomach was hard to ignore now. The sun was setting, and with it, my patience.

Manakel must have sensed the shift in my energy because he stood up and sat in a chair in the corner of the backyard. It was almost comical how small it seemed beneath him, like it was struggling to contain him. He didn't say anything, though. Just sat there, watching me in a calm and calculating way.

The silence stretched, and I couldn't take it anymore. "So where exactly did you say my grandmother went?" I asked, my voice more clipped than I intended. "I just want to check on her quickly. She's been gone most of the day, and I'm starting to worry."

Manakel didn't hesitate. "I lied before." His voice was flat, matter-of-fact. "She didn't go to get herbs. But she *is* at a friend's house."

The air in the yard seemed to thicken with the weight of his words, and I froze. *He'd lied.* He admitted it so easily, and for some reason, that hit me harder than anything else.

My mind raced. Maybe I was being paranoid, or maybe my hormones were messing with my judgment today, but I had always been good at reading people. In assessing their character, their motivations. And right now, everything in me was telling me that I should be cautious.

Manakel continued, oblivious to the way my unease was growing. "I only lied about the herbs. She didn't tell me why she was going, or which friend, only that she wanted me to assist you today and assess your skills. Without you holding back."

I could see the discomfort on his face now, but it wasn't from the chair. It was the conversation. He didn't know how to handle this, how to deal with the question of trust that had just been opened between us.

"I knew if I'd said she was at a friend's, you probably wouldn't have been inclined to stay," he added, his voice softer, almost apologetic. "So I said the first thing I could think of, which, considering the variety of herbs right here, was probably not the smartest thing."

His words hung in the air, and all I wanted to do was storm out of the backyard and search for her. But where would I even start? She had so many friends, some who didn't even live in Laochra. I wouldn't know which direction to go in.

I felt trapped—caught between the confusion of the lies, the worry gnawing at me, and the ever-present question of who Manakel really was and what my grandmother had asked of him. His eyes searched mine, looking for something, maybe answers, maybe reassurance. But I couldn't give him any of that yet.

Before I could say anything, before I could make any decisions, the sound of shuffling at the back gate broke the tension. My heart lurched in my chest, and I turned toward the sound, my breath catching in my throat.

There she was, my grandmother.

13. A World Turned Inside Out

The sight of my grandmother stepping through the back gate hit me like a wave—relief that she was safe, anger that she'd been gone all day without a word, and confusion about her connection to Manakel. She didn't seem to share any of my anxiety as she strolled in, a soft smile on her face, and her long golden braid swaying with every step. As if she hadn't left me to stew in worry for hours, or left me here alone with this giant stranger.

"Well, looks like you two survived," she said lightly, giving me a knowing look, and then turning her attention to Manakel. "How'd it go?" she asked, completely ignoring my stunned silence.

Manakel stood with a slight groan, the small chair creaking as it was released from his weight. He nodded once, that same stoic expression settling back into place, but his eyes flicked toward me briefly. "She has potential," he said flatly, as if I weren't standing right there, as if he weren't assessing me like some kind of object.

"Potential?" The word was out of my mouth before I could stop it, and I scoffed, finally finding my voice. "What is going on here? And why was he assessing me? You've been gone all day without saying a word, and now you just waltz in like nothing happened?"

My grandmother's expression softened at my frustration, and she reached out to place a calming hand on my arm. The touch felt like it came from a lifetime ago, something that belonged to a world where everything was simple and safe. But I was done with comfort, done with the lies. "I didn't mean to worry you, dear," she said, her voice low and soothing. "I know you're confused, but there are things I need to explain. Important things, and I needed a moment to collect myself before telling you everything."

Her eyes darted toward Manakel, then back to me, and I could feel a shift in the air like the world was holding its breath. There was something ominous behind her words now, and it made the hair on the back of my neck stand on end.

I shook my head, stepping back from her touch as the confusion morphed into frustration. "Explain what? Why you left me with a stranger? Why he's been lying to me all day?" My voice rose, tight with the rawness of my emotions.

Manakel, of course, remained unfazed. His eyes met mine with that familiar intensity as if I was the one out of place here.

"He's not a stranger," my grandmother said quietly, her words barely above a whisper. "Manakel's been watching over you for some time now."

Watching over me? I froze. The words didn't fully register. What was she talking about? I glanced at Manakel, who stood still, his eyes still fixed on me, but something was unsettling about it now. Something I hadn't noticed before.

There was a moment of silence as I tried to make sense of her words, my mind scrambling to connect the dots. Watching over me? Had he been here all this time, and I hadn't known? Had he been observing me, waiting for this? I felt like the walls were closing in, like I was trapped in a story I didn't understand.

"Raine." My grandmother's voice cut through the fog in my mind, and I turned to look at her. "There's so much more at play than you realize. Just know, I kept it from you to protect you, but the time has come for you to understand your place in all of this. And Manakel is here to help guide you through what's coming next."

"What's coming?" The question slipped from my mouth before I could stop it. My throat was dry, and the words barely made it past my lips. I hadn't realized how desperately I wanted an answer, how much I needed to know what this was all about.

My grandmother's eyes softened, but the seriousness in her focus never wavered. "Your eighteenth birthday isn't just a rite of passage. Not for you. Not for our family." She paused as if gathering her thoughts. And for the first time, I saw her flustered, her calm demeanor faltering in the face of whatever she was about to say. She was scared—she was scared.

A cold feeling washed over me. Something in the pit of my stomach told me that whatever she was about to tell me was going to change everything. And I wasn't ready for it. I wasn't ready for more changes, for whatever this was that had my grandmother so shaken. After what happened in the forest yesterday, my mind kept racing to the worst-case scenario—death. I wasn't ready for that.

Manakel cleared his throat, breaking through the growing tension between us. He gave my grandmother what I could only assume was a reassuring nod, but it didn't reassure me. It only made my unease deepen. What did he know that I didn't? This stranger who had somehow been in the shadows of my life, watching, knowing more about me than I did about myself.

This was wrong. All of it was wrong. If something this monumental was coming in just five days, why hadn't my grandmother told me sooner? Why had she waited this long to prepare me for the truth?

I racked my brain, trying to recall the endless drills she'd made me go through over the years. The training, the tough love, the constant attention to detail. And then I remembered something—the tally in her book. Had that been for this? For whatever was coming? I had always thought it was just her way of teasing Wren, watching him get frustrated every time she added a point to my name, making him push harder, and lose focus. But now I wasn't so sure. Now, I wondered if there was something more to it. Something I didn't understand, and no one seemed willing to explain.

Done with the glances and the silent communication between Manakel and my grandmother, I couldn't take it anymore. The tension between us had been building for far too long, and I was done being left out.

"So, is someone going to fill me in on what's going on or what?" My voice was sharper than I meant it to be, but I was done with the mystery. "You both keep saying there's more at play here, but you haven't shared what that is. Please, for the love of whatever I just witnessed, get this over with. It's glaringly obvious by the looks you two are sharing that it's not going to be good news, and I'm tired and hungry, so let's move this along."

I wasn't proud of the way my tone had risen, but I didn't care anymore. I was beyond the point of being patient, beyond the point of trying to make sense of whatever was happening. It felt like I was the last one to know anything, and I was sick of it.

My grandmother's gaze shifted back to me, her expression torn, her hands twisting together. I'd always known her to be strong and confident—an unshakable pillar in my life. But now, seeing her this way, something shifted in me. I didn't know if I was scared or just confused, but the feeling churned in my stomach. Manakel stood next to her, his presence like a stone wall—imposing and steady. But that was the thing: he looked like he knew everything while I was left in the dark, drowning in uncertainty.

"You're right, Raine. You deserve the truth," she said, her voice barely above a whisper, trembling with emotion. "The reason I haven't told you sooner is because I didn't want to burden you with it unless absolutely necessary." She paused, her eyes searching mine for any sign that I understood. "When you turn eighteen, it's not just a milestone for you.

It's when you can decide if you want to awaken… another part of you—an immortal part."

I blinked, her words hanging in the air like a cruel joke. Immortal? That word didn't even make sense in my mind. It felt like I had just been hit with something too heavy to grasp, my heart thumping louder in my chest.

"What?" I stammered, the word escaping like a breath I didn't mean to let go. "What do you mean, 'immortal'?"

Her eyes drifted toward Manakel briefly, a glance laden with something I couldn't name. "You carry my blood, Raine—and with it, the gift of immortality."

I shook my head, disbelief flooding my senses. My grandmother had always seemed different. Sure, her timeless looks were unmarked by the years and had always been something I couldn't fully explain, but I'd always chalked it up to some secret tonics or her unyielding energy. Not… immortality.

No, this explanation was absurd. A cruel, twisted joke. My mother, Baren, and Wren weren't immortal. I'd seen them age over the years, so it was highly unlikely. But what if I'd missed something? What if the family I thought I knew, this world I thought I understood, was all based on a lie?

None of it seemed to make sense anymore. I couldn't think straight or even concentrate on the questions plaguing my mind. I shook my head, the words escaping me in a disjointed blur. "Does that mean… Mom, Baren," My voice faltered as I whispered my brother's name, "and Wren are too?"

She looked at me, sadness clouding her face. She had to know the betrayal I was feeling. And yet, even as I wanted to comfort her, I couldn't—because right now, she felt as much of a stranger to me as the silent, looming figure beside her.

"No, no one else knows," she said softly. "Not even your mother. This is a secret I've kept tightly because I didn't want to burden any of you with this choice. Not unless it was absolutely necessary."

A choice?

More like a life-changing LIE! And now, she was dumping it all on me. My stomach twisted with a surge of anger that burned hot. "So why tell me? Why keep this secret for so long just to suddenly spring it on me now?" My mind was reeling, "I mean, why the need to finally share something as little as, I don't know, THE FACT THAT OUR FAMILY CAN'T DIE?" My voice rose, the frustration seeping out in sharp waves. "And what about the river? Isn't that supposed to keep your kind out? But I guess considering Manakel's appearance, that was a lie too? Something to make us feel safe while immortals could just cross it leisurely?"

The words spilled from me before I could stop them. I didn't care. This was insane. It had to be. Everything I thought I knew was collapsing around me, like a house of cards, and I couldn't breathe. Was my whole life a lie? A lie to try and think we were safe on this side of the river?

My grandmother's eyes were soft, but they were filled with something else now—guilt, perhaps? I didn't know anymore. She placed a hand gently on my arm as if that could make everything better. "The river's magic is very real, and that's why this is so important, Raine." Her voice was steady but filled with a sense of gravity that made my skin prickle. "When you turn eighteen, you'll have to decide if you want to accept this burden. You're the only one who can save us—save this village."

My mind reeled. Save the village? I couldn't make sense of it. Save them from what? What kind of power could I possibly have?

Before I could ask, Manakel spoke, his voice low but certain. "The river... It's losing its strength. Every day it weakens. It seems the Queen of Dermaine left out a crucial part of the treaty when creating the river. We don't know if she never told your King or if he simply chose not to tell his people."

He glanced at my grandmother for approval before continuing. I didn't know what to make of him now, but the way he spoke made me uneasy. Like he wasn't just a messenger but someone who had more to do with all of this than I could see.

"The Queen intended for the river to last only a hundred years. After that, it would lose its magic, no longer able to stop the immortals from crossing over."

The weight of his words hit me like a cold gust of wind. "No," I whispered. "That doesn't make sense."

"There's still a chance to stop it," Manakel continued, and his eyes hardened. "It's risky, but it's possible. The hundred years will be up in sixty-two days. We have sixty-one days left to get to Dermaine and beg the Queen to extend the river. If we don't, the immortals will be able to roam free, and you're the only one who can stop it."

I blinked, my heart pounding as everything began to spin out of control. "Wait… you want me to go with you? After all this, you think I'm just going to—?"

I couldn't even finish the sentence. The thought of traveling with him, back into the forest, was insane. Every part of me screamed against it.

Manakel seemed to read my hesitation and paused as if weighing his words. I could see that he was trying to gauge me, trying to figure out whether I was worth the effort. But right now, I didn't care what he thought. I was drowning in this mess.

My grandmother, ever the steady hand, spoke up again, her voice soft but firm. "You don't have to do anything you don't want to, Raine. I'll start with that. Even if you choose not to do anything, I'll answer all your questions. I know you must have a lot."

Understatement of the year. I nodded, but my thoughts were spinning so fast, I wasn't sure I could follow all the details she was giving me.

"If," she said, her voice tightening with purpose, "you choose to go through with this, you won't automatically become immortal. The imbe rite is a choice, one that every immortal must make at your age before awakening the magic." She gave me a hard look, waiting for me to argue. "You only have half the gene, so it's not strong and pulsing like a full immortal gene would be, but it's still there, small but ever present." She swallowed nervously as if someone had just shattered her life, but I listened anyway. "If you choose not to do this, then it won't affect you past your birthday, but to reveal your full power and step into immortality, you must undergo something called the imbe rite."

Manakel nodded in agreement, and this time he spoke with more authority. "Yes. The imbe rite is a tradition of my people. It was created millennia ago to control immortals and stop unnecessary breeding. The rite is something you choose to participate in, but if you do, there is no turning back. No way to reverse it, so it's a choice I advise you don't make lightly."

I stared at him, my mind screaming. Immortal? Me? I still couldn't comprehend it. I had so many questions and so many doubts, but one thing stood out above all else.

"You've known this my *whole life*? And you just chose *not* to tell me?" I croaked, my eyes darting to my grandmother as my voice cracked with the weight of everything. "How could you—how could he know before I did?"

Manakel stepped forward, his eyes softening for the first time. "I've been watching over you, Raine," he said quietly, his deep voice steady. "Your grandmother chose not to tell you about your immortality because it's more of a curse than anything." He looked towards her now before continuing, "But when I found you in the forest last night, I questioned if you were training for the rite. I asked her if it was because of the upcoming deadline and realized she, like you, had no idea."

I felt a surge of anger, but before I could lash out, he added, "I know this is a lot. But with your eighteenth birthday only six days away, you need to decide if you're ready."

I clenched my fists, the pressure of it all threatening to crush me. "Before I agree to anything, I need to know exactly what I'm agreeing to." I tried to steady my voice but failed. "I've been living a lie, sharing a room with this liar. And now, I get to decide if I want to be part of it. How nice of you to offer me a choice in my death."

Manakel's eyes were steady. "It's not deadly. The imbe rite tests your character and your worthiness, and if you pass, you will be granted immortality. With it, you'll gain power—more than you can imagine. But it's not a gift—it's a responsibility."

I swallowed hard, barely able to process the weight of his words. "What happens if I don't pass?" I asked, voice trembling.

His expression was intense. "If you don't pass, you'll lose everything you know. Not only your future, but your family's safety. Immortals will cross the river, and there will be bloodshed all over Luminara."

My chest tightened, the suffocating weight of his words threatening to swallow me whole. "No pressure." I tried to laugh sarcastically, but I was trapped in a nightmare I hadn't asked for. A nightmare I didn't know how to survive.

The choice before me seemed impossible. And no matter what I decided, there was no escaping this secret now.

"Why didn't you prepare me for this?" My voice cracked as I demanded the answer, though I already knew the weight of her guilt would crush me. "Why didn't you tell me?" The question echoed through the quiet, raw, and desperate. Hurt laced every syllable, but I didn't care. She needed to understand how deeply this had cut into me.

My grandmother's eyes dropped to her trembling hands, and I could see the guilt etched into every line of her face. Her shoulders sagged as though the weight of a thousand years pressed down on her. "I didn't know about the treaty expiring," she murmured, her voice thick with regret. "I thought I could protect you from this, just like I did with your mother and brothers. But now it seems you may be our only hope to save this village and all of Rioga." Her voice faltered, and she met my eyes, remorse flooding her expression. "I'm so sorry, Raine. This was never supposed to be your burden."

Tears threatened to spill from my eyes, but I blinked them back fiercely, refusing to show any more weakness. My mind was already spinning with the weight of everything I had just learned. It was too much. I couldn't wrap my head around it all. How had everything been a lie?

"And the forest?" My voice shook, and I hated the vulnerability that slipped through. "Yesterday… that was connected to all of this, wasn't it?" My throat felt tight, as though I couldn't breathe properly.

Manakel nodded, his expression somber, his eyes dark with something

I couldn't quite place. "The forest is pulsing with magic, and it's drawn to you, Raine. There are ancient forces at play, some of them wanting to stop you from fulfilling your destiny. You've already been marked by the forest. It's why I intervened."

Marked. The word slithered into my thoughts like ice, sending a cold shiver down my spine. I wrapped my arms around myself, a feeble attempt to ward off the chill that now seemed to fill the air. It wasn't cold, not really, but my body shuddered in reaction to the weight of his words. The forest. Marked. What did that even mean?

I wanted to run. Escape. I wanted to scream until everything made sense again; until this impossible nightmare ended, but I couldn't. There was nowhere to run. I had to face it.

"So… what now?" I forced the question out, my voice barely steady. I felt like I was teetering on the edge of a cliff, unable to find solid ground beneath me. "What do I do?"

My grandmother's voice cracked as she stepped closer, her touch gentle but firm on my cheek. Her eyes softened with something I couldn't name. "You decide and then we prepare," she said, the determination in her voice unmistakable. "You have six days until the rite, and we will make sure you are ready. We will face this together, as a family."

Family. The word tasted bitter in my mouth. How could she even say that word to me right now, after everything that had been kept from me? The family she had lied to my entire life… the family I now had to lie to as well? How could I look my brothers in the eye and pretend that this wasn't all a huge mistake?

I turned away, my stare locking on Manakel. I still wasn't sure what to make of him—should I trust him? Or fear him? He was the reason I even knew any of this, the one who had come into our lives like a shadow, knowing things I couldn't even begin to comprehend. "And what about you?" My voice dropped, barely a whisper, "Are you here to protect me?"

His eyes met mine, and for a moment, it felt like the world paused. There was a flicker of something in them—regret? Guilt? Or was it understanding? I couldn't tell, but his stare held me steady as he spoke, his voice calm and unwavering. "And to prepare you for what's ahead."

My life, everything I had thought I knew, had just been shattered in an instant. He was part of the reason for that destruction. But, for all the anger I felt, there was also a part of me that wanted to believe him. Wanted to believe that somehow, he had answers and would help me. But then again, what if those answers led to even more danger?

I nodded stiffly, my heart heavy in my chest. I couldn't bring myself to speak, couldn't express the whirlwind of emotions churning inside me. Six days. Six days to prepare for something I wasn't even sure I could ever be ready for. To learn how to face magic I hadn't known existed. To face a future that seemed darker and more dangerous than I could ever have imagined. I wasn't ready—not by a long shot—but for the sake of my family, for the village I had grown up in, I would do what I had to. No matter how terrified I was.

I had no choice. I couldn't let them down.

14. The Edge Of Loyalty

I barely slept. My body twisted and turned under the weight of the impossible truth I had just learned. Everything I thought I knew felt like it was being ripped apart and rewritten. Immortality. Powers. Secrets buried so deep they'd reshaped the foundation of my entire life. How could my life be turned upside down in a single day?

My thoughts swirled, relentless and unyielding. Manakel and his cryptic intentions, my grandmother's half-truths, the looming reality of my imbe rite. Five days. In five days, I would cross the river, and my life would never be the same. Would I be able to do it? Would I survive whatever challenges were thrown at me? And if I did, and somehow got the Queen to reconsider, would I even be able to come back home? I didn't know the answers to any of it, and couldn't help but wonder if, when all was said and done, I would still be myself. Would the people I loved recognize the change, or worse, fear me for what I had no choice but to become?

I rolled over instinctively, expecting the soft, steady rhythm of my grandmother's breathing beside me, like it had been on so many sleepless nights before. But the other side of the room was cold. Her bed empty. I sat up, the dim light from the lantern on the vanity catching her figure. She was perched at the edge of the table, her journal open, her pen moving steadily across the pages. The sight of her calm, methodical focus lit a spark of frustration in me. How was she okay with all of this? Not only keeping this secret, but with giving me no real choice in the matter either.

I didn't even stop to think before the words came tumbling out. "So I assume I'm expected to lie to Mom and Wren about everything, right?" My voice was sharper than I intended, my emotions too raw to contain. "Just what, act normal while I'm hiding this huge life-changing thing from everyone?" I scoffed bitterly, unable to hold back my hurt. "Unlike you, I'm not exactly *comfortable* lying to my family."

Her hand stilled, the pen hovering over the page, and I saw her entire body tense. She didn't look at me right away, taking a few moments to breathe before turning, but when she did, her calm demeanor made my anger flare even hotter.

"You can tell whoever you want, Raine," she said, her tone maddeningly measured and soft. "It's your secret now, too. But you do need to understand what that would mean." She exhaled before continuing, "Most people in Laochra, all of Rioga, actually, fear anything to do with immortality. If this gets out, it won't just affect you; it will also put all of them in danger. Wren, your mom, even your Dad, and Baren on their travels."

Her words hit like a punch to the gut. I hadn't thought of that. What if my secret brought them pain? What if my actions made them targets for hate? Up until yesterday, the only knowledge of immortals was what had been shared in the stories, and that didn't exactly paint them in a favorable light. Finding out one lived among us all along was sure to cause an uproar, and as much as I was angry at my grandmother now, I didn't want a secret she had been able to hide for over a century to affect her life here. Or my family's life. I clenched my fists, swallowing hard against the rising tide of guilt.

I sighed, my anger ebbing into resignation. "I guess I can see *why* you kept it hidden," I said, my voice quieter now. "But *how*? How did you keep this secret for so long without… breaking, without telling someone?"

She closed her journal slowly, resting her hands on the cover as though drawing strength from it. When her eyes met mine, there was a softness that hadn't been there before. "It wasn't easy," she admitted, her voice lower, almost tender. "It was lonely. Crushing, at times. But I knew it was the only way to keep everyone safe. The only time I ever told anyone was when your grandfather was dying." Her voice faltered for a moment, and I saw the grief flicker across her face. "I owed him the truth. He gave me a life and a love I never thought possible—with a human, no less. And when I told him… he didn't even flinch." She smiled softly, as if reliving the moment in her mind, "He looked at me like he always did, like I was still his Leighna. Like my immortality was just another piece of me to love."

Her words softened the edges of my frustration, cutting through my anger with something much harder to face: understanding. She paused, drawing in a slow breath before continuing. "I almost told your mother that day, too. You were just two years old, and even then, I could see the strength in you, the spark. The difference between you and your brothers. But I couldn't do it. Losing your grandfather…" Her voice broke, and she glanced down at the journal, her hands tightening around its edges. "I just… I couldn't risk losing anyone else I loved. So I kept it hidden. For you. For our family. For all of us."

The room felt heavy with her words, the air thick with the weight of everything she'd carried for so long. I hadn't seen it before, the toll her silence had taken on her. The loneliness. The sacrifices. And now she'd passed that burden on to me.

I pressed my palms into my eyes, the exhaustion crashing over me like a wave as the truth of it settled around us. "I think I'll try to get some sleep," I muttered, my voice tight and fraying at the edges. I couldn't bear to keep talking, to keep feeling the enormity of everything. Morning would come too soon, and with it, another impossible day with decisions I wasn't ready to make.

I hesitated before lying back down, a question slipping from my lips before I could stop it. "What happens to me after I cross the river?" My voice was quiet but insistent, trembling with the weight of what I feared the answer might be. "And if the Queen agrees to extend the treaty… will I ever be able to come back here? Back home?"

The knot in my chest tightened as I spoke, the thought of leaving my family, of never seeing them again, threatening to suffocate me. How could I leave them behind? How could I leave this behind?

My grandmother froze for a moment, her pen poised mid-air. Her expression softened as she turned to face me, her eyes filled with a sadness I couldn't quite decipher. "I wish I had an answer for you, Raine," she said gently, her voice laced with regret. It was the kind of regret that spoke of years of pain, of choices made when there was no right answer. "Only you can decide what's best for you. And whatever choice you make, it will be the right one."

Her words hung in the air, offering me little comfort, but she continued anyway, "The world outside this village is vast, endless even," she whispered. "You've always had a restless heart, my Wildheart. Even if you *can* come back… I don't think you'll *want* to. There's so much more out there waiting for you to explore."

Her words twisted something deep inside me. She meant to reassure me, to remind me of the dreams of freedom I'd nurtured all my life, but all they did was deepen my confusion. How could I choose between the family I loved and the promise of a life beyond the borders of Laochra? Between the world I'd always known and the one that was being thrust upon me now?

I had spent years dreaming of what lay beyond this village and the forest, of places I'd only heard of in stories. But now, with that world suddenly within reach, it didn't feel like freedom—it felt like another prison. A cage, gilded with promises of power and immortality but locked with choices I didn't feel ready to make.

I stared at the ceiling long after she turned back to her journal, my thoughts swirling in endless circles.

Waking up, I hoped—*prayed*—that this was all just a terrible dream. But the ache in my muscles, the dull throb in my head, and the hollow pit in my stomach reminded me that it wasn't.

I wasn't just turning eighteen, I was becoming something else entirely. Something I hadn't even known was a possibility until yesterday. Something I wasn't ready to face. *Immortality*. A fate that had always been painted as dangerous. Evil. Soulless. And now, it was going to be mine.

A few days ago, I dreaded being forced to find a job in Laochra, being stuck here longer than planned. But now, I was facing something much more difficult—leaving my family and embracing a new life as an immortal.

I pressed my face into the pillow, willing the tears to stay hidden. The weight of my grandmother's words, of the choices looming before me, felt impossible to bear. It felt like a death sentence in its own way—the death of my normal life, and the birth of a new one that I wasn't sure I wanted at all.

In five days, I would cross the river. And nothing—*nothing*—would ever be the same again. Not who I was, not my family, or even the small village I resented. In five days, whether I was ready or not, the life I knew would no longer exist. And it no longer felt like a dream to leave it all behind.

I didn't understand why it had to be me.

Why the weight of everything, this prophecy, this power, this impossible future, was suddenly resting on my shoulders. It felt like a mistake. Like someone had pulled the wrong thread in the loom of fate, and now I was tangled in something far bigger than I could ever hope to carry. I wasn't ready. I didn't think I ever would be.

And sure, I had Manakel's help—his guidance, his relentless calm in the face of my spiraling thoughts—but it wasn't like we could exactly train in the backyard. Not without raising questions. Big, impossible-to-explain questions.

There was no universe where I could casually explain the existence of a towering immortal man with shadows in our garden, no matter how quick I was at improvising.

I stepped into the kitchen, hoping for a distraction, something grounding. But the moment I saw Wren's satchel slumped on the table, daggers catching the light, my chest tightened again.

He must've gotten in late last night and dumped everything in his usual storm of exhaustion and carelessness. It should've felt normal. Comforting, even. A piece of everyday life that hadn't cracked beneath the weight of everything I'd learned. But I couldn't find peace in the clutter. *Not today.*

My mind wouldn't stop racing, every thought tripping over the next, skipping ahead to questions I wasn't ready to ask, let alone answer.

My stomach tightened as I heard the faintest rustling outside, the calm before the storm of whatever I was being thrust into today. I peeked out the window and saw Manakel waiting for me in the garden, lounging like it was just another lazy morning, the kind where nothing was amiss. But nothing felt normal anymore.

I stormed outside, irritation bubbling in my chest, a tidal wave of frustration crashing into me as I approached him.

"You can't just be here hanging around in plain sight!" I snapped, gesturing toward him. He was far too relaxed, far too confident with his infuriating smirk. Didn't he understand the kind of trouble he could get me into? I was already juggling a dozen lies, and I couldn't add explaining his presence to the list. My family would never buy it. Especially not Wren. He'd never believe Manakel was from here, especially with his otherworldly aura hanging around him like a dark cloud of shadows.

Manakel chuckled softly, completely unfazed, his calmness infuriating me further. I swatted his arm in annoyance. "This isn't a joke," I muttered, crossing my arms, suddenly feeling too small to be scolding someone like him.

"We need a new plan if this is going to work. My brother and mother are home today, and they're *definitely* going to ask questions if they see you. I'm not sure I can lie to them about anything else. Not now, not after everything. I'm already keeping too much and have to leave in five days with no real reason why." I sighed, feeling the weight of the world on my shoulders.

Instead of laughing at my melodrama like I expected, he simply stood, his towering figure making me feel even more insignificant. "Well, good thing today's training was meant to focus on history and information," he said, his voice smooth but firm. "We can do that in the forest. It actually might help you understand what you'll be up against." He looked at me with an authoritative expression before pointing behind us, "Meet me behind that tree in an hour. Don't be late."

His words were like a command, and the authority in his tone made it clear that disobeying wasn't an option. My chest tightened. If I didn't show up, he would probably come back here and drag me into the forest himself.

He offered only a nod in parting, as if what we were preparing for wasn't about to shatter the reshape my entire life. And then, as if it were the most casual thing in the world, large black wings appeared behind him.

Not imagined.

Not hinted at in shadow.

But real wings.

Dark as obsidian, vast as storm clouds, they unfurled from his back like shadow and smoke woven into something living. They stretched from his back with a quiet power that made the hairs on my arms rise. I took a step back without meaning to, breath caught somewhere between awe and sheer confusion.

He didn't even flinch. Just unfurled them fully, glanced once over his shoulder, and launched into the sky like gravity meant nothing.

And then... he was gone. Vanished into thin air like I'd imagined it all. As if the towering, winged being that stood in front of me seconds ago had been part of a dream I hadn't yet woken from. And I was reminded how little I understood about the world outside of Laochra.

I stood frozen, the world tilting beneath my feet, as silence rushed in to fill the space he left behind.

Manakel had wings.

I knew I'd seen them once before, flickering through the trees the night of the attack, cloaked in moonlight and doubt. I'd convinced myself it was my imagination, a trick of fear or desperation holding onto the impossible. But I wasn't imagining anything now.

The world I thought I understood was starting to come apart at the seams. If men could grow wings and vanish into the sky like it was nothing…What else was out there? What else was real?

Suddenly, my village felt too small, and everything beyond it felt impossibly large. Unknown. Dangerous.

I hadn't asked for any of this. Not immortality. Not the secrets. Not walking straight into a rite that could kill me. And certainly not him.

But here it was anyway—unraveling around me, pulling me into a life I hadn't chosen, and somewhere deep in my stomach, the dread I'd been trying to ignore finally settled in, heavy and cold.

I knew nothing about the world outside of Laochra. And I was starting to think that ignorance had been a luxury I could no longer afford.

I rushed back into the house, trying to act as if it was just another morning in the garden. The smell of breakfast wafted through the air, and I found my mother's back turned toward me, busy preparing food. Wren was sitting at the table, looking impatient as usual, a scowl on his face.

"Finally," he grumbled as I entered. "Mom wouldn't let me start without you, and I feel like I've been sitting here for hours, starving." He rolled his eyes before whispering, "Where were you, anyway?"

I scrambled for an excuse, my mind going blank. I needed to keep things normal, to convince him I hadn't just seen a winged immortal vanish into thin air. "Oh, I was cleaning my daggers by the side of the house," I said quickly, trying to sound nonchalant. "You were still sleeping when I woke up, and I needed something productive to do while you slept the day away."

Wren eyed me skeptically, the look in his eyes sharper than usual. He had a keen sense of knowing when I was lying, but thankfully, he didn't press. "Really?" he asked, his voice still carrying a trace of doubt. "Well, that's convenient. I was going to suggest heading out back today, it's been a while since we trained together, and I want to see where you need improvement. But let's eat first so my stomach will quit grumbling."

If only he knew that my need to clean my daggers was not out of boredom, but rather an attempt to erase all traces of the intense sparring session I had with Manakel yesterday. I also didn't feel like explaining the new skills I had acquired overnight and who taught them to me.

"Ohh…uhh," I stuttered, not sure what I could say to decline his offer. I never passed up an opportunity to train with him, and I felt heat rise to my cheeks as Wren's questioning gaze bore into me. "I wish I could," I said, flustered. "But I have other plans today. Ones that might take all day."

He didn't seem convinced. The way he tilted his head and studied me, his eyes narrowing with suspicion, made it clear that he wasn't buying my excuse. "Other plans? Really? Where are you headed?"

My heart skipped a beat. What could I possibly say that wouldn't raise alarm bells? I forced a shrug, hoping it looked casual. "Just some errands around the village. A few supplies and things I need to pick up before the end of the week." The lie tasted bitter on my tongue, but I couldn't afford to let it show. Not with Wren watching me like a hawk.

His eyes didn't waver. His lips twisted into a smirk. "Supplies and things? Sounds interesting! Want some company? I'll even offer to hold them for you."

I laughed too quickly, trying to deflect the conversation before he could dig deeper and spot the obvious lie. "It's not *that* interesting, Wren. And besides, I'm not a kid anymore, you don't have to follow me around like a chaperone."

He studied me a moment longer before nodding in agreement. This was getting dangerously close to a confrontation I didn't want. Thankfully, my mother chose that moment to turn around, carrying plates of food to the table. "Enough chattering, both of you," she said, her voice light and playful. "Eat up before breakfast gets cold."

Grateful for the brief reprieve, I focused on the food in front of me and hoped that my brother would drop the subject. But I knew him too well. He wasn't done with the questions yet, and as much as I wanted to confide in him and tell him everything, I also knew, for his safety, that was the last thing I should do.

We finished our breakfast in silence, sneaking glances between bites. Wren could read me like an open book, and he could no doubt tell I was hiding something from him, but didn't know what. If I was going to pull this off and keep them safe, I needed to get better at lying. At least for the next five days.

Once breakfast was finished, I excused myself quickly, eager to escape another interrogation, and hurried upstairs to change. Knowing I had exactly one hour to meet Manakel, I couldn't afford to be late. There was no way to lie my way out of who he was or why he was here.

I slipped into a fitted tunic, the sleeves brushing my wrists like whispered reassurance. My trousers—plain, worn, soft, and easy to move in—were the kind of nondescript that promised I'd draw no questions. Not that I had any answers worth giving. I wasn't exactly given any more information since the *"you're an immortal"* secret was dropped in my lap.

My fingers worked through my hair with practiced ease, braiding it back with quick, familiar motions. It was something to do, something to keep me from falling apart as the ache in my chest pulsed louder. I hated lying and secrets. It was one of the reasons I asked as many questions as I did. Yet, here I was keeping the biggest secrets of all and actively lying to keep them.

I understood it was to protect my family, but when did lies, even necessary ones, become a good thing? And what would happen if Wren saw through the lies like he usually did? What if he followed me into the woods?

There would be no explaining that. No harmless excuse for venturing into the trees alone—not when he knew me well enough to be suspicious. Curious, yes. But not reckless.

I laced up my ankle boots and reached for my cloak—deep emerald, lined with soft wool and heavy enough to shield against the creeping autumn chill. I fastened it at the throat, and the fabric fell around me like a shield: quiet, concealed, forgettable. Just another curious villager slipping through the shadows of the trees.

I cracked the door open and stepped into the corridor, each footfall deliberate, measured. I didn't breathe until I reached the end of the hall, afraid that any noise would announce my departure. Wren's voice drifted from the hearth room, warm and full of easy laughter as he spoke with my mother. I clung to the sound—his distraction, my salvation.

I offered a silent prayer to the gods for their mercy. Or their timing.

This was my chance to escape unnoticed. It was now or never. I moved through the kitchen in silence, every step deliberate, every breath held tight in my chest. My hand curled around the back door's handle, and I winced as it creaked open, sharp and accusing in the quiet.

When I was finally outside, I exhaled in relief, but the weight of my actions hung heavy. I couldn't let myself be seen or followed.

Not now. Not with everything on the line. Not with everything I was risking to keep my family safe.

So I ran. I ran as fast as I could through the shadows of my own backyard and into the forest that had once taken me, feet flying over soil I used to fear, heart thundering like a warning.

And with every step, I prayed I wasn't running straight into a trap.

But the truth was… I wouldn't know until it was too late.

15. Unraveling

Manakel's piercing stare met mine as I approached, his brow furrowed in a deep scowl that made my heart skip. The tension in his jaw made it clear he wasn't thrilled that I was almost late. But even with that irritation etched on his face, there was no denying how magnetic he was. His presence was overwhelming—not just because of his looks, though that was a distraction all its own—but because the confidence radiating from him wasn't arrogance, but certainty. He knew exactly who he was, and more importantly, what he was capable of. It was that knowing, that calm power, that made him stand out in a world of uncertainty.

I couldn't help but wonder what it must feel like to carry that kind of certainty in your bones. To walk through the world with a presence so sure of itself, it never had to demand attention. It simply was.

But I caught myself, heat rising in my cheeks before the thought even finished forming.

I wasn't here to fawn over him. And I reminded myself—*again*—that whatever Manakel was, he wasn't human. Still... I'd never met anyone like him. Not in Laochra. And trying to compare him to the boys in town felt ridiculous, like holding up a flickering candle beside a star and pretending they gave off the same light.

He would always win. Not just in strength or stature, but in the way he carried himself. Calm. Collected. Confident.

I wasn't immune to his looks, but this wasn't about attraction. It was more… a fascination. Curiosity. He was unlike anyone I'd ever known. And that made him dangerous because my curious nature wanted to know everything. Not just about surviving the rite, or what I'd expect to face in the river, but about him, too.

"You're almost late," he growled, his voice a low rumble that seemed to reverberate through the air, making the leaves at our feet tremble.

I shrugged, trying to maintain an air of nonchalance, though the buzz of nervous energy under my skin told a different story. "Well, I'm here now, aren't I? And with a couple of minutes left to spare."

He raised an eyebrow, clearly unimpressed with my casual response, but he looked like someone who wasn't going to waste their time scolding me. "Let's get started. We have a lot to cover and not enough time to do it in." He said with a frustrated growl.

I nodded, my stomach tight with nerves, but I forced myself to focus. Whatever this training was going to entail, I needed to be sharp. Manakel may have been fascinating, but he was also intimidating, and my only way to understand the new world I was being thrust into. That is, if I even decided to go through with the rite. I still had a choice in the matter, even if it didn't really feel like it.

"Okay, so," he began, his voice more serious now, "I'm not sure how much you know about Immorro or the types of immortals and their unique gifts, but this training isn't just about surviving your rite. It's about what to expect when you come out of it."

I shuddered involuntarily at the word "rite" and everything that suddenly felt too real. All my life, I'd been taught that immortals were dangerous. Unnatural. Gifted with power they didn't deserve and cursed with hearts that couldn't feel the way ours did. They were the villains in every story, the shadow lurking beyond the border.

And yet, here I was standing beside one, and unknowingly, sleeping beside one my entire life. It was a lot to process. Too much, maybe.

I was still struggling to accept that my grandmother—the woman I trusted more than anyone, the one who taught me how to braid my hair and combine herbs for tonics—wasn't just an elder. She was one of the things she warned me about. An immortal.

And in five days, I would be too.

The thought alone felt like it might split me in half. I didn't know what that made me, what I'd become once I decided to accept my imbe rite, and I wasn't sure I was ready to find out.

Manakel's eyes narrowed as he noticed my discomfort, but he continued. "I know it seems like a lot we have to cover, but I want you as prepared as possible."

I nodded, noting that being prepared *was* important, so I should probably be listening instead of internally spiraling.

"You'll encounter a few Eldren along this side of the forest as you make your way toward the river," Manakel said, his tone calm, almost dismissive. "Most are harmless, curious more than anything. But the ones who may be of use to you..."

He glanced past me, toward the trees. "...you'll find them beyond the river, deeper within the woods that border Dermaine."

"Eldren?" I repeated the word, unfamiliar.

He gave a small nod. "Eldren were created with old magic. Creatures born of the wilds—of river and root, cave and flame. They're not immortal like me or human like you. They're something else entirely."

I stared at him, my mind racing to stitch the truth into something coherent. I'd grown up on stories, yes—warnings about the forest, whispers about the river—but never this. No one had ever named them or talked about any creatures beyond immortals as a whole. Every warning or story only generalized them.

"And these Eldren, they can help me during the rite?"

He paused, "The Eldren may choose to help you, or test you. It's entirely up to them as they don't owe us allegiance."

"So, the Eldren in the woods beyond the river will *also* be trying to test me?" I asked out loud, mostly to make sure I was understanding. Not only did I have to survive a deadly river and *its* creatures, but also whatever lived and lurked within the trees before and after it? It sounded insurmountable.

"Probably. As will some immortals that have settled in Dermaine. News of your rite will no doubt be whispered and known," he said casually.

I blinked. "I thought Dermaine was primarily human lands… apart from the evil Queen in the castle, of course." The words slipped out before I could think better of them. Manakel's expression darkened, and I could tell he didn't appreciate the term.

His jaw tightened, irritation simmering just beneath the surface. "Well, yes, it's mostly humans. At least it *used* to be. But lately it's become more complicated than that."

I frowned, confused. "What do you mean, 'complicated'?"

"There are parts of Dermaine, near the main city, that are still inhabited mostly by humans, or humans with immortal partners who try their best to blend in. But other parts, especially the outskirts or closer to the woods, have been infiltrated by more immortals since the rumors of the river magic expiring surfaced," he explained, tensing more with each word. "Most immortals want to live quietly and in peace, but there are others who are biding their time, waiting for the river to lose its power. *Those* are the only immortals you should fear."

"How will I know if I've encountered one?"

He paused, exhaling softly, and said, "Trust your instincts and pay attention to your surroundings. If you feel uncomfortable or scared, it probably means you're in danger and shouldn't trust them."

The knot in my stomach tightened. "So… I'm supposed to trust *some* immortals, but not others, and trust I know the difference?" I asked, my voice a little shaky. The idea of navigating a world where I couldn't even tell the difference between friend and foe felt terrifying.

Manakel sighed, rubbing his temples as if my confusion was exhausting him. "Yes. Not *all* immortals are dangerous, Wildheart. But those who are… they've been shaped by centuries of fear, jealousy, and loss." He met my stare, his eyes intense. "You'll need to be careful who you trust, but know not everyone will be against you."

That explanation didn't make me feel any better, but I nodded. It's not like I'd be able to tell the difference or know their intentions, but I didn't say that out loud. "I get it," I whispered, more to myself than to him. "I think. But can we start from the beginning? I haven't been taught much about your kind, besides," I shot him a smirk. "You know, all immortals are evil, soulless, bloodthirsty killers that hate all humans."

He shook his head in what I assumed was disbelief, but at least he wasn't mad about my jab. "I expected you wouldn't know the specifics, but clearly you know nothing at all."

Manakel folded his arms and leaned back against the tree, his annoyance at my ignorance simmering. I guess he wasn't happy about having to explain the basic history of immortals, but I wasn't exactly doing this willingly either.

"Some, like us, Sciathain, and most of the Eldren were created with old magic by the gods and had no choice in becoming immortal. For us, it's just… life, the way we were made. But for others, most of Immorro, actually, immortality is a choice. The same as it is for you."

I was trying to focus and pay attention to everything he was saying, but my head was still spinning at why none of this was ever taught or spoken about in the stories. Did no one besides my grandmother really know what lived beyond our borders?

Manakel studied me for a moment, his usual calm demeanor returning. But now I could see the weight in his eyes. He wasn't just talking about immortality in abstract terms.

"A common misconception is that becoming immortal happens by accident, but it's not like someone can just be *turned* into one." He laughed like the concept was absurd. "You must be born with the immortal gene," he explained, his voice low but deliberate. "But blood alone isn't enough. That potential must be claimed, *chosen,* through the Imbe Rite. And the choice must be made on the eve of their eighteenth birthday."

I blinked at him, "And after that?"

"After that," he said, eyes darkening slightly, "the window closes. The gene goes dormant, and you stay a human and live out a normal life. Whatever spark the gods placed in your blood fades back into silence, and you can never go back and reclaim it."

My throat tightened. "So… that's it? One chance? One decision you're supposed to make to change your entire life?"

"One chance," he confirmed. "That's why most take years to decide. Some never go through with it at all. It isn't a ritual you complete on a whim. The Rite doesn't just grant immortality, it anchors your soul to a power most mortals were never meant to wield. Once you begin the Imbe Rite, there's no going back. It's a life-changing choice."

The wind shifted in the trees above us, rustling like whispered warnings. I tried to steady my breathing, but the truth of his words pressed against my chest like a weight I hadn't asked for.

One chance. One choice. One path that could never be undone.

I opened my mouth to speak, but the words caught in my throat. How could I make such a decision when I had so little understanding of what it meant to be immortal? To choose immortality? It felt like jumping into the unknown with only days, not years, to prepare.

"So, choosing immortality doesn't automatically mean you get a life full of glamour and riches? Got it." I tried to lighten the mood with sarcasm, but the words felt heavy as soon as they left my mouth.

Manakel straightened, his eyes narrowing with a sharpness that made my skin prickle. "This is going to become your real life if you choose it. And a lot is riding on your success, so pay attention."

The scolding tone hit me harder than expected, and I couldn't help but feel like I was back in classes getting reprimanded for not doing my homework. My smirk faded, and I nodded, clamping my mouth shut.

He continued, "Now, going back to Dermaine, rumors of the weakening river have drawn hordes of rebels and cursed immortals to its border, eager to make their move. They see it as their chance to reclaim control and to stop hiding. But not all of us want that."

I shifted uncomfortably at the mention of rebels, my thoughts spiraling. There was so much to absorb. "And what about the Queen?" I asked, my voice tentative. "I mean, she's immortal and created it…what does *she* want? If I'm supposed to convince her, I should probably know where she stands."

He nodded, his expression grim. "That's complicated, and no one really knows. I'm assuming you've heard the river creation story, but what wasn't mentioned, I'm sure, is that in creating the river, she also bound her powers to it."

I gasped in shock, but he continued unfazed. "When she brokered the treaty and agreed to create the river to keep immortals out of Rioga, she created something that not only helped humans but would kill her own kind. The gods saw the implications of her intentions and power and decided to bind her magic to the river's."

A flicker of something—astonishment, maybe—washed over me. We all knew about the Queen creating the river, but had no idea her power was so intricately tied to it. My thoughts were spinning, struggling to keep up with the flood of new information.

He continued, "Once the river weakens fully… no one knows what will happen. Whether she'll regain her full powers or lose them forever. But there are rumors that once the river stops flowing, she'll lose all of her power, and with it, her reign as Queen."

I wanted to ask what that would mean. If an immortal had ever lost their powers before, and if that was how they were able to die? But I didn't. I stayed silent and listened.

"Her son has been preparing to take his place as the sole heir and the new King of Dermaine if that does happen. But no one knows for sure, and no seer can predict it either."

I swallowed hard, grappling with this new piece of the puzzle. Why did everything feel like it was teetering on the edge of something bigger than anyone expected?

I hesitated before asking, "So if I cross the river and make it to her castle, would she even consider agreeing to reinforce it? And if she doesn't have full access to her power, would she even be able to?"

Manakel's eyes narrowed slightly, calculating. "It'll be up to you to convince her, and up to the gods if she can fulfill it. I know she won't go against the immortals and her family again without a good reason."

And I could understand why, since she no doubt had been receiving backlash since its creation. But what could I, an insignificant human from Laochra, say to convince her? If no one here listened to me, why would an immortal queen?

As if sensing my inner turmoil, Manakel looked me in the eyes and said, "If a human, one brave enough to face the woods and the river, makes it to her and pleads to save their people, then maybe she'll use that plea as her fuel. Not only to continue providing safety for all of Rioga, but to save her position on the throne."

It felt like a mountain of "maybes" and "what ifs," and my stomach churned at the uncertainty of it all, but I forced myself to focus on what we *did* know.

"Okay, so putting the Queen agreeing aside, we should probably focus on what I'm going to be facing in these woods. Because I'm going to have to make it through these tests unscathed before I even *think* about asking for her assistance, right?" I looked to him for reassurance, but his face remained detached.

"Precisely," he said, his voice steady. "You're not just walking through a magical forest or a river primed to kill. You're entering a world where the balance of power is about to shift. And if you make it across..."

He winced, probably hearing the uncertainty he'd been trying to avoid showing me. "I mean, *when* you make it across, not everyone will be happy about it. Some will see you being able to cross the river as a threat, and they'll try to intervene before you even make it out of the woods."

My stomach dropped. The idea of being a target for vengeful immortals didn't exactly fill me with hope. I rolled my eyes, trying to hide the fear gnawing at me.

"*Great*. So, I'm basically walking into a giant target zone. Hopefully, their aim is as good as mine and they never get a bullseye." I smirked at my attempt at a joke, but Manakel seemed less than amused.

Sighing, I asked, "What about the immortals in Immorro? Are they different from the ones camping out in Dermaine? How do *they* feel about the river's magic potentially ending?"

Manakel hesitated, clearly weighing his words. "Immorro is... complicated. It's where most immortals, who were born outside of the human lands, ended up, but not everyone shares the same views. Like any territory, some areas are peaceful, but there are also dangerous places—places ruled by the same rebels who believe they should be in control of roaming both realms."

I tried to keep up, nodding slowly as I processed his words. It all sounded like a world of danger, and I was about to be right in the middle of it. "So, the odds are stacked against me in most scenarios. Tell me again why it's a good idea for me to do this? Because all I'm hearing is danger, danger, death, vengeance, more death."

His lips tipped slightly, and I mentally checked off that that was eight. But I still wasn't counting.

"In all seriousness, what now?" I asked.

His expression softened slightly, a flicker of something almost... sympathetic in his eyes. "Now, we train. You need to be prepared for it all. The journey, the Eldren you'll meet along the way, the choices you'll have to make, all of it. Your life is about to change in ways you can't even imagine, Wildheart. But you won't have to go through any of it alone. I'll be here every step of the way to guide you."

I took a deep breath, grounding myself in his words. If I wanted to ensure my family's safety, I knew what I had to do. There was no turning back now. No matter how uncertain or overwhelming this was, I *had* to be ready.

I looked around at the forest, its shadows no longer as threatening as they had felt just days ago. But the deeper I got into this world, the more I realized how much I still didn't know.

"So you mentioned Eldren as being creatures of the forest, but what kind of creatures are we talking about?" I asked, needing more details.

"And which of them would want to hurt me? Oh, and how about in the river? Are those creatures also Eldren? And are you certain none of them will harm me as long as I cross during the night of my rite? Also, how far exactly *is* the river from here? And then, how far from the river is Dermaine, or more specifically, the castle? I just need to know—"

I froze, startled as Manakel's hand gently pressed against my lips, shutting me up. My heart stuttered in my chest, caught between the unexpected touch and the intensity of his stare as he examined me. Slowly, he lowered his hand, his expression calm but focused. I swallowed the flood of questions in my throat, realizing how fast I'd been speaking and that I hadn't given him a chance to answer any of them.

Manakel gave me a faint smile, but there was no humor in it, just an unspoken message I clearly understood: *Slow down. You're in over your head now, but I'll guide you through it.*

"First," he began, his voice low and steady, "there are different types of Eldren, the same way there are different types of immortals. Let's start with immortals, as after the Rite, you will become one. Each type is unique and has its own strengths, weaknesses, and gifts."

I nodded along, wishing I'd brought a journal to write this all down. I'd need to remember that for next time, or maybe I could ask if he had something to take notes with. But no, why would he? And why wasn't I paying more attention so I could actually *retain* this information?

Unaware of my mental spiral, he thankfully continued. "I'm a Sciathain, a rare breed with not many of us left in Luminara. We have the ability to move freely between lands. Our wings make that possible, and a lot easier to get around."

His black wings twitched, the motion almost imperceptible, but it made my heart beat faster. I was still in awe that men with wings actually existed and that he was able to use them to fly. It was surreal.

"I was *also* gifted the ability to shift and bend shadows, but that's not a power an immortal can possess. It's more of a gods' thing." He seemed almost reluctant to speak about it, but it was hard not to be fascinated by his power and what he was capable of.

I nodded, wanting to ask more, but I couldn't tear my eyes away from his wings. They were so much more imposing up close, their black feathers shimmering in the light like a liquid shadow, stretching wide and powerful behind him.

I shook my head, trying to focus on something—*anything*—other than his wings. "How did you hide them before? I mean, back at my house when we first met, you didn't have them, and then this morning they just *appeared.*"

Manakel shifted, a hint of another smile on his lips, but it didn't quite reach. He shrugged as if what he was about to say was no big deal. "It's not exactly *easy* to hide wings as big as these," he said with a faint laugh. "But I've had plenty of practice, since like my parents, I'm a Shifter."

I froze. "A Shifter?" The word sounded foreign in my mouth, like a piece of a puzzle I couldn't even begin to fit into place. "What do you mean, you're a Shifter?"

He looked at me curiously, a look that made it clear he found my confusion almost endearing. "Shifters, Wildheart. Immortals who can change their appearance and become entirely different beings."

He stepped closer, and I caught a glimpse of the way his wings rippled as he moved—like they were part of him, but not entirely.

"They mostly take the form of animals, and their power is fluid and ever-changing, but it requires a deep connection to the animal world, one that takes years to master. My parents could shift into creatures of the air—one into a bird, the other into something much more dangerous. But instead of shifting entirely like they could, I can just shift to hide my wings. It's a fragment of their gift, not the full thing, but I'm grateful all the same."

And then to prove his point, his wings disappeared entirely, leaving an open space where they used to be. And then before I could blink, shadows curled around him once more, and they reappeared.

I blinked, trying to wrap my mind around what just happened. "Wait, you mean there are immortals that can *shift* into other beings? Other *creatures?*"

The words slipped out before I could stop them, my voice small and full of disbelief. If I thought him producing wings out of thin air was cool, what would happen if I saw someone turn into a sheep or a bird?

His chuckle was low, rich, almost dark. "Yes. It seems there's a lot you still need to learn, but I guess that's what today's lesson is for, right?"

His eyes glinted with a masked emotion, amusement, and something that made me feel like I was standing on the edge of a cliff, about to fall into something vast and unknown. But safely, because he was with me.

"So could I become a Sciathain too after the Rite?" I asked, hating my naivete and how little I actually knew about his world.

He shook his head, "No, we're not *just* any type of immortal, we were technically the *first* immortals in Luminara. Sciathain are angel-type beings created by the gods and sent to Luminara centuries ago as protectors of humans," he added quietly, almost as if the next words hurt to say. "But it was also Sciathain who defied the gods and created the first immortal hybrid with the humans."

I wasn't expecting that, but I stayed silent, giving him the space to speak, but it didn't seem like he was going to continue.

"Okay, so I won't be getting my own set of wings as a Sciathain? Noted. But what kind of powers *could* I get? What types of immortals could I become?" I asked.

"All immortals are *technically* descendants of Sciathain, and gifts were passed down, but over time, they were narrowed down and given specific gifts. The gods used the Rite to decide and eventually sorted them into a type based on their abilities. There are healers, like your grandmother," he said, his tone shifting. "They can manipulate life itself, mend wounds, and even slow down death… but never stop it. Their powers are necessary but not limitless."

I nodded, remembering the story of the healer in Rioga who couldn't save the Queen.

"Then there are elementals—immortals who control aspects of nature. Like fire, water, earth, and air. Most elementals only have the ability to manipulate one, but I've known a few that can manipulate multiple.

Elementals and healers are the most common gifts granted, but elementals who possess more than one element are rare and can be as dangerous as they are powerful. Especially if they've lived long enough to master their abilities."

I took it all in, the weight of this new knowledge pushing down on me. There was so much I still had to learn, and I barely felt ready for any of it. But Manakel was here to make sure that the next five days were spent preparing for whatever I was going to face.

"Then there are the cursed ones," he said, his voice darkening. "They completed their rite but weren't deemed worthy by the gods to possess any gifts. Greed, envy, hatred—they're consumed by it, feeding off fear, chaos, pain. And they usually live out eternity in hiding, or as a part of the rebels. Determined to undermine any laws set forth by the gods out of spite."

I shuddered, a chill creeping up my spine, thinking of the rebels in the story and the ones Manakel mentioned were waiting it out for the river to expire.

"The creatures that live in the river? Are they cursed ones too?" I asked, my voice barely a whisper.

He shook his head. "The river is guarded by Eldren, born of water, shadows, and ancient magic. Like myself, they're not immortals, but something older, something tied to the land itself. Like I mentioned, Eldren don't have any allegiance with us, but because the Imbe Rite was created by the same gods that created the Eldren, you will be protected from them during it."

I exhaled in relief, not even realizing I was holding my breath, hoping to hear something positive.

"But if you fail…" He didn't need to finish the sentence for my face to pale.

"Wait…Fail?" My voice cracked, betraying the fear rising in me.

"If you hesitate, or lose focus, if doubt creeps in, the Eldren could turn on you. But as long as you complete the Rite with purpose, knowing who you are and why you chose to embark on it, they won't be able to kill you."

I swallowed hard, trying to steady myself. They might not be able to kill me, but that didn't rule out seriously harming me. And none of that sounded reassuring. I needed to switch topics before I started spiraling again.

"Okay. And from here, how far is the river on foot?"

"Around a half a day's journey through the woods," he replied, pointing behind us. "And then Dermaine is about a few hours beyond that."

I bit my lip, trying to process everything. Powers, creatures, immortality—it all felt too overwhelming. But Manakel's calm presence, his steady voice, kept me tethered to the reality of this conversation. He was offering me answers about this world I was about to enter, and though it made my head spin, it also grounded me in a way that made me want to listen.

I took a deep breath, focusing. "Okay, so there are five types, but I can't become a Sciathain like you. So that only leaves four. And I doubt I'll fall into the cursed category, so I could either become a healer, a shifter, or an elemental. Those choices sound pretty good to me."

Manakel's lips quirked upward into a smirk. "Those are just a *couple* of the types, Amadán. I didn't know how much information to provide today, but I can tell you about the rest if you think you can handle it all."

I scoffed, putting my hands on my hips. Me? I could remember details from stories told a decade ago—of course, I could handle more. "I can handle more than you think, so give it to me, Teach. I'm ready." With that, I plopped down on a nearby rock and crossed my legs, trying to get comfortable, even though the weight of what he was saying made the air feel thick.

Manakel smirked again, and I couldn't help but notice how the corners of his lips lifted—just a little. My stomach tied itself into knots at the sight. It wasn't even a full smile, but it made my pulse race like I'd sprinted a mile. I quickly fidgeted with my hands, then sat on them to keep them still, trying to focus on his words. He looked amused but thankfully didn't comment on my flustered state.

"So, besides healers, shifters, elementals, and cursed ones, there are also seers and hunters. It may not seem like much more, but they are the rarest types. And then there are the Eldren, who have their own types, too. Most Eldren have been around for millennia and breed within their own kind, like the creatures in the river and the fairies. No new immortal can *become* one of these types during their Rite. And most have never even encountered the ancient beings, but no doubt you will."

I rolled my eyes and muttered *"Lucky me"* under my breath, but thankfully, Manakel didn't hear.

"There are many Eldren that dwell in the forest or just outside of it, but the ones you could encounter and should know of are Dryads, Osiris, and Fairies. They're mostly harmless unless provoked or feel threatened."

I leaned forward, the rock beneath me suddenly feeling a lot less comfortable. The Eldren were a mix of Dryads, Osiris, and Fairies. The forest had felt strange already, but now, knowing these ancient beings were hidden within it, the air around us felt charged and electric, as if the trees themselves were watching my every move.

I glanced up at Manakel. His expression was unreadable, but his eyes were steady as he continued. "Seers can glimpse fragments of the future, but their power is unpredictable. Some have visions that are crystal clear, while others… Well, let's just say the future is tricky to see, even for them."

"And Hunters?" I asked, my curiosity slipping out before I could stop myself. I needed to know as much as possible, and there wasn't much time left.

Manakel's eyes darkened slightly. "Hunters are exactly what they sound like—immortals with heightened senses and incredible strength to hunt. They were created to track and eliminate threats in Luminara, whether those threats are human, immortal, or something else entirely. They are feared, even among the fiercest immortals."

I swallowed hard, trying to picture myself as one of these beings. My mind raced through images of what each might look like—Seers with their distant gazes, Shifters whose forms could twist into something else entirely, and Hunters with their deadly, unwavering focus.

"So, any of them could become my type after I cross the river? And how will I know what it is?"

Manakel nodded, his expression serious. "The gods will choose what type suits you best based on what they see in you during the Rite. You may feel a pull toward one or the other, but ultimately, it's not up to you. The only thing you *can* control is how you use the power once it's gifted."

I shifted nervously on the rock, still processing everything. His words echoed in my mind, but I wasn't sure how to absorb them all. When he spoke again, it was like he could see the conflict in my mind.

Manakel's eyes swept toward the trees, his voice lowering as if not to disturb them. "As for the Eldren I mentioned earlier, Dryads are forest spirits, bound to the trees and the earth. Most days, they appear as ordinary trees—still, silent, rooted in place. But beneath the bark, they're always listening. Always watching. When the forest stirs with magic, they shift... not suddenly, but like something waking from an ancient dream. Bark becomes flesh. Limbs twist into arms. Faces take shape in the wood. They are the memory of the land. They do not speak often, but when they do, the forest listens."

He paused, eyes narrowing slightly. "They are not cruel, but they are not easy either. Show them respect, and they may show you wonder. They're peaceful unless their home is threatened."

I looked around, trying to spot any differences in the trees surrounding us. Trying to see a glimpse of something otherworldly, but they all remained eerily still.

Bringing his focus back to me, Manakel continued, "Osiris are harder to explain... but they're ancient beings, and don't follow the same rules as we do. Their gifts are vast and unknown, and their motives unpredictable. But thankfully, they mostly reside in bodies of water, and there aren't that many left besides those in the river."

"That sounds comforting... since I'm going to be in that river in less than a week," I muttered, sarcasm slipping from my mouth before I could catch it. Of course, there had to be more mysterious beings lurking around, waiting to shake things up and *hopefully* not kill me.

Manakel's lips twitched again, and he ignored my sarcasm, continuing. "Then there are Fairies. They are mischievous but mostly harmless. They can be helpful if they choose to be, but they also enjoy playing tricks on humans and immortals alike. Nothing deadly, but it's best to keep your wits about you when in the presence of one."

I couldn't help it. A laugh escaped me—soft, at first, but growing as the absurdity of it all hit me. Fairies. Dryads and Osiris. It sounded like something from a made-up fairy tale story, but here I was, about to cross into a world where these beings not only existed but were an integral part of it.

"I know it's a lot to take in," Manakel said, his voice softer now. "But you're strong and capable, Amadán. You've handled everything thrown your way so far. You'll handle this, too."

I looked at him, brow furrowed. *Amadán?* He'd called me that a few times now. What did it mean? My mouth opened to ask, but before I could speak, I decided I didn't need to know right now. I was already overwhelmed by everything else—there was no room for another question. I would just have to remember to ask him later.

"Guess we'll find out soon enough," I murmured, meeting his eyes.

There was something steady there—a quiet, unwavering confidence that felt almost foreign in the shadow of my uncertainty. I didn't know how to summon that same certainty in myself, not yet. But if a Sciathain, an immortal warrior who had seen more lifetimes than I could fathom, believed I could do this, then maybe I owed it to both of us to try. To at least *pretend* I was capable until the lie softened into truth. Until the weight on my shoulders felt less like a burden and more like purpose.

16. A Test Of Faith

Manakel extended his hand, his expression guarded as he silently urged me to stand and follow him further into the trees. The gesture seemed simple, but as I stared at his outstretched fingers, memories of the last time I'd been in this forest crashed over me like a wave. I could almost feel the groping branches clutching at my limbs, the suffocating grip of the sinking earth around my legs, the eerie whispers that seemed to taunt me from the shadows. Even now, with the forest calm and still, those sensations lingered just beneath my skin like echoes taunting me.

I reached for his hand, hesitant, and as our palms connected, a strange jolt raced through me, sharp and fleeting, like a spark of electricity. I flinched, startled, and quickly glanced at him, but his face betrayed nothing. He didn't even react, like he hadn't felt anything at all. Maybe it was just me, nerves fraying in the silence, or maybe the result of anxiously rubbing my palms on my thighs for the last few minutes. Either way, I shoved the feeling aside as he helped me to my feet.

The second I was upright, he dropped my hand abruptly, as though the contact had been as unwelcome for him as it was unnerving for me. He began walking ahead, and I stayed a few steps back as I followed.

The silence between us grew heavy as I trailed behind him, my feet crunching over the forest floor with each step. I had no idea where we were going or why, but there was no denying that the further we ventured into the forest, the more unpredictable. It was coming alive in ways I couldn't explain.

The quiet was oppressive, gnawing at me until I couldn't bear it any longer. "So… after I cross the river," I started, my voice cutting through the stillness, "What then? What happens to me?"

Manakel stopped so suddenly that I almost bumped into him. He turned to face me, his piercing eyes locking onto mine, his expression flat. "After you cross, you will be fully immortal," he said, his tone measured, deliberate. "But your powers will remain dormant. The gods will decide what gifts you receive, based on the challenges you face during the Rite. The trials will test your strength, your resolve, your character, and your very essence. Some gifts can manifest quickly, while others… take time. Either way," he said, stepping closer, his voice lowering into something just above a whisper, "you'll need to be ready for whatever comes."

There was a weight in his tone that hadn't been there before, like something unspoken lingered behind every word.

"That's why we're here. To prepare you… as much as we can before the Rite." His eyes held mine, impassive. "There's not much time left, and even less room for hesitation. Ready or not, it's coming."

I swallowed hard, the air suddenly feeling thinner.

As much as we can. Not enough time. Ready or not.

All these words rushed through me, shaking my resolve. It was like even *he* wasn't sure it would be enough to face whatever was coming. And that scared me more than anything he could've said outright. Because I knew I was in over my head and there wouldn't be much time to ask questions, no room left to uncover the truth before stepping into the unknown.

Whatever this was, whatever I was being pulled into, it had already started. And I couldn't turn back. Not without letting everyone down.

I watched him, really watched him, as the shadows shifted across his face—too calm, too certain. There was no fear in his expression, no hesitation, just that quiet intensity that made him unreadable. And maybe that was the first time I wondered… who exactly had chosen me for this?

Was it fate? Or was it him?

Because for someone claiming to be my guide, he held too many secrets in his silence. And for all his cryptic truths and half-offered reassurances, not once had he asked me what I wanted.

Not once had he asked if I was willing.

The thought lodged sharp beneath my ribs. Was I ever really given a choice when my family's safety was brought into question?

Maybe I hadn't been dragged into this kicking and screaming, but that didn't mean I'd walked into it freely. It felt more like falling, slow at first, then suddenly. And now I was tumbling into a life that had been waiting for me long before I knew it existed. A life I didn't think I'd ever understand.

A root twisted out of the forest floor like a hand reaching to pull me under. I didn't see it until too late—my boot caught, and I stumbled forward with a sharp gasp.

Before I could hit the ground, Manakel's hand closed around my arm, steadying me with effortless strength.

"Thank you," I breathed, embarrassed by how shaken I felt over something so small.

But he didn't let go right away. His grip lingered, and when I glanced up, his eyes weren't on the path—they were on me.

"Don't thank me," he said, voice low. "Just be more aware of your surroundings. And don't rely on others to help you."

Manakel tilted his head, something hidden within his stare. "Be careful where you place your trust, Raine," he said softly, like he wasn't just offering advice, but issuing a warning. "Even the noblest of causes can hide treachery in its roots. Don't trust that the things in this forest always have your best interests in mind. This is *your* journey, and only you can decide where to go next."

My heart stuttered. The way he said it—it wasn't just about the trees or the creatures we might meet. It felt like a deeper warning, coiled in something unspoken. Like maybe he was including himself in that statement.

He released me then, and I swallowed hard and straightened, even as doubt twisted in my gut. "I'm ready to continue."

I wasn't. *Not really.*

But this was my path now, whether I'd chosen it or not. And if this was the only way to keep my family safe, then fear and every thread of doubt curling in my chest would have to wait.

Manakel's gaze met mine, quiet but piercing, as if weighing the truth behind my silence. Asking if I was sure. If I was truly ready.

I gave a slow nod, forcing the movement past the lump in my throat. "Alright," I said, my voice barely above a whisper. "Let's go."

The words wavered, fragile as glass. I wasn't ready, and both of us knew it. But I had someone willing to guide me—for now—and I knew that wouldn't last forever.

So I stepped forward.

Because sometimes, stepping into the unknown isn't about being ready. It's about choosing to move forward, one trembling step at a time

And for now, that would have to be enough.

Manakel's eyes lingered on me for a moment longer, a look of silent approval crossing his face before he nodded, as if satisfied with my resolve. Without another word, he turned and began walking deeper into the forest. I followed closely behind, the soft crunch of our feet the only sound breaking the stillness. But the silence now felt different—charged, expectant, as though the very forest was holding its breath, waiting to see what I would do next.

The trees around us were older here, their trunks thick and gnarled, the branches twisting together to form a canopy so dense that only fragments of sunlight broke through, casting shadows across the forest floor. The deeper we went, the more alive the forest felt, as though it were awakening to our presence. The air was thick with the scent of moss and earth, the weight of magic hanging in the breeze. Then, the sound of moving water reached my ears, distant at first but growing louder as we continued.

Manakel slowed his pace as we neared a small creek that wound through the trees, its waters sparkling faintly in the dappled light. I knew it wasn't the Queen's river—*that* river was still half a day's journey away—but there was something peculiar about this creek, a quiet power emanating from it. The surface shimmered in a way that felt more than just a reflection of the trees above. It felt as though it were reflecting something deeper, something I couldn't yet understand.

"This is where we'll start," Manakel said, stopping at the water's edge. His voice was steady, but there was an intensity to it that sent a shiver down my spine. "It's not the same magic as the river, but it, too, has been enchanted for centuries. The Queen's magic might have created the river, but her elemental power touches every waterway near Dermaine. This creek can help prepare you for what you might face at the river."

I crouched beside the water, gazing into its depths. The creek looked shallow enough that I could probably touch the ground without being submerged. But the way the water moved, faint ripples dancing across the surface, made it *feel* impossibly deep. I looked up at him, uncertainty creeping in. "What exactly am I supposed to do in there?"

Manakel crossed his arms over his chest, his wings shifting behind him with a soft rustle. He didn't look at me directly, his eyes instead focused on the surface of the water, as though he could see something in it that I couldn't. "This water will test your will. It's harmless now, but step inside with the promise of magic in your veins, and it will transform. It will show you your worst fears, your doubts, and your weaknesses, hoping you'll crack under them."

I shuddered at the concept of having to endure whatever it thought was my biggest fear. Before this week, not much beyond staying stagnant in a small town scared me, but now, my eyes were being opened to danger so close to home I never anticipated.

"This isn't about your physical abilities; it's meant to strengthen your mind. You'll need to have control over both your mind *and* your body to survive the river's magic during the Rite."

I swallowed hard, a knot of apprehension twisting in my stomach. This wasn't what I expected. The uncertainty that had been building inside me since the moment I set foot in the forest suddenly felt a thousand times heavier. "And if I can't handle it? If it shows me things I don't want to see, will I fail?"

For the briefest moment, Manakel's gaze softened, his usual stoic expression giving way to something gentler. "Not today. This is a test of your resolve. A trial of things you *may* face, but anything you experience here will be trivial compared to what awaits you in the river."

He paused, his eyes locking onto mine, his voice lowering, almost as if he were sharing a secret. "But remember this: if you learn what haunts you now, it can't break you later."

I took a deep breath, trying to steady my racing heart. His words didn't ease the tension in my chest, but I knew he was right. I couldn't back down now, no matter how scared I was of what I'd see. The only way to prepare was to do, and completing the Imbe Rite was inevitable. So maybe facing the powers of the creek today was a way to prove, not only to myself, that I could do this.

Steeling myself, I untied my boots before removing them with my cloak, and stepped forward, the cool water immediately lapping at my toes. It was deceptively calm, like a mirror reflecting the world around it. I placed one foot in completely, waiting for a shift that never happened. But as I submerged my second foot, a sudden jolt of energy pulsed through my body, and the world around me shifted.

The creek, the forest, and even the sunlight all faded away. The water, now a tangible force beneath my feet, seemed to pull at me, dragging me forward and luring me deeper. Panic surged through me as the temperature of the air dropped, and I realized that I wasn't standing in the creek anymore. I was drowning in a suffocating void, darkness pressing in from all sides, its cold tendrils wrapping around me, pulling at my limbs to drag me under its weight.

The forest sounds were gone, replaced by a low, humming noise, a chorus of whispers that grew louder and louder until it felt like they were inside my head. I gasped, trying to breathe, but the air felt thick and foreign, like I couldn't catch my breath no matter how hard I tried.

Manakel's voice broke through the chaos, calm and steady, reminding me where I was. "Stay focused, Wildheart. This is a test of your will. Face what comes and do not waver. You are strong enough to face whatever it's showing you."

I nodded, even though I wasn't sure he could see me, as I couldn't see anything but the oppressive darkness. But his voice, steady and unwavering, somehow anchored me.

This isn't real. None of this is real.

I repeated as I reminded myself this was a trick and none of it was actually happening, not the water dragging me down, not the shadows suffocating me. It was all an illusion—a test.

I clung to that thought and began focusing on things that were real. Like the memory of the time Wren had blindfolded me during training, and I'd nearly stabbed him with a dagger because I couldn't see. That blindfolded fight had been a test of trust, to trust my instincts. And now, I had to do the same. I had to trust myself to walk through this darkness, just like I'd trusted my instincts wearing a blindfold that day.

Imagining Wren ahead of me, waiting like he always had in those games, I took a small step forward. My feet, once weighed down by the pressure of the water, now felt lighter. The shadows tried to pull me back, but I fought against them, pushing forward, one step at a time. Focusing on following my instincts instead of what my mind was feeling.

The grip on my arms loosened, the oppressive pressure beginning to lift. With each step, I felt more in control, like I was regaining something that had been lost in the dark. I wasn't drowning anymore; I was walking through it.

And then, just as my chest squeezed too tight to breathe, a sliver of light broke through.

It wasn't comforting. It was unnerving.

A golden thread of afternoon sun filtered through the trees above, cutting across the water like a spotlight. Too sharp. Too still. Like it had been staged as the rest of the forest was steeped in shadow, damp, hushed, watching. I couldn't tell what was real anymore, but the light led somewhere, and right now, that was all I had to guide me.

Then I saw him. Or… at least it *looked* like him.

Manakel stood at the far bank of the creek, haloed by sunlight, still as stone. His wings were tucked in tight, dark against the light. His expression was calm, almost kind. And there was a faint smile on his lips, but it felt too soft, too inviting.

Relief flooded me at his presence; I wanted it to be him. Gods, I *needed* it to be him, but something in my gut twisted with unease.

Still, I moved toward him, my steps slow, testing. The current pulled at my legs, sticky and cold, but I pressed forward. When he extended a hand, I didn't hesitate; I reached for him, needing to feel something solid and hopefully be done with this useless test.

But the moment our hands connected, it wasn't skin I touched, but heat. Burning, living fire, sliced up my arm, wanting to devour me whole. His hand twisted in mine, hardening, warping, until it felt like I was holding raw lava, branding my skin with every heartbeat.

I cried out and tore away, stumbling back into the creek with a splash that sent icy water rushing up my spine. My skin screamed. My breath hitched. The shadows snapped inward.

The moment my hand broke contact, the world around me blurred, the light vanished, and the man in front of me shifted. His face, once gentle, turned cruel, his smile curling into a sneer. His eyes, no longer familiar, turned black, gleaming with something ancient and unkind. His wings unfurled in jagged, unnatural angles, more bone than feather now. The shadows around him thickened, curling around his shoulders like armor.

The Manakel I was starting to know, however briefly, wasn't who was standing before me. The real Manakel didn't look at me like prey. He didn't smile like that. This was something else. Something wearing his shape and full of twisted evil. My stomach turned as whispers swirled through the air like smoke, brushing against my ears with too many voices.

"You're not real," I whispered, voice trembling.

The thing wearing his face tilted its head, amused. "And yet... You still reached for me."

I froze. Because it was right. I had. Even now, some part of me wanted to believe it was Manakel. That he'd come to help. To pull me free.

The shadows around his feet writhed, slithering into the water like tendrils. I tried to still my breathing, to push down the panic clawing up my spine. The creek surged around me. The water thickened, dragging at my legs like hands made of current. Around me, the forest was swallowed in darkness. Trees swayed without wind, and whispers curled through the air like smoke, snaking past my ears.

You don't belong here.

You'll never survive the Rite.

Only foolish humans trust this easily.

My breath came in shallow gasps. I couldn't tell what was real anymore, couldn't trust the sun above, the roots beneath, even my own voice felt like it echoed from someone else's throat.

Still, the thing that wore Manakel's face didn't move. It waited. Watched.

My heart was screaming. My instincts wanted to run. But I knew better now. If this were truly a mental test, running away wouldn't get me any closer to the end. This wasn't a test of strength, either, but a test of certainty. And right now, I had none.

I dug my fingers into the water lapping at my sides, grounding myself in something I could feel. Something real. Even if it was cold and wet and ugly.

Looking up again, I instinctively knew this wasn't the real Manakel. Steeling myself, I took a deep breath, and despite the terror crawling up my spine telling me I was being misled, I stepped forward. The darkness around him thickened, wrapping itself around him like a cloak, but I wasn't afraid. I couldn't be. Not now, when every decision could be used against me.

"I'm not afraid," I lied, because the truth would only feed it.

The growl that echoed back wasn't his usual quiet intensity. It was darker, cruel, something twisted. And then a laugh cracked through the stillness, low and mocking.

"You should be." The voice wasn't his. It was hollow. Splintered. Like it had been dragged from the bottom of a well.

I closed my eyes for a breath, but didn't flinch. I couldn't afford to. I wouldn't run. I couldn't. Because this wasn't about trusting him. This was about trusting myself.

"You trust too easily," it said softly. Too softly. The cadence was familiar. Almost gentle. "And that," it added, stepping closer, the water around it turning black, "is how you'll break."

The shadows surged again, curling tighter around my legs, the water now sticky with dread.

But something inside me snapped, not in fear, but in resistance. Because those weren't his words. They hadn't come from him. Manakel had never promised safety. But he'd never used my fear against me, either.

I took a shaky step back, my voice rough but steady. "You can mimic his voice all you want, but you're not him."

It stared at me before vanishing completely, and silence answered me. Real silence. The kind that meant something had changed. The veil was cracking, or maybe I was getting closer to the truth, but I had to find the real Manakel.

I lifted my chin and forced a playful edge into my voice, trying to channel the mischief I used as armor when Wren and I played childhood games of hide and seek. "Manakel, where are youuu?" I called out, sing-song and defiant. "Come out, come out, wherever you are."

The shadows thickened, pressing in like smoke, but I swore the air shifted, something drawing closer. I kept walking, blindly, water rising around my ankles, vision cloaked in darkness. I couldn't see him, but I had to trust something would guide me.

"I figured, being a brooding giant with wings, you'd be terrible at hiding," I said, feigning a smirk. "But I'll still find you."

The shadows didn't speak, but they pulsed with quiet menace. Every step dragged like I was walking through molasses. The creek wasn't wide—maybe a few meters—but it felt like a never-ending void. My limbs ached. My pulse thudded against my ribs like a warning bell, and the only thing I focused on was getting out of the creek one step at a time. I counted my steps in my head, trying to steady my breath, but the darkness around me wasn't letting up. With every step, the shadows seemed to grow thicker, more oppressive. I could feel the weight of them pressing in, thick and suffocating. Still, I kept going.

"Manakel," I called again, my voice more confident than I felt. "You know I'm going to find you. You might as well save us both the suspense."

The shadows curled tighter around my legs like ink in water, thick and endless, whispering doubts I wasn't strong enough to name. My breath came slower now, more focused, but the silence was what unnerved me most—too complete, like the forest surrounding us was holding its breath.

No answer. Not even a rustle. Just an eerie stillness that made the forest feel dead. A flicker of nervous energy tickled my spine. I shifted tactics.

"I mean..." I cleared my throat. "Unless you're just standing there trying to look intimidating again. In which case, congratulations, it's working. Very broody. Very mysterious. I'd give it a ten out of ten, if I wasn't currently blind and knee deep in an enchanted creek."

Still nothing. *Wonderful.* Now I was flirting with a hallucination. Or worse—being ignored by one.

There was only silence. Complete stillness. Not even a rustle in the trees. The panic clawing up my throat tried to convince me I was alone in here. That I'd already failed. That I'd walked straight into a trap.

I let out a shaky laugh, heat rushing to my cheeks despite the cold of the water and afternoon air. "Come on," I murmured, quieter now. "You're really going to make me crawl out of this alone just so you can smirk at me from the shoreline and say I told you it wouldn't be easy?"

The water lapped higher, cold and relentless. Still no sign of him. Still no end in sight, either. I wasn't sure what this test was showing me, other than that I wasn't great in the dark or quiet, and was getting increasingly uncomfortable the longer my senses were being denied.

"If you're just hiding to see how long it takes me to beg for help, I hate to break it to you, but I'm really stubborn. And possibly a little prideful. My mind is an endless place of thoughts that can keep me company, so unless you want me to keep talking nonsense until you show yourself..."

A branch cracked behind me. I spun, breath caught in my throat, but there was still nothing to see. Not even a hint of anything, just trees and deeper blackness. But a small smile curved at the corners of my mouth as I leaned into my other senses. Somewhere in that silence, I swore I heard the faintest exhale, a breath, maybe. Like someone stifling a laugh.

I doubled down, not willing to give up or admit defeat.

I tried a different tactic, my tone more playful, maybe even a little more flirty, though it felt like I was fumbling. "You know," I said, hesitant and breathless, "when I get out of here, I'm going to be wet. Soaked actually, and possibly in need of... warming up. Not sure if you have any ideas on how to help with that? It's slightly uncomfortable being wet and all alone."

It came out shakier than I meant it to, and my face burned. But I pressed on, voice faltering into a whisper. "I was wet and alone all of last night, too, but for a completely different reason."

Even as I said it, mortification flared. I winced, cheeks flushed, praying he wasn't actually there to hear that. But somewhere in the shadows, I swore I heard a cough—no, more like a choking sound.. Almost like—

Was he... laughing?

I strained to see through the darkness, my heart pounding in my chest. The noises stopped, and the eerie silence that followed made my skin crawl. Something was wrong. I didn't know what, but everything suddenly felt off.

"Manakel?" I called out, quieter now, suddenly unsure. The silence that followed was thick with something I couldn't name. And each passing second seemed to stretch longer than the last. My next step was shaky, my feet unsure as I tried to keep steady. The edge of the creek had to be near now, but every step felt like it only led further into the void. I didn't know how long I'd been here, the darkness surrounding me removing any illusion of time.

"Manakel, come on," I pleaded, my voice a little frantic now. "If you're out there, say something. *Please.* You should probably know... I can't stand the quiet."

Then, I heard it. A faint rustling, followed by a low growl. It wasn't a playful sound or the mocking snarl I'd heard earlier, but something far more dangerous, more primal. My pulse quickened, my breath coming in faster. Whatever this test was supposed to prove, I wasn't sure how much longer I could hold it together.

I took another shaky step, and the ground shifted beneath my feet, soft and cold. The water of the creek lapped at my legs, and I could feel the power of the water's enchantment swirling around me, debating if I was worthy to leave unscathed.

My foot slipped on something slick beneath the surface, and I stumbled. The water caught me—cold and cruel—but just before I fell face-first into it, something solid met me halfway.

Grass, lush and firm, where there had been only dirt and water. I collapsed face-first onto the bank, my legs still dangling in the water, heart pounding against wet earth. I tried to push myself upright, but the world tilted. My vision blurred. My limbs refused to obey.

What just happened? Where was I? And why was my head spinning? But before I could pass out, strong and steady hands came out to catch me. They were unfamiliar, yet unmistakable, and belonged to Manakel.

But as soon as the warmth of his grip met my skin, a cascade of memories surged—those snarling shadows, the monstrous face that wore his features like a mask.

My body tensed beneath his touch, and I recoiled, yanking myself away from him. My heart was pounding again, and I struggled to breathe.

The man I was supposed to trust, who admitted to watching me and being here as a guide, had shifted in the shadows into something I didn't recognize. I didn't know why, but the darkness hadn't just tried to break me. It had used him to do it.

The darkness may have lifted, but the fear of this being an illusion, too, still gripped me.

"Get away from me," I whispered, my voice a little broken, but firm. I backed away, stumbling as I tried to steady myself. My body shook, still trembling from what I'd just faced, or *thought* I had faced. I still didn't know what was real or imagined.

Manakel didn't move, but I felt his eyes on me, studying me, his expression guarded. He didn't try to come closer, but I could see the confusion or maybe hurt in his eyes. I wasn't sure which, and it made everything worse. He looked like himself, the same Manakel I was getting to know, but I couldn't shake the snarls or the evil in his eyes that felt so real in the moment.

"What the hell was all that?" I asked, my voice trembling now. I couldn't stop the fear from slipping through. "What happened to you back there? One second, you were helping me, and the next—" I stopped, the words failing me.

How could I explain what I had seen, what I had felt? How could I tell him that I wasn't sure I could trust him or what was real anymore?

He sighed and took a small step forward, but I held my hand up, not wanting him to get any closer.

"Your mind was tested," he said quietly. His voice was calm, too calm for how I felt. "The water's magic doesn't show you things traditionally like a dream or nightmare. It forces you to face what's inside you—your fears, your doubts, sometimes things you don't even know about. It twists reality until you're questioning if your very existence is real."

I shook my head in disbelief. "Okay, but it was you I saw. You changed. You—" My voice cracked, and I swallowed hard, fighting the panic rising in my chest. "You wanted to hurt me."

Manakel stepped back, his expression softening. "I didn't change, Amadán. What you saw was your mind playing tricks on you. The water's magic feeds off fear, and it made me into what you feared most in that moment."

I stepped back again, not sure if I could face him right now. Everything still felt too real, too raw. "Then how do I know this is real?" I asked, my voice small. "How do I know you're really you right now?"

He met my stare, steady and unflinching. "You don't. But you made it out on your own. You passed the first test, the shadows are gone, and you're still standing."

Barely, I thought, but the word lodged in my throat. I couldn't say it. Couldn't admit how close I'd come to unraveling. So I said nothing. Just stood there, dripping and trembling, staring at the person I hoped was him and not another illusion. The truth was, I didn't know what to believe anymore, not about this trial, not about myself, not even about him.

The shadows may have vanished, but they'd left something behind. A doubt that clung to my skin like the water's chill. And maybe that was the worst part of all—knowing I'd made it through, but I didn't feel stronger. I felt fractured. Like something inside me had shifted, and I wasn't sure who I'd be when the pieces finally settled.

17. Wild Lies, Wilder Truths

I trudged forward, aiming for what I hoped was the direction of my house. Every step felt heavier than the last, the weight of the creek, the darkness, and my doubts pressing down on me. Manakel walked a few paces behind me at first, his presence a quiet shadow. Then, without a word, he moved ahead, taking the lead. The silence between us was thick, but for once, I welcomed it. I didn't trust myself to speak—not with the lingering embarrassment from my earlier attempt at flirting or the raw edge of fear still clawing at my chest.

The air around us was damp, the earthy scent of the forest mixing with the faint metallic tang of the creek water still clinging to my clothes. My boots squelched with every step, and I was painfully aware of how utterly exhausted I felt. If wading through that tiny creek had drained me this much, what chance did I have against the river?

Manakel broke the silence first, his tone lighter, no doubt trying to dispel the lingering tension. "So… you were right about being wet, but were you still needing assistance with it?"

I didn't even have time to feel mortified by his attempt at a joke before a coughing fit took over. It was sudden and violent, water I hadn't realized I'd swallowed forcing its way out of my throat and nose. My chest burned, and I doubled over, clutching my knees for balance.

"Raine!" Manakel was at my side in an instant. His hand pressed against my back, steadying me as the coughing subsided. I wanted to pull away, to keep my distance after everything that had happened, but I was too tired to fight him, and his touch, surprisingly, didn't feel unwelcome. It anchored me, keeping the panic from spiraling out of control.

"Easy," he said, his voice softer now. He rubbed small circles against my back until I caught my breath.

When I finally straightened, I wiped my mouth with the back of my hand and groaned. "That was disgusting." My voice was hoarse, and I could feel the heat rising to my face again. *Perfect.* As if this day wasn't humiliating enough already, the guy I wasn't sure what I was feeling towards had just seen me cough up half the creek.

But Manakel didn't laugh or tease me. He stayed quiet, watching me carefully with an expression I couldn't quite read. There was no smugness, no shadow of the darkness I'd seen in him before, just a quiet sort of concern. I hated that it made my chest tighten in a way I didn't want to analyze, and even more that I enjoyed him looking out for me. Besides Wren and my grandmother, no one else really had.

I nodded faintly, a signal that I was ready to keep moving. He didn't ask about it or push me to talk, and I was grateful for it. The silence returned, but this time, it felt less suffocating. Still, the tension between us lingered, unspoken but heavy.

After a while, I forced myself to break it. "I'm… sorry," I said, my voice low. "About earlier. I shouldn't have freaked out like that when you were only trying to help."

Manakel glanced at me, his gaze steady. "You have nothing to apologize for," he said simply. "Anyone would've reacted the same way, and I'm glad you're learning not to trust so easily."

I wasn't so sure about that; he was a stranger, and yet I trusted him enough to lead me into the woods I'd feared my whole life, but I didn't argue or admit that. I kicked at a loose stone in the path, my thoughts circling back to the creek, to the magic, to the river waiting for me in five days. "Five days," I muttered, more to myself than to him. "Five days until I'm set to face the river, and I can barely handle a creek with a fraction of its power."

Manakel slowed his pace, turning slightly to look at me. "When the time comes, you'll be ready," he said with certainty. His voice was calm, but there was an edge of conviction in it that caught me off guard. "That was just the start, your first glimpse into this, and you handled it better than most. You're stronger than you think, and you proved that today. Yes, the river will test you, but you'll make it through. I know if anyone can, it'll be you."

I wanted to believe him, but doubt gnawed at the edges of my resolve. I knew I needed the confidence, seeing as how I didn't have much of my own, but I also wanted to be realistic. "And if I don't?" I asked, trying to hide my worry and insecurity.

He stopped walking and turned to face me fully. His hazel eyes met mine, steady and unwavering, and for the first time, I saw something in them that silenced my fears. It wasn't just confidence he was radiating; it was confidence in *me*. "You will make it," he said firmly. "I'll make sure of it anyway I can."

The weight of his words settled over me, not heavy like the doubts I carried, but steady and grounding, like the promise of solid ground beneath my feet.

Maybe he was right.

Maybe I *was* stronger than I thought.

Maybe I *could* do this.

And maybe when all was said and done, after saving my family and my village, I'd get the chance to finally explore the world outside of Laochra.

We finally broke through the treeline, and the clearing near my house came into view. Relief washed over me as I caught sight of the familiar chimney and the curl of smoke rising into the sky. It felt like we'd been wandering the forest for days, not hours. My legs ached, my clothes and boots were soaked, and the sun was still stubbornly hanging in the sky as if mocking my sense of time.

"How long were we in there?" I asked, my voice laced with exhaustion. "And how long do you think the river portion of my Rite will be?"

Manakel didn't stop walking, but his focus shifted back to me briefly. "We were gone three hours, Amadán."

There was that nickname again, the one I *still* didn't know the meaning of. Before I could ask, he opened his mouth to speak, but then hesitated, his eyes falling to the ground as if weighing his next words carefully.

"As for the river…" Manakel's voice cut through the stillness, measured and low. "No one knows how long it'll take. Each Imbe Rite is shaped differently. Yours will be the first to ever take place in the river, and it'll keep you as long as it needs to. Until you've proven whatever the gods need to see."

That wasn't comforting. At all. I frowned, the weight of it pressing in. "That's not really an answer."

He didn't flinch at my tone, just met my gaze evenly, something unreadable passing behind his eyes. "I know," he said quietly. "But it's the truth. The Rite doesn't follow a timeline and is shaped by the person taking it. There's no way to predict what yours will entail or how long it will take, which is why you need to be prepared for anything."

I didn't know how to respond to that. I wasn't even sure if it was meant to comfort me or remind me that I was already in too deep.

So I shifted, reaching for something I *could* ask, and hopefully get an answer to. "You keep calling me a name, Amadán, or something, but I have no idea what it means."

I caught the way his lips twitched, just barely.

He didn't answer right away, just lifted a brow like he was enjoying my confusion. Typical. That was quickly becoming a theme with him. "You wouldn't, it's a word from the old language."

"That's not an answer either," I said, placing a defiant hand on my hip. If I was supposed to trust him, to rely on his guidance, none of these half-truths were going to get me there.

His chuckle was low, rough around the edges. I hated that I kind of liked the sound of it. "It's just a nickname, Amadán. Don't overthink it."

I hesitated, unsure if he was mocking me or protecting something. "Is it… a title? An insult?"

His steps slowed, just barely. "It's how I see you, and a word I don't use lightly," he said finally, with a calm certainty that left no room for argument.

I blinked, caught off guard by the quiet power in his words. He didn't elaborate, didn't look at me again—just kept walking, as if he hadn't unraveled something quietly significant in the space between us. And even though I still didn't understand the name, or what it meant to him, I carried it with me like a stone warmed by fire. Because somehow, I knew it mattered, or at least I wanted it to.

As we reached the edge of the clearing, I walked ahead and stopped short, turning to face him. "I'll see you tomorrow, then?"

The teasing in his expression faded, replaced by the serious resolve I'd grown accustomed to. He nodded, "Same time. Same tree. It's safer than me showing up here again."

I nodded, already dreading whatever tomorrow's lessons would entail. I knew I needed to be prepared, to know and understand everything I could face, but it was a lot to undergo. My muscles ached at the thought of it, but I didn't have a choice if I wanted to be ready.

"See you," I muttered, turning toward the house.

When I reached the back door, something made me pause. A flicker of instinct, like a string being tugged deep inside my chest.

I glanced over my shoulder, and there he was. Manakel stood at the edge of the trees, half-shadowed by branches, as still as stone. His dark eyes held mine across the clearing, cool and steady. I gave him a small nod, half thanks, half questioning why he was actually helping me.

Without acknowledging it, he moved. A powerful beat of his wings stirred the air, rustling leaves and sending a shiver down my spine. Shadows curled around him like smoke, wrapping him in their familiar shroud before he lifted into the sky and vanished into the light above the trees.

I stood frozen, watching the last ripple of movement fade into the clouds.

And then it hit me.

Not like a gentle realization, but like something cracking open inside me, exposing a truth I had never thought to question when first seeing his black wings.

He could fly. And right now in the sky, he looked a lot like Onyx, my guardian bird. I'd always believed the bird was just that, a large bird. A rare black-winged creature I'd caught glimpses of when I was alone, either at home or walking the streets. It had been my secret protector, my silent companion. But now I was starting to wonder if it wasn't a bird at all, and was actually Manakel.

From the moment I saw Onyx, I'd felt a connection, an odd comfort. I'd always felt less alone when I spotted those wings cutting through the clouds, and it might have been him all along.

Manakel. My guardian. My teacher. The stranger I was still trying to figure out.

I let out a breath I didn't realize I was holding, the pieces clicking into place. This is what he meant. What my grandmother meant when she said he had been watching over me... protecting me.

He hadn't just shown up to warn us about the river. He had always been there, silently watching from above.

A soft smile crept across my lips, shaky but real. Maybe the gods really had been watching. Maybe he was their answer to my prayers all those nights I thought no one was listening.

Maybe I wasn't as alone as I thought I'd been. And maybe… just maybe… Manakel wasn't a stranger at all.

Stepping into the house, the warmth of the kitchen enveloped me, and the familiar scent of freshly baked bread filled the air. I could hear Wren's voice in the next room, chatting with Mom. I knew he was probably filling her in on my sudden disappearance this morning, but I didn't have the energy to defend my whereabouts.

I closed the door behind me with a sigh, leaning against it for a moment. *Five days.* There were only five days until I faced the river. Five days until I had to leave this house, this life, and the family I loved. Five days to figure out how I was going to lie to them and leave without questions. To uncover the truths Manakel was still keeping, and admit the ones I was hiding from myself.

I set the kettle under the tap, craving the small comfort of tea, but my hands moved on autopilot. My thoughts wouldn't stop circling, fraying at the edges. Any minute now, Wren would walk in, ask about my day, and every word out of my mouth would be a lie.

I hated lying; hated the way it scraped against my ribs, no matter how small the deceit. But what choice did I have? I couldn't tell them about the river or the Imbe Rite without admitting to things that would put them in danger. And if I told the truth, consequences be damned, they'd try to stop me. Try to convince me there was another way.

But there wasn't. My grandmother and Manakel had both made that clear—it had to be me. I was the only one who could keep the river's border from expiring, the only one who could safely cross the river and make sure the immortals stayed out of Rioga.

I'd already accepted that invoking my immortality and facing the Queen was the price I had to pay. I just wished I could pay it without lying to my family. But the truth would shatter us in ways I couldn't fix, and that was a break I wasn't willing to cause.

The whistle of the kettle snapped me out of my thoughts just as Wren walked into the kitchen.

"Oh, you're back," he said, eyeing me suspiciously. "How were your errands? Did you get everything you needed today?"

I froze for half a second. I had been so caught up in the *idea* of lying, I hadn't actually come up with a convincing one. I plastered on a casual smile, hoping it wasn't suspicious, and let my mouth do the talking. "Uh, yeah. But they're holding everything for me because I couldn't carry it all."

Wren looked smug. "So my earlier offer to come with you might have come in handy?"

I chuckled, trying to deflect, "Yeah, probably. I didn't realize how many things there would be."

He raised an eyebrow and asked, "Why? Prepping for your birthday *already?*"

"Something like that," I said quickly. My mind raced, trying to come up with a plausible excuse for needing material items I usually didn't care for. "Actually... It's for my new job." I saw him tense, so I added, "In Ceannairí."

"Ceannairí?" Wren's face twisted in surprise. "Since when did you get a job? Let alone one in Ceannairí?"

"Since *recently*," I said, forcing a laugh, like it was no big deal, I was digging myself into a deeper hole of lies. "It's an apprenticeship, actually. I'll be helping a local blacksmith with logistics."

Wren stared, his piercing eyes questioning and suspicious, but I held my ground. Lies or not, I had to make him believe this because denying it now would cause more questions.

"Logistics?" he said finally. "You? Managing things? Ha. That's surprising."

I shot him a look but didn't rise to the bait. "It's *temporary*," I said firmly. "And it's a good opportunity now that I'll be of age."

Wren didn't look convinced, no doubt wanting to ask more about this fictional apprenticeship, but after a moment, he sighed and pulled out a chair at the table. "Hmm... it just came out of nowhere."

I nodded before grabbing a second cup for him and said, "It did, but also at the perfect time. You know I didn't want to stay here long."

As I steeped the herbs, I felt his eyes on me, quiet but probing. I handed him the cup, hoping he wouldn't ask more questions I couldn't answer without lying.

Five days, I thought to myself, taking a seat across from him. Five days to prepare. Five days to say goodbye without really saying it. And five days to become the liar I never thought I'd need to be.

As we sipped our tea, his eyes lingered on me for a moment longer, searching, and I prayed he wouldn't see the lies lurking just beneath the surface. Wren had always been good at reading me, better than I liked to admit, but for once, I needed him to trust my words and not the unease that threatened to slip through the cracks.

He took another sip of his tea, his face softening, and relief started to creep in when he finally nodded, appearing convinced, at least for now. Before he could probe further, I stood abruptly, muttering something about being tired and needing a nap, and made my escape upstairs.

As soon as the door to my bedroom clicked shut, the composure I'd managed to hold crumbled. My back pressed against the wooden frame, and I slid down to the floor, my legs folding beneath me as the weight of everything settled heavily on my shoulders.

Manakel kept insisting he believed I could do this, but how could he know that? Especially when everything in me screamed otherwise. My heart raced as dread coiled tightly in my chest.

I wasn't ready. I wasn't strong enough. I couldn't even keep a straight face while lying to Wren. How could I face the river—an unknown force that would test me in ways I couldn't even imagine—when I'd barely managed to stumble across a creek today?

The memory of the creek surged forward, uninvited and razor-sharp. The shadows dragging at my legs. The weight of water pressing down on my chest. The panic clawing its way up my throat as I gasped for breath that wouldn't come. And his face, twisted and wrong. Familiar features warped into something cold and cruel. A stranger wearing Manakel's skin.

Even now, the thought of it made my skin crawl. My chest tightened at the phantom sensation of drowning, of being completely alone with something that wanted to break me. But still… something deeper, quieter, urged me to trust him.

Because my instincts had known the truth, even then. That *thing* in the water might've worn his face, but it wasn't him—not really. Not the version of Manakel I was coming to know. The real one was still a mystery, yes, but one wrapped in quiet steadiness and sharp, knowing glances. He had been patient when I pushed, careful when I stumbled, protective when I didn't realize I needed it.

The creature in the creek had felt real in the moment—terrifying and unrelenting—but it didn't match the man who had waited for me on the riverbank. The one who didn't offer false comfort, only the truth. The one who stayed and offered his assistance.

Whatever I saw in that water was meant to shake me. And it had. But it hadn't broken me. Because even when the world is twisting around you, sometimes your gut knows what your eyes don't. And mine was starting to trust him.

I leaned my head against the wall and let out a long breath, grounding myself in the silence. For the first time in what felt like hours, I let the fear loosen its grip. Just a little. Just enough to breathe.

The truth was simple—I'd made it across the creek. It hadn't been pretty or graceful. It hadn't been fearless or easy. But I did it. And maybe that was what mattered most. Not how strong I appeared, or how steady I felt. Just that I kept moving forward, even when everything in me wanted to turn back.

That had to count for *something*.

Maybe I didn't trust the path ahead yet. Maybe I didn't even trust myself to succeed. But Manakel did. And until I could find that kind of faith in myself, maybe borrowing his would be enough.

For now, surviving today was enough.

And tomorrow… I'd try again.

18. Lessons In Shadow

The soft click of the doorknob jolted me out of my thoughts. My heart skipped as I shifted to the side, making room for whoever was entering. The door creaked open, and my grandmother slipped inside, shutting it gently behind her. She didn't say anything at first, just walked to her bed and pulled the worn, familiar journal from her pocket. She set it down carefully before sinking to the floor beside me.

"Raine, honey," she began softly, her voice warm but measured, "I know things have been overwhelming since…well, since the other day. I just wanted to check in, see where your head's at, and how you're holding up with all of this."

How I'm holding up? The casual tone of her words landed like a stone in my chest. She said it so easily, as though she hadn't just dropped the weight of a whole other world onto my shoulders. My first instinct was to snap back, to unleash all the questions and anger and confusion that had been swirling inside me since I found out the truth. But I knew her too well, and if I came at her too hard, she'd shut down. I couldn't afford that—not when I still had so many questions I needed her to answer.

I took a slow breath, steadying my voice. "I'm…okay," I said, though the word felt hollow and untrue. "As okay as someone whose entire life has been turned upside down in just a few days." I tried for a small, tight smile, but it didn't quite reach my eyes. "It's just…been a lot to take in. I feel like there are a hundred things I don't know, and not nearly enough time to learn them. Everything's moving so fast, and I'm just trying to keep up."

My voice wavered at the end, and her sharp eyes caught it. She scooted closer, resting a hand on my knee—a touch that was meant to comfort me but only reminded me how far apart we actually were right now. I'd never felt this distance and broken trust between us before, and it was as if the woman beside me was a stranger, not my grandmother and best friend.

"I told you I'd answer any of your questions, and I meant it," she said gently. "What has Manakel told you so far? Why don't we start there, or is there something else you're curious about?"

Something I was curious about? That didn't even begin to cover it. I wanted to know it all. My head was full of tangled questions, each one pulling me in a different direction. I searched for a place to start, something I wanted to know more than anything else, but the one question I'd been avoiding bubbled to the surface before I could stop it.

"How did you end up here…In Laochra?" I blurted. "How long has it been, and do you still have any family across the river?"

Her expression froze, her face shifting from surprise to something heavier—regret, maybe? "That is…a complicated truth," she said, her voice quieter now. "And a long story, far longer than we have time for today."

Of course. Another deflection, another lie. Frustration clawed at my chest, and I looked away, biting down the urge to press her harder and demand she tell me. But I held my tongue, not exactly surprised. She was never one to offer a straight answer right away without a cryptic meaning or lesson behind it, so why would this be any different?

But then she sighed, her shoulders slumping slightly in defeat. "To answer your first question, I've been here a *long time*, Raine," she admitted, her voice barely above a whisper.

"I arrived shortly before the river was created. I came to Rioga for what I believed was a quick job, but the journey stretched on longer than anticipated. And without knowing the river was being created until it was too late, there was no way to return home."

Her words carried a weight I couldn't fully understand, but there was something in her eyes—a shadow, a pain—that made me pause. For a moment, I wanted to reach out, to take her hand and tell her it was okay. That everything worked out for the best. But then I remembered all the years of secrets she'd kept from me, and the impulse dissolved. Maybe she had a good reason for keeping this hidden, and I had to trust that in time she would reveal the truth.

I cleared my throat. "I'm sorry. That must have been hard, leaving the only life you'd ever known and realizing there was no way back," I said softly, realizing the similarities we were about to share. When I completed my Rite, I too would be facing a new life, a new reality, and would have no one I knew to help guide me through it.

"I'm also curious about my Imbe Rite and don't fully understand what will be entailed. Manakel vaguely explained some aspects, but I still don't understand the tests I'll have to face, or what the gods expect out of me. And it's only five days away."

The questions tasted bitter in my mouth as I came to terms with the truth of them. *Only five days left.* My chest tightened at the thought of leaving without saying a proper goodbye to my family. To let them know I loved them and had no choice but to leave with a trail of lies in my wake. I just hoped, one day they could understand and hopefully forgive me.

My grandmother stood and crossed the room, retrieving a sheet of paper and a pen from the vanity before handing them to me. Her eyes softened as they met mine, the familiar crease between her brows appearing—the same one that always showed when she was trying to protect me from something she couldn't stop.

"The imbe rite isn't meant to scare you, Raine," she said gently as if sensing the storm already gathering in my thoughts. "It's a test, yes. But it's also a new beginning. It's an opportunity to *choose* your path and your future. It's you choosing to accept your immortality and the gifts that come with it. Everyone's test is different, tailored by the gods to reveal your strengths, and then determine what gifts you'll carry into your immortal life."

I nodded slowly, unsure why the gods would bother testing someone like me, but I kept my questions to myself and started jotting down notes that might be useful.

"At midnight on your eighteenth birthday," she continued, "you'll drink a protection tonic. I've already started preparing it, but you'll finish mixing it the day of. You'll carry it with you into the forest, and take it just before stepping into the river."

I paused my writing and looked up at her. "So my test doesn't actually start until I drink it?"

She smiled, a small, knowing curve of her lips. "Not exactly. The truth is… it begins the moment you decide to step into the woods with the intention of completing the Rite. Maybe even before that. We're assuming the bulk of your tests will be faced within the river, but the rite is as much about the journey as it is about the outcome."

I was still confused, but she continued, "The forest will probably be a big part as well. It will watch you, listen to you, and even learn from you. You will need to be prepared the minute you take your first step within the trees and know that the gods are assessing the way you handle each test on your path."

A shiver worked its way down my spine. I scribbled that down, too. *Be ready before the river*, and *they are watching everything.* It felt a little ominous if I was being honest. But I was happy I was finally getting something tangible, answers I could hopefully use.

She reached out and touched my knee, grounding me. "But listen to me when I say this—the tonic is meant to protect you, but it doesn't make you invincible. Once you drink it, you'll enter an in-between state where you won't quite be human anymore, but not immortal yet either. For about twelve hours, you'll be safe. No human or magic can kill you during that time. The gods grant you that advantage, at least."

My throat felt tight. "But the tests… they can still hurt me?"

"Yes, but the Rite was never designed to break you or kill you. It will challenge you, scare you, even force you to face things you've been trying to outrun. It was created to reveal your true nature and to reveal your hidden strengths and weaknesses. To see what's inside you when there's nowhere left to hide."

I swallowed, my voice barely more than a whisper. "And what if I'm not strong enough?"

She smiled softly, brushing a strand of hair from my face. "You are. You always have been. But strength doesn't mean you won't feel afraid, my Wildheart. It just means you need to be strong enough to keep going, even when you don't know how."

I held onto those words, trying to lock them somewhere deep inside me. The knot in my stomach tightened. "And the gods just what, watch? Decide what I'm supposed to become based on how well I do on tests I can't prepare for?"

She nodded. "Sort of. They'll see what you fight for, what you protect, and how you endure through each challenge. And from that, they'll see your truth and grant you a gift to complement it. The powers gifted after each Imbe Rite are not only to determine the kind of immortal you're meant to be, but to reveal your true nature and potential."

"And after it's over?" I asked. "Are those gifts like a job? A role I'll have to follow forever?"

She shook her head. "Not exactly. It's more like it'll become… a part of you, woven into your very existence. Extensions of what's already there." She squeezed my hands and offered me a genuine smile. "Just know that the gods don't make mistakes. Whatever you're given, it will be a *gift*—a reflection of who you are and who you're meant to become. Like something you've been carrying inside you all along, just waiting for the right moment to surface."

That should have been comforting. And maybe, in some small way, it was. But as I glanced down at the paper in my lap, scribbled with a few notes that still felt muddled, the only thing I could think was *what if there was nothing beneath my surface at all?*

But I didn't say that part aloud.

The thought of being assigned a destiny I couldn't change made my skin crawl. It was one more thing I couldn't control. I nodded, more to signal that I was done talking than to show I understood.

Exhaustion was pressing down on me like a heavy blanket, and my grandmother noticed, offering her hand to help me up.

"What's it like?" I asked as I sank onto the edge of my bed. "Being immortal?"

She hesitated, then shrugged. "It's just normal life, Raine, except mine seems to last longer than most. It's not as black-and-white as the stories make it out to be. There's no clear indicator of good or evil, no more than with humans, anyway. We're all just trying to survive, but with fewer things that can kill us and more time to figure it out."

That sounded *anything* but normal to me, but whether I was ready or not, it would become my new reality soon.

"One last question," I said, stifling a yawn as I burrowed beneath the covers. "Do your teas and tonics work because of the herbs you grow or because of…magic?"

She chuckled softly. "No magic powers here. The herbs do most of the work on their own, like I have always taught you. However, I *am* a healer, and my healing gifts can help the plants grow stronger and be more potent. But I still had to learn all the remedies and blends like any other human healer would." She met my gaze, her expression serious again. "But don't worry so much about your gift because it's something you cannot control. Focus on clearing your mind because if today was any indication, your test will likely be one of mental strength."

Her words settled over me like a weight, pressing down on my chest. I nodded and crawled under the covers, but even as exhaustion tugged at me, my mind stayed restless, caught in a storm of what-ifs.

There was so much I didn't understand, so many unknowns I couldn't comprehend, but whether I was ready or not, my life was going to change. And there was no way of stopping it or slowing it down.

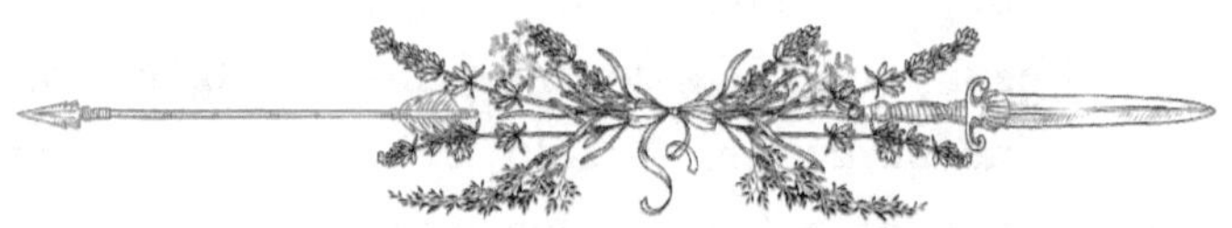

I lay awake, staring at the ceiling for what seemed like hours already, the weight of my grandmother's words and my upcoming Rite pressing down on me like an anchor. *Mental strength.* The words circled my thoughts like a predator, hunting every shred of confidence I had. No matter how hard I tried to shake the fear twisting in my stomach, it wouldn't budge. Every answer she gave me only unearthed more questions, each more unsettling than the last.

My mind drifted back to the creek, to that moment I felt the shadows crawling in, suffocating me under layers of terror I hadn't even known existed. It was a small taste of what the Imbe Rite would bring. A test of my mind. My resolve. My ability to endure and face my fears.

I sighed, turning my head toward the window. The forest stretched out beyond the glass, dark and alive under the silver glow of the moon. The trees seemed closer tonight, the jagged branches clawing at the edge of the clearing like they were reaching for me. I shivered as the shadows shifted, but my eyes caught something—a figure moving between the trunks. It stopped just at the edge, and the glint of gold in the moonlight made my chest tighten.

Manakel.

I sat up, my heart thudding in my chest. There was no time to waste. Curiosity burned hotter than my fear as I slipped quietly down the stairs and out the back door. The cool night grounded me in the moment, though my nerves still hummed like a live wire.

"Manakel," I called softly, not wanting to disturb the fragile stillness of the night or wake anyone up. Human or otherwise.

He turned slowly, his golden flecked eyes catching the light in an almost mystical way. For once, his watchful stare wasn't distant or guarded. There was something softer there, an expression I couldn't quite name.

"Couldn't sleep?" he asked, his voice low and steady, like a thread pulling me back from the edge of my spiraling thoughts.

I shook my head. "I can't stop thinking about it. The rite, the gods deciding my future, everything you and my grandmother said—it's like I'm being asked to prepare for something I can't possibly understand." My voice faltered, betraying the tremor of fear I tried to suppress. "Not in five days at least."

He stepped closer, the shadow of the forest clinging to him like a second skin. "No one feels ready to face the unknown. Not even those of us who've lived as long as I have, but there's a difference between being fearless and being brave. Being fearless means you don't see or focus on the danger. Being brave, however, means you see it and choose to continue anyway."

I tilted my head, searching his face for any sign of insincerity. "And do you think I'm fearless or brave?"

His focus shifted past me, toward the forest, and I saw a flicker of something rare in him, vulnerability. "When I first met you, I would have said fearless, reckless even…But I also see hidden bravery beneath the surface. And the more we prepare, the more I can start to understand why you are the only one who can do this."

My cheeks heated with the rare compliment, and I bit back a smile even though I knew he could feel the effect his words had on me.

"The gods test you in ways no one can predict and force you to grow in ways you can't imagine, but it's no different than everyday life. Things are unpredictable and scary. I've been terrified more than I care to admit." A faint, almost wistful smile touched his lips. "Sometimes, I'm no braver than a human."

Hearing those words from him, someone who seemed so untouchable, so steady, felt like a lifeline. The fear in my chest loosened, just a little.

The night pressed close around us, the forest alive with the quiet hum of unseen creatures. Shadows stretched long between the trees, and the air felt thicker here, like the woods themselves were holding their breath. I traced the curve of a leaf with my thumb, pretending not to notice the way Manakel watched me from where he leaned against the trunk of an old tree.

"My grandmother thinks my test will be mental," I said softly, half hoping the night would swallow the words before they reached him. "She said the gods will force me to face the things I try to bury. The fears I won't even name out loud."

For a heartbeat, he was silent, his focus fixed on the dark beyond the treetops. Then his eyes slid back to mine, and the intensity there made my breath hitch.

"You're stronger than you think, Raine," he said, his voice low and sure, as if it wasn't just a belief but an unshakable truth. "That fear you try so hard to hide? The uncertainty you hate so much? Those aren't weaknesses. They're exactly what will get you through this. You question everything. You see what others overlook. That hunger for truth, your determination…it's all part of what makes you dangerous. And if the gods are watching, they'd be fools not to see it too."

I didn't know what to say to that. No one had ever called me dangerous before. And certainly not like it was a compliment.

A slow, crooked smile tugged at the corner of his mouth, as if he knew exactly what he'd said to me. "Just remember who you are," he added, softer now, almost like a secret meant just for me. "Who you've always been. It'll be enough. More than enough. Trust me. You're stronger and more stubborn than most people I've crossed paths with in all my years."

We stared at each other silently, tension radiating between us. I looked away first. I had to. His eyes were too much, all sharp edges and warmth at once, and I felt like if I looked too long, I'd give something away I wasn't ready to admit. Not even to myself, and as much as I hated to admit it, I wanted to trust him.

He gestured toward a patch of grass nearby. "Come. I want to show you something."

But even as I turned to follow, his words lingered like the echo of a promise I hadn't realized I needed. And for the first time in days, hope stirred inside me, quiet but steady. Because if someone like him could believe in me... maybe everything *would* work out.

We settled on the cool earth, the dampness seeping through the fabric of my clothes, but for once, I didn't care. The air between us felt delicate somehow, like the whole forest might crack if we spoke too loudly. Manakel shifted beside me, his knee brushing mine as he leaned in slightly, his voice low and even.

"Close your eyes," he said. "And breathe."

I obeyed, the darkness behind my lids matching the night around us. At first, my thoughts fought it. My mind was a storm—memories, doubts, what-ifs spinning too fast to catch. But then his voice cut through it, smooth and steady as a river's current.

"In," he guided, the word slow, deliberate. "Out. Follow the rhythm. Feel the ground beneath you. Focus on the air around you. Let everything else go."

And somehow, I did.

With each count, the tension I'd been gripping like armor began to slip away. The weight on my shoulders lightened. For the first time in days, I wasn't waiting for the next bad thing to happen. I wasn't bracing for the fate of the gods or the river or whatever nightmare waited in the shadows. I was just... here. Present.

When I opened my eyes, I found him already watching me, his expression warm and knowing.

"There you are," Manakel said quietly, a faint smirk tugging at the corner of his mouth. "Knew you could do it."

And there it was, that familiar flutter low in my stomach. The start of something dangerous.

Before I could gather a reply, a sound split the stillness. Sharp. Sudden.

Like a branch snapping somewhere just beyond the edge of our little clearing.

I stiffened, the calmness from a moment ago vanishing. "What was that?"

Manakel's head tilted slightly as he silently scanned the shadows beyond us. His hand brushed against mine, just briefly, just enough to remind me I wasn't alone this time.

The forest had shifted. I felt it in my bones. The air grew heavy, thick with unseen magic, and then in the distance a humming melody started— soft at first, curling through the leaves like a whispered secret. It wound its way around us, sweet and sharp and old. It was beautiful. *Too beautiful.* And slightly familiar.

I barely noticed myself leaning toward the sound. It felt like something I knew, something I'd heard before, though I couldn't place it. Goosebumps rose on my skin as the sound intensified and swirled around me, familiar yet elusive.

I didn't know why, but I needed to get closer, needed to figure out how I knew the sounds I was hearing. Before I could get up to follow it, Manakel's hold on my hand, one I hadn't even realized was still holding mine, squeezed, bringing me back to the present. I stilled, frozen, my eyes wide as I started to place the familiarity. The sound I was hearing was the same one I'd heard many times in my dreams. And it was the same haunting melody that lured me into the forest that very first night.

"Don't. Stay present." Manakel's voice was sharp, and his hand reached out to cover mine. A grounding warmth, steadying me. "Remember your breath and don't follow it."

But the song called to me, drawing me closer, willing me to get up and follow it further into the trees. I stared ahead, torn between staying at Manakel's side and answering that instinctive pull. But when he tightened his grip again, I finally tore my eyes away and took a steadying breath.

I let him pull me back to the here and now, even as the echo of the melody lingered in my ears. I was actively trying not to focus on the memories and fear linked to the haunting melody, and focusing on it being another trap.

When Manakel finally spoke again, his voice was softer than the rustling leaves, and I knew he saw what I was holding back when he said. "Fear doesn't define you, Raine. What you choose to do in the face of it—that's what truly matters."

I tore my focus from the dark, blinking as if waking from a dream. "But what is it? Why does it call to me?"

"This time, it's friends of mine coming for a visit," he said, cryptic as ever. But then his expression softened. "They're curious. Not dangerous. But I can't say the same for all of their kind, which is why you need to be alert whenever you hear it."

Before I could ask who he meant, the trees around us lit up. Tiny orbs drifted down from the treetops, glowing like captured stars. I held my breath as they floated closer, tiny, glowing lights flickering like fireflies. But they weren't fireflies. These were faeries. Real, living, breathing faeries. Not like in the bedtime stories my father used to read to us as folklore and fiction. Not the impossible creatures I'd always thought were just myths.

They were here.

"They're... they're really real," I whispered.

Manakel's smirk deepened. "Told you."

I couldn't look away. Their green and gold light illuminated their delicate, winged forms, and my awe deepened with each flutter of their gossamer wings. Their laughter, high and chiming, was like the wind slipping through bells. They circled us slowly, studying me with wide, gleaming eyes. It was surreal, like stepping into the pages of an ancient storybook.

"She's taller than I remember," one of them remarked with curiosity, her voice light as air. "And older. But yes...it's her."

I blinked. "Me?" I asked. My voice felt too small, too human for this moment as I looked between them and Manakel, confused. "But we've never met."

The golden faerie hovered just above us, her iridescent wings beating slow and steady. "Oh, it was a long time ago, so you probably wouldn't remember," she said with a shrug, as if that explained everything. "But it's nice to see you again, not-so-tiny human. I was beginning to think you'd never come back."

I froze. *Come back?* When had I come here in the first place? And what did she mean a long time ago? I had so many questions, but when I opened my mouth to ask what she meant, the words stuck. I'd never been this deep in the forest before. And certainly never met a faerie. I was sure of it. I was also certain I would have remembered if I had.

Manakel's gaze flicked toward me with a stillness that revealed nothing. "Ignore her. She's just excited to meet a human girl this deep in the woods," he said lightly, though something in his tone made me wonder if even he fully meant it. "This is Dela," he said, gesturing toward her golden figure. "She's an Eldren, and in these woods, she's a garden faerie who has called this forest home for a few centuries." He smiled a her and nodded to the ground in the distance. "See all those flowers? That's all her doing; her magic is unlike any other, but it doesn't do much for her sense of time. See, when you've been in the forest as long as her, time begins to all blur together."

Dela winked, darting down to pluck a wildflower that was almost her size, and twirled it between her fingers. "Oh, sure. Blame time, but I know what I know. And I *know* she's been here before."

She darted away quickly, and I followed her movements, gasping. Beneath the towering trees ahead, she hovered near a sea of wildflowers. They were so vibrant and unruly that even under the dark sky, it looked like the forest itself was bleeding color. Blues, yellows, purples— the flowers stretched out in an endless, chaotic tapestry, shimmering under the faeries' light. Bees buzzed lazily between the blooms, their wings catching the moonlight. The scene was so alive, so otherworldly, especially in the dark canopy of the forest, and I felt unworthy just standing here, being able to experience it. It was truly magical.

Dela flitted among the flowers, her iridescent wings catching the light as if she were dipped in starlight. She moved with deliberate grace, her golden curls bouncing with each flutter. When she glanced up at us, a mischievous glint lit her eyes as she flew our way again. With a playful swat of her wings, she struck Manakel's cheek, laughing as he swatted back half-heartedly.

"Still cheeky as ever, I see," Manakel muttered, but the fondness in his voice was unmistakable.

"Only because you deserve it, Manny," Dela replied, her voice light and melodic. She perched on his shoulder as though it were her rightful throne, her golden wings fluttering softly as she rested.

I smiled shyly, watching their familiarity. "It's nice to meet you, Dela," I said, my voice smaller than I intended. "I'm Raine."

Manakel shot me a look of curiosity, and I couldn't help but wonder if he was thinking of the first time we met, which felt much longer than just a few days ago. I hadn't offered him my real name then, but I also didn't know him, yet now, I'd willingly offered it without question to Dela. I smiled back at him, hoping he understood that this trust I was handing over had everything to do with him being here.

The moment felt like standing on the edge of something monumental. This was my first glimpse into the woods without the feeling of suffocating fear surrounding me. Dela's earlier words were still a mystery I wasn't quite brave enough to ask about, but couldn't stop thinking of, either.

She somehow thought she knew me, or at least a younger version of me. But maybe she was remembering my grandmother walking through these very trees. Manakel *had* said she'd been here for centuries. But before I could dwell on it or ask, another flicker of light zipped into view, moving so fast I blinked as it stirred the air around us. I barely had time to track the source before another faerie was circling my head, her wings a blur of gold and green light.

She paused close to my face, her wings fluttering to hold her in place. "I'm Fern," she declared proudly, her voice high and lilting, like the chime of a distant bell. Despite her small size, there was an undeniable boldness about her as she held her chin high and looked me straight in the eyes. She studied me, as if she too recognized me and had been waiting for this moment far longer than I could understand.

She hovered inches from my face, her wide, sage-green eyes glinting with mischief and knowing. Before I could reply, she moved closer and flicked her wing against the tip of my nose—a feather-light tap that caught me off guard.

I gasped and blinked in surprise, and so did she, immediately darting backward as her cheeks glowed a faint, shimmering green color.

"Oh! Sorry," she stammered, wringing her tiny hands, the green hue extending like an embarrassed blush. "I've never been this close to a human before, and… well, I always wondered what your faces looked like up close."

As the sliver of light from the moon danced across her cheeks, they glowed with a radiant warmth. The shadows created by the trees above cast a delicate pattern on her bronze skin, highlighting the golden freckles that adorned her arms and cheeks like glistening stars in a night sky. I couldn't help but be captivated by her unique beauty. Unlike the ethereal, porcelain faeries portrayed in fairy tales, she looked more like a miniature human with striking features and glowing wings.

A crown of tiny fern leaves and twigs was woven into her dark brown curls, adding to her earthy charm and perfectly reflecting her name. Her nose was small and button-like, while her heart-shaped lips gave her face a gentle softness that balanced out her boldness. But it was her eyes that drew me in the most; large and wide with curiosity, they seemed to hold endless secrets within their sage-green depths. And right now, they were staring at me with the same fascination I felt for her.

As I realized I'd been openly staring, I smiled sheepishly. The absurdity of this entire encounter pulled an unexpected laugh from my throat, light and unguarded. "It's quite alright," I managed, smiling despite myself. "I've never seen a faerie up close either."

From beside me, Manakel let out a quiet snort, reminding me we weren't alone. "What's the difference between me and a human?" he muttered under his breath, though just loud enough that I caught it. "It's not like she's never seen someone on two legs before."

A laugh slipped from me before I could stop it, warm and unexpected. Fern's glowing cheeks deepened as she shot Manakel an exaggerated glare.

"I meant *her*," Fern huffed, pointing her tiny hand at me as if to make her case. "She's... different. Besides, you're hardly the same, especially when you unfurl those wings of yours."

Manakel raised a brow, his lips twitching. "Careful, Ferny. You're dangerously close to admitting you like me better with my superior wings."

Fern scoffed and tossed her curls. "Hardly. You're tolerable at best. And your giant wings just make you clumsy and noticeable. Hardly an advantage in these woods."

Dela let out a sharp laugh from Manakel's shoulder while he rolled his eyes. "Oh, she's got you there, Manny," Dela teased with a smile.

Fern's attention shifted back to me, and despite her attempt to redirect, her blush lingered. If I had seen the coloring on anyone else, it would have looked like she was seconds away from hurling, but the soft green blush climbing her neck and cheeks complemented her coloring.

"Anyway," she said, her voice a bit higher as she smoothed her tiny skirt, "I'm sorry for the flick, but it's not every night we get someone like you wandering this deep in the woods. I was just... curious."

Her words were soft and apologetic, even though she had nothing to apologize for. I was curious too, so I completely understood. Manakel glanced in my direction—quick, thoughtful, like maybe he knew she wasn't the only one who was intrigued. His eyes wordlessly told me to trust them, to let them in, and maybe I'd create an unlikely alliance.

Fern's glow softened, her wings slowing as she floated nearer again, the tension easing as quickly as it had sparked. There was something undeniably calming about her presence—a gentle steadiness beneath all her restless energy, like the plant she was named after. Closed off before opening to their full beauty. Resilient, rooted, protective, and impossible to ignore once you notice them.

She tilted her head, her crown of tiny fern leaves and twigs shifting slightly in her dark curls. And as much as she was studying me, I realized I was doing the same—memorizing every impossible detail as though proof of this night might dissolve come morning.

Fern leaned in slightly, lowering her voice as though we shared some long-held secret. "You're...definitely different, alright," she whispered. "The woods haven't seen someone like you in a very long time, but we've all been waiting for your arrival."

The weight of her words landed softly but firmly, unsettling the quiet in my chest. Manakel's eyes shifted sharply toward Fern, something unnerving flashing in his eyes. But he said nothing.

Dela, still lounging across his shoulder, like it was her usual resting place, snorted. "Don't scare her off already, Fern. She's barely found her feet and is probably overwhelmed."

Fern bit her lip, then smiled anyway, small, unsure, but genuine, before her shoulders lifted in a half-shrug. She landed lightly on a branch hovering near my shoulder, "I'm only repeating what the whispers in these woods are already saying. We all heard rumblings that your time for the Rite was approaching, but no one expected you to *actually* do anything about it."

I swallowed, unsure how to respond to that, or why they all knew about it. "How did you know that?" I asked, simply.

A faint smile flickered on her face, bashful and uncertain, like she wasn't sure she was allowed to say it. "The Eldren in these woods know everything that goes on within it. There's not one flower blooming around these parts that we don't know about."

I was starting to learn that the answers I wanted to know weren't going to be said, and all immortals preferred cryptic answers. It was frustrating, but I figured if I wanted to know more, I'd just have to ask questions they *would* answer directly.

I nodded before asking, "So do you all have specific roles? Responsibilities within the woods?"

Fern perked up instantly, her wings fluttering so fast they hummed in excitement. "Oh, absolutely! When it comes to moss, soil, or sprouts, I'm your girl. I keep the earth soft and steady, and help new things grow."

"And I," Dela interrupted with a dramatic toss of her curls, "make sure the flowers bloom just right, with plenty of room for the bees and butterflies to pollinate them. And sometimes," she shot Manakel a pointed look, "I chase off anyone who thinks rearranging my work is a viable prank."

Manakel smirked, wholly unbothered by her obvious frustration. "It's not my fault you get so worked up and are easy to tease. Besides, someone needs to keep things interesting around here."

Dela rolled her eyes but ducked her head as a quiet grin betrayed her.

"Well, the flowers… they're truly beautiful." The wildflowers seemed to dance and sway at the compliment, creating a magical scene that I could hardly believe was real.

Dela's cheeks flushed, her golden glow brightening as she beamed with pride. "Thank you. I'm glad *someone* appreciates my hard work. Unlike Manny," she teased as her wings fluttered. "Sometimes, he'll pick flowers and hide them in other parts of the forest just to mess with me. Then I have to go back and replant everything so things can keep growing as they should." She circled him with a huff, but I could see there was no real malice there. They were more like old friends teasing each other.

Manakel smirked, rolling his eyes. "You know it's all in good fun, D. Someone's gotta keep you sharp in your old age."

The two of them bantered like old friends—effortless, familiar, a rhythm I had no part in but couldn't help leaning into. Their laughter rang through the trees like the woods were listening, like it too remembered what it meant to laugh freely. I let out a soft chuckle without meaning to, and when Fern giggled in return, something inside me eased.

I wasn't just standing on the outside, watching. I was here. In the woods. With a winged immortal and faeries I'd been raised to fear, and I felt safe. That alone was surreal enough to steal the breath from my lungs.

Most of my life, I'd felt a step removed from the world around me. Like I was too much or not enough, never quite the right shape to fit the spaces people tried to press me into. But here, under the heavy hush of the night sky and the hum of unseen magic, I didn't feel too big or too small. I just… was.

Their teasing was light, harmless, and grounding. A kind of magic of its own. And yet, beneath their smiles was something more, something ancient and watchful.

The woods haven't seen someone like you in a very long time…

We've been waiting.

Their words clung to me, whispering promises I wasn't sure how to interpret. I had questions, so many, but I kept them quiet, tucked behind my teeth where they couldn't ruin the fragile spell of the moment. There would be time for answers later. *Hopefully.*

I glanced at Manakel. He wasn't laughing, not exactly, but there was something softer in his eyes. Steady. Grounding. Like he was reminding me that no matter how strange the world became, I wasn't walking through it alone anymore.

The night pressed closer, warm and alive. The scent of wildflowers and mossy earth wrapped around me like a cloak. I could feel the magic in every breath I took, threading through my limbs, settling beneath my skin, blurring the lines between who I'd been and who I might be becoming.

Maybe I didn't belong here. *Not yet.* Maybe I never truly would. But the faeries hadn't turned me away and had been kind, friendly even. The woods had whispered my name. And somehow, without realizing it, this place, this whole night, had already begun to feel less scary and intimidating than it once did.

For the first time in a long time… I didn't feel like a stranger in my own story, and I was ready to face whatever came next.

19. Friends Of The Forest

I definitely spoke too soon.

Not even five minutes had passed since I'd dared to think this night felt… manageable. Safe, even. That I was ready for what came next. As if the forest might not be as terrifying as I'd imagined.

But then the air shifted.

The warmth and familiarity that lingered from Fern and Dela's presence drained like someone had plucked the sun from the sky. The wind sharpened. The trees, once humming softly like a quiet chorus, seemed to hold their breath in anticipation.

"Well, well, what do we have here?"

The unfamiliar female voice slid through the dark like silk over a blade, smooth, mocking, and cold enough to send a ripple of goosebumps down my arms. I turned sharply, but the shadows remained empty.

Empty…until they weren't.

Dela's wings flickered nervously as she abandoned Manakel's shoulder, her glow dimming as if trying to shrink herself from sight. Fern tucked herself behind a low branch, her bravado and fearlessness nowhere to be found. The air had thickened, humming with something sour and ominous. My pulse quickened, and my fear returned. Whatever had spooked them had to be powerful enough if it unsettled even these magical beings.

"I thought I warned you to stay away, human. You are not welcome here," the voice said again, sharper this time. It was everywhere and nowhere all at once, the words wrapping around me like a chilling fog.

I spun, trying to locate the source of it. My breath hitched as the voice whispered again, closer now, like it was brushing against my ear. *"You're stubborn. And I don't repeat myself for fun. If you value your life, you'll turn around and leave."*

Chills ran down my entire body, and my stomach dropped. The icy command dragged me back to the memory of the first time I'd stepped into these woods. That voice—*this voice*—had been there too, taunting me, chasing me out, filling my nightmares ever since. Only three days had passed since that moment, but it felt like a lifetime. So much had happened since, and yet here I was, face-to-face, or rather, ear-to-whisper, with the same debilitating fear.

Manakel's posture shifted just slightly beside me, nothing dramatic, just the faintest shift of his weight, but it was enough to notice. He felt it too. Whatever, *or whoever*, wasn't here to play nice or offer more opportunities to leave unscathed.

I was beginning to wonder if the voice belonged to the forest itself, some disembodied taunt carried on the wind. No creature stepped forward. No shadow peeled itself from the trees. Just silence and tension stretching tighter with every breath. Even the faeries were still now. And beside me, Manakel's expression had shifted, shoulders tense, jaw clenched. That alone set my nerves alight.

Then she appeared.

One moment, there was only shadow and trees. The next, something drifted into view like a blossom on the breeze—if flowers had razor-sharp edges and looked like they might cut you open for fun.

She was another faerie, that much was obvious, but nothing like the others. Dela and Fern were wild and lovely in their own way, but this one? She was stunning. Dangerously so.

She was draped in fabrics in shades of rose and gold that clung to her like light. Her wings shimmered like sunlit frost, thin and glimmering like spun glass, that stirred the air with every shift of her body. They trailed glittering gold dust with every flutter. Golden hair cascaded down her back in gleaming waves, woven with tiny rosebuds and berries that crowned her like an ethereal queen. She looked like something from a forgotten fairytale. Beautiful. Enchanting. Lethal.

But then she smiled, and it ruined everything. It was the kind of smile meant to draw blood. Sharp. Slow. Measured. Like she already knew our secrets and was bored waiting for us to admit them.

Her eyes swept over us with something colder than curiosity— calculation. And just like that, the fairytale cracked.

"Faerie got your tongue, little human?" she purred, her sharp stare slicing straight through me. "No screaming this time? No tears? No begging...how disappointing."

I swallowed hard, fighting the instinct to shrink back or turn and run. She was smaller than the others, tiny, in fact, but it didn't matter. Her presence alone filled the entire clearing, her power humming through the air like the low vibration of a storm on the horizon.

Manakel must have sensed the slow-burning resolve building in me, or maybe it was the venom simmering just beneath her smile, because he stepped forward with practiced ease, slipping between us like a drawn blade. His tone was dry enough to slice the tension in two.

"Alfreda," he said coolly, with the faintest tilt of his head. "I'd say it's nice to see you, but we both know I'd prefer not to lie."

Her smirk sharpened, curling at the edges like smoke fanning a dying flame. She folded her arms, her eyes flicking over him with a lazy sort of disdain. "Oh, Manakel," she purred, voice dripping with indignation. "Still playing the dutiful guard dog? Tell me, is helping the girl *really* worth all the trouble she'll bring?"

"She has every right to be here," he said evenly, though the air shifted with the subtle ripple of his magic as his wings unfurled wider. His shadows extended and wrapped around us, dark and quiet, like the dark promise of a gathering storm. "She's under *my* protection. In the woods by *my* invitation."

Alfreda laughed, a sound too light to carry so much venom. She floated closer, trailing golden dust that shimmered like embers on the wind. "Your protection? How… precious." She tilted her head, her piercing gaze darting between him and me. "Don't forget, shadow boy… you're not the *only* god-made being in these woods. And you're far from being the strongest."

Manakel's jaw clenched, and I saw his fist tighten as his wings tensed. She looked at me, her attention settled on me as she looked me up and down curiously. She was sizing me up, and I felt it land like a weight, cold and unrelenting, wrapping around my ribs like invisible hands tightening with each breath. But I refused to give her the satisfaction of fear. I had a feeling she thrived on it and was expecting me to cower.

So instead, I stepped out from behind Manakel's shadow, even as I felt the slight stiffening of his body, as if some part of him wanted to stop me but refrained. I didn't let him and wouldn't. Not this time.

I met Alfreda's eyes head-on.

Let her look. Let her see that I wasn't some trembling, delicate thing waiting to be chased back into the shadows. "I'm not leaving," I said, forcing each word past the knot in my throat. "I'm here to prepare for my Rite. Whatever problem you have with that… it's yours to keep."

Her smile twitched, just barely. But I saw it falter before she caught it, sharpening it into something meaner.

"Brave words," she murmured, her voice as smooth as it was cruel, "for such a fragile thing."

She glided forward, wings brushing the air beside my cheek. The scent of roses bloomed around her, sweet and cloying, twisting into something bitter underneath. Like rot hidden beneath beauty.

"Let's see how long that bravery lasts when the woods decide you're no longer welcome," she whispered, circling me like smoke. "It only takes one misstep, little human. *Just one.* And you'll be crawling back out. Crying. Begging, even." Her smile widened. "That is, if you make it out at all."

The words cut deeper than I expected. The memory of the night in the forest rushed up like a ghost, the floor dragging me down, shadows pulling at my limbs. She had seen it. She knew.

A shiver crept down my spine, but I locked it down. I was scared. Of course I was. But I was also stubborn, and she'd have to do a lot more than throw pretty threats and poisoned smiles to make me run this time.

I kept my eyes steady, unflinching, even as the air between us crackled with something sharp and ancient, like a wire drawn too tight, waiting to snap. For a breath, I thought she might strike. That she *wanted* me to flinch. But instead, she gave a little flick of her wrist—and in a swirl of petals and golden dust, she vanished. Gone, like a dream turned nightmare. But the chill of her presence stayed behind, clinging to the trees, the air, my skin.

The silence that followed pressed in like a warning, and I wasn't naive enough to think that was the last I'd see of her. Whatever Alfreda's motives were, it was clear: she didn't want me here.

And now...I was starting to understand exactly what Manakel meant when he said not all Eldren could be trusted.

I exhaled slowly, only then realizing how tightly my hands had curled into fists. The pulse pounding behind my ears slowly eased as Manakel turned toward me, something unknown lingering in his expression.

"Now *that* was reckless," he said, though there was a glint of something else beneath the reprimand. Admiration, maybe, or something dangerously close to it. "Alfreda doesn't tend to forget things. And you've just made yourself very... *memorable.* That's something you don't want to be, especially not to her."

Fern fluttered out from behind her hiding spot, her sage-green glow still dim. "She's just a bully," she offered, though the shake in her voice made the words feel thinner than she intended. "Beautiful and powerful, but still a bully."

Dela's wings flickered, her earlier playfulness nowhere to be found. "Just… stay sharp and try not to wander the forest alone, especially at night," she added, her voice quiet. "Alfreda doesn't make threats for fun, and it seems she's determined to run you out of here and watch you squirm in the process."

I nodded in understanding, though their warnings sat heavy in my chest. Maybe I *had* gone about that encounter all wrong, but I was trying to stand my ground. I was attempting to show her I wasn't afraid of her, even though it couldn't be further from the truth.

The moment might have passed, but the taste of her threats lingered. Alfreda wasn't finished with me. I felt it as surely as I felt the damp cold in the air surrounding us. And whatever the woods had planned next… she'd make certain it hurt and made me never want to set foot in these parts again.

Dela and Fern whispered their goodbyes, and the last of their glow faded into the trees. It left the path ahead darker, quieter, as if the forest itself had been waiting for them to leave. I missed their laughter and easy banter as their lightness was replaced by the weight of the woods closing in.

Manakel stepped closer, his movements almost quick and silent despite the dry twigs and leaves crackling beneath his boots.

"See?" he murmured, voice low and smooth, quiet enough to belong to the night itself. There was something behind it, too. Not quite warmth, or praise, but close. "Not all faeries are bad."

A beat of silence passed between us, the kind that held more weight than words.

"But not all of them are good either," he added, his eyes drifting toward the shadows Alfreda had vanished into. "The difference here is learning who you're facing before it's too late. Trust is… dangerous. Even those who seem harmless can turn on you without warning."

There was something else in his voice now, something that made my skin prickle. He wasn't just warning me about faeries or the Eldren. His words felt layered, like they were meant to teach me something deeper. Or maybe… confess something he didn't know how to say outright.

Maybe he wasn't just talking about *them*.

Maybe he meant *himself*.

Or maybe… he meant *me*.

I nodded, slow and thoughtful, letting his words settle. They wound their way through me, heavier than they should've been. I couldn't tell if the tightness in my chest was fear or understanding. Maybe both. But I didn't let it show. I'd spent enough time letting fear drive my reactions; I wasn't ready to give it the reins again.

We kept walking. The trail narrowed, trees arching together above us like clasped hands, thickening into a canopy that swallowed the sky. Time felt different here. The path could've looped back on itself a dozen times, and I wouldn't have noticed. There was no moonlight, no markers, no sound but the hush of our breath and the steady rhythm of our steps.

It felt like we were moving through something more than just a forest. Like we were walking through some in-between place that didn't belong to day or night. A place outside of certainty.

I stayed close to him, too close, probably, but I didn't move away. I didn't want to. I didn't trust the woods. I didn't trust the silence, or the way shadows curled around every branch like they were waiting for a misstep. I wasn't even sure I trusted myself—*not fully*.

But him?

Somehow, despite everything, I was starting to trust him, and I didn't know what had changed. Maybe it was the steadiness in his voice, or the fact that he hadn't tried to soften the truth, hadn't tried to lie and make this easier. Maybe it was the way he'd stood between me and a threat that could've swallowed me whole without blinking. Or maybe it was something deeper. Older. Like the kind of knowing that doesn't make sense on paper but sits quietly in your chest, whispering: *This one. You're safe with this one.*

I didn't understand it. Not yet. But I followed him anyway. Because out of all the uncertain things around me…He felt the least like a lie.

"Are you…" I started, but the words caught in my throat. I hated the way my voice softened, hesitant, like I was asking for something I shouldn't. "Are you allowed to stay with me? During the Rite, I mean. If something goes wrong… will you be there to help me?"

The question hung between us like thick fog. Before coming here, I would've mocked the idea of needing anyone. But now? Now, the thought of being left alone in this place made my skin prickle.

He looked at me then, *really looked*, and something in his expression shifted. The sharpness I'd come to expect dulled, and for the first time, I thought I saw something like conflict flicker behind his eyes.

"During the Imbe Rite, no one can interfere," he said carefully. "Not even me. It's something between you and the gods, and if anyone tried to step in… it would risk more than just failure."

I swallowed, unsure if the knot in my throat was from his words or the way he said them. He looked away, as if considering whether to keep going or if I could handle it. But continued, quieter, "But if something unnatural happens, something that threatens you beyond the Rite itself—I'll stop it. I can offer you that much."

The promise wasn't spoken loudly, but it landed with the weight of something that could shatter the very ground we walked on. His voice was steady, his gaze unwavering, but I saw the truth in it. The cost of his words. The danger of helping me if it came to that.

My chest tightened. "So basically I'll be on my own," I whispered, half to myself.

His focus drifted back to me, and this time the corner of his mouth tugged up, the smallest hint of a smirk hiding beneath his usual restraint. "Not entirely. I'll still be nearby to guide you. Besides, you're stronger than you think, Raine. You've made it this far, and you only found out about an entirely new part of your world days ago. That already says more about you than you realize."

There was something in the way he said my name, like it meant more to him than it should have. Or maybe I just wanted it to.

I tried to focus on the path, but my heart was beating loudly now, drumming in my ears as a faint pink blush crept up my neck. I cleared my throat, desperate to steady myself. "You're pretty good at this, you know," I muttered.

"At what?"

"Making people feel like they're not about to face an untimely death in a magical forest where everything goes against logic and reason."

He huffed a soft laugh, and the sound did something to me I didn't expect. "It's part of the job. Something required of all Sciathain. Except it's usually from afar and a hands-off approach."

"Right. Just part of your job." I muttered because maybe that's all I was. All he saw me as. Another task he needed to complete. The poor, helpless human girl struggling with her new future. One she didn't even know existed, let alone prepare for.

But a part of me also wasn't sure I believed that. Not with the way his eyes lingered. Not with the way his steps slowed whenever mine did, like some invisible tether refused to let me fall behind. Manakel hardly seemed like the type of person to do anything he didn't want to. Especially not out of obligation. So that had to mean he wanted to be here.

Didn't it?

We continued walking, the forest curling tighter around us, shadows twisting long across the ground. The wind shifted, carrying the scent of damp earth and something sweeter beneath it, like wild honey and rain-soaked wood. I thought about asking him what it was. But then he spoke again, low and thoughtful, the words threading straight into me.

"During the Rite," he said, "there will be moments when you feel completely alone. That's part of the test. But remember… the woods are never truly silent or asleep. The forest watches. The wind listens. And if you pay attention, you might realize you're never really alone."

I didn't know if he meant himself or the forest. Maybe both. Maybe neither. But the thought of him lingering somewhere in the shadows while I faced whatever came next eased something restless in me.

"Thank you," I said softly, meaning it more than I expected. "For... this. For being here and for helping me navigate it all."

He looked at me as if every thought was securely locked behind stone walls, I saw the edges of his restraint falter. The tiniest crack. The ghost of something warmer waiting just beneath.

"It's my duty, Raine," he said at last.

But I couldn't stop the thought from creeping in. *What if it wasn't just duty anymore?*

He'd said it was his role, his responsibility, but responsibilities didn't usually show up in the middle of the night, unannounced, and wait in silence, hoping you'd show up. They didn't linger in shadows or step between you and the things trying to hurt you, like it was instinct. That had to mean something more. *Didn't it?*

I told myself not to overthink it. Not to twist something simple into something it wasn't. But every time I tried to convince myself it was nothing... it felt a little less like the truth. And the longer we walked, the more the forest seemed to press in, tall and watchful, like it was holding its breath. Watching and waiting. But with him beside me, that weight felt easier to carry. The path didn't feel quite so impossible. The dark didn't seem quite so endless.

Maybe it was still duty. But a big part of me was starting to hope it was something else, too.

20. One Step From Falling

Manakel came to an abrupt halt, and I nearly walked into him before catching myself. He stood in front of a tree so massive it looked like it had been carved into the earth itself. But *"massive"* didn't feel like the right word. This tree was ancient—its trunk impossibly wide, its bark dark and furrowed with age, like it had witnessed lifetimes I couldn't begin to comprehend. When I craned my neck upward, its limbs vanished into the canopy, merging with the sky like the forest had built its own shield.

I swallowed hard, a slow unease settling into my bones. My grandmother once told me you could tell a tree's age by the thickness of its trunk. If that was true, this one might've been the first to ever grow. It didn't just feel old, it felt aware. Like it was watching, listening, and judging everything within these trees.

Manakel didn't speak, his expression as stoic as always, so maybe it was only me who felt unease around the large tree. He simply knelt, a little off to the side, fingers moving with unexpected gentleness as he gathered a few wildflowers growing in the mossy shade. From what I could see, he chose goldenrod and violets, and handled them with care as he bundled them into a bouquet. His hands hovered briefly before he placed them at the base of the tree with something that looked like reverence.

Something in me stilled. My breath caught, a flicker of memory rising unbidden—my grandmother's hands guiding mine, soft and sure, as she taught me the quiet language of flowers. Not just what they looked like, but what they meant. What they whispered, when words were too fragile and intentions too pure. Most flowers carried a meaning, a quiet language that could convey emotions, promises, and secrets if you knew how to listen.

"Flowers speak," she once said, pressing my fingertips against a velvet petal. *"Not everyone knows how to listen. But they always mean something, so be mindful when choosing them for others."*

I'd asked her, *"But what if the person you give them to doesn't understand?"*

She only smiled, brushing soil from her palms like the answer was simple.

"Then it's not for them to understand. It's for you to give. The intention is the gift, not their knowledge of why you chose it."

Goldenrod meant encouragement. Good fortune.

Violets meant loyalty. Devotion.

I stared at the gathered blooms resting at the foot of the ancient tree and wondered if this was still about the Rite… or if, somehow, it was about something more important. Another lesson perhaps?

My eyes lingered on the small bouquet, each bloom startlingly vivid against the muted forest floor. The goldenrod caught the moonlight in delicate threads of gold, while the violets nestled low and quiet, their deep purple petals nearly swallowed by shadow. *Why these flowers, specifically? And why place them here?*

The questions pressed against my ribs, heavy and insistent. But before I could give them a voice, the earth beneath my boots shifted. Not dramatically. Not like in stories where the earth cracks open with a roar. No, this was quieter. Slower. But somehow, that made it worse.

A low groan rippled through the roots beneath my feet, ancient and primal. I froze, breath caught in my throat. The towering tree before us seemed to exhale, as if it had just remembered how to breathe.

Roots stirred, slow and deliberate, curling like fingers stretching awake after centuries of stillness. The trunk, so solid a moment ago, began to move.

I stumbled back, a startled cry caught in my throat. A hand reached out and steadied me, and I flinched, only to find Manakel beside me, his grip firm and grounding. Even still, my heart raced. I wasn't imagining this. It was really happening.

The bark began to ripple, and I blinked, certain my eyes were playing tricks on me, but no—there it was again. Right in front of me, the bark rippled like water, forming lines, hollows, and ridges that slowly took shape. Grooves shifted, knots stretched, and pulled. My pulse skittered as the rough surface began to reshape itself, forming what looked unmistakably like… a face. *There was a face… inside the tree.*

I stumbled back, air snagging in my lungs. My heart beat hard against my ribs like it wanted to run. Branches above rustled without wind, as if the forest itself was watching and listening.

The face blinked, and the eyes opened. Not carved. Not symbolic. Real eyes. Deep-set and impossibly warm, blinking slowly with a patience that made time feel irrelevant. They were a unique shade of brown, layered with age and polished like wood soaked in wisdom. I couldn't look away.

It blinked again, and I suddenly realized I hadn't taken a breath.

The face was gnarled and weathered, grown from the tree itself, sculpted into furrowed brows and hollowed cheeks that resembled an elderly man. A thick beard of roots spilled downward, tangling into the forest floor. Moss and leaves blanketed his head like a wild mane.

It was terrifying. And beautiful. And impossibly, undeniably… alive.

And then, as if the transformation from ordinary tree to talking tree man wasn't shocking enough, a sound echoed from deep within the trunk. A groaning sigh that stirred the air before he spoke.

"Manakel."

I flinched. His voice was deep and resonant, like the earth itself was speaking. The sound vibrated through the ground, the trees, and the very air around us. The forest quieted around us, like even the birds and insects knew to listen.

"It has been many ages since you last visited me. And I see you've brought… a guest."

Me. He was looking at *me*.

His stare was quiet and assessing. Not unkind, but not entirely safe either. I opened my mouth and closed it again, unsure how to speak to something that felt like a living myth.

I glanced at Manakel, unsure, but he gave me a small, almost amused nod. So I stepped forward, my voice barely more than a whisper. "H-hello," I stammered, wincing at how small my voice sounded. "My name is Raine. I… I didn't know trees could… well, come to life or talk, so excuse my shock."

The ancient being chuckled, a sound like rustling leaves in the wind. "There is much that lives in this forest you do not yet know, young one. I am Caden, Keeper of the Forest. It is my role as a Dryad to preserve the balance and bear witness to those who seek truth or passage through these woods."

His eyes flicked briefly to Manakel, then back to me. "And you…you've come hoping to prepare for your Rite?"

The weight of his truth, about knowing everything within the woods, settled heavily on my shoulders, and I swallowed hard. "Yes," I whispered. "I… I don't know what I'm walking into exactly, but I've been told these woods are the place to start."

Caden inclined his head slowly. "The forest will show you what you need to see. But beware, its truths are rarely what you expect. It will test you. Not with tricks, but with revelations. It'll reveal strengths you didn't know you had and prey on weaknesses you thought you'd buried, even from yourself."

His stare pierced through me then, sharp enough to make me shift on my feet. "Every Eldren and shadow here has a story. Some are guides, others deceivers. But it's up to you to learn the difference, or lose yourself to the wrong one."

Manakel stepped forward then, his voice quiet but steady. "Caden, I bring her to you not just for a blessing to pass through, but to seek your guidance."

Caden's eyes twinkled with something between amusement and fondness. "You know the rules, old friend. I offer no direct answers. But I can give… insight."

He leaned closer to me, his face filling my view, bark and moss and age. The bark around his mouth cracked into what I could only describe as a smile.

"Raine, remember this—what you seek lies in both the questions and the answers. In the space between what you think you know and what you're willing to discover. Keep your heart open and your mind clear. The woods will give you what you need, but not always what you want."

His words rooted themselves in my chest, sharp and strange and true.

"Thank you," I murmured. It felt small, but I had so many questions, and could sense this was all he would give.

Caden began to draw back, his face slowly dissolving into bark once more. The ridges flattened, the lines blurred, until he was almost indistinguishable from the tree itself. Just before he disappeared completely, his voice drifted once more into the silence.

"And do not fear the shadows, Raine. They are as much a part of you, and these woods, as the light."

The forest fell silent, and I stared at the tree, half-expecting him to reappear. The wildflowers remained at the base, untouched, still glowing softly in the moonlight, like they'd always been there.

I turned to Manakel, my voice barely above a whisper. "Uhh…what just happened?" I was still in shock and awe that a tree could come alive and talk, let alone that it spoke to *me.*

He looked at me with a detached demeanor. "You met the Keeper. He's one of the eldest Eldren in these parts," he said simply. "And you'd do well to remember his words and warnings. These woods are always listening and hear more than they're willing to repeat."

We kept walking, but Caden's voice echoed in my mind, each word settling into me like seeds pressed into soil—quiet now, but certain to grow and thrive.

I paused, then spun on my heel to face Manakel. My heart still beat too fast, the woods still felt too alive, like the veil between the real and the impossible had torn open, and I was standing on the edge of everything I didn't understand. Every shadow now felt suspicious, every branch a potential secret waiting to reveal itself. But when I looked at him, my chest settled a little. He didn't look shaken, not even fazed. Just calm and steady. Like nothing out of the ordinary had happened.

His hand found my arm when I wavered on a root, grounding me as we began walking back the way we'd come. For once, I didn't flinch or pull away. Instead, I found myself leaning into his touch, letting the contact linger longer than I should've, maybe longer than it needed to, but I didn't care.

He glanced down, his expression flickering with something I couldn't quite name. But he didn't move. His hand lingered, gentle but sure, and we walked in silence that felt oddly natural.

"We're heading back to your house now," he said eventually, his tone softer than usual. "I don't need your family waking up and wondering where you wandered off."

"Thanks." I managed a small smile, grateful for his consideration, and relieved I didn't have to come up with another lie to explain my absence.

He returned the smile, faint but genuine, before adding, "But don't think this means you're off the hook for the rest of the day. We still have a lot to cover today, and I'll need you back in the forest no more than an hour after you're home."

The shift in his tone was subtle, but it left no room for argument.

I rolled my eyes to break the tension. "Alright, boss," I teased, shooting him a sideways glance. Then, before I could second-guess it, I added, "Or should I say... Manny?"

I was surprised when I first heard Dela call him the nickname, thinking it was too soft and sweet for him. But I was also starting to see many more sides to him than my initial observations.

His reaction was immediate. A hint of pink crept up his cheekbones, quickly masked by a tight exhale and a flicker of exasperation. "Please don't. I actually *hate* that name," he muttered, almost to himself. "But it's been centuries, and the fae don't listen. At some point, it stopped being worth correcting, but I'd prefer it if you didn't call me that."

I tapped my chin with mock thoughtfulness. "Hmm. Interesting."

He groaned and dragged a hand down his face, which only made me grin wider.

"I *could* never say it again," I offered sweetly, leaning a little closer. "But... what's in it for me?"

He glanced over, a slow smile curving his lips—equal parts amused and something else, something that made my breath catch.

He leaned in, just close enough for his breath to graze my cheek, and murmured, "I'm offering you my time, guidance, and a better-than-average chance at survival." His voice was low and velvet-smooth. "But if that's not enough, Amadán... what more do you want?"

The warmth of his breath sent shivers down my spine, and my breath caught. The word *Amadán* curled through me like a secret. I still didn't know what it meant, but the way he said it, warm, teasing, quiet, made something in my chest clench. It sounded... personal. Like it was something meant just for me.

Heat flooded my face, and my heart raced, but for an entirely different reason. The space between us had shifted, charged with something I didn't know how to name. And maybe it was reckless, maybe it was naive, but for the first time in a long time, I felt like I wasn't just someone he *had* to help. I felt like something was shifting between us, and he would never be the first to admit it.

So I said it. Before I could second-guess or retreat into logic, the words tumbled out, soft and certain.

"I want you to kiss me."

The forest held its breath. His smile vanished, and the playfulness was no longer evident. For a second, the world went still. Even the leaves overhead stopped stirring.

Shock flickered across his face, so quick I might have missed it if I weren't holding my breath, watching his every move. He stilled, his fingers loosening against my arm. He took a small step back, as if he needed space to process the shift in gravity between us.

And suddenly I wasn't so sure anymore.

Had I misread everything? Had I just made this unbearably awkward? Ruined things with the one person who made me feel safe in all this strangeness?

The silence between us felt louder than Caden's voice had moments ago. And my heart, traitorous thing that it was, just kept waiting for his answer.

His silence stretched. And the longer it lasted, the more foolish I felt. My heart pounded in my ears, heat prickling at the back of my neck. I opened my mouth to take it back, to laugh it off before he could shut me down, but then he finally spoke.

"Raine..." His voice wavered as he said my name with barely more than a breath. The way he said it made my breath hitch, sent a shiver rolling down my spine. He was being careful. As if trying to piece the words together before he spoke them, reluctant, and heavy with something unspoken. "That's not something we should do."

Not *can't*. Not *don't want to*. Just... *shouldn't*.

It wasn't rejection. *Not yet*. It was mindful, measured, like he was stepping into unfamiliar territory and didn't want to make a mistake he couldn't take back. I swallowed hard, forcing a smile even as something inside me sank.

"You deserve someone who can give you more than—" He exhaled sharply, jaw clenching as if he couldn't bring himself to finish the thought. His gaze dropped for a breath, and when it returned to mine, it was raw. "I can't be that person for you."

The words landed exactly where I feared they might. There it was, the warning, the denial I expected. But underneath it was something that felt like wanting or regret.

"Relax," I said lightly, waving a hand like it was no big deal. "I was joking. Mostly. I just figured if I'm going to potentially die sometime in the next few days, I might as well check first kiss off the list."

He huffed out a short laugh, the tension in his shoulders easing just a fraction. "You're not going to die, not on my watch. Which is also why this can't be anything more."

I took a shaky breath, summoning every ounce of courage I had left. "Maybe I'm not asking for more," I whispered. "Just… this. One moment. One kiss. That's all."

I tried to laugh, to lighten the air, but the tension between us only thickened. "I'm not asking you to marry me…just one kiss."

His expression shifted, his ever-present walls cracking just enough for me to see the conflict in his eyes. The moonlight filtered through the trees, highlighting the golden flecks in his eyes, and I thought, just for a moment, that I saw him waver.

Then he stepped closer. So close I could feel the heat of him, steady, quiet, impossibly grounding.

I raised a brow, and his lips twitched, but his eyes didn't leave mine. "One kiss. One time," he said, his tone soft, careful. "But only if you understand it can't mean anything more."

The words should have stung more than they did. But something in his voice, almost too gentle, told me they weren't entirely true. Not for him. And surely not for me. But I wasn't about to ruin the moment by admitting that.

"Sure," I said, shrugging, even as my pulse raced. "One-and-done. No emotional side effects or expectations. It's just a little kiss, no big deal."

His expression twitched again, somewhere between amusement and agony. "I wouldn't exactly call anything I do *little*."

I coughed, not expecting the abrupt shift, and countered with a teasing smirk, stepping closer, "I wouldn't know since you're still talking."

The moonlight filtered through the trees, catching on the edges of his hair, the faint shimmer in his eyes. He didn't move as I came to stand in front of him. Didn't retreat. Just watched me with that same unreadable expression that made my breath catch.

For a heartbeat, I wasn't sure if he would do it. If he'd back away. If he'd vanish again like smoke and leave me standing in the dark, wanting this more than I'd be willing to admit. His hand slid up my arm, slow and feather-light, the kind of touch that gave me a final chance to pull away. I didn't.

"One moment," he echoed, his voice barely more than a breath. "One kiss."

His hand rose, slow and certain, and cupped my jaw, his thumb brushing a line just beneath my cheekbone. He leaned down, the world stilled, and my eyes fluttered shut.

The first brush of his lips was so gentle it felt like a secret, like something fragile, fleeting, a moment stolen from time itself. But it wasn't hesitant. I barely had time to process it before my body reacted instinctively. The rest of the world, the forest, the Rite, the weight of everything unknown, faded into nothing.

There was only him. Only the warmth of his touch, the steady, grounding presence of his hands against my skin. The feeling of his lips pressed to mine.

He pulled me closer, but there was restraint in the way he held me, in the way his fingers lingered but didn't press, as though he was afraid of giving or taking too much. That restraint made my heart ache in a way I hadn't expected. I wanted to chase this feeling, to capture everything he was willing to give me before it slipped through my fingers. A moment suspended in time, tender, impossibly delicate, and over too soon.

He pulled away first. Slowly, carefully, his forehead resting gently against mine as he took a slow, shaky breath. I opened my eyes to find him already looking at me, waiting, and clouded with regret. But there was something else, too. Something deeper. Something he wasn't letting himself feel, but couldn't quite hide. His fingers still lingered at my jaw like he didn't quite want to let go yet.

"One time, Raine," he said, his voice lower now. Rougher. "This can't happen again. You know that, right?"

I nodded, even though my heart screamed otherwise. I swallowed, the ache in my chest settling like fog.

"One time," I echoed.

It felt like a lie. But I mean it, too. At least part of me did. Even if this was all we'd ever have... it would be enough.

His thumb brushed my cheek—soft, slow, reluctant—before he stepped back completely. And just like that, the distance returned. The silence folded in between us, but the ghost of his touch stayed with me.

My first kiss.

Not a promise. Not a future. Just a moment, impossibly fleeting, painfully beautiful, and already slipping through my fingers like the shadows surrounding us.

21. Cloaked In Shadows

I couldn't stop thinking about that kiss.

I was supposed to be listening to Wren recount his patrol from the castle, nodding along and sipping tea like nothing had changed. But instead, I sat motionless, eyes fixed on the loose leaves at the bottom of my cup, my thoughts miles away.

I kept replaying it, every second of that fleeting moment. The softness of his lips. The way his hand had cradled my cheek like I might vanish if he let go. The restraint in his touch, like holding me too tightly, might undo something he wasn't ready to face.

It had felt perfect. Like something pulled from a dream.

Except it wasn't. And now I was spiraling, because even though we'd agreed to "one time," I wanted more. Had it even meant anything to him? Or was it just pity? A favor for the reckless, pathetic human girl who practically begged to be kissed?

I stirred my tea, hoping the leaves would offer some kind of answer, a sign, anything to explain what came next. Like, how was I supposed to face him again, now that I knew how his lips felt?

A throat cleared sharply, and I blinked, jerking my eyes up to find Wren, my mother, and my grandmother staring at me. My stomach dropped. I'd clearly missed something.

Wren leaned forward, brow furrowed. "So… the job?"

I froze, recounting my lie from yesterday. The flimsy excuse I'd spun about a position in Ceannairí suddenly felt paper-thin under their scrutiny. I forced a smile, hoping they wouldn't catch on to me stalling.

"Right. The job," I said quickly, my words tumbling out faster than I intended. "It's just a temporary position. A few months to start."

I winced as my mother's expression shifted from confusion to hurt. "A few months?" Her voice cracked slightly.

"Yeah," I rushed on. "I thought it'd be a good opportunity to get out of Laochra, try something new, before I decide what to do now that I'm of age."

I hadn't expected her to cry. But she wiped at the corner of her eye, and the guilt hit hard. When I told Wren, I didn't think he'd mention it, at least not before I had my story straight or was able to tell her first. But now, seeing the hurt I caused by not telling her myself, I knew I'd messed up. I understood where I went wrong, but I couldn't take it back. I'd let the lie form, let it shape itself into something I thought sounded reasonable, but in reality, I was blindsiding her. And soon, I'd have to face my father, too.

He'd see right through it, though. He always did and was able to pick apart even the tiniest lie. I needed a better story. A believable reason for a job I hadn't mentioned. A job I hadn't applied for. A job that didn't even exist. I just didn't know how much time I had to figure it all out, not with my birthday and Rite only days away.

Across the table, my grandmother met my stare, her expression guarded but edged with concern. She knew the truth. Knew where I was *really* headed. And though she said nothing, I saw the warning in her eyes—*if you can't sell the lie, everything falls apart.*

But it was easy for her to judge, considering she had perfected the art of lying to her family for over a century with no remorse. She probably had a backlog of excuses to pull out if someone got too close to the truth. But I had felt cornered and blurted the first thing that came to mind yesterday, not fully focusing on the consequences of the lie.

She glanced at the clock, subtle but deliberate. My hour was nearly up, and Manakel would be waiting.

I swallowed, my heart drumming against my ribs as I pushed back my chair abruptly. "I should get ready. I have a lot to finalize today," I muttered, barely paying attention to the way Wren was still watching me like he knew something was off.

But before I could make it to the stairs, my mom's voice stopped me.

"Raine, promise you'll be back for dinner."

I froze.

"Your father and Baren will be home early. They'll want to hear your news, too."

I hesitated, not sure if I could endure another round of questions. Especially without a solid plan in place to keep up the ruse of my fake job opportunity. My family trusted me. And I was lying to them. *On purpose.*

I nodded quickly, avoiding her gaze as I fled upstairs.

The moment my bedroom door shut behind me, I leaned against it, heart pounding. My lie was unraveling faster than I could patch it. The pressure was building, and this was starting to feel too real. My father would see straight through every lie. Baren, already suspicious about everything I did, would dig until he found the truth.

I was in over my head, with the lies, the Rite, Manakel, my grandmother's secret…everything.

And worst of all, I wasn't sure I could stop any of it now.

I caught my reflection in the mirror as I pulled my shirt over my head. My hair was a tangled mess, nothing new, and faint shadows clung beneath my eyes, reminders of too many restless nights spent battling thoughts that refused to settle. I ran a hand through the knots, exhaling, but my mind slipped again.

To him.

To the way Manakel looked at me before he kissed me—soft, intent, like I was the only thing anchoring him to the moment. Whether he regretted it the second it ended. If it meant anything to him? Or if it was just a fleeting indulgence, easily forgotten the moment he vanished into the trees?

I shook the thought off. There wasn't time for this, no time to question it since it wouldn't be happening again. I dressed quickly, splashed water on my face, and headed for the stairs.

Halfway down, my foot caught the edge of the step, and I nearly collided with Wren. He caught me by the arms before I could fall. "Whoa there, Wildheart," he said with a crooked smile. Light and teasing, but there was a weight behind it, too.

He knew.

Maybe not the full truth, but enough to sense I wasn't being honest. And that stung more than I wanted to admit. Because until now, Wren had always been the one person I could tell anything. But some truths were bigger burdens than even he could help me carry.

"Where are you rushing off to this time?"

I swallowed hard, pulling away. "Just errands, grabbing some things I didn't get to yesterday."

I gave a small shrug, keeping my face neutral. "Nothing exciting. But I'll see you later, okay?"

I didn't look back. *I couldn't.* But I knew he nodded, because we both knew each other better than anyone else. Wren had always been by my side, and I just hoped that after everything, he'd understand why I needed to do this, why I had to lie, and that all that mattered was his safety.

I reached for the door handle, but before I could step outside, my grandmother appeared, my satchel in hand. She placed it on my shoulder without a word, her knowing smile already in place.

"There's some food and tea in there," she said simply, placing a folded blanket into my arms.

I frowned, glancing up at her, trying to decipher why she'd given me these things, but I was already going to be late. "Gran—"

"No fussing, Raine." Her tone was firm, but warm. A steadying force. She tucked a stray curl behind my ear, fingers resting gently against my cheek.

"You have a habit of overthinking everything, of carrying the weight of the world before it's even yours to bear," she murmured. "Always trying to solve what hasn't happened yet. But not everything in life is meant to be understood before it's lived."

I swallowed, my fingers tightening around the satchel.

"Use your time today wisely," she continued. "Ask your questions. But don't be afraid to listen, too. Sometimes, the answers we seek don't come in the form we expect."

Something inside me tugged painfully at her cryptic advice. She was right, but I was still so unsure. And I was running out of time to get it right.

"I just… I don't want to make the wrong choice or focus on the wrong things." My voice was quieter than I meant it to be, but she heard me anyway.

Her expression softened. "We don't grow by standing still, Wildheart." She brushed a kiss against my temple. "You're meant for great things. But even greatness requires risk. Trust yourself to lead you where you're meant to go."

The words settled somewhere deep, lingering in the spaces where doubt lived. I nodded, unable to find my voice, shoving the blanket inside the satchel and gripping the strap tight.

As I stepped outside, the crisp morning air greeted me, sharp with dew and promise. I hesitated, glancing back at the house. The weight of it all pressed down—the lies, the looming Rite, the feeling that everything familiar was slipping through my fingers.

But I couldn't afford to think about any of that now.

Manakel was waiting, and time waited for no one.

I moved quietly through the trees, my pulse thrumming against my ribs as I felt the eerie feeling of being watched. I glanced over my shoulder, but no one followed.

Mom and Wren were still inside. I'd made sure they were distracted before slipping away, but the unexpected weight of my satchel tugged heavily against my shoulder. Not from the food or tea packed neatly inside, but because of everything else I was carrying with it.

Lies. Secrets. Choices I wasn't ready to make.

The shadows shifted around me as branches stretched overhead and rustled in the wind like skeletal fingers grasping the air. The moment I passed the first cluster of trees, I exhaled, allowing myself to breathe a little easier and steadying my steps.

This was our meeting spot: the hidden clearing behind the large twisted tree. Where the edges of my world had begun to unravel, only to reshape into something else entirely.

But it was empty. No familiar silhouette. No gleam of golden brown eyes. No shadows or wings in sight. Just stillness.

A strange tension settled over my shoulders, and the silence pressed in. This was all wrong. It was *too* still. *Too silent.*

My steps slowed, and a prickle of unease crawled up my spine. It hummed with the wrongness of it all. Not of something dangerous, but just *off*. Like the moment before lightning strikes, when the air changes direction. The same feeling I used to get as a child when I wandered too close to the woods and sensed that the shadows weren't just shadows but something lurking just beyond sight.

I looked around, searching for any sign Manakel was close, but just as I was about to turn around and leave, I saw a flicker of black wings in the distance. Relief bloomed, and I exhaled, the shadows not feeling quite as suffocating now that he was here. But it curdled almost instantly. The air warmed unnaturally, thickening around me, choking each breath from my lungs like a snuff to a flame. A prickling heat built low at the base of my skull, subtle at first… then spreading, blooming like embers catching flame.

I took a hesitant step forward, and the forest moved with me. A gust of wind snapped through the trees, sudden and sharp, a branch swung out its leaves brushing the back of my arm in a soft caress, and my senses were on high alert. I tried to turn and leave, but couldn't.

A pressure wrapped around me, invisible but suffocating, like the air itself had hands, pressing against my skin, holding me in place.

"Well, well."

The unfamiliar voice uncoiled in the air, low and deliberate. The words slipped past my guard like smoke through a keyhole, curling around my throat, my wrists, my spine. The whisper brushed so close to my ear it felt like a part of me. Every instinct bristled at the wrongness of it, yet beneath the resistance, something deep in me leaned toward it.

"What do we have here? A girl, wandering all alone in the woods?"

My breath hitched as the words slid around me. My eyes darted around to try and track the source of the voice, but there was no one in sight. *How was that even possible?* Panic clawed its way up my throat. Was this another trick? My mind conjuring up voices? A faerie game? A test to see how long I'd last?

"Look at you," the voice murmured, amused. *"So far from home. So far from safety. So utterly helpless, and…human."*

The word *human* dripped with contempt, laced with venom, and curled around me like a vice. Something twisted in my chest. A flicker of something hot, an instinctual urge to fight, but my body couldn't move.

"Tell me—are you lost, or just foolish, straying into places you don't belong?"

The whisper brushed my ear, too close, threading heat down my spine. A laugh followed, hollow and mocking, circling me like a predator who had all the time in the world to corner me.

"Look how easy it was to corner you." The words coiled in the shadows, heavy with amusement. *"To take hold of your mind… to still your body*

without even touching you."

My breath stuttered, shallow and uneven, the air in my lungs thick as if it no longer belonged to me. Invisible restraints tightened around my limbs, not crushing, but unyielding, holding me in place with an ease that made my pulse hammer against my throat.

"I could break you faster than you could even think to scream."

A slow beat of silence followed, heavy enough to make my skin prickle.

"And no one would hear you...or care."

Every nerve tuned to the curl of that voice, the heat of it sliding through my veins as I let the truth sink its claws in.

It *had* been easy for him to corner me, to ensnare me, and hold me hostage. I didn't even know who was doing this, yet he had me exactly where he wanted. Scared, helpless, and holding onto hope for someone or something to help me. My breathing turned ragged; my body strained, but I remained immobile.

Where was Manakel? And why hadn't he come like we'd planned?

All I could hear was my heartbeat, pounding like a war drum, each beat rattling through my ribs. The invisible shackles cinched tighter, winding around me like a spider spinning its final thread.

The prickling at the back of my neck began as a whisper, a faint warning skimming over my skin. It lingered, building, each pulse of it sinking deeper until it threaded down my spine. Unease rippled through me, sharp at first, then melting into something heavier. The air seemed to thicken, charged, and changing.

Then came the heat. A slow, deliberate exhale ghosted over the curve of my neck. My skin tensed beneath it, every hair standing on end, as if my body recognized the danger before my mind could. The closeness wasn't imagined—it was everywhere, seeping in, claiming the space around me.

Something cold pressed against my mouth, stealing the gasp I hadn't meant to give. I tried to scream but couldn't. Tried to jerk free, but my body wouldn't obey. Terror tore through me in jagged bursts, every nerve raw and screaming while my muscles stayed locked.

My thoughts scattered, clawing for anything—an escape, a weapon, a way to fight—but each possibility dissolved before I could hold it. There was nothing. No way out. Only the weight of him everywhere, and the certainty that he had me completely at his mercy.

"See, Raine?" The voice hummed, close—*too close. "I told you if I got close, you wouldn't be able to scream."*

The sound of my name on his tongue startled me. This wasn't a stranger, and he somehow knew who I was. A storm of panic rose inside me, frenzied and untamed, but still, I couldn't move.

Then fingers, real or imagined, slid across my cheek, trailing lower toward my lips. I was still silenced by the invisible force holding me captive. In any other circumstance, the touch might have been gentle, intimate even. But this wasn't that. It was wrong. Deeply, viscerally wrong.

My skin crawled beneath the touch. My stomach turned, and I couldn't breathe. My body was trembling. Whoever, or *whatever* this was, wanted me scared, and they were succeeding.

I could feel him, his presence pressing in close now, tracing over me with an attentiveness that made my stomach twist. They were thriving on my discomfort, taking in each hitch of my breath as they got closer. Assessing me, like a wolf sizing up its kill.

Then, like the snap of a breaking chain, a low growl echoed through the trees.

"Leave her alone, Aeron."

Manakel.

Relief hit like a gasp of air after drowning. His voice sliced through the suffocating tension like a blade, sharp and unmistakable. My knees nearly buckled at the sound of him. But it wasn't just his voice; it was the fury in it. And then he stepped through the trees. His jaw was tight, shoulders rigid, his wings half-unfurled, as his frustration crackled in the air. Moonlight glinted along the sharp lines of his face, illuminating the storm in his eyes and making him seem more intense.

This was a side of Manakel I hadn't seen before. And I felt sorry for whoever was on the receiving end of it. *Whoever this Aeron was.*

My heart pounded, caught between the flood of relief that Manakel was here and the icy realization that Aeron wasn't letting me go. He stepped closer, tension radiating from him like a blade drawn halfway from its sheath.

"I said," he growled, voice coiled and sharp, "Let her go."

The invisible grip around me tightened. I gasped, every nerve in my body screaming, but still, my body was locked in place.

Behind me, the voice only laughed, sharp and laced with mockery. "You're always so predictable, dearthár. Needing to be the *Savior*. The *Protector*."

Venom dripped from his voice, and my stomach twisted. That word, dearthár, hung in the air like smoke.

Brother?

The weight of it hit me hard. This wasn't some nameless threat. This was someone Manakel knew. Someone who knew *me. His brother?*

Aeron's tone darkened, curling around me like a vice.

"But don't you know...she's just a fragile *human* girl," he sneered, dragging the word out like a curse. "No need to guard her so fiercely when she can just turn around and leave. Spare herself the heartache, before all of this becomes something she can't undo."

My stomach twisted. Manakel's face had shifted, still and impassive. Fury, yes, but something deeper settled beneath it, and that almost scared me more than Aeron's threats.

"I know, Aeron," Manakel bit out, voice flat, refusing to meet my eyes. "I've got it handled here. No need to intervene."

Aeron's laugh was low and cruel, soaked in something darker than amusement. "Oh, come now. You know how good I am at helping. Please, let me assist you in breaking her."

Without even looking, I instinctively knew his focus had shifted back to me. "Let me show her why entering these woods was a mistake—and not one she should think about repeating."

Every word scraped across my skin like iron. My limbs wouldn't move. My mouth still silenced, every instinct screaming that this wasn't just about fear, it was a test. A warning. A game I didn't know the rules to.

Manakel wasn't looking at me either, but I could feel the difference in his stance, the sharp restraint in his voice.

"Don't worry, *brother*," he said at last, cold and biting. "If I need help breaking her, I'll let you know."

Every muscle in my body locked. The words felt like a slap, each syllable scraping against my skin like iron. I felt eyes on me. All-consuming. Like I was already falling apart under a gaze I couldn't even see. The air was thick, charged with something I couldn't place, but my instincts screamed that I was in more danger than I even realized. And I didn't know who to trust.

The realization of my situation settled like lead in my chest. Aeron wasn't just being cruel; he seemed to be enjoying this. Watching me feel helpless, playing on Manakel's protective instinct, saying things that would have me doubt them. The way he spoke, the way he sneered, made me feel like I was some fragile little plaything, insignificant enough to be discarded at their whim. And naive enough to trust blindly.

The air around was charged with tension and silence. Then, without warning, the pressure on my lips vanished. I choked on a gasp, air rushing in too fast. My throat burned. My legs threatened to give out, but before I could speak, Manakel's eyes snapped to mine. Like a blade cutting through the dark, and something in that look stopped me cold.

Not now. Don't fight this.

His stare was fierce. Sharp and pleading. Begging me to cooperate. So I stayed quiet. I clenched my jaw, forcing the words that had been clawing at my throat back down.

Even if I'd wanted to push him, *demand answers*, I couldn't. Not when my body still trembled, not when Aeron's presence still lingered in the air, recovering from whatever spell he'd had me under. Slowly, I turned, heart pounding so hard it drowned out everything else.

The air shifted, taut and expectant, as though the forest itself was holding its breath. A weight settled over my chest, cold and crushing, like something unseen was watching. Waiting for the right moment to strike.

And even though Aeron was no longer touching me, I could still feel him surrounding me.

Every instinct screamed at me to run before I saw him, before I could put a face to the voice I felt all around me. Then, as though the very forest itself had exhaled, he stepped into view, and every coherent thought I had crumbled like ash in the wind.

This was Aeron.

Seeing him was like a thunderclap—instant, jarring, shattering every thought and scattering my breath into the air between us. The forest fell away. I couldn't think. I couldn't even blink to look away. Every sound, every whisper of wind through the leaves dimmed until the only thing that existed was him.

He wasn't simply tall; he towered. A presence more than a man, as if the trees bent subtly around him, not out of fear, but in reverence. His broad shoulders bore the kind of power that didn't need to be announced. It simply was, the way mountains simply exist—immovable, undeniable. Shafts of light broke through the canopy, like the sun itself couldn't resist touching him, gilding his golden skin. Shadows clung to him like loyal companions, casting him in shifting contrast. Half-light, half-storm.

He moved with deliberate slowness, each step an act of possession— of the earth beneath him, of the space between us, of my pulse. The air seemed to shift to accommodate him, reshaping itself around his presence.

His face was unnervingly perfect. Too sharp. Too symmetrical. Like something carved by the gods with a clear, arrogant intention—to be admired. It was wrong because someone this flawless shouldn't exist. His chiseled jaw was dusted with the faintest shadow of stubble. Full lips curved in a knowing, infuriating smirk, the kind that said he knew *exactly* what effect he had on me and was entertained by it. Unruly dark hair broke the flawless symmetry, softening his brutal beauty just enough to make him look both chaotic and somehow entirely in control.

But it was his eyes that held me captive. Grey, like rain clouds pressed low against the horizon, streaked with threads of silver that caught the fractured light. They didn't just look *at* me. They saw *through* me.

There was no warmth there, no interest, only the quiet, devastating acknowledgment that I was something fleeting and hardly worth his attention.

A sliver of black ink crept up from beneath the collar of his shirt, curling across his skin like smoke. A secret inked onto his skin, one that beckoned closer inspection. It disappeared under the fabric before I could make out the shape. I shouldn't have noticed. I shouldn't have *cared*, but it called to me. Everything about him did—like an unspoken invitation I desperately wanted to reject.

He was dressed in black, nothing ornate, yet on him it wasn't simple. It was intentional. Perfectly fitted, tailored by something more precise than human hands, as if the clothes existed to amplify him. On anyone else, it would have been unremarkable. On him, it was a warning of his power.

And then his wings unfurled.

The movement was slow, ruinous, a sweep of shadow that seemed to steal the air from my lungs. Vast, inescapable, their feathers ink-black, each tip brushed with gold that caught the light and sparked like embers. They shimmered when he moved, as though the night sky had lent him its stars.

I'd seen beauty before. This wasn't that.

This was terrifying. This was divine.

A reminder that whatever he was, he wasn't human. And no matter how badly I wanted to look away, I couldn't.

My heartbeat betrayed me, pounding louder, faster, the more I stared. Aeron didn't speak; he studied. Watched me with a detached sort of interest, like I was a puzzle he was moments from solving, or discarding. The air thickened, and I felt it then, the battle happening in the space between him and Manakel. Tension crackled between them like a silent war, and it felt deafening.

"I'd say it's a pleasure to finally meet the human who's been keeping Manakel busy," he said finally, his voice smooth as smoke. "But I'm not a liar."

The sound of his voice cut through the silence, too calm, an unsettling charm wrapped in the promise of something far darker.

"He mentioned you once or twice," Aeron went on, his eyes never leaving mine. "Though I see now why he spared the more interesting details, like how small and fragile you are."

Then, before I could react, he stepped closer and took my hand in his. Not rough. Not rushed. Just… deliberate. I froze at the contact. Cool fingers, calloused and strong, slid against my skin like silk fraying at the edges. My breath hitched. Something in the contact, subtle as it was, unraveled a thread inside me I hadn't known was pulled tight.

He raised my hand slowly, eyes steady, and full of knowing. I should've pulled away. I meant to. But my body had stopped listening. Then his lips brushed my knuckles, barely a breath of contact, and everything shifted.

A hum, low and ancient, sang through my veins like a forgotten melody stirring to life. It wasn't romantic. But it felt familiar in a way that made my skin buzz and my stomach twist. The world didn't fall silent. It rang. My pulse stuttered. My knees wobbled. The forest around us blurred, lost in the sudden, searing clarity of him.

His mouth lingered a breath too long, too much intention in the way he did it. Too intimate. It wasn't a greeting. It was more of a warning. A threat. I didn't breathe. I couldn't. I fought the instinct to yank my hand away, and when I thought the air between us might fracture from the weight of whatever this was, I forced myself to meet his eyes. He tilted his head slightly, studying me, not in admiration, but like a question poised on the edge of a blade. As if he were curious to see why I *hadn't* pulled away yet.

The spell shattered. My cheeks flamed, and I gently removed my hand from his. He stepped back with a low, knowing smirk, like he'd peeled back a piece of me and was tucking it into his pocket for later. Like he knew exactly what I was feeling.

I stared at him, jaw clenched, heat crawling up my neck, "Funny," I said, voice steady despite the roar in my head. "I'm not exactly pleased to be meeting you either. But lucky for you, I don't have to lie, since Manakel never mentioned you. You must not be all that important."

It was a deflection, one I hoped landed, because something about Aeron made me feel unsteady. He assessed me with curiosity shining in his steel-grey eyes, like he'd never been spoken to this way, least of all by a human.

I flicked a glance at Manakel, searching for something, *anything*, to anchor myself. But his expression was stoic. No flicker of reassurance. No spark of familiarity. Just blank. His jaw tightened, his shoulders subtly shifting as he stepped closer, slow and deliberate, placing himself between us like a shield.

"Aeron was just leaving," he said, voice low and sharp. There was no room for argument. Only warning.

But Aeron didn't budge; he only smirked, keeping his eyes fixed on me. "Oh, dear brother," he drawled, "don't be so quick to chase me off. Can't I admire the human you've become so… invested in?"

His voice slithered through the air, velvet-laced malice coiled beneath every word. "You've been training her," he mused. "Or is it considered torturing? The line's always been a bit blurred with you."

Manakel's body tensed beside me, the shift subtle but unmistakable. A low sound built in his chest—too soft to be a growl, too raw to be anything else. It startled something in me.

Possessiveness.

Aeron chuckled, low and knowing. "Easy deartháir. In case you've forgotten, *I* was the one assigned to these woods. So it just seems sort of *convenient* that you got here first."

He tilted his head, his smile twisting. "And even more fitting that she hangs on your every word."

Heat flared up my neck. Embarrassment. Confusion. A sharp awareness of the space between us, and how little of it there was. Aeron was toying with me. And Manakel was letting him. I turned to him again, needing, *hoping*, for something in his face that made this make sense. But his eyes were cold. Distant. Walls slammed shut.

My chest tightened.

"Leave. Now." Manakel's voice was barely more than a whisper, but it was lethal. And I felt the weight of it settle in my bones.

"I won't say it again. Whatever you're playing at, it ends now. Stay out of this. Stay away from her."

Aeron's smirk didn't waver as he raised his hands in mock surrender. "As you wish, *brother*," he said lightly. "I only swooped in because she looked so… frightened and helpless. All alone in the scary woods." His eyes glinted as they flicked back to me. "I thought I might offer a little guidance. A reminder, really, of the true dangers that lurk in these parts."

His smirk deepened. "Which, apparently, today, have turned out to be us Sciatháin."

Then, with a taunting dip of his head, he vanished into the trees, dissolving into the darkness like smoke curling back into the shadows. The forest exhaled. But the unease remained, lingering like a stain I couldn't wash away.

I turned to Manakel, desperate for some kind of explanation, but he just sighed and dragged a hand through his hair, his composure cracking at the edges.

"We should get going," he muttered, already turning. His tone was clipped, frustration radiating off of him in waves, but I followed. My mind was spinning. Aeron's words echoed in my skull like footsteps behind me.

Training her—or torturing her?

All alone in the scary woods.

The most dangerous things today are us Sciatháin.

Each sentence coiled tighter, sharper. More damning. And still, Manakel said nothing. No explanation. No reassurance. Just silence.

And suddenly, I wasn't sure which silence unsettled me more, Aeron's appearance, or Manakel's refusal to answer why. There was so much I didn't understand, and the longer we walked, the heavier the doubt became.

I couldn't shake the feeling that my grandmother had been right—

The answers I sought wouldn't come from asking. At least not directly.

22. Weapons Of Choice

We walked in silence. Manakel kept ahead of me, his shoulders tense, his pace deliberate. The air between us felt thick with unspoken words neither of us dared to say. I wasn't about to admit how shaken I'd been, facing someone like Aeron, and it was clear Manakel wasn't in the mood to explain who, or what, Aeron truly was.

I hated the quiet. So I tried to cut through it.

"So…" I offered lightly, "looks like you were the one running late today. Do I get a prize for being here first?" My voice was teasing, an invitation to bring back the banter that usually lived between us.

But Manakel didn't take the bait. Just shook his head and kept walking, eyes fixed on the path ahead, his expression locked in an uncharacteristic silence.

I scowled. I was the one who had been ambushed, blindsided by Aeron's arrival, and basically held hostage while Manakel played silent witness. If anyone deserved to be upset, it was me.

Frustration burned in my chest as I quickened my pace, cutting in front of him and planting myself squarely in his path.

"Alright, enough," I snapped, crossing my arms. "Don't shut me out like this. Talk to me."

Manakel sighed, stopping as his shoulders slumped like the weight of the world rested on them. His eyes dropped to the ground, avoiding mine, and for a moment, I thought he might push past me. But something bold in me took over. I stepped closer and reached out, gently lifting his chin until his eyes met mine.

And I faltered. There was pain in his gaze. Real, unguarded pain. Sadness. Longing. Guilt. Something else too, something deeper I hadn't been expecting, and it threw me off balance. My first instinct was to comfort him, but then I remembered the wall he'd put up after our kiss, the way he'd shut me down as if none of it mattered. Embarrassed by my boldness, I drew my hand back, but before I could step away, his hand caught my arm.

Not rough. Just enough to keep me still. Warmth bled through his grip, grounding and confusing all at once. The contrast between the physical connection and the emotional distance he kept was maddening. I searched his face, willing him to say something, anything.

"Manakel," I said softly, my voice trembling despite myself. "I deserve to know what's going on. If you want me to trust you, you need to do the same and stop treating me like I can't handle the truth."

His eyes held mine for a moment, his fingers tightening slightly, like he was bracing himself for something he didn't want to say. Finally, he spoke, his voice low and heavy. "You weren't supposed to meet Aeron. Not like that. Not yet."

"Not yet?" I echoed, a sharp edge creeping into my tone. "So what, you both planned to gang up on me later, or something?"

He stilled, and I pushed further, needing to know what was going on. "Are there more surprises? More *brothers*, I need to worry about ambushing me?"

He flinched, guilt flashing briefly in his eyes. "Things with Aeron are... complicated. He *calls* me brother, but it's not blood that binds us. It's obligation. A bond neither of us chose." He paused, his jaw tightening.

"He's dangerous, and you should stay away from him. That's the only thing you need to understand right now."

"I figured that out when he stalked me like prey. But *why* is he dangerous? What does he want, and why does he even care about you training me?"

Manakel's jaw flexed. His expression shifted, softening for the first time, though it was laced with unease, like he was choosing his words carefully.

"Because you're a threat," he said. "To everything he believes in. To the balance he wants to protect."

He paused, like weighing how much more to give me.

"Aeron serves those who want the current ways burned to ash. To him, you're a complication. A reminder of what was taken over a century ago… and what could rise again if you succeed."

His words sank in slowly, filling me with a heavy mix of dread and confusion. "What does that even mean? Is this because of my Rite?" I asked, but Manakel's guarded expression slipped back into place.

"It means you need to be careful," he said, releasing my arm and stepping back. "Aeron won't be the only challenge you face, Raine. Others will try to come for you. To break you. And you need to be ready."

The abrupt shift in his tone, from careful to commanding, left me reeling, but I didn't have time to push further. He turned and started walking again, a clear signal that the conversation was over.

My mind raced with unanswered questions as I followed him into a part of the forest I didn't recognize. We stepped into a clearing, the canopy thinning above us to let in scattered shafts of sunlight. Golden pools dappled the forest floor, soft and warm against the otherwise shadowed world around us. Manakel stopped, turning to face me with an unreadable expression.

"I had a different plan for today," he said. "But after what happened with Aeron, I think we'll start here instead."

I raised an eyebrow, skeptical. "Where exactly is *'here,'* and what did you have in mind?"

Instead of answering, he gestured to the bag slung over my shoulder. "Take out the first thing you think you'll need during the rite."

Confused, I lowered the bag to the ground and opened it, scanning the contents: two daggers, a folded blanket, sandwiches, a thermos of tea, two cups, and a small pouch of herbs—sage, rosemary, mugwort.

I reached for the daggers without hesitation. "Obvious choice. What's next?"

Manakel didn't react. "Look again. Are you sure there's nothing else that could be more helpful?"

I frowned. "What else would I need more than these? The rest is just food and… herbs. A dagger is *obviously* more useful."

"Protection comes in many forms," he said evenly. "This isn't just about defending yourself with steel. Look again, and think about what you've learned, and not just by me."

His eyes held mine with quiet insistence. I sighed, rifling through the bag again until my fingers brushed the pouch of herbs. *My grandmother's herbs.* They carried her energy, her lessons, and if you knew their properties, you *could* deem them useful.

With a sigh, I picked up the pouch and held it out. "This?" I asked, doubtful. "You're telling me herbs are more important than a blade?"

A flicker of approval crossed his face, and he nodded. "Weapons don't always come with sharp edges. The Rite will test more than your strength and skills, Raine. It will test your mind, your spirit, your heart. These herbs hold power—protection, cleansing, guidance, and those are just as useful as a dagger, if not more so."

I stared down at the pouch, something heavier settling in my chest. This wasn't about survival in the way I'd imagined. It was about knowing who I was and what I carried with me.

A memory stirred as I stared at the small bundle of herbs in my hand— my grandmother's hands in the garden, deftly plucking leaves and stems, her voice soft in the summer air. *"Every herb, flower, and plant has a purpose, Raine. When you understand their meanings, you'll understand more of what you'll face in the world. You'll understand yourself."*

Back then, I hadn't understood the gravity of her words. Not really. I was too busy dreaming of wielding swords and charging into battle like the heroes in stories. I'd wanted swords, not stems. Action, not intention.

But now, with Manakel watching me, the weight of her wisdom settled on me in a way it never had before.

I turned the pouch in my hands, trying to recall their meanings. Sage for cleansing and protection. Rosemary for focus and strength. Mugwort for intuition and dreams. Each one carried a unique energy, its own quiet power. I knew they weren't just plants; they were also tools. Weapons, in their own way. Intentional and quietly powerful.

"It's not just about defense or offense, is it?" I asked, my voice softer now as understanding dawned. "It's about... balance."

Manakel's expression softened, the edges of his face warming. "Exactly," he said. "In the Rite, you'll need more than strength or sharp blades. Your greatest weapon is here." He tapped his temple. "And here." He pressed a hand to his chest.

I nodded, swallowing the unease rising in my throat. For all my bravado, I suddenly felt wildly unprepared. But somewhere buried deep was also a burning determination. Like maybe, with each lesson, I had already begun.

Manakel tilted his head, a faint smirk playing at his lips as he gestured to the satchel again.

"So," he said, "what else did Leighna pack for you?"

I opened the bag and pulled out a neatly wrapped sandwich, a thermos of tea, and the blanket. The tension between us eased slightly as I glanced over. His focus shifted to the sandwich, and a quiet growl escaped his stomach.

I smirked, seizing the opportunity to tease him. "Hungry?" I asked innocently, holding up one of the sandwiches.

He shook his head, "I'm fine," he said flatly.

His stomach, however, betrayed him with another growl, louder this time, and I bit back a laugh as I spread the blanket out and took a seat.

"You're terrible at lying, you know that?" I said, offering the sandwich again.

With a sigh that sounded more like resignation than denial, he lowered himself onto the blanket with practiced grace. "I said I'm fine."

"Sure," I said, unwrapping it and taking an exaggerated bite. I chewed slowly, eyes fixed on him. His expression didn't shift, but the flicker of longing was unmistakable.

After a few silent bites, I asked, "Still not hungry?" Reaching into the bag, I pulled out another sandwich. "Because I'd hate for this to go to waste…"

Before I could finish, he snatched it from my hand with lightning speed and unwrapped it without a word.

"Fine," he said, smirking. "If you insist."

I rolled my eyes, biting back a laugh. "I thought you weren't hungry."

He took a bite, his eyes slipping shut for a second, savoring it. For a moment, the weight of everything faded, replaced by the simple, absurd image of Manakel—this powerful, winged enigma of a man—devouring a sandwich like he hadn't eaten in days.

But just as I started to relax for the first time all day, he leaned closer. His hand brushed along my jaw, tilting my chin. His thumb dragged across my bottom lip, slow and deliberate.

"You missed some," he murmured, his voice low, teasing, almost intimate. His thumb lingered. And then, without breaking eye contact, he brought it to his mouth and sucked it clean.

My breath caught. I blinked, trying to re-calibrate, but my brain refused to cooperate. I was caught between shock and… something else. His smirk widened, a glint of mischief in his eyes as he leaned back, clearly pleased with himself.

"You…" I started, my voice faltering as my mind scrambled to form a coherent sentence. "You're insufferable."

He chuckled, taking another bite of his sandwich like he hadn't just completely disarmed me and set off fireworks in my chest. "And yet, you're still here choosing to share your food with me."

I glared at him, but the effort lacked any real heat. He wasn't wrong. As maddening as he was, I couldn't seem to stay away.

And as much as I hated to admit it, I didn't want to.

I handed Manakel the third sandwich, and we ate in silence, broken only by the rustle of leaves and the distant hum of the forest. Though neither of us spoke, something lingered in the air—a charge, quiet but palpable. Every glance felt like a pull, a thread tightening between us. But I forced myself to focus. To remember why I was here and what was at stake. I needed his help to cross the river and survive the Rite. Whatever else existed between us… It would have to wait.

Still, my thoughts drifted. If—no—*when* I made it through, maybe I'd let myself explore whatever this was. But for now, I tucked the feeling away, making a silent promise to myself to focus on the Rite, which was only days away.

I cleared my throat, breaking the quiet. "Earlier, you mentioned there are only a few Sciatháin Angels left. How many were there originally? And… what happened to the rest?" My voice was quiet, unsure if I was overstepping, but my curiosity wouldn't let me hold back my questions.

Manakel's gaze drifted, his expression turning distant, as though he was searching for something far beyond the trees. "Your village… they never told you the story of us? Of the original immortals in Luminara?" he asked, his tone soft but guarded.

I shook my head. "No one in my village has even heard of your kind." I hesitated before admitting, "But growing up, I used to see this huge bird flying over the trees, sometimes over our house. I even named it Onyx. It was the biggest bird I'd ever seen, and I kept it a secret, like it was my guardian. Something just for me, watching over me and protecting me, or something."

His eyes sharpened, locking onto mine with an intensity that made my heart stutter. "And now you're wondering if maybe it wasn't a bird at all," he said, voice low. "If it was one of my kind?"

I nodded, the admission feeling both foolish and oddly significant if it had been him. "The thought crossed my mind. Especially when I saw your wings for the first time..." I trailed off, heat rising to my cheeks.

To my surprise, a faint blush colored his face as well, softening his sharp features. Instead of deflecting, as I'd expected, he turned toward me fully, his dark hair illuminated by the rays of sunlight and casting a dark halo around him. I wanted to bottle the moment—every flicker of light, every shadow, every unspoken feeling between us.

"It wasn't me," he admitted quietly, "but it could've been another. We've always stayed hidden, though clearly not as well as we thought."

He shifted, his expression growing heavier. "There were hordes of us once, sent to Luminara by the gods to protect humankind. We weren't meant to be seen, just to guide and defend from the shadows using our powers if needed."

"What happened?" I asked, barely breathing as I leaned closer.

"Over five hundred years ago," he began, his voice careful, "the Sciatháin lived among the gods. Our kind was originally created, not born, and made using some of the most powerful magic and gifts in the ether. We were the link between the ether and Luminara, since our wings allowed us passage through both realms. From stories passed down through the centuries, we know that the first Sciatháin were sent here to protect humans from a looming darkness. They were given clear orders: protect the humans from afar but don't intervene or interact directly."

I hung onto every word, absorbing this piece of history I'd never known.

"At first, there were around a hundred sent here, and they settled in the Dearmadta Mountains. Isolated, safe, and hidden enough to stay out of sight." His lips twitched, almost a smile, though it didn't quite reach his eyes.

"But over the years, some grew tired of following the gods' orders. They believed it had become a sentence to live their days being isolated in Luminara. Out of rebellion, or loneliness, they began to interact with humans, at first just making our kind known, but any interference was considered forbidden." He looked down at the blanket and began picking a piece of grass nearby, and I stayed silent, hoping he would continue.

"Eventually, they started forming connections. Some even fell in love and bred with humans, creating lives completely separate from those in the mountains. Those babies were the first immortals born in Luminara."

He still wasn't looking up towards me, but I leaned closer, enraptured by everything he was sharing. I'd always been curious about the origins of the immortals. If they were born or made? But hearing it like this, from someone who'd seen it all happen, in a way, felt like uncovering a hidden chapter in a story I'd known my whole life.

I held my breath, scared to interrupt him but unable to silence my curiosity. "And… were you one of the originals sent here?" I asked, my voice barely above a whisper, scared that he would stop talking.

He chuckled softly, shaking his head. "No, I wasn't. I guess I was lucky, in a way, since this is the only home I've ever known. Both of my parents were originals. They were sent here, like all the others, but somehow they found each other, fell in love, and eventually, had me." His expression softened, his mouth lifting into a faint smile as if he were remembering something he hadn't thought of in a long time. "But that was a long time ago."

I could see it, the mixture of pride and sadness in his eyes. There was a deep-rooted history within him, one I assumed he rarely shared. The weight of his story hung in the air between us, making the forest seem quieter, almost reverent.

"That does sound lucky," I said softly, resting my hand on his arm, pulling him gently back from his memories. "But what happened to them all? Did they get sent back?"

His face changed, shadowed by something painful. "No. Our kind wasn't meant to interact with humans, let alone mate and create an entirely new breed. The gods were furious when they found out, and punished all Sciatháin who broke the rules, who dared to love or be with a human. The gods saw the children as abominations, so the ones that created them weren't just banished, they were killed." He paused, letting that heavy truth settle between us.

A chill ran down my spine. "Killed? By who?"

"A Sciatháin hunter," he said quietly. "The gods forged weapons capable of destroying our kind. Nothing made in this world could harm us, so they created something that could. And someone to wield it. The ultimate immortal hunter, I guess." He laughed sarcastically as if the thought alone was one he still couldn't comprehend.

I couldn't imagine the kind of betrayal that must have been—one of their own, turned into a weapon against them. The thought of a god-made executioner made my stomach twist.

"But the firstborn immortals… what happened to them? Were they punished too?" I asked.

Manakel's shadows seemed to darken around him, stretching longer as the sun dipped lower. "At first, the immortal children were lost; they didn't understand what they were. Their Sciatháin parents were killed, and their mortal parents didn't always survive long enough to guide them. Most had no understanding of the power they were able to wield. Immortality comes with a degree of darkness. A shadow we all carry." His eyes flicked to his shadows, the tendrils curling and shifting like they had a mind of their own.

I shivered. I'd felt the pull of darkness in myself before, in fleeting moments of anger or despair, but never understood where it came from.

"Their powers emerged without warning, without a way to control them, and without guidance; they became reckless," he said, his voice heavy with something I couldn't name. "They hurt humans. Killed them, even. They didn't understand what was happening to them as their gifts and powers manifested. There was no limit to power then; the firstborn inherited multiple gifts based on their lineage. They weren't aware of their limits or the consequences of having that much raw power."

I felt my pulse quicken with each word, absorbing secrets I hadn't known existed.

Manakel looked up, our eyes meeting, and his voice lowered, "The gods saw the firstborns as proof of our failure in Luminara. Failure to not only remain hidden, but also protect humankind. See, our powers and gifts were never meant for humans, but it was too late to stop the creation of immortals. So they created a way to contain what they couldn't destroy. A trial. A reckoning."

The weight of his words settled over me, the forest around us growing impossibly still.

"That's why they created the Rite?" I whispered.

And he simply nodded.

23. Echoes Of Forgotten Truths

The forest breathed around us, the wind threading through branches like a whispered warning. Manakel's shadows stretched long behind him, curling at the edges like smoke, an extension of something he couldn't fully outrun.

"Living without consequences tends to bring darkness to the surface," he said, his voice quiet but heavy, as if the words carried centuries of weight. "When the first immortals grew reckless, the gods had no choice but to intervene and take back control."

There was something in his tone, hurt or shame, maybe both. It clung to each word, unspoken but impossible to miss. I wondered if he was speaking from experience, but didn't want to assume. Something told me silence was safer, that if I interrupted, he'd close himself off again.

"The Imbe Rite was their solution to curb the chaos," he continued, eyes locked beyond the trees. "They thought if immortals had to wait to earn their gifts when they came of age, it would control the defiance. The Rite gave the gods a hand in deciding who was worthy of what gifts, and how much power they deserved."

His voice cracked slightly like he was holding back something deeper, something that had lived inside him for too long.

"To this day," he said softly, "some immortals still blame us, the Sciatháin and the gods, for the Rite and the rules they're now bound to."

His shadows flickered restlessly, as though they, too, felt the weight of the moment. I shifted, the coolness of the afternoon wind pressing against my skin.

"I was only a hundred years old when the Rite was created," he added, quieter this time. His gaze dropped, fixing on the forest floor, but I felt his mind was far away. "And my parents, they paid the ultimate price for their allegiance to the gods that year."

His shoulders slumped, the grief in his expression raw and unguarded. I wanted to reach out, to place a hand on his arm, to offer even a sliver of comfort. But something about the way he stood, tense as if holding himself together by sheer will, kept me frozen.

This wasn't just a story. It was a confession. And I wasn't sure he'd ever spoken these words aloud before.

His grief poured out like acid, burning through the space between us, and I felt it, every ounce of it.

"It was my hundredth birthday," he said, his voice brittle with nostalgia and regret. "My father was meant to be on patrol duty that day, and he'd promised to take me with him, to teach me."

A faint smile tugged at his lips, but it didn't reach his eyes. I could almost see the image, the younger version of him, eager and proud, standing tall beside his father.

"I told everyone I saw on the mountain," Manakel continued, shaking his head as if he could still see his younger self making that mistake. "I didn't think anything of it. I didn't realize not all Sciatháin were on the same side."

His shadows darkened, stretching further as his voice dropped lower.

"There were some who resented my parents. Blamed them, *blamed me*, for the fate of their own families."

I held my breath, the pieces of his story fitting together like jagged glass.

"Some believed that if every Sciatháin defied the rules and had children with humans, the gods would have no choice but to spare them all," he said, the words bitter in his mouth. "But there were eight who refused. They stayed loyal to our kind, marrying each other and having full Sciatháin children, preserving their bloodlines."

Four families. Eight originals.

The numbers sat heavily in my chest. And if what he said was true, those families were all that stood between the gods' wrath and the Sciatháin bloodline fading into myth.

I swallowed, feeling the weight of it.

"And now from the eight originals, there are only six pure Sciatháin left," Manakel said, answering the thought I hadn't voiced aloud. His eyes met mine, a flicker of understanding passing between us. "All of us descended from the few who didn't break the rules."

A cold ache settled over me, and I realized the depth of his loss, of what the Sciatháin had endured just to survive in Luminara.

The forest around us felt heavier, the weight of Manakel's words anchoring the space between us. His dark wings barely stirred, but his voice carried the weight of years—centuries—pressed into each syllable.

"My parents didn't realize," he began, voice hushed but sharp, "that some of the original Sciatháin had brought weapons made by the gods when they first arrived in Luminara. They had all been united when arriving here, friends even. But when alliances were tested, people chose sides, furious with the gods and anyone who sided with them. They waited patiently and kept their intentions and weapons hidden until the perfect opportunity arose to avenge those who had been killed."

His focus drifted to the treeline, distant, as though he could still see the moment playing out in the shadows.

"And that day," he continued, the words heavy with memories that had long refused to fade, "must have seemed perfect for them to go after my parents. They knew exactly where we would be, since I made us an easy target." Manakel's jaw tightened, and for a moment, I thought he might stop sharing. But he continued.

A shiver crept down my spine, and I braced myself, sensing the shift—the inevitable part of his story that I wasn't sure I was ready to hear.

"The day started beautifully," he said softly, almost as if he were reciting something fragile. "I woke up to my mother's famous birthday breakfast, and by mid-morning, I was soaring above the trees with my father. I remember the wind, how it felt against my wings—strong and steady."

His eyes softened, but there was something else behind the faint smile tugging at the corner of his lips. A shadow of hurt and loss.

"I was young," he murmured, the bitterness creeping in like a ghost, "so of course, flying around all day, I tired faster than he did. I begged to take a break, so we flew down to rest."

The air shifted, and I felt the weight of the memory settle like a cold stone in my chest.

His gaze darkened, distant. "While we were on the ground… someone came up behind my father and lunged. Before either of us knew what was happening, they used a god's weapon on him." His voice faltered for a breath, the edges of his words sharp with grief. "They sliced through his wings, immobilizing him before stabbing him in the stomach, and then he vanished—instantly."

The world around us seemed to slow, the space between heartbeats stretching unbearably long. Manakel's face didn't change, but the tension that gripped his body radiated like a storm ready to break.

"I didn't have time to react," he admitted, the words cutting through the quiet. "Or even look to see who did it. I knew if I faltered, I would have been next, so I did the only thing I could."

His wings shifted slightly, the memory rolling through his muscles as if his body still carried the instinct.

"I shot into the sky," he said, his voice barely louder than a whisper. "I flew home as fast as I could—to warn my mother."

A tear slipped down my cheek before I realized it was there, and I moved to brush it away, only for his hand to lift, his thumb gently wiping it aside. His touch lingered for just a second, grounding me in the moment.

"I didn't understand back then," Manakel continued, his eyes meeting mine, grief unmasked. "I didn't know how deeply my parents' bond ran—or how fast a gods' weapons worked."

I swallowed the knot forming in my throat, hanging on every word as his voice grew softer.

"When I burst through the door to our home, my mother only had minutes left," he said. "Her life was tied to his. Their connection—" His voice cracked slightly, and he took a steadying breath. "She already knew what was happening the moment she saw me."

The ache in his expression twisted something inside me, and I gripped my hands together tightly to keep from reaching out.

"She didn't even panic," Manakel said, almost to himself. "She just… smiled. Told me she loved me. Told me I was the greatest thing that had ever happened to her and my father. And that if I were lucky, I'd find a love or a soul connection like theirs one day."

His voice softened further, the words carrying a fragile weight that made my chest tighten.

"That was her final wish for me."

Silence lingered in the air, but I couldn't bring myself to break it. I wanted to ask him if he had ever found that kind of love. If someone was out there now, waiting for him. But the question felt too personal, too intrusive against the rawness in his voice.

Instead, I waited. And after a moment, he continued.

"I never forgot the feeling of losing both of them at once," he said, the quiet tremor in his voice undeniable. "And all because of their bond. One they didn't even choose for themselves."

I held my breath, sensing what was coming before he said it.

"So, I made a vow," Manakel whispered. "I would never find my soul-connected mate, if there was ever one destined for me."

I swallowed hard, his words pressing down like stones.

"I couldn't bear the thought of succumbing to the same fate, of putting anyone else through it either," he finished, his voice rough but steady.

His pain rippled through the air like an unspoken warning, and I felt it more than I understood it. The ache, the fear of losing someone so completely that it broke a part of you forever.

I thought of my parents, of the love they shared, and the thought of losing them both sent a sharp ache through me.

I reached out instinctively, my hand brushing his arm. "I'm sorry," I whispered. "I can't imagine how painful it must have been."

His eyes held mine, steady but full of sorrow.

"The memories don't fade," he replied quietly. "They linger, just like the scars they left behind, but I've learned to live with them."

"You can't live in fear, though," I said, my voice stronger than I expected. "We all have scars, but that doesn't mean we stop living. You've been carrying this alone for too long, and maybe after centuries, it's time to let someone else in."

His lips quirked into a faint smile, one that didn't quite reach his eyes. "How did a human get to be so wise?"

I smiled back, determined to lighten the moment. "We have our moments."

For a brief second, the weight between us lifted, replaced by something fragile and unspoken. Something that felt like hope.

The warmth of his arm beneath my fingertips grounded me, tethering me to the words I couldn't leave unspoken.

"I was lucky. To be raised around real love," I admitted. "It hasn't always been easy, knowing I might never have a love like my grandparents or my parents do. But I've realized I'm not afraid to try anymore. I don't want to let fear keep me from something real. You shouldn't either."

He stilled under my touch, and our eyes locked. The weight of his stare sent a blush creeping up my neck, but I refused to look away.

"You shouldn't have to go through life alone because you're scared," I continued, my voice barely above a whisper. "I'm not willing to live that way, and neither should you."

The world around us seemed to hold its breath as he stared at me. I felt the heat of his gaze and dared to meet it again. His eyes searched mine, filled with questions and a feeling that made my chest ache in the best way.

I dropped my eyes to the ground, feeling my cheeks burn, but the words wouldn't stop. "Maybe we can get past this… together."

His eyes softened, the lines of tension in his face easing just slightly. For a moment, I thought I saw a flicker of hope there, fragile but real. He hesitated, slow and deliberate as if he were testing the weight of the idea. "Maybe."

The air between us seemed to hum with unspoken understanding, an electric charge that made my pulse quicken.

I broke the silence with a small smile, wanting to ease the heaviness. "But we should be focusing on the here and now. I've got a river to cross in a few days, and still so much to learn."

The corners of his mouth curved into a smile, breaking through the shadows of his pain. The warmth of it struck me hard, and I marveled at the way it softened his features, making him look even more beautiful, if that was possible. "Right," he agreed, his voice lighter. "I guess we should be focused on that."

He rose and offered me his hand. I took it, the simple gesture making my chest flutter. We packed the blanket in silence, but it was a different kind now, comfortable and almost familiar.

Our hands brushed as we walked, and each accidental touch felt more deliberate than the last. I wondered if he noticed it too; if the quiet glances and soft smiles meant as much to him as they did to me. I didn't know what any of this meant yet. But as he looked at me, uncertain, unguarded, I found myself hoping.

Whatever this was, wherever it led, I wouldn't face it alone.

Not anymore.

I might not know what the future held—for me, for him, for us—but I dared to believe my earlier words were a prophecy and we would be able to get through all of it together.

The afternoon sun bled gold through the treetops, slicing through the canopy in shimmering ribbons that danced across the forest floor. The light painted the leaves like tiny lanterns, their flickers guiding our path, but the beauty did nothing to ease the tight coil in my chest.

Be home by dinner, Raine.

My mother's words from this morning echoed louder now. It should've been simple—a curfew, a reminder. But there had been something in her voice. Something weighted. Like she already knew that between morning and night, everything could change.

I glanced at Manakel. He walked ahead, half-shadowed by the dark tendrils that trailed behind him like a second skin. A stray beam of light caught the sharp angle of his jaw, glinting off features carved in silence. He looked distant, his focus fixed somewhere far beyond the trees, as if haunted by something only he could see. I wondered what lived in the quiet between his steps.

This man wasn't the boy from the story he told me. He wasn't the wide-eyed angel who flew over mountaintops with hope stitched into his wings. Just like I wasn't the girl who once ran barefoot through the village, chasing adventure and believing she could be anything but ordinary. That girl felt like a memory now. Fading a little more each day, each secret stripping away a piece of her.

The River treaty ending, the looming Imbe Rite, immortals and gods, no longer fables but facts clawing their way into my life. Secrets unraveling everything I thought I understood.

I missed the simplicity of not knowing. I missed the girl I once was. I missed her freedom, the simplicity of dreaming without the weight of destiny pressing in from every angle.

But I knew there was no turning back.

I breathed deep, trying to tether myself to the present, but the weight of it all clung like mist. Maybe if I made it through tonight, through dinner, through pretending everything was fine, I could hold on to a sliver of who I used to be.

Even if it was only pretend.

I slowed, letting the forest draw closer, its quiet rustle wrapping around me like a cocoon. Manakel was silent again, and I didn't know if he felt the shift in the air too, but I did.

Something was coming.

"Manakel," I said softly, not wanting to startle the quiet. His head turned, hazel eyes catching mine with startling precision. The way he looked at me, alert and unwavering, made me wonder if he sensed more than he let on.

"I need to head back soon," I continued, brushing stray leaves from my sleeve. "I promised my mom I'd be home for dinner."

He studied me for a long moment, then nodded once. "Understood. We can continue later. You'll need every ounce of strength for what's ahead."

The calm in his voice settled something restless inside me, but the lingering tension didn't quite fade.

I hesitated, shifting my weight between steps. "Do you think I'll be ready in time?" The vulnerability in my voice caught me off guard. "What if I'm not prepared?"

It felt strange to say out loud, like admitting I was afraid would somehow give the fear more power.

Manakel stepped closer. His voice was low, steady. "You have more strength than you know, Raine. Trust it. Trust yourself. When the moment comes, you'll rise."

I wanted to believe him, and the conviction in his tone helped, but beneath it, the worry still lingered.

"I just… I don't want to let anyone down," I admitted quietly.

"You won't." He said immediately, unwavering. "You're already becoming who you were meant to be. Just keep going, and take it one step at a time."

I nodded, holding onto his words as if they could keep me steady. We walked in silence, the path to home stretching ahead, winding and quiet. But the weight of everything unspoken pressed in at the edges.

His shadows moved differently today, less like an extension of him and more like something watching. I wasn't sure if that made me uneasy or just more aware of how little I knew about him. When we reached the edge of the clearing, I paused, brushed dirt from my hands, and tucked wild strands of hair behind my ear.

"I'll see you soon," I said, offering a small smile. "And… thank you for everything today. I mean it."

His eyes lingered on me, something masked flickering behind them.

"Stay safe, Raine."

My pulse quickened, but I nodded. And without looking back, I stepped toward the place that used to feel like home, knowing that in a few days it no longer would.

The clearing appeared ahead, my backyard just beyond the thin veil of trees. The house stood quietly beneath the fading sun, its windows glowing softly against the dusk.

I slowed, ears straining for footsteps, rustling, anything. But the yard was still. No Wren waiting at the back door. No sign of Dad's watchful eyes from the kitchen window. Not even my grandmother hanging around in the garden.

Good.

I wasn't ready to explain *why* I was stepping out of the forest. I'd barely come to terms with the answer myself.

I edged closer to the tree line, careful to stay hidden in the shadows. One more step and—

A hand shot out, cold fingers clamping around my arm. Before I could cry out, I was yanked back into the trees. A strangled gasp caught in my throat, and another hand, gentler this time, covered my mouth.

Panic surged, and I was gearing myself up to fight, until a familiar voice whispered in my ear.

"Calm down, Raine. It's just me."

I twisted free, heart still hammering as I came face to face with my grandmother, her silver blonde hair catching what little light filtered through the leaves. Her expression shifted between amusement and urgency, though the glint in her eyes suggested she'd been expecting this reaction.

Her hand lingered over my mouth for just a second longer, and I swear she could feel how fast my heart was beating with worry.

"Everything's fine," she assured me, voice low but calm. "Everyone's safe. I just needed to catch you before you went inside."

I exhaled a breath I didn't realize I was holding. "What's going on?" I whispered, glancing toward the house, hoping I was quiet enough not to raise suspicions.

A sly smile tugged at the corner of her lips as she brushed a stray leaf from my shoulder. "Saving you from a lie that could spiral fast," she said, voice low and even. "We need to talk."

I stilled. "Is something wrong?"

"No," she said quickly. "But you telling Wren you were working in Ceannairí wasn't exactly a smart thing to do."

The heat of embarrassment crept up my neck. I'd been hoping to avoid this conversation altogether.

I winced. "That obvious, huh?"

She gave me a look. "It was bold. And reckless. Ceannairí is close enough that Wren, or even your father, could decide to visit. And if they do, and don't find you there, what do you think they'll do?"

"I didn't have time to think of a better excuse," I muttered. "He was asking a lot of questions, and it was the first thing I thought of. It just… came out."

"As most dangerous lies do." Her voice softened, but the warning stayed beneath.

I exhaled slowly, biting the inside of my cheek. She wasn't wrong. I'd known it was reckless the moment the words left my mouth, but desperation made strange choices for you.

I glanced toward the house, guilt coiling in my gut. "So what now? I can't exactly take it back and say I was kidding."

"I have a plan," she said, with the sort of pride that made me nervous. "It *should* keep us covered."

My brows rose in question. "You always have a plan."

"Yes, and it's a good one." She leaned in. "I visited Ceannairí this morning. An old friend of mine, Lugh, owns a blacksmith forge there. I told him your predicament, and he agreed to vouch for you and say you're working there. If anyone asks, he'll back up your story."

Relief hit me hard and fast.

"There's more," she continued. "He also has a private cottage on his land that's vacant. It's secluded and far enough from the main road to keep curious eyes away. If the boys get suspicious, we can say that's where you'll be living, free of charge as part of your wages."

I stared at her, absorbing every word. The tension that had been knotting my stomach for days began to loosen, even if just a little. For the first time since this all started, I felt like the ground wasn't crumbling beneath me, and maybe something would finally work out.

But a flicker of doubt remained.

"But why would he do all that? What does this *friend* of yours want in return?" I asked carefully. "Because favors like *that* don't come free."

A knowing smile tugged at her lips. "You're right to ask." Her voice dipped slightly, quieter now. "Lugh owes me a debt from a long time ago when I helped him out of a situation that could've cost him his life. He's been waiting for the chance to repay it."

I narrowed my eyes. "And you trust him?"

"With my life," she replied without hesitation.

I wanted to question it further. Ask if she was sure we could trust him, and how long he would keep up the ruse? Something about it felt too easy, too convenient, but my heart couldn't argue with the way tension had started to ease from my ribs.

Still, I nodded slowly.

"Thank you," I whispered. "For everything lately. I was starting to lose track of everything I had to keep straight. And needing to explain it to my Dad was stressing me out all day." I smiled sheepishly, my cheeks staining pink, but she smiled, pressing a reassuring hand to my arm.

"We'll say you came with me to Ceannairí today to settle it all. That you met Lugh during an herb delivery a few weeks back, and he offered the position. We'll say we saw the forge and toured the cottage today. Simple and not too much information. That'll be our story."

I exhaled, nodding, my relief tangible now.

"Now, let's get you inside before your dad starts asking questions about where you've been all day," she said, moving back towards the house.

As we crossed the clearing, the scent of bean stew drifted from the kitchen window. It wrapped around me like a blanket, grounding me in the familiar comfort of home.

For a moment, I let myself pretend.

Pretend I wasn't lying to everyone I loved. That I wasn't sneaking through forests with stolen truths tucked beneath my skin. That I wasn't carrying a secret that could change everything.

I imagined it was just another ordinary day. One without shifting loyalties, vanishing treaties, or men with wings stirring in the dark.

But the moment passed, fragile and fleeting. And the truth was still there, waiting for me on the other side of it.

My life was no longer normal. Maybe it never had been. And no matter how tightly I clung to the idea that it could be again, I knew I was only lying to myself.

And I wasn't sure how much longer I could keep it up because, like I had told Aeron, I wasn't a liar.

24. Bound By Secrets

The late afternoon light filtered through the kitchen window, casting a golden warmth across the room. The scent of stew hung thick in the air, herbs, garlic, and something heartier, wrapping around me as I stepped inside.

I froze at the sight before me—my parents swaying gently in the middle of the kitchen, their bodies moving in quiet rhythm to the soft hum of music that wasn't actually playing.

I lingered by the doorway, unseen and unwilling to break whatever spell had settled over them. They moved like two halves of the same whole, perfectly attuned to each other as if dancing together was second nature.

Mom's head rested on Dad's chest, her hand curled in his, her laughter soft and effortless. He twirled her once, grinning like it was easy to forget the world outside. Like nothing could touch them here.

A quiet ache bloomed in my chest.

Dad looked like he always had—solid and grounded and entirely present. His sleeves were rolled to the elbows of his worn plaid shirt, and his dark slacks dusted with flour, no doubt from helping with the bread I could smell in the oven. His damp hair curled at the nape of his neck, silver catching in the beard I used to tug on as a child. He looked every bit the protector and provider I'd always known, the kind of father who could shield us from storms with just a smile and steady hands.

And mom…she was the light that balanced him. She was radiant, glowing in the warm light of the kitchen. Her forest-green dress caught the soft breeze drifting through the open window, the fabric clinging gracefully to her frame before flaring at her calves. I watched as her eyes crinkled with joy, the same soft gold flecks reflecting in her piercing blue eyes that I saw in my own. My mother had always been the heart of our home, displaying quiet resilience beneath her gentle nature.

I pressed closer to the door frame, letting the moment settle around me like a secret I wasn't meant to see. They looked so… happy. So blissfully unaware of the things shifting around us. Of the truths I hadn't spoken, and the weight I was learning to carry alone.

I wanted to stay in this threshold forever, where everything still felt whole. Because the thought of leaving this, of walking away from it, from them, for whatever waited ahead, felt like a quiet kind of breaking.

I shifted my weight, announcing my presence when the wooden floor creaked beneath me.

Dad's head lifted immediately, his eyes finding mine like it always did. "Alright, Wildheart," he said with a teasing smile. "If you think you can sneak past us without being noticed, you're in the wrong house."

Mom turned in his arms, her face flushed, eyes bright and sparkling with quiet delight. They looked like something out of an old love song, faded edges, worn smooth by time, but still glowing.

I stepped into the kitchen, folding my hands behind my back like a child caught spying. "Wasn't sneaking," I said, voice light. Just… observing. It's not every day I witness an epic romance in my kitchen."

Mom laughed, brushing loose strands of hair from her face. "Oh, sweetie," she said softly, "yours will come too, one day."

The words landed heavier than I expected, stirring the quiet ache I'd been keeping at bay.

I offered her a small smile, trying not to let the weight show. "I hope so."

Dad grabbed a ladle and poured stew into a bowl, blowing over the top dramatically. "Here," he said, sliding it toward me with a smirk, "a little magic to keep you grounded. I've heard you've been more distracted than usual."

It was meant to tease, but his eyes lingered, searching, maybe even suspecting or waiting for a reaction. I reached for the bowl but paused. Did they sense it? That I wasn't the same girl who left this kitchen days ago before the bonfire? That something was shifting beneath my skin, and I was slipping further into a world they couldn't even comprehend?

I swallowed hard and forced a laugh. "I think I'm just tired. It's been a long day."

Mom reached out, taking the bowl back with a soft cluck of her tongue. "Not so fast," she said with a wink. "Wash up first, and when you're done, bring your brothers down too. We're eating together tonight—like a family."

I smiled, grateful for the small distraction and excuse to escape. There was comfort in her words, even if they unknowingly hinted at what I feared. *This might be one of the last times we did this all together.*

As I turned toward the stairs, the light hum of laughter and clinking bowls followed me like a tether I wasn't ready to cut.

In my room, I caught a glimpse of myself in the mirror. My braid had loosened, stray strands curling around my face, softened by heat and humidity. I tightened it, fingers fumbling as I tried to anchor myself to something—*anything.*

The weight pressed down harder than before. The lies. My grandmother's plan. The Rite. Everything I hadn't said and all the things I couldn't.

Tonight, I would pretend. I'd sit at the table, surrounded by the people I loved, and smile at stories, pass the bread, and act like nothing had changed. I would pretend I wasn't about to step into something unknown.

Pretend every word out of my mouth wasn't a lie.

A noise outside the door made me pause, and I opened the door just as Wren's fist hovered midair, getting ready to knock.

He blinked. "Oh. You're ready." He scratched the back of his neck. "I was coming to get you. We're all starving."

I smiled and swatted his arm playfully. "You and your food. Is that all you ever think about?"

His grin came easy, but the worry in his eyes didn't quite fade. "Only when Mom's cooking. Let's go. You know I'm not responsible for my actions when I'm hungry, and she insisted we all wait to eat together."

I followed him down, tucking the truth and my unease deeper inside where no one could see it.

Tonight, I could still pretend everything was normal. Even though I knew nothing ever would be again.

The stairs creaked beneath our feet as Wren led the way down, each step felt heavier than the last, like a quiet reminder of what I was about to do. His usual carefree energy was dimmed by the silence between us, a tension he either didn't notice or chose to ignore.

I kept running over the story in my head, smoothing out the edges of the lies I'd carefully stitched together. But no matter how polished it sounded, it couldn't silence the churn in my stomach. By the time we reached the kitchen, I'd chewed the inside of my cheek raw.

Dad and Baren were already at the table, bowls of untouched stew steaming in front of them. Mom placed a dish of warm bread in the center, her face lit by the golden flicker of soft light above us. When she looked up and saw us, her smile was soft and bright, like sunlight after rain.

"There you are," she said, gesturing for us to sit. "We were waiting on you two."

I slid into my seat, trying to appear relaxed even as my heart pounded against my ribs. I avoided Dad's stare and reached for the bread, tearing into it like it might anchor me. Or save me from his line of questioning, even temporarily.

"So," Dad said, reaching for the dish himself. "Wren tells me you've taken a job. In Ceannairí, of all places."

I forced a smile, meeting his gaze with as much confidence as I could muster. "Yes. I'll be working with a blacksmith there. He's looking to expand into training equipment, so my knowledge of weapons from Wren might *actually* come in handy."

Wren nudged me under the table, his smirk almost smug. I could practically hear the unspoken *'you're welcome'* loud and clear. His curiosity, however, betrayed the amusement on his face.

He raised a brow. "I don't remember you ever mentioning wanting to work in a forge."

I shrugged, playing it off. "It wasn't exactly the plan, but the opportunity came up and felt like a good fit. Plus, I'll mostly be handling the records and supply orders, not forging or working directly with the tools."

Baren leaned forward, his arms crossing over the table, and his dark eyes narrowed slightly. "And you'll be living there too? His voice was low, skeptical. "Ceannairí isn't exactly next door. Seems a bit far for someone your age to take on alone."

"Well, I won't be alone," I replied, keeping my voice light. "He has a small cottage on the property for apprentices, and I'll stay there. It'll be safe and easy to go to and from."

Dad's hand slowed as he tore a piece of bread. His brow furrowed, the playful glint in his eyes dimming as they searched mine. "How did you even apply for this position, and do you even know or trust this man? It's a big move and you've never been that far from home."

My throat tightened, but I willed my voice to stay steady. "Gran actually knows Lugh," I said carefully. "She helped arrange it, so if she trusts him, then I do too."

The mention of my grandmother gave him pause. I saw the shift in his expression, the way his worry pulled taut and then, just slightly, eased.

"If Leighna's involved, I suppose that's more reassuring," he said, nodding slowly, "Just remember, this doesn't have to be permanent. If something doesn't feel right, or you want to come home, just say the word and we'll come get you."

The gentleness in his voice made the guilt twist harder. I managed a small smile. "I know, Dad. I'll be careful, but thank you."

We fell into a quiet rhythm, bowls clinking softly, spoons stirring. But I could still feel them watching—Wren's occasional glance, Baren's furrowed stare. Not accusing, just... noticing something was off. I could feel them trying to pick at the seams I hadn't sewn tightly enough.

And all I could do was keep smiling, keep eating, and pretend I wasn't already drifting further away from everything I loved and lying every step of the way.

After dinner, we gathered in the hearth room. Baren added a few logs to the fire. The flames crackled to life, casting a golden haze across the room as we settled in with blankets and chairs pulled close. The smell of smoke curled into the air and filled the quiet between us.

I loved nights like this—wrapped in the warmth of family, sharing stories and laughter by firelight. It was the kind of evening that made the world feel small and safe. But tonight, that warmth felt fragile, like glass that could shatter at any moment.

I shifted, feeling eyes begin to drift toward me. I leaned forward, forcing a smile, searching for something, anything, to deflect the attention.

"Dad," I said, feigning excitement, "you know Ceannairí better than anyone here. Once I'm settled, where should I go? What should I explore first?"

His eyes lit up instantly, the familiar spark of storytelling lighting his eyes, and the weight on my chest eased a little.

"Oh, Ceannairí," he said, reclining into his chair like he was slipping into a memory. "That city is full of stories. There's an inn near the old gate called The Harpy's Nest. Looks like nothing special from the outside, but it's a gathering place for all kinds—travelers, guards, even the occasional noble." His grin curved knowingly. "The innkeeper's an old friend, and the first time I stayed there, he showed me a hidden tunnel out the back that leads right into the market square."

Wren raised a brow, nudging me with his elbow. "A secret tunnel? Sounds like the kind of thing you'd need with the trouble you get into."

Dad chuckled, shaking his head. "It's more for dodging crowds than stirring trouble. Ceannairí is a maze, full of twisting streets and hidden paths. You'll get lost a few times, but that's part of the fun."

I smiled, letting myself relax into the rhythm of his voice, the fire casting flickers of light across his face. But when he looked at me again, something in his expression shifted; his playful spark softened into something tender.

"Just remember, Wildheart, no matter how far you go, this will always be your home, and we will always be right here to bring you back to it."

His words hit deeper than I expected. I nodded, unable to say much more.

Baren shifted forward, resting his elbows on his knees. His eyes, sharp as always, found mine and were filled with accusation and hesitation. "So, what made you even want to take this job, Raine? It just seems… sudden."

My stomach tightened. I dropped my focus to the frayed edge of the blanket in my lap. "I guess… I wanted to prove I could do something on my own. Step outside the village and experience what else is out there."

Wren grinned, "Well, you'd better come back with stories of your own. And they'd better rival Dad's. He added with a wink. "If I'm ever stuck in Rioga late, maybe I'll come stay with you, and you can show me around."

I laughed and nodded. That sounded nice, Wren and I exploring a new city together. Too bad it would never happen.

Dad clapped a hand on Wren's shoulder, still smiling. "If she experiences even half of what I have while traveling, she'll have more than a few tales. Though I imagine there'll be one or two she keeps to herself." He turned that knowing look on me, his voice light but layered. "Just be safe, my

Wildheart."

I held his gaze for a beat longer than I meant to. Then forced a chuckle. "I'll try. But no promises."

Everyone laughed, and the conversation drifted into easier territory, stories and teasing warming the edges of the evening. But I couldn't shake the weight in my chest—the ache that came with knowing this was one of the last nights I'd sit here like this. Surrounded by my family. All of us safe and sound.

So I memorized it. Every flicker of firelight. Every smile. Every story. Every laugh.

Because no matter where I was headed, this—*they*—would be the one thing I'd carry with me.

The fire had burned down to glowing embers by the time we called it a night. Hours of laughter, stories, and songs had filled the house, wrapping it in the kind of warmth that only comes from being surrounded by the people you love most. I lingered by the hearth for a moment, reluctant to let the feeling slip away, before following Wren and Baren up the stairs.

But as I passed the kitchen, the scattered cups left on the table caught my eye. My feet paused before my thoughts could. Silently, I crossed the room and began collecting them, letting the rhythm of small tasks keep my thoughts from unraveling.

The house had quieted to a hum, floorboards settling, distant footsteps creaking above, but the lingering scent of stew and fresh bread still clung to the air, like the home itself was reluctant to let go of the night the same way I was.

The soft click of footsteps didn't startle me. I felt her before I saw her.

Mom stepped beside me, quiet as ever. She rarely interrupted moments like this. Dad was the voice that filled a room, the storyteller, while she was the steadiness behind him, quiet and grounding him with her presence. But something in her silence tonight felt different. Heavier.

I glanced at her, noting the distant look in her eyes. She was physically here, standing inches away from me, yet I could tell her mind was someplace else. I offered a small smile, hoping to deflect whatever emotion I saw building behind hers. I didn't have the energy to face whatever she was about to bring up or muster up another lie in the moment. My chest was already too full—overflowing with secrets I couldn't share and a growing ache I didn't know how to name.

But then her hand touched my shoulder, gentle, lingering, weighted, and I knew. Whatever she carried was something she couldn't keep to herself anymore.

"So," she said softly, her voice catching even on the first word, "your birthday is a couple of days away, and I wanted to make it special. I know things are moving quickly with the new job and… the unexpected move, but I still want to do something all together. I just wish we had more time."

Her voice cracked, and when I turned to look at her, tears were already slipping down her cheeks. The cup slipped from my hands and clattered into the sink. I didn't even register it. I just pulled her into a hug.

She wrapped her arms around me tightly—tighter than usual—like she wasn't just hugging me, but holding on to the moment itself, memorizing the feel of it. I rested my head against her shoulder, feeling the soft rise and fall of her breath. She smelled like bread and rosemary, like all the nights she tucked me in after long days in the kitchen. The weight of her hand on my back, the faint tremble in her arms… it felt like she knew I was hiding something and that my leaving was inevitable. A thing neither of us could stop or delay.

"It's all happening so fast," she whispered, the words brushing against the side of my head. "I knew this day would come, but I didn't think it'd be this… soon. You were just eight years old yesterday, and now here you are, turning eighteen in two days and getting ready to leave home."

I stayed silent, afraid that if I opened my mouth, I might let too much slip—too much truth, too much fear and uncertainty.

She gently pulled back, framing my face with her hands, brushing a piece of hair behind my ear like she used to when I was little. Her eyes, glassy and full, searched mine.

"I know you're ready," she said. "Ready for this job, for whatever comes next. But I need you to remember—no matter how far you go, or how much time passes, you'll always have us. You'll always have this. Your family and your home."

The knot in my throat tightened, and I nodded, swallowing against the weight pressing down on me. "I'll miss you more than you'll ever know," I whispered, forcing a smile. "But I'll be okay. And I want you to be okay too, even if it takes me a little while to find my way back."

The words tasted hollow as they left my lips. I wanted them to be true—to believe them with the same certainty I once believed the world was small and safe. But nothing felt certain anymore, and the truth sat too close to the surface.

She smiled, but I saw the sadness still there, quiet, watchful. Like she saw the truth anyway.

After a moment, she straightened and exhaled. "Alright," she said, wiping her cheeks with the back of her hand. "We'll just have to make the next few days count. Tomorrow we're celebrating—one day early, I know, but I want us all together. Just promise me something?"

I nodded, holding her a bit tighter.

"Just promise me, no matter where life takes you, you won't lose touch with who you are and where you came from."

She reached up, her fingers tracing the braid over my shoulder. "Laochra will always be your home, and you will always have a place here."

The word *home* settled deep inside me, heavier than I expected. I nodded again.

"I promise," I whispered. And I meant it. Even if I couldn't say *when* I'd return, I meant it. I would do anything I could to get back here, back to them.

We stood in the kitchen a moment longer, the silence wrapping around us like a familiar blanket.

Then she reached into the sink and picked up the cup I'd dropped, drying it with slow, steady movements. I watched her, seeing the small tremble in her hands as she dried it, knowing she was trying to stay strong, too.

"Now, off to bed," she said gently, placing the cup back on the shelf. "We've got a big day tomorrow. And I need my almost birthday girl bright-eyed and well-rested."

I smiled, squeezing her hand. "Goodnight, Mom."

As I climbed the stairs, the warmth of her touch lingered on my skin. The ache in my chest deepened, bittersweet and familiar, like the feeling of holding onto something precious that you know you're about to lose.

But as I paused at the landing and glanced back, the flicker of light still glowing from the kitchen, I felt it—the strength in her words, in this home, in the love that filled every corner of it.

No matter what lay ahead, no matter how far I had to go, I would carry that with me—etched into my bones, my breath, my determination.

And I knew that even if everything else fell apart, this, *my family, this home,* would always be the piece that held me together.

25. Eyes In The Dark

Sleep clung to the edges of me, but never fully arrived. The forest stirred beneath my skin, quiet, restless, and tugging me back toward consciousness like it didn't want to let me go. And when I finally drifted off, it wasn't peaceful.

Shadows chased me through the trees. Branches clawed at my clothes. No matter how far or fast I ran, something followed, something ancient and watching. I jolted upright, breathless and trembling, the remnants of the dream still clawing at the edges of my mind. My heart was hammering loud enough to drown out the creaking bones of the house settling around me.

Moonlight slipped through the window in thin silver ribbons. I forced my breathing to slow, but the tightness in my chest didn't ease. But then, just beyond the glass, I saw it.

A flicker of movement beyond the tree line, shadows bleeding into the clearing like smoke, stretching outward with quiet purpose. A figure stood just beyond the edge of the light, and I didn't need to see his face to know.

Manakel.

His presence was a tether, dark and steady, threading through me even from this distance. I pressed my hand to the cool glass. His shadows moved like they had minds of their own, weaving through underbrush as though they were searching for something—*or someone.*

Though he was barely more than a smudge in the night, I could feel the weight of his stare pressed against me from across the distance, familiar and unsettling all at once. His shadows weren't simply lingering—they were waiting. *Calling me.*

My eyes flicked to the bed beside me. My grandmother lay still, her breath even and undisturbed. The quiet of her sleep made the chaos inside me feel louder. I slipped from the covers, careful not to stir her, and reached for my cloak. My bare feet barely made a sound as I padded across the floor, through the doorway, and out into the night.

The cold met me like a warning. Wet grass kissed my toes, the earth soaked and unforgiving, but all I felt was the magnetic pull of him. He stood at the clearing's edge, moonlight catching on the dark edges of his wings. He looked carved from shadow—part protector, part predator— and somehow neither felt wrong.

"You're out here late," he said softly, his voice cutting through the silence.

I pulled the cloak tighter around me, shivering as much from his stare as the cold. "I could say the same to you. Your shadows... they woke me."

"They were meant to," he replied, a small smirk tugging at his lips. "I didn't want you waking up alone in fear."

Something about the way he said it, casual but careful, knotted my breath. The words should've unsettled me. Instead, they made something inside me exhale.

"Were you watching me?" I asked.

His head tilted slightly. "Not watching. Just staying... nearby."

His honesty wasn't defensive. If anything, it was quiet. Matter-of-fact. Like he didn't see anything strange about lurking in the shadows, waiting for me to wake up and notice him. I should've felt uneasy by his admission, by the silent guardianship he'd taken upon himself. I should have backed away. But instead, my shoulders eased, and a strange warmth brushed through me.

"I don't know why," I murmured, "but knowing you're out here makes it easier to sleep."

He stilled, and in the silence that followed, I felt it—his control slipping for just a second. His shadows flinched, and there was something like relief in his eyes.

"Then I'll stay close, Amadán," he said, quieter now. "Until the time comes for you to walk through the river, I'll make sure you're never truly alone."

The name lingered in the air between us. A softness cloaked in something still. I tried to suppress the blush rising to my cheeks, but as the wind nipped at me, I shivered again, pulling the cloak tighter around myself. Before I could secure it, Manakel's hand brushed past my shoulder. He stepped closer, reached behind me, careful not to touch my skin, and caught the tie that had come loose. The air between us thickened as his fingers worked in silence, looping the knot with practiced ease. He didn't touch me, not allowing his skin to graze mine. But I felt every inch of space between us like it was strung tight on a wire.

I stood there, frozen under his dark gaze as it dipped, lingering on my face with a kind of intensity I hadn't felt before. Not from him. Not like *this*. My body reacted every time he was close, but this feeling was completely different; there was something primal about the way he was looking at me. Like a predator stalking its prey, but instead of being scared, I *wanted* to invite him in.

I shifted slightly, the cold from the earth creeping up my legs. It took me a second to realize I'd forgotten to put on shoes. Noticing my movements, Manakel's focus drifted downward, his eyes narrowing when he caught sight of my bare feet. A muscle jumped in his jaw, and a sigh slipped out, laced with something akin to irritation. Before I could take another step, his arms hooked under me, lifting me effortlessly off the ground.

A startled gasp escaped me, but I didn't fight it; part of me was too stunned to react. His hold was firm, one arm beneath my knees, the other around my back, as though carrying me was second nature.

"You'll catch a cold wandering without shoes," he muttered, his voice a low rumble against me.

"I didn't realize you were such an expert on footwear," I replied breathlessly, unable to keep the sarcasm at bay. I bit my lip, "And I didn't exactly *plan* to come outside."

He glanced down with a mask no crack of light could slip through. "And yet here you are."

I looked up. His face was closer than I expected—cheekbones sharpened by moonlight, a shadowed crease between his brows. I felt the heat of his breath, smelled the strange scent of ash and storm that clung to him like a second skin.

My pulse stumbled. My breathing hitched at his closeness. Even the forest was still as his solid arms were wrapped around me. And for one terrifying, comforting second… I let myself lean into him.

We slipped into a comfortable silence as he carried me back toward the house, his strides slow and measured. I could feel the heat of him through my cloak, the quiet rhythm of his breath brushing my temple with every movement.

At the door, he lowered me carefully, his hands lingering a fraction longer than they needed to. When I looked up, his gaze didn't waver.

"If I'm going to protect you," he said, voice low, "let's at least keep you from dying of something stupid before even starting the Rite."

The smirk that tugged at his mouth softened the words, and despite my embarrassment, I smiled.

"Thank you," I whispered—hoping he understood it was not just for the warmth or the rescue, but for the steady calm he carried like armor. A stillness I kept finding myself drawn to.

Something in his expression shifted at that. His features softened, but the shadows were already pulling at him, beckoning him back into the trees.

"Try and get some sleep," he murmured. "I'll see you in a few hours."

Then, with a final glance, he vanished into the night, without sound or shape, as if he'd never been there at all—except for the warmth still clinging to my skin, and the quick, uneven rhythm of my heart.

I stood there a moment longer, breath caught between relief and something far more dangerous. Because I was starting to rely on him, trust him even, and I didn't know if that made me smart or naive.

I lingered in the cool night air, letting the breeze wrap around me like a thin veil, hoping it might dull the restless stirrings in my chest. My house had gone still. The faint hum of life inside softened by distance, but out here, beneath the stars, with the moon casting long shadows across the clearing, everything felt sharper. The stillness carried weight, pressing against me, and I wasn't sure if it was comforting or suffocating.

My attention was pulled toward the woods before I could stop it, searching for the familiar flicker of shadow, the telltale shape that had somehow become a comfort. I told myself it wasn't about him. That it was just the forest—the dream that had unsettled me. The need to know he was somewhere nearby.

But the forest remained quiet, his dark form nowhere in sight. He'd said he wouldn't stray far. I believed that. And yet, his absence was prickling under my skin, like a tether pulled too tight, ready to snap.

I didn't see him. But a soft pink glow caught the corner of my eye, flickering between the trees—too delicate to be firelight, too fluid to be anything natural. It moved like silk through the underbrush, elusive and alive.

I swallowed hard. *Alfreda.*

I knew it was her before I even had time to think. Her presence carried something unmistakable: power disguised as grace, mischief hidden in stillness.

I stared too long, waiting for something—proof he had left me to go to her, maybe. And that's when it struck me. The tightness in my throat. The uncomfortable pull low in my stomach. The heat rising behind my eyes even though nothing had been said.

I didn't know what I was feeling. Not really. Just that I hated the idea of her being near him. Of them being together in the quiet, close, familiar, comfortable in a way I didn't understand. In a way I couldn't be. I didn't have the history, the knowledge, the power. All I had were flickers, glances and shadows and the steady sense that I wasn't imagining what passed between us when he looked at me.

But maybe I was. I told myself it didn't matter, and yet, the way my heart twisted betrayed me. Alfreda had known him longer, that much was obvious. She probably understood the layers beneath his carefully guarded exterior and had chipped away at those walls in ways I hadn't even begun to. That realization felt like a thorn pressed under my ribs, small but sharp enough to linger.

I shouldn't care. I knew that. He wasn't mine to worry over. This wasn't about romance or feelings or—

Gods, what even was this? A crush? My very first?

The word felt too small for what was happening inside me, too flimsy to hold the sudden ache, the heat, the irrational pull that made me want to wander into the woods just to see if she was alone.

And yet…I couldn't look at that glow and not feel something sharp settle behind my ribs. A jealous sting that felt foreign and wrong and too loud. Maybe it was because I *didn't* trust her, or because some part of me had started to trust him.

I tore my eyes away. It didn't matter. It *shouldn't* matter. He was only helping me get through my Rite. After that, we probably wouldn't even see each other again.

Still, the bitterness clung to me as I stepped back inside, the worn door groaning faintly in protest. I leaned against it, letting it shut behind me, the cool wood pressing against my spine. My hands wouldn't stop trembling.

I told myself to breathe. That I was being foolish. That I had more important things to worry about than whether the dark-winged stranger I barely knew was standing in the trees with the stunning faerie who could already hold her own.

I closed my eyes, willing the feelings away, willing myself to focus. In two days, everything would change, and I needed to be ready. I needed sleep to focus.

But the truth was, no matter how tightly I wrapped the cloak around my shoulders or how deeply I buried my thoughts…I didn't feel safe or prepared unless he was near. And that scared me more than anything because I was never one to *need* anyone before.

I wanted to believe tomorrow would bring clarity. That sleep would erase the ache burrowing into me now. But deep down, I knew nothing would.

I lay tangled in my blankets, the heat of the day still clinging to my skin like a second cloak. The pillow beneath me felt too firm, the silence too loud, and every time I closed my eyes, I saw the soft flicker of Alfreda's glow in the woods. Her presence had stirred something sharp and unfamiliar in my chest, an ache I didn't have the words for.

I should've been worrying about the Rite. The river. The weight of everything I still didn't understand. Instead, I was here, restless and burning with something dangerously close to jealousy. Eventually, exhaustion won. My mind drifted, still knotted around half-formed thoughts, until I slipped into sleep.

And there in the quiet, I dreamed of wings.

Not the delicate shimmer of fae or the soft feathers of a guardian bird. These were vast, black wings that filled the sky, powerful enough to stir the wind and silence the world. They moved with purpose, not menace. Like they had always known where they were going—and now, they were circling back for me.

I stood beneath them, barefoot in a field washed in gold. The light shimmered in small threads, curling around my arms like silk spun from the sun. I couldn't see his face, only the outline—tall, cloaked in shadow and light both. But I felt him.

His presence didn't frighten me. It calmed me.

Even with the unknown still stretching before me like an open wound, I felt… safe. Not because the world was suddenly easy or certain. But because he was there, standing beside me like a promise. Like the chaos would come, but I wouldn't face it alone.

Something warm unfurled in my chest. I reached out, fingers grazing where his hand might be, just barely brushing the edge of his light.

Everything will work out.

The thought didn't feel like mine. It felt like a whisper. Like a vow. And I wanted to believe it more than anything.

I slipped out of bed just as dawn began spilling through the cracks in the curtains. The house was still cloaked in silence, save for the soft creaks as I eased down the stairs. For the first time in days, my chest wasn't tight with dread. The ache of uncertainty hadn't vanished, but it had dulled, replaced by something quieter. Steadier. A fragile resolve I hadn't felt in a long time.

I moved to the kitchen window, watching the sun inch its way over the treetops, bathing the backyard in soft amber light. The world felt suspended, like it was waiting alongside me. Today, I wanted to anchor myself in the simplicity of being with my family, letting their presence pull me back into who I was before all of this: before immortality, the river, the Rite, and the truths I hadn't told.

Mom had asked that we spend the day together. Everyone else, Dad, Baren, and Wren, would leave tomorrow for their own paths. So I would spend my actual birthday with only Mom and Gran before leaving.

That quiet, unspoken truth of where I was truly headed sat between us like a fragile thread, but I wasn't ready to unravel it.

I grabbed my bag from the chair, the familiar weight anchoring me. The thermos inside clinked against two cups, nestled beside my twin daggers. A strange mix of normalcy and necessity. With Manakel, I had learned to expect the unexpected. Even on a calm morning like this, the blades felt necessary—just in case.

Outside, the air was sharp with dew, the grass shining like glass beneath my boots. The forest ahead was hushed, reluctant to wake. The faintest rustle in the distance highlighted the morning breeze, and I followed the narrow path into the trees, my cloak drawn tighter around me.

There was a stillness to the air, one that made me feel as though the world was waiting with me, listening for whatever might come next. I was approaching the clearing just ahead when two small figures darted from the branches in a blur of iridescent wings.

"Raine!" Dela's bright, high-pitched voice broke the stillness as she zipped toward me, Fern close behind. Their wings caught the morning light like threads of spun glass, their presence crackling with energy as they hovered close to my face.

"Thank the gods you came back," Fern grinned, her dark hair catching the light as she spun midair. "We thought Alfreda and Aeron scared you off for good."

Dela shot her a warning glance, sharp and quick. It was the kind of look Wren and I exchanged when one of us was about to reveal too much.

But Fern, oblivious or unconcerned, kept going. "Alfreda said you'd never come back, let alone start your Imbe Rite. Then she told Aeron you wouldn't last a day alone in the woods."

I arched a brow, unable to help the smirk tugging at my lips. "Well, here I am." I looked around us, exaggerating my movements as I spun in place, "And it looks like I'm alone and still alive and well."

Fern's wings stilled for a second, wide-eyed surprise lighting her features. "You're *really* not scared of them?"

I leaned in slightly, lowering my voice with a conspiratorial edge. "Bullies don't scare me. I won't let anything stop me from crossing the river. I'll finish the Rite, no matter what they throw at me."

Dela's expression softened, something like admiration flickering across her face. "Good," she said. "It takes more than strength to survive the rite. You have something that scares them. That's why they're trying to get under your skin."

Fern nodded eagerly. "Alfreda is *totally* scared of you. So is Aeron. They'd never admit it, but we see everything in these woods, and it's obvious you're a threat to them."

Their words warmed something inside me. Even if they were small, their confidence in me felt massive. A little flame of confidence I hadn't realized I needed. "Thank you," I said sincerely. "Knowing I have you two on my side means a lot."

Fern giggled. "Oh! Don't forget Manny's rooting for you, too. He's waiting for you just past those trees." She winked, a mischievous glint in her eyes. "He's been pacing since sunrise for you to finally arrive."

She and Dela exchanged conspiratorial looks, and I smiled at their playfulness, nodding before I continued through the woods.

The moment I stepped into the clearing, I spotted him instantly. Manakel stood at the edge of the trees, his back to me, shadows curling faintly at his feet. His posture was still, but not relaxed, and his presence felt heavier, as if the quiet around him carried the weight of something unspoken.

"You're early," he said without turning, his voice low but steady.

"I couldn't sleep," I replied. "I thought I'd make the most of the morning."

He finally faced me, his eyes sweeping over me with a quiet intensity—like he was peeling back the layers of who I was without needing to ask.

"That's good," he said simply. "We'll need all the time we can get."

I adjusted the strap of my bag. "My family is planning to spend the afternoon together for my early birthday celebration. So, I'll need to be back by lunch."

"Then let's make it count. We're heading back to the creek. You'll need to strengthen your mind for what you'll face in the river, and this will help you tap into your control, even when you can't decipher what's real."

We walked in silence, the trees parting as the creek came into view, sunlight dancing over the current. I edged closer without hesitation, the cold biting through my clothes like needles, but I didn't flinch. Manakel was beside me, so focusing on his steady presence was enough.

"During the Imbe Rite," he said, "your mind will deceive you. It will reveal things you fear the most, and you'll need to learn to tell the difference between what's real and what's not."

I nodded, bracing myself as I stepped closer to the water's edge. His eyes held mine for a second longer, a silent warning that whatever lay ahead wouldn't be easy. But I was ready to face it. And this time, I meant it.

The forest exhaled around us, the hush of leaves and distant hum of crickets folding into a stillness that mirrored the quiet between us. I sat on the mossy bank, letting out a breath I hadn't realized I was holding. The silence wasn't empty—it was full and steadying, but it didn't erase the unease inside me. It merely dulled the edges of it, made it easier to breathe.

Beside me, Manakel stood with his back half-turned, eyes fixed on the slow-moving creek. His eyes tracked the water's path like it carried answers I couldn't yet see. His presence grounded me, but it didn't erase the unease that stirred beneath my skin.

"Does it…" I hesitated, tightening the cloak around me like it could shield me from the question I wasn't sure I wanted to ask. "Does it ever stop? Will facing the forest on the other side of the river be like this, too? Will I continue being tested until they decide I'm worthy?"

The words hung in the air, fragile and uncertain, but I needed to voice them. I needed to know if this relentless push and pull —the battle between fear and resolve —would ever let up.

Manakel's gaze shifted toward me, his expression sharp beneath the dim light cutting through the canopy. He studied me carefully, his eyes lingering as if weighing how much truth I could bear. When he finally spoke, his voice was low, each word measured and deliberate.

"Yes. No one fully knows what the gods look for in the Rite when determining your gift, but there will be multiple trials. And not just in the river."

I waited, but the pause that followed stretched too long.

"The forest on either side will provide different trials," he added, glancing toward the trees, like the forest itself might be listening. "Here, the tests are designed to break you, but only if you let them. They'll dig into your fears, and force you to confront every shadow you've tucked away."

Different. The word gave me little comfort. I swallowed hard. I remembered the visions I'd seen in the water last time—the flickers of grief and truth I hadn't been ready for. They still clung to me like damp smoke.

I swallowed hard, remembering the visions I'd seen in the water last time we were here—visions that still clung to the edges of my mind like ghosts unwilling to let go.

"But on the other side…" he continued, quieter now, "*that's* where the unknown waits. It won't prey on fear the same way. It'll demand something else. Everything you've learned, everything you are. Strength, yes—but also clarity. Purpose. Because the gods aren't the only ones waiting there."

He turned to face me fully then, his face heavy with warning. "The immortals will be waiting. And some of them will be hoping for you to fail."

A cold prickle ran down my spine at the mention of the immortals. I had imagined their presence during the Rite, and once crossing over into Dermaine, but hearing him confirm their presence made the threat feel more tangible, more dangerous.

I nodded slowly, the weight of his words pressing into me like stones in my pockets. It wasn't the answer I'd been hoping for, but deep down, I knew it was the one I needed. No sugar-coated promises. No comforting lies. Just the truth—stark and unforgiving, so I could go into this knowing what I'd be up against.

I pressed my palm to the earth, grounding myself in the cool, damp moss. "Then I have no choice but to be ready," I murmured, the quiet declaration more for myself than for him.

Manakel's eyes softened, just slightly, as if he recognized the shift happening within me—the way the fear was slowly hardening into resolve, fragile yet growing.

"You will be," he said. "Or you wouldn't have made it this far."

The wind picked up around us, tugging gently at my hair as I turned my focus back to the water. The creek mirrored the canopy above, the reflection of the trees rippling in and out of focus with each passing current.

I didn't know if I fully believed him yet. But I knew more than anything, I needed to.

"Are you ready to try again?" he asked, voice soft but anchored with certainty, and already knew I wasn't. "It's okay if you need more time."

"No," I said, the word rasping out, torn between defiance and truth. "I'm *not* ready. And I don't think I ever will be. But the Rite isn't waiting for me to be ready."

I drew in a slow breath, straightening. "In a day and a half, I'll be standing at the edge of that river, whether I'm ready or not. Time isn't a luxury we have."

My voice wavered, but the truth in it felt solid beneath my trembling hands. He studied me for a long moment before his fingers uncurled, releasing me with the faintest brush against my skin. There was no disappointment in his eyes, only understanding; a quiet acceptance that I didn't need coddling.

Then he nodded. "Okay. If you're sure." A pause, then gently: "Let's try this again."

I wasn't sure. I didn't know what *sure* felt like anymore, only that I couldn't falter. Not anymore. Not when every step I took forward was one more inch between danger and saving the people waiting for me back home.

I gave a faint nod and inhaled sharply, closing my eyes as I turned back to the water. My legs ached, my pulse a slow echo of fear, but I kept walking anyway. The waves greeted me like an old memory, cold and constant. The forest quieted around me, as if the trees themselves were holding their breath, watching to see if I would shatter or endure.

I let the cold seep in. I let myself sink, not physically, but somewhere deeper, surrendering to the flow of the water as it tugged at me like it wanted to pull me under entirely.

Manakel stayed on the bank, his shadow stretched across the water, a silent tether behind me. He didn't speak. He didn't need to. I knew this choice was mine alone.

I closed my eyes.

In, out. In, out. I focused on my breath, letting the world fall away as I waded deeper, the creek swallowing my knees and chilling me to the core. I sank again, surrendering to the pull of the water, willing myself to stay calm even as I felt the familiar shift of reality slipping away.

The world around me blurred. The creek, the trees, the distant chirp of birds, all of it faded into silence.

At first, the visions came softly, like a whisper at the edge of my mind. They weren't hazy or distant like a dream but sharp. Vivid, like I was standing in the heart of them, experiencing it through my own eyes. I stood at the edge of Laochra, the gentle hum of the village wrapping around me. For a moment, everything was still. Familiar. The scent of burning wood, the rustle of barn animals in the morning, and the warm voices of neighbors exchanging stories.

I was standing in the village that had always been my safe haven, but it also wasn't. There was something different, too; this wasn't the village I knew. The air was thick with tension and fear, and I innately knew something was wrong. Smoke curled from rooftops, and darkness loomed over the cobbled streets while the faint cries of voices floated toward me. But my feet felt rooted to the ground, unwilling to carry me forward.

As if taking me closer into the vision, I saw my family standing in the center of the village square. My father, his broad shoulders hunched protectively in front of my mother like a shield. Baren and Wren were flanking their sides, expressions grim but determined. But they weren't alone.

Figures draped in black cloaks circled them, their faces hidden beneath hoods, but all I could focus on were their hands. Hands slick with red, they were closing in around my family. Thick ribbons of crimson dripped from their fingers like ink, and I knew without a doubt what the cries had been about.

I tried to scream. The force of it burned in my chest, but no sound escaped. The water swallowed my voice, wrapped around my lungs, and trapped me in suffocating silence.

I looked around frantically, trying to find someone who could help, who could get to my family in time. But they weren't screaming. They weren't even running. They just... stood there, silent and frozen, as if resigned to whatever fate approached them.

Wren's eyes lifted, locking on mine as the look he gave me sank like a blade into my chest. It wasn't fear or panic. It was blame. And I innately knew that I must have failed if this was their fate. I could feel his disappointment a a voice that sounded like his crept into my mind.

You should've been stronger.

If you'd been prepared, this wouldn't be happening to us.

Our fate should never have been left in your hands.

Our blood is on your hands.

I looked down frantically, my hands shaking as I tried to get closer or intervene. Anything to stop the exact thing I was fighting to prevent. And then, like a beacon of hope, I saw my grandmother. I stretched to get a closer look, to urge her to intervene, but she too felt different. Instead of her usual earthy dresses or aprons, she was wearing the same dark hooded cloak and was standing on the wrong side of this.

She lingered behind the cloaked figures surrounding my family, her face hidden in shadow except for the faint trace of blood that lined her lips. She let the figures around her lunge for my family as I screamed in horror.

Why was she just standing there? Why wasn't anyone stopping them?

She shifted slightly, her icy blue eyes gleaming as they locked on mine while she lifted a blood-slick dagger to her lips and smiled while licking it clean.

I tried to move, to run toward them, but my feet refused to move. I was anchored in place, the cold pressing against me until it felt suffocating. I looked around and saw the piles of bodies, all brutally drained of their blood and life force as these creatures grew stronger and stronger.

A cold, hollow terror spread through me. I thrashed against the current holding me in place, but no matter how hard I pushed, I couldn't move. Couldn't change anything. The scene before me repeated, looping endlessly—the same helpless struggle, the same pitiful failure.

I squeezed my eyes shut, fighting the panic rising like a storm in my throat. *This isn't real. My family is safe. This isn't real. My family is safe.*

I repeated the words in my head, knowing it couldn't be. Even if it *felt* more real than anything I'd experienced before.

Manakel's words echoed faintly in my mind: *'Your mind will deceive you. It will reveal things you fear the most.'*

I struggled against the restraint of the water, trying to break free, but remained frozen, forced to watch as my family's blood pooled beneath them and watch the life drain right before my eyes.

I let out a shuddering breath, remembering the truth—the thing that mattered most. *My family is safe. This is fear, not truth.*

The thought cracked something open, and the vision flickered. The cloaked figures faltered, and the darkness began to fray, unraveling at the seams.

The village dissolved, and I was standing on a riverbank. The once-lush forest surrounding the water withered, its vibrant green draining to lifeless gray. The flowing water dried before my eyes, revealing the cracked, barren earth below.

More hooded figures emerged from the far bank, hordes of them and their shadows stretching endlessly toward me. They crept forward, closer to the village, closer to everything I cared about and what was left of my home.

I dropped to my knees, desperately digging into the earth, trying to restore the barrier, to reach the water that had kept them out all these years. My hands clawed at the dirt, but when I looked down, instead of being covered with mud, they were soaked with blood. And it wasn't my own.

I stumbled back, staring at the crimson stains dripping from my fingers. Fingers that were no longer mine, or human, but elongated, clawed, and pale as bone. These were hands that belonged to an immortal. Proof I had become one of them. The very thing I feared.

I looked down to find the lifeless body of someone I knew all too well. My brother Wren, my best friend and confidant, was lying beside me, dull and hollow. His blood was on my hands.

I was an evil, bloodthirsty, immortal. The monster parents whispered about when warning their children not to stray too far from home. The vile creatures in the old stories who brought destruction and death to our lands.

Bodies were piled at my feet. Familiar faces. Neighbors. Friends. Silence settled over the wreckage, and as I looked beyond it, there was nothing left but silence, shame, and failure.

This isn't real, a voice whispered through the fog in my mind.

Not all immortals are like this. I am not evil.

I gripped onto that thought like a rope, desperately repeating it over and over. It wasn't just something I was hoping was real; it was something I felt deep inside, something I clung to as truth.

I *would* stop this.

I *would* cross the river and make sure this never happened.

I *would* prove that fate wasn't set in stone and that not all evil won in the end.

The hooded figures drew closer, trying to lure me in and join them. I squeezed my eyes shut, blocking them out. A faint song being hummed called out to me, and everything in me wanted to go to it. To follow the familiar sound, but I couldn't. I knew the minute I did, I would seal my fate.

Instead, I tried to drown out the melody, repeating over and over, *This isn't real. I am not evil.*

The more I chanted the words, the truer they felt, and then all of a sudden the vision cracked. Shattered like glass.

I gasped, breaking through the surface of the water, breath tearing from my throat, and eyes blinking rapidly before coming back to reality. My lungs were heaving like I'd been underwater for hours. Out of nowhere, Manakel appeared, his hand reaching to steady me as I stumbled forward.

"Breathe," he said, calm but firm.

His hands were gripping my arms as I swayed. I hadn't realized how weak my legs had become, trembling beneath me like they could give out at any moment.

He guided me toward the bank, and I collapsed onto the grass, shivering despite the warmth of the rising sun. My pulse thundered in my ears, and I felt lightheaded. The vision clung to me, damp and suffocating like the creek still hadn't let go.

"Here," he murmured, retrieving the thermos from my bag. He pressed it gently into my hands, his fingers brushing over mine briefly. The warmth was instant, not just from the tea but from his touch, like an anchor tethering me back to reality.

I took a slow sip, the familiar, earthy taste of yerba mate grounding me. The taste reminded me of home, of my grandmother humming softly while brewing it. I kept drinking, the warmth chasing away the icy grip of the vision, still shaken from what I saw.

Manakel crouched beside me, watching closely. His presence was calm, but I could tell he was assessing, reading every slight tremble, every exhale, each flicker of doubt lingering in my eyes.

"You saw something," he said quietly.

I nodded, setting the thermos down carefully. "I saw them. My family. The village. Everything was destroyed, and everyone was dead. I saw the river drying up, and…" I hesitated, struggling to voice the rest. "I was one of them. One of the monsters responsible for it."

He didn't flinch. "The water shows what you fear most, Raine. It isn't a prophecy, but it's not a lie, either. That fear exists inside you; it's what you fear becoming. And coming to terms with your new identity as an immortal is part of your Imbe Rite."

I swallowed the lump in my throat, meeting his gaze. "I refuse to become a monster. I won't let it happen or let immortality control me."

His eyes met mine, and a small, almost imperceptible nod of approval crossed his face. "Good. Hold on to that confidence. You'll need it."

His tone was quiet. Steady.

But something about it unnerved me because I knew there were still things he was holding back. Truths he hadn't shared. And we were running out of time.

The creek hummed in the background, water slipping over stones like a lullaby meant only for the trees.

"You did well." He said, and I simply nodded. There wasn't much else to say.

I reached for my bag, but Manakel handed me the blanket, helping me pull it over my shoulders without a word. His eyes stayed fixed on me, studying me like he was waiting to see if I would shatter or hold together.

"So…" I hesitated, pulling the blanket tighter around me. "Will it feel like that when I'm in the river? Will it pull those same fears out of me, or will it be something different?"

The words felt heavy as they left my mouth, like speaking them aloud might somehow make the river more real, more dangerous.

"The river is a threshold," he said carefully. "Whatever you face will be born of the unknown on the other side, showing you things you've never experienced, creating fears you never thought possible. That's why these practice tests matter. So that when you face the unknown, you'll know you have the strength to meet and conquer it."

I nodded, the weight of his words settling deep in my bones. It wasn't the answer I wanted, but it was the truth. And I could live with the truth, even if it left a bitter taste behind. The image of my family—still, helpless, drenched in blood—clung stubbornly to the edges of my mind. I gripped the thermos tighter, grounding myself in the heat radiating through the metal.

I could feel Manakel's focus on me, quiet and steady as if he could sense the thoughts racing behind my eyes. There was something about his presence that made it easier to breathe, even as fear clawed at the edges of my chest.

After a moment, I glanced at him, searching his expression. "Did you see it?" I asked hesitantly. "What I saw in the water… did you see any of it too?"

His gaze lowered slightly, regret flickering behind his dark eyes. "No, Amadán," he said softly. "I don't have the ability to see what you see. But by your screams and thrashing, I can only assume it was meant to torture you. I've heard screams like that before, but not in a long time." His voice dropped at the last part as if the idea alone unsettled him.

"Pretty much," I muttered, forcing a weak smile. I could see the empathy in his eyes, the way they softened despite the sharpness of his features. And in that moment, it hit me—how much he must have endured and seen to be standing here now.

I thought of his story. His parents. The way his world had crumbled in front of him without warning. There had been no illusions for him, no twisted reflections in the water, just cold, unforgiving reality and loss of the two most important people in his life. And yet, here he was, helping me face shadows of something far less real but just as terrifying. No one was ever prepared to lose their family, and I wasn't about to make my vision a reality. That was why I was completing the Rite in the first place. To save them from that fate. I only wish Manakel could have had the same option before losing his own family.

A pang of guilt tightened in my chest, and I lowered my eyes. "I'm sorry," I whispered, the words slipping out before I could stop them. "I didn't mean to pry into your past earlier. I can't imagine what it was like for you. Seeing your parents…I mean, seeing them vanish for real," I hesitated, unsure if I should say more. "I didn't mean to bring it up again. I just—"

His eyes darkened slightly, and for a brief moment, the mask he always wore cracked, letting something unspoken slip through. He looked away, his jaw tight as if weighing how much to say.

"The past leaves marks on all of us," he said finally, his voice quiet and rough. "But every scar reminds us we're still here and is proof we survived."

He glanced at his hands, calloused, worn, then flexed them slowly.

"Gather enough scars," he continued, meeting my face, "and your skin will become thick enough that nothing else can get through."

The words lingered between us, sinking in like stones dropped into the creek. I wasn't sure I believed that, not fully. But somehow, his quiet resilience, his refusal to let his scars break him, sparked something in me. If he could endure, maybe I could too.

I nodded once, slowly. And held onto that small glimmer of hope, because sometimes hope was all you had.

26. A Lesson In Survival

The sun had shifted, dipping through the trees and turning the creek gold. Streaks of light slipped between the trees in long, fading ribbons, and shadows pooled across the mossy banks, stretching wider by the minute. And still, I hadn't moved.

I didn't know how long I'd been standing there. Time had blurred the moment I stepped into the water, and now the day was already slipping away. But the longer I stalled, the less of it I had. Two hours. That's all the time I had left before I needed to be home. The knot in my chest tightened. Two hours wasn't a lot of time to gain control and learn how to silence the visions threatening to shake me, but it was all I had left.

With it being the day before my Rite, I didn't feel any more prepared than I had a week ago, though I still wasn't sure what exactly I was supposed to be preparing for.

I wiped the lingering drops of water from my skin, pushing damp hair back from my face as I stood. The creek's icy bite still lingered in my bones, but I wasn't finished. Not yet.

When I tucked the thermos back into my bag, he handed me the blanket without a word. I wrapped it around my shoulders, the gesture anchoring me in a way I didn't expect. He didn't look away. His eyes stayed fixed on me, studying me like he was waiting to see if I would shatter or hold together.

Feeling a renewed surge of purpose, I asked, "So… what's next? More visions in the water? Or do we do something a little less terrifying, like sparring with daggers?" I tried to muster up a grin, a thread of humor, but it was barely masking my nerves.

He arched a brow, that ever-serious expression softening just enough to spark a glimmer of amusement. "If you're up for it," he said, "we'll go back to the basics. Technique. Footwork. Control. Assuming your adrenaline isn't still crashing from the visions."

I nodded, already reaching for my bag. The familiar weight of my twin daggers met my palms like old friends. I gripped them, letting the metal's cool solidity ground me further. "I'm good," I said, more conviction in my voice than I actually felt. "I've got about two hours left to outsmart my mind, slash illusions in half, and maybe learn a new move or two on defense."

His mouth quirked into something close to a smile. "Ambitious. Let's see what you've got, Amadán."

Despite the lingering tremors in my limbs, I squared my shoulders and held the blades up, determined to face whatever challenges came next. Feeling steadier, I pulled the daggers free, their blades catching the dim light as I held them out to him.

Manakel stepped closer, taking the blades with practiced ease, turning them over in his palms as if reacquainting himself with old friends. His fingers brushed against mine for the briefest moment, sending a small shock of warmth through me.

"Before we start with these, maybe we should talk about what you should pack for tomorrow. You'll only be able to bring what you can handle carrying, and trust me, a lighter bag is better, especially while you wade through the water."

He leaned in slightly, lowering his voice as if sharing a secret. "But the good news is… I'll be nearby. Close enough to help if you need it. There's no rule against *that*."

I couldn't help but smile at the whispered offer of his help; gods knew I needed it.

"Good. I'll take all the help I can get," I replied, feeling a small but welcome lightness settle over me. The thought of Manakel nearby, even if I had to cross the actual river alone, made the whole thing feel a little less daunting. Like he was an anchor just out of reach but tethered to me all the same.

His eyes pierced into mine, but he gave a small nod of approval before setting my daggers down. "Let's focus on essentials first. It'll keep your mind occupied on what you *can* control. That might help balance out the unknowns I can see weighing you down." His calm tone wrapped around me like a shield, something steady to hold onto.

I listened intently as he rattled off items. Dried food, pouches I could fill with water to hydrate, loose herbs, and healing salves. He also mentioned I bring a personal item to ground me in case the river tried to play tricks and deceive me. My fingers drifted instinctively to my pocket, where the flint stone from my grandmother usually stayed tucked, smooth and familiar against my skin. It was a gift from her on my thirteenth birthday, and I never left home without it, keeping it hidden in my pocket like a silent good luck charm.

I hesitated. "Not my bow?"

His reply was instant. "No. You won't need to hunt; you just need something to protect yourself. Daggers are lighter to carry and faster to wield."

I forced a nod, even as irritation prickled beneath my skin. Lately, I'd spent more time with the bow than the blades, convincing myself the hours mattered. But archery had proven just as insignificant—at least for me. My aim never quite found its mark, and the bow wasn't even mine to bring. It belonged to Wren.

It was probably for the best, anyway. Daggers had always been the thing my hands trusted most, the weight I could wield without second-guessing.

Still, there was a difference between sparring in the safety of home and carrying steel into the unknown. One I suddenly wasn't so sure I was ready for.

Completely ignoring my internal battle, he added, "Your cloak might weigh you down in the water, but with the autumn weather approaching, you'll need it to ward off the chill. And you should pack some dry clothes to change into, too."

I mentally filed each instruction away like a checklist I couldn't afford to forget. Once we'd gone over the list three times, having me repeat it back to him like a petulant child, he returned his focus to the daggers. He plucked one off the ground, twirling it between his fingers with ease before holding it out to me.

"Now," he said, a flicker of amusement crossing his face, "show me what you've got. Your stance wasn't terrible last time, but we need to work on that grip. I was able to disarm you way too easily."

I groaned, but there was no denying it. "You don't have to sound so smug about it."

"Just an honest observation." He grinned as I rolled my eyes.

The next hour passed in a blur of repetition. Stance. Strike. Reset. I practiced, feeling the burn in my arms and the ache in my fingers as we went over the same moves again and again. His voice was quiet yet commanding, correcting my form with the brush of a hand on my elbow, the nudge of his foot against mine. They were subtle, but controlled, and little by little, I felt myself improving. His presence beside me felt like a shield, reinforcing my resolve every time I started to doubt.

The clearing was quiet, save for the rhythmic rustle of leaves and the occasional clink of steel meeting steel. I adjusted my grip on the dagger, *again*, feeling the familiar bite of its hilt against my palm. Sweat clung to the back of my neck, and my breath came quicker than I'd like to admit.

"Widen your stance," Manakel said, circling me. "You're too narrow, you'll lose balance the second someone pushes off-center."

I rolled my eyes but obeyed, shifting my weight onto the balls of my feet. "You say that like someone's planning to shove me."

He didn't answer, just lunged. His blade caught mine with a sharp tap, the force jolting up my arm. I twisted to block the second strike, then stumbled as his foot hooked behind mine and sent me flat on my back.

My breath came out in a grunt as I stared up at the sky, dagger still clenched in my hand. "Unnecessary."

"Realistic," he replied, offering a hand. I ignored it and pushed myself up instead.

He waited until I found my footing again, then nodded. "Again."

This time, I was ready. Our blades met with a satisfying clang, and I moved faster, lowering my center, watching his shoulders, adjusting my grip the way he'd shown me. But even then, his dagger slid up my blade and knocked it clean from my hand with a swift twist.

I stared at the weapon skidding across the dirt, lips tightening. "Okay. I don't get it. If the Rite is mostly mental, visions, illusions, or whatever, why am I spending my time getting taken down with dagger drills?"

He didn't look amused. "Because the journey to and from the river still counts. The threats you face along the way will be very real and very physical."

I bent down, retrieving my blade. The metal felt heavier now, like it knew how useless I was with it. "Right. So I'm supposed to just fend off shadow monsters and Eldren with steel blades and a half-decent pivot step?"

His face remained expressionless. "Regardless, you'll need to be able to defend yourself."

That caught me off guard. I tried to pass it off with a crooked smile. "But why? You'll be there and you've got wings, and big, scary shadows remember?"

He tilted his head, gaze sharpening. "You need to be prepared for anything that can happen, Raine. The Rite is unpredictable, and I can't promise I'll be there every moment. You have to be able to hold your own. *That* is part of the test, too."

Unease settled in my chest, but I nodded. "Okay. Let's go again."

We reset, circling. My fingers ached from gripping the hilt too tightly, but I forced myself to relax, to move in smoother steps. I watched his feet this time, not his blade, and when he feinted left, I pivoted fast, stepping inside his reach and ducking low.

Then, just to mess with him, I let my hand brush lightly across his waist, like a distraction, and smirked as his eyes flicked down in momentary confusion. That second was all I needed. I swept my blade up in a mock strike to his ribs, not enough to hurt, but enough to catch him off guard and drop his blade.

He froze. Then stepped back, eyebrows raised. "Not bad."

"Not bad?" I said, grinning, "How about admitting I got the upper hand on that one?"

"You got lucky." He murmured, but his mouth twitched like he wanted to smile.

I sheathed the blade, chest rising and falling with exertion. "Luck doesn't exist without preparation meeting the right moment, right?"

He didn't answer right away. Just looked at me, a flicker of something unreadable passing behind his eyes. Then quietly, he said, "You're closer to being ready than you think."

I couldn't stop the smile that crept onto my face. His quiet confidence in me felt dangerous, like it might become something I started to rely on and couldn't bear to lose. *Even after this was all over.*

"Alright, Amadán," he continued, brushing the dirt from his hands. "It's almost midday. I don't want you to be late for your own birthday celebration."

I blinked. "Right." I slid the daggers into my bag, cheeks flushing as a pang of guilt twisted through me. They'd notice if I was late. They always did. "They'll probably send a search party," I joked weakly.

A pang of longing twisted in my stomach. In a different world, maybe I'd invite him along, say he was a new friend from Ceannairí. But that was too risky. Besides, I wasn't sure he could even pass as human, even if he hid his wings and shadows. Still, I felt the tug of something forming between us, something that had grown steadily over the past few days.

Especially since our kiss.

And then, before I could say anything else, or beg him for one more time, I blurted, "It's an early celebration anyway. I'll be with you tomorrow on the real day. Stuck in the in-between, completing the Rite and trying not to drown or die."

I meant it as a joke, but the words hung a little too heavy in the air. His expression shifted, quieting into something almost tender.

"You won't die," he said softly. "The river will try to shake you, but it won't break you. You're stronger than you know."

His words lingered in the space between us, wrapping around me like armor. Quiet. Sure. Steady.

And I wanted to believe him. Gods help me, I *really* did.

The sun hung low, casting an amber glow over the clearing as I followed Manakel through the trees. The quiet rustle of leaves beneath our boots felt peaceful—an echo of peace in a world that hadn't offered me much of it lately.

I hadn't realized how much I needed this, the distraction, the stillness, the steady rhythm of training. It was something I could control, something I could focus on besides the looming weight of crossing the river and becoming something I still feared.

Still, as my hand brushed the hilt of one of the daggers tucked into my belt, a question crept in.

What was the point of all this? Nothing I'd learned could outmatch the river. A dagger wouldn't protect me from the Eldren, or from whatever nightmares the crossing might conjure. I doubted it would even slow them down.

The river had taken countless lives before, both mortal and immortal, so why would I be any different? And did they know for sure, the protection tonic my grandmother was preparing would actually work?

But I didn't ask. I didn't want to ruin the moment or remind either of us how little time I had left, and how much I still didn't know.

I shifted, fingers tightening on the strap of my satchel. "I appreciate everything you're doing for me, Manakel. I really don't know what I'd do without you."

His expression shifted slightly, "You'd manage. I'm just here to guide you. The rest... that's all you."

I swallowed against the lump rising in my throat. There wasn't anything I could say to that. So I didn't. I clutched the bag on my shoulder and let out a slow breath.

"I should go," I said instead, voice rougher than I intended. "Before my mom starts wondering if I'm lost in the woods or something."

I turned toward the edge of the woods leading to my backyard, only to stop short. My family had already gathered outside, circled around the fire pit. I could hear their laughter before I saw them, warm, familiar, real. They were facing away from me, starting to roast food. But if I walked straight out of the trees, someone would see me. They'd ask where I'd been. Ask questions I wasn't ready to answer.

Pacing, I tried to think of a solution to get around them, but nothing came to mind. Behind me, a rustle of movement stopped my movements.

"Problem, Amadán?"

I didn't answer. Just stared at the flicker of firelight ahead.

"Ah," he murmured, stepping up beside me. "You can't exactly stroll out of the woods without raising suspicion, can you?"

I shot him a look. "It would definitely... complicate things."

He smirked, stepping in close enough that I could feel the warmth of him as he whispered in my ear. "If only you knew someone with wings."

I gasped and my eyes widened, but before I could react, I was swept into his arms without warning. The ground vanished beneath us as air rushed past my ears, trees blurring into streaks of green and gold. I let out a startled yelp, instinctively clutching his neck for safety.

By the time I caught my breath, we'd landed on the opposite side of the house, shielded from view. I stumbled, grabbing his arm to steady myself.

"Next time, a little warning would be nice," I muttered, still shaken.

He chuckled softly, steadying me with a hand. "Where's the fun in that?"

I huffed, brushing down my cloak. "Yeah, *fun*, sure," I grumbled, rolling my eyes, but a reluctant smile tugged at my lips. I paused, "Thanks," I said softly, looking up at him. "For everything."

His expression softened. "You're welcome," he said, his voice barely above a whisper. "I'll see you tomorrow. Or tonight... if the shadows call you back."

I hesitated. Then nodded once before turning toward the house. The sound of my family's laughter grew louder, melding with the lingering echoes of my racing heartbeat. I forced one foot in front of the other, following the smell of roasted vegetables and pine smoke.

As I stepped into view, my mother looked up, her face flashing with relief. "There you are! We were about to send out your brothers with torches."

I smiled, forcing calm into my voice. "Got caught up with preparations. But I'm here now and am starving."

My father handed me a skewer of vegetables, and I took it with a grateful nod, sinking into the low seat beside him. The warmth of the fire soaked into my skin, but it was the closeness of my family that soothed the restless part of me.

Their company reminded me why I was doing the Imbe Rite in the first place. It was all for them, to protect them.

Yes, tomorrow everything would change, but for now, just for tonight, I had my family. And that was enough.

27. A Birthday Like No Other

The sun dipped behind the treetops, casting streaks of violet and amber across the sky. Hints of pinkish gold hues lingered on the horizon, slowly surrendering to dusk. Overhead, the moon emerged, bold and bright, a waxing gibbous.

I'd never paid much attention to moon phases before. But something about the timing of this one tugged at me, like the sky was in on a secret I hadn't quite pieced together. Waxing moons meant growing, pulling toward a breaking point, but not fully there yet. It felt ironic, fitting even, that the moon was stuck in the same limbo I was. Not quite ready, but moving forward anyway.

We huddled closer to the fire pit, wrapped in thick blankets that smelled of cedar, wool, and lingering smoke. The flames danced in the growing dark, casting dancing shadows on the ground as my father turned the skewers with practiced ease. The scent of roasted lamb, sweet root vegetables, and the creamy weight of Mom's coddle filled the air, familiar and grounding.

I stretched my legs out toward the fire, the heat licking at my boots.

These were the kinds of evenings I wanted to freeze in time, the simple, quiet ones when the world felt small and safe. Where nothing else seemed to exist beyond the circle of warmth and laughter.

Wren sat across from me, his cheeks flushed with laughter, a half-burnt piece of squash skewered on a stick between his fingers. "You know," he started, eyes dancing with mischief, "I was just thinking about that time we trained all day, and before we knew it, we were at the edge of the woods, practically touching the trees. Remember that?"

My heart stilled for half a beat. Why was Wren mentioning the woods right now? I tightened the blanket around my shoulders, careful to keep my expression neutral. I knew exactly what story he was talking about, but I gave a nonchalant shrug. "Which time?"

He jabbed the stick toward the trees lining the edge of the clearing, where I had *just* stood with Manakel. "You were maybe twelve, and couldn't even look at a dagger without flinching. But as we loomed closer to the trees, something changed." His eyes glinted with the weight of the memory. "I saw it happen, like a switch flipped, and all of a sudden, you weren't scared anymore. I swear, something clicked, and you finally realized you were allowed to be dangerous."

A soft blush crept up my cheeks, though I wasn't entirely sure if it was embarrassment or pride. "Dangerous might be a stretch," I muttered, fiddling with the edge of the blanket.

"No, he's right," Dad chimed in, his deep voice steady and full of fondness. "I remember that day, too. You weren't the same after that, like you'd finally stepped into your purpose and saw you were a force to be reckoned with."

Wren chuckled, nudging me with his elbow. "And honestly, I was a little worried. You nearly knocked me flat on my back. I wasn't ready for you to get that good that quickly; it was like you were fearless. I refused to spar with you for over a week after that."

I rolled my eyes, shaking my head with a laugh. "You were caught off guard. That's the only reason I got the upper hand."

Baren, who had been quietly listening, leaned forward, his face softening as his eyes filled with nostalgia. "I remember you being fearless long before that. Even before you knew what it meant." His voice carried a quiet affection, "You were maybe six, standing at the window while Wren and I raced in the yard. I think you were supposed to be inside helping Mom, but all I remember is you bursting out the back door, determined to join us because you didn't want to be left out."

I smiled faintly, the memory filtering back with surprising clarity. I had pressed my palms to the cool glass, heart pounding with longing, watching them run until the temptation to join in became too much. The second Mom sighed and nodded toward the door, I was gone, racing right alongside them. I remember us running for hours, my grandmother holding her journal in her lap, tallying up our wins for each round. My legs were shorter, but I was determined to win, at least once.

Baren's lips curved as he added, "I'll admit it now, you won fair and square that day. Wren and I tried to outrun you, but you were too fast."

I raised an eyebrow, staring at them both. "Wait… are you telling me you didn't *let* me win? That you didn't slow down because I was your little sister?"

Wren snickered, raising his hands in mock surrender. "We figured it was about time we told you. You earned that victory fair and square."

I groaned, swatting his arm playfully. "Unbelievable. I held onto that for years, thinking I got pity points and mad you never gave me the chance to truly prove myself."

Baren grinned slyly. "To be fair, you got your revenge by ruining dinner that night, remember? We came in starving, hoping for something hearty, but the pies you helped Mom make were so salty we nearly passed out."

The memory of earlier that day flooded back, and I laughed despite the heat rushing to my cheeks. Mom chuckled along, shaking her head fondly, as if she too was reliving the moment. "Yup. That was the last time I let your sister help me cook unsupervised."

The warm echo of laughter filled the air, wrapping around us like a second blanket. I leaned back, watching the flames flicker higher, and let the familiar sound of my family wash over me. Moments like this felt like treasures I wanted to lock away, like glass figurines too fragile to touch but too beautiful to forget. I didn't know how many more nights like this I'd get in my life, so I wanted to savor tonight as much as possible.

I caught my mom watching me from across the fire, her gaze soft but distant, as if she were memorizing my face the way I was memorizing hers. I smiled back, hoping she wouldn't see the tightness and dishonesty lingering behind it.

The truth gnawed quietly at the edges of my mind; my Imbe Rite was only a day away. But for now, I held onto the present. To the feeling of being surrounded by the fire and my family. The looming challenge of facing the river and all its uncertainties felt a little less daunting at this moment. I wasn't focused on my future; I was celebrating the time I had left with the people I loved most.

I would be leaving home tomorrow, and although I wasn't headed to Ceannairí, I still hoped our last night together would be one we'd always remember. As the evening air cooled, my mom and grandmother slipped into the house, returning moments later with dessert. They held a platter with my favorite carrot loaf, topped with a layer of thick frosting and three candles. The familiarity tugged at something deep inside me, a bittersweet ache I wasn't ready to confront.

This was our yearly ritual and had been since I was born. Three candles, three wishes—one for the present, one for those around me, and one for my future.

Dad rose first, his voice carrying the weight of tradition as he began the familiar toast, his words warm and steady like they always were:
"May your heart be light and happy,
May your smile stay big and wide,
And may a wild heart like you,
always know you've got family by your side."
The corners of my mouth tugged into a soft smile as I leaned forward, letting the warmth of the candles brush my cheeks. My eyes fluttered closed for a brief moment as I blew them out, each breath carrying with

it the weight of my wishes.

One for the present—to get more answers, to feel prepared for what I'd face in the rite.

One for those around me— for their safety and ignorance while I was gone.

And one for my future— that I would make it across the river, have the gods deem me worthy of immortality, and grant a useful gift, so I would make it to the Queen.

My grandmother disappeared inside to slice the loaf, and just as the quiet settled around us again, Wren stretched, cracking his knuckles with a mischievous glint in his eye. "Alright, Wildheart," he said, crossing his arms. "Ready for your birthday bumps?"

I groaned dramatically, shooting a pleading glance toward Mom, who shrugged but smiled knowingly, like this wasn't a ridiculous part of my birthday each year.

"Aren't we a little old for this?" I pleaded.

Wren shrugged, already motioning for Baren to join him, and as they stood, I threw my hands up, trying to stall them so I could bargain a way out of it. "*Technically*, I'm not eighteen yet. Twenty-six more hours to go! Bumps before the actual day? That has to be bad luck, right?"

Wren feigned thoughtfulness, stroking his chin. "Hmm… Maybe. But it's worth the risk."

I shot to my feet, taking a step back, but their grins told me I wasn't escaping this. At least not without a fight. It was all in good fun, and the playful chase around the fire pit left us breathless and laughing by the time she returned with the sliced loaf. She set it down just as my brothers caught me, lifting me off the ground and proceeding to flip me upside down. Each of them held a leg and then slowly, and gentler than any previous year, they 'bumped' my head on the ground, counting from one to eighteen.

I don't know when or how the birthday bumps tradition started, but they had been doing this every year for as long as I could remember. As a kid, I found it hilarious to be flipped upside down, and usually tried to squirm my way out of their hold before they reached my number. But this year, as much as I protested, I wanted to hold onto the memory also. It was probably the last time I'd ever experience this.

As we settled back down to eat dessert, the atmosphere shifted subtly. The fire burned low, plates were passed around, and the conversation drifted into easy reminiscing. Stories of past birthdays, funny adventures, and shared memories that made up every moment of my life before today. But beneath the lightheartedness, a strange sense of finality crept in. This was the last night I'd have with them before the rite. Tomorrow night would bring everything to the edge of change.

I lingered longer than usual as we packed up, trying to absorb every sound, every look, and every flicker of familiarity. When I finally hugged Dad, Wren, and Baren goodnight, I held on just a little tighter, hoping they didn't notice the slight tremble in my grip.

I turned to head toward the house, but Dad's hand found my shoulder, pulling me back gently. His light brown eyes were soft but searching. "Is everything alright, my Wildheart?" he asked, patting the seat beside him.

I hesitated but sat next to him reluctantly, watching the fire's final few sparks in front of us. The rest of my family had gone inside, and suddenly the air between us felt heavy with unspoken words.

"You've seemed different lately. Like you've been off, which isn't like you," he said carefully, his tone light but questioning.

I swallowed hard, trying to weave together an explanation that didn't reveal too much. I hated lying, but I couldn't say anything that would make him suspicious, either. "I guess I'm just thinking about leaving home. I've always wanted this, you know? Something bigger than a life in Laochra, somewhere I can truly grow. But now that it's here, I don't know if I'm ready for it after all."

Dad's gaze didn't waver. He let my words settle in the space between us before responding. "Can I tell you a secret I've learned over the years?"

I nodded, the lump in my throat making it hard to speak.

"No one's ever fully ready," he said, a quiet smile tugging at his lips. "But that's what makes the journey worth taking." His words settled over me like a warm blanket, grounding me in a way I hadn't known I needed.

"There were plenty of times I doubted myself," he continued, his voice low. "Even now, there are moments when I wonder if I've done enough, been home enough over the years for you all. But stepping into the unknown is the only way to find the pieces of yourself you haven't discovered yet." He tapped two fingers lightly over my heart, his touch steady and reassuring. "And you, my Wildheart, have everything you need right here. Just waiting to be unleashed."

Tears welled unexpectedly, but I blinked them away, smiling softly. "Thanks, Dad. I'll remember that." And I knew I always would.

We stood, and he pulled me into a strong, unwavering hug. I let myself sink into it, hoping I'd remember the strength in his arms when I stood at the river's edge. Remember how his words made me feel confident and capable, and how he'd never been afraid of seeking the unknown.

I lingered out there a couple more moments, alone, taking in everything that happened today, and knew that no matter what I faced, I would make it. I was my father's daughter, and that honor meant more to me than the immortal blood running through my veins.

When I finally slipped inside, my grandmother was waiting in our room with a folded cloak and warm clothes resting neatly on my bed. She looked up with a knowing smile, more reserved than usual, but still familiar.

"Tomorrow is the big night," she said, gently smoothing the fabric of one of my shirts. "You'll appreciate having everything packed and ready to go."

I felt the weight of her words settle somewhere deeper. She didn't need to explain why she was helping me; she knew exactly why I was leaving and the lies I was keeping to ensure my family's safety.

"I'm assuming you'll want to see Manakel again tonight?" she asked, eyes twinkling conspiratorially, since she knew exactly where I'd been sneaking off to the past few nights. "Go on. I'll cover for you if anyone comes looking."

I blinked, surprised but grateful for the offer. "Thank you. I won't stay out too late."

She tucked a strand of hair behind my ear, her touch tender. "We'll always be here for you. Even if the others don't know the full truth of where you're headed or why. Family is forever."

The weight of those words carried me out into the night, where the cool air met me like an old friend. The woods called to me softly, and I somehow knew Manakel would be waiting. Tonight, I'd ask the questions that needed answers, because tomorrow night I would begin my Rite, and there would be no turning back.

28. Something Like A Warning

The cold bit at my cheeks as I moved deeper into the trees, my boots pressing faint imprints into the damp earth. The air was sharper here, cleaner, cut through with the weight of anticipation and the fear of being in the woods at night. I pulled my cloak tighter around me, though it wasn't the wind I was bracing against. It was the eerie silence and the feeling that I wasn't alone.

I'd expected to find Manakel here, waiting. That strange sense of gravity he carried always seemed to announce him first, like the space around me shifted to make room for him. I wondered if he was already watching, hidden somewhere between the trees, waiting, but the clearing remained empty. No ripple of shadow. No flicker of movement in the dark. Just the creeping thought that maybe he *wasn't* here.

The woods felt alive tonight, more than usual. Shadows twisted along the edges of my vision, curling around tree trunks and skittering across branches. Tiny flickers of light, like distant stars, blinked through the darkness. Faeries, probably. But the strange energy in the air made the hairs on my neck rise, prickling with something cold and ominous.

My steps slowed, uncertainty creeping in where excitement had been moments before. Was he late? Or had he actually decided not to come?

I took a hesitant step back, trying to shake the unease settling over me so I could head home before I got cornered. But I collided with something solid behind me.

Panic shot through me like lightning. My heart stammered, my breath caught, and for the briefest moment, I thought it was just a tree, until it shifted.

Warm breath tickled the back of my neck, but before I could react, a low voice curled around me. "Looking for someone?"

The voice was smooth, but it carried that sharp edge I recognized immediately. I spun around fast, so fast the world tilted for half a breath before a steady hand caught my arm.

Aeron.

Of course, it was him. His eyes, sharp and glinting like shards of ice, met mine with a calm I didn't trust. His hand lingered longer than necessary before letting go, his expression unreadable but far too entertained.

"Aren't you a little far from home?" Aeron's lips curved into a smile that didn't reach his eyes. He leaned in, his eyes narrowing as he studied me with fascination.

I forced myself to stand straighter, pulling away from his touch as subtly as I could while tension coiled through me. I searched the trees again but came up empty once again.

"Where's Manakel?" I asked, my voice was steadier than I felt, even as my pulse pounded loudly in my ears.

The name landed heavily between us. Aeron's smile didn't waver, but there was something calculating in the way he held my gaze.

"Ah, Manakel," he mused, tilting his head as if the thought amused him. "*That's* who you were hoping would be here? You'd do well to remember he won't always be there to save you."

I swallowed hard, the darkness pressing closer around us as I hoped for the telltale ripple of shadows that signaled Manakel's arrival. But the woods remained silent, save for the faint rustle of wind through the leaves.

"You shouldn't be wandering out here alone," Aeron added, taking a slow step toward me. "You never know what might be lurking within the trees, trying to get to you."

I took a step back, careful not to let him see how rattled I was by his mere presence. "Like you?" I asked tightly.

His grin sharpened. "Someone *exactly* like me."

Aeron shifted closer, his hand brushing against the edge of my cloak as if testing how far he could push before I recoiled and ran away. His hand just hovered, as if daring me to flinch.

"I can handle myself. Now, let me pass," I said, even though my voice betrayed a sliver of doubt.

He didn't miss it. His eyes dipped lower, lingering far too long as if searching for something hidden beneath the layers of my clothing. A spark of irritation flickered through me.

He tilted his head and smirked. "What's the rush?"

I clenched my fists, willing myself to stay calm, but the weight of his stare left me feeling exposed. Vulnerable. I hated it.

"I *said*, let me pass," I repeated, this time with more force behind my words, willing him to listen.

Aeron's smirk deepened, and instead of stepping aside, he leaned in closer, his lips brushing against the shell of my ear. "Don't worry, I'm only here to keep an eye on you and make sure you survive at least until tomorrow night."

"That's not your job," I said, quieter now.

He looked at me for a long moment. Then said, simply, "I think you have no idea what you're walking into and should be glad *someone* is concerned."

I sucked in a sharp breath, his words striking like cold steel. It wasn't *just* his words, though; it was the *way* he looked at me. As if sizing me up for something beyond my control. Like *he* was the danger I needed to be wary of. My heart pounded, panic flaring with the sudden awareness that I had walked into these woods unarmed.

Why hadn't I thought to bring my daggers? I cursed silently at my stupidity.

I had waltzed through the trees with no daggers or a plan. Just the naive assumption that Manakel would be waiting for me. But he wasn't. Aeron was.

Well, tonight would be the last time I ever wandered into these woods without a weapon or some form of defense. Lesson learned.

"You don't even know me, so save me your *concern*," I snapped, needing the deflection like a lifeline. "I doubt you even know my name."

His smirk barely wavered. "Raine, isn't it?" He tilted his head. "Though I'll admit… It's a bit plain for you."

I scoffed at the audacity, "*Plain*? Like the name Aeron is any more unique?"

His mouth twitched, showing a hint of white teeth, and his eyes lingered too long. Not on my mouth or my clenched fists, but somewhere deeper, like he was reading a thought I hadn't spoken yet. Then, just as I drew breath to ask him to move aside again, a low murmur slid across the back of my neck.

"You're playing with fire, Banríon."

I froze. The words coiled through the air like smoke, warm and intimate, the kind of whisper meant to slide under your skin and stay there. But I had been looking right at him, and his mouth hadn't moved. A strange prickle sparked at the base of my skull, creeping up the back of my neck like the ghost of a touch. I swallowed hard.

"…What did you just call me?" I asked, swallowing thickly.

A flicker of something passed across his face, surprise, maybe. But it vanished so quickly, replaced by that infuriatingly smug expression he wore like armor.

"Not sure what you mean?" he said, amusement dancing in his face.

I blinked, trying to remember the strange term I heard whispered, clear as day. "It was something like, *Banríon*."

He eyed me curiously, "Hmm. Where did you hear that?" he said casually, but his tone had changed. It wasn't teasing now. It was cautious and questioning.

"You said it. I heard *'you're playing with fire, Banríon,'*" I replied slowly, trying to understand the prickling heat that bloomed along my spine as I repeated his words.

He said nothing at first, just observed me a little closer. "Interesting," he murmured.

"Well, what does it mean?" I asked, pulse hammering.

He didn't answer right away. Instead, he took a step closer, his eyes darker than before, watchful and measured.

"It's just a pet name, Banríon. One that suits you perfectly," he finally said aloud, the word curling off his tongue with quiet authority. "But don't worry. You'll grow into it. I promise."

I hated the way my chest tightened at the sound of it again. What was it with both Sciathain men deciding on unknown nicknames without any explanation or meaning?

"But what does it *mean*?" I asked again.

Another flick of a smirk. But I noticed something this time— how his jaw tightened just slightly after he said it. How his eyes lingered, not on my face, but somewhere deeper. Like he was trying to read an unseen part of me, only he could decipher.

"You worry too much, Banríon," he said, the word again, slicing through the space between us like silk-wrapped steel. His lips barely curved, but the glint in his eyes sent a chill crawling down my spine. "I don't plan on eating you."

I exhaled, just barely, until he leaned in that fraction closer and gripped my arm again. His voice whispered against my ear, "…even if you do look rather delicious."

My breath hitched, a sharp knot of panic and fury forming in my chest. *Where are you, Manakel?*

Aeron's grip loosened just enough to keep me uncertain. But his eyes stayed locked on mine, watching, weighing. He wasn't just standing in my path. He was testing how far I'd go to claim my own ground.

I fought the instinct to shove him away, knowing full well it would be useless. Aeron was too close, too solid, his presence pressed in like gravity, impossible to ignore. He loomed, not just in stature but in the quiet confidence of someone who didn't need to exert force to dominate a moment. He was the threat, and he knew it.

I straightened my spine, meeting his stare head-on. If this was a line being drawn, then I'd meet him at the edge. A sharp awareness settled in my chest—a realization I should have grasped long before now. I had relied on the invisible tether of Manakel's presence, the certainty that he would always be near, always watching, ready to intervene if I was faced with danger. But maybe this was the moment I needed to understand that he *wouldn't* always come, and I would have to start looking out for myself.

"If you think you can intimidate me, you're wrong," I said, my voice low but deliberate, each word sharp with defiance. "I'm not scared of you, Aeron."

Something shifted in his eyes, a brief pause before his lips curled, slow and deliberate, into an amusing smirk. His head tilted just enough to be mocking, as if I was the most entertaining thing he'd seen all week.

But his grip didn't loosen. His fingers remained coiled around my wrist, heat pressing into my skin, a reminder that no matter how much space I tried to reclaim, he still held a part of me captive.

His smirk was lethal. Not just because of the way it sent an unwanted jolt through my chest, but because I knew, *I knew* he had seen it. The smallest, most imperceptible shift in my breath. The way my pulse betrayed me as it kicked too hard against my throat. He felt it. Every subtle shift I hadn't meant to give away. He knew *exactly* what he was doing to me and was enjoying it.

My jaw tensed. I tried to glare, to scowl, anything to reclaim the space he was taking from me. But he didn't flinch. The more I fought *against* it, the more entertained he seemed.

Fine. If he wanted a reaction, I'd give him one.

I moved fast. Twisting sharply, I yanked my wrist from his grip with a sudden snap of motion. My knee shot up fast and hard into his ribs before he could react. It caught him off guard, and his body jolted, breath catching as a strangled groan escaped him. One hand flew to his side, his stance buckling as pain darkened his features.

Satisfaction surged through me like a strike of lightning. But I didn't stop there. Before he could straighten, the shock that I escaped his hold still evident, I stepped closer, stomping down on his foot and pinning him in place. His hiss of pain slipped past his lips and cut through the night air, sharp and bitten off.

Then, with every ounce of momentum coursing through me, I swung my hand his way. The sound of flesh hitting flesh cracked through the silence, the sound of my slap sharper than I expected, echoing through the trees.

For a moment, everything paused. Even the forest held its breath, as if the very air around us quieted to watch what would happen next.

My heart was pounding, no, *slamming*, against my ribs, so loud I was sure he could hear it too. The adrenaline surged through me in waves, making my hands tremble at my sides, but I clenched them into fists, grounding myself in the aftershock of what I'd just done. *How was it even possible? How had I landed three moves without interference?*

The thought of Wren came through sharp and clear. That exact sequence—disengage, strike, move—he'd drilled into me over and over. A flicker of gratitude shot through me because I originally thought I would never need to use it. But like muscle memory, my subconscious remembered, along with his warning that defending myself might be the difference between walking away and not walking at all.

I hadn't believed him until now, and almost smiled. I *should probably thank him. Hopefully, I'd still get the chance to.*

But all happy thoughts vanished the moment I dared to glance up, because Aeron was already looking at me. He straightened slowly, eyes locked on mine, impassive at first, until something darker slid into place. Something slow, amused, and razor-edged. A muscle flexed along his jaw before a smile tugged at the corner of his mouth. Not angry, but intrigued.

That look was *dangerous*. And not in the way that promised retaliation.

No, this was something else entirely. Something worse. Because the way he was looking at me now, like I had just become infinitely more interesting, made me wonder if I had just made a mistake. *One I couldn't take back.*

A laugh clawed up my throat—sharp and breathless. I hadn't expected to land the hit. I'd expected him to catch my wrist, to block me. I'd expected to fail. But the flicker in his eyes told me he hadn't seen it coming either. And that was the problem because I doubted Aeron had ever been caught off guard, least of all by a human girl.

Before I could turn and run, his hand lashed out, faster than I could react. His fingers wrapped around my wrist like iron, his touch searing with restrained strength. All amusement vanished from his face, leaving something cold and sharp behind.

The flicker of triumph I'd felt a heartbeat ago disintegrated. He clenched his jaw, and it bled into something far more menacing. A slow, dangerous smile tugged at the corner of his mouth, like a predator intrigued by its prey.

"Bold, aren't you?" he murmured, voice so soft it made the steel beneath it more dangerous. His grip flexed. Not enough to bruise, but enough to say he could. To remind me exactly how much stronger he was, and show me he was *choosing* not to break me.

My breath faltered, and I yanked against his hold, but he didn't so much as flinch. His fingers held firm, as unmovable as the trees, ancient and sturdy. The woods felt smaller now, closing in around us.

The world had narrowed, leaving only him and me. Maybe I'd underestimated him. Maybe I'd been reckless trying to fight back. But there was no undoing it now.

Aeron leaned in, slow and deliberate, until his breath skimmed my cheek. He didn't touch me anywhere but my wrist, but the air shifted, thick, pressing. His presence threaded around me like smoke, blurring the line between distance and closeness until I wasn't sure where I ended and he began.

"But boldness only gets you so far, Banríon."

A shiver licked up my spine, and I stiffened. It wasn't just the unknown meaning of the nickname; it was how he said it. The sound of it, the way it found me. Like a whisper I didn't remember hearing, curling low and warm at the base of my skull before blooming up the back of my neck. He'd taken my name and changed it to something unknown. Something he said I would grow into, but I didn't see how, if I didn't know the meaning.

I forced my chin up, ignoring the way my pulse battered against my ribs, refusing to let him see just how much he had rattled me. But his eyes—Grey like smoke curling over embers—searched mine like he could see through every defense I had. Like he could peel me apart layer by layer and find something I didn't even understand myself.

His grip still held both of my wrists in one, his strength coiled but controlled. He could snap them if he wanted to. He didn't. Instead, his thumb brushed against my skin, absentmindedly, like he was testing something. A silent reminder that I was still tethered to this moment, *to him*, no matter how much I wanted to pretend otherwise.

I told myself to move. To pull away. To fight harder. But I didn't. Or maybe…I didn't want to.

His head tilted slightly, those sharp eyes flicking down, lingering too long on my mouth before dragging back up to my eyes.

"Curious, are we?" he drawled, the quiet mockery in his voice making my skin prickle. "I wonder… do you look at Manakel this way, too?"

Heat burned a path up my face instantly. I jerked my eyes away, too fast, but it was too late. His chuckle, dark and deep, curled around the space between us like smoke. He'd seen it. My hesitation. My reaction. My stupid blush. And he *liked* it even though *I* hated it. Hated that my body betrayed me, that he could read me so easily, that I was so affected by his presence alone.

Aeron leaned in closer, his breath brushing the shell of my ear. He was too close; the feelings creeping up were too much.

"The difference is," he murmured, "I don't pretend to be your protector." His voice was a slow, deliberate unraveling of every single thought I had left. "I don't *pretend* to be anything at all."

A sharp exhale pushed from my lungs. His words threaded through me, unwelcome and unrelenting. My mind scrambled for steady ground, for anything that would keep me from drowning in the storm that was him. But when I turned back, when I *forced* myself to meet his eyes again, I caught the edge of his smirk. He was waiting. *Testing me.* And this felt like one I would never win.

"Do you think I'm scared of you?" I asked.

Aeron didn't blink. Didn't look away. "I don't know, *are you?*"

"No," I said, sharper than intended. "You might be dangerous and unhinged, but I'm not *afraid* of you. I'm not afraid of most things."

"Oh?" His head tilted slightly, the silver flecks in his grey eyes catching the faint light as they narrowed, assessing, like he was peeling back my words and weighing them against the truth. "Then I guess we'll just have to see how fearless you really are."

And just like that, his fingers loosened, and he released me. The sudden absence of his grip was jarring. One moment, his fingers were unyielding, his touch a brand against my skin, and the next—emptiness. My arms dropped to my sides, the absence of his hold somehow just as disorienting as the weight of it had been.

A beat of silence stretched between us, and his eyes never left my face.

He lingered, guarded, like he was waiting for something I didn't know I was supposed to give. I should have turned and walked away. Should have taken the distraction as my chance to leave. But I didn't, and for the life of me, I wasn't sure why.

The air between us hummed, thick and charged, every nerve in my body still caught in the intensity of his stare. Frustration curled tight in my chest, thick and bitter. At him. At myself. At the strange way my pulse still hadn't settled.

Then, without a sound, he was gone.

A rush of air, the sharp beat of wings slicing through the night. His dark form rose above the trees, curling into the shadows like smoke, higher and higher until he was nothing but a memory against the stars.

But I still felt him. Even now, with the forest stretching wide and empty around me, he was still here. Even in the silence he left behind, Aeron remained. In my pulse. In my breath. In the echo of his voice.

In the places I wasn't sure I wanted him to be.

I exhaled slowly, but it did nothing to calm the frantic beat of my pulse. The night pressed in, thick and soundless, cloaked in shadow. No wind, no rustle of leaves, just the echo of my own steps and the phantom grip of Aeron's fingers still burning into my skin.

No matter how many times I flexed my wrists, I couldn't shake the imprint. And his smirk—that infuriating smug smirk—had carved itself into the back of my thoughts, sharp and knowing, like he had seen something in me I hadn't meant to reveal.

I should have run the second he released me. Should have left. But my feet had stayed rooted, trapped in the weight of something I didn't understand.

Even now, my steps were hesitant. The trees grew thinner as I moved, but the dark stayed close, thick with tension I couldn't name. It curled at the base of my spine, settled between my shoulder blades like a weight I couldn't shrug off. The woods felt colder. Emptier. The fireflies had vanished, and the stars above blinked cold and far away, silent witnesses to my hesitation.

I quickened my pace, unsteady and eager to put as much distance between us. From whatever strange pull he had over me, whatever twisted game he was playing. But even as I pressed forward, the sensation didn't leave, a tension curling at the base of my spine, making the space between my shoulders feel too tight.

I exhaled sharply, releasing a breath I hadn't realized I'd been holding.

And that's when I felt it, a prickle of heat against the back of my neck, the sensation of being watched.

"Giving up already?"

The voice curled at my ear, low and amused, too close. My breath hitched, and I froze mid-step, heart lurching in my chest. I looked around, but he wasn't behind me. He wasn't anywhere. But I heard him. *Felt him.*

"Wow," his voice drawled, smooth as sin. *"I expected more of a fight from someone with your reputation."*

I turned in a slow circle, eyes scanning the trees, heart pounding. There was nothing. No movement. No wings. No flash of dark clothing against the night. Just darkness, and shadows, and silence. Yet somehow, he was everywhere. It felt like he was right next to me, his presence thick in the air, a weight pressing against my skin, but I couldn't see him.

"Just because you're hiding doesn't mean I'm afraid," I muttered, more to myself than anything else, willing myself to believe the words.

"You sure about that?" The words slid beneath my skin like a blade. *"I thought your guardian angel might've warned you about the things that lurk in the shadows. Guess he's been... distracted."*

I clenched my jaw. Where was he, and how could I hear him? I turned, my fingers clenching into fists at my sides as the feeling of being hunted sank into my bones. I didn't know much about immortals and their powers yet, but I was fairly certain invisibility wasn't one of them.

"Distracted or not, I don't need him to deal with the likes of you," I snapped, more to myself than anything. But I knew he could still hear me.

A chuckle echoed through the trees—low, dark, laced with mockery. *"Mm. Confident. I like that. But what makes you so certain?"*

The prickling sensation at the base of my skull deepened, a slow, pulsing warmth just beneath my skin. I didn't understand what it meant, only that every time I heard him like this, it preceded the same strange heat, like a thread had been pulled taut between us and all of him was surrounding me, inside and out.

"What do you even want with me?" I bit out. "If this is just some game—"

"I don't play games, Banríon," he whispered, like a promise or a warning, I wasn't quite sure. *"Not unless I intend to win."*

There it was again. That name. *Banríon.* It unfurled inside me, curling around my ribs. I didn't know what it meant, only that it felt like something I shouldn't ignore, especially coming from him. I swallowed hard, forcing down the sharp retort burning my tongue. I would not let him see how much he was getting under my skin.

I tried to push past the rising heat in my chest, tried to ground myself in the dirt under my boots. "If you're not going to help me, then leave me alone. I don't need riddles. I don't need—"

His laugh rippled through the silence, low and mocking. *"Now, where's the fun in that?"* he continued, his voice dipping lower, *"Besides, I never said I'd help you, did I?"*

I gritted my teeth, my fists curling tighter. His words slithered around me, teasing, taunting, coiling around my throat, like a velvet noose.

"You just blindly assumed I would. So I'll let you in on a little secret, Banríon... assumptions will get you killed in this world."

I forced in a slow breath, ignoring the way my pulse clawed at my throat. He was enjoying this far too much.

"Enough," I snapped, my voice ringing out into the trees, cutting through the night like a blade.

"But I'm not done yet. For someone who isn't scared, you sure look adorable standing there, all tense and on edge, glaring into the dark like I might jump out at any second."

I felt a whisper of breath at my neck, but didn't turn around. I knew he wouldn't be there, and this was just another way to weave me into a trap. One he was enjoying far too much.

My voice didn't waver this time as I said, "Well... *I'm done.* This little game of yours is over."

I took a step forward, then another. I was ready to leave it all behind, leave *him* behind. But the second he sensed my determination to end this back and forth, a sudden rush of air greeted me.

I jerked back just as Aeron appeared in front of me, as if he'd stepped through the dark itself. One second, the path was empty, the next, he appeared out of nowhere. Leaning against a tree, arms folded, gaze fixed on mine like he'd been waiting for this exact moment.

My breath caught. He didn't say anything right away. Didn't move. Just watched me with those pale, storm-washed eyes and the faintest tilt of his head, half-curious, half-dangerous. The shadows clung to him like they belonged to him. His wings, barely visible, curved against the dark.

"This is far from over, Banríon," he said out loud at last, voice velvet-smooth. "We've only just begun."

A chill danced down my spine, and I should have hated the way he said it. The problem was…I wasn't sure I did.

The moonlight carved sharp lines along his jaw, catching on the silver flecks in his eyes—dangerous, deliberate, impossible to look away from. I should have felt it then; the prickle of fear, the instinct to step back, to move. To pull away from the strange gravity of his presence before I got caught in it.

But I didn't.

Instead, curiosity coiled tight in my chest, a reckless thing refusing to let go. My feet stayed planted, my pulse drumming a steady war beneath my skin as I squared my shoulders and held his gaze.

"What do you want with me, Aeron?"

His head tilted as he studied me in silence, his perusal slow and assessing. Not the kind of silence that felt careless, but the kind that felt heavy and weighted with meaning. The kind that said too much.

"Wouldn't you like to know?" His voice lowered, curling around me like smoke, slow and deliberate. "Let's just say… you're more interesting than I expected."

I narrowed my eyes. "That's not an answer."

"It wasn't meant to be."

Of course it wasn't. I resisted the urge to roll my eyes, to let the frustration bubbling under my skin show. A smarter person would have turned and left, ignored whatever cryptic nonsense he was playing at. But I wasn't feeling particularly smart tonight.

"If I'm so *interesting...*" I said, lifting my chin, "I'd think you'd have figured me out by now."

Aeron moved slowly and deliberately, his steps circling me like a predator testing its prey. He assessed me, lingering just a fraction longer than he should have, taking me apart piece by piece.

"See, that's the problem," He said, his voice soft, threading into the air like a whisper curling at the edges of my mind. "I can't quite put my finger on you."

I arched a brow, forcing myself to look unimpressed. "Well, try and keep your hands to yourself then. I don't want your finger on my *anything*, thank you."

He blinked, startled—just for a moment. A cough slipped past his lips, small and unintentional, like he hadn't meant to let it escape. It was the first crack in his composure.

Good. Maybe I was getting to him the same way he was getting to me.

I could have left then. Should have taken my small victory and gone. But before I could take a single step back, his hand was on my chin, tilting my face up toward him with an infuriating gentleness that did nothing to mask the strength behind it.

My breath caught, and the playful flicker in his face darkened, thick tension settling into the space between us.

"Oh, Banríon," he murmured, his voice dipping lower, smoother. "If I got my fingers on you, you wouldn't know what to do with yourself... except maybe beg for more."

Heat slammed up the back of my neck, spreading like wildfire to my cheeks. I hated how fast I flushed. How quickly my body betrayed me. And Aeron? He watched it happen. Drank it in. His smirk curled wider as though he'd won some invisible game.

Then he leaned in, slow and deliberate, close enough that I could feel the brush of his breath at my ear.

"I wonder how far that blush would lead me and my *unwanted* fingers..."

My stomach tightened, every nerve sparking with a treacherous mix of irritation and something dangerously close to anticipation.

Move.

Say something.

Step back.

Do anything except stand here like an idiot while he was flirting.

Was this even flirting?

But I didn't move. Or maybe I couldn't. All I knew was that this was humiliating. His words tethered me, pulsing with something dangerous and electric, and worse, some part of me liked it.

I exhaled slowly, forcing my feet back a step. Needing distance. Needing clarity. But his eyes followed me, sharp as ever, like I hadn't moved at all.

Get it together, Raine. This is all a game, and he's waiting for you to crack.

That damn smirk still hadn't faded. But there was something else behind it now. A flicker of something quieter, more calculating—like he was studying me. Trying to figure me out.

"I think you're enjoying this a little too much," I said, forcing as much indifference into my voice as I could manage.

"Maybe," he said, the corner of his mouth lifting. "But I can't help it. You're entertaining and endearing when you're flustered."

He thought I was flustered? Fantastic. What else was he planning on pointing out in my wake of humiliation?

"Well, I'd hate to bore you by being predictable," I muttered, rolling my eyes.

He chuckled, a low sound that sent an unwelcome shiver through me. "Don't worry. You haven't yet." He paused, and then continued, softly, almost to himself, "Which is surprising in itself." Something about the way he said it made my skin crawl and heat all at once.

Still, I pressed on. "So what now? More cryptic riddles? More games? Or are you going to tell me why you're really here?"

He stepped closer. Not enough to touch, but enough to feel. His presence was too much. Like he took up more space than he should've been allowed.

"I told you already," he murmured, his voice dipping into that smooth, velvet tone again. "I'm… curious."

I narrowed my eyes. "About what exactly?"

A flicker of hesitation crossed his face, brief but noticeable.

"You." The word was simple, but the way he said it wasn't. "You're not like the others. *Definitely* not what I expected."

I blinked. "Others?"

He glanced to the side, scanning the shadows, like he saw something in the dark I couldn't.

"You'll find out soon enough."

There was weight in his words, something unspoken but heavy. Something that left a hollow and ominous feeling in my stomach.

"You're being cryptic on purpose," I accused.

Aeron's grin widened. "Did you expect anything else?"

I groaned under my breath. This was going nowhere. He was being infuriating just to taunt me, and I was done being his entertainment for the evening. Turning away, I started down the path, this time determined to leave this encounter behind, but I'd barely taken three steps when his voice—infuriatingly smooth and taunting—drifted after me.

"So you're really not scared of me, are you?"

I didn't stop walking, but I glanced over my shoulder, catching his eyes through the shadows.

"Should I be?"

Aeron's smirk remained, but something darker rested behind it, and the hairs on the back of my neck rose to attention.

"Not yet. But this has only just begun, Banríon."

Another chill ghosted down my spine, but I ignored it, pushing forward.

I could still feel his eyes on my back.

Watching.

Waiting.

But this time, I didn't look back.

29. Allies Or Enemies

The forest pressed in around me, the air dense and oppressive, like even the trees were holding their breath. Shadows stretched long beneath the slivered moonlight, every step I took sounding louder than it should have. My heartbeat thudded in my ears, too loud, too fast, and I wondered if the entire forest could hear it, too.

I tried to convince myself that I was alone, and it was better this way. I'd left Aeron behind and was headed home, where I could forget tonight ever happened. That he had his fun taunting me and would now leave me be. But the farther I walked, the more it felt the weight of his lingering presence trailing behind me. And even though I told myself his games were over, that what I was feeling was just nerves from his cryptic words and searing touch, I didn't quite believe it.

I paused, pulling my cloak tighter around my shoulders. The cold nipped at my exposed skin, but a deeper chill came from something else, the feeling that I wasn't as alone as I hoped to be. I exhaled just as a flicker of pink and gold caught the corner of my eye.

"I thought I warned you never to come back here."

Alfreda.

I spun too fast and nearly lost my footing, stumbling over a root in the process. She hovered near a branch just above my head, arms crossed over her chest, and a cruel smirk tugged at her lips. Her wings shimmered faintly, catching the moonlight like glass, but there was nothing delicate about the way she carried herself.

I opened my mouth to speak, to make up some excuse for why I was here again, but nothing came out.

"Faerie got your tongue?" she purred, tilting her head as if studying a bug she was about to squash. "Or did you think a human girl sneaking around in my woods at night would go unnoticed?"

I swallowed, feeling the weight of her stare boring into me. My heart kicked into a frantic rhythm, and I tried to step back, but a voice slipped into my mind like silk laced with thorns.

"Hold your ground. Don't let her see your fear."

I stiffened, jerking my attention toward the shadows. *Aeron.* But he wasn't here, or at least, not where I could see him. His voice *was.* Taunting me as if he were standing right beside me.

I clenched my jaw, trying to steady my breathing. Maybe I was imagining it, but his voice hadn't come from the trees. It had come from inside me. Or perhaps this was just another trick. Another game. Another test. And I was already failing.

"Planning to run?" Alfreda sneered, drifting closer, her pink glow pulsing across the clearing. She circled me slowly, deliberately, as if scenting blood. I forced myself to stay still, even as the muscles in my legs begged to flee.

If Aeron could see Alfreda circling me and cared enough to warn me, why wasn't he stepping in? Why bother telling me anything at all and then disappear? *Coward.*

She leaned in, her breath warm against my ear. "Nothing to say now? Well, you should've listened. I was generous last time with my warning, and that won't happen again."

I swallowed hard, resisting the urge to shrink away from her.

"I don't scare easily," I managed, though my voice lacked the conviction I wanted.

"*Liar*," Aeron's voice echoed, laced with amusement as my breath hitched at the intrusion. He sounded far too pleased with himself.

Alfreda's eyes narrowed as her wings fluttered louder, and she began twirling small sparks between her fingers before a flame flickered to life in her palm. It danced delicately, bright and almost playful. But the malice behind her sneer made my stomach knot.

I grit my teeth. I didn't need Aeron infiltrating my head and confusing me with his disappearing act while I was trying not to get torched by a psychotic faerie. I needed to focus and get back in control so I could walk out of here in one piece.

"*She's more dangerous than she looks,*" Aeron warned, his voice colder now, closer. "*Don't underestimate her. Fire magic is the least of your concerns—her real strength lies in time manipulation. She could trap you in this moment, and make you live it over and over.*"

Time manipulation? My stomach twisted. I had no idea faeries were capable of that. How much more was out there that I still did not understand?

"*I can feel you doubting yourself,*" Aeron's voice hummed. "*Can hear your heart beating out of control. You need to calm down because she can sense it, too.*"

I forced the panic down, locking it away, willing my body to still even as every nerve screamed. Alfreda's eyes lingered on me like she was waiting for something—some tell, some crack to show she was winning. But I wouldn't give her that satisfaction.

She twirled the flame higher, her smirk deepening. "How do you expect to complete the Rite when you can't even protect yourself from your own fear?"

Before I could respond, tell her I wasn't scared, Aeron's voice cut in sharply, louder this time. "*Don't engage. Focus on finding your power.*"

But I don't have any power, I thought bitterly, clenching my jaw as I stood there silently. All I wanted to do was fight back, or run, whichever would get me the furthest away from her.

Alfreda chuckled softly as if she'd heard that thought herself. "You look like you're about to break. I wonder if Manakel knows just how fragile you are."

Her voice was all venom, but it was the name, *his name*, that snapped something in me.

"I'm not fragile," I said sharply before I could stop myself.

Aeron's sigh curled through my thoughts. *"And there it is. You're going to have to learn how to listen one of these days. You gave her exactly what she wanted."*

Alfreda tilted her head, mock-pity in her eyes. "You shouldn't be here, human. I think it's time someone taught you a proper lesson." Her eyes flicked past me. "Don't you agree, Aeron?"

A gust of cold swept through the clearing. The hairs on my arms rose, and instinct pulled my shoulders tight.

"Look at you," Aeron's voice rang out, too casual to be comforting. He stepped from the shadows, movements smooth, his expression calm, almost bored. But tension rippled beneath the surface. His stare cut toward Alfreda, the glint in his eyes equal parts mischief and menace. "Caught between smoke and water…one will choke you, the other will swallow you whole."

He strode toward us and smiled, slow and sharp, then shifted his focus to me. "Choose your next move wisely. No one's coming to save you."

Alfreda's expression darkened at his words, but I wasn't sure if that made me feel better or worse.

"And you're getting ahead of yourself with the threats," he told her, voice silkier now, but laced with warning.

She pouted, spinning the flame between her fingers. "But it's been ages since I've had a little fun."

Aeron stepped closer, slowly circling me, his presence looming over both of us. "Don't ruin this for me," he said, voice soft but firm. "I'm not finished with her yet."

Something in his tone made Alfreda hesitate. Her smirk faltered. His eyes locked onto mine for half a second, and though no words passed between us, the weight of his message was clear in my mind. *"Stay still. Don't provoke her."*

The thought wasn't mine, but it hummed behind my eyes, low and steady. I didn't understand how he'd done it, how I'd heard it, but swallowed hard and obeyed.

With a sharp snap of her fingers, Alfreda extinguished the flame. "Fine," she huffed. "But don't expect me to clean up your mess if you don't end this."

"I wouldn't dream of it." Aeron's voice dropped an octave, his words low and laced with threat.

The clearing vibrated with unspoken tension, and for a heartbeat, I thought she'd defy him, push him further. Instead, her wings flared, catching the moonlight like shards of crystal. She gave me one last venomous look, then vanished into the dark.

The silence that followed felt heavy, like something sacred had been disturbed.

Aeron's voice broke it. "Well, Banríon," he drawled, the nickname coiling in the air between us. "Looks like it's just us now."

I exhaled shakily, my heart still racing. *"Great,"* I muttered, rolling my eyes instinctively.

He chuckled, stepping closer, faint amusement curling his lips. "I told you, you're too interesting to leave alone."

I took a step back, but he matched it with ease.

"Are you afraid yet?" His tone was playful, but there was something darker beneath it.

I met his gaze, lifting my chin despite the shiver that ran down my spine. "Not enough to run."

His smirk widened. "Good."

I narrowed my eyes. "So are you two teaming up now or something?"

He gave the faintest shake of his head. "Hardly. But if you fight her, you'll lose." The bluntness of it sank deep.

"She's more powerful than she appears," Aeron added, his voice lower now, more serious. "And she wants you to underestimate her."

I swallowed hard, keeping my face neutral. The forest closed in around us, its darkness pressing against my skin like a second layer. The air crackled with tension, the faint hum of magic lingering where Alfreda had vanished. I could still feel the ghost of her presence, the echo of her mocking laughter curling around the edges of the trees.

Aeron watched me closely, head tilted, reading more than I wanted him to see. The intensity of it was like chains wrapping tight around my ankles, rooting me to the spot. I took a slow breath, trying to steady the hammering in my chest. But the forest felt alive in ways I couldn't explain, as if the very ground beneath my feet was listening—waiting for its cue.

Aeron gestured lazily to the woods around us, his hand cutting through the stillness. "The Witrial Woods has secrets," he said softly, the words laced with meaning I couldn't yet decipher. "Ones you're not ready to understand."

A silence wrote itself across his features, somewhere between a warning and a taunt, and it left me feeling even more off balance. I glanced toward the empty path Alfreda had taken, hoping she wouldn't return. Aeron's head tilted as if reading the thought directly from my mind.

"Oh, don't worry about her," he mused. "She won't be bothering you again. Not tonight." His smirk deepened, sporting a grin as sharp as his words. "But that doesn't mean you're safe."

I folded my arms across my chest, masking the unease curling in my stomach. "You're terrible at reassuring people."

"I'm not trying to," he said, and laughed, the sound low and vibrating in the hollow space between us.

I hated how calm he was. How easily he slipped between teasing and threatening, like it was all part of some elaborate game I didn't know the rules to. Everything about him was a contradiction. Threat and protection. Humor and danger. His eyes dragged over me, lingering, like he was trying to peel back layers I didn't want him to see.

"What is it you're really looking for out here, Banríon?"

I stiffened at the nickname, heat prickling across my skin.

"I'm not looking for anything," I lied.

He smiled knowingly, tilting his head as his eyes glinted like he could hear every unspoken truth screaming beneath the surface.

"You're a terrible liar," he murmured, stepping close enough that I had to crane my neck to meet his eyes.

The space between us seemed to shrink, the air heavy with something I didn't have a name for other than tension. *There was definitely a lot of that.*

"You think this is a game," I said quietly, more to myself than him.

He leaned in, voice brushing the shell of my ear. "It is a game," he said softly. "The only question is… are you ready to play?"

His words coiled around me, tightening like vines as I searched his face for some flicker of truth. I swallowed hard, forcing myself not to flinch, not to move, even as every instinct screamed to run. To escape him. Or maybe just the pull he seemed to have on me. But Aeron gave nothing away, other than his infuriating smirk and the glint in his eyes that promised danger.

"What if I say no?" I challenged, lifting my chin slightly.

His eyes dropped to my lips, lingering for half a second longer than necessary. "Then I suppose," he said slowly, "I'll have to make the game more… enticing."

A shiver trailed down my spine, but I didn't let it show. Didn't give him the satisfaction.

"I don't trust you," I said bluntly.

He straightened, the corner of his mouth tugging into something between a smirk and a shrug. "Good. You shouldn't."

And gods help me, I hated how much I knew the truth of those words.

Before I could respond, the air around us shifted. The forest, which had been holding its breath, suddenly exhaled, long and low and cold. Shadows curled tighter around the clearing, thickening like smoke at my heels.

I took a step back, but Aeron didn't follow. Instead, his focus slid past me into the trees. The change was subtle, his shoulders tensing, the edge in his jaw hardening, but it was the first time I'd seen him look... serious.

Aeron reached out, fingers brushing my arm as he stepped forward, placing himself between me and the shadows. The gesture was so instinctive, so quiet, I almost missed it.

But I felt the shift. In him. In the forest. Whatever was out there wasn't part of his game. For the first time since I'd met him, I saw something other than arrogance in his expression. *Caution.*

I swallowed, instinctively moving closer to his side as the shadows deepened around us, so thick I could barely see anything in the distance.

"What is it?" I whispered, not sure I wanted the answer.

He didn't answer right away, but when he did, his voice was low and unflinching.

"Something far more dangerous than me."

Aeron's grip on my wrist was light, but his presence made it feel heavier than it should have. His touch wasn't threatening, not exactly, but the heat of his palm sent my pulse skittering in ways I didn't care to admit.

"There's not much time before your Imbe Rite," he said, voice smooth, edged with something colder. "And if tonight proved anything, it's that you still don't understand what you're up against."

The truth of it hit harder than I wanted to admit. I forced my shoulders to square, to show I was unaffected, but the weight of his words coiled in my chest. I knew I was unprepared. I just didn't expect him to see it so clearly.

"I'll figure it out," I said, keeping my tone steady.

"Will you?" His smirk tugged at the corner of his mouth, but his eyes, sharp and controlled, held no trace of humor. "You're playing in shadows you don't even know the owner of. And the river, it isn't just water. It's alive. It will test you, strip you bare and peel back every lie you've ever told yourself, and if it finds you lacking…"

He didn't finish the sentence, but he didn't need to.

I swallowed hard, feeling the prickle of unease crawl up my spine. "I already know it's dangerous. I understand the risk."

"You *think* you know," Aeron corrected, his voice lowering as if the trees themselves were listening. The path narrowed, and the air grew heavier around us, thick with magic I could almost taste. "But knowing and surviving are two different things."

He was right, and that unsettled me more than I cared to admit.

I glanced up at him, searching his face for any sign of deception. I didn't know much about him, other than his fascination with taunting me, but tonight there was something different in the way he spoke—like this wasn't just another game and he was giving me a warning.

"Then tell me, what should I expect?" I asked, my voice quieter now, almost hesitant.

His gaze slid to me, unreadable in the darkness. "The river doesn't just test your strength. It tests *you*. Your fears, your guilt, every doubt you bury deep. It will twist them, turn them into illusions so real you won't know what's true. And if you can't tell the difference…"

"I'll drown," I finished for him, feeling the word stick in my throat like a stone.

Aeron nodded, but his expression softened slightly. "Not just in water, Banríon. It's drowning in yourself."

The weight of his words lingered long after he stopped speaking, settling like lead in my chest. Silence stretched between us, broken only by the rustle of leaves underfoot as we walked. Every step carried us deeper into the woods. Farther from anything that felt safe.

I took a shaky breath, feeling the pulse of my heart echo in my ears as his fingers still held my wrist, the sensation of his skin on mine doing nothing to calm it. Nothing about tonight made sense. Not Manakel leaving me in the woods alone, not even bothering to show up. Not hearing Aeron's voice in my head, like he somehow had a direct line of communication to me. Not Alfreda letting me go as easily as she did. I didn't understand any of it, except that each thing involved the person beside me.

I drew a slow breath. "Why are you helping me?"

Aeron's hand tightened around my wrist ever so slightly, a flicker of hesitation I almost missed if I wasn't so in tune with his movements.

"I didn't say I was." His voice was quieter now. "But if you die in that river…You'll never get to see what you're truly capable of."

I blinked, startled by the honesty in his answer. Or maybe the fact that he wasn't trying to hide it.

"You don't want me to fail?" I asked, more to myself than to him.

He chuckled under his breath. "I want to see if you'll surprise me more."

A breeze swept through the trees, like they had drawn closer without moving. "And if I don't?"

His eyes met mine. No smirk this time. Just a blunt truth.

"Then you won't make it out of these woods alive."

His words hung there, heavy and unyielding. But I didn't look away. I didn't back down. Instead, I met his stare head-on, feeling the fire inside of me that flickered beneath the fear.

"Then I guess I'll just have to surprise you."

I swallowed hard, the chill crawling beneath my skin as Aeron's gaze lingered. His eyes, a grey that seemed plain until you noticed the silver floating through them, seemed to hold too much knowledge, truths he wasn't quite willing to share. And for a moment, I wondered just how much he already knew. How much he wasn't saying. And why he was even helping me in the first place.

I drew in a breath, pushing past the weight in my chest. "So, do you have anything that's *actually* helpful to share? Or is this all just cryptic warnings meant to scare me off before I begin?"

Aeron's lips curved slightly. "You want step-by-step instructions?" His voice dipped lower. "This Rite isn't a typical trial or human test. The river will pull from your mind, your memories, your fears, your doubts, and craft illusions meant to break you. And believe me, those illusions will know exactly where to cut the deepest. No one can help you, not really. Because no one else will see what you see. The trials are already living inside of you, just waiting to emerge."

His perusal swept over me, sharp and calculating. I didn't flinch, but I felt the heat of it. "You can prepare all you want, but in the end, only you can help yourself, Raine."

"So you *do* know my name," I said, lifting a brow. "I was starting to think you just liked calling me nicknames to be difficult."

His smirk widened, but his eyes never left mine.

"I call you Banríon because it suits you," he said as if that answered anything.

I shifted uncomfortably, feeling the weight of the forest pressing closer. Aeron's smirk faded, and the playful edge in his tone had morphed, replaced by something heavier, something real.

"You want to know what's waiting for you before reaching the river?" he asked, eyes still locked on mine.

I nodded, ignoring the prickling unease curling at the edges of my mind.

"It's not just the water that'll try to keep you from crossing," he said, his eyes darkening like storm clouds. "There are others who hope to see you fail before you ever reach it."

The chill that ran down my spine had nothing to do with the cold.

"You've made enemies just by existing here—by being the first human on this side chosen for the Rite in decades," he continued. "Some of the obstacles will be obvious. Others trickier. They can disguise themselves in shadows or blend into the night itself. They'll smile as they try to destroy you."

The wind shifted, rustling the leaves overhead. I glanced around, but nothing moved in the trees. Still, the feeling of being watched gnawed at the edges of my senses.

"Even the ground beneath your feet will work against you to try and stop you from succeeding," Aeron added quietly. "It'll find your weaknesses and widen the cracks just as you start to find your footing."

"You make it sound like I'm doomed before I've even started," I murmured, barely able to keep the tremor out of my voice.

He stopped abruptly, forcing me to turn toward him. His eyes met mine, and for a moment, there was something like understanding in them.

"Not *doomed*," he said quietly. "But definitely unprepared."

The words hung in the air like a stone sinking into the water, rippling through me in ways I couldn't ignore. I clenched my fists, trying to suppress the creeping dread.

"How… how am I supposed to know who or what to trust?" I asked softly.

He let out a quiet laugh, humorless. "You don't."

He stepped closer. "Think of everything in the woods being against you. The faeries might smile and flutter, but don't be fooled. The trees may come alive and whisper, but their words are not always useful. Most of the Eldren take joy in watching humans fall. Especially ones like *you*."

"Ones like me…" I echoed. "Meaning what exactly?"

"Meaning you still haven't figured out why you're doing this. Yes, to save your family and your village, but what about for you? Are you here to prove something, to make a change, or merely survive an ancient Rite you felt forced to do?"

I stubbornly held his gaze. "Is protecting those I love not enough of a reason? Now, not only am I trying to save them, but everything will be working against me, and the only person I can rely on is myself?"

"For now," Aeron said softly. "But that's the point of the Imbe Rite. To prove you can stand on your own, and come out the other side changed."

I exhaled slowly, the weight of his words sinking deep. "Anything else I should know?"

Aeron's focus flicked to the shadows, as if sensing something just beyond the edge of my sight.

"Just this," he murmured, meeting my eyes once more. "Even the warmest winds can turn, and drag you straight into the heart of the storm. Fear only fuels those rooting for your downfall. They want you to fail, expect it actually. But don't let them win. Don't give them that power."

He leaned in closer, voice barely a whisper. "Because I promise you, they will enjoy every second of watching you break."

The air between us felt stretched thin, like a thread pulled too tight. I could still feel the ghost of Aeron's touch on my wrist, his fingers long gone but their imprint lingering like heat after flame. He hadn't held me hard, but the weight of his presence made it feel heavier than it was.

His eyes held steady, sharp as a blade, and for once, there was no trace of the usual smug amusement that followed his every word.

"There's more to your Imbe Rite than getting to the river and surviving," he said, his voice low but cutting through the silence like a crack of thunder. "Don't mistake crossing it for the end. That's just the beginning, and I wouldn't be surprised if the Royal Court is waiting for you the second you think you're safe. Your decision to partake isn't exactly a secret."

I swallowed the knot rising in my throat. "That's reassuring."

"I'm setting you up with realistic expectations. The Imbe Rite is a lot for *anyone* to undergo, let alone a human girl who had no idea of its existence a week ago. It's not for the faint of heart, and I'd say good luck, but you'll need more than that."

I let out a shaky breath, the corners of my mouth tugging into something that wasn't quite a smile. "Not exactly motivational," I muttered, forcing lightness into my tone. "But I guess it's more than I expected from you."

His mouth curved, *barely*, but there was no mockery in it this time.

"And you mean Dermaine's Royal court?" I asked, narrowing my eyes slightly. "Or Callix's? I don't know much about either, but our stories say he's fair, or at least he *was* before the river."

Aeron's head tilted, surprise flashing across his face for the briefest second before he masked it completely with indifference.

"Callix hasn't been King for almost a century," he replied, and his tone held the weight of something bitter. "The river was his undoing. Some say it broke him until he finally stepped down and handed over the crown."

I straightened, the hairs on the back of my neck prickling.

"Then who—"

"His daughter," Aeron cut in, his eyes darkening. "Verena."

He said her name like a curse. Quiet, but heavy and full of malice. I had never heard the name Verena; the stories never mentioned her, or any of his children besides the Queen of Dermaine, but the way he said it made my stomach tighten in fear.

"She's not like her father," he added. "And you better hope you never have to meet her. She's not what one would call... pleasant or forgiving."

A cold silence wrapped around us. I didn't know whether to ask more or just be grateful he was sharing anything at all.

"Do you think she knows about me?" I asked anyway.

Aeron's eyes met mine, but he didn't answer. "Yes. And as a leader, she is ruthless and controlling. She demands the death of anyone she suspects is working against her, so steer clear from anyone with the royal insignia."

I swallowed the lump forming in my throat, not wanting to add that I wouldn't even know what that looked like since Immorro had been a complete mystery to us.

"If anyone from her court comes sniffing around," Aeron added, stepping closer, "Lie. And make it believable. It might be the only thing that can save you."

My breath hitched. He wasn't trying to scare me; he was trying to prepare me. I could only nod, the image of this unknown queen forming like smoke in my mind, beautiful, cold, and deadly.

I glanced toward the trees, sensing the shifting shadows that seemed to move in closer. For a long moment, we stood in silence, and I wondered what Aeron saw when he looked at me. Did he see me as the fragile human he mocked a couple of days ago, or did he see something else now? Someone stronger? Someone who could fight back? Someone who was trying to save the people she loved and would do anything to protect them?

I wasn't sure why it mattered, but for some reason, I wanted him to see the latter.

Aeron cleared his throat and turned, the movement fluid as he began to melt back into the forest. "Well, if there's nothing else, I'll be on my way," he said over his shoulder. "Tomorrow is going to be a long day for you."

The thought of going home didn't feel comforting. The idea of lying in bed, staring at the ceiling, and counting the hours until the Rite felt worse than staying here in the dark.

"Wait," I blurted out, surprising even myself.

Aeron paused, one foot already disappearing in the shadows. His wings twitched, and his head turned slightly, his demeanor smooth as calm water, betraying no current beneath as he studied me from the corner of his eye.

"Can I ask you one more question?"

He let out a soft sigh, turning around and crossing his arms like he didn't have time to entertain one more thing from me. "Fine," he said with a reluctant nod. "One more question, Banríon."

I hesitated, the words catching in my throat. "Why do you care if I make it? If I survive this? I know you said you don't, but you wouldn't be helping me if you didn't. Even if it's a backwards way of helping."

It sounded ridiculous out loud, but the question had lingered between us all night. Aeron tilted his head, amusement flickering in his eyes as he studied me.

"*That's* your question?" he asked, stepping toward me once more. "You're about to face one of the most dangerous Rites imaginable, and instead of asking about what you'll encounter, or how to survive, you're asking about *me*?"

My cheeks flushed, but I forced myself to hold his stare. It might not have been the most important question, considering I was running out of time, but it was. At least to me, it was.

"Maybe I just want to know who's on my side. Who I can rely on in all this?" I whispered.

He chuckled softly, the sound low and unsettling. "Who's on your *side*?" Aeron repeated, inching closer. "Banríon, this isn't about sides. There are no teams, no allies. Just you, your strength, and whether you can handle what's thrown your way *alone*."

His words hung heavily between us, but I already knew he was right.

"So then why did you come? Why did you share all of that with me if it wasn't to help or gain my trust?" I asked.

He paused, his eyes locking with mine. "I have my own reasons for my actions. Reasons you wouldn't understand. Even if I told you… which I won't."

My brows furrowed. "So you're helping me because it benefits *you*?"

His smirk returned, but there was something distant about it. "Not exactly *helping*, remember? Let's just say I have an interest in seeing you succeed."

For the briefest moment, something like concern brushed across his face—so quickly I almost thought I imagined it.

"Now," Aeron added, his expression hardening once more, "get some rest. Tomorrow, when everything feels impossible, remember this— the only person who decides if you make it… is you."

And just like that, he vanished—swallowed by the dark, leaving me alone with the cold, the silence, and the weight of his words and everything to come tomorrow night.

The woods behind me pulsed with quiet danger, but it also felt… honest. Its threats didn't pretend to be anything else. They were wild, raw, and laid bare—sharp-edged truths in a world that so often wore masks. I wasn't ready for them. Not truly. But I didn't have the luxury of waiting to be.

The wind whispered against the branches, and I found myself leaning into the whisper of the three wishes I had made earlier.

My wish for the present: to get more answers, to feel prepared for what I'd face in the Rite.

Aeron, as infuriating as he was, had given me that much. Maybe not in the way I had imagined, but his warnings had filled the gaps in my knowledge with sharp edges and heavier truths. And I somehow felt more prepared than I had when entering the woods tonight.

My wish for the people around me: for my family's safety and ignorance while I was gone.

I exhaled slowly, picturing their faces, my father's quiet, watchful eyes, my mother's gentle but knowing smile. Baren and Wren teasing me, blissfully unaware of how different things would feel come tomorrow.

And lastly—

My wish for my future: success in crossing the river, having the gods deem me worthy, and making it to the Queen.

I knew that might be a bit harder to predict the outcome of, but I was finally feeling confident and steady when I thought of everything I would be facing before and after my Rite.

I glanced over my shoulder one last time, eyes searching the tangle of shadowed limbs and hollow stillness. The trees stared back, vast, unblinking, and full of looming threats.

And yet somewhere in that darkness, I felt him. Not in the way you see someone in the distance, but in the way you feel heat after the flame is gone. A prickle at the base of my neck. A presence that lingered in the dark like smoke after a fire. Aeron. I couldn't explain how I knew he was still there, watching. But I did. And strangely, that knowing didn't scare me. It steadied me.

I turned away and stepped forward, the familiar crunch of the earth beneath my boots grounding me in the moment. With each step, I carried more than just what I'd learned tonight. I carried the weight of every warning, every unspoken truth, every new piece of information or advice, and every flicker of fear.

Tomorrow night, I would walk back into the woods. I would stand at the edge of the river and face whatever waited beyond it.

And I would not break.

I would cross.

I would survive.

I would succeed.

30. Ties That Bind, Ties That Break

The quiet hum of the house kept me awake. Soft and familiar, the creak of the wood beams, the faint groan of the old pipes, the sigh of wind pressing gently against the windowpanes, it was a song I had always known. One I wanted to remember, just in case this was my last night here.

I lay still beneath the quilt, eyes fixed on the ceiling's shifting shadows, committing every sound to memory. This house held so many pieces of me: whispered secrets, stolen moments, the rhythm of childhood, and the quiet ache of growing up. Leaving it, even for something as monumental as my Imbe Rite, felt bigger than I could handle.

Eventually, sleep found me, but it didn't hold me long.

The soft rustle of a page turning and the steady scratch of pen on paper stirred me from the edges of a restless dream. I blinked, groggy, and turned toward the sound. My grandmother sat upright in bed, a worn leather journal balanced on her knees. The moonlight cast a silvery sheen across her hair, and for a moment, she looked ethereal—like some ancient scribe writing truths the world had long forgotten.

"What time is it?" I asked, my voice still thick with sleep.

Her pen stilled mid-word, and a soft smile tugged at her lips, as if she'd been expecting me to wake at this exact moment.

"I didn't mean to wake you," she said gently, lowering her pen. "How was your evening in the woods?"

The question settled heavily between us. I pushed myself upright, the blanket still clutched around my shoulders like armor. Flashes of earlier tonight clawed their way back—Alfreda's haunting voice, Aeron's cryptic warnings, and Manakel's absence, like a phantom wound that hadn't stopped aching. I swallowed hard, unsure how much I should share or how much she already knew.

"I didn't stay long," I said, carefully. "But I learned a few things… enough to feel more prepared, I think."

Her brow lifted, amused and discerning, as if she could taste the half-truth behind my words.

"Is that so?" she murmured, folding her hands over the journal. Her posture was casual, but her eyes held the weight of something heavier than her light tone suggested.

The air in the room thickened, but she didn't press further. Instead, she set the journal aside with gentle care, folding her hands neatly in her lap as if settling into an unspoken ritual.

"The forest has a way of preparing you," she said after a beat. "Even if it's not in the way you expect."

She exhaled softly, and there was something distant in her tone, like she was speaking to herself as much as to me. I watched her face, the flicker of old memories moving behind her eyes, and I knew— she'd walked through her own shadows once, too.

I hesitated, the words catching on the edge of my tongue. I wanted to tell her everything. About Alfreda's strange magic. About Aeron. About the way the forest had felt alive beneath my feet. But something in me recoiled. I wasn't sure if it was fear… or pride.

"I didn't realize how little I knew," I admitted, tugging the blanket closer around my shoulders. "Even after everything I've learned this week, I thought I had a better understanding of what I was stepping into. But I didn't. Not really. And now I just hope I'm truly ready."

Her eyes softened, and the corner of her mouth curved into that quiet, knowing smile that always made me feel like a child again—like she held all the answers but was letting me stumble toward them at my own pace.

"Sometimes," she said gently, "it's the unexpected that shows us what we're made of. And no amount of preparation can help with that."

Her eyes shifted to the window, where the moonlight cut through the curtain, illuminating the edges of her face in gold.

"Tell me, what happened? What did you learn?"

I hesitated, chewing the inside of my cheek. There was something in her voice, light as it was, that told me she wasn't just curious. She already knew pieces of the answer and wanted the words to come from me.

So I told her.

Piece by piece, I laid it out, the flickering shadow that seemed to breathe with the darkness, the way Alfreda had taunted me like she'd been expecting me to cower in fear, and Aeron's guarded warnings that left me with more questions than answers.

She listened without interruption, her expression calm and steady, though I could see brief flickers of emotion that passed through her eyes. Pride, maybe, or worry, it was hard to tell, but there was definitely restraint. Her silence only fueled my curiosity and that gnawing feeling that there were pieces she still wasn't sharing, truths she wouldn't reveal. I knew it. I could feel it in my bones.

There had always been a quiet understanding between us, a sense that she knew more than she let on, and I'd always trusted that, trusted *her*. Knowing that when the time came, she would share, but now, with everything shifting and life changing truths being revealed, I felt the sudden urge to know *everything*. Still, I couldn't bring myself to ask what she was hiding. Not directly.

"You don't seem surprised," I said slowly, watching her face for a reaction. "It's like... You *knew* I'd face them."

I shifted uncomfortably as her lips pressed together, and for a heartbeat, I thought she might brush it off or change the subject entirely. But instead, she smiled faintly, like I'd caught her in the middle of a secret she hadn't meant to reveal, and there was no turning back now.

"There are some things we can't control, Raine. Only prepare for, and that is what I'm trying to help you see."

The words felt like a half-truth, and the cryptic tone of them bothered me more than it should have. I wanted to ask more, wanted to push, to demand she stop hiding things from me like everyone else had been since this all started. But the way she looked at me, tired and tender, proud and protective, made me pause. Maybe she wasn't holding back out of secrecy. Maybe it was out of love. Maybe I wasn't ready for the answers. Or maybe she wasn't ready to give them.

"Trust your instincts," she whispered, reaching across our beds to give my hand a gentle squeeze. "They'll serve you better than anything I can tell you."

I nodded, even as I swallowed the knot forming in my throat. I held onto her fingers a second longer than I needed to. Just to feel something certain. Tomorrow, everything would change, and I didn't know when or if we'd get moments like this again. But it was almost morning, so by this time tomorrow, my Imbe Rite would begin. I would take the tonic, and the river would call me to it so I could step into a trial no one could prepare me for.

The weight of it hung over me, pressing down with every breath. I wasn't sure what terrified me more, that I might not be ready, or that I might have to face whatever came next entirely on my own.

I swallowed. Then asked the question I hadn't been able to let go of.

"Aeron said not to trust anyone once I enter the forest," I said softly. "Even those who've helped me before. What do you think?"

She didn't answer right away. Her eyes met mine, soft but sharp in that way only hers could be, like she was seeing all of me at once. I watched as she weighed her response carefully, choosing her words with the same precision she used when tending her garden—delicate but firm.

"I think that's useful advice," she said, her voice low and thoughtful. "You'd do well to remember it, especially while you're still undergoing your Rite."

That was it? That was the only answer I was going to get? No deeper explanation, no follow-up insight? I frowned, irritation tightening the muscles in my shoulders. I sank back into the bed, trying not to let my frustration show.

Lately, every immortal I met seemed to speak in riddles. Like truths were something they got to ration, even if they were the very thing I needed to survive this. But I wasn't a child anymore. And by nightfall, I wouldn't be the human girl lying in this bed, staring at the ceiling, memorizing the way home felt. I would be something else entirely.

I shifted on the bed, pulling my knees to my chest as the weight of her vague answer settled uncomfortably around me. "Why does everyone feel the need to be cryptic?" I muttered, half to myself. "I'm not asking for some ancient forbidden secret, just… honesty."

Her eyes softened, but there was something else behind them now. Something heavier. Like she'd carried the same question once and never got the answer she wanted either.

"The truth isn't always straightforward, Raine," she said quietly. "Sometimes it's hidden, sometimes it's given in pieces, and sometimes it's the thing you have to find for yourself, but only when we're ready to see it."

I huffed quietly and looked away. That wasn't the answer I wanted or needed right now. I needed facts, a map to follow—something solid I could cling to. But lately, all I'd been given were half-truths and shadows of information. The unknown stretched out ahead of me like a dense fog, thick and unforgiving.

"I don't like going into something like this blind." I admitted, "There's too much I still don't know, and no time left to prepare."

Her hand drifted to the edge of her journal, tracing the worn leather cover with the same care she always did when she was deep in thought.

"And what about after?" I asked quietly, lowering my knees. "Will you still be here? I mean, after the Rite. Does that change anything for you?" I hated how small my voice sounded, how vulnerable the question felt hanging between us.

A flicker of shadow crossed her face, subtle but noticeable, like she hadn't expected me to ask that. But the look passed as quickly as it came, replaced by the soft, familiar warmth she always gave me.

"I'll always be here for you, my Wildheart." She stood and crossed the room to sit beside me, her palm pressing gently against my leg. "No matter what happens, nothing changes that."

I wanted to believe her. But there was a tremor beneath those words that made me wonder if she was trying to convince herself as much as me. I wanted to believe that this Rite wouldn't shift the foundations of everything I knew. But deep down, I wasn't so sure.

"What should I hold onto?" I asked. "When I drink the tonic, when everything starts… shifting. What do I cling to when it gets hard?"

She glanced toward the window again, as if searching for answers in the distance. "Hold onto what matters most," she said. "The anchor points you've been noticing all week. Memories that ground you. People who remind you who you are. The things you love. Those things will guide you back to the present when everything feels like it's unraveling."

I nodded, my mind replaying everything from the past few days. I thought of Wren. Of the laughter we shared before everything started to change. Of my family and their unwavering love and support, even as I lied to them. I thought of this house, this bed, this woman beside me who until this week had been my greatest anchor, and how I didn't want to forget any of it.

"Thank you," I whispered, though I wasn't entirely sure what I was thanking her for. Maybe just for being here. For staying beside me when it would've been easier to let me go. For not making me feel like I had to face this alone.

"You've always had more strength inside of you than you give yourself credit for," she said. "I know this feels overwhelming, and it will be. But you were chosen for a reason, Raine. You're one of the only humans to undergo this Rite in a century, and as much as it might feel like a burden, it's also an honor."

I took a steadying breath, letting her words wrap around me like armor—*an honor*. Not a burden or a punishment, but a chance to carve something new out of the unknown. A chance to prove that I was capable of more than surviving, not just to the immortals or my family, but to myself. That I could stand at the edge of this ancient Rite and step forward, not because I was forced to, but because I *chose* to.

Still, doubt slithered in, curling at the edges of that fragile belief. I shifted slightly, glancing down at my hands where they rested in my lap. The faint scars from years of sparring with Wren traced my knuckles—small reminders of past victories and losses. And yet, as I flexed my fingers, they suddenly felt too small to carry the weight of everything ahead.

"It's hard to believe I'm leaving already," I admitted quietly. "It just feels like… a lot, all at once, and I wish I had more time."

She came to sit beside me and reached for my hand, not to hold it tightly but just enough to remind me she was with me, that she had always been there. Like a tether grounding me to something solid when everything else felt like it was shifting beneath my feet.

"Strength isn't about how prepared you are. It's about how you move forward when you're not. You have a good heart, a sharp mind, and instincts that will guide you when you need them most. Trust yourself."

I nodded slowly, letting the quiet fill the space between us again. A question tugged at me, something I hadn't fully allowed myself to ask until now. I hesitated before meeting her gaze.

"Do you think…" I paused, unsure how to phrase it without sounding ridiculous. "Do you think a seer would already know what happens to me?"

My grandmother straightened, her hand retreating from mine as her expression shifted—subtle, but still noticeable.

"There hasn't been a seer that skilled in over a century," she said, her tone too even. "And the strongest seers are part of the royal court. I doubt Callix or anyone in Immorro would concern themselves with the fate of a human girl from Laochra."

I frowned as she mentioned the former immortal King.

Callix. Hearing the name, knowing it was no longer his court, felt like I finally knew something she didn't. And yet instead of triumph, the truth felt out of place.

"It's actually Queen Verena running the royal castle now," I said, slowly.

Her reaction was immediate. A flicker of surprise crossed her face, sharp and undeniable, though she masked it as quickly as it appeared.

"I didn't know that," she said after a beat, her tone lighter, but I could sense the wheels turning behind her eyes. "But it doesn't matter. You're destined for Dermaine, not the royal court of Immorro."

She said it with such certainty, but there was something in the way her eyes shifted away from mine that left me unconvinced. Her hand returned to rest on the bed beside me, though this time the gesture felt more like a reassurance for herself than for me.

"Then why does it feel like there's more going on?" I asked, the words sharper than I meant them to be. "More than you're telling me."

She looked at me for a long moment. "Because there always is," she said simply. "But what you're facing tomorrow? That's yours alone. No one else can walk through it for you. So instead of letting the unknown paralyze you, try to focus on the smaller things. Face it one task at a time."

I looked toward the window. The sky had begun to pale at the edges, night bleeding into dawn.

"You're going to be fine, Wildheart," she said softly. "You can handle more than you think. You just need to remember that only you can decide your future."

The confidence in her words sparked something—small but undeniable. A flame flickering to life in the center of my chest. She was right. I didn't need to know every answer, didn't need to untangle every mystery right now. Maybe this wasn't about finding clarity beforehand, but about embracing the uncertainty and facing it step by step. Maybe the questions would answer themselves in time.

I met her stare, feeling that quiet shift inside me—the steady hum of determination taking root. Her smile was faint but genuine as she patted my leg, her eyes filled with a kind of love I couldn't put into words.

I nodded, swallowing against the lump rising in my throat. Whatever came tonight, whatever the Imbe Rite revealed, would just be one more part of my future story. Not the ending or beginning.

I knew I should have focused on getting some sleep, but when the morning light finally stretched in long shadows across the room, I realized we had been up all night talking.

She pulled me into a strong embrace, the kind that felt like it lingered just a little longer than usual. I held on tighter, breathing her in, the familiar scent of herbs and smoke, and something faintly floral. Savoring the quiet moment between us before she stepped back. She crossed the room to the chair in the corner and picked up the worn leather satchel slung over the back.

"I know your birthday isn't until midnight," she said softly, smoothing a hand over the satchel's surface. "But I thought I could help you pack what you'll need. A sort of early birthday gift, if you will. Tools to prepare you for what's to come."

There was something tentative in her voice, like she wished she could give me more but knew this was the best she could offer. Her eyes flicked to mine, catching the soft morning light pouring through the window.

There was a gentle uncertainty in her voice, like she wanted to do more but knew this was the best she could offer. Her eyes met mine, catching the early morning light as it streamed through the window and turned them to sea-glass, stormy and soft, all at once. That familiar blue-green shade had passed through the veins of every woman in our family, but in that moment, it didn't just feel like shared blood—it felt like shared memory. She looked at me like she saw a younger version of herself, and I looked at her like I was staring into my future. The lines at the corners of her eyes deepened, etched there by time and wisdom, and I found myself wondering if mine would one day mirror them.

I nodded. "I'd appreciate that... more than you know."

Relief softened her face, a faint smile tugging at her lips. "Good. But first, let's have tea and breakfast. I still need to gather the last of the herbs. The tonic's been steeping for five days, but a few ingredients need to be added fresh, just before you drink it. So I can explain all of that, too."

I watched as she slung the satchel over her shoulder, moving with the same graceful ease I'd admired for years. She gave me a look, a silent nudge, to follow her downstairs.

The kitchen was quiet, save for the morning birdsong drifting through the window. Sunlight fell in warm streaks across the counters, brushing over bundles of rosemary and lavender resting in a woven basket. The air smelled of dried herbs, honey, and something sweet and floral I couldn't name.

She moved with practiced ease, pulling jars from the shelves and lining them up with precision. Her neat handwriting marked each label, a familiar comfort.

"These will calm your nerves and keep your senses sharp," she said, setting the rosemary and lavender aside. She glanced at me with a spark of quiet amusement. "You'll thank me later."

I managed a soft smile and leaned in, watching her work. There was something oddly soothing about watching her work, the careful way she handled each ingredient as though they held more than just healing properties. I realized then that I hadn't noticed her preparing the rest of the tonic. She must've done it at some point this week while I was distracted, quietly tending to things in the background, carrying the weight I hadn't even noticed slipping from my shoulders.

Our breakfast was simple—roasted meat leftover from last night's fire, thick slices of bread, and creamy yogurt dusted with cinnamon. As we ate, she pulled a small wooden box from her satchel and slid it across the table.

"There are a few other essentials you'll need," she said, watching me closely.

I opened the lid slowly. Inside were several small glass vials filled with herbs and powders in muted earth tones. A faint shimmer caught my eye as I noticed a tiny vial, no larger than my thumb, containing fine silver dust.

"You know all of these herbs and their uses already," she gave me a knowing wink. "But that one," she added, nodding toward the shimmer, "is river stone dust. Keep it close, and if you find yourself in danger, *especially in the water*, sprinkle it around you. It will help ward off anything trying to harm you."

My stomach twisted at the thought of even needing protection in the river, but I was glad she had known to add it. The stories of the creatures that lurked beneath its surface were woven into every bonfire story I'd ever heard. Creatures that craved not just flesh, but the unraveling of something deeper. Immortality splintered. Souls peeled apart like bark from a dying tree. Taking from those who were only seeking more.

I swallowed, rubbing my hands together to shake the sudden unease. It must have been noticeable because she leaned in slightly, "Remember," she whispered, her tone gentle but firm, "the tonic will protect you. For twelve hours after you take it, nothing magical can actually kill you." She paused, "But you should wait and drink it as close to crossing the river as possible."

I froze mid-bite, suddenly realizing what she was implying. "Wait," I said slowly, "that means I have to walk through the woods unprotected?"

Her nod came without hesitation as if the answer had always been obvious to her.

"It's the smartest option," she said. "You don't know how long the river will keep you, or what will happen once you enter. The most danger you'll face should be in the water, so the longer you are protected there, the less room you'll have for mistakes. This way, the tonic covers everything during and until you safely cross into Dermaine."

I swallowed. The thought of walking through the woods at night—alone, vulnerable, unprotected until the moment I drank—tightened something in my chest. But her voice held no fear. Just confidence. Quiet, unwavering belief. There was a certainty that made me trust her, even if the idea itself felt daunting.

She reached for my hand and gave it a small squeeze. "You're ready,

Raine. Whether you feel it or not. I've taught you everything I know. And the things I couldn't… you'll find those within yourself when the time comes."

She handed me a small wooden box, her eyes softening in a way that made my heart ache.

"Use the river stone dust wisely," she said, fingers tightening gently around mine. "And remember, when you step into that river, you're not just crossing to the other side—you're letting go of the girl who stood on this shore. Every version of you that hesitated, that wondered if she was enough, that waited for permission… leave her with the current. What waits beyond is yours to claim, but you have to meet it as the person you were always meant to become."

Her words settled heavily in the space between us. I could feel their weight, the significance of what she wasn't saying out loud. I wasn't just doing this for my family, I was doing it for myself, too. For who I would become.

"Thank you," I whispered, and this time, I knew exactly why I was thanking her. For every lesson, every secret she'd kept until now, and for believing in me even when I struggled to believe in myself.

For the sleepless nights spent grinding herbs by candlelight. For the warnings disguised as bedtime stories. For the way she taught me to stand still when the world shifted, and listen before I spoke.

She never asked for praise. She never demanded obedience. She simply offered knowledge like a gift, wrapped in patience and silence—waiting for me to be ready.

And now, I was.

Even if I didn't know who I'd be on the other side of the river, I knew what I carried with me. Her wisdom in my hands. Her strength in my shoulders. Her love in the spaces between every breath.

No matter who I became, whatever version of me stepped out of the woods, I would not walk forward empty.

I would carry her with me.

Always.

31. The Hardest Goodbyes

The plan was simple on the surface. Pretend today was like any other. I'd say goodbye to my father, Baren, and Wren as they rode toward Rioga, just like I had a dozen times before. No fanfare. No long looks. Just another farewell before we all head to separate places.

But this time *was* different.

After they left, I was supposed to pack like I was heading to Ceannairí later with my grandmother. We'd say goodbye to my mother by early afternoon and slip away under the guise of settling into the blacksmith's apprentice cottage. In truth, we'd head straight for the woods. She'd walk with me until Manakel arrived, and from there, he and I would travel the half-day journey to the river. If everything went according to plan, we'd reach it just before nightfall. Just in time to rest for a few hours before midnight. Just in time to drink the tonic and step into the unknown.

It was going to be a long day. Possibly the longest of my life. But there was no turning back.

My boots crunched softly along the gravel path as I made my way to the stables, where Baren stood adjusting the straps on his horse. His shoulders were squared, his movements steady, but there was tension in the way his hands lingered over every buckle, every line of rope. He was stalling.

He glanced up, and the moment our eyes met, the weight in my chest tightened. His face softened, but worry still clung to the edges of his smile.

"You're really leaving for Ceannairí today?" he asked, his voice low and quiet.

I nodded, but before I could reply, he stepped forward and pulled me into a firm hug. The kind of hug that said everything he couldn't, because he'd never been one for long goodbyes. His arms wrapped around me like they could shield me from what was coming.

And for one fleeting moment, I wanted to tell him everything. That I wasn't heading to Ceannairí. That I might not come back. That I was terrified, more for them than myself. But I didn't. I couldn't.

Instead, I whispered, "You've trained me well, Baren. I'll be fine. I can handle myself."

He huffed a soft laugh against my hair, but when he pulled back, his expression was sharper than before. "I know you can, but I've always been close by. Watching your back, making sure you didn't get into too much trouble. Covering for you if you did. Who's going to do that now?"

His eyes searched mine, and the weight of his words pressed heavier than I expected. Wren was always my sidekick, but Baren was the one who watched over us, like a protective cloud just hovering nearby, and I never fully appreciated his role in my life until now.

I blinked back the sting in my eyes, forcing a small smile. "I'm not a kid anymore. I'll be eighteen tonight. I think that makes me an adult. And besides, I can't stay here forever. You know I'd drive everyone mad."

Baren's lips twitched, but the humor didn't quite reach his eyes. "Doesn't matter how old you are. You'll always be my little sister." He reached out, tapping the top of my head gently. "Just keep that stubborn head down, will you? Don't go making enemies."

I laughed softly, though my heart felt heavier by the second. "I'll try.

But no promises, big brother."

His chuckle was soft, almost fond. But the silence that followed was heavy. Neither of us wanted to break it. So we didn't. For a moment, we stood there, lingering in the unspoken. I wanted to say more, to ease his worry, but I didn't have the words. He nodded once, turned, and resumed strapping the last of the supplies to the carriage. Like he needed something to do with his hands, because if he didn't, he might say more, or stop me from leaving. And we both knew neither of us could handle that.

Then I saw my father.

He stood near the wagon, arms crossed, his weathered face breaking into a wide grin the moment he spotted me. That grin had always been my anchor, my constant. His familiar warm presence, the silver starting to streak through his hair and beard, made something tighten in my chest.

"There she is," he said, voice bright. "My Wildheart."

The nickname caught in my throat. I stepped into his arms, and he wrapped me in a hug that smelled of earth and smoke and cedarwood. Safe.

"Packed and ready for your grand adventure?" he teased.

"Almost," I murmured, not quite ready to let go.

He pulled back and cupped my face in both hands to study me.

"Any last words of wisdom?" I teased, but a part of me needed anything he was willing to give me in this moment.

"You already know the best advice I can give," he said with a soft smile. "Stay true to who you are. Trust yourself and don't let the world dull your fire."

A playful glint sparked in his eye. "And remember, don't start any fights you know you can't win."

I smirked. "Oh please, win or lose, when have I ever backed down from a fight?"

He laughed, low and gravely and familiar. "Just be careful, and know that no matter how far you go, you'll always have this, *us*, in your corner."

His kiss landed gently on my forehead, but lingered—just long enough to tell me he knew. Maybe not the exact details, but enough to sense this goodbye was different. That this hug might have to last a little longer than usual. And clinging to his embrace, I bit down the sting of tears that threatened to rise.

Last was Wren.

I found him standing alone, leaning against the barn with his arms crossed, watching me with an intensity he always had when something weighed on his mind. Like he'd been waiting for this moment and dreading it in equal measure.

He waited until I reached him, his hand gently catching my arm as he pulled me just far enough away to speak in private.

"Raine," he said quietly. "I know this is just a temporary job, but… something about it feels off. And not just the way you've been acting this week."

I sighed, shaking my head softly and looking down. I didn't trust myself to meet his eyes. "I'll be fine, it's only Ceannairí. It's not the end of the world."

He held my gaze, his eyes flickering with something deeper.

"It is for me." His voice cracked. "You're my best friend, Ray," he admitted, voice rough with emotion. "Always have been," he looked down at the ground and kicked a rock. "I know Baren and I are supposed to be the closest, being brothers and all, but you've always been the one I felt most connected to."

My heart twisted at the vulnerability in his words. I squeezed his hand, grounding both of us and hoping he understood why I had to leave.

"I just need you to know, I'll always be here. If you ever need anything, or if things get tough out there, I want you to know it's okay to come back. Don't try to handle everything on your own."

I nodded, "I'll be okay." I wanted to promise, but something about that felt too big a lie, so I added the only thing that mattered, "I love you too, Wren. You know that, right?"

He nodded, pulling me into one final hug that didn't feel like a farewell, but a tether—like he was trying to anchor me in place just a moment longer. And I let him.

Then, too soon, it was time for them to leave.

I stood by the fence and watched as they climbed into the carriage—Baren glancing back one more time, Wren pretending not to, Dad waving with that big, bright grin that had lit every childhood memory I had.

I didn't wave back. I couldn't.

The ache in my chest was too sharp, too real. It felt like something was breaking. I stayed there, staring after them until the carriage disappeared into the trees, swallowed by the morning fog.

And when they were gone, I whispered the words I hadn't dared say aloud: *Please let this not be the last time.*

I took a slow, steadying breath as I laid everything out across my bed.

Four daggers. Two of them were mine—slim and well-balanced with carved wooden hilts stained a deep chestnut, the grips wrapped in dark leather softened by years of use. The other two were Wren's, borrowed from the shed in a silent, guilty rush. His were heavier, forged from darker steel with pale etchings along the base—symbols I never learned the meaning of but had always admired. I figured I'd ask for forgiveness later. *Hopefully.*

Beside them, I set a bundle of herbs tied tightly with twine, the vial of shimmering river stone dust, the tonic my grandmother had spent days coaxing to life, an extra pair of clothes, my lucky flint stone, and a scattering of small supplies—items I wasn't sure I'd need, but couldn't bring myself to leave behind.

None of it looked extraordinary. But tonight, they weren't just objects. They were pieces of preparation. And in my hands, each one felt heavier than it should—like they knew, better than I did, what was coming. An unspoken promise that they'd agreed to take part in whatever lay ahead.

My grandmother moved quietly around the room, the familiar rhythm of her steps muffled by the creak of old wood. She ran her fingers along the blades with a kind of reverence, checking edges without speaking. I noticed the slight tremble in her hand when she reached Wren's daggers, and something inside me pulled taut.

She never said much when she worked like this. I watched her with a mix of gratitude and unease twisting together inside me. There was something in her silence, something unspoken, as if she too felt the finality of packing this bag with me.

"You'll need this as well." Her voice was soft as she pressed a small linen pouch into my palm, her touch lingering just long enough to settle me. "Inside are the final herbs needed for your tonic. Mix them in just before you take it at midnight."

I ran my thumb over the worn fabric, nodding. It was small enough to fit in my palm, the fabric soft and worn with use, its scent earthy and sharp with a hint of something sweet and unfamiliar. I tucked it securely into the leather corded belt pouch at my hip.

The pouch was dark brown, oiled until the hide gleamed faintly in the low light. My grandmother had given it to me earlier without a word, fastening it around my waist like a quiet ritual. The leather was etched faintly with a unique pattern—old symbols I couldn't name but felt familiar all the same. It hugged close to my side, tied with a loop of sinew cord, the kind that wouldn't easily slip or snag.

I tightened the knot once more for good measure. The herbs had to stay safe. If I lost them, the tonic couldn't be completed. And without the tonic… the river wouldn't just test me. It would consume me.

"Raine," she said, stepping closer, her eyes steady and unflinching. "The river isn't called forbidden because it's dangerous. It's called that because it changes you. No one has survived those waters, and once you cross that threshold, there's no going back—not to who you were, or what you thought you knew."

Her hand settled on my shoulder, firm and grounding, as if she was anchoring me in place before the current could pull me away.

"Getting there unscathed is its own trial. The woods will test your courage. The river will test your soul. And not all dangers will wear fangs or claws. Some will look like friends and speak things that sound like truth."

I swallowed hard, but she wasn't finished.

"You'll want to cling to what you've been taught, trust what you know. But trust your instincts above all else. They'll be your compass when the world tilts sideways. They'll keep you alive when everything else falls away."

Her thumb brushed my jaw gently, the weight of her words sinking into my skin like a second heartbeat.

"Supplies can be lost. Paths can vanish. But you? You carry your power within you. Never forget that."

I nodded, holding her gaze even as something inside me coiled tighter. I wanted to believe that was enough, that trusting myself could carry me through whatever waited in those trees. But deep down, I couldn't shake the feeling that instincts didn't chase away shadows and wouldn't stop whatever lurked beneath the water.

When everything was packed, she held my cloak out to me. The wool-lined cloak settled over my shoulders, its emerald folds whispering against the corset tied tightly around my chest. I smoothed the fabric, feeling its weight, heavier than it should have been—like the secret I carried pressed into every seam. The silver clasp clicked into place at my throat, gleaming like a quiet confession. Too fine, too deliberate for a simple move to a neighboring town.

That was the lie everyone believed—that I was leaving Laochra for an apprenticeship, that a carriage waited just beyond the village gates with trunks of books and tools for some noble craft. And in a way, it wasn't entirely untrue. I was leaving. I was learning. Just not the lessons they imagined.

I fastened the last buckle on my corset, the supple leather hugging my ribs like a second skin, restrictive but reassuring. Each strap cinched tighter than the last until breathing felt like work. Beneath it, my fitted tunic peeked through, sleeves bound at the elbows with slim cords, my fingers trembling only when they brushed the edge of the dagger sheath strapped to my hip.

The boots came last—sturdy, mud-brown, laced just above my ankles for terrain far rougher than a cobbled city street. Their leather was worn, pliant, and still bore faint scuffs from the few training sessions I'd stolen under starlight. I told myself they were practical, but deep down I knew what they made me look like: a girl dressed for battle, not for life in someone else's tidy workshop.

Would my mother notice the extremity of my outfit? Would she tilt her head in that way she did, eyes narrowing like she was searching for the pieces of truth I'd hidden? She thought my grandmother was simply escorting me to a new town, a safe life, and a job that awaited. Maybe that was why I'd stayed silent around her today, why the words clawing at my throat refused to surface. If I told her the truth, which I knew wasn't possible, I'd see the fear bloom in her eyes. And I wasn't sure I could bear that or that she would let me leave.

I slung the satchel across my shoulder, its weight biting into the curve of my spine. Bigger than anything I'd carried before, its contents rattled softly—tonics, dried herbs, a flask of water, all nestled alongside something colder, heavier. Two daggers rested against my hip, their weight a small comfort. A quiet reminder that I wasn't going in unarmed, even if I still felt entirely exposed. But the mix of both mine and Wren's blades felt like an anchor, a truth I couldn't shake, no matter how many lies I told myself.

I raised the hood last, letting the emerald fabric shadow my face. My wisps of hair spilled free from my braid and framed my face, wild and defiant against the ordered lines of leather. In the reflection of the vanity mirror, I caught a glimpse of myself and froze. I didn't look like a girl headed for an apprenticeship and leaving home for the first time. I looked like someone preparing to cross a threshold she could never return from.

And maybe that was the truth of it. This wasn't just a journey. It was a severing of the life I'd always known.

I took a deep breath and squared my shoulders. "I think I'm ready," I said, though the words felt small in the face of what loomed ahead.

My grandmother studied me for a moment longer before a faint smile softened her features. "Come. Let's take one last walk around Laochra. It'll help settle your nerves to walk through somewhere familiar."

The village stretched before us, bathed in blue skies and shimmering sunlight. Laochra had always been a quiet place, the kind of village that held stories in the creak of old wooden fences and the worn paths beneath our feet. But today, everything seemed sharper—more vivid, like I was seeing it through fresh eyes.

The dusty paths that wound between small cottages, the fire pit still blackened from the last gathering, the faint slapping of the kissing barn's weathered doors in the wind—it all rooted me in a way I hadn't expected.

Even the animals along the fences seemed louder. Chickens clucked and pecked at the ground while soft bleats echoed from the neighboring pasture, where sheep grazed lazily under the sun. Children's laughter rang out from the far side of the village, tangled with the sound of bare feet slapping against packed dirt as they raced past their homes, wild and free.

I watched it all—burned it into memory. Because I didn't know if I'd ever walk these paths again. And if I didn't... I wanted to remember them exactly like this.

By the time we circled back, I found myself lingering in front of our house, breath caught in my throat like it knew what came next but still wasn't ready. My mother waited on the steps, framed by the soft gold light of early afternoon. Her arms were folded loosely across her chest, but her eyes, glistening with unshed tears, were fixed on me with an intensity that almost undid me.

She didn't say anything at first. Just stepped forward and wrapped me in her arms like she meant to keep me there, to hold me in place with nothing but the strength of her love. I sank into her without hesitation, burying my face in her shoulder, breathing in the familiar scent of lavender and baked bread that clung to her skin. It felt like home—anchored and warm and desperately hard to leave.

"My sweet girl," she whispered, her voice trembling. "I've never known anyone as brave as you."

The words sank into me, hitting somewhere deep and aching. I clung to her tighter, wishing I could bottle this feeling, carry it with me like a second heartbeat.

"I'll be okay, Mom. I promise," I whispered, as if saying it aloud would make it true. "I won't be gone forever."

She nodded against my hair, but I felt the falter in her breath. Her fingers curved around the back of my neck like she could still protect me, like she could still keep me small and safe and untouched by the world I was walking into. When she pulled back, her hands found my cheeks, cupping them gently as she searched my face like she was trying to memorize every freckle, every line of me, before I slipped out of reach.

"I know you will. I just…" Her voice caught, and she pressed trembling fingers to her lips, trying to catch the words before they could escape. But the tears came anyway, slipping down her cheeks unchecked. "I just don't want you to go through any of this alone. You're my baby girl, Raine. And out there, I can't protect you. I can't help you if something goes wrong."

Her words wrapped around me like a fragile thread, one tug away from unraveling completely. I covered her hands with mine, holding them tightly against my face, willing her to feel the truth in what I said next.

"I won't be alone," I whispered, hoping the weight of those words was enough to anchor her fear. Even as uncertainty stirred inside me, I held onto the only thing I could promise her. "I'll carry all of you with me. Every word. Every lesson. Every part of this life and home."

She let out a shaky laugh, soft and watery. "You sound just like your grandmother," she murmured, wiping her eyes with the edge of her sleeve. "You always have. Stubborn, poetic, and too brave for your own good."

I managed a small smile, even as the weight in my chest grew heavier.

"Must run in the family."

Her laugh cracked like glass. "You should go," she said quietly, her thumb brushing beneath my eye. "Before I change my mind and tie you to that bedpost with my apron strings so I can keep you here forever."

She kissed my forehead—once, twice—her lips lingering longer than usual. I let the warmth of her sink into my skin, pressing it into memory, into bone. I didn't want to move. I didn't want to leave this porch, this house, this version of me, the one who had only ever known her love as a constant. I wanted to fold into her warmth and cling to the safety of home just a little longer. But the pull of the forest was stronger, a quiet calling I couldn't ignore.

With a final squeeze of her hands, I stepped back, slowly, afraid that if I moved too quickly, I'd lose the courage I'd worked so hard to build. I bit the inside of my cheek to try and stop more tears from spilling over. She didn't say anything more, just let her eyes follow me, as if trying to etch every detail of me into her memory.

When I turned, my grandmother was already waiting near the door, leaning casually against the frame with the satchel I was bringing draped over her shoulder. Her face was more guarded than I was used to, but there was a softness in her eyes that told me she understood just how hard this goodbye was.

She silently held out her hand, not rushed, not expectant, just steady. I reached for it, letting her fingers curl around mine. No words passed between us, but none were needed.

We walked in silence, our footsteps the only sound echoing down the long road out of Laochra. The village around us seemed suspended in amber, the shadows longer, the colors warmer, as if the town itself understood this was a farewell. It all felt surreal, like I was seeing Laochra through the lens of a memory, even though I hadn't left yet.

It was home. Imperfect, simple... and yet, I couldn't shake the feeling that I was already starting to miss it.

And maybe that was the hardest part. It wasn't just my family I was leaving behind. It was me—the girl who had grown up chasing fireflies between cottages and stealing bread from the cooling racks in the kitchen. The girl who had never truly outgrown her wild nature. With every step I took, that version of myself felt further away. But I still carried her with me, just as I carried my mother's tears, my father's laughter, my brothers' teasing words, and my grandmother's steady strength. Because no matter what waited across the river, I wasn't doing this for me. I was doing it for all of them.

By the time we reached the tree line, Laochra had disappeared behind us, swallowed whole by the looming hush of the woods. The softening rays of sunlight clung to the trunks, casting long golden shadows that stretched like fingers across the earth. The trees stood tall and unyielding, guardians of a path I couldn't yet see, their silence heavier than I remembered.

My grandmother finally stopped, her focus sweeping the woods ahead as if reading secrets in the spaces between branches. Then she turned to me, her hands finding mine— warm, calloused, grounding. The way they had always been.

"My Wildheart," she said softly, though her voice still held its familiar steel, "there's nothing more I can give you that will truly prepare you for what's ahead. But know this—you are stronger than you believe. And there is more inside you than any test, any magic, any ancient Rite could ever break."

Her words lodged somewhere deep inside me, where doubt had long made a home. I swallowed hard, forcing the lump in my throat down. I wouldn't cry. Not now. Not here.

She must have felt it, my effort to hold steady, and pulled me into a tight embrace. Her hand slid through my hair, slow and familiar, the same way she used to soothe me after nightmares or scraped knees. Except this time, I wasn't a child, and the monsters weren't just in stories.

"When the world expects you to fall," she whispered, "stand a little taller instead."

I closed my eyes, clutching her like I could anchor myself in that one sentence. I didn't want to let go.

"Thank you," I murmured, the words catching on the sharp edges of emotion in my chest. "For everything. For the lessons, the protection, even the silence. I know now… how hard it must have been to keep this from us. And I think I'm starting to understand why you had to."

She stepped back just far enough to meet my eyes, and for a moment, hers shimmered with something vast and unspoken. Pride, or maybe grief. Or a quiet knowing that some goodbyes don't come with certainty.

"I know if anyone can face what the gods have in store, and convince the Queen," she said, brushing her thumbs along my cheeks, "it's you. My little Wildheart."

The name curled through me like firelight—soft, warm, alive.

"Remember—add the herbs to the tonic just before midnight. Drink it all in one go, and it will protect you. But be cautious, it won't make you invincible. You'll still be vulnerable… even if nothing can truly harm you."

I nodded quickly, burning every word into my memory like scripture.

"Manakel will meet you soon, and he'll guide you the rest of the way. Listen to him—but more importantly, listen to the forest. It will speak to you if you know how to hear it."

She squeezed my hand tighter.

"Everything around you will be watching, but don't be fooled. Even familiar faces can betray you when magic tests your will."

"Got it," I whispered, holding her hands as tightly as I dared, as if I could absorb a piece of her courage before I let go.

She hesitated then—just for a breath—but I felt the shift. A flicker of softness. A final offering.

"One last thing," she said softly. "Trust yourself. Even when everything else feels wrong. You'll know what to do when the time comes."

That was the part that scared me the most—that it would be me, alone, making the choices. That no spell or blade could save me from the moment I hesitated.

But still, I nodded.

And then, without another word, I wrapped my arms around her and held on one last time, burying my face in her shoulder and letting the weight of everything settle.

She pulled me in close, one hand cradling the back of my head, the other curled tightly around my waist like she could hold the moment still.

"Be safe, my Wildheart," she breathed, her lips brushing my temple like a blessing, like a goodbye she didn't want to say. "Go forward with fire in your heart and steel in your veins. Face the river, face yourself… and come back changed."

Her voice cracked, just slightly, but she didn't pull away.

"I can't wait to meet the version of you who makes it to the other side."

When she finally stepped back, her hands lingered on my cheeks, thumbs swiping away tears I hadn't realized had fallen.

"You were never meant to stay small," she whispered. "So go now. Be bold. Be brave. And don't look back."

I didn't speak as I stepped away. I couldn't. My throat was thick with everything I hadn't said, everything I wasn't sure I'd get the chance to. She stayed behind, her silhouette framed by the trees, watching as I walked forward into the shadows. I didn't need to look back to feel the weight of her stare or the warmth of her love pressed against my spine.

The path ahead was narrow and uneven, the kind of trail that didn't care who you were before you took it. I took a breath that didn't quite steady me, squared my shoulders anyway, and stepped forward.

The river was waiting.

32. Into The Unknown

I didn't know what I was walking into. I only knew that today would alter the trajectory of my life in ways I wasn't ready to comprehend.

Growing up, I used to imagine leaving Laochra at eighteen, stepping beyond the narrow paths and quiet expectations to chase something bigger. Something that belonged to me alone. But I never imagined it would happen like this. Not with the weight of the unknown pressing so heavily on my shoulders, as I stepped into unknown territory with nothing but instinct to guide me.

The trees thickened as I moved deeper into the woods. Branches clawed at my sleeves, and low brambles tugged at my boots like the earth itself was reluctant to let me go. I hadn't walked this part of the forest before. Few had. There was no path to follow, no footprints or worn trail carved by those who came before. I was alone in a place that felt untouched—not just by people, but by time.

I pushed forward, brushing aside the undergrowth, the soft hush of late afternoon settling over everything like a held breath. The sun slanted through the leaves in golden ribbons, illuminating specks of pollen and dust as they drifted through the air. It was beautiful in that strange, otherworldly way beauty often is—sharp-edged and unsettling.

And yet, the further I went, the steadier I felt. Everything I had ever known was behind me, and the only way out was forward.

I could do this.

I would do this.

I had to do this.

I adjusted the strap of my bag, its familiar weight pressing against my side like a silent companion. Inside was everything I would need to survive this place. Every item chosen with purpose. Every item a promise I would succeed.

I glanced around, searching for any sign of Manakel, though I already knew he wouldn't be here waiting. He hadn't come last night either, and I was starting to realize maybe it was for the best.

Maybe some journeys had to begin alone, and this was the start of me relying on myself.

Still, the thought of going forward without him, or anyone, felt like standing at the edge of a cliff, staring down into a fog-drenched abyss. Scary and unsettling. But I pushed those doubts away, forcing one foot in front of the other. I could figure this out. I had no other choice.

The river was somewhere ahead. I just had to find it.

The forest here felt different—ancient in a way that made the hairs on my arms rise. The damp earth cradled my steps, muffling the sound of my boots as if the ground wanted to swallow any trace of me. I hadn't noticed how quiet it had become until now. No chirping birds, no scurrying animals in the underbrush. Just silence. And the hum.

I told myself this was a good sign, something meaningful. Maybe it was the forest acknowledging me, recognizing the purpose that carried me forward.

I could *almost* believe that, even if it sounded far-fetched.

My grandmother's voice echoed softly in the back of my mind. *Trust your instincts.* I wanted to. But the truth lingered, clawing at the edges of my resolve— I had no idea what I was walking into.

The path I'd envisioned for myself had changed the moment I stepped into these woods. There was no going back, no return to the safety of home. And maybe that was how it was meant to be.

I paused beneath the sprawling branches of an oak tree, tilting my head as if the forest might whisper some hidden direction in return. Nothing. The undergrowth thickened ahead, wild and undisturbed, but I could feel it, the quiet invitation urging me forward.

Then a branch snapped beneath my foot.

The sound shattered the stillness like a crack of thunder, and I flinched, my heart hammering in response. I held my breath, waiting, listening for anything; movement, a voice, anything that might suggest I wasn't alone.

But the woods gave nothing away.

Exhaling slowly, I scanned the area around me. There was no hint of familiarity, no landmarks I could recognize, just endless trees stretching in every direction. The quiet didn't feel welcoming anymore.

I swallowed the lump forming in my throat and pressed forward, each step heavier than the last.

I didn't know where I was going. I didn't know if Manakel would find me. I didn't even know which direction the river was.

But I kept walking.

Because even if I didn't understand the destination, something in the pit of my stomach told me I was exactly where I needed to be, and I wanted to believe in that feeling.

I had been walking for what felt like hours, though it had likely been no more than a few minutes. The forest had a way of distorting time, making every step feel stretched and elongated like I was wading through the currents of something ancient and unseen. The thick canopy above muted the light, draping the woods in a green-tinted twilight that felt neither day nor night. I could still recall the lingering chill of my first journey through the forest, the way the shadows felt heavier, how the trees whispered in ways they shouldn't. The memory tried to root itself in my mind, but I shoved it aside.

Fear wouldn't help me now. I had to keep looking ahead, keep my focus on where I was headed. *That* was the only way through this, but as I started walking, the faint murmur of voices caught my ear.

I froze, pressing myself behind a nearby trunk. The bark was rough beneath my palms, and I held my breath, tuning my ears to the sound drifting through the trees.

It was distant but approaching, threaded with tones too distinct to be carried by the wind. I strained to listen, hoping for the friendly banter of Fern and Dela, or at the very least, anyone but the sharp-edged wrath of Alfreda.

I leaned into the shadows, keeping my breathing shallow.

Three voices. I counted three, each distinctly different.

I should have announced myself, but curiosity anchored me in place. I needed to know what, *or who*, I was walking into before risking exposure. They drew closer, the sound of their voices louder as I held my breath and listened.

"—told her to wait," grumbled the first voice, low and irritated. A man's voice, by the weight of it.

A second, female, soft and melodic, replied, "You think she'll make it? The River hasn't let anyone through in years."

The hair on the back of my neck rose. There was something haunting in her timbre, like her words weren't meant to be heard out loud. Like she was used to whispering to the trees while they carried her secrets in the wind.

"She has to make it," a third voice cut in, calm but urgent. "There's more at stake here than she probably realizes… especially for the Sciatháin."

My heart stilled.

If they were talking about them, then it had to also be about me.

I peered around the trunk. Three cloaked figures glided between the trees, their steps soundless. Their garments shimmered with faint movement, like mist caught in fabric, and though I couldn't see their faces, I felt their presence like heat from a flame. Something about them felt… old. Not in the way of age but in presence, as though they belonged to this forest as much as the roots beneath my feet.

"If she doesn't reach the river by midnight, she will fail her Imbe Rite," the first voice hissed, low and urgent, "and then everything we've set in motion will be for nothing."

There was no mistaking the desperation threaded through his tone. Not fear for *me*, but for what I carried. For what my failure might uncover or cause.

A second voice answered, smoother and steadier. "The river is only the beginning. If she can't reach the Queen… *then* it's all for nothing."

Something in my chest twisted.

"Don't be so quick to doubt," the calm one replied, his gaze drifting around the area as though sensing something unseen. "Leighna prepared her well. Maybe even more than we hoped."

My breath caught.

They knew her. *My grandmother.*

My grip tightened on the tree trunk beside me, grounding myself against the creeping unease spreading beneath my ribs.

Then the first voice again, quieter this time, like he feared the forest itself might overhear. "Let's just hope she remembers who she is when it matters most."

"And let's pray the Sciatháin don't tip the scales before she does."

Silence fell like a stone. No footsteps. No movement.

I didn't dare breathe.

Their voices had vanished like mist, leaving behind only the crackling hush of the forest. But the silence wasn't still. It throbbed with warning, like the air before a storm.

A sudden rustle to my left snapped through the quiet—sharp and deliberate. I spun, heart hammering. But there was nothing. Just trees and shadow.

Then a burst of motion ensued overhead.

Three birds, sleek, black-feathered, shot through the canopy above me. Wings slicing the air in perfect unison, not a single cry between them. They moved with uncanny precision. Not wild. Not free. *But Purposeful.*

I followed their path until the last one vanished into the thick branches, a chill curling down my spine.

They were shifters. I didn't have proof, not really. But something inside me, something older and instinctual, knew.

The voices. The watching. The warning. They weren't just Eldren or figments conjured by the Rite. They were real. Flesh and feather and something more.

And they were watching me.

I stayed hidden, holding my breath until their silhouettes flew out of sight. Before I could decide whether to step out or keep hiding, the tree I was leaning against shifted.

Branches curled swiftly into vines around my waist, lifting me effortlessly off the ground and holding me out for inspection. I gasped as a face emerged from the wood, ancient and feminine, her amber eyes glowing with the knowledge and weight of centuries.

"Normally, people greet me with an offering," she mused, tilting her head. "And yet, you throw yourself against me with neither warning nor gift. How… unceremonious."

I froze. "Uh—sorry," I said quickly. "Didn't realize you were… well, you." I tried to keep still, though the tips of her fingers brushed my arms and legs, the texture rough and tickling against my skin. I bit back the urge to squirm.

Her bark-textured brow arched, if dryads could even do such a thing. She leaned in, breath warm and earthy, stirring the loose strands of hair around my face.

"You carry the scent of river stones and ancient magic," she murmured, her eyes narrowing. "The Imbe Rite?"

"Y-yes," I stammered, my mind racing. "I'm on my way to the river. I'm—well, I'm supposed to cross it tonight." I gave a cautious nod, careful not to move too much in her grip.

Her branches tightened for just a second, the pressure firm but not painful. "Do you understand the weight of what you are facing, child?"

Her warm voice carried an ominous tone, like a warning buried beneath the layers of her curiosity.

I swallowed. "Not exactly," I admitted, feeling small under her unblinking focus. "But I'm ready. My grandmother—she made sure of that."

The dryad's bark creaked in a sound that could have been a sigh or a laugh—maybe both.

"Ready?" she echoed. "No one ever truly is. The woods will test more than your courage. And the river—it takes something every time it gives."

Her words made my stomach twist, but I lifted my chin, determined. "The tonic will protect me."

She studied me, then slowly, with a low groan of wood, her branches began to lower me back down.

"I see," she said, "but protection is not the same as permission."

As my boots met solid ground again, her form began to blend into the tree once more.

"But heed this advice—should you encounter another like me, bow your head and offer respect. Not all dryads are as…forgiving."

I exhaled shakily. "Thank you, and I'm sorry. I'll be sure to remember."

The dryad smiled faintly, her form already fading back into the trunk.

"Go on then. The river waits, and it's been a long time since it welcomed someone like you."

And just like that, she vanished back into the plain bark of her tree. Leaves rustled overhead, stirred by a breeze that hadn't existed moments before. They twirled in a slow spiral, scattering like breadcrumbs along a narrow opening in the trees.

And I followed, hoping they led me where I needed to go.

The leaves stirred ahead of me, their spiral dance purposeful, as if they knew the path ahead better than I did. They shimmered in the late afternoon light, twirling in silence, their rustling soft but insistent. It felt less like wind and more like guidance.

I hesitated, glancing around, searching for anything, anyone, that could explain the strange pull in the air.

Nothing.

I exhaled slowly and tightened the strap of my bag across my chest. "Trust the forest," I whispered to myself, trying to believe it. Or at least, pretend to.

I stepped forward, following the rhythm of the leaves. The air thickened around me, clinging to my skin with a quiet tension. The trees stretched higher here, their bark darker, the canopy overhead so dense it nearly sealed off the sky. The light dimmed to a dusky haze, casting everything in a green-tinged twilight.

The moss softened my steps, but every footfall still felt heavy, the earth damp beneath my boots. Wildflowers bloomed in scattered bursts, their colors too vivid against the creeping shadows curling between roots.

And then, the hum returned, low and insistent, no longer a feeling but a sound. It pressed against my ribs, then split. It wasn't the wind. It wasn't the rustle of leaves. This was something else.

"You don't belong here," a voice whispered, close but invisible.

I froze, my breath catching.

"Turn back, human, before it's too late," another voice echoed, sharper this time, coming from behind me.

I whipped around, but there was nothing. No one. Only trees and the hum vibrating in the air. Roots shifted beneath me. One curled around my boot, and I stumbled, catching myself just before I hit the ground.

Calm down. Breathe. Keep moving.

I pushed forward, ignoring the phantom voices, but it was as if the trees had closed in tighter, their shadows flickering strangely, and the air felt thick enough to choke on. Fog crept through the underbrush, curling around my ankles like smoke.

A flicker of movement to my right, and I froze.

It was my father.

My breath caught in my throat. My dad, his tall frame unmistakable, stepped from between the trees, eyes wide with panic as he scanned his surroundings.

"Raine, turn back now!" he called out, his voice full of desperation, his face etched with worry.

I took a shaky step toward him, a multitude of questions flooding my veins. *Why was he here? How had he found me? Had he followed me from Laochra? Did he know my job in Ceannairí was a lie and was here to bring me home?*

"Dad?" I screamed, but the sound barely broke the surface.

He moved closer, his steps unnaturally smooth, the forest parting around him like it welcomed him. Like it recognized him.

My heart pounded, panic rising in my chest. My mind was spinning. He shouldn't be here. I was doing this for *his* protection, his safety—all of theirs. I needed him to turn around and go back home before he got hurt, or worse, *killed.*

I opened my mouth to warn him, but the words got trapped by the heavy, suffocating air pressing down on me.

"Dad!" I called, my voice cracking.

Could he even hear me? If I walked toward him, I'd be going in the opposite direction of the river, but right now, all I cared about was his safety.

I took another step forward, reaching for him, but his body flickered, the edges of him blurring like smoke drifting through the trees. The illusion dissolved, his image fading, like he had never been there at all.

I swallowed hard. It wasn't him. It was a trick.

I clenched my fists, forcing the tremor in my hands to stop. "Nice try," I muttered under my breath, as much to myself as to the woods. I wasn't about to let them see me falter. But the forest wasn't finished.

I didn't have time to fully recover before I saw him—Wren. He was leaning against a tree, arms crossed, with his familiar cocky smirk.

"You're going to fail, Ray," he called out casually, as if he were commenting on the weather. "Might as well turn around now before you embarrass yourself."

I swallowed hard, ignoring the flare of frustration boiling under my skin. But the forest didn't let up.

To my left, my mother stood still as stone. Her arms were folded, disappointment etched across her face. I knew that look. I'd worn it myself.

"You're not ready, Raine," she said softly. "You should've stayed home."

I gritted my teeth and kept walking, refusing to blink. Refusing to cry. Both visions dissolved like mist, but their words lingered, embedding themselves in my thoughts like thorns.

Then I heard Baren's voice.

"You're not strong enough."

He didn't say it with anger. Just certainty. The kind that settled into your bones and made a home there.

My steps faltered. I closed my eyes, let the ache rise—and fall.

I wasn't turning back. They could send ghosts of my past, dig up every buried fear, twist every doubt into a weapon, but I wasn't giving up.

I would keep going.

Because maybe they were right.

Maybe I wasn't ready.

Maybe I wasn't strong enough.

But I was here anyway. And I wasn't walking away.

The voices wrapped around me like unseen hands, their whispers sharp as glass, each syllable slicing through what little resolve I had left. They didn't shout; they didn't need to. Their words were soft, precise, and cruel, unraveling me thread by thread. I dug my nails into my palms, grounding myself.

Don't listen. Don't let them in.

But the whispers slithered beneath my skin, weaving through my thoughts like ivy, squeezing until my chest felt too tight to breathe.

Turn back. You can't do this. You're not strong enough.

A sting burned behind my eyes. My throat tightened. I bit down on the inside of my cheek, hard enough to taste copper. I couldn't give in. Not now. Not after everything I'd risked to be here. All I could do was put one foot in front of the other and hope that was enough.

I kept walking.

Then, without warning, I stumbled, colliding into something solid. Unmoving. My momentum halted, breath knocked from my lungs. Strong hands caught me, steadying me before I could stumble. I snapped my eyes open and came face-to-face with Aeron.

He stood before me, his wings slightly unfurled like shadows edged in gold lining. His expression was carved from something colder than stone. But beneath the sharp angles of irritation, something unreadable settled in his stormy eyes—a quiet intensity that set my nerves on edge.

"Running already?" His voice was low, laced with disdain and disappointment.

His grip lingered, fingers like anchors around my arms. Not painful. Just… refusing to let go. He studied me, eyes flicking across my face like he was cataloging weakness.

I swallowed hard and tried to step back, but he didn't release me right away.

"Let go," I said, quieter than I meant. Finally, he did, but he didn't step away.

"You should know better by now. You can't outrun the woods," he murmured, the corner of his mouth tugged into a smirk, and his wings twitched behind him. "Or an immortal—especially one with wings."

He gestured lazily, like *I* was the one being ridiculous. *Why is he always like this?*

I rolled my eyes, irritation flaring. "I wasn't *running*," I muttered, straightening my shoulders, though the heat crawling up my neck betrayed me. "I was…walking fast. I need to reach the river before midnight."

His smirk deepened, teeth just barely showing like he was already enjoying this too much.

"Is that so?" he drawled, stepping closer—*too close*. His voice dropped, brushing against me like smoke curling against bare skin. "Well, you might want to turn around."

I froze. "What?"

"The river's that way," he said, nodding behind me, amusement sharpening in his eyes.

My stomach dropped.

No. *How had I been walking in the wrong direction this entire time?*

My heart stuttered, panic slamming into me like a cold wave. Aeron caught it instantly and smiled wider.

"Did you not listen when I said the woods would test you, too?" he mused, tilting his head slightly. His voice was calm, but something about the way he looked at me made my breath catch, like he was deciding just how far to push. "It can twist your path, warp your sense of time, and show you things meant to break you. That's the point."

I clenched my jaw.

"And *you*," he added, stepping closer, "followed the first lie it offered— like a lost little human."

The sting of embarrassment burned beneath my skin. I had blindly followed the leaves. They'd felt like a sign, gentle, guiding, but the startling realization that I'd been led astray hit like a blow to the gut. This was a test. And I had already failed.

"I thought I was being led," I admitted, my voice quieter now, ashamed.

His expression shifted—just for a blink. A flicker of something almost… sympathetic. Then it vanished.

"You need to start thinking for yourself," he said, and this time, it wasn't teasing—it was a lesson. "Think of the forest as being against you. Trust no one. Nothing. Things here will deceive you, or throw you off course. And if your instincts don't sharpen, they'll bury you here."

I clenched my fists. I wanted to believe him, but doubt gnawed at me. What if *he* was the test, here to throw me off course and confuse me further? I needed time to think, to question his words, but I didn't have it. If I *had* been walking in the wrong direction all along, I'd just added hours to my journey—hours I couldn't afford if I wanted any rest before stepping into the river.

"What if you're the one deceiving me?" I countered, searching his face.

That earned me a pause. And then his smirk grew, like he was proud of me for asking.

"Now you're learning," he murmured, stepping close enough for his voice to brush my thoughts instead of my ears. *"Listen carefully. But don't believe a word I say out loud. These woods respect those who can untangle lies from truth. Prove yourself to them, and maybe... just maybe... you'll find allies when you need them most."*

Then, aloud—sharp and taunting—his voice sliced the air. "You know, I could make this easier for you," he taunted, circling me like a predator. "Spare you the river's cruelty. Believe me—it won't be nearly as generous with you."

I held my ground, even as every part of me tensed. I knew he was playing a part, but that didn't soften the razor-sharp tone in his voice or the way his eyes searched mine with a kind of intensity I couldn't place. There was a weight behind his words like he wouldn't hesitate to follow through if I so much as flinched.

The air between us thickened as his circles moved closer, his presence pressing against me, brushing too close. My pulse pounded in my ears. Every instinct screamed at me to run.

But I didn't.

My inner voice screamed at me. *Trust nothing. Not even him.*

No sound passed his lips, but his voice echoed in my mind, laced with warning. *"Everything in these woods is watching. I need them to believe I want you to truly fail."*

I didn't flinch; I couldn't let it show that he was somehow warning me silently. Out loud, his voice was mocking.

"The forest eats the weak, Banríon. Let's not pretend you haven't already thought about running and giving up."

I swallowed hard, forcing myself to meet his gaze, though every inch of me itched to step back. My instincts screamed at me to fight or deny, but I kept my footing steady. I had to remember his whispered warning—to do the opposite of what he said aloud. I straightened, tightening my grip on the straps of my satchel as I lifted my chin in defiance.

"I'm not afraid of you," I said evenly. "And I'm not afraid of these woods."

His face darkened. A spark flared—approval, or warning, I couldn't tell.

I took a breath. "Unless you're here to help, get out of my way. I'd say it was nice to see you again, but we *both* know I'd be lying."

His smirk stayed, but his expression sharpened. "Then I guess I'll see you on the other side...*if* you make it. Considering you *have* been walking the wrong way this whole time."

I turned. His hand shot out, his fingers wrapping around my wrist like iron wrapped in silk.

My breath hitched. A flicker of something crossed his face—a wink, or a dare. Was he telling the truth? Or was this just another layer of his twisted game? My head spun, each of his cryptic words pushing me further into doubt. I glanced around; the sun was beginning to dip behind the trees, casting shadows that stretched across the forest floor. Time was slipping, and I needed to get moving. *Fast.*

Without another word, I yanked my wrists free, turned my back on his taunting smile, and walked away, desperately trying to shake the fog of confusion he'd left me in.

But I could still feel him behind me, the press of his warning, the heat of his hand, the weight of his words. The shadows seemed darker now, the forest quieter, as if holding its breath.

Still watching.

Still waiting.

Trust no one. Not even him.

33. Claws In The Dark

The sun bled into the horizon, its orange and pink hues dissolving into the creeping darkness, but none of its warmth reached me. Shadows stretched long and thin across the forest floor, slithering between the trees like unseen hands grasping at the edges of my resolve.

I pulled my cloak tighter, my fingers clenched around the fabric as I forced myself to keep moving. The crackle of leaves beneath my boots felt too loud, like the forest itself was listening, waiting for a misstep.

It was watching. I could feel it.

I told myself it was paranoia, that exhaustion was making me imagine things, but the weight of unseen eyes refused to fade.

Think, Raine. Stay focused.

I tried to retrace my steps, but everything looked different in the fading light. Aeron's words haunted me, twisting in my mind—*trust no one, nothing*. But then he had whispered that I could trust the things he didn't share out loud.

He had done this before—offering cryptic half-truths that felt like riddles more than guidance. And still... a small part of me wanted to believe him.

I swallowed hard, frustration burning in my chest as I pushed forward. Manakel should have been here by now. We'd prepared for this all week, trained together, had a plan. He was supposed to guide me to the river, but he didn't show up last night, was nowhere this morning, and I was left wandering blindly through an unfamiliar forest that wanted me dead.

The doubt crept in like a slow poison, curling into my ribs. I closed my eyes, inhaled deeply, and searched for something, *anything*, that might help me.

Then something shifted. The air turned cooler, crisper—carrying a scent that stirred something in me.

Water.

My eyes snapped open, my pulse surging. I couldn't hear it, couldn't see it, but I felt it. Like a magnetic pull buried deep in my bones, beckoning me to its waters. The river was close.

Renewed determination burned beneath my skin, and I quickened my pace, trusting the new feeling to guide me. The woods seemed to shift around me, shadows dancing at the edge of my vision. I couldn't shake the feeling of being watched, of unseen eyes tracking my every move.

The forest came alive with new sounds. The rustle of unseen creatures, the eerie hoot of an owl, and whispers that seemed to come from the trees themselves. Flickers of light danced in the distance; possibly from faeries, but I tried to block it all out, focusing only on my goal. The river. *I had to reach the river.*

As I pushed through a dense thicket of evergreen trees, my foot caught on something, possibly a root. But when I looked down, a glint of metal caught in the fading light. *A trap.* I froze. My pulse slammed against my ribs as I took in the small trap just inches from my boot. I stepped aside carefully, realizing how close I'd come to being ensnared.

"Well done," a voice slithered from the unknown.

My spine stiffened before I even turned. *I knew that voice.* I spun around to face Aeron as he emerged from behind a twisted oak, darkness clinging to him like a second skin. His movements were effortless, fluid, smooth, like a shadow slipping free from the night.

His wings shimmered faintly behind him, half-furled. And those sharp steel-dark eyes, sparked with flecks of silver, drank me in.

"You're learning, Banríon." His smirk was maddening. And something in it, something beneath it, unraveled a thread I didn't know I was gripping.

I exhaled sharply, my fingers twitching for my dagger on instinct. He caught the movement, his eyes dropping to my hand before returning to my face with a slow, deliberate drag that made my skin warm beneath the cold.

"Easy now," he said, raising his hands in a slow, exaggerated show of surrender. "I'm not here to hurt you." He paused, assessing our surroundings, "Quite the opposite, in fact."

I didn't relax, not when the weight of his earlier words lingered in the air between us. I could still hear his warning—*trust no one.*

But hadn't he whispered later that I could? My head spun with the contradiction. What was real? And who was I to believe or count on? I was honestly losing track now.

"What do you want, Aeron?" I asked, my voice sharper than intended.

He stepped closer, and I didn't flinch. I held my ground, refusing to give him the satisfaction of seeing me retreat.

"I'm here to assist," he said easily. "And to observe, of course." His lips curled, that infuriating edge returning. "What kind of guide would I be if I let you wander too far off course?"

I narrowed my eyes. "But you're not my guide, are you?"

He smiled like I'd just said something particularly amusing.

"So what exactly are you observing?" I pressed.

Aeron smiled in amusement. "Your progress. Your instincts. Your mistakes." He tilted his head, letting the silence hang. "How you play the games in these woods." Then he shrugged casually. "Not all guides can be as gallant as Manny."

The name landed like a blow to the chest.

Manakel.

My *actual* guide. The one who was supposed to be here, but was nowhere to be seen.

Something sharp twisted in my gut, but I swallowed it down and met his gaze with steel. His smirk widened, slow and infuriating. The weight of his stare pressed down on me, and I shifted uneasily. His words danced the line between mockery and something far more dangerous. I remembered his earlier warning—to ignore his surface words, to prove myself through action.

"Well, I don't need your guidance."

He took another step. The space between us shrank. I could feel the heat of him, like standing too close to a fire that didn't burn.

"And why should I believe anything you say?" I challenged, forcing my chin higher.

"You shouldn't." His voice dropped, a whisper just for me. "That's the point, isn't it?"

The dagger on my hip felt useless—*he* was the weapon here, and I was already caught in his aim. The woods around us stilled, as if waiting for one of us to make the next move.

"Fine," I bit out through clenched teeth. "If you're here to *observe*, then do that. But I'm not some helpless human waiting to be rescued."

He chuckled softly, the sound more menacing in the quiet. "No," he agreed, "you're something far more interesting."

Then he looked toward the treetops, to where the last gold of the day was bleeding out.

"You're running out of time," he said, voice casual. But the words sank in like stone. "The river doesn't wait for stragglers. And the woods at night don't take kindly to uninvited guests."

My stomach twisted. He wasn't wrong—dusk was slipping quickly into night, and I was no closer to the river than I had been hours ago. Still, I refused to admit that to him. I turned on my heel, jaw tight with determination, and took a step forward, but the ground betrayed me.

Roots curled around my boots like fingers, dragging me down. I stumbled, catching myself on a low branch, heart racing.

Aeron's laugh behind me was low, dark, and unsettlingly amused.

"Still so sure you don't need my help, Banríon?" he taunted, his voice laced with something sharp.

I whirled on him, my frustration bubbling over. "What did you do?"

He raised his hands, feigning innocence. "Me? I didn't do a thing." He tsked and gestured to the tangled mess of roots writing at my feet. "The woods have a mind of their own. I'm merely here to witness their mischief."

I tore my eyes from him and back to the ground. The roots were now still, blanketed in moss and shadow, as though they hadn't just come alive or tried to drag me under.

"I can handle a few roots and uneven ground," I snapped, brushing off my cloak. "I've made it this far on my own."

Aeron tilted his head, watching me with a knowing glint in his eyes. "Have you, though? Or has luck simply run alongside you until now?"

His words struck a nerve, and I hated the flicker of doubt they ignited. How much of this journey so far had been skill, and how much had been chance? I straightened my shoulders. "Does it matter? I'm still standing."

He stepped closer, the space between us shrinking to a breath. "For now," he said quietly. "But the night is still young. And you haven't even reached the hardest part."

His voice dropped lower—like a secret meant only for me. "Do you even know if you're heading in the right direction this time?"

I clenched my jaw, forcing my feet forward without answering. Because I wasn't sure. I *didn't* know. But I couldn't just blindly *trust* him now, the same way I couldn't ignore the gnawing feeling that he might be right, either.

"You said it yourself, I still have time," I muttered, more to convince myself than him. I met Aeron's stare, determined to mask the nervous tremble in my hands. "I'll make it on my own... I have no other choice."

The last part slipped out softer than intended, but his sharp hearing caught it anyway.

"I won't ask you to trust me, or even expect it. Because, unlike Manakel,

I can see that you're stubborn enough to do exactly what you want, no matter who warns you otherwise."

"You're right. I *won't* trust you, and have gone eighteen years doing what I want, so what's a few more hours?"

He tilted his head, that infuriating smirk curving at the corner of his lips, equal parts amused and annoyed. "Stubborn to your core," he mused, almost fondly.

Then, with a slow, deliberate step backward, he melted into the dark like a shadow retreating from fire.

"Alright," he whispered, voice dipping so low I couldn't tell if it was out loud or in my mind. *"Go on alone then."*

And just like that, he was gone, but his presence lingered.

The air hadn't shifted. The silence hadn't returned. He was watching—maybe not with eyes, but I could feel him near in the marrow of me.

The forest exhaled around me. But I couldn't.

Manakel should've been here.

That thought had been looping in my mind ever since I stepped into the woods and realized I was alone. And with every passing second, it became heavier—more suffocating. He was supposed to lead me to the river, just as we had planned. He had promised to be here with me every step of the way.

A sick feeling curled in my stomach. Had something happened to him? Had someone, *or something,* prevented him from coming? Or had I been a fool to think he ever intended to come?

Trust no one. Nothing.

Aeron's words slithered back into my thoughts, unbidden but impossible to ignore. And with them, the stark reality that they extended to him and his trustworthiness.

In Laochra, I had mastered the art of wariness. It was second nature to be cautious, to question, to guard myself against deception. But I'd stepped into these woods hoping, foolishly, that someone might show up for me.

That was the mistake. The fear and desperation made me soft and desperate. Made me forget I had no one to rely on but myself.

I clenched my fists. I couldn't afford to be careless anymore. Aeron was right; whoever, or whatever, was waiting for me in these woods wanted me to break.

But I would not break. I would not fail.

I forced one foot in front of the other, the forest whispering with every step. The scent of water had faded, swallowed by the damp, earthy tang of moss and rot. The trees had grown denser, their trunks thick as stone pillars, their canopies blotting out the last of the sky.

No stars. No moon. Only shadow.

Was I heading in the right direction this time? I had no way of knowing.

I didn't know where I was or where I was going.

But I knew this—I wasn't turning back.

My breath came faster now, each exhale curling into the cool night air. My boots crushed brittle leaves and twigs beneath me, the only sound in the suffocating silence.

Then I heard it.

A snarl. Low. Deep. Close.

I froze. My pulse slammed against my ribs. The sound hadn't been distant—it had come from behind me. Slowly, I turned, my fingers twitching toward the dagger strapped to my hip.

But there was nothing. The trees stood still, the underbrush undisturbed. The air had shifted again, charged with something unseen, something waiting, something that hadn't made its presence known yet.

Then came another growl. Closer this time.

A sharp, guttural rasp that wrapped around the trunks like smoke. My breath hitched. My chest rose and fell in shallow bursts.

Something was out there and was hunting me.

I took a step back. A branch snapped beneath my boot. The growl that followed was a rumbling exhale, like whatever was out there had just grinned. Terror carved a path through me, sharp and cold.

My mind raced. I didn't know what it was, but it was close. And it wasn't afraid. *What kind of creatures roamed these woods at night?*

I'd trained. I'd prepared. And evidently hadn't asked the right questions. But none of that mattered now. Not with something unknown stalking me through the dark, and no insight on how to defend myself.

My fingers tightened around the hilt of my dagger, but my legs locked in place, frozen by an instinct older than thought itself. I felt the prickle of unease creep up my neck, sending shivers through me.

"Run!"

A voice that wasn't my own bellowed. Aeron's voice.

"Now, Raine. Don't look. Just run."

Panic collided with confusion in my chest; his voice held an edge of urgency I had never heard before.

I didn't have time to think. I ran.

The forest blurred around me, branches clawing past as I pushed my legs harder. The ground shifted beneath every frantic step, unsteady and wild. My breath tore from my lungs in ragged gasps, the sound of it tangled with the thunder of my heartbeat, loud and uneven in my ears.

Behind me, something crashed through the trees. Fast. *Too fast.* Branches snapped. Heavy footfalls pounded the earth.

It was chasing me.

I risked a glance over my shoulder and caught a glimpse of it.

A towering shadow surged through the trees, dark fur bristling, its massive form moving with impossible speed. Glowing yellow eyes locked onto mine—twin moons burning in the darkness—piercing, unblinking, and terrifyingly aware. Its elongated muzzle twisted into something almost human, an unnatural mimicry of expression that made my blood run cold.

It moved like a bear, broad and powerful, but its form was all wrong. Too lean. Too fast. Its shape shimmered, flickering between solid and smoke, as though the world itself couldn't decide what it was. One moment it seemed tangible, muscle and bone pounding the forest floor; the next, it blurred, shifting at the edges like a nightmare I couldn't fully wake from.

As it drew closer, I caught the sharp lines of a wolf's snout, stretched and exaggerated, but it was too massive to be any kind of wolf. Too fluid to be flesh alone. Its razor-sharp claws, long as daggers, scraped against stone and root with each step, sparks hissing in its wake—each sound a promise of how easily it could tear me open.

It wasn't a creature of this world. It was something caught in between. A beast born of shadows and broken boundaries.

Something that should not exist.

"What is that?" I panted, though I didn't expect an answer out here alone.

"That is something you can't face on your own," Aeron's voice replied, edged with warning. *"And precisely why I suggested you might need my help."*

Another snarl rang out, louder this time— close enough that I felt it in my chest.

"I'd really like to know what I'm up against, Aeron," I muttered under my breath, pushing harder through the underbrush, lungs burning with each labored inhale. "You know—for preparation."

Silence. Then—

"As if you'd stand a chance. Prepared or not."

His voice threaded through my mind like smoke—dry, unimpressed, maddeningly calm. No footfalls beside me. No figure in sight. Just that familiar presence curling around my thoughts like a shadow I couldn't shake.

Somewhere to my left, a faint sound, like a sharp exhale or the scrape of leather, slipped through the trees. He was nearby. Watching. Always watching.

"But, fine." The word slid into my mind like a blade. *"It's a Barolf. A rare*

Eldren and a guardian of this stretch of the woods."

I stumbled, more at the unfamiliar name than the terrain beneath my feet. "That's not exactly helpful," I muttered, mostly to myself.

A huff—this time close enough I could almost feel the breath on the back of my neck. But when I twisted to look, nothing stirred behind me but mist and branches.

"They hunt at night," he continued, the tone colder now, stripped of even the hint of amusement. *"Not for food. For trespassers. For those foolish enough to get this close. The river is called forbidden for a reason—it's not meant to be reached. Not easily. The Barolf ensures that."*

I stumbled to a halt, dragging in a breath as the weight of his words settled. The trees seemed darker now, shadows pooling between trunks like ink. A predator was out there, watching. Listening. Waiting.

"So… it's hunting me," I whispered, pulse rising.

His voice dropped, as if the trees themselves could hear our minds. *"It knows why you're here. And no, it's not here to get acquainted or become friends."*

That chill I'd been pretending wasn't creeping down my spine finally took hold. I hesitated, scanning the tree line—hoping for a glimpse of him, something solid to anchor me, but all I caught was movement at the edge of my vision. A darker patch of shadow that vanished before I could focus.

"You've dealt with one before?" I asked aloud, though I wasn't sure if it mattered whether I said them aloud or not.

No answer. Only stillness. Then, the faintest sound, a scoff in the dark. Not cruel, but clipped. Impatient.

Which meant yes.

And still, he said nothing more. No warning. No instructions. No way to fight back or hide. Just that same cool presence tucked like a whisper behind my ribs. My chest tightened, not just with fear now, but frustration. He was holding back. Feeding me slivers of truth while the rest stayed buried in shadow. Like he was testing me. *Again.*

I clenched my fists and picked up my pace, brushing low-hanging branches aside with a trembling hand. I wouldn't ask for help. Not again. I'd said I didn't need him, and I'd meant it. Even if every step forward made it clearer, I didn't know what I was walking into.

And I was running out of time to figure it out.

A sudden roar ripped through the trees, raw, ancient, and unmistakable. The kind of sound that didn't just strike fear, but remembered it. I flinched, the sound of snapping twigs and heavy footsteps following close behind.

It was going to kill me.

I ran harder, my lungs burning, my legs screaming as the ground sloped downward. The air changed, damp and sharp. Water. I could smell it again, which meant the river was close. I pushed forward with everything I had.

Behind me, the Barolf roared—a sound not meant for mortal ears. My legs nearly buckled beneath it.

"Faster, Banríon." Aeron's voice wasn't teasing now. It was raw, sharp, edged with something dangerously close to fear.

I surged forward, branches clawing at my clothes, the ground itself shifting under my feet. Roots tried to snag me. Shadows tried to hold me. The forest wanted me to fail. Twigs snapped beneath my boots, echoing far too loudly in the suffocating quiet of the trees. The sound of my breath, ragged and uneven, roared in my ears.

The Barolf let out another bone-rattling snarl.

I forced my legs to move faster, my heart hammering against my ribs in a desperate, frantic rhythm. My fingers clenched around the hilt of my dagger, but I knew it would be useless against something so massive.

The river. I had to reach the river.

"Don't look back. Don't hesitate. Just run."

Aeron's words slammed into me, right before a sound unlike anything I'd heard before split the air. A scream that sounded like agony, pain, and death all in one- a sound I had never heard before, not even in my nightmares.

A large hand suddenly reached out, rough and strong. It gripped my arm and yanked me sideways while another clamped over my mouth.

"Don't move." Aeron's breath was hot against my ear.

I froze, barely breathing as the sounds of pursuit grew louder. The Barolf crashed into the clearing behind us. Heavy, furious footfalls. Leaves exploded into the air.

"And maybe get your dagger ready," he whispered. "Just in case."

"What in the world *is* a Barolf?" I gasped, unable to tear my eyes away from the terrifying beast not far from us.

Aeron's grip on my wrist tightened, bringing me back to the present. "Something you don't want to go up against. Part bear, part wolf... all deadly."

I turned just enough to see it. It was towering. Hulking. I watched in horror as the Barolf stood up on its hind legs, towering over Aeron, who was already well over six feet tall. Its muscles rippled under its thick fur as it let out a guttural growling howl into the night sky.

My heart pounded in my chest as I watched it scan its surroundings for any sign of us. Its eyes glowed, its claws tore through bark and soil with every step. It was a creature made of nightmares—except worse. Because it was real.

My foot shifted, and a twig snapped beneath my heel. The Barolf's head swung toward us. Aeron's eyes flashed as he shot me a warning glance, and I shrank back. He pressed a finger to his lips as his voice slithered in my mind, *"I'd suggest staying still, but it's too late for that now."*

The Barolf let out a snarl, taking another step forward. Its nostrils flared, massive head tilted, and it growled a low, deep rumble that shook the tree we were hiding behind. I held my breath, pressing myself between Aeron and the rough bark of the tree, willing myself to become invisible.

"We can't outrun it forever. What's your plan exactly?" I whispered, trying not to concentrate on how close he was and deciding which predator was *actually* worse to be trapped with right now.

Aeron's lips quirked, not a smile, not quite. "Who said anything about running? We just needed a distraction for you to catch your breath."

I stared at him in disbelief. "Are you insane? You just said I wasn't ready to face it alone!"

"You're not. I guess it's a good thing you're not alone then," he said simply, moving closer to my side, his body a wall of heat and steel.

"Now, listen carefully. When I say run, you need to—" he stopped, eyes narrowing.

"Run!" he panted and shoved me forward.

I bolted. But he didn't follow.

Behind me, the sound was immediate. The sharp, gut-wrenching noise of claws tearing through flesh, followed by a furious roar. I gasped, my instincts screaming at me to turn back. To make sure he was okay. *Alive.*

But I didn't. I couldn't afford to hesitate. Not when the river was so close. The scent of water grew stronger, crisp and cool against the humid, metallic tang of copper in the air, and I knew I was almost there. Aeron had just risked everything to buy me time.

A flicker of movement appeared in my periphery—dark and massive. I tried to move out of its line of sight, but barely had time to shift before something slammed into my side. The world tilted. My body wrenched violently off course, my breath stolen from my lungs as I hit the ground with bone-jarring force. Leaves and dirt scattered beneath me, my dagger slipping from my grip, vanishing into the underbrush.

Pain sliced through my ribs, sharp and blinding. I gasped, rolling to my side. But Aeron was gone. No longer beside me. The panic came swiftly, curling up from my chest like smoke.

A shadow moved in front of the fading light. Towering. Silent. Patient. *The Barolf.*

It had circled ahead—waiting and watching.

Its yellow eyes burned like twin torches in the dimness, locked onto me with the stillness of a creature that knew it had already won. Its massive shoulders coiled. A low, guttural growl rolled through its chest, vibrating through the earth beneath me.

I reached blindly, fingers searching the dirt until they closed around the cool, familiar hilt of my dagger.

The Barolf lunged.

I threw myself sideways. Its claws sliced the air where my throat had been seconds before, gouging deep grooves into the earth. A cry tore from my lungs as I scrambled to my feet, adrenaline dulling the pain screaming from my ribs, but not by much.

The Barolf stalked toward me, slower this time, savoring the moment, like a predator toying with its prey.

I raised the dagger, my grip unsteady but firm. The blade felt too small, too useless in my shaking hand.

I wasn't going to win this fight. And I knew it.

The Barolf lunged again, faster than anything its size had any right to be.

I braced myself, too slow to dodge—

But then, in a blur of movement, Aeron collided with the beast mid-air, knocking it sideways with a brutal, calculated force. They slammed into the earth in a blur of teeth, claws, and dark wings.

I staggered back, breathless, heart in my throat.

Aeron moved like fury incarnate. His wings unfurled in a violent sweep, ripping the air into chaos. Shadows wrapped around him as he struck, a blade flashing silver with each deadly arc. The Barolf snarled, lashing out, claws aiming for his throat, but Aeron twisted, dodged, and countered with supernatural grace.

Every movement was precise.

Controlled.

Deadly.

I could only watch, stunned, as he forced the Barolf back step by step. He's winning, I thought, foolishly—for half a second. Then the Barolf feinted.

A calculated lurch. A stuttered step.

Aeron shifted left to dodge, his eyes frantically urging me to run, to flee. But I was frozen with fear and doubt. Every instinct screamed at me to help, *to fight.* He was only here because of me. Because I'd been reckless. Because I'd needed him and couldn't admit that before now.

Could I really leave him now?

The Barolf twisted, claws raking close to Aeron's side. His face contorted, but he didn't cry out. He turned sharply, eyes locking onto mine—

"Run." His voice echoed through my mind, sharp and unrelenting.

"Don't worry about me. Go. Get to the river before it's too late."

He stumbled back, wings dragging through the dirt, his blade barely raised in time to deflect another strike.

And still, his voice pressed into my mind—

"Banríon. This is not your battle. Not yet. Go."

My throat burned. My grip tightened on the dagger. But my feet finally moved. Not toward him but toward the river.

Because if I stayed, he wouldn't survive. And if I failed, none of this would matter.

So I ran.

Tears stung my eyes. The sound of the fight faded behind me, claws and steel, roars and wings, and I forced myself not to look back.

Not even once.

I didn't hesitate. As soon as Aeron's pleading voice sliced through my mind, I ran.

The forest blurred around me, a chaos of shadow and silvered moonlight. Branches whipped my skin, tearing at my clothes like clawed hands, but I didn't slow. Behind me, the Barolf roared, a guttural, bone-deep sound, followed by the brutal clash of steel and fury. Aeron was holding the beast back, buying me time.

I forced my legs to move faster. My heartbeat thundered in my ears, drowning everything else out, but his voice still rang clear.

"Don't look back. Keep going."

But gods, I wanted to go back. I wanted to make sure he wasn't being torn apart by the creature he'd thrown himself against for my sake.

No. Focus Raine. He can handle himself.

I continued running and kept my focus up ahead, blinking hard as the forest twisted unnaturally at the edges. The trees leaned too close, casting long, reaching shadows, conspiring to keep me in their grasp. The path narrowed and pitched downward, and I had to adjust quickly to avoid stumbling over roots that jutted out like jagged traps.

A howl split the night, sharp and vicious, far too close.

My foot caught on an exposed root, jerking my body forward. I lurched, my arms flailing as the ground tilted beneath me. I had one breath to brace before the ground vanished beneath me entirely.

A scream tore from my throat as I plummeted, the wind shrieking in my ears. My arms flailed, fingers clawing at empty air, desperate for something, *anything,* to stop my fall, but there was nothing but darkness and the cold, yawning abyss swallowing me whole.

The impact stole every breath from my lungs.

Water—ice-cold and merciless. crashed over me, closing around me like stone walls. My muscles seized violently, pain ripping through my chest like fire, the cold suffocating in its sudden grasp.

Surface. Get to the surface. Breathe.

I thrashed blindly, clothes dragging me down like chains. Panic gripped me. My limbs moved sluggishly, every movement harder than the last.

Stay calm. Don't fight it.

My boot struck something solid beneath me, and I shoved upward with everything I had.

I burst through the surface with a ragged gasp, water erupting from my mouth as I choked and sucked in the sharp, frozen air. It hit my lungs like knives. I coughed hard, spluttering, each breath more a fight than a relief. My whole body trembled, jolted by the shock of cold and the terror still clinging to me like a second skin.

The water surged around my waist, dark and frigid, pulling heat from my limbs with every second. My teeth chattered as I blinked droplets from my lashes, the world above me dim and distorted. My heart thundered so loudly I could barely hear the slap of water against stone.

I looked around, eyes adjusting to the darkness. A pit. I was in a pit—deep and narrow, carved into the earth like a wound. Steep, slick walls loomed on all sides, their surfaces clawed with tangled roots that jutted from the mud like broken fingers. The jagged rim was barely visible overhead, swallowed by shadows and distance.

This wasn't an accident. It was a trap. And I had walked straight into it. *Again.*

Panic clawed up my spine, sinking its teeth in. I stumbled forward, boots scraping slick stone beneath the water, nearly slipping. My muscles ached, heavy and sluggish from the fall and the freezing cold, but I couldn't stop moving. Couldn't let myself freeze here, paralyzed and helpless.

The walls pressed in. The cold seeped through.

I had to get out.

A low growl rolled through the air like thunder beneath the earth, vibrating through my bones like a warning bell. I froze, my pulse hammering against my skin. Slowly, as if any sudden movement would shatter the fragile illusion of safety, I lifted my eyes toward the rim of the pit.

Two glowing yellow eyes stared down at me.

The Barolf.

A new wave of terror surged through me. My hand gripped my dagger, even knowing it wouldn't save me. The beast prowled along the edge, claws carving trenches in the mud, gauging whether it could reach me. Its heavy pants came in snarling exhales, visible in the cold night air. The longer it paced, the clearer it became—it was looking for a way down.

I pressed myself against the mud wall, flattening into it, hoping I could disappear, as if that would make me less of a target. My breath came in quick, sharp bursts, and I fought against the rising panic clawing up my throat. I was trapped, and if the Barolf managed to find a way in, I was dead.

My lips were already numb from the cold, my body trembling uncontrollably. I wouldn't last long in this water. The Barolf knew that. It was waiting, anticipating my weakness. The rustling above grew louder. I braced myself, half-expecting the beast to leap down.

I closed my eyes, waiting for the inevitable splash I'd hear, but a darkness blanketed the pit, covering my only way out. I tensed, the grip on my dagger tightened, waiting to strike.

"Banrion?"

Relief slammed into me so violently my knees almost buckled. I exhaled shakily, clinging to the sound of his voice like a lifeline.

"Took you long enough to find me," I rasped, trying and failing to sound irritated. My voice was raw. I was frozen to the bone.

Aeron crouched at the edge, his eyes sweeping over me with an expression caught between amusement and assessment. His eyes flicked from me to somewhere up ahead in the distance.

"You seem to have a habit of walking straight into traps," he said dryly.

"I'd argue I was distracted trying to outrun a beast." I glared up at him, shivering violently. "Maybe if my *guide* had shown up like he was supposed to, I wouldn't be waist-deep in freezing water waiting on you to help me."

Aeron's smirk deepened, a shadow of something like smoke, slipping through his grasp as he tried to hide his amusement. "No one ever said this was going to be easy."

A low, guttural growl echoed through the pit. The Barolf had no doubt turned its attention toward Aeron again. Even from down here, I saw the faint yellow from its glowing eyes narrowing with interest.

My relief turned to dread. If Aeron was busy distracting the Barolf… there would be no one to pull me out. And I couldn't get out on my own. Not without anything to hold on to or climb. I sucked in a breath, my mind racing through every possible outcome. Aeron could fight off the Barolf, but then what? Even if he won, I would still be stuck down here like prey just waiting for the next monster. And if he lost—*if he lost*—I wouldn't stand a chance on my own.

The Barolf let out a snarl, its hulking form shifting as it crouched, preparing to pounce. Aeron stood slowly, his wings unfurling. The moonlight shimmered along their golden edges, casting his silhouette in shifting light and shadow.

"Don't do anything stupid," I whispered, voice trembling more from cold than fear.

Aeron's lips twitched, but his lips didn't move. Still, I heard him; the words pressed into my thoughts, soft and sardonic.

"Define stupid."

Before I could answer, the Barolf lunged. Aeron shifted in a blur, his wings slicing through the air as he dodged, twisting away from the beast's snapping jaws. The pit shook from the impact as the Barolf landed where he had stood moments before.

I threw my arms over my head, barely dodging as rock and mud pelted the water around me.

"Aeron! Are you okay?" I shouted, stumbling backward.

"Working on it," came his infuriatingly calm reply.

I gritted my teeth. If he got himself killed while I was stuck down here, I'd drag him back just to yell at him properly before killing him myself.

Above, they circled with slow, predatory steps—shadow and fury, steel and claw. Aeron dodged low, rolled, then lashed out with the hilt of his blade, striking the Barolf's side with vicious precision. It roared out in fury.

Aeron crouched slightly, his fingers flexing at his sides, his wings twitching as if considering whether or not to take flight. He wouldn't, though. If he flew, the Barolf would come straight for me, and even though I wasn't supposed to rely on anyone, in this moment, I foolishly did.

Aeron exhaled slowly, calling down to me—mind to mind, *"I suggest you be ready to climb. Quickly."*

I blinked, breathless. "There's nothing to climb with!"

"Then improvise. Since when have you let something challenging stop you?"

I hissed through my teeth but obeyed. My hands searched the wall, roots, mud, stone, anything that reached the top and would be strong enough to hold my weight.

Above, Aeron lunged his body, now only visible through the myriad of shadows he and the beast were creating. His body moved like liquid shadow, dodging the Barolf's massive claws as he spun, his wings folding close to his body before snapping open again. He was fast. So much faster than I'd ever realized.

The Barolf snarled, swiping at him, but Aeron ducked low, slipping beneath it, wings folding in, then exploding outward again to slam the beast off balance.

"Now, Raine! Climb!" he shouted aloud.

I sucked in a breath and moved.

My fingers dug into the roots, the slippery mud coating making it almost impossible to get a grip. My muscles screamed in protest, my ribs ached, but I forced myself higher.

The Barolf shrieked in fury.

And still—I climbed. Hand over hand. Mud-slick fingers digging into the wall like claws. My breath tore from my throat. I didn't look down. I didn't look back.

I climbed for my life.

34. Borrowed Time

My arms trembled with effort as I hauled myself upward, inch by miserable inch. The roots were slick beneath my hands, and my boots struggled to find footing along the crumbling wall.

I was nearly halfway when my hand slipped, and I fell with a loud splash back into the freezing water below.

The cold was brutal, but the humiliation burned hotter. I coughed and looked up to see Aeron, crouched lazily at the rim of the pit, wings tucked and silhouette backlit by moonlight and trees. He hadn't moved. Not even an inch. I didn't need to see his face to feel the smirk dripping from him.

"Seems you're in a bit of a hole," he called down, voice infuriatingly casual. "I thought you'd be halfway to the river by now. Or are you sightseeing? Anything good down there?"

I gritted my teeth, forcing myself upright to keep hold of the slick roots. "If you're here to help, then help. Or are you just going to stand there and watch me freeze to death? I can't get out. I already tried."

Aeron hummed, leaning slightly over the edge. "But I already told you,

I'm not really here to help, but observe."

"I bet you're really enjoying *observing* this, then," I muttered, fingers finding the root again and pulling to see its stability.

"Oh, absolutely," he said, not even pretending otherwise. "It's not every day I get to watch the girl who 'doesn't need help' beg from the bottom of a pit."

His laugh reverberated through the pit, and it took everything in me not to vault up and haul him down with me so he could see how frustrating this was.

I shot him a glare. "I am *not* begging."

"Not *yet*." He leaned in slightly, eyes gleaming. "But I figure a bit more time down there and you will."

I shot him a glare before shaking the water from my hands and starting over. This time, I moved slower, anchoring my grip with every inch. I couldn't afford to fall again. The roots trembled beneath my fingers, mud slick and untrustworthy. I looked up, finding him still there staring, and even though it should have bothered me, it felt oddly soothing that I wasn't truly alone.

"You know," he added, "for someone who keeps claiming she *doesn't need me*, you're surprisingly demanding."

"I wouldn't be *demanding* anything if you stopped hovering in the shadows, distracting me, and were actually useful."

"Touchy," he mused. "Didn't you learn manners in your village? Normally, someone would at least say *please* when begging?"

I rolled my eyes, ignoring him because I was still not begging. Nor would I. But I *did* need his help if I wanted out of here, and was just within reach of his outstretched hand when I stretched to grab it. The root I was clutching in my left hand snapped, and I gasped. Slipping with a jolt that left me dangling by one arm, my body was straining under the weight of holding itself up. Mud crumbled beneath me. My boots scrabbled for purchase, but the wall kept giving way the more I kicked and tried to find my footing.

"Hold still," Aeron barked, all teasing gone as his jaw clenched.

I barely had time to process the command before his hand shot out, gripping my forearm in one swift motion. His grip was unrelenting, strong enough that it sent a jolt of reassurance through me.

"Let go," he said, nodding to the crumbling root I still clung to.

I hesitated, glancing up to meet his gaze. *Don't trust anyone.* Those were his words, were they not?

"I've got you," he said softly, like a promise. His expression had shifted— no smugness, no amusement. Just certainty.

I took a deep breath and let go, the root snapping as I did. And for a breathless moment, I hung suspended, held by nothing but his grip and blind faith he wouldn't let me fall.

Aeron pulled me up with startling ease, dragging me over the edge and onto solid ground. I collapsed there, gasping, soaked and shaking, but before I could speak—

A gust of wind. A flash of claws. The Barolf's paw swiped through the air behind us, narrowly missing Aeron's wings.

"Move," Aeron snapped, yanking me to my feet.

We ran. Crashing through the brush, lungs burning, the sound of pursuit like thunder in the trees behind us. I pushed myself harder, trying to match Aeron's pace, trying not to stumble. Every sound, every snap of a twig, made me flinch, fear surrounding my awareness that the Barolf might emerge from the shadows again.

It felt endless—until it wasn't.

Aeron slowed near a dense cluster of trees, pulling us into shadow so I could catch my breath out of sight. I collapsed against a trunk, chest heaving, the forest pressing close.

"You could've warned me that you hadn't taken it down," I panted, voice ragged.

"Didn't realize I needed to?" he murmured from the dark, that damn smirk curling in his tone again.

"Besides, if you plan to make it to the river intact and on time, you should stop relying on others to steer you in the right direction. I told you, trust is fickle around here, but that doesn't mean you can't ask for help either. Just think twice before you take it."

His tone was calm, but his eyes cut straight through me—no smirk this time, no mocking edge. Just a sharp, unshakable stare that felt like he saw of me than I wanted him to.

"The woods aren't just testing you for fun," he added. "They're watching. Assessing. Deciding what kind of immortal you'll be by how you face the challenges in your path. And sometimes, knowing when to ask for help—that's the real measure of strength and character."

I ran a hand through my damp hair, heart still pounding, breath shaky. "Well, it would've been nice if you'd warned me about potentially falling through the ground into a pit *before* it happened."

Aeron's smirk slid back into place. "You wouldn't have learned anything if I had."

I let out a groan, half-frustration, half-exhaustion, but he was already pulling a small pouch from his belt. With a flick of his wrist, he tossed it toward me. I caught it, *barely*.

"What's this?" I asked, opening the pouch to find a fine, glittering green powder.

"Barolf repellent," he said, far too casually. "Use it along its scent trail if you see it again. Should buy you enough time to run."

I stared at him, incredulous. "And you've had this the whole time?"

"I did," Aeron shrugged, unbothered. "But honestly, I forgot about it until right now. Running for our lives makes for a much better story, though, doesn't it?"

I shook my head, biting back a reluctant smile as I tucked the repellent away, hoping I wouldn't need to use it. "Well… thanks, I guess."

He nodded his head, already stepping back, his figure retreating into the shadows like he belonged to them. "Not quite the praise I deserve for saving your life by risking mine, but I'll take it."

I watched his silhouette fade, that flicker of a smirk still visible even as he vanished into the trees.

"*Good luck, Banrion,*" he called, voice fading with him. "*Hope I see you on the other side.*"

And just like that, he was gone. His presence was replaced by the hush of the forest, the cold bite of reality, and the reminder that I wasn't safe yet. I wouldn't be until I reached the river. And then it was a whole other set of things I needed to conquer.

I exhaled slowly, turning toward the faint glimmer of light breaking through the trees ahead. The river was out there somewhere. Waiting. And I'd reach it.

One way or another.

The trees above swallowed the moonlight, making it impossible to see more than a few steps ahead. Each sound, branches creaking, leaves shifting, seemed amplified, as if the woods were breathing around me. Echoes bounced between trunks, making it impossible to tell what was real and what was imagined. I kept moving, each step light but wary, my senses straining for any sign I wasn't alone.

A faint shimmer flickered up ahead—black wings catching the faintest trace of moonlight. My heart lurched. Relief hit too fast, too recklessly, and I fought the impulse to sprint forward. Wings. Was it finally Manakel? Or Aeron returning?

Hope curled inside me like a lit fuse, sharp and unwelcome. This day had been a tangled knot between the two of them, one leading, the other shadowing. I thought I'd trusted Manakel. Needed him, even. His steady guidance had kept me grounded when the forest threatened to pull me under. But that trust now felt fractured. Raw. He'd promised to meet me at the river. Promised I wouldn't face this alone. And yet—he wasn't here.

The wings vanished as quickly as they'd appeared, swallowed by the dark.

I froze. The silence that followed pressed in tight, like the forest itself was watching. Waiting. Pleased by my hesitation.

I hated how disappointment rose so quickly, so sharply. I should've known better than to let hope in.

Trust no one. Aeron's warning echoed in my mind.

I'd been raised to stand on my own, to forge my own path, but somewhere along the way, I had leaned into Manakel's presence. Let it steady me. And now… without him, I felt unsteady.

I swallowed hard, forcing the sting of disappointment away. Maybe the forest had held him back, turning him against me the same way it had twisted every step I'd taken tonight. Or maybe he'd never meant to come, and relying on him had been another test.

A flicker of warmth teased the corner of my vision. I spun around, dagger raised, heart hammering. But nothing was there—just the endless darkness and faint pinpricks of fireflies bobbing lazily in the air. I exhaled slowly, lowering the blade a fraction, but the unease stayed. Heavier than before.

Focus.

I adjusted the dagger at my side, forcing the ache in my limbs down. I couldn't afford to dwell on the absence, not Manakel's or Aeron's. Whatever waited ahead, I would face it alone.

But then I heard it—the faint rustling. It was close. Too close.

I turned, scanning the trees looking for whoever disturbed the woods.

"Manakel?" I called, voice low, uncertain.

The leaves whispered back like they were mocking me. I stepped forward cautiously.

"Manakel, is that you?" I tried again, quieter now.

No answer. Just the breath of wind slipping through branches. Then, in the distance, a laugh rang out. Melodic and familiar. It echoed from every direction, bouncing between trees as if the forest itself were taunting me.

Alfreda.

Her voice twined through the air like smoke, curling around me in invisible coils. My chest tightened. I clenched my fists, shoving aside the exhaustion creeping in. Every muscle burned, but I refused to stop. Not when the river felt so close.

Flames sparked in the darkness ahead—soft orange and pink flickers illuminating the silhouette of a small figure. Wings of fire and silk stretched wide, curling at the edges like burning parchment.

Alfreda hovered before me, delicate and deadly, her smile glowing in the flickering embers.

"Oh, how gullible you are," she purred, drifting closer. "Did you really think the shadow of wings meant salvation? That your precious protector would swoop in and carry you to safety?"

Her words dripped poison as she watched me stiffen. But I didn't respond. Wouldn't give her the satisfaction.

"You think you're getting close," she went on, circling lazily overhead. "But you're not the only one the river calls to. And unlike you, I know things about this forest you couldn't begin to fathom."

A sudden burst of heat flared from above. I looked up to find Alfreda lounging effortlessly on a low branch, one knee propped up while the other leg dangled. Her pink wings shimmered faintly, casting tiny embers into the night like falling stars.

With a flick of her fingers, a ring of fire erupted around me. I stumbled back as the flames licked the earth, encircling me in heat and licking at my heels. I forced my breathing to steady, gripping the dagger tight enough for the hilt to bite into my skin.

A small flame hovered just beyond the ring, suspended like a star.

"Ready to give up yet?" she teased, voice syrup-sweet.

"Not even close," I muttered, shifting my stance.

"Oh, little human," Alfreda purred, her voice dripping with mock sympathy. "You're practically *begging* for me to step in and help. Look at you—soaked to the bone and wandering in circles, lost, confused, and exhausted. You can't possibly think you'll reach the river before midnight like this."

She wasn't wrong. I *was* all of those things. But I refused to let her see it.

"Why not rest?" she coaxed, wings unfurling like petals. "Stay a while.

I'll even keep you company and tell you stories about every soul I've watched lose their way in these woods. You'll love it."

Embers drifted from her wings, spiraling to the ground around me. Where they touched the ground, flames bloomed, tightening the circle, trapping me inside a ring of fire.

"Alfreda," I called, keeping my voice steady, "I don't have time for this. I need to keep moving."

Her laughter echoed through the trees. "*Time*, my dear, is the one thing you *do* have. You humans are always in a rush, but I can help slow things down for you. Make it feel like you have all the time in the world. Doesn't that sound nice?"

With a flick of her wrist, the flames wavered, stretching unnaturally. The world around me shifted. The fire slowed, each flicker elongating as if it danced in syrup. The crackling of the flames dulled, becoming distant. Even the forest around us seemed to warp, branches twisting at odd angles as if time had been pulled thin.

I tried to take a step, but the air thickened, clinging to my limbs, holding me down. My breath felt heavy in my chest, the thudding of my heart like slow echoes in a cavern.

Alfreda's voice curled around me, distant yet suffocating. "Do you know how hard it is to fight when time betrays you? When every second stretches longer than the last? There's no need to be scared, you're already running out of time, so there's no way you would have made it anyway."

She looked at me with a sickly sweet smile that felt false and menacing, but a part of me wanted to believe her words. Maybe she was right. Maybe I was too late. Maybe this had all been for nothing, and I had failed before I even began?

I blinked my exhausted eyes and gritted my teeth, forcing myself forward, but my body moved sluggishly as though the forest was pushing back.

"Stop it, Alfreda!" I snapped, though the words stretched apart, sluggish and distorted. "It seems like you're the scared one. If you didn't think I would succeed, then you wouldn't be working this hard to keep me from reaching the river."

Her eyes narrowed, the faintest flicker of irritation slipping through her smug facade. Her smile was sharp, false, beautiful. And for a moment, it felt so easy to let go, to succumb to her tricks.

Anchor yourself.

My grandmother's voice stirred in my memory. *Illusions unravel when you remember what's real.*

I fumbled inside my pocket, my fingers leaden and slow, until they closed around cool stone. The flint stone. I closed my eyes, focused on it. Let its familiar feel and weight ground me. I let it block out Alfreda's voice, the flames, and the heavy air pressing down on me. The fire around me flickered, a small break in her grip.

"If I weren't a threat, you wouldn't be trying this hard," I said, voice hoarse but steady.

Alfreda's wings faltered. Just a beat.

I pressed on, my fingers tracing the smooth edge of the flint. The stone cold and real in my palm.

"You're scared I'll actually make it, aren't you? *That's* why you're here. That's why you're stalling."

The flames quivered, noticeably this time, and I closed my eyes, envisioning the fire receding, feeling the embers cooling to ash around me. I focused on the cold, the earth, the weight of my own breath. One by one, I imagined the flames dying out, the ground beneath me solid and cold.

I exhaled, slow and steady, and opened my eyes. Alfreda was in front of me again, her perfect face twisted in irritation as the fire vanished, leaving behind only a faint haze of smoke curling into the night.

"I don't know how you resisted that," she hissed, wings snapping closed. "But this isn't over. You're on borrowed time, and I'm not the only one against you."

She dissolved into a swirl of embers, fading into the dark, leaving nothing but smoke and scorched leaves. The light dusting of gold glitter sprinkled on the ground was the only reminder that this was real. That *she* was real.

I lingered, chest heaving, staring at the space where she'd been. "I might be on borrowed time," I muttered into the night under my breath, "But it's still mine."

Steeling myself, I brushed lingering ash from my cloak and pressed forward. The distant murmur of the river grew louder with each step, steady and flowing, just beyond the trees.

The trees closed in around me, colder and darker than before, but I forced myself to keep going. Alfreda's laughter still echoed in the shadows, filling the silence with doubt, but I didn't stop. I couldn't.

Despite the exhaustion, despite the fear, I pressed on, one stubborn step after another. The river was waiting for me—*I could feel it*—and nothing, not even Alfreda's tricks, would keep me from reaching it.

Because I wasn't done yet.

35. Truth And Treason

The forest had settled into an uneasy stillness. Not the kind that whispered peace, but the kind that watched. Silence curled around me, save for the occasional whisper of leaves brushing against one another overhead. The air grew colder the further I pressed on, each step muffled by the damp undergrowth beneath my boots. The distant hoot of an owl echoed somewhere far off, low and hollow, then fell silent.

I navigated the narrow path, weaving between low branches and the tangled mess of roots clawing their way out of the ground. I adjusted the strap of my satchel, the wet fabric pulling at my shoulder like dead weight. The ache in my ribs flared again, but I pushed through it. I was close. I could feel it—that pull, steady and magnetic, like the river was calling to something buried inside me.

Stay along the perimeter of the clearing. Don't walk through it unless you want to invite attention. Don't linger.

Manakel's warning echoed in my memory as the trees thinned ahead, revealing a break in the forest, wide and still, moonlight slicking the grass in silver. My breath caught. This had to be it. The clearing he described.

Relief settled in my chest, small but real. I moved closer, careful to stay tucked in the shadows of the trees.

Then something shifted.

A sharp rustle broke the silence. I stopped. On a low-hanging branch, directly in my path, sat a raven.

Its feathers shimmered like oil, dark and absorbing light rather than reflecting it. It tilted its head slowly, watching me. black as ink and bottomless, pinned me in place. Not curious. Not afraid. Just…waiting and far too omniscient for any ordinary bird.

The hairs on the back of my neck rose.

I stared at it, my heartbeat thudding loudly in my ears.

"It's just a bird," I whispered to myself, fingers tightening around the hilt of my dagger. "You've dealt with worse in these woods."

The raven let out a deep, guttural caw that reverberated through the clearing. The wind died. Even the insects fell quiet.

I exhaled slowly, removing my dagger from its sheath, hoping the sight of the blade would scare it off. Because this wasn't *just* a bird. If it was in these woods, it was anything but.

Its feathers began to ripple. Shift as if stirred by an unseen breeze.

The transformation was fluid—unnatural. Talons stretched into slender fingers, wings narrowed and pulled inward, folding into a cloak of silken black. The shimmer of feathers bled into fabric, and in the bird's place stood a woman.

She was tall, draped in a robe that shimmered like smoke and shadow. Her hair was long, wild, and tangled with stray feathers, her skin pale as frost beneath the moonlight. But it was her eyes that froze me in place.

Unchanged. Still sharp. Still watching. Still not human.

My heart pounded so loudly that I wondered if she could hear it. I didn't lower the dagger, but didn't move either.

"You're a shifter?" I asked, my voice steadier than I felt.

She stepped forward, her bare feet whispering against the forest floor, barely disturbing the carpet of damp, mottled leaves. The woods seemed to retreat from her, branches bending subtly, shadows parting, as if even the trees knew better than to stand in her way.

"Very perceptive," she cooed, voice light and lilting with mock praise, like someone humoring a child who thought they'd outsmarted an adult. "But not perceptive enough, it seems. You've wandered deep into these woods, Raine. Far deeper than you were meant to."

My breath caught.

"You know my name?"

Her smile unfurled slowly, sharp, predatory, and too pleased. "I know more than just your *name*."

Her tone begged me to ask more, to engage, but I didn't answer. *Couldn't.* Something cold and ancient slid down my spine, pooling in my gut like ice.

She tilted her head, studying me with idle curiosity, like I was some fragile, flickering thing she could snuff out with the curl of a finger. "I know who you're searching for," she said, almost sing-song. "And where you think you're meant to go. I *also* know how this all ends." Her eyes gleamed, catching the moonlight like blades. "And it's not in your favor."

I straightened, jaw tight, refusing to let my uncertainty show.

How did she know? Had she seen it play out because she was a seer as well? No, Manakel had made it clear. You only received one gift after the Rite, and she'd already revealed herself as a shifter. So how did she know so much, or was this yet another trick?

"I don't need anyone to guide me, but thank you."

"Oh, but you do." Her smile didn't falter. "You just haven't realized it yet. I'm Corvina, and against my better judgment, I'm here to inform you that you're heading into danger. The kind you won't return from. But there's still time to turn back."

"I think I'll take my chances, Corvina," I said, letting her name linger on my tongue like a challenge. I didn't need another so-called *guide,* not after today's mess of half-truths and blurred loyalties. I might not know who to trust, but I knew I didn't trust *her*; that was easy enough to decipher.

"You don't trust me, do you?" She tsked, as if disappointed I was onto her deception. "Let me guess, Aeron warned you not to trust anyone in these woods." She looked at me pointedly, "Right?"

My silence must have been answer enough, because her grin widened. "So he *has* been helping," she said, her cloak twitching slightly, feathers flashing before vanishing again.

"Aeron always had a weakness for lost and broken things. And that curiosity has gotten him in trouble a time or two."

My fingers clenched around my dagger. "I'm not lost or broken."

"No?" She stepped closer, closing the distance between us in an instant. I didn't retreat, but my body tensed like a drawn bowstring.

Her face searched mine, something ancient flickering behind her eyes. "You stand at the edge of something vast," she said softly. "And you have no idea what waits beneath the surface of that river and beyond. Are you prepared to leave everything behind? To let go of the parts of yourself that won't survive the crossing? To become something else entirely?"

I didn't answer because I didn't know. But I also didn't have much of a choice if I wanted to ensure my family's safety.

"I thought not," Corvina said, voice sharpening. "And no amount of guidance from Aeron or orders from Manakel will save you from what comes next. You walk this path alone, whether you see it or not."

The truth in her voice felt like a knife twisting in my chest. But I wouldn't let her see it.

"I know what I'm walking into," I said, lifting my chin defiantly. "And I'll get there—with or without anyone's guidance."

Corvina's eyes darkened, shadows flickering behind her irises. "So certain for a naive human," she murmured. "We'll see how long that certainty lasts."

Then, without another word, her form began to shift. Feathers scattered like smoke in the wind as her wings reappeared. Her face elongated, the lengthening of her mouth and nose starting to form the outline of a beak. But before she fully shifted into her raven form, her voice echoed through the trees.

"Be careful what you find at the river's edge. Some things were never meant to cross without great sacrifice."

And then she flew up into the sky and was gone, leaving me alone. A gust of wind swept past, carrying the scent of something wild and ancient. I stood there, shivering, not just from the cold, but from the unknown.

I didn't know if her arrival was a warning, a test, or something else entirely, but one thing was certain. I had no intention of turning back, even *if* she made me doubt everything. And I didn't know why, but that unsettled me more than anything I'd faced up until now.

I kept to the edge of the clearing, each step deliberate, quiet. But even the softest rustle beneath my boots felt thunderous in the unnatural silence that surrounded me. My heart pounded as I tiptoed along, senses on high alert, practically holding my breath. Every snapped twig sent a spike of panic down my spine, and the darkness around me seemed alive, like it was waiting to pounce if I made one wrong move.

Manakel had warned me to stay on the perimeter of any clearings. Not to walk through or linger. And for once, I listened.

Relief sparked as I reached the far edge of the clearing, but it didn't last—it never did. The moment I caught my breath, voices drifted from the trees ahead. Low. Close. *Too close.* They blocked the path I needed, standing between me and the river like sentinels of fate.

I stilled, slipping into the crooked shadow of a leaning elm, the bark damp against my shoulder. My breath hitched. Even the wind seemed to hold still. My fingers closed around the dagger at my hip, pulse hammering beneath my skin as I inched forward. I couldn't make out the words, only the cadence—casual, confident, dangerous.

A twig snapped behind me. Close enough to raise the hairs on the back of my neck.

I spun without thinking, pivoting low on my heel as my blade swept up in a clean arc and struck true, plunging into warm flesh with a sickening give. A sharp breath escaped the figure, more startled than pained, and in the next heartbeat, the shadows peeled back just enough to reveal his face.

"Manakel?" I choked out, voice barely more than a whisper, horror rushing in faster than my blade had.

His face blurred before it focused—his dark eyes locked on mine, half-lidded with pain and surprise. I barely registered his form as I stumbled back, horrified, releasing the dagger still buried in his arm.

"Amadán," he murmured with a half-smile. "I was hoping for a warmer welcome."

I blinked, disoriented, as he pressed his palm to the wound. Light pulsed faintly beneath his fingers, sealing the flesh and any trace of my blade.

"You... you didn't say anything. Just snuck up behind me and I didn't know who it was." I stammered with an apologetic glance.

He chuckled. "I thought you'd sense me. *Apparently not.*" Manakel lifted his arm, now healed, and tilted his head, studying me with familiar eyes.

"You've grown jumpy," he said, lips quirking. "But I'm glad to see you defending yourself."

I looked down, embarrassed but defensive. "I thought you were something dangerous." I tried to keep my voice steady, though the adrenaline still coursed through me. "There are... creatures everywhere, things trying to stop me, and I'm tired of running and feeling defenseless."

His smirk sharpened, and something in his expression... shifted. The warmth receded as his eyes lingered on the dagger in my hand with curiosity.

"And you would have done well if I were really a threat. Although..." he looked down at his arm, arching a brow, "maybe a little warning next time?"

I let out a shaky breath, almost laughing at the absurdity of stabbing an immortal angel, but it couldn't have been too bad since he hadn't bled and had been able to heal himself. "I'll try to keep that in mind."

He nodded, his face turning serious as he stepped closer. "The river is close, but the woods aren't finished with you yet."

The change was instant. One second, we were teasing like normal, and the next, his voice lost its usual cadence, twisting into something venomous. Cruel. Wrong.

He stalked around me in slow, deliberate circles, his presence a cold, suffocating weight against my skin. The warm, steady guide I'd trusted was gone, replaced by something darker, something that enjoyed watching me cower.

"Did you *really* think I'd come to your rescue, Amadán?" he asked, voice dripping with mockery. "That I'd swoop in and lead you gently to the river like some noble guardian?"

Each word felt like a slap, sharp and precise, landing where my confidence was thinnest. I tightened my grip on the dagger, hating the way my stomach twisted at the sound of his voice. I told myself it wasn't the real him—*it couldn't be.* This had to be another test. But the magic surrounding us was powerful, and the lines between real and illusion blurred too easily when it wore the face of someone I'd once believed in.

He stopped in front of me, eyes narrowing as if he could see straight through the cracks in my resolve. "I was here the whole time. Watching your every move, every fumble, every misstep. The way you hesitated, the way you looked for me and waited. Pathetically clinging to the hope that I'd show up."

Shame seared through me before I could stop it. His smirk deepened, crueler now. "So predictable."

I clenched my jaw, but his words burrowed deep, settling in the spaces where doubt already lingered. But I forced myself to meet his stare head-on.

"Are you really that naive?" he said, his voice sharpening, colder than before. "That you'd think the woods wouldn't challenge your little rebellion, your stubbornness, your—" he paused, the next word laced with venom, "desperation to believe someone might choose you."

That one carved straight through bone. I flinched, *barely*, but forced myself to straighten. My heartbeat thundered in my chest like a warning drum, urging me not to falter.

"Did you seriously expect me to be your knight in shining armor?" he sneered, stepping closer. "To personally guide you to the river that easily?"

I clenched my jaw, swallowing the ache building in my throat. This wasn't real. It couldn't be. It was just another illusion, another trick meant to shake me.

And yet…His hazel eyes, usually flecked with warmth, now looked darker, but somehow still his. Familiar in a way that made it worse. His wings weren't visible, no trace of black feathers curling behind, just a tall, lean figure in the moonlight, echoing the Manakel I'd first met in the woods. The one who'd helped me. The one I'd come to trust.

But this version twisted that memory into a weapon. He wasn't like the illusions of my father or Wren—ethereal, vague, untouchable. No, this Manakel was grounded, solid, and close enough to reach. Close enough to hurt if I let him. And he was saying things only the real Manakel would know.

"Stop it," I whispered, the words barely catching on my breath. They quivered as they left my lips, soft but raw, like something splintered from inside me. "I didn't *ask* for your help, remember? You're the one who came to *me*. You needed me."

I straightened, or tried to. My legs wobbled beneath me, leaden and trembling, but I forced myself upright, spine stiff despite the ache crawling through my limbs.

"I don't need you," I said, quieter now but firmer. "I've made it this far without you, and I'll keep going. Alone, if I have to."

His gaze sharpened, something dark flickering behind it, and for a breathless second, he didn't move, his dark eyes just assessing. Then he leaned in slowly, his presence folding over mine like a shadow. His face was so close I could feel the warmth of his breath, could see the faint flecks of amber in his otherwise onyx eyes. Eyes that once felt safe. Now, they stared through me like I was little more than an inconvenience, taking up his time.

"Oh, really?" he murmured, voice dipped in ice, each word delivered with precise, mocking cruelty. "Then show me. Show me how little you need me."

I didn't flinch, but I didn't move either. Because the truth was, I *did* need him once. Maybe I still did. And hearing those taunting words in his voice, even if it wasn't his true self saying them, shattered something small and tender inside me that I didn't realize was still waiting for him.

I should have looked away, should have severed whatever invisible thread was holding me in place. But I held his stare, even as the weight of his challenge threatened to crush me.

I knew this wasn't him. I knew it was an illusion—another trick, another test designed to make me doubt everything I thought I trusted. But doubt was a tricky thing.

I straightened, drawing in a slow, deep breath. "If this is the game you want to play, then let's play," I said, my voice stronger now, talking more to believe the words myself than to him. "But I know who I am. *Why* I'm doing this. And regardless of what stands in my way, I *will* reach that river. No matter what it takes."

His smirk faltered, just for a breath, and I caught the barest flicker of irritation behind his eyes. Then just as quick, he laughed, a cold, mirthless sound, and took a step back, vanishing into the shadows as if the forest itself had swallowed him whole.

I exhaled slowly, forcing my muscles to relax as the silence crept back in.

Keep moving. Don't stop.

I reminded myself how far I'd come and how close I was to reaching the river. I just needed to keep going.

The trees whispered around me as I pressed forward, each step heavier than the last. The air grew thick, and the weight of exhaustion began to settle deep in my bones.

I walked faster, driven by the distant hum of running water I couldn't quite hear but felt. And then the voices returned, softer, and no longer wearing Manakel's face but slithering through the trees like echoes of my own doubt.

You're not strong enough.

You're just a girl pretending to be brave.

You'll never make it alone.

I squeezed my eyes shut for a moment, shaking the words loose from my mind. "I *am* strong enough," I whispered under my breath, repeating it like a mantra until the edges of doubt began to fray.

But the forest wasn't done with me yet.

Something hard wrapped around my ankle, yanking me to a sudden stop. I looked down, and a root, thick and knotted, had coiled itself around my leg, snaking higher with each passing second. Another snared my wrist. Then another coiled around my waist, yanking me downward.

I thrashed, yanking at the roots twisting around me like ivy, but more appeared, curling tightly and pulling me down, further into the soft earth.

You're not ready.

Turn back.

You're never going to survive this.

I grit my teeth, struggling against the tangle of roots, but they held firm.

"No," I growled, twisting, struggling, "Let go." I twisted the dagger in my grip, the blade slashing through the nearest root, cutting it clean in half. Dirt sprayed as it recoiled, writhing away from my body. It loosened just enough for my wrist to break free.

I hacked at the other tendrils, adrenaline surging as the last root snapped and slithered away, disappearing into the ground.

I stumbled forward, gasping. I stood there for a moment, panting, staring at the dirt clinging to my legs and hands, the leaves tangled in my hair. But I was free.

"I *am* ready," I affirmed, louder this time. Letting the words ring out like a blade drawn in defiance.

And then, as if answering, the faint sound of water rushing over stone drifted toward me—soft, but unmistakable.

I straightened, brushing off the dirt and fixing my eyes on the path ahead, which was still dark and dangerous.

The river was close. I could feel it. And nothing was going to stop me from reaching it.

Not now. Not ever.

36. Rise Or Fall

I didn't know how much farther the river would be. The forest had a way of stretching distance, turning every step into a guess and every shadow into a dead end. I'd long lost track of time; there was no sun to guide me, only the pale glow of the moon threading through the trees in thin, silvery strands.

Last night, I remembered staring up at it, round and swollen, just shy of full, thinking it looked like a coin flipped by the gods. Now, it hovered directly above, indifferent and watchful. I didn't know how long I'd been walking. Hours? More?

But then the trees began to thin, and there it was—the river, shimmering under the glow of the moon, catching the light like a thousand shifting stars. I froze at the sight, the breath catching in my throat. Relief washed over me in waves strong enough to soften the ache that had settled in my bones. The weight I'd carried through the forest—fear, doubt, exhaustion—fell from my shoulders like a cloak sliding to the ground.

I stepped forward, drawn by the river's calm, inviting stillness. The woods had been relentless, but this—*this* felt like a reward.

As I edged forward, a figure appeared at the water's edge, arms folded, bathed in silver light. His posture seemed relaxed, but even from here, I caught the familiar glint in his eyes and the smirk tugging at his mouth.

"About time, Amadán. I thought you might've gotten lost."

Manakel. His voice rang out, light and teasing, like the night hadn't been heavy with danger just moments ago.

A shaky laugh slipped from me before I could stop it, and I lowered my guard. Not entirely, but enough to let the familiarity of his presence settle around me like a shield.

The woods could conjure shadows, mimic voices, and play at my deepest fears, but it couldn't replicate *this*. The real Manakel stood before me, solid and steady. The warmth in his eyes, the slight tilt of his head as he watched me approach—this was him. Not some illusion stitched together to torment me.

"Well," I called back, brushing damp strands of hair from my face, trying to steady my breath, "I might've gotten held up, but I made it."

"Obviously nothing you couldn't handle," he replied, a sliver of pride threading through his voice.

I started to nod, to let it go at that, but the words slipped out before I could stop them, quiet and half-muttered.

"Wouldn't have, if someone hadn't stepped in to help."

The words slipped out before I thought them through, and the moment I said them, Manakel's expression shifted, just slightly, but I saw it. The humor in his eyes dulled, and he straightened slightly, stepping toward me with quiet intent. I didn't clarify, but the damage was done. The truth had escaped, and the air between us shifted, tighter somehow. Tense.

"Help?" he echoed, his voice losing its playful edge.

I hesitated. I could've lied. Should've, maybe. But Aeron risking his own life with the Barolf, or warning me of danger more than once, still lingered in my head.

"Aeron," I admitted, his name barely more than a breath. "He showed up right when I needed help."

I didn't elaborate. I couldn't, when I still didn't know what his presence had meant. I still didn't know if he'd helped me, tested me, or simply enjoyed watching me squirm.

Manakel's reaction was instant. His smirk vanished, jaw tightening. His eyes flicked toward the woods, sharp and searching, like he expected Aeron to emerge from the shadows behind me.

He muttered something I couldn't catch. Then, "You shouldn't trust him, Raine." His voice was low and weighted with something close to anger.

"He's kept things from you—things that…" He cut himself off, his eyes narrowing. "Let's just say Aeron isn't the guardian he pretends to be. His loyalty is only to himself, so whatever he's doing, it's not for your sake. It never has been."

A shiver crept down my spine. I wanted to believe him. Wanted to take comfort in the simplicity of his certainty. But nothing about this path, about Aeron, had ever been simple.

"I'll remember that," I said quietly. "And I'll be more careful."

It wasn't a lie, but the words felt thin, lacking conviction. Because the truth was, I wasn't sure who or what to believe.

Manakel studied me, like he could see the cracks I was trying to hide. Eventually, he sighed, tension bleeding from his shoulders like he'd finally decided to let it go, at least for now.

"Good," he murmured. "But come. Sit. You look exhausted and like you've been through a war already."

I flushed, not because he was wrong, but because I was embarrassed. Looking exhausted was hardly a compliment from someone you liked, and Manakel had always been honest, so if he pointed it out, I must have looked *rough*.

Before I could come up with a response, he stepped forward and gently slipped the bag from my shoulder. His touch was brief, but grounding, warm fingers brushing my arm before he set the satchel down on the ground. Something inside me eased. Just a little. And for the first time in hours, I let myself exhale.

I watched, bemused, as he rifled through my bag with the ease of someone who'd done it a hundred times before. His fingers closed around a thermos I didn't remember packing. He twisted off the lid with a knowing smirk.

I blinked. "Where did that come from?"

He didn't answer, just gestured toward the grassy riverbank and sat, his movements fluid, purposeful. Like he belonged here.

"Planning to stay awhile?" I asked, arching a brow as I hovered a few feet away.

He glanced back, grinning. "Someone's got to keep an eye on you."

Steam rose as he poured the tea into the cap, the scent of honey, mint, and something darker curling in the cool night air. I recognized the blend, her apothecary's signature. Perfect for calming and grounding.

I sank to the ground beside him, cautious but too tired to care, and accepted the makeshift cup. The warmth seeped into my fingers, chasing off the last of the cold the woods had buried in my bones.

"I didn't even know she packed this," I murmured after a sip. The tea slid down smooth and sweet, like something meant to lull.

"She probably knew you'd need it," Manakel said, settling back on his hands beside me. He kept a careful distance, but his presence still curled around me.

The silence stretched. Not heavy, just… still. The tension from earlier blurred at the edges. For a heartbeat, it almost felt normal. Like this, sipping tea under stars, the river humming beside us, wasn't borrowed time before the storm I would soon face.

"You really made it here on your own. With no map or guide," he said finally, glancing at me with something softer in his eyes. "It's impressive. Most wouldn't have managed half that trek, even immortals."

I shrugged, exhaustion tugging at my limbs. There was something about his tone, like he was surprised I was here. "I didn't have much of a choice." I stretched my legs, the ache sharp in my joints. "Considering I was left to fend for myself in the woods and didn't know where I was headed or how to get here."

The bitterness slipped through before I could stop it.

"I honestly didn't expect to find you waiting," I added, meeting his stare. "Especially not looking so… calm. Did you forget you promised to meet me?"

He chuckled low, the sound brushing against the edges of my irritation. "Straight to the point. But I shouldn't be surprised."

Manakel smiled as if this was a normal night, and he hadn't gone back on his word and left me alone. He leaned in slightly, hand lifting to tuck a stray piece of hair behind my ear. His fingers lingered, just long enough to shift the air between us.

"I told you I wouldn't let you go through this alone," he murmured. "Not even for a second."

His voice was velvet and iron. A promise that dug in, even as doubt still curled beneath my skin.

"But I couldn't intervene—not directly," he added, his hand fidgeting at his side. "That was part of the test. I wanted to tell you… But I couldn't."

The confession should have comforted me. Instead, it tangled with everything Aeron had warned about trusting people, even those who had helped me in the past. Still, Manakel's presence radiated certainty, steady and warm beside the chaos I'd crawled through to get here.

"But none of that matters now," he said, his voice low. "You made it. Just like I knew you would."

His smile, small but bright, disarmed me in a way I wasn't prepared for. I didn't respond, but I smiled back. Because despite the shadows still trailing me, despite the questions I wasn't ready to ask, he was right about one thing.

I did make it.

The river stretched out before us, its surface calm and glass-like beneath the moon, shimmering with deep shades of blue that made it seem endless. The soft hum of the water filled the space between us, reminding me that soon, I'd drink the tonic and cross to whatever awaited me in its depths and on the other side.

Everything was falling into place, just as Manakel had said. But somewhere beneath the surface of my relief, Aeron's voice echoed.

Question everything.

I stole a glance at him, catching the way his gaze shifted toward the river, distant and guarded for just a breath of a moment.

"Well," he said, glancing at the sky, "it's officially midnight." His lips twitched into something softer. "Happy birthday, Raine. Eighteen suits you."

I blinked, caught off guard by how casually he said it, like it was just another passing moment, not the beginning of the Rite that could alter the entire course of my life. "I guess it is," I murmured, suddenly aware of how fast the time had crept up on me.

I turned the cup in my hands, watching the steam curl upward like tendrils of smoke offering silent omens. Midnight. My eighteenth birthday. The beginning of something I could never return from, and the end of… something else. Something softer. Simpler.

Manakel glanced over, his face giving nothing away before quietly softening. My breath caught. I looked away too quickly, brushing at a loose thread on my sleeve like it had any power to ground me. His hand lifted to my chin, gently tilting my face up to meet his stare. His touch was light, but purposeful, holding me in focus as if to make sure I didn't drift away with the weight of my thoughts.

The silence stretched between us, not uncomfortable, but laden. The kind of quiet that makes you feel like something important is waiting just beyond it.

"This is the part where I tell you how ready you are," he said, voice barely a whisper. "But I think you already know that."

The look in his eyes sent a quiet shiver down my spine, not fear, but something else I couldn't name. Longing, maybe. Or the echo of something I wasn't ready to admit lived in me, too. His thumb brushed along my jaw, featherlight, and my heart stuttered in my chest.

I thought, just for a moment, he might kiss me.

The space between us crackled, shrinking with every breath. I couldn't tell if I was leaning in or if he was. But the space between us narrowed, the warmth of his breath grazed my lips, and I forgot how to think at all.

Then, just as quickly, he smiled, soft and knowing, and pressed a kiss to my forehead instead.

It was a simple gesture, yet somehow it left me more breathless than anything else. I closed my eyes as his lips lingered just long enough to make me feel the absence when he pulled away, his fingers brushing mine before falling back to his side.

"Happy birthday," he murmured, and though the words were light, something heavier lingered beneath them.

I kept my eyes closed for another breath, steadying the thrum in my chest. When I opened them, he was still watching me with that same flicker of something I didn't yet understand.

"There aren't many things worth breaking the rules for," he said quietly. "But I think you might be one of them."

I swallowed hard, unsure how to respond to that. The weight of his words settled over me, heavier than I expected, and I felt myself inching backward, needing space to breathe before I let myself think too much about what he meant.

The river shimmered ahead, calm and indifferent to the tension curling between us. I turned to it, desperate for a distraction.

"So," I said, trying to sound lighter than I felt, "are you going to explain how this works? Or are we just pretending the river isn't waiting to swallow me whole?"

Manakel chuckled, the sound rich and familiar, and some of the tension in the air finally eased.

"There's no rush," he replied, his gaze following mine to the water. "The river isn't going anywhere, and neither am I." He glanced sideways at me.

"But since you're so eager—" He leaned closer, his voice dropping slightly, "—just know it's less about the water and more about what you take with you when you cross."

I frowned. "That's vague."

He laughed again, shrugging. "I wish I could tell you more, but I know you can figure the rest out on your own."

Despite myself, I smiled, *definitely sticking to vague answers then.*

But then his expression shifted, turning serious. "You'll be tested, Raine," he said, "but it's not the river you should fear. It's everything the magic will try to convince you is true."

His words tugged at something deep inside me, a quiet echo of Aeron's warnings. I tightened my grip on the edge of my cloak, suddenly cold despite the warmth of his presence.

"I'll remember that," I murmured.

Manakel leaned closer, reaching for my hand, his palm resting gently over mine in reassurance.

"I'll be with you the whole way," he said, eyes steady. "I promise."

But I wasn't sure I believed him, not completely. Not after being left to wander the forest alone. Not with everything still unsaid.

Still, I didn't pull my hand away or tell him.

I took a slow breath, letting Manakel's words root deep inside me. Beside us, the river whispered a low, uneasy sound that curled through the night air like a secret. It felt alive, humming with something ancient beneath the surface, an unspoken promise of transformation, but also danger.

Soon, I would step into those waters. And when I did, nothing would be the same. But for now, I let the quiet settle between us, just for a moment longer.

"So," I whispered, reluctant to break the stillness, "what happens now?"

Manakel rose in one smooth, unhurried motion and extended a hand toward me. His palm, calloused but warm, stood in sharp contrast to the night's chill.

"Now," he said softly, reverent almost, "you mix the tonic. Then you step into the water and let it guide you. I'll be waiting on the other side."

I hesitated before placing my hand in his, letting him pull me to my feet. His grip was steady and sure, like he'd done this a hundred times before. But this was my first. The weight of that truth pressed hard against my ribs.

My legs felt unsteady beneath me, but his hand never wavered as he led me toward the water's edge. Each step on the cool, damp earth reminded me how real this was. No longer a distant idea, no longer something to prepare for. I was finally here, and the river stretched before me like a threshold I wasn't certain I could cross.

"Remember," he said, his voice dipping lower, "the river will test you. Whatever you see, whatever you experience, won't always be the truth. You have to be able to know the difference. You'll have to trust yourself."

I nodded, though the reminder twisted tight in my stomach. Everyone kept warning me about the river. But it wasn't the water I feared; it was what it might show me.

I dropped to one knee, reaching for my satchel, but Manakel crouched first and held it open for me. His eyes met mine in the low light, silent, steady, as if to remind me I wasn't doing this alone.

I reached in, my fingers brushing the glass vial of the tonic my grandmother had been preparing for over a week. But as I dug deeper, a faint shimmer caught my eye. I paused, feeling the material of the pouch with the river stone dust. I hadn't meant to grab it, but my hand closed around it instinctively, and I slipped it into my waist bag when I took out the final herbs needed for the tonic.

I arranged the herbs I needed to add on the ground, carefully setting each one in place. My grandmother's instructions echoed in my head. *"The herbs carry intention. The intention carries power."*

I whispered the mantra under my breath as I worked, like a spell meant to anchor me to this moment, to her guidance.

The tonic itself already held strength—oregano for luck, basil for success, sage for wisdom, and mugwort to guard against illusions. But I knew it wasn't enough. The final herbs had to come from me, chosen for this exact moment, infused with my intent.

I reached for the herbs she'd ground fresh this morning, and with careful hands, I sprinkled the lavender in first, its soft scent curling into the night air like a protective veil. A calmness settled over me with every breath, steadying my nerves.

Next came rosemary—sharp, grounding, anchoring me to the present moment and pulling me out of my spiraling doubt. I needed that focus. If I was going to make it across, I couldn't afford to lose myself to fear or second-guessing.

And finally I added mint. Bright and crisp, it shimmered faintly as it settled into the tonic, the leaves curling in the liquid like they recognized their purpose. Movement. Safe passage.

I sealed the vial and shook it gently, watching the herbs swirl together like memories, like prayers filled with intention. For a moment, I imagined every woman who had done this before me, kneeling at this river's edge, carrying their own fears and hopes into the current. I felt them in my blood. I felt them in the water.

Manakel stood beside me, quiet, watchful. His silence spoke louder than words. He hadn't said much while I worked, but his presence alone was enough to ease my nerves.

I lifted the vial to my lips and closed my eyes, pausing as the cold glass pressed against them. One more breath. One more heartbeat.

The tonic was bitter, sharp, and heavy with the weight of everything I'd poured into it. It slid down my throat like a dare and bloomed in my chest like a second heartbeat, warming everything it touched and weaving into every corner of my being.

The air changed. So did the river.

I felt it. Not just the sensation of water against the shore but a pull, subtle yet insistent, as if the river recognized the tonic, recognized *me*.

"It's ready for you now," Manakel said quietly.

I rose to my feet slowly, letting the warmth settle through my limbs. When I looked over, he held my bag in one hand, the thermos now tucked inside, before slinging it over his shoulder. "I'll carry this across for you," he said with a faint smile. "Less weight to pull you down."

My heart softened at the gesture. "Thank you," I whispered.

I stepped forward. With one step, my foot slipped into the water, cool but not unbearable. The river seemed to welcome me, swirling gently around my ankles as if testing my resolve.

I took another step. Then another.

The current pressed against my legs, rising to my knees, then my thighs, each step forward pressing against me with an unseen force and testing my resolve.

I glanced over my shoulder just once.

Manakel stood where I left him, half-shadowed by moonlight. His expression was soft, but distant, like he was with me, but a part of him was already waiting on the other side.

I turned back, eyes fixed on the water, the river stretching endlessly ahead, ready to meet whatever lay beyond.

Whether I was ready or not.

37. Reflections In The Water

The moment my foot slipped beneath the river's surface, the cold seized me.

It wasn't an ordinary chill. It was deeper, heavier, something ancient burrowing beneath my skin, curling around my bones like frost threading through marrow, curling around my bones with eerie precision. The water lapped at my ankles, gentle on the outside but wrong beneath, like unseen fingers tracing my skin.

Assessing. Waiting.

The warmth of the tonic still lingered in my veins, but it pulsed faintly now, no match for the river's ancient pull. It had tasted me, and now it was deciding if I was worthy.

I pressed forward. The opposite side shimmered in the moonlight, looking close and unreachable all at once. Each step dragged, like I was wading through something sentient. Something watching.

Then, a flicker moved beneath the water. A shift in the dark depths.

Before I could react, something coiled around my ankle. Panic slammed into me as I yanked my leg back, but the grip tightened. It wasn't like stepping on a stray root or slipping into an unseen current. This was deliberate. This was a force, something *alive*.

The hold tightened. My other foot slipped, and before I could cry out, the river swallowed me whole. Cold slammed into my chest like a thousand frozen knives. I gasped, inhaling a rush of water that scorched down my throat. I thrashed, reaching blindly for the surface, but the unseen force yanked me deeper, pulling me down, down, down.

Above me, the world dissolved into darkness. The moon vanished beneath the weight of the river's depths. The deeper I sank, the heavier it became, like I was being dragged into something older than time itself.

The river wasn't just water. It was a gate. A threshold of change. And it had been waiting for me.

Shadows slithered through the depths, smoke-like and shifting. Figures emerged, not of the current, but within it, shifting between liquid and solid, their forms slipping between nightmares. Fingers brushed my skin. Not just one pair. Dozens.

Clawed hands, skeletal and rough, gripped my arms and legs, dragging me farther. I kicked hard, panic flaring bright and hot as they pulled me deeper and deeper into the darkness, their grips like ice and iron.

Through the swirl of onyx, a face appeared—Pale, hollow-eyed, and ancient. It appeared before me, its features sharp yet blurred, shifting between something human and something entirely otherworldly. The longer I stared, the more I felt myself unraveling, like the river was stripping me down piece by piece, to see what was underneath.

Its eyes, two burning orbs of silver light, locked on mine.

The river had a face.

And it wanted me to drown.

I screamed, but the water stole my voice, devouring my fear whole. My lungs burned as I fought harder, kicking and thrashing, clawing at the hands pulling me under. They raked at me, nails dragging across my skin, leaving behind trails of searing cold that spread like fire.

The hands tightened, dragging me deeper.

No. No. No.

I kicked harder, fighting against the hands pulling at me, but they were everywhere—tracing my arms, gripping my shoulders, clawing at my legs.

Strength. Focus. Courage. Truth.

My grandmother's words of what I'd need to survive this rang through my mind, cutting through the panic like a blade. I wasn't just drowning; I was being tested, and I had to fight.

I reached for anything—my fingers scraping the thick, muddy floor. If I could just find something to hold onto, I could find a way out. But there was nothing. Only darkness.

And then a weight. Heavy. Ancient. Overwhelming.

It slammed into me, pressing down like an invisible hand crushing my chest. Not water. Not the river's current. Something bigger. It wasn't trying to drown me; it was taunting me.

The presence sifted through my mind, pushing at my thoughts, at the fractures in my will. It wasn't just seeking weakness. It wanted to know who I was and why I was here.

Panic threatened to consume me, but I forced it down. I wouldn't break. *I couldn't.*

My fingers curled around something solid in my pocket—the flint stone.

My grandmother's gift. The thing I had kept with me for luck since I was thirteen. I clutched it like a lifeline, its smooth, solid weight anchoring me to something real. Reminding me who I was and where I came from. Leaning into it to ground me.

I am Raine. I have people who believe in me. I believe in myself. I am strong. I am courageous. I am a fighter. I do not belong to this river. I do not belong to the hands dragging me under.

The pressure intensified, sensing my resistance. My lungs screamed. But I gritted my teeth and held on. A moment stretched, endless, but I refused to break.

The weight around me paused. Shifted. The hands fell away. The crushing pressure eased. And slowly, I rose, pulled upward as if the river itself had decided to let me go.

I broke the surface with a gasp, air flooding my lungs in desperate, shuddering gulps. Water streamed down my face as I blinked against the sudden light. My limbs trembled. My heart thundered.

But it wasn't over.

I had barely regained my breath before the next threat came. The water around me thickened, growing heavy—like I was wading through tar. I tried to move, but every step forward fought against me.

Then, a voice rang out around me. Soft, melodic, and far too sweet to be trusted.

"Rest now."

"You're tired. Just let go. We know you want to."

"Let the water carry you to sleep."

The words coiled around my mind like mist, warm and lulling, a fog seeping into the corners of my mind. The exhaustion I'd been keeping at bay unfurled, dragging my limbs with a heaviness.

I could stop. Just for a moment. Close my eyes and let the current take me. The edge of the riverbank would still be there to catch me. Wouldn't it?

No.

I bit the inside of my cheek, hard, the sting cutting through the haze and reminding me this was yet another test I needed to conquer.

The voice hissed, retreating, but not gone. It was lurking. Waiting.

I forced myself to keep moving, step by step. The river nipped at my heels, unrelenting in its pursuit to drag me back down into its grasp. Then it struck again, hitting like a tidal wave and driving the breath from my lungs.

I stumbled, crashing beneath the surface again. It was overwhelming. This wasn't the subtle, insidious pull of the river. This was raw power, ancient and heavy as the world itself was pressing down on me until I thought I might break apart beneath its weight.

But it wasn't trying to kill me. It was trying to see me. I could feel it, sifting through my mind, testing the cracks in my strength. The fractures I tried to hide.

Panic threatened to bloom, but I forced it down. I gritted my teeth and refused to succumb to it. The pressure pushed harder, testing, demanding, and I held the river stone tighter. It's cool surface an anchor. A reminder of something solid and real.

Truth, I reminded myself, gripping it tightly.

I had come this far. I wouldn't let the river turn me away. I wouldn't fail.

The suffocating weight bore down, seeking weakness, but I didn't yield. I didn't look away. I didn't let go. Eventually, like mist burned off by the rising sun, the weight began to lift.

My head broke the surface, the night air pouring in like salvation with each gasp. Stars blinked overhead, quiet witnesses to my survival.

The far bank loomed ahead now. Closer.

The river hadn't let me go.

But it had allowed me to continue.

I wiped the water from my face, breath ragged, every inch of me trembling. My legs moved as if wading through molasses, each step forward a silent challenge. It felt like the river was watching, measuring, deciding if I was worthy of crossing at all.

Panic clawed at the edges of my mind. The tonic was supposed to protect me, to be a safeguard against the river's magic. But the current clung to me like invisible chains, its chill sinking into my bones, ancient and sentient. The warmth in my veins flickered, waning like a dying ember. It should have been impossible to breathe, but the tonic was keeping me tethered to this world, even as something darker threatened to pull me under.

But I refused to let it.

I would reach the other side and face whatever waited there.

Then the current shifted ahead, and two figures emerged—fluid and graceful, gliding through the water like they belonged to it. Which, I realized with a slow thrum of unease, they did.

I froze.

They weren't human. Their bodies were long and sinewy, shimmering with otherworldly light. One had skin the color of sun-warmed earth, her platinum braids trailing like silver ribbons through the water. Scales rimmed her neck and arms, deep, stormy blue, and caught the moonlight like shifting metal. Her eyes were gold, sharp and steady.

The other was smaller, more delicate, with pale skin and hair like rippling ink streaked in shades of green and blue. Her scales gleamed like river glass, a kaleidoscope of blue and green along her arms and down her spine. Her expression, cold and glacial, locked onto mine. It was unsettling, not threatening, but impossible to look away from.

They circled me slowly. Observing. I should have been afraid, but instead, I was drawn in, caught in the unnatural stillness of their presence.

They didn't look hostile, but something about them, about the graceful way they glided through the water, like living reflections of the river itself, kept me tense.

"I am Meriol," the golden-eyed one said, her voice rippling through the water like a current over stone—clear, echoing, unburdened by breath.

"And I am Kaia," said the smaller one beside her. Her voice was softer, crystalline. "We are Osiris. The Seers of the water and these woods."

They circled me in tandem, their slow, deliberate movements making my skin prickle with unease.

I was still sinking, the water thick around me, but somehow, their presence held me captive. The panic that had threatened to consume me was ebbing away, replaced by something colder. Older. A presence I couldn't name, like I had stepped into a place not meant to be seen.

The moment the Osiris appeared, I knew I was not in control anymore. They moved through the current like shadows, fluid and effortless, their forms shifting between light and darkness. Their scales shimmered beneath the surface, iridescent like the river itself, as if they had been born from its very essence.

"You've come farther than most," Meriol said, her stare never wavering. There was weight in her words, like she wasn't only speaking to me, but to something watching beyond us.

Kaia drifted closer, her pale eyes searching mine. "But do you understand *why* the gods have led you to us?"

Her voice sent a ripple of dread down my spine. It wasn't quite a question; it was more of a warning that I didn't know the full truth of things.

I struggled to make sense of what was going to happen, to stay focused even as my chest struggled for air. But then, like a breath from the depths, a strange warmth spread through me.

I inhaled. I shouldn't have been able to, but I did. Water filled my lungs as if it were air, flowing smoothly without resistance or pain. I froze, stunned, but the sensation felt natural, like the river itself had shifted to sustain me. I could somehow breathe underwater. My eyes widened.

"You can breathe now," Meriol said gently as if reading my thoughts. "The river has accepted your presence…at least for now."

I swallowed thickly, the new weight of the water pressing against my skin, yet no longer suffocating me. "I don't understand," I admitted, my voice wavering but steady enough.

Kaia tilted her head. "Few have had the opportunity."

Their presence felt ancient, like something woven into the very fabric of the river's existence. I could sense their power, not aggressive but heavy with the weight of centuries, layers of forgotten stories etched into the current. They drifted beside me, no longer circling, but guiding.

"We've witnessed many try to cross," Meriol continued. "Immortals. Beings long forgotten. Each of them carried gifts and abilities shaped by those who walked before them, and left fragments of them behind when they decided to enter the river's clutches."

Kaia lifted her hand, and the water shifted. Light rippled outward, swirling until faint, shimmering figures began to appear—ghostly echoes flickering in the dark current. Warriors, scholars, healers, each face unfamiliar, but filled with the same defiance and desperation I felt now. Their eyes met mine across the veil of time before fading into the dark.

"We were the first to see," Kaia continued. "To collect the thoughts and gifts left behind. Their sacrifices fed the river, so their knowledge and memories remain within it. We keep all of them safe until the river decides the time has come to reveal the truth."

I stared into the shadows. How many had failed? How many had sunk beneath the surface, their stories sealed in the current? And what would the river take from me if I couldn't prove myself? I hardly had anything of substance to offer it.

The cold pressed closer like the river could hear my thoughts, whispering promises of the depths that still lingered below.

"Why are you telling me this?" I asked, gripping the river stone in my pocket until my knuckles ached.

Meriol studied me for a long, breathless moment. "Because the river has been waiting for you, Raine. You are not like the others who have come before, and therefore, the river is choosing to offer you what it has never offered before."

Kaia's voice softened, but there was a weight to her words. "It's offering you a chance, and wondering if you are strong enough to leave a mark or become one that never returns."

I swallowed and squared my shoulders, the weight of their words wrapping around me like the river's current. "I'm not planning to stay," I said, voice steadier than I felt.

Meriol's lips curved. "Let's see if the river agrees."

I nodded, forcing down the rising tension in my chest. Whatever this was, whatever they were about to show me, I had to remember it was all part of my Rite and needed to keep moving forward. I couldn't let the river claim me, not like the others who now lived only as memories in its depths.

The Osiris drifted beside me as I moved forward, their luminous eyes never leaving mine. I could feel it again, that quiet, patient power gathering beneath the surface, bracing for the next test.

Whatever it was, I would meet it head-on. Because I wasn't here to be remembered.

I was here to survive.

The river stirred, and suddenly, I was no longer standing in the water. I gasped, staggering backward, but the current around me had become something else—a memory.

One that was not mine.

The world shifted and formed around me, clearer than dreams, vivid and unnatural. A field stretched in every direction, wild and windswept, under a sky heavy with the promise of rain. I didn't recognize it, yet every breeze through the grass whispered and felt too real to be anything but truth.

Then, a blurry figure appeared. As she came closer, I recognized my grandmother.

She stood alone in the field, younger than I'd ever known her. Her golden hair blew loose around her shoulders, and both hands cradled the curve of her pregnant belly.

The sight stole the breath from my lungs. A quiet ache bloomed inside me, like the sudden pull of a string I hadn't realized was connected to my soul. But before I could make sense of it, the scene shifted.

The field dissolved into a large apothecary shop. I inhaled sharply, looking around—the walls were lined with shelves of herbs, the air thick with the scent of dried flowers and tinctures. I had never seen this place before, but my grandmother moved through it with practiced ease, gathering vials, grinding roots, preparing mixtures with the precision of someone who had done this for years. She looked… at peace.

But this wasn't in Laochra. *So where was this?*

Then again, the vision bent time and changed.

She was older. Still pregnant, and this time, a child trailed behind her, a little boy with fiery hair and wide, curious eyes. He couldn't have been older than four, clinging to the hem of her dress.

I tried to move closer, to reach out, but the vision pulled me further, faster, flashing through time, showing me glimpses of a life I had never known she'd had.

My grandmother sat in the heart of a modest home, the fire crackling gently beside her. Two children sat in her lap now. The boy, maybe ten, held a carved wooden dagger with fierce pride, his hand tightening protectively around it. The little girl beside him, no older than four, had soft blonde hair that tumbled in waves around her shoulders. Her wide, curious eyes matched the boys', both with an unmistakable shade of blue that made my stomach twist.

My breath caught.

I knew those eyes.

They were the same blue as *mine*. The same blue as *hers*.

They held the same depth that marked my family, the color passed down like a thread connecting us across generations.

I stared, frozen, as the scene unfolded and switched to the children stirring a pot as my grandmother's hand guided theirs. Then, to laughter echoing as they chased each other, weaving between thick tree trunks. The boy whispered into the girl's ear, and she clung to his arm, trusting him implicitly. I smiled, reminded of my own relationship with Wren and the similarities.

My throat tightened.

The way my grandmother looked at them, how her hand lingered on the girl's cheek, it was unmistakable. This wasn't kindness. It was love. Family.

But who were they and where were they now?

I swallowed, my mind racing. My grandmother had always said family was everything. It was the only thing worth fighting for, and that blood was sacred, binding us through time.

I tried to reject it, to deny the truth staring back at me. Tried to tell myself it was a trick, that the river was testing my belief in what I knew of her. But the images stayed. Solid. Unyielding.

Her arms wrapped around them, her face relaxed in a way I'd rarely seen. She had been happy. Peaceful. And the longer I watched them interacting, the more I realized how much this version of her differed from the woman I knew.

A flicker of doubt crept in. Had she hidden them from us? Had they died? Or... did she abandon them?

This didn't look like Laochra, so what had happened for her to move across Luminara and leave them behind to start over?

I took a step back, shaking my head. This wasn't real. It couldn't be real. I knew my grandmother, and if these children *were* family, she would never have left them. This had to be a test to discern truth from lies, the river playing tricks on me and testing me. *It had to be.* My grandmother might have lied to me my entire life about her immortality, but she wouldn't knowingly leave her family behind. I knew that much as absolute truth.

The visions fractured like glass, the world tilting, and suddenly, the images were gone. Darkness stirred beneath us, and suddenly, I wasn't standing in water anymore. The current shifted, changing form, turning into something else.

I stumbled, blinking rapidly as images flickered through the depths. At first, they were blurred, like reflections distorted by a restless tide.

Then, they became clearer and I saw my home. Laochra stretched out before me, its rolling green hills bathed in morning light, the scent of damp earth and fresh rain lingering in the air.

For a moment, I forgot to breathe. I could see everything. The rooftops of our small village, the winding paths leading through the streets, the distant barn where I used to hide as a child.

Then, faces emerged. Familiar. Unbearably familiar. My father, his steady gaze searching for something beyond the horizon. My grandmother, standing in the greenhouse, her hands stirring herbs, her face lined with quiet worry. And Wren.

My breath caught in my throat. He was laughing, teasing me in that effortless way of his, his dark curls falling over his eyes as he nudged me with his shoulder. I could almost feel his presence. Hear his laugh. But before I could catch my breath or reach out to him to let him know I was okay, the river roared. The tide turned violent, slamming into me like a force of fury.

Darkness swallowed me whole, and a scream pierced the silence—raw and filled with agony. My heart stopped. I whipped around, my pulse hammering. I couldn't see him, but I could hear his gasps, his desperate struggle.

"No—NO— let me go!"

I thrashed toward it, but the river was no longer water. It was sand, and it was clinging to my legs, pulling me deeper, slowing every step as Wren's cries grew more desperate.

Then I saw him. Knees in the muck, clawing at his throat, as though something was strangling the life from him. In an instant, the sand around him turned crimson and began pouring towards me like a thick river. The unmistakable metallic tang filled the air and my senses. It was blood. *My brother's blood.*

My stomach turned.

My grandmother ran toward him, desperate. I tried to warn her, call out to her, but my voice was gone. I saw her reach Wren and attempt to claw him out of the thick grips of his blood that was trying to swallow them both whole. Her eyes, usually so full of life and mystery, met mine, but they were not her own.

They were empty. Hollow. Unrecognizable. The same shade as my brother's lifeless eyes beside her. That was the last thing I saw before she vanished, and they were both swallowed up by the dark crimson tide.

The silence that followed was worse than any scream. I couldn't move. Couldn't breathe.

Was this the future the river wanted me to see? What it *needed* me to see? If the river lost its magic, if I failed, Wren would die. My grandmother would die. And no doubt everyone else I cared about.

I screamed their names, tearing at the water where I last saw their faces. I was furious at the river for showing me something I didn't want to see.

Couldn't allow it to become true. I dove for the place they'd vanished, but my hands met only water.

Still. Cold. Empty.

The moment shattered. The vision completely cleared. Wren was gone. My grandmother with him. And I was alone again.

I gasped, my lungs burning as I fought to breathe again. The Osiris watched silently, their expressions still as a blade sheathed in darkness, promising danger in its restraint. They were watching. *Waiting*. I didn't want to confront what I was feeling, but as the water calmed around me, the storm raged inside me.

I turned to them, my hands shaking, my breath ragged. "You showed me a lie," I said, voice low and shaking. "Something that hasn't—*won't*—happen."

Meriol's golden eyes did not waver. "Are you sure about that?"

Kaia stepped forward, tilting her head as her eyes assessed mine. "The river does not *lie*, Raine. We merely showed you what you were meant to see. What you do with that vision is now up to you to decide."

I clenched my jaw, my hands curling into fists.

"It wasn't real," I whispered, more to myself than to them. "It can't be."

Meriol's lips curved into something almost sad. "Perhaps not yet. But again, that is up to you to decide."

The current loosened around me, like the river had taken what it wanted. It had shown me what it wanted me to see and taken hold of my mind, my fears, and now it was letting me go. The weight of the vision lingered in my bones.

"You are not meant to carry the past like a shackle or the future like a burden. You must decide whether to wear it like a chain that holds you back or let it be the fire that forges you." Kaia added before disappearing into the water.

I nodded once, not fully understanding but knowing the weight of the words would reveal themselves in time.

I swallowed hard, my fingers tightening around the stone in my pocket—an anchor tethering me to the very alive people I loved on the other side of these trees. I wasn't sure what I had just faced or seen. What was truth and what was deception? But as I took another step forward, closer to the other side of the river, one thing was certain.

I would fight. For Wren. For my grandmother. For the ones who still had a chance to live. I was doing this for the people I loved, and no matter what was thrown my way, I would succeed. Because strength wasn't born in the absence of fear, but in the decision to continue despite it.

The current thickened around me, no longer just water but something sentient—alive and coiled like a beast tightening its hold with every step I took. It was done watching. Done waiting.

I pushed forward, limbs aching, lungs straining, the weight of the current clinging to my skin like chains. Moonlight fractured across the mist, barely illuminating the bank ahead, and for a breath, I thought I was alone.

But then I saw them. Two figures waiting at the water's edge.

Manakel and Aeron.

I stopped cold. My breath caught. The river climbed higher, curling around my waist, my ribs, my chest like it meant to claim me for good.

The two Sciathain stood side by side, still, silent, each with an outstretched hand. *They were giving me a choice.*

The river urged me forward, pressing cold fingers into my spine, whispering promises I couldn't hear but could feel in my bones. My gaze fell to Manakel first.

His face was illuminated in the pale light, calm and familiar, the same steady warmth I had come to rely on. There was a flicker of a smile on his lips, just enough to remind me of every moment before this one. The times by the creek, the gentle strength in his hands during training, the quiet reassurance when I was doubting myself. His lips on mine.

He had been there through everything regarding my Rite and was the one to save me multiple times already. If I could trust anyone, it should be him. *Shouldn't it?*

But then there was Aeron.

He stood tall, rigid. His hand extended, his shoulders squared. His grey eyes locked on mine, sharp and steady, like he knew exactly what I needed even if it wasn't always the easiest option. He didn't move, didn't beckon. There was no coaxing in his expression; it didn't soften or try to convince me. He simply waited with his hand extended. Didn't reach, didn't beg, just waited.

It wasn't a plea for trust. A challenge. An invitation. A test. A choice. *My choice.*

I swallowed hard, the current tightening like a noose. My pulse pounded in my ears. Aeron had never been easy to read. His words were sharp-edged things, laced with riddles and truths wrapped in thorns. He had helped me in his own way, but it felt like he was always testing me, taunting me, or waiting for me to give up.

And yet… his eyes now held something different. Something raw, that told me he wouldn't stop me if I reached for him. *Chose him.* But he wouldn't protect me from the consequences, either.

I turned back to Manakel, heart aching with doubt. His fingers shifted forward in a silent invitation. I forced myself to breathe, to drown out the storm of doubt in my chest.

Trust the truth. Trust your intuition.

But my intuition wasn't answering. It twisted, torn between the memory of safety and the weight of suspicion I had been pushing away since last night.

Manakel had been the one to guide me this week. He had trained me, laughed with me, and made me feel safe when the shadows lurked too close. My grandmother trusted him. I trusted him, and my heart had started to as well.

He was safe. Sturdy. Reliable. And the most logical choice.

My hand moved before I could think twice. I reached for him. And for the briefest moment, warmth flooded through me when our fingers met.

Then everything shifted.

His lips curved into a smile, one that didn't belong to the Manakel I knew. It was sharp. Cold. Menacing. Something hollow lurked in his eyes, twisting the warmth I thought I knew into something darker.

"Did you *really* think it would be that easy?" His voice curled through the air, soft yet sharp enough to cut through me like ice.

My stomach plummeted. His grip tightened around my hand. Too fast. Too strong. Fingers like shackles closed around my wrist, and panic surged through me as he yanked me forward. I tried to pull away, but his grip was like stone, unrelenting and crushing.

"Manakel?" My voice wavered, barely above a whisper.

His smile twisted further, amusement flashing across his face, but there was no kindness left in it. A stranger wearing the face I had trusted.

This was another trick. A lie. A deception. And I had fallen for it. *Again.*

I jerked back, but his hold was iron. Then all of a sudden, he shoved me backward at the same time he released his hold on me.

I gasped as the river rose to meet me like a beast waiting to swallow me whole. The surface shattered around me, cold knives slashing across my skin as I plunged beneath the water. The pain was immediate. Piercing. The cold burned like fire, wrapping around my chest, my ribs, my lungs until every breath felt like razors. I twisted, kicked, fought, but the river had me now. It spun me in the dark, dragging me, disoriented and drowning.

The world above fractured into shadow, but a sliver of light cut through the black water. I could barely make out anything around me, my eyes burning. Blinking a few times, I saw a figure standing above me.

Aeron.

He was still there. Still waiting. His steel grey eyes locked onto mine, but they didn't hold anger. Only disappointment.

It hit harder than the cold. I clawed at the water, my chest aching with betrayal as much as the need for air. I reached for him, for anything, but the current dragged me down. My chest heaved. My vision blurred.

I had chosen wrong.

I had failed this test.

The river knew it, and it would make me pay.

My lungs screamed, and so did my heart. The worst part wasn't the pain or the cold; it was the trust I had so willingly placed into the wrong hands. I had mistaken safety for truth. Familiarity for certainty. I thought I could tell the difference. *But I was wrong.*

The river strengthened its hold on me, pulling, yanking, breaking. I kicked harder, muscles straining, the darkness stretching longer, the current wrapping tighter.

No. Not like this.

I refused to give up. Even if it broke me, even if the cold carved me hollow, I would not let this river be the end of me.

Because now I knew what betrayal looked like.

And next time, I would not reach for the wrong hand.

38. When Legends Fall

The river's grip clamped around my ankles like icy chains, dragging me under before I could scream. My limbs flailed, kicking against the current, but the water twisted around me, ruthless, alive, pulling me deeper into its black depths.

Panic surged. My lungs shrieked for air. I clawed upward, but the river shoved back. Water flooded my mouth, silencing my cry, and pressure built behind my eyes, my ribs, my ears, every part of me screaming as the darkness wrapped tighter.

It was useless. No matter how hard I fought, the river was stronger. They'd told me I couldn't die here. That the river was a passage, not a grave. But in that moment, with the weight of the current crushing my chest and the cold gnawing into my bones, it didn't feel like survival. It felt like succumbing to death.

But the moment I stopped fighting, when every last shred of breath had fled my lungs, the river released me.

I plummeted like a stone, plunging into a hollow pool. The sudden change in pressure spat me out violently, and I broke the surface, gasping and sputtering as air rushed back into my lungs.

Slick stone met my trembling hands, and I pushed against it, the surface slippery as I forced myself to stand.

Moonlight spilled in from a narrow slit high above; the silver ribbon was the only thing illuminating the space. I turned in slow circles, heart hammering, trying to make sense of where I was. It seemed impossible, but I was in a cave.

The walls rose around me in smooth, glistening towers of wet stone, glinting with moss and tiny rivulets that trickled down into the pool I'd just emerged from. There were no stairs, no ledges, no visible way out besides the narrow opening stretching up at least twenty feet and far out of reach. I was trapped.

I turned in a slow circle, water pooling at my feet, heart still thundering. The realization struck like a slap to the chest: I was buried beneath the river. Panic tightened its grip again. I pressed a shaking hand to my ribs, steadying my breath as I took in the sheer impossibility of where I stood.

None of this made sense. The river shouldn't have led me here. Logic didn't stretch far enough to explain what I was seeing.

Which left only one explanation.

Magic. And I had learned by now that magic was unpredictable, wild, and dangerous.

I waded toward the wall, hands skimming across the damp stone. Slick and unyielding, there wasn't a single handhold. The walls curved upward like glass, impossible to climb.

My eyes drifted to the narrow slit of moonlight above, my breath fogging in the faint chill that hung in the air. I wasn't sure if I was too far down for anyone to hear me or if the cave simply swallowed the sound the way the river had swallowed me.

But I had to try.

Tilting my head back, I cupped my hands around my mouth and called out, "Hello?" My voice cracked as it echoed, bouncing off the stone. "Can anyone hear me?"

I held my breath, listening, waiting for something, anything. But the cave gave nothing back.

My shoulders slumped, and the weight of the silence pressed down harder, heavier. Just the hush of water and the slow drip of condensation falling off the walls. The silence pressed in heavier. I slumped against the wall, throat tight, legs trembling from cold and exhaustion.

Then I felt it. A ripple. Gentle. Barely there.

I looked down, and the water lapped at my ankle, too slow, too smooth. My muscles locked. The water stirred unnaturally, thick and heavy, as though something vast had just shifted beneath the surface. A low, sloshing sound echoed around the cavern, reverberating off the walls.

I spun, breath catching, eyes fixed on the black pool.

The water rippled again, and then, slowly, almost deliberately, something began to rise. At first, I thought it was part of the cave wall, jagged and dark, slick with algae. But as it unfurled, I saw the scales, slick and glistening, the thick coils of its body, shimmering in hues of green and black, beneath the water. Shadows shifted unnaturally as the creature peeled itself free from the depths.

Its head broke the surface last, and I froze.

It loomed, impossibly large, its massive form stretching upward toward the slit of moonlight like it could tear through the rock and sky alike. Spines like jagged obsidian ran the length of its serpentine back. A thick mane of slick fur trailed along its back, clinging to its body in heavy matted tendrils. Wings, small and leathery, hung uselessly, too small to lift its hulking body, but sharp enough to be their own weapon.

Twin horns curved back from its skull, framing glowing red eyes that pierced through the darkness like burning coals—two burning orbs of sickly red, locking onto mine with cold, hungry precision that paralyzed me where I stood.

A word crashed through my thoughts, sharp and certain.

Oilliphéist.

The river serpent. The destroyer.

I had heard the stories. Whispers of a beast dragged from the marrow of old nightmares. Said to haunt the deepest lakes and caverns, devouring mortals, swallowing ships whole, and drowning those foolish enough to cross its path.

And now… it was here. *It was real.* And it was staring directly at me.

Its maw opened slowly, deliberately, revealing jagged teeth the size of my forearm, chipped, yellowed, and cracked like they'd chewed through more than bone. Water spilled from between them, steaming in the cold air. It didn't move. Just watched. Like it had all the time in the world to decide my fate.

I edged backward, my boots slipping on the wet stone. There was nowhere to go. No exits. No crevices to hide in. Just me, alone and cornered in a giant open cave, trapped as easy prey for this predator.

The Oilliphéist tilted its head slightly, eyes glowing like embers in the dark, calculating. But I didn't wait for it to decide.

The moment it lunged, I dove, barely clearing its massive jaw as it snapped shut with a deafening crack that shook the cave around me. The sound rang in my skull as I hit the ground hard, skidding across the stone. My dagger scraped free from its sheath, more reflex than strategy.

Not that it would do me much good. Against this beast, my dagger was no more than a needle.

The Oilliphéist coiled back, preparing to strike again. Its head snapped forward, and I rolled beneath the blow, the rush of air and water blasting past me as its jaws crushed the space I'd just occupied. I scrambled upright, lungs heaving, heart pounding so loudly it drowned out everything else.

It was toying with me.

I spun, desperate for an exit. There was none.

A deep rumble echoed from its chest, more vibration than sound, and the stone beneath me trembled. It slithered forward, the bulk of its body coiling around the pool like a wall of living armor, cutting off any escape.

Think, Raine.

My gaze darted wildly, scanning the cave, but there were no crevices, no ledges, no way out but up. The walls were too smooth to climb, and the tiny opening above was too high. The Oilliphéist lined the chamber, filling every breath with the scent of wet stone and something metallic, old blood. It darted its tongue out to lick its upper teeth in a taunting show of power, and if I didn't act fast, I'd be torn to shreds before I could think of a way out.

And then it hit me. The only thing in this cave tall enough to reach the surface was the Oilliphéist itself. Maybe I could use its size to my advantage and get myself out.

My pulse thundered. It was reckless, maybe even suicidal, but it was the only chance I had to survive this.

It lunged again, but this time, instead of dodging, I charged toward it. I hurled myself at its side, seizing the coarse, matted fur along its spine. My hands burned as the sharp edges of its scales bit into my skin. It screamed, a shriek of rage, and thrashed wildly, bucking and twisting to shake me off its back. I held on, *barely*. My grip slipped, its scales wet and slick, and for a terrifying second, I thought I'd fall.

My fingers burned as I clung to the short fur, nails digging into its skin as I was whipped side to side. It reared up, dragging its massive body from the water, lifting me with it, rising toward the mouth of the cave.

I was closer, but the opening was still too far.

Frantic, I fumbled in my pocket, cold, soaked fabric clinging to my hand, searching for anything that could help, anything that could help me survive this or upset it enough to roar to its full height.

My fingers brushed against the small pouch I'd slipped into my pocket just before Manakel took my bag. My breath hitched.

'River dust.' My grandmother's voice echoed in my mind, soft but firm. '*Use this when you feel like the river will devour you.*'

I'd dismissed it then, thinking I wouldn't need it. But now with the Oilliphéist's jaws nearly closing around me, I realized I had never been more wrong.

I couldn't outrun this. Not without some help.

Below me, the serpent hissed, its body coiling upward as it reared toward the small opening above. I struggled against the wind from its surprisingly strong wings, gripping tighter to its mane as it bucked beneath me. With shaking hands, I fought to keep hold of the dagger in one hand, deflecting its snapping jaw while fumbling in my pocket to grab the pouch with the other.

The Oilliphéist twisted sharply, nearly hurling me off its back again. A startled cry escaped my throat as I yanked the pouch free, tearing it open with my teeth. A fine shimmer of dust spilled into my palm, and I flung it across its back as my dagger clashed against its thick scales.

For a moment, nothing happened.

Then the Oilliphéist let out an ear-piercing shriek, the sound reverberating through the cavern and stabbing into my skull. Steam hissed from where the dust touched its scales, sizzling like hot iron plunged into water.

It writhed in agony, rising higher, wings flapping wildly as it tried to throw me off. I nearly lost my grip and slid down its back, my feet landing dangerously close to the razor-sharp ridges along its tail. My muscles screamed in protest. I couldn't hold on much longer.

My focus shifted to the narrow opening high above. It was barely wide enough to squeeze through, but it was my only chance to escape. But to do that, I had to get higher.

The Oilliphéist reared back, its body stretching as it tried to shake off the burning dust still clinging to its flesh. And I took its distraction as my chance.

Clenching my jaw and planting my foot against the slick curve of its spine, I lunged, driving my dagger into a crevice between two uneven stones in the cavern wall. The blade sank deep, holding firm. I gripped the hilt with both hands and hauled myself upward, fingers bleeding, arms shaking.

The cavern spun around me, but I focused solely on the opening that held the sliver of moonlight like a beacon of hope. My arms screamed in protest, the cold sapping my strength. The dagger trembled beneath my weight, and I knew it wouldn't hold for long.

The Oilliphéist lunged below. Its jaws snapped at my feet, slamming into the wall with enough force to shake loose dust and mud. My fingers scraped against the jagged rock, nails splitting as I scrambled to haul myself higher. The stone was slick beneath my grasp, wet from the river spray, and my boots skidded, barely finding purchase.

I could see it—freedom. The narrow opening was just above me, inches from my outstretched hand. Light filtered through the crack, tantalizingly close, but the Oilliphéist wasn't finished with me yet.

A guttural snarl tore through the cavern, low and violent, vibrating through the stone and straight into my chest.

I shouldn't have looked down, but I did.

The Oilliphéist twisted below, its slick, serpentine body coiling tighter, muscles rippling beneath iridescent scales as it prepared to strike again. The water churned violently beneath it, frothing with rage.

My fingers screamed from the strain, wedged into a narrow crevice in the rock slick with water and blood. The dagger in my other hand trembled, jammed into a crack just wide enough to hold my weight, but it wouldn't last long. My body dangled over open water, soaked and shaking, ribs burning with every breath.

And then it lunged. A flash of green and black scales and teeth. I yanked my legs up just in time, but not fast enough. Its jaws snapped shut around my boot, teeth scraping rubber and leather as I cried out, the shock slamming through me like a lightning bolt. My grip slipped an inch. My heart stuttered.

No, no, no—

I kicked wildly, gritting my teeth, driving my heel into the creature's maw again and again until it snarled, thrashing violently.

"Let go!" I screamed, more animal than human.

The dagger wrenched in the stone, slipping, but I didn't stop. I slammed my foot into its face, using every ounce of strength I had left. With a final, furious kick, the Oilliphéist released me, crashing back into the water with a deafening splash that echoed off the walls like a war drum.

I clung to the rock, breath ragged, chest heaving. The cavern pulsed with silence for a beat, then I heard it again: the wet slap of its tail disappearing into the depths.

Retreating. But it wasn't gone. I knew it couldn't have been that easy to defeat it, and I had seconds, *maybe,* before it came for me again.

I dug the dagger in deeper, gritting my teeth as I hauled myself higher, fingertips bleeding, lungs on fire, and only one thought driving me upward. Climb or die.

My muscles screamed with each movement, but I didn't let go. I couldn't. The dagger was my lifeline, wedged deep in the slick crevice of stone. My fingers clung to the crack above it, nails bending, tearing. The sharp sting barely registered; there was no room for pain anymore. Only survival.

The edge of the opening was close. I could see it now, a jagged lip of stone about a foot above my head, rough and uneven, but wide enough to hoist myself over. *If* I could reach it. If my arm didn't give out. If the creature didn't rise again from the churning dark below.

I thought back to the first pit I had been in tonight, the way Aeron had pulled me up and out. But no one was coming this time. This time, *I* had to climb, and the only one I could rely on was myself.

I shifted my weight, slowly, carefully, ignoring the tremble in my shoulders. My foot found the edge of the dagger's hilt, shaky but steady. I used it like a step, gritting my teeth as I pushed upward.

Another inch. Then another.

My fingers scraped the edge, and I let out a choked sob, rage and desperation mingling in my throat.

One more push.

I slammed my knee against the wall, bracing with every bit of strength I had left, and lunged upward, my fingertips just catching the lip of the rock. The motion jolted through my entire body like I'd been struck, but I held on. The stone was rough and cold beneath my palms, but it was there.

I gritted my teeth, forced my legs to push, and dragged myself up, inch by agonizing inch, arms burning, legs numb. My chest scraped along the stone, and for a breathless, terrifying moment, I thought I was going to slide back down.

With a final, desperate heave, I thrust my arm up, fingertips brushing the edge of the opening. I hooked a hand over the lip of the cave and hoisted myself up with everything I had left. My shoulders screamed in protest, but I kept going, legs scrambling to push off the wall until I was out.

My body collapsed in a heap, soaked and shaking, face pressed against the blessedly solid ground. For a few seconds, I couldn't move. Couldn't think. Just breathe.

Rolling onto my back, my chest heaved as I sucked in gulps of cool air. The dirt beneath my palms felt more real than anything ever had. The cold seared into my skin, but it was real. It wasn't water. It was solid, dry land.

My fingers flexed against the dirt, just to be sure. They shook uncontrollably, scraped raw and bloodied, but they moved. I stared at the stars above me, letting the weight of what I'd escaped settle into my bones.

I was alive and out of reach. *For now.*

A laugh bubbled up in my throat, sharp and wild and breathless. It escaped before I could stop it, echoing hollowly through the air around me like a dare. A challenge to the woods surrounding me.

I'd made it.

Battered. Bruised. Half-drowned and half-mad.

But still—alive.

I was no longer in the river. I lay on dry land, lungs aching, skin burning, but the fleeting sense of safety that came with solid ground was short-lived.

The air around me thickened, the trees beyond the river's edge groaned as they bent and twisted, their branches cracking like joints coming undone. A low howl rippled through the stillness, threading between trunks and roots like a warning.

The forest was alive.

But not in the way the river had been. This wasn't a breath or a whisper, and didn't feel welcoming; it was as if the trees themselves were waiting for me, testing me again.

I swallowed hard, pushing to my feet, heart still thrumming from the escape. The sense of safety I'd felt moments ago faded, replaced by the familiar weight of unease. The river had nearly devoured me, but I wasn't free. The Rite wasn't over; it had only just begun.

I stepped forward, boots crunching on the damp leaves, but the feeling only grew stronger. The Oilliphéist might have vanished beneath the surface, but something else waited here. I wasn't drowning anymore, but I wasn't safe. I was prey.

The sky overhead was still shrouded in the dim gray-blue veil that came just before dawn. Time had continued moving while I was underwater. I tried to gauge how long I'd been in the river—an hour? Two? The tonic's protection only lasted twelve hours at best, and I had to be running low. I may have had five hours left? Probably less.

Don't think about it.

I straightened, brushing damp hair from my face as I surveyed the forest ahead. The land on this side of the river was unfamiliar, wild in a way that felt older, untouched. The trees loomed taller, their branches twisting together like skeletal fingers, blotting out the morning light. The path ahead, if it could be called that, was little more than a thread winding through gnarled roots and tangled underbrush.

A shiver ran along my spine.

I froze, instincts prickling.

Something was... off. The air had stilled completely. No wind. No birdsong. Just the slow curl of mist wrapping around my ankles like it meant to tether me here. My eyes narrowed, scanning for movement, but I saw nothing. Still, the feeling persisted, the undeniable weight of eyes, of being watched from somewhere beyond the shadows. Someone was out there.

I exhaled slowly, forcing myself to focus. I needed supplies, something to steady my nerves, even if it was just the comfort of knowing I had tools to defend myself.

My hand drifted automatically toward my bag, but my fingers grasped at nothing but air.

My stomach dropped when I remembered.

Manakel.

He'd taken it, offered to carry it before I stepped into the river, probably assuming I wouldn't survive long enough to need it again.

I bit down on a bitter laugh. All I had were the two daggers on me, a flint stone, and the sheer will that had kept me alive this long.

I reached for the sheaths at my hips and found only one blade. The second dagger, the one I'd used to fight the Oilliphéist, was gone, still embedded in the cave wall, my last foothold before escape.

I muttered a curse under my breath and tightened my grip on the remaining blade, the worn leather handle grounding me. It wasn't much. But it would have to be enough.

The mist crept higher, slinking through roots and pooling along the ground like it had weight. The forest held its breath.

Somewhere, a branch cracked.

I whirled, blade raised, every muscle coiled. But there was nothing. Just trees and silence. I steadied my breath and kept moving.

Each step deeper into the forest felt like a descent into darkness. The shadows grew thicker, clinging to the bark like old bruises. The air was heavier now, laced with something I couldn't name, a faint vibration, like magic pressed against my skin.

Was this still a part of my Imbe Rite?

Manakel had said no one's trial was ever the same. My grandmother had warned me that the gods carved each test to expose something hidden, something buried. Some faced illusions, others monsters, but none had ever crossed the forbidden river.

Was that what made my Rite so different? I didn't know what I had been expecting, but so far, the things I had faced were not even in the realm of possibility when I was preparing.

I gripped the dagger tighter, forcing myself to keep walking.

The forest ahead felt darker. Shadows moved where they shouldn't. Too fluid. Too aware. My steps slowed, muscles coiled tight, every sense prickling. And I couldn't shake the feeling that something waited for me within it.

I barely had time to register the dread curling under my skin before I heard it. A melody, soft, distant, and chilling in its familiarity. It wound through the trees like a whisper half-remembered, lilting and strange, a lullaby wrapped in smoke. My breath caught.

I knew that song.

Not from this forest, but from my dreams, the ones I hadn't shared with anyone in years. The ones where the music lured me deeper into the woods until I woke gasping, heart pounding, and drenched in sweat. Now, hearing it with my eyes wide open, my blood turned to ice.

I shifted, the damp soles of my boots pressing against moss-slick ground as I weighed my options. But my body betrayed me, drawn forward as if by invisible threads, the melody slipping beneath my skin, threading through my ribs.

It wasn't just a sound. It was a summons.

My pulse thundered. *Don't listen.*

I tried to shove the thought aside, to drown out the melody's pull, but the tune wound tighter around me, wrapping itself into the cracks of my resolve. But my feet moved on their own, one step, then another. Leaves crackled beneath me, each step hazier than the last. It felt like walking through water, distant from my own limbs, unable to stop.

I gritted my teeth, blinking hard to refocus. *No. Not now. Don't let it control you.*

I clenched my fists and dug my nails into my palms, but even pain didn't break the trance.

The wind stirred. First a whisper, then a hiss. It twisted through the trees in a spiral, pulling the fallen leaves into a dance, until I realized they weren't just circling me. They were climbing.

Tendrils of brittle foliage curled around my ankles, brushing up my legs like living vines. I stumbled back, kicking hard to shake them off, but they coiled tighter.

Panic bloomed in my chest.

The forest was alive. The branches around me creaked, their spindly limbs shuddering as if in response to the melody.

"Stop it," I rasped, voice trembling.

But the leaves didn't heed my plea. They climbed higher, winding around my knees, my hips, soft, deliberate, and inescapable. Like the forest had chosen me, and it wanted to keep me.

I thrashed, wild and desperate, but the more I fought, the more they constricted. The music swelled, no longer a lullaby but a command, pressing into my ears, into my lungs, like weight made of sound.

I sucked in a shaky breath, heart pounding like a war drum.

If I didn't break free now, I wouldn't.

With trembling fingers, I reached for my dagger. The hilt was slick against my palm, but real. Solid. Mine. And I let its familiar weight ground me, just for a second, long enough to draw it with a sharp hiss of steel.

With a fierce cry, I slashed at the leaves, tearing them apart in desperate strokes. They fell away, brittle and lifeless once more. The wind hissed through the clearing, a sound that felt eerily like a wounded gasp.

I didn't wait to find out what would happen next. I ran, forcing my legs to move despite the lingering pull of the music. The melody faded, but the weight of it lingered, like hands pressed against my back, like eyes in the dark tracking my every move.

The forest wasn't done with me. *Not yet.*

I spun in a slow circle, breath heaving, eyes scanning the warped landscape. I tried to piece together my surroundings, but everything felt wrong. Trees stretched taller here, their limbs skeletal against the dim light, reaching skyward like they were trying to snatch what little light managed to break through the thick canopy. Shadows pooled unnaturally beneath the underbrush, stretching and shifting, like they moved when I wasn't looking.

Dermaine.

The thought came sharply, grounding me. I had to reach Dermaine.

The Queen's castle. My destination. My purpose. The reason I was here.

I imagined the towering gates, the cold stone walls, the look in the Queen's eyes as I begged her to renew the river's magic. If she refused, the barrier would fall, and everything I'd risked, everything I'd left behind, would be for nothing.

That couldn't happen. I wouldn't let it.

Nothing would stop me. Not even this forest. I gripped the dagger tighter, its hilt biting into my hand. The forest could stalk me. It could try to claim me. But it wouldn't stop me.

Still… a part of me, small, stubborn, and bone-deep, hoped Manakel would appear. I could almost see him stepping out of the trees, casually unbothered, my satchel slung over his shoulder, smirking like he expected me here, waiting for him. He'd say something sarcastic or something half-concerned about surviving the river or being reckless.

But the forest answered only with silence.

I rubbed my arms, soaked to the skin and shivering as wet clothes clung to me. Each movement felt slow and heavy, every brush of fabric against my skin amplifying the cold that had settled into my bones.

I just need warmth. Something dry to soothe the aching chill. A fire. A blanket. Even tea.

My mind ached for those quiet comforts, the ones that felt like home. My grandmother's calming brews, the scent of her herbs surrounding me. The weight of a blanket over my shoulders. Small things. Insignificant to most, but they anchored me, reminders of the life I had left behind. The one that felt further away with every step.

Now, I had nothing but a blade, a forest determined to break me, and a mission that demanded everything I had left. And still, I kept walking.

The shadows crawling at the forest's edge shattered the fragile grip I had on those memories.

I froze, searching for anything familiar, any semblance of wings in the shadows. Instead, something darker shifted between the trees. It materialized from the shadows, tall, silent, cloaked so completely it seemed woven from the woods itself. A figure. Silent. Still. Watching.

I narrowed my eyes, trying to anchor the shape to something human, something familiar. But it stayed just far enough away to blur the lines between reality and nightmare.

My throat tightened. I had seen this before.

The visions from the creek surged back like a tidal wave, crashing over my thoughts. Hooded shapes, faceless and cruel. Crimson blood glinting off blades. Screams swallowed by the night. The sear of heat, the ache of loss, the sound of steel slicing through the people I loved.

I couldn't breathe. My hands trembled, and I staggered back until bark scraped against my spine. The tree was real. Solid. But everything else felt like a dream unraveling into a nightmare.

It's not real. But it felt real, *too real.*

I squeezed my eyes shut, willing the images away, but they clung like burrs beneath my skin. Somewhere in the back of my mind, my grandmother's voice whispered, *The tonic will protect you,* but her words felt fragile now, stretched too thin to hold.

The vision bled into the present, the panic swirling inside me blurred every thought, marring the lines of what was real and what was just fear. I clutched the dagger, pressed the blade's tip into my palm until pain bloomed sharp and bright, grounding me with the sting.

Anchor yourself.

Fear won't save you.

I exhaled shakily and shifted, inching sideways along the tree's edge. My heart pounded like war drums beneath my ribs, and slowly, I risked a glance around the trunk.

The figure had moved closer.

It glided, not walked, with a slow, methodical grace, savoring the moment, each step deliberate and soundless.

It wasn't a hallucination. It wasn't a memory.

My legs screamed at me to run, but the music, that same soft, melodic hum I thought had disappeared, drifted faintly through the trees, curling around the figure like smoke.

I clenched my teeth. It was just like the visions, except this wasn't a *vision*.

It was here.

And it was watching me.

Move, Raine.

I pushed off the tree in a sharp burst, heart hammering as I forced my legs to carry me forward. Every rustle of leaves behind me sent another spike of panic lancing through my chest.

I didn't look back. I didn't need to.

Because I already knew.

The figure was following.

39. Footsteps In The Dark

The figure crept closer, each step deliberate and silent, as if it had all the time in the world. Its eyes burned red, twin coals glowing through the dark, locking onto me with a hunger that drained the air from my lungs. Around us, even the forest seemed to hold its breath.

I was frozen, spine pressed against the bark of a tree, every instinct screaming at me to run, except I knew I wouldn't get far. My heart pounded so violently it felt like it might shatter against my ribs. Run. Every nerve screamed for me to move, but I couldn't. Not with those eyes pinning me like prey.

It stepped forward, pale skin catching the faintest slivers of moonlight. Its face twisted into a cold, satisfied smirk, and I saw the glint of fangs beneath its lips.

My fingers curled around the dagger at my side, but my palm was slick with sweat. The blade felt useless, laughable, against the predator standing before me.

Blood-drinker. Hunger without end.

The name echoed in my mind like a curse. *Abhartach.*

And I knew—this was the monster I'd imagined with every childhood warning whispered on bonfire nights. This was the shadow I saw behind the stories, when the elders spoke of the immortals who once ravaged the lands, who hunted humans for sport or hunger or vengeance. This was what I pictured, even before I knew its name.

The cloaked figures from my visions. The faceless horrors from the creek. I'd seen them in nightmares and smoke and fire.

And now one stood in front of me.

Real. Breathing. Watching.

The stories rushed back in fragments, nightmares whispered about pale demons that slipped through villages at night, draining the life of anyone caught in their gaze. My father had stopped telling those kinds of tales when I was a child, my mother cutting him off abruptly when the details grew too dark and we refused to settle. Now I understood why. Because this was more terrifying than any story could convey.

It wasn't just a myth. It was real.

But the stories had never mentioned how staring into its eyes would feel, like hooks buried beneath my skin, like it could hear my heartbeat and was already imagining how it might taste. I swallowed hard, my mind scrambling for what came next in those stories. How to kill it. How to survive it. But we'd never gotten that far.

It was always just the warning of staying out of the forest, of the threat of the river, and immortal creatures like this. Nothing solid or concrete on how to defeat it, if there even *was* a way.

The Abhartach stepped forward, savoring the moment. Its head tilted, like it was listening to the chaos unraveling inside me.

I won't die here. I won't let it take me.

With a burst of panic-laced adrenaline, I shoved off the tree and lunged. My dagger cut through the air—

And struck nothing.

The Abhartach vanished, and I stumbled, nearly falling face-first into the dirt. The laugh that followed wasn't loud, but soft and cruel, echoing through the clearing like thunder in my ears. I spun just in time to see it reappear at my side, too close, so close I could see the faint cracks splitting its lips, like dried blood.

I tightened my grip, forcing a smirk onto my face. "Really?" I rasped, voice thinner than I wanted. "Vanishing and reappearing? A bit dramatic, don't you think?"

It tilted its head again, eyes glittering with curiosity. For one brief second, I thought I'd surprised it, maybe thrown it off balance. But its smirk widened, colder this time, and I wasn't fooled.

This was a game, and as the Abhartach closed the distance slowly, I knew they were savoring it. Its hand lifted, pale fingers reaching toward my throat.

Move.

I pressed back harder against the tree, willing my body to obey, but fear locked every muscle in place. I couldn't outrun this. I couldn't fight it and win. Not like this.

It leaned in, close enough for me to feel the unnatural warmth of its breath against my skin. I squeezed my eyes shut, my heart slowing as a cold acceptance settled in.

This was it. It would all be over soon.

I held my breath waiting for the inevitable pain. But a sudden, gut-wrenching howl split the air. Wild. Deep. Terrifying.

I snapped my eyes open just as the Abhartach jerked away, snarling. A massive shadow burst from the trees behind it, all fangs and muscle and fury. And before I could register what was happening, the Abhartach was dragged to the ground, its bone-like fingers scraping against the dirt as it writhed in the jaws of a massive black wolf.

I staggered back, hand to my chest, gasping.

The wolf was enormous, its fur pitch black except for the stark white dusting along its chest and jaw. It towered over the Abhartach, moving like a living shadow, all power and precision, pinning the pale creature without effort.

The Abhartach writhed beneath it, its red eyes wild with fury. It let out a piercing, inhuman screech that rattled through the clearing. The sound cracked the air like splintered bone, loud enough to make the trees shake, but the wolf didn't flinch. Its jaws clamped tighter.

For a breathless moment, the Abhartach's blood-red eyes met mine, wide and pleading. I thought it might have been begging—not for mercy, but for help. But I didn't move.

It thrashed harder, but the wolf growled, a deep, rumbling warning that sent shivers down my spine. Then it wrenched the creature sideways, driving it hard into the ground, snapping bone against earth. The Abhartach's body convulsed, once, twice, then collapsed. Its cloak unfurled in the dirt, dark mist unraveling into shadows that vanished through the trees. What remained was a lifeless body that was eerily human. Small. Fragile. And hopefully dead.

I exhaled sharply, only then realizing I'd been holding my breath. My legs trembled beneath me, the rush of adrenaline wearing off like a fading tide, and I sagged against the nearest tree for support.

The wolf remained still, towering over the Abhartach's body, where its darkness had disappeared, leaving behind pale flesh. Its chest rose and fell in slow, steady rhythm, unshaken. Then its focus shifted from the spot where the Abhartach lay to me.

I froze, hoping I wasn't next, and wishing that if I was, it would be just as quick and painless.

Golden eyes, bright as molten light, held mine in a way that stripped the fear from my limbs, replacing it with something gentler. Not safety, exactly, but understanding. There was no malice in those eyes, no predatory gleam. Only something watchful. Measured. As if the creature wasn't just seeing me, it was reading me, searching for something invisible beneath the surface.

The forest seemed to lean into the silence, holding its breath with me.

"I… thank you," I said quietly, the words catching on the rawness in my throat.

The wolf tilted its head slightly, as if in acknowledgment. Then, without a sound, it turned and vanished between the trees, melting into the darkness as if it had always belonged to it.

But the stillness didn't last.

From the very place the wolf had disappeared, a woman emerged from the shadows like she was part of them, woven from the forest itself. Her presence shifted the air, bending the stillness around her like a storm about to break. For a moment, I wondered if I was still seeing the wolf, if the creature hadn't disappeared, but had shifted, stretched, and reshaped itself into the woman standing before me. Because she didn't feel entirely human.

I stood there, paralyzed by the sudden, unshakable realization that the wolf hadn't just been a *beast*. It had been *her*.

Her skin, rich and deep as polished mahogany, glowed faintly beneath the last remnants of moonlight. Her face was all sharp edges and striking beauty—full lips, a defined jaw, high cheekbones, and eyes the color of wildfire trapped in amber. There was something ancient in her gaze, something that made the hair on the back of my neck prickle.

Her hair spilled over her shoulders in a riot of thick, dark curls, but the ends faded to a ghostly white, as if the transformation from wolf to woman hadn't fully left her.

She was beautiful, but not in a fragile way. She was the kind of beautiful that felt dangerous, like the calm before a storm or the flicker of lightning too close to where you stand.

Her eyes met mine, and I knew I'd been staring too long.

"Well, that was fun," she said, her voice low and husky, curling around me like smoke. "I haven't caught an Abhartach in a while."

I stiffened, unsure if she was talking to me, the empty forest, or perhaps to the lifeless husk of the creature lying a few feet away. Her tone was too casual, like this had been some sort of game, not a nightmare dragged from the darkest corners of old fireside stories. She glanced toward the tree line, as if expecting more shadows to rise.

Then her eyes locked with mine.

A knowing smile tugged at the corner of her mouth, slow and deliberate. Not unfriendly, but it wasn't exactly comforting either. Like a fox who found a mouse with just enough fight left to be interesting.

My heart thumped loudly in the stillness as she moved closer and extended a hand. Her fingers were long and graceful, but there was strength in the way she held them.

"I'm Arella," she said, the amusement still glinting in her voice. "And you must be the human everyone's been whispering about in these woods."

I stared at her hand like it might bite me, some part of me convinced that touching her would trigger something irreversible—a bargain struck without realizing the terms.

She cocked her head, and the white-tipped ends of her hair shimmered like mist. "Did you really crawl out of the river unscathed? I suppose its power truly *is* fading, if you survived that… only to cower before an Abhartach."

The words weren't sharp, more a passing thought than a mockery, but they still burrowed beneath my skin like a thorn.

I hesitated too long before finally reaching out and taking her hand. Her grip was cold but steady, the kind of firmness that anchored something fragile rather than crushing it. The sensation rippled through me, grounding me even as my fingers trembled.

"I—I guess so," I stammered, feeling foolish for the crack in my voice. I tried to swallow down the lingering fear. "Are you… Are you a shifter?" The question slipped out before I could stop it, and I immediately regretted how naive I sounded.

She laughed, a low, rich sound that rumbled deep in her chest. It didn't echo in the same way the Abhartach's screech had. No, this sound felt warm, almost electric.

"Of sorts," she replied, releasing my hand and folding her arms. "But some might say calling me a shifter doesn't quite capture it."

Her eyes trailed over me, assessing me, lingering too long on the places I tried to hide—my fear, my doubt, the lingering tremble in my bones. I felt transparent under her stare.

"You've barely stepped foot in these woods, and already you've attracted more trouble than most do in a lifetime," she said, voice curling into something close to a purr.

"I hope you're ready for a *few* more encounters. You've wandered into dangerous parts, little river-crosser."

I stiffened at the name, but the unease coiling in my chest had already begun to bloom. Because she was right. And worse, I didn't know what else I would face, or how much fight I had left in me.

I glanced toward the horizon, where the thinnest slivers of dawn threaded through the trees. The light dappled the ground in patches, painting the forest floor with soft golds and grays, but it felt far away. Fragile. Like the calm before a storm.

Arella followed my stare and offered a crooked smile. "Don't let the sun fool you," she murmured. "Not everything in these woods sleeps when the moon fades."

Her words sent a chill down my spine, an unshakable sense that this reprieve wouldn't last.

"I suppose that means… you're not planning to kill me too?" I asked, managing a breathless smile that tasted more like desperation.

Arella's smile widened, and this time it was all teeth.

"No, I think I've had my fun. *For now*," she said, but the way she said it made something in me twist. As if she hadn't decided not to kill me, only that she wasn't ready yet.

Her expression shifted, amusement fading as her gaze flicked to the path of trees behind me, then back to the crumpled form of the Abhartach on the forest floor.

"But we do need to deal with this vulture," she said, voice dipped in something darker.

"Vulture?" I echoed, blinking. My eyes followed hers to the pale corpse, sprawled like discarded linen against the dirt.

Her eyes twinkled with mischief. "I suppose I'll have to be the one to teach you this lesson, in case you come across any more." She gestured with a small nod toward the Abhartach. I watched her with growing curiosity as she moved forward with fluid grace, bare feet silent against the damp moss. Then, without warning, she began to shift.

I stood there frozen, watching the transformation.

It was unlike anything I'd ever seen. The change wasn't violent. It didn't splinter or tear. It was seamless, a fluid ripple that flowed over her like a shadow caught in a breeze, soft and elegant. One breath, she was human, the next, a massive wolf, cloaked in midnight fur brushed with white that glinted in the early morning light. Her golden eyes held the same fierce intelligence, determination, and playfulness.

Then, to my utter surprise, her voice echoed into my mind, a steady, calm voice that seemed almost surreal.

"We need to bury it. That's the only way to prevent it from rising back to life."

The sound rang like a bell inside me, jarring and clear. Her mouth hadn't moved, only a faint whimper escaped her, yet the words were unmistakable.

I stumbled back a step, pulse kicking. "How can I hear you? How... how are you speaking into my head?"

Arella didn't answer, at least, not aloud.

"The Abhartach are blood-drinkers. Vultures of flesh and memory. They hunt humans and immortals alike. There aren't many left, but the ones that remain are cunning, lingering in these woods, waiting for anyone foolish enough to stumble upon them."

I swallowed hard, the weight of her words pressing into my chest. My gaze drifted to the twisted corpse at our feet, bile rising in my throat. The way its limbs curled, its lifeless face slack in the dirt, I couldn't stop the shiver that rippled through me. If Arella hadn't come when she did...

"After years of dealing with their kind, we discovered there was only one way to stop them from coming back. They have to be buried upside down, nose deep in the earth. They track blood by scent, so by blocking their sense of smell, they are as good as gone. But that alone isn't enough."

I looked up, gripped the hilt of my dagger tighter, knuckles whitening as I waited for the next part.

"We'll need a stone. One with magic and power," she echoed, the intensity in her voice unwavering. *"That's what seals them. Binds them to the earth. Without it, they can claw their way back eventually."*

I nodded slowly, but a hollow ache unfurled in my chest. I didn't have anything like that, no enchanted relic, no spell-laced weapon. Just a blade and the feeling of being unprepared.

Arella, however, didn't wait for me to dwell on it. She turned, paws slicing through the soil like knives through silk, scattering clumps of dirt as she dug into the earth. I stood there uselessly for a moment before dropping to my knees and clawing at the dirt with my bare hands. My fingers scraped at roots and rocks, every motion clumsy and slow. Beside her, I looked like a child playing at survival.

"I wish I could be more helpful and just create a grave using magic or something," I muttered under my breath.

The moment the words left me, the ground shifted beneath us.

The earth rippled like water, parting beneath Arella's paws. The hole widened and deepened in seconds, far beyond anything we could've managed on our own.

She froze, ears twitching. Her head turned slowly toward me, eyes narrowing in surprise.

"That… wasn't me," I said, stumbling back slightly.

Her eyes lingered on me, something curious flickering in her face.

"Maybe it was," she said at last, tone unreadable.

I stared into the freshly dug grave, the smooth, dark walls of it unsettling. This wasn't me. There was no way. It was the forest responding to a plea I didn't even know I'd made. I wasn't sure how or why, but I wasn't about to question it either. If the forest wanted to help us, I would gladly accept.

Arella nudged the Abhartach's corpse toward the pit with her snout. I hesitated, then stepped closer, the chill of its skin prickling against my fingertips. It took both of us to roll the thing in, its body folding awkwardly as it slumped face down into the earth.

Arella nudged the loose soil at the edges with her paw, and the dirt obeyed, sliding back into the grave as if it, too, wanted the creature buried.

A heavy silence followed, but Arella's eyes didn't leave the spot.

"Now we need a stone. It doesn't need to be large, just powerful enough to bind its body to the grave."

I scanned the forest floor, but every stone looked the same, mud-caked, dull, ordinary. I had no way of knowing which, if any, carried the magic we needed. Panic itched at my throat.

"I don't know what I'm supposed to be looking for," I admitted, voice low with frustration.

Her expectant gaze lingered on me, calm but heavy with the weight of anticipation.

My hand slipped instinctively into my pocket. My fingers brushed against my flint stone, smooth, warm, familiar. A gift from my grandmother that I'd carried for years, always more out of comfort than use. Its warmth seemed to pulse faintly beneath my fingertips, grounding me, as if some small part of her still lingered with me.

I pulled it free, turning it over in my palm. It shimmered faintly in the early light, catching the soft gold of dawn.

Arella's head snapped toward me, her eyes widening.

"Where did you get that?" Her voice, usually so controlled, held a trace of something else, something close to disbelief.

I frowned, lifting the stone slightly. "My grandmother gave it to me for my birthday… years ago."

She stepped closer, sniffing the air before meeting my eyes. Something in her expression shifted as she looked between me and the stone I held in my palm.

"That flint carries magic. Old magic," her voice echoed, nodding toward the grave. *"It's more than enough to seal the grave, if you're willing to part with it."*

I looked down at the stone in my hand, feeling the warmth of my grandmother's presence in its smooth surface. It wasn't just a lucky stone I had carried with me every day; it was a piece of home, an anchor I always kept close, no matter how far I'd strayed.

But as I glanced toward the grave, the decision became clear. My grandmother had given it to me for protection. And perhaps this was exactly why she'd given it to me.

I knelt at the edge of the grave and pressed the flint into the soil with both hands. The earth trembled, accepting it like an offering.

Arella's eyes softened, a quiet reverence settling over her features as she stepped toward the grave. No words were spoken. None were needed. With slow, deliberate movements, she pressed her massive paws to the earth, scooping loose soil over the embedded flint. The dirt cascaded in gentle rivulets, cloaking the stone inch by inch until the wound in the ground disappeared completely, erased as if no blood had been spilled, no monster slain.

And then, for the first time since the Abhartach arrived, the clearing stilled. The usual rustle of leaves, the distant cry of birds, all of it seemed to pause in quiet acknowledgment.

I exhaled slowly, the tension in my chest finally loosening. Cold morning air slid down my throat, crisp and grounding. For the first time since I'd crossed the river, my chest didn't feel like it was being squeezed by invisible hands. For the first time, I could breathe without scanning the shadows for something lurking and waiting to strike.

But the feeling didn't last long.

As I pushed to my feet, Arella turned toward the tree line, her attention sharpening like a blade as she scanned the trees. Her presence, though still powerful, felt further away somehow, like she was already preparing to disappear.

Her voice brushed my thoughts without warning, soft but firm.

"These woods are full of things that want to hurt you. You'd do best to remember that when walking through it."

My spine straightened at the weight of her words. Her golden eyes met mine, ancient and impassive, and for a moment, I felt like a child being lectured by someone who had lived a thousand lives longer than me. Small, mortal, and foolish.

"Use your wits, and if you don't know how to defeat something, call on the woods. Maybe the creatures on your side will answer."

Her gaze lingered, a truth in her words I hadn't expected to hear.

"Be smart... but don't be afraid to ask for help. We all need it at some point."

I swallowed the lump in my throat, nodding even though I wasn't sure I fully understood if her words were a warning or a gift.

She tilted her head slightly, ear flicking as her voice threaded through my mind again, this time, more curious than stern.

"The Abhartach's song—it's meant to lure people in, take hold of their minds, and hollow their will. But you resisted. How?"

I hesitated, caught off guard. "I… don't know," I murmured.

Arella huffed, a sound that almost resembled a laugh.

"Well," she said, with something close to amusement, *"I suppose now I know why you were chosen."*

Chosen? Chosen for what?

The word snagged on something inside me. But before I could ask, Arella tipped her head back and howled. The sound shattered the stillness. Low and melodic, it rolled through the trees like thunder wrapped in music. It vibrated in the earth, in the roots beneath my feet. It wasn't just a call, it was a claim. A declaration that something had been done here, something sacred. The trees seemed to sway in response.

When the final note dissolved into silence, Arella looked at me one last time. Her assessing stare lingered, full of things she didn't say, before she turned.

And then with one smooth bound, she slipped into the underbrush, her dark coat vanishing between branches like a shadow returning home. Within seconds, she was gone.

The forest closed behind her. As if she'd never been there at all.

But her words remained. *Don't be afraid to ask for help.*

I stood in the quiet she left behind, then slowly knelt beside the grave. I pressed my hand to the freshly packed soil. The ground felt warm beneath my fingers, pulsing faintly, like a heartbeat. Or maybe that was just mine. Either way, it felt alive, almost like the land itself had acknowledged our offering. I traced small circles over the dirt, letting the pulse of the forest wash over me.

Had I unknowingly called for help earlier when the ground opened up to create the grave? Or had it acted on its own, choosing to aid me for reasons I didn't understand? I wasn't sure, but I bowed my head anyway.

"Thank you," I whispered to the soil. To the stone. To whatever ancient force had listened.

I rose, brushing dirt from my palms. The woods still loomed dark and tangled, but something had shifted. They no longer felt entirely hostile. Still dangerous, yes, but not entirely against me.

Maybe Arella was right.

Even in the darkest parts of the forest, there could be allies.

I turned away from the grave, letting the finality of the moment settle over me. Then, with one last look at the place where a monster was buried, and something older had stirred, I stepped toward whatever came next.

Because I would face it and was no longer afraid to ask for help.

40. An Unwanted Gift

After what felt like hours walking aimlessly through the trees, I pressed my back against the rough bark, breath catching as the ridges bit through my shirt and into my spine. It was the only thing holding me upright. My eyes swept the forest, darting between branches and shadows, scanning for movement, anything that might be a threat, or salvation.

I couldn't stay here.

The castle was somewhere ahead, but the forest made a game of direction. Every step I took twisted the path behind me until I wasn't sure which way I'd come from, let alone where I was going. If there was any hope of Manakel finding me with my satchel, it would happen by luck alone.

I needed to rely on something more than luck.

Dryad.

The word surfaced like a spark in the fog. I clung to it.

Caden's calm voice echoed in my memory. The way he had emerged from the tree, effortless, as if it had been his skin all along. He had helped me, quiet, ancient, and watchful. Maybe he could help me again, or another of his kind.

I whirled around, scanning the trees. Could any of them be Dryads? Were they watching me now? Hidden deep within the trunks, waiting for the right gesture, *an offering*, to draw them out? I remembered the way Manakel had placed something at the base of the tree before Caden appeared. And the way the female had balked when I approached empty-handed. *They expected something.*

But I had nothing to give. My satchel was with Manakel, and I was left with only the clothes on my back, a single dagger, and a rapidly fraying sense of direction.

I ran a hand through my tangled hair, eyes flicking around for anything I could use. *I needed something, anything.*

A splash of color caught my attention.

Clusters of wildflowers peeked from beneath the low branches, pale and delicate in the dim light, their petals dusted lightly with morning dew. I crouched closer, fingers brushing over the petals as I tried to remember what they were.

Bittersweet. Wild Angelica. White Alyssum. Bluebell. Wild Clary. I whispered their names aloud, my grandmother's voice filled my mind like smoke curling from an old hearth as she taught me the meanings of each.

Truth. Inspiration. Calmness. Gratitude. Vision.

Each flower meant something, held sacred intent, and maybe that was enough.

With the tip of my dagger, I clipped a few stems of each and wove them into a small bundle. The ritual steadied me. The cool touch of petals. The focus of my hands. It gave my fear somewhere to rest.

When I finished, I stood and turned to the nearest tree, broad and weathered, bark cracked with age, its branches twisted high above like they were reaching for something just out of sight. There was something about it... a hush in the air around it. Like it was listening, or at least aware.

I knelt, placing the bouquet at its roots.

"Please," I whispered, feeling slightly foolish for speaking aloud to a tree and hoping it would answer.

"I seek guidance and truth. I need help finding my way to the Queen."

I stepped back, arms crossed tight over my chest, staring up at the bark as if it might blink, hoping—waiting.

But nothing happened.

The forest remained silent, and the tree stayed exactly as it was.

I bit the inside of my cheek, trying to ignore the sinking feeling in my chest. Maybe it wasn't the right tree. Maybe I hadn't said the right words and just needed to keep trying.

I picked up the bouquet and moved deeper into the woods, approaching another tree, this one with thicker roots and sprawling limbs that stretched like protective arms over the forest floor.

I placed the flowers down again, quieter this time, more reverent, and waited. And still, nothing.

A faint breeze stirred the leaves overhead, and I heard it, soft at first, then unmistakable. A sound like a sigh, trailing between the branches.

A chuckle.

It drifted, the sound light, and mocking, as if the forest itself was amused by my naivete. My stomach twisted.

My fingers tightened around the bouquet until the stems bent. Frustration flared, hot and bitter. I was stumbling through customs I didn't fully understand, grasping at half-formed teachings of rituals. I could feel it, the gap between me and the magic of this place. It was wide, and I was just a fool trying to bridge it with wildflowers.

Tears stung at the corners of my eyes, but I blinked them back. I clenched my jaw and threw the bouquet on the ground with a defeated thud, the flowers hitting the dirt with a soft thud and scattering across the forest floor.

I sank to the base of the nearest tree, knees pulled to my chest, arms wrapped tightly around them as I buried my face in my hands. The cool soil pressed into my skin. And I let it, let the chill of it seep into me. I sat there, listening to the faint rustle of leaves and the distant drip of water somewhere far off, trying to shake the weight of failure pressing down on me.

I had tried. But maybe that wasn't enough. Maybe I wasn't meant to reach the castle. Maybe I was never meant to make it through these woods at all. Maybe the forest had been waiting, quietly, patiently, to swallow me whole.

The rough bark pressing against my back shifted, sending a ripple of sensation through me. At first, it was subtle, a faint ripple, like wind moving through branches, but it deepened, and the earth beneath me seemed to hum in answer.

My head shot up, breath catching as I twisted to look behind me.

The tree—no, the dryad—was changing.

Bark twisted and stretched, as if molded by unseen hands, sculpting itself into a face with slow, deliberate grace. High cheekbones pushed through the wood, a slender mouth curved in a faint smirk, and deep hollows bloomed into eyes glinting faintly in the fractured light.

I scrambled to my feet, my pulse thudding against my ribs.

She was beautiful in the way wild things are, untamed, unyielding. Vines tumbled from her head like hair, their leaves brushing her collarbones, and her eyes, dark as rain-soaked soil, studied me with the knowing gaze of something that had been watching far longer than I realized.

"Well," she said, voice carrying the weight of mild amusement, "that's one way to present an offering.

My gaze dropped to the wildflowers scattered in the dirt at her roots. My cheeks burned with embarrassment, realizing I must've looked like a sulking child throwing a tantrum.

"I… I'm sorry," I managed, brushing my palms against my thighs. "I thought I'd never find another dryad."

Her laugh was soft and melodic, like chimes caught in a shifting breeze. It felt too rich, too alive for something born from bark and soil.

"Oh, the other two trees were dryads too. But they didn't care for your offering," she replied nonchalantly.

I blinked, disbelief settling like a stone in my stomach.

"They were?" My voice caught slightly as I glanced back toward the trees I had knelt before earlier.

"We dryads prefer gifts with a little more substance," she continued, the corner of her mouth twitching as if she enjoyed watching my confusion. "Things that nourish—worms, mushrooms, insects, things that feed the soil and keep our roots strong. Flowers are lovely, but fleeting. You gave them sweetness, not sustenance."

The flush on my cheeks deepened, heat prickling along my neck. If I'd known that earlier, maybe I wouldn't have wasted my time wandering from tree to tree with a bouquet of useless petals.

"I didn't realize," I admitted softly, lowering my gaze to the forest floor.

"How could you?" She shrugged, the motion sending a ripple through the vines draped over her shoulders. "Humans rarely speak the forest's language, but if you plan to keep wandering these woods, it wouldn't hurt to learn what we deem useful." She arched a brow, if that was even possible with bark for skin. "We don't get many offerings. Most aren't foolish enough to walk this deep or offer so blindly."

I nodded quickly, tucking the lesson away in the back of my mind. "Understood."

She seemed satisfied with that and straightened, the vines draped over her shoulders shifting softly in the wind. I half-expected her to retreat into the bark, fading away without another word. But instead, she tilted her head toward the flowers at her roots.

"I suppose it's the thought that counts. I doubt you went to the trouble of gathering those flowers just to throw them in the dirt, or awaken a dryad on a whim. So, what is it you really want?"

Her eyes pinned me, dark, perceptive, and expectant, far too ancient for me to hide anything from. I hesitated, caught off guard by her bluntness. But this was my opportunity to ask for help, and I wasn't about to waste it.

"My name is Raine," I began, my voice softer than I intended. "I've come from Laochra, a small village in Rioga."

Her brow rose slightly at the name, but she stayed silent.

"I'm here for my Imbe Rite. I crossed the river and braved these woods, but my final task is to reach the Queen of Dermaine." I exhaled slowly, eyes lowering again. "The problem is… I don't know how to find her castle."

Silence fell, stretching between us like a pulled thread. The weight of those words hung between us, a quiet confession of inadequacy that I hated admitting.

Her gaze narrowed, and something like recognition sparked. "You're the human they've been whispering about?"

I stiffened. "I guess so…?"

"No one expected you to make it to the river. Let alone cross it and survive long enough to reach these woods," she said, the teasing gone from her voice, replaced by a note that felt dangerously close to respect.

I opened my mouth to respond, but no words came.

She bowed then, slow and deliberate, the leaves and vines in her hair rustling softly as she dipped her head.

I stared in disbelief. The forest knew about me. The forest had been watching. And somehow, in all my stumbling, bleeding, and nearly drowning, I'd become someone worth whispering about.

The dryad's voice cut through the stillness like a blade through fog. "It's been a pleasure meeting you, Raine. Though I imagine your journey's been… unpleasant, it's a feat that you are here."

"Does that mean you're willing to help me?" I asked with a hopeful nod.

The lines in her bark twisted subtly, what I assumed was a smile. "Perhaps. But just so you know, you'll need more than flower offerings to survive what lies ahead."

Relief pulsed through me, loosening the tight knot in my chest. "Thank you," I whispered, though the words felt fragile, too small to carry the weight she'd just lifted.

She leaned forward, her wooden frame creaking softly. "There are two ways to reach the castle."

She gestured left with a gentle shift of her branches, toward a narrow trail swallowed in shadow. I squinted at the path and immediately shivered. The trees in that direction stood close together, hunched like watchmen whispering to each other. The light barely reached the moss-covered ground.

"That way winds deeper through the woods. It's slower, will take at least a few hours on foot, but it keeps you hidden. At least, from most things."

"Or," she continued, turning her gaze to the right, "you can cross through the clearing. It leads to the city's edge, and from there, it's a short walk to the path leading directly to the castle."

My gaze followed the direction she pointed, spotting a break in the trees where traces of dawn spilled onto patches of grass and thickets beyond. The idea of emerging from the woods and stepping closer to civilization was tempting. The idea of sunlight, of city streets and people, stirred something inside me that longed for ease. It felt safer than braving the wilderness alone.

But then her voice sharpened, pulling my attention back to her.

"The city streets may feel more inviting," she warned, "but they are filled with immortals and rebels alike. Any one of them could sense you're still part human, and won't hesitate. Until your immortality is fully awakened, you'll be seen as a threat. Or worse, an opportunity—to challenge you, to hunt you, or capture you."

She held my gaze with a steady, knowing weight. "Word of your crossing has already spread further than you know. And those who seek to stop you from reaching the Queen are waiting." She gestured toward the sunlit clearing. "The easier path is exactly what they're hoping you'll take."

I looked again. What once looked like freedom now felt like bait, its golden glow stretched too bright, too open. Like a trap laid in daylight, and exactly where they'd be waiting for me.

"So... the forest path it is," I muttered, forcing steadiness into my voice. "I've made it this far. A few more hours through the woods won't stop me."

The dryad studied me for a moment. Her expression softened,

something like quiet approval blooming behind her bark-dark eyes. "A wise choice," she said. "But don't confuse perseverance for protection. The deeper parts of this forest hold creatures more ancient and cunning than any you've faced so far. And they are not always kind to outsiders."

I nodded, spine straightening. "I'll be ready," I said, because I had to be. "I didn't come this far to turn back now."

A small, knowing smile tugged at her wooden lips. "Your spirit may carry you through, Raine of Laochra. But even the boldest travelers have sought guidance."

She paused, and for a heartbeat, the forest seemed to still with her.

"Before you go, I can offer one more last truth, if you choose to accept it."

I nodded immediately, desperate for any advantage she could offer. "Please, I'm listening."

She leaned forward slightly, her branches swaying gently. "Keep to one side of the path. The center is too open, too inviting. Anything lurking in the shadows will watch your every move if you give them a clear line of sight."

I nodded, committing the warning to memory.

Her voice softened. "Trust your instincts, Raine. If something feels wrong, it likely is. The woods are not without mercy, but they do not favor hesitation. Be swift, but be cautious."

"Thank you," I said, my voice thick with gratitude for her help and her warning.

She dipped her head in a slow nod. "May the forest guide you. Now go—before the sun claims too much of the sky."

As the last word left her lips, her features began to shift again, folding back into the bark of the tree. I stood silently, watching the intricate patterns of her face blend seamlessly into the rough surface until she vanished entirely, leaving behind nothing but the outline of her form in the knots of the trunk.

Silence returned. But the forest no longer felt empty. It felt like it was watching.

And now, I had to decide to be brave enough to keep walking under its gaze.

I let out a slow breath I hadn't realized I'd been holding, my gaze flicking once more toward the clearing bathed in sunlight to my right. It definitely felt like a trap.

I took the opposite way, bathed in thick trees and shadow. I stayed close to the edge of the path, letting the trees shoulder some of my weight. Their trunks stood like sentinels, rough against my fingers, their branches leaning low enough to tangle in my hair. Above, the canopy twisted tight, only letting through thin slivers of light, as if the forest rationed what little warmth it allowed in.

With every step, the silence grew heavier, interrupted only by the wind whispering through the leaves, a sound almost too intentional. Beneath it, something sharper lingered in the air. A scent like iron. Like blood and smoke, faded and faint.

I'd been warned, but the silence that hung between each rustle of the underbrush felt louder than anything else. It was as if the forest itself was holding its breath, waiting to see if I would stumble.

I didn't know if it was paranoia or the dryad's lingering words, but the sensation of being watched prickled along the back of my neck.

Someone, *or something*, was out there.

I exhaled slowly, trying to steady myself. I had crossed the river. I had defeated ancient Eldren and buried an Abhartach. I refused to let shadows unravel me.

But the dryad's caution echoed in my head.

Creatures far more ancient and cunning than the ones you've met.

The deeper I walked, the thicker the shadows became. The trees pressed in close, and I adjusted my steps to hug the trunks, staying well away from the open center of the path. It felt strange to stay on the edge like this, but I trusted her words.

A few more hours. That's all I had to endure, and this would all be over.

A root jutted across the path, forcing me to slow. As I stepped over it, I caught it, softer than a breath, too shapeless to be a voice. A whisper, curling through the leaves.

I froze, my breath catching in my throat.

It wasn't a voice exactly, more like the sigh of the wind through the leaves, but it felt different. Intentional. I slowly turned my head, scanning the dense underbrush.

Nothing. Just stillness.

But the sensation of being watched pressed down harder, coiling low in my spine. I moved again, slower now. Each step deliberate. The dryad's words hummed behind my ribs—*Trust your instincts. If something feels wrong, it likely is.*

Ahead, the trees parted slightly, revealing a break in the path. Not a clearing, but just enough space for sunlight to slip in and paint the moss in gold. I hesitated before stepping into it. The hairs on the back of my neck stood on end. The light felt unnatural. Too precise.

I crouched low, keeping close to the trees, the rough bark scraping my shoulder as I hugged the curve of the opening. The ferns ahead didn't stir. The stones were still, slick with dew. Even the insects had gone silent.

Something about the space felt off.

Then a flicker of movement caught my eye to the right.

I spun, blade drawn, heart leaping—

But it was only a fox.

Its amber eyes met mine from beneath a bush, unblinking. Its tail curled behind it, motionless. I didn't lower my weapon right away. Something about the way it looked at me was too focused. Too knowing. Then, it turned and padded silently back into the undergrowth.

I waited, eyes fixed on the place it had disappeared, wondering if something else would emerge, if it was another shifter. But the area remained still. Only the sound of my breath and the quiet thrum of the forest returned.

I didn't know how far the castle lay beyond these trees, but I knew better than to hope the quiet meant safety. I knew better than to let my guard down. The silence wasn't peace—it was presence. Every creak of the woods, every flick of wind through the leaves reminded me I was not alone.

The deeper I went, the more the forest seemed to shift around me, shadows stretching unnaturally long, as if reaching for me with invisible fingers. Each rustle of leaves sent a jolt through my spine, my nerves raw and strung tight.

I kept my hand near the dagger at my hip, though I knew it was little more than a comfort. Steel meant nothing to shadows.

Just as I was beginning to convince myself that I was imagining things, a flicker of green shimmered ahead, soft and deliberate, too slow for a firefly. It hovered in the air, pulsing like breath.

I blinked, squinting toward the light. It felt too deliberate, too alive, to be a mere trick of the forest. The glow drifted closer, and a familiar shape emerged, wings humming, small frame silhouetted against the dimness.

"Fern!" I breathed. Relief flooded through me, and the tension in my shoulders eased.

She hovered at eye level, arms crossed, iridescent wings shimmering in shades of green that danced across the bark behind her.

"You look like you've seen a ghost," she teased, her eyes dancing with mischief.

"I wasn't expecting to see you out here," I replied, unable to help the quiet smile tugging at my lips. "How did you even find me?"

Fern rolled her eyes and gave a dramatic twirl midair, her wings catching the light like stained glass. "Wings, remember? I don't need to worry about things like crossing rivers."

I shook my head with a soft laugh. "Right, how could I forget?"

She grinned wider, then floated backward with theatrical flair, crossing her legs mid-air like the forest itself had offered her a throne. "Besides, all the faeries on our side took bets on how far you'd make it. And guess what? I'm winning."

I blinked. "You what?"

Her cheeks flushed the faintest shade of green, quickly looking away. "It's not a big deal or anything. I just happened to say you'd make it all the way to the castle. And well… everyone else bet you'd either drown or get eaten by something before you made it this far."

A laugh escaped me before I could stop it, light and strange in the heavy silence of the woods. "Wow, thanks for the vote of confidence," I said with a wry grin.

Fern shrugged unapologetically. "I believed in you. Someone had to."

The warmth in my chest caught me off guard, and for a brief moment, I didn't feel so alone in these woods.

I tilted my head. "Seeing as how you're personally invested in my success… any chance you'll stick around? Maybe warn me if something with claws gets too close?"

I meant it as a joke. But Fern's smile slipped. Her wings slowed, and she shifted, fidgeting with the hem of her skirt.

"I can't," she said quietly, eyes dropping to the moss below. "We're not allowed to interfere. Not directly."

The weight of those words settled uncomfortably between us, and I felt the first tug of disappointment claw at my chest.

She hesitated, the gleam in her eyes dimming. "I'd get in serious trouble if I helped. But I meant it," she added quickly, offering a half-hearted smile, "I really do hope you make it. I've never won anything before."

The faint blush returned, turning her skin a deeper shade of green. Her voice was soft, but the honesty in it pressed against something raw in me. She'd bet on me. Not because she had to, but because somewhere, somehow, she believed I could survive this.

I smiled gently. "Then I hope you win too."

Her wings fluttered brighter, casting flickering green light over the bark and leaves. "Stay safe, Raine," she said, hovering just a little closer. "Don't let the forest swallow you whole. You're stronger than you think. And people who were hoping you'd fail know you're here. They've been whispering about you."

I stiffened. "What do you mean?"

But she was already drifting back, eyes gleaming. "I probably shouldn't have said that. Just be careful, okay?" she whispered, more to herself than to me. Then with a cheeky salute, she zipped upward and vanished into the dark, her glow trailing behind like a fading wish.

I stood still, watching the last shimmer dissolve into the trees. The silence closed in again, but it wasn't empty. It felt like the forest was listening.

Still, Fern's words lingered, soft but steady, like a thread wrapped around my spine, holding me upright. I took a deep breath, letting that belief settle into something solid beneath the fear and uncertainty.

She believed in me.

And surprisingly, I believed in myself too.

41. Wings Of Freedom

The exhaustion gnawed at the edges of my strength as I dragged myself through the dense thicket, each step heavier than the last. My throat was raw, lips cracked from thirst. Every breath scraped my lungs like sand, but I kept going. I had to.

Then out of nowhere, like I conjured it from thought alone, I heard the soft murmur of running water. Relief surged up, hot and reckless, but it tangled with a thread of dread. My grandmother's warnings echoed through my memory: *Nothing in this forest comes without consequence. Water could lure as easily as it could soothe.*

But the thirst burned too deep to ignore.

I veered toward the sound without hesitation, weaving between thick trunks and tangled roots, my feet moving faster with each passing second. The sound grew louder, closer as I chased it, until, just as abruptly as it had appeared, the sound stopped.

I turned in a slow circle, straining to catch even the faintest trickle of water. But there was nothing but stillness and trees, as if they had swallowed the sound whole.

Had it been real? Or simply a mirage my mind conjured up because of my thirst?

Panic tightened its grip on my chest. I had been so focused on following the sound of running water that I hadn't been watching where I was going. Now the trees around me felt unfamiliar, and the path behind me had vanished. The forest didn't want to be retraced.

I was lost.

I closed my eyes, fingers brushing the coarse bark beside me, grounding myself in the one solid truth I could find. "I wish there was a stream here," I whispered, my voice barely audible. "I just… I need water. I'm so thirsty."

The ground stayed dry.

I swallowed hard, remembering Arella saying, *"Don't be afraid to ask the forest for help."*

Then spoke again, clearer this time, hoping the forest might listen if I just *asked* and was more specific.

"It would be helpful if the ground would open and create a stream I can drink from."

The moment the words left my lips, the ground trembled, shifting with a low groan. My breath caught as a slender channel formed, carving through moss and root, and filled with glistening water. It looked too clear, as if it had always been there and yet was completely out of place.

I dropped to my knees, hands trembling as I plunged them into the icy current. The chill bit my skin, sharp and clean. I drank deeply, greedily, letting it carve the ache from my throat. With each sip, the world around me steadied, grounding me in a way I hadn't felt since entering the forest in Laochra.

I drank until the ache subsided, lingering beside the stream as the gentle hum of the water filled the air.

"Thank you," I whispered to no one in particular. I wasn't sure if the words were for the forest, for whatever magic had answered me, or for something else entirely.

The soft clearing felt peaceful, the weight in my chest easing for the first time since crossing the river. For a moment, I let myself believe I was safe.

Until I heard it.

A soft, deliberate throat-clear.

I froze. Water dripped from my cupped hands before I wiped my hands on the grass. I reached for my dagger, unsheathing it without thought, heart hammering against my ribs.

I turned sharply, eyes scanning the shadows between the trees, but the forest stared back, silent.

Was I imagining things?

"Who's there?" I whispered, eyes raking the shadows.

No answer. Only the low hum of leaves and tension crawling beneath my skin. The forest had a way of playing tricks—turning your own fears against you. I had to believe that was all this was. The hairs standing on end at the back of my head had me on alert as I crouched to cup another handful of water.

"Banríon."

Aeron's familiar voice echoed, not spoken aloud, but in my mind. A presence threading through my thoughts.

"I need to warn you. Keep going; don't stay here. You're only drawing attention to yourself."

I rose slowly, blade in hand, spinning in place. "Where are you?" I hissed, my eyes darting through the trees. The forest remained still, but the weight of his presence lingered, unseen but there.

"Watching from a distance," Aeron's voice replied, softer now. *"I can't be near you openly, not without being seen. But I'm keeping an eye out. Trust me when I say you're making yourself an easier target near running water."*

My instinct said listen. But a part of me still hesitated. Was he truly helping me? Or was he helping himself?

The forest watched me, and though I couldn't see Aeron, I felt him—just beyond the veil of trees, and something about him looking out for me even after I didn't choose him in the river made me feel safer.

I sheathed my dagger with a sharp click and took one last, lingering glance at the stream. Of course, he would warn me to keep moving after I did something as monumental as summoning a stream of water when I was thirsty. He always knew the worst times to show up.

I heard the throat-clearing again, soft but unmistakable, like someone trying far too hard to suppress a laugh. I scoffed, cheeks heating as I bent down for one last sip of water, more out of spite than need.

"You always show up when it's convenient," I muttered under my breath, brushing damp strands from my face.

Aeron's laughter echoed faintly in my skull, low, amused, and frustratingly calm. *"Look up."*

My breath caught. Slowly, I tilted my head. At first, I saw nothing but the web of branches and shifting leaves casting dappled patterns on the forest floor. Then I saw it. A shadow gliding in lazy circles. I narrowed my eyes, trying to make sense of the shape—broad wings, sleek movements, too large for any ordinary bird.

Recognition struck like a lightning bolt through my chest. His wings stretched wide as he soared overhead, and though I couldn't make out his face, I felt his stare. It was strange, the sensation of being watched usually put me on edge, but this wasn't the same. His presence settled over me like the sun peeking through the trees, warm and lingering, as if he had been circling for some time.

A small, involuntary smile tugged at my lips, and I felt ridiculous for how reassuring it felt to know he was out there keeping an eye on me.

"I see some of your gifts have already begun to reveal themselves, Banríon," Aeron's voice murmured in my mind, his tone edged with something like pride. *"It takes most immortals years to master their elemental gifts, yet here you are, not even fully immortal and already creating streams."*

My breath hitched, and I lowered my eyes to the stream of water trickling beside me, the memory of how it appeared from the earth like a mirage flashing in my mind.

That couldn't be right. I hadn't *created* anything—I had simply asked, and the forest responded. It was the earth's kindness, not a reflection of something within me. *Wasn't it?*

"You called water from the earth without knowing how. That power isn't the forest's alone. It came from you."

"No," I whispered, shaking my head. "I asked. That's all. The land responded, not me."

"Is that what you truly believe?"

I clenched my jaw, the weight of what he was implying sinking in like stone.

"An elemental?" I whispered to no one, the words tasting foreign and uncertain as they left my mouth. The idea seemed too big, too distant from anything I had ever imagined for myself.

My mind spun with possibilities. I wanted to deny it, but this wasn't the first time the earth had answered me. The grave. The stream. What else might rise if I called? But I didn't feel powerful or worthy of such a gift.

The sky above had cleared; Aeron was already gone. I debated calling out to him, asking him to explain how he knew, or if it was too early to tell. I was still in the middle of the Rite, so nothing was certain, except his warning of moving away from water.

"Go. Don't stay here. Predators lurk in the distance, waiting for you to falter."

I stiffened. Predators? As soon as the thought emerged, a faint rustling sound drifted through the trees nearby, barely a breath, but enough to ignite the quiet alarm that hummed under my skin.

I moved before I could second-guess, slipping into the nearest shadows, pressing my back against a tree, and trying to stay out of sight of whatever was approaching. My eyes scanned the forest, watching for movement, ready to react.

Whatever was out there, whatever hunted these woods, knew I was here now. And I was done waiting to be found.

A figure emerged through the underbrush, wings folding with quiet precision against his back. *Manakel.* His sharp eyes swept the clearing, landing briefly on the stream, as though sensing something out of place.

His expression was calm, but there was something in the way his face shifted across the clearing that told me he was searching for something—

most likely me. Relief settled in my chest, loosening the fear that had been coiled there since Aeron's warning. But I didn't move. *Not yet.*

I hesitated, watching him from behind the thick trunk, weighing my options. The urge to step forward was strong, but Aeron's voice returned, louder than before, urgent, almost sharp.

"Don't share what your gift is just yet. Catching your enemies off guard is your greatest defense."

I swallowed, torn by the unspoken command.

But Manakel wasn't the enemy. *I trusted him.*

I knew he and Aeron weren't exactly friends, but they were both Sciathain. Didn't that mean they were on the same side? Both sworn to protect humans and guide me through my Imbe Rite?

And yet, Aeron's tone held an edge I couldn't ignore, and doubt slithered into the space where trust should have been. Was there something he knew that I didn't?

And who was I supposed to trust? Manakel had said something similar about Aeron's motives, so I didn't know what to believe or *who*.

My hand slipped to the hilt at my hip. The dagger's cool bite grounded me.

Maybe Aeron was right. Until I understood what had happened, until I was certain this power belonged to me, it was better to say nothing at all.

I stepped from the shadows, the soft crunch of leaves under my boots betraying me. Manakel's head lifted instantly, his eyes snapping to mine like he'd been waiting for me all along. The sharpness in them softened for just a breath, a flicker of something almost like relief, but it passed too quickly to name.

"Amadán," he greeted, voice smooth and controlled. "I was beginning to think the forest had swallowed you whole."

His eyes traced over the bruises on my arms, the damp fabric clinging to my frame. "You held your own," he added after a beat, the words tested before he committed to them. "Impressive."

I gave a small shrug, forcing a smile I didn't quite feel. "Still standing."

He studied me, gaze lingering too long, as if trying to peel apart the truth behind my answer.

"You've made it further than most even attempt," he said, gesturing slightly toward the stream, as if it marked some invisible threshold. "Tell me... what have you encountered and overcome?"

I hesitated.

The Barolf. The Osiris. The Oilliphéist. The Abhartach. Shifters. Aeron.

I met his eyes, searching for any trace of intent or hidden motive behind the calm exterior. Nothing. Just polished stillness, as smooth and unyielding as glass.

"Nothing I couldn't handle," I said lightly, the words slipping from my tongue with practiced ease. "A few surprises, but nothing you didn't train me for or warn me about."

His eyes narrowed, just slightly. He heard the lie. I was sure of it. But he only nodded, slow and deliberate.

"Then I did my job," he murmured. "Seems everyone underestimated you."

The praise settled over me like warmth, unexpected and heavier than I expected. I looked away before the warmth rising in my cheeks gave too much away. I hadn't realized how much I wanted that approval, *needed* it.

"Do you have my bag?" I asked, desperate to fill the silence with something practical. "I could use some dry clothes."

He pulled the satchel from his shoulder without a word. His fingers brushed mine, brief but steady, and for reasons I couldn't explain, I held onto that touch longer than I should have.

The familiar weight of the bag grounded me, and I exhaled, quickly rifling through things until my fingers wrapped around the extra clothes I'd packed. I held them against my chest before glancing at him, "Give me a minute to change?"

He nodded, stepping back with the casual grace of someone who'd spent a lifetime pretending not to watch every move someone made around him.

Behind a tree, I stripped the sodden layers from my body. Cold air kissed my skin, but the thick navy thermal and black pants I pulled on quickly chased away the lingering chill.

When I tried to untangle my braid, I winced. It was a knotted mess—wind, water, and exhaustion wound tight into each strand. I sighed, fingers working through the knots as best as I could. A comb was one of the many things I hadn't packed, and my efforts to tame the mess were proving fruitless. Eventually, I gave up and let it fall loose around my shoulders. The air would dry it faster this way—hopefully.

When I stepped back out, Manakel was watching, not in an obvious way, but just long enough that I noticed.

His gaze drifted over my hair, his head tilted ever so slightly, noting the change of clothes, the flush on my skin. His face didn't betray much, but something shifted.

"You look…" he began, then smirked faintly. "More comfortable."

I let out a soft snort. "Not exactly a high bar. But yeah. Thanks for the rescue…And returning my things."

He tilted his head, like he was still trying to figure me out. "Of course. Wouldn't do to lose you now, would it?"

I tried to laugh, but the words sat strangely between us. Something had shifted. I couldn't tell if it was him or me, or just the fact that, for the first time, I realized how little I actually knew about the man standing beside me.

"Does this mean you're here to bring me to the Queen?" I asked, smoothing my hands over my sleeves just to give them something to do. "I assume that's where we're headed next."

He stepped closer, gently taking the damp clothes from my arms, tucking them back into my satchel with practiced ease before slinging the strap over his shoulder once more. His movements were seamless, as if the weight of the bag was nothing at all to him.

"Yes," he said, his voice smooth but carrying that same faint edge of something I couldn't quite place. "I promised to make sure you safely got to the Queen, didn't I?"

It should have comforted me. Maybe it did. But there was something about the way he said it, like the words were part of a larger truth I hadn't been told.

"Let's go," he added, his fingers brushing my arm as he turned. A brief, grounding touch, like an unspoken reminder to keep moving.

We fell into step, side by side, his pace matching mine without effort. Sunlight bled through thinning trees ahead, casting long beams across the mossy ground. The path glowed faintly, golden and soft.

For the first time in what felt like days, I let hope slip in. Maybe this meant the worst was over. Maybe I was close.

I glanced at Manakel. His dark hair was unruly beneath the moonlight, each lock drinking the silver until it shimmered like something wild and untouchable. Golden flecks stirred in his hazel eyes as they scanned the forest, guarded and unyielding, like a predator certain the shadows would answer to him alone.

I was grateful for him. For not being alone now, and feeling safer with someone watching my back, especially in uncharted territory.

"Thank you," I said quietly, unsure if I meant for holding my satchel, his guidance, or the fact that he'd shown up at all. He had no obligation to tell us about the river or offer to help me train, but did anyway, and I would always be grateful for that.

Manakel glanced sideways at me, his smile small and fleeting but undeniably real.

"You don't need to thank me, Amadán," he said, voice low and certain. "Just stay close. You're not out of danger yet."

Something about the way he said it made me believe he wasn't just warning me about the forest, but about something far more dangerous.

42. The Veil Of Silence

We stepped into the light, the dense canopy thinning behind us as golden sun broke through the trees. But the moment didn't feel like relief. If anything, it felt heavier, like something unseen had turned its attention on me, pressing against my shoulders with invisible hands.

Without thinking, I reached out.

My fingers curled around Manakel's arm, stopping him just before we crossed into the open clearing. His head turned, smooth and slow, eyes dropping to my hand before meeting mine. There was a flicker of surprise there, quiet and guarded, but he didn't pull away.

And for reasons I couldn't explain, I didn't let go.

The warmth of his skin bled through the fabric, grounding me in the moment when the rest of the world felt too vast, too uncertain.

"So…" The word caught on my tongue, barely more than breath. "We're almost out of the forest. That means the tonic's going to wear off soon, right?" I glanced down, suddenly aware of how tightly I was still gripping his arm. "When am I supposed to receive my gift? How will I even know what it is or when it happens?"

I hated the way the questions sounded, small and unsure. But the closer we got to the end, the less certain I became. Of the tonic working. Of the gods deeming me worthy of a gift. Of myself.

Manakel's brow furrowed, and for a heartbeat too long, he didn't answer. The silence stretched, thick and expectant, the clearing holding its breath right along with me. And then he exhaled softly, like the question had been heavier than it should have been.

"The gods don't favor clarity," he said finally. "Some feel it instantly, like a fire igniting inside their chest. A rush of power so strong it's impossible to ignore." His focus drifted toward the horizon, far away. "For others, it comes softly. A slow stirring beneath the skin. A whisper instead of a roar."

I bit my lip, my mind flicking back to the stream I'd conjured… or at least *asked* for.

"And what if…" I hesitated, the thought fragile, ridiculous even as I said it. "What if it's already happened? What if I was gifted elemental magic without realizing it?

That got his attention. His eyes narrowed slightly, not in suspicion but interest.

"Before I saw you," I continued, forcing the words out before I second-guessed myself, "I needed water, so I asked the forest to create a stream. And then it did."

He didn't speak right away. Just watched me, his golden eyes raking over me in silent assessment. "Did it?" he asked, like the words themselves were a test.

Aeron's warning to keep it to myself echoed faintly in the back of my mind, but I couldn't shake the feeling that I needed to hear what Manakel thought, even if I didn't reveal the entire truth.

I shrugged, feeling suddenly foolish. "I don't know. I needed water. I asked. And then it appeared. Like the ground opened up to make it true."

For a moment, he just studied me, "It's possible," he said finally. "Or maybe the forest heard you and decided to help. Either way, the tonic's still in your blood. The magic that surrounds you now bends more easily, responds faster. But it isn't permanent or necessarily yours."

I nodded, letting his words sink in. There was something in the way he said it that tugged at the edges of my thoughts, as if there was more meaning beneath his words, hidden just out of reach.

I swallowed, tucking loose strands of hair behind my ear. "And if it never comes?" The words escaped before I could stop them. "What if I leave the forest and nothing happens? How do I protect myself if I don't know what I'm meant to wield?"

Manakel stepped closer, his hand brushing lightly against my shoulder. The contact was brief, careful, as if he wasn't sure how long he was allowed to linger.

"It will come when you need it most," he said quietly, his gaze holding mine like an anchor. "That's the only truth you can count on. The gods don't grant gifts by mistake. Whatever they see in you... It's already there, waiting. It will reflect your strengths, even the ones you haven't discovered yet."

A rush of warmth spread through me at his words, comforting, steady. But still, something beneath his calm unnerved me, like a warning disguised as reassurance.

"You're the first to cross the river in over a century," he added, softer now. "That alone says more about your strength than anything I could tell you."

The words hit harder than I expected. I'd heard them before, but coming from him, they felt different. He made them sound real. Like maybe I was something more than the scared girl I'd been when I first stepped into the woods the first night he found me.

I finally released his arm. But the warmth of that contact lingered as we stepped into the clearing. Light poured across the hills ahead in soft, glowing sheets.

It should have felt like victory. Like the hard part was over. But I couldn't shake the brittle edge of unease.

"And when we meet the Queen?" I asked, unable to keep the question from slipping out. "What happens then? Is getting her to agree part of my Imbe Rite, too?"

Manakel's expression dimmed slightly, a shadow slipping behind his calm.

"The Queen is… complicated," he said carefully. "She values strength, but not in the obvious sense. She'll look for what's beneath it. The things people hide when they're afraid to be seen. This was never just about survival. It was about who you become while surviving."

He glanced back at me with a mask polished to perfection, offering no seams to pry open.

"Just be honest with her. And with yourself. She will see through any pretense. If there is weakness in you, she will find it. But if you face her as you are now…with the same resolve you've shown in surviving this forest and the river, you'll do alright."

It wasn't exactly an answer. But it was all I was going to get. This wasn't just about me. It was about protecting those who couldn't protect themselves, the people I'd left behind in Laochra, *my family*. It felt bigger than anything I'd ever carried before. But I had no choice with my family's safety on the line.

We walked in silence for a while, the trees thinning behind us as sunlight opened the path ahead. I glanced sideways. The wind caught in Manakel's dark hair, the color a mirror to his wings. His face was angled forward, expression neutral, eyes sharp. He looked like someone built to survive storms.

My mind drifted back to the first time I saw him, standing in the clearing behind my house, his dark figure blending in with the shadows surrounding him. I had been terrified then, unsure whether he was friend or foe. Now, as he walked beside me, the quiet protector who had guided me this far, that fear seemed almost laughable.

Still, I knew better than to believe I'd come this far alone. My determination had carried me through the rite—the strength I'd drawn from memories of my grandmother, from the promise I made to myself to survive for my family. But Manakel's presence, unwavering and constant, had been a lifeline I didn't know I needed while preparing.

I glanced at him, noting the ease in his steps, the quiet confidence that seemed to radiate from him as if he belonged in every world, both light and dark.

"I'm happy I found you," I said, the words slipping out before I could elaborate on what exactly I meant. For showing up in the woods that first night. For coming to Laochra to warn us. For training me and bringing me this far.

His gaze flicked sideways. A small, brief smile curved at the edge of his mouth, barely there, but enough to warm the edges of my chest. "Let's get you to the Queen," he replied, his focus fixed ahead. "I have a feeling she's been waiting for you."

Manakel stayed a step ahead, guiding us up the hill, but the air between us felt different now. He hadn't done anything to cause the change, not really. But the easy comfort I'd felt in his presence before was shifting, curling into something quieter. Something watchful.

We crested the hill, and something blue caught my eye. A cluster of delicate wildflowers shimmered faintly, their petals tinted like twilight. I crouched down, wanting a closer look, and realized I'd never seen flowers like them before. Maybe they only grew on these hills, or were native to Dermaine, but either way, there was something unmistakable about them. Something I could not ignore. I brushed my fingers over their soft edges, feeling the faint pulsing hum of energy beneath the surface.

These flowers weren't ordinary, but I didn't have time to figure out why.

When I looked up, Manakel had stopped several paces ahead, his posture gone still. Rigid. Staring toward the far horizon.

"Manakel?" I called.

He didn't answer, so I stepped forward, following his stare.

At first, I saw nothing, just the hills rolling softly beneath the sky, grass bending with the breeze. But then there was movement. Shadows, long and thin, gliding through the field with an ease that made the earth seem weightless beneath them. A horde of dark, slender figures was moving steadily toward us.

A uneasy feeling prickled beneath my skin.

"Friends of yours?" I said, trying to lighten the air, but it didn't reach.

Manakel didn't answer at first. Didn't laugh or smile either. His jaw tightened, and the steady calm I'd come to depend on was nowhere in sight. Instead, there was calculation in his eyes. Tension across his shoulders. A stillness that felt like the moment before lightning splits the sky.

"Something like that," he murmured. No comfort in the words.

A chill worked its way down my spine, settling deep and low. I stepped back a step, not far. Just enough to feel the space between us stretch. Enough to test whether the safety I'd once felt standing beside him still existed. *It didn't.*

I watched him carefully, waiting for the glance, the grin, the reassurance he always offered. Anything familiar. But he didn't even look at me. He didn't have to. Because I already knew. This had to be the warning I kept hearing over the over since starting the Rite.

The figures were still too far to make out clearly, but the flicker of unease in Manakel's stance told me enough. The pull in my gut sharpened. The same silent warning my grandmother had taught me to listen for, the one the river had whispered into my bones.

Trust your instincts, Raine. The sky is always quiet before a storm.

"Who are they?" I asked, forcing my voice to stay steady.

This time, his eyes found mine. And in the brief moment our eyes locked, something passed between us. A quiet, undeniable truth. The recognition. The dread. The decision. He knew exactly who they were. And he wasn't planning to tell me.

Manakel hesitated, and the weight of that pause pressed heavier than anything he could have said aloud. And for the first time, I realized how little I *actually* knew him.

He turned before I could press him further, his stare lingering on the figures who moved like shadows over the hill, steady and silent and far too controlled to feel like a friendly welcome.

"Let's keep moving," he said, quieter now. "We wouldn't want to be late."

Late?

The word lodged in my chest like a splinter.

Late for what?

And why did it suddenly feel like I was being delivered—not guided?

I had a sinking feeling that wherever we were headed was no longer leading us to the Queen, but toward a fate I hadn't agreed to.

This doesn't feel right. The thought crept in like a whisper, coiling around the base of my spine and tugging with invisible fingers.

I slowed a half step, casting one last glance over my shoulder at the forest behind us, but the trees stood silent and indifferent. But their shadows had already retreated, too far now to offer any protection. Going back wasn't an option anymore. Not alone. Not now.

And yet, the ache in my chest told me I hadn't left the danger behind. I was walking straight into it. But what was the alternative?

Run?

Demand the truth?

Turn on the only person who had gotten me this far?

No. I couldn't do that. *Not yet.*

So I pushed the doubt down. Swallowed it whole and buried it beneath the hope that maybe I was imagining things. Maybe exhaustion was making ghosts out of nothing.

But I didn't trust the ground beneath me, or the silence between us. Something in Manakel had shifted the moment he saw them. Something I couldn't name but couldn't ignore.

So I followed, but kept my distance, just enough to remind myself that the person leading me forward might not be doing it for my sake.

Because even if I didn't know who was heading towards us…Every part of me knew we were being led straight into another trap.

The formation crested the hill in eerie unison, each step deliberate, silent, too controlled to be human. They didn't walk through the land so much as command it to part before them. A tide of cloaked figures, shadows cut from emerald and obsidian, moving with the slow inevitability of something that had already decided how this would end.

My pulse quickened.

As the group neared, the formation shifted, parting just enough to reveal three figures at the forefront. It was clear from the way the others stepped aside that these were the ones in charge, the ones who truly commanded the power radiating from this legion.

At their center, one figure rose above the rest, taller, broader, crowned in flame, his presence impossible to ignore. His emerald cloak swayed with each stride, the gold embroidery flashing like blades under the pale morning light.

A pelt, rust-red and coarse, was slung across his shoulders—fox fur, or something similar. But it was the fire of his hair that stole my breath. Vivid red streaked with gold, it spilled past his jaw like wildfire breaking loose, framing his face like a halo of fire. While the others blended into the dark, their forms swallowed by black and gray, he stood like a flame in the night—unmissable, undeniable. His gloved hands rested idly at his sides, not bothering to reach for a weapon; he didn't need one. It was clear why he led them. Beyond his towering frame, he demanded attention simply by existing, as if the season itself had crowned him in fire and dared the world to look away.

My eyes drifted from him to the woman flanking his right—ethereal, cold, too perfect to be real. Her blonde hair cascaded down her back in soft waves, and an intricate braid was woven like a crown of sunlight against the dark forest behind her. Her emerald cloak mirrored his, though hers shimmered with vine-like gold along the sleeves and hem in a more intricate embroidery pattern. Even from afar, she seemed untouchable, her pale hair and lithe form making her look like a figure plucked from the oldest myths, where beauty always came laced with a quiet sort of command.

The authority they carried came naturally, as though the forest itself bowed in recognition of their passage. The blonde woman's faint smile was polite, but not warm, and I might have been comforted by her lack of overt malice if not for the third figure. It was her presence that stopped my breath entirely.

To the man's left, moving with lethal grace, a woman with black eyes absorbed the light as if the sun itself feared to touch her, leaving the space around her dimmer, colder. She was striking in a way that felt almost unnatural, like shadow in flesh—sleek, silent, deadly. Her skin gleamed with an unnatural chill, too pale, too still, gleaming white that belonged to things buried in frost and never meant to thaw.

Her long, jet-black hair cascaded in perfect waves over her shoulders, but it was her eyes that held me captive, black, starless eyes, void of warmth. Just endless, depthless black. They swept over the hill with cold precision, as if she were already calculating the best way to eliminate every living thing in her path. There was no softness there, no trace of humanity to cling to. Just perfection. Something too precise, as if each detail of her appearance had been carefully curated to unsettle.

And when her eyes met mine, they didn't waver. They locked onto mine, piercing straight through me as if she'd been waiting for this exact moment, this exact meeting.

I swallowed hard, resisting the urge to shrink behind Manakel. A chill slid down my spine, prickling beneath my skin as if my body understood the danger before my mind could name it. My fingers twitched at my sides, instinctively curling into fists, though what I thought I could do against someone like her, I had no idea.

And she knew it. The faint curve of her lips wasn't a smile so much as a warning. One I hadn't even heard yet, but already feared. She didn't have to speak to make her point clear. The longer I looked, the more certain I became that whatever fury lived behind those eyes hadn't dimmed in centuries. It waited—*coiled, quiet, patient*—watching me like prey that had already lost the fight.

The air felt heavier with each step they took. There had to be at least fifty of them. Fifty immortals, all draped in shadows, weapons glinting beneath their cloaks—swords, bows, daggers. But it wasn't the weapons that unsettled me. It was the silence. The stillness. The way they moved, so tightly packed and in sync.

My eyes looked to Manakel, then back toward the treeline behind me, weighing my options. I wasn't sure which direction held more danger, the woods I had barely escaped, or the deadly procession closing in with deliberate steps.

I searched his face for anything familiar, the steady calm I'd come to rely on, the quiet anchor he'd been through the shadows and storms of the last few days. I felt him shift beside me, tension rippling through his frame like a silent alarm. But he didn't offer any explanation or reassurance. Just silence. Careful. Measured. Neutral.

Then I saw why.

Her.

The dark-haired woman's eyes didn't leave me. She moved forward, unhurried, and the others followed. Her eyes sliced straight through us like a blade drawn in daylight. Correction, it sliced through *me*. Because the venom in her stare wasn't meant for Manakel. It was meant for anyone standing beside him.

The air shifted, and so did I. My instinct screamed to step closer to him, to bridge the sudden, invisible divide growing between us. But Manakel didn't move. Didn't tense. Didn't shield. He just watched her approach with a stillness I couldn't quite decipher. Not fear. Not surprise.

Expectation.

As if he'd been waiting for her.

The trio parted the ranks like a blade parting water, their emerald cloaks billowing against the muted black of the others trailing behind them. A pack—silent, sure, inevitable. The air thickened with every step they took, pressing down on my ribs until breathing felt like a conscious effort.

Strength. Courage. Focus. Truth.

I repeated the words in my mind like a mantra. Armor to shield me from what was to come, but they didn't quiet the doubt, or stop the fear. They barely dulled the unease gnawing beneath my skin. I flexed my hands at my sides, nails biting into my palms, the sting keeping me tethered while a cold, sour knot twisted in my gut.

I wasn't ready for this.

But I would have to be. Because what other option did I have?

The formation of cloaks fanned out with practiced ease, slipping into the treeline like shadows cast from some older, crueler world. Weapons caught the light in flashes—swords sheathed, daggers strapped to hips, each gleam a quiet promise of violence.

But the woman, *the predator*, carried none. She didn't need them when her stare was a weapon all its own. She didn't walk beside the others. *She led.*

Her green cloak moved like water around her, whispering across the earth as if the ground itself bent to her will. And her black eyes—starless and vast—fixed on Manakel with an intensity that made the space between them feel like a thread pulled taut, stretched thin enough to snap.

Then, with the barest flick of movement, her attention cut to me.

Not curiosity. Not interest. A glance, as fleeting and dismissive as a stray thought.

"She doesn't look like much of a threat," she said, her voice soft and low, silk laid over steel. It didn't rise to be heard, but it didn't need to. Each word curled around us like smoke laced with poison.

I kept my chin high, but my fists clenched to keep from shaking.

"She isn't," Manakel replied, his tone flat and clipped, the words slipping easily from his mouth. *Too easily.*

Something shifted then, not in the air, but in me. A crack, subtle and sharp, running right down the center of my chest.

The woman smiled, cruel and knowing. "Is that why you're still babysitting her?"

He didn't answer, but he didn't need to. I already knew I was outmatched when it came to her. She stepped forward, slow and certain, lifting onto the tips of her boots to press a kiss to his cheek.

It wasn't the kiss itself that knocked the breath from my lungs; it was the way he let her. Like the interaction was effortless and familiar. Like it had happened before.

Something inside me twisted sharp and hollow. I took a step back, stomach sinking, unsure what hurt more—the intimacy of it, or the way she glanced at me while still so close to him. Her smirk deepened, like she'd been waiting for the moment I realized just how far outside the circle I truly stood.

"Oh, Manakel," she purred, brushing nonexistent dust from his shoulder, fingers too practiced. "You're right. She's not a threat. She's even more helpless and human than you described."

The laughter that followed from the shadows behind her was low and cruel and not nearly as distant as I wished it was.

My thoughts snagged on one word: *Described.*

That meant he'd talked about me. To her. Told her things. But about what? About how easy it had been to get me this far? How naive I was to follow along and believe him? How I had begged him to kiss me?

The ache in my chest sharpened. And then, as if the blow hadn't landed hard enough, he wrapped an arm around her waist, pulling her closer before kissing her.

Not a polite kiss. Not indifferent or hesitant. But full, possessive, and certain. Like someone claiming what was his. And the worst part was he didn't once look at me. Not once. Because why would he when I was just a helpless human?

The bitter sting of betrayal flooded my veins, but I forced myself to stay still. To stand there and watch. I refused to turn away, to give them that satisfaction, even as I felt the weight of humiliation digging into my bones.

Manakel had kissed me once, too. And now I realized just how little that moment meant to him. *Nothing.*

I clenched my jaw, swallowing the lump rising in my throat. I wouldn't let them see me break. Not here. Not like this.

He pulled back from her, *finally* meeting my eyes, and if there was any trace of apology in his eyes, I couldn't find it. They held nothing. No apology. No regret.

Just expectation. Like he was waiting to see what I'd do next.

So I stepped forward. Not because I knew what came next or where I was heading. But because standing still wasn't an option anymore.

The blonde woman and the red-haired man exchanged a look, something wordless and wary passing between them. It struck me as strange, like they were reading a secret in the silence, but I forced myself to ignore it, even as the hairs at the back of my neck prickled in warning.

Instead, I stepped forward.

Toward *her*. The dark-haired woman.

She watched my approach like a hawk circling prey —cold, precise, patient. Her mouth curled in something too close to a smile, but there was nothing warm in it. Nothing safe.

I closed the distance between us until we were only a breath apart. My heart pounded so loudly I was certain she could hear it, but I wouldn't give her the satisfaction of seeing me falter.

"I don't believe we've met," I said, extending my hand with practiced calm. "I'm Raine Roghnaithe. From the village of Laochra."

She stared at my hand like I'd offered her poison, but I didn't lower it.

The tension stretched, so taut it felt like the entire hillside held its breath. And then, with deliberate slowness, she finally took my hand in her own. Her grip was like steel dipped in ice.

The moment lingered long enough for me to lean in, my voice dropping low enough that only she could hear. "And you must not have been informed," I murmured, sweet as honey, sharp as glass. "But I'm no longer human."

Her fingers tensed around mine, pressure building, like the urge to crush my bones simmered beneath her perfect, polished exterior.

I smiled wider. "I completed my rite. So I'm immortal now. Just like you... I assume?"

She yanked her hand back, wiping it on her cloak as if my touch had stained her.

"Oh no," she sneered, her voice low and lethal. "*You* must be mistaken. You and I are *nothing* alike. And thank the gods for that."

The words hit their mark, slicing clean and deep, but I didn't let it show. I tilted my head, letting the edges of my smirk sharpen. "Really?" I shifted my focus, just enough for her to follow. "You should tell *him* that. He didn't seem to notice the difference when he kissed me."

It was petty. Reckless, maybe. But the flicker of irritation that flashed across her face made it worth it. Rage sparked behind her eyes, flickers of fire dancing at her fingertips like a promise. She was fire personified. But I had survived being burned before, and I wasn't afraid of it now.

The circle around us tightened, shadows pressing in. Every pair of eyes locked on me now, expectant and hungry, the air charged like the breath before a storm.

They watched me like a pack circling its weakest link.

But I wasn't weak. *Not anymore.* Because fear didn't own me anymore. And I wasn't broken, I was irate.

Because Manakel stood there in silence, offering no defense. No explanation. Not even a second glance to check if I was okay beneath the weight of her fury and their stares. It hit harder than any blade could have, and I had to force myself to breathe. To stand taller. To not care.

Because I could brace for enemies. I could see betrayal coming when the knife was held in a stranger's hand. But Manakel? I trusted him, and that was my mistake.

Focusing on the memory of his hand brushing against mine, the way he'd smiled at me beneath the stars by the river, the way he'd made it seem like he wanted to kiss me again but couldn't. But all of it had been a lie. Every touch, every word, was a carefully placed piece in whatever game he was playing. A trap I hadn't even known I was stepping into.

I thought I'd been cautious, too guarded to let him in. But the truth cuts deeper than any blade, and some wounds never heal.

There was no way to forgive someone who made you feel safe, only to destroy it the moment you let your guard down. So instead, I stood tall, breath steady, even as everything inside me cracked. I swallowed the knot in my throat, lifting my chin as I tried to even my breaths.

Don't let them see you break.

Because I wasn't broken. *Not yet.*

43. Roots Of Rebellion

A flicker of movement at the edge of my vision pulled me from my thoughts. I turned, instinctively tracking the two figures who lingered behind the dark-haired woman. The others had faded into shadow like ghosts, but these two remained—watching.

They didn't look at me with the same contempt the others did, but with something sharper. They were assessing, studying me like I was something unexpected, something they hadn't planned on finding, looking at me with recognition.

The blonde woman and red-haired man moved slowly, deliberately, like they were testing the air for threat, or memory. As they approached, I began to make out the finer details. The man's face was rugged but kind, lined with age but softened by a glint of warmth in his features. Laughter lines cut across his cheeks, framing a mouth that hadn't forgotten how to smile, even if it hadn't done so in a while. His beard was the color of wildfire, coppery gold catching in the morning light, and framed a strong jaw. His expression held no threat, but there was a steady, weighted look in his eyes—eyes that, even from several feet away, felt oddly familiar.

And then the woman stepped closer. Her beauty was delicate and ethereal, so perfect it barely felt real. Her skin seemed to glow faintly beneath the morning light, too smooth to be marked by time. Around her throat, a thin silver chain glinted where it caught beneath the edge of her cloak. She offered me the smallest of smiles, gentle but cautious. But it wasn't her face that stopped me cold.

It was her eyes. The same color as the striking man's beside her.

Blue-green, ringed in silver.

The exact color I'd seen in my own reflection since childhood. The same eyes as my mother. My grandmother. The ones that marked our line—rare, unmistakable.

The same eyes as me.

I went still, the blood in my veins rushing all at once to my ears.

No. No, that wasn't possible.

I blinked once, twice, desperate to clear the illusion, trying to convince myself it was a trick of the light, but the color didn't change. The familiarity didn't fade. Those weren't ordinary eyes. That hue, that shimmer, was unique. It had always been part of my family line.

They knew something. I could feel it in the way they looked at me, not with threat, but with recognition. Both their eyes held the exact color and depth as the eyes I had inherited, the same eyes I'd seen staring back at me my entire life.

I stumbled back a step before I could stop myself, the movement small but not subtle. My fingers curled into fists at my sides.

And then, almost against my will, I turned to Manakel. Looking for something, *anything,* to explain how this was even possible.

A flicker of guilt. A spark of truth. A hint of who they were. Why they looked at me like that? How they had *my* eyes.

But he said nothing. Not a word.

Just watched. Like this moment had always been inevitable, and I was exactly where I was supposed to be.

I had no idea who they were. But I couldn't escape the feeling that somehow, they knew exactly who I was.

And had been expecting me.

It was impossible, yet undeniable. They had my eyes, and I didn't know how or why they were here.

I tried to keep my face neutral, to keep the shock buried just beneath the surface, but it burned hot and restless. My gaze darted between them, two strangers standing too still, watching me too closely, desperately searching for an explanation.

The red-haired man's stare didn't waver, his intensity like a weight pressing down on me. There was something there—recognition, curiosity... maybe even disbelief.

The blonde woman carried herself differently. Her sharp blue-green eyes lingered on me with caution, as if unsure whether to trust what she was seeing. I could feel her scrutiny like a blade skimming just beneath the surface of my skin. She wasn't just looking at me; she was studying me, piecing together a puzzle she hadn't realized was missing a piece.

I wanted to ask. Who they were. Why they looked like me? If this was some divine accident, or another secret buried beneath my grandmother's ever-growing silence. But the words caught behind my teeth, too heavy, too dangerous.

Even if I asked, I wasn't sure they'd answer.

Whatever connection existed between us, it had shifted something in the air, something fragile and delicate. I could only hope they were as curious as I was, curious enough to keep me alive long enough to figure it out.

A rustle broke through the stillness.

I turned just in time to see Manakel and the dark-haired woman striding back toward the group, tension crackling between them like lightning through dry air after a heated argument. Their movements were sharp, voices hushed, but I caught the tail end of his whisper.

"We'll discuss this later, Elea."

So *that* was her name. *Elea.*

The word settled on my tongue like ash.

She was beautiful in a way that didn't invite admiration. Sharp-cheeked and sharper-eyed, with lips stained a bruised red that only made the malice beneath her calm exterior more unnerving. And whatever they were discussing must not have been pleasant because the subtle flush of pink on her cheeks did nothing to soften the edge of her expression.

But it wasn't her expression or their approach that twisted my gut.

It was the lingering stares of the others—the pair with two sets of identical eyes that had followed me like a tether, unblinking. Unwavering. But there was something else there, beneath the quiet. Something bordering on longing or searching.

Elea's voice sliced through the quiet, snapping their focus away from me.

"Carmenta. Roan." Her irritation simmered, words sharp as iron. "What is so fascinating about this human that you've completely forgotten why we're here?"

I stiffened at the words. I could almost feel the smugness radiating off Elea as she crossed her arms, eyes narrowing in satisfaction.

Carmenta's head tilted just slightly in response, but she said nothing. Her expression remained neutral, betraying nothing to Elea. The man, Roan, simply gave a short nod and took a small step back, positioning himself closer to Carmenta's side.

I studied their reactions carefully, my mind trying to recall if I'd ever heard those names. *Carmenta and Roan.* I turned them over in my thoughts, combing through the fragmented stories my grandmother had shared over the years. But nothing surfaced. No tales, no mentions. Just emptiness and confusion.

I clenched my fists at my sides, frustration biting at me. My grandmother had kept so much from me—her immortality, her past, the truth about who I was—and now, I wondered just how deep those secrets ran.

Was it possible they were more than strangers and somehow a bigger part of my story?

I felt their eyes still flicker toward me as they moved as if drawn by some unspoken force. Neither of them seemed to know what to make of me, but there was no mistaking the intensity of their focus.

And then, like a wave collapsing around me, things began to shift. The cloaked ones began to spread out, fanning into a wide arc that curved around me like a tightening noose. I tracked the motion with rising dread, watching as every escape route slowly disappeared behind dark figures and gleaming blades. Their red scars caught the light, flashes of crimson against the black. Their hands rested on the hilts of daggers and swords, ready—waiting.

My heart thudded. I was surrounded.

I felt it then, the inevitability of whatever was coming. This wasn't some passing encounter. This was a trap.

And I'd walked into it willingly.

I resisted the urge to look at Manakel, to search his face for regret, or even guilt. But I couldn't bear it. Not now. Not after the silent betrayal that still burned beneath my skin.

Instead, I fixed my stare on the only two who hadn't looked at me like prey, holding tight to the thin thread of recognition between us. Carmenta and Roan.

Maybe they wouldn't save me. But maybe they wouldn't let Elea destroy me either. And I'd take any small mercies I could get.

I kept my eyes on the path ahead, but the weight of Manakel's betrayal pressed heavily against my chest, threatening to choke the breath from me. I told myself I wouldn't look back at him. That I wouldn't give him the satisfaction of seeing the hurt he'd left behind. But despite myself, I looked anyway.

Just a glance. A flicker of weakness, searching his face for even the faintest glimmer of guilt or hesitation. But there was nothing

His eyes, once warm with quiet understanding, were distant now. Cold. Expressionless. A stranger in familiar skin. Whatever sliver of hope I'd still harbored, the foolish belief that maybe, somehow, he'd meant what he said about protecting me, died right there. Snuffed out like the last ember of a dying flame. How could I have been so blind? So naive to miss his blatant betrayal?

I faced forward again, my throat tight, the sting behind my eyes sharp and hot. The crunch of footsteps swallowed what remained of the silence. Cloaked figures walked in a loose formation around me, their presence a cage I couldn't escape. A rough hand pressed between my shoulder blades, shoving me forward, not cruel, but firm enough to remind me I wasn't free.

I stumbled on a patch of uneven earth but caught myself before I could fall. Every instinct screamed to run. To shift, to twist, to fight. But I knew I wouldn't make it far. I was surrounded, cloaked figures pressing in from every side, their weapons a stark reminder of my fate if I attempted to flee.

The castle loomed in the distance, its dark stone towers stretching skyward like jagged claws scraping against the clouds. Its silhouette was foreboding, casting long shadows across the land, but I felt a sliver of hope take root despite myself.

Maybe this had been the plan all along. Maybe they *were* taking me to the Queen.

I exhaled slowly, carefully guarding the fragile hope building in my chest. If I could just reach her, speak to her directly, perhaps I could convince her to hear me out. Maybe there was still a sliver of mercy left in this world, hidden beneath the crown.

I began rehearsing words I might say in my mind. Not pleas, exactly. But truths. Sincere and carefully chosen. She would hear the desperation in my voice. She'd see the truth in my eyes. I wouldn't beg. But I'd make her understand why I was here.

I stole a glance to the side, catching Carmenta and Roan watching me. They weren't subtle about it. Every few steps, Roan's eyes flicked back, brow furrowed like he was trying to place a face he should already know. Carmenta's expression was more restrained, but I could feel her eyes on me like the brush of cold wind across exposed skin.

I forced myself to remain composed, but every time their eyes lingered, the same unsettling realization clawed at the edges of my mind.

I somehow knew them.

Not by name, not in person. But I'd seen them before, I just didn't know where or how.

The vision from the river slammed into me like ice water down my spine.

The Osiris… the image of my grandmother.

The two children on her lap, a younger blonde girl and an older fire-haired boy. They were younger versions of themselves, but the resemblance was uncanny.

My breath caught. It was them. I knew it as surely as I knew my own name. But how? If they were the children from my vision… then the river had shown me something real. A memory. A fragment of a past that wasn't mine, but somehow belonged to me.

My grandmother hadn't just known them. She'd loved them. Carried them. Protected them.

I struggled to keep my face neutral, but my heart raced wildly in my chest. This wasn't a coincidence. The connection I felt, the familiarity woven into their faces—it wasn't imagined. They were linked to me. Linked to my grandmother.

I needed answers, but I knew better than to ask. Not here. Not now.

My mind spun, trying to decipher what their presence here could mean. If they had been part of my grandmother's past, why didn't she mention the possibility of running into them when I crossed? Unless… she'd been trying to protect them. Or maybe she'd been protecting me. It was somehow all connected.

I swallowed, casting another sideways glance at them. Roan's stare lingered a moment too long, his brows knitting ever so slightly as if he too was trying to solve the same riddle.

What do you know?

The unspoken words were communicated with a look, and I wished I could reach out to him, to ask what he knew, too. But the circle of immortals walking beside us made that impossible.

Elea's voice broke through the silence. "Eyes ahead, Roan. You can admire her later."

Her words were like acid, sharp and cutting, but Roan barely reacted. His expression hardened, but he said nothing. Carmenta's eyes flicked briefly toward Elea, her lips pressed into a thin line. It was subtle, so quick I almost missed it, but there was tension there. Disdain, perhaps. Or something more complicated.

They don't trust her.

I tucked the knowledge away. A small truth buried in a mountain of questions, but a truth all the same.

As the castle loomed closer, I reminded myself to stay calm. There was more happening here than I could see, threads being pulled behind the scenes, and I needed to play this carefully.

Wren's voice echoed softly in the back of my mind. *Preparation before action is the key to any battle.*

I took a deep breath, falling in line with the group as we crossed the field. I didn't know who Roan and Carmenta truly were, why they shared my eyes, or why the river had chosen to show me them.

But one thing was certain.

I wasn't giving up until I found out.

The closer we drew to the castle, the heavier the air became, like something ancient pressing down on my chest, warning me to turn back before it was too late.

Dermaine rose in the distance like a city carved from storm clouds and stone. The castle's towers pierced the sky, casting long, skeletal shadows over the earth. Spires loomed like jagged spears, their tips lost in the mist that clung to the horizon. Each step forward felt like crossing an invisible line; the earth itself seemed to resist our approach.

The castle wasn't just large. It was immense. Its stone walls, darkened with age, seemed to thrum with memory. Power. Conflict. Blood. Every weather-worn block whispered of things that had come before, and warned of things that would come again.

I forced myself to breathe steadily, but the farther we walked, the more it felt like the walls ahead weren't welcoming me; they were swallowing me. Sealing me in. My escorts kept a tight formation, silent and steady, their footsteps synchronized like a single heartbeat echoing across the hills.

It was strangely beautiful here. The fields behind the castle were untouched, like something from an old legend—lush with wildflowers that bloomed in vivid bursts across the grass. The wind carried their scent, sweet and intoxicating, laced with something I couldn't name. Something heavier.

Part of me wanted to turn and run into the field. To lose myself in the colors and let the open air swallow me whole because it felt safer than anything we were walking towards.

I glanced back, my eyes trailing over the hills we had taken out of the forest. The trees in the distance stood tall, their canopies swaying gently in the breeze. The woods had never been safe, but at least I understood their danger, or at least expected it. The path ahead was something else entirely. Something I wasn't ready for.

The feeling crept over me slowly, the unsettling realization that I was crossing into a world I had no control over. Whatever lay beyond those walls would not yield to me, not like the river, or the earth opening up in offering.

I swallowed hard, resisting the urge to slow my pace.

Manakel hadn't spoken once since we left, but I could feel his presence just ahead of me, commanding without speaking. Shoulders squared, gait steady, as if he hadn't just torn the ground out from under me. My satchel hung from his shoulder like a cruel reminder of just how little control I had over my circumstances. I hated how easily he carried my belongings, my only anchor to my home, like it meant nothing.

We crested the final slope, and the city of Dermaine unfurled below us in sharp contrast to the stillness behind. The streets ahead shimmered with activity even from this distance—a thousand lives moving on as if mine hadn't just shifted irreversibly.

A surge of panic rose in my chest.

I needed to be smart, my mind racing through every scenario. Once we reached the city, I might have a chance to escape through the dense crowd. If I cried out too soon, I risked drawing the wrong attention, but if I stayed quiet for too long, my window of escape could slip away entirely. Maybe someone, *anyone,* would see the fear on my face or notice the strange formation surrounding me and intervene.

I could only hope.

The archway ahead towered over the path leading into Dermaine city, weathered, cracked, and looming like a gate to another world. Its height alone was unsettling—twenty feet at least. *Who or what had once needed that much space to enter?*

My stomach turned at that.

I cast another glance at Manakel, searching for anything, an unspoken sign, a flicker of remorse, but he didn't offer any. The warmth I'd once seen in his eyes had vanished like a lie exposed to sunlight.

The arch swallowed us in shadow as we passed through it, the bustling city stretching out beyond in a wave of color and sound. Dermaine was unlike any place I had ever been.

Nothing like Laochra, where the streets were quiet and familiar, where every face had a name, and the land belonged to the people. Here, everything moved too fast, breathing with a constant hum of activity.

The cobbled streets shimmered as if washed clean by rain, glinting gold in the afternoon light. The air was thick with the scent of fresh bread and roasted meat, but underneath it lingered something metallic, sharp, like steel warmed by blood. A warning woven into the flavor of the city itself.

Shops lined the main road, doors flung wide to display goods like vibrant fabrics, painted ceramics, and blades that caught the light with dangerous precision. Brightly painted signs creaked, swinging on their hooks, some offering services or products I didn't recognize. Other shops were more discreet, their darkened windows cloaked in shadow and hiding the mysteries within.

People moved quickly, parting as we passed. They stepped off the road, clutching baskets or children, casting wary glances at the figures surrounding me. Some lingered, openly staring with curiosity, but when Elea moved past, her cloak brushing the ground, they quickly averted their gaze.

I kept my head down, but my eyes scanned the crowd. Some were human, others unmistakably immortal—the glow in their eyes and the elegant way they moved making that obvious. Yet none of them stepped forward to interfere. No one dared.

Maybe they knew better.

The further we pressed into the city, the more the streets filled, bustling with life. Vendors shouted above the noise, children weaved between carts, and the scent of spice and smoke clung to the air. A flicker of hope sparked in my chest. This was my chance. If I could just create a diversion or bring attention to myself, this *could* work.

A firm hand pressed against the small of my back, harder this time, steering me forward with silent finality. I stumbled, caught myself, and bit back a curse.

Elea led the group, cutting a path down the middle of the street like she owned it, and for all I knew, she probably did. Her presence tethered the group like an invisible chain, keeping the group tightly bound to her. No one strayed. Especially not me.

Carmenta and Roan kept pace just ahead, no longer leading with Elea, but still bound by the same current. They weren't like the others. Something in the way they kept glancing back at me, watchful and almost wary, unsettled me. Carmenta's brow furrowed, like she was trying to place me or recall a memory she didn't know she had.

I couldn't dismiss the vision the Osiris had shown me—my grandmother with two children on her lap, a boy with fire-kissed hair, and a girl with pale braids wrapped in sunlight. I didn't initially believe it, chalking it up to another illusion to trick me. But standing here now, I couldn't deny the resemblance.

It had to be them.

But why were they here, marching with the people who were kidnapping me?

I bit the inside of my cheek, holding down the swell of questions. Now wasn't the time to ask, not yet. If they were tied to my family, maybe I could use that to my advantage somehow.

Roan's eyes flicked toward me, guarded with the kind of silence that swallows words before they can form, but there was something else there, too. For a moment, I wondered if he felt it too, the strange pull of recognition, like a thread tugging taut between us, neither of us knew how to unravel.

Elea's voice cracked the moment like a whip. "Keep moving."

I straightened instinctively, locking my emotions and questions behind a mask I didn't fully trust.

I couldn't shake the eerie sense that they weren't just leading me to the Queen. There was no clear path to the castle gates from here. We didn't stay on the main roads for long. Instead, we slipped down narrow alleys, weaving through backstreets where fewer eyes could follow.

They weren't taking me to the Queen. This wasn't protocol; it was something else. Something carefully concealed.

My head spun, echoes of whispered warnings swirling in my mind. Aeron, Arella, Fern, even the Eldren, and the forest itself had hinted at something unusual about my Imbe Rite. Each one had looked at me like I was something more than I understood. Had more power than I believed.

Manakel and my grandmother had alluded to the same notions as well, but I'd thought they were being kind. Providing a false confidence to help me feel prepared, something to cling to in a world I barely understood.

But now, with each forced step forward, I wondered if they'd known this would be my outcome all along. Because I wasn't just being guided, I was being delivered, and my destination was still unknown.

My pulse quickened, every step harder than the last. I didn't know why I mattered, or what they thought I could offer. I was no one, an untested immortal, newly bound to this strange and ruthless world. I wasn't powerful, not like them. I wasn't royalty or born to a noble family. I wasn't trained and didn't even know the full extent of my power. Whatever this was, it wasn't about acquiring a ransom or politics, yet here I was, being escorted like a prisoner

My steps faltered, dragging against the uneven stones. I couldn't keep the thoughts from tangling, tightening, until my body moved slower than my mind could keep up with.

The first shove came without warning.

My shoulder clipped someone ahead of me, and I stumbled forward, catching myself on instinct. Carmenta turned sharply at the commotion, her eyes lingering too long. I muttered a soft apology, cheeks burning, but it didn't matter. The entire group had stopped, and every set of eyes was on me—*again.*

The air grew heavier, thick with unspoken tension. My throat tightened, and the dryness in my mouth made it nearly impossible to swallow. I coughed, the sound harsh in the silence, but no one moved. No one said a word or reached for me.

Manakel stood behind Elea, my satchel still draped over his shoulder like it belonged to him. His hand idly traced the strap, fingers brushing leather like he was taunting me with everything that was no longer mine. His eyes found mine, calm and unshaken, but the subtle shift of his lips, that slight smirk, felt like a slap to the face.

He knew.

He knew I was tired and thirsty. Knew I'd been dragging my feet. And he wanted me to see it, to see the power he held over me. My belongings, my voice, my autonomy, all reduced to something he could dangle just out of reach. If he was waiting for me to break and beg for them back, he'd be waiting a long time.

I clenched my fists until my nails bit skin. I wouldn't beg. I wouldn't break. Not here. I wouldn't give him the satisfaction.

I didn't know what they wanted from me, but I knew one thing: I wouldn't give it to them on my knees. I wanted to scream that I was just as lost as they were, that whatever answers they were looking for, they wouldn't find them in me. Instead, I stood there, silent and small beneath their scrutiny.

Elea's eyes narrowed, sharp as glass, before flicking behind me. "Keep moving," she ordered, her voice cold as iron. "We don't have time for this."

The second shove hit harder, sending me stumbling forward, barely catching my footing. The urge to scream pulsed in my chest, but I swallowed it down like poison.

My legs obeyed, falling back into the rhythm of their march, but the unease rooted deeper with every step.

The closer we got, the narrower the streets became. The crowds that had filled the market had thinned, leaving only quiet alleyways in their place.

I didn't know where they were taking me, or what awaited me behind those castle walls. The Queen, a prison cell, or something worse, something final. But I knew one thing: whatever this place demanded of me, whatever it wanted to take, I wasn't ready. Not to fight. Not to bow. Not to break.

But maybe survival didn't wait for readiness. Maybe it only waited for the moment you chose to keep going anyway.

So I breathed once.

And then again.

And I continued walking.

44. The Other Side Of Loyalty

The moment we veered off the main path, every trace of hope I'd clung to shattered like fragile glass. The castle, once a beacon of promise, of answers, shrank behind us, swallowed by the thick tangle of trees that pressed in beyond the city's edge. I stared at it, willing it to stay in view, but it kept retreating behind the rising line of forest. I'd been a fool to believe this was the end of my journey. That I was anywhere near safety.

My steps faltered, the hair at the nape of my neck prickling.

"Why are we leaving the road?" I asked, voice tight but steady.

Manakel glanced back, his hazel eyes lighting up like a storm held at bay, but he said nothing. I could have been mistaken, clinging to any scrap piece of hesitation, but he looked almost conflicted, like he *wanted* to say more but couldn't.

"It's a shortcut," Elea called over her shoulder, not bothering to conceal the amusement in her tone.

I didn't believe her. Not for a second.

The castle walls were still in sight, but with every step, they grew smaller and further away. I could feel the shift, the way the air thickened, the sunlight filtering through the thick canopy as it swallowed the light whole. The road beneath our feet narrowed, cobblestones giving way to packed dirt as the city fell behind us and shadows stretched ahead.

I swallowed the lump rising in my throat and pressed forward, not because I trusted them, but because I had no other choice. My legs kept moving, but my chest screamed to turn around. To run.

The moment the path dipped toward the edge of another forest, this one darker, older, and hung with a silence so heavy it rang in my ears, I stopped walking.

Dug my heels into the earth, forcing the cloaked man behind me to halt. His hand, rough and unrelenting, clamped harder around my upper arm, but I twisted, panic rising swift and sharp in my chest.

"No!" The word cracked from my throat, loud and sharp, too raw to be reasoned. "I need to see the Queen. You said—" My voice broke. "You said I'd be taken to her."

My voice rang out over the murmuring of the group, louder than I'd intended, but I didn't care. I thrashed, clawing at the hand pinning me in place, but the more I struggled, the harder he pressed, forcing me to stumble forward in his wake.

The castle was behind me, a new expanse of trees was ahead, and I was being pulled toward the wrong future. I had come all this way. Survived the river. Fought against everything the woods had thrown at me. Defeated creatures that nightmares were made of. And now, I was being led away from the one thing that mattered most. The reason I was even here.

No. I wouldn't let this happen.

I reached for my dagger. The hilt met my palm, the cool metal against my palm offering a flicker of reassurance. I could fight my way out—cut through the group and disappear into the streets. I might not make it far, but I'd make it far enough.

I tugged the blade free, the faint whisper of steel barely audible beneath the crunch of footsteps, but the second the tip cleared the sheath, a hand shot out and caught my wrist.

Manakel.

I froze, my breath hitching as I met his stare. His grip wasn't rough, but there was no mistaking the threat in his eyes, the silent command that warned me to drop the blade or face the consequences.

He was different now. Colder. The warmth he'd once let slip in brief moments, the tenderness that softened his sharp edges, were gone. And in its place was someone I didn't recognize, someone who watched me like a predator, toying with its prey just before the kill.

"Let. Me. Go," I said, quieter now. The fire was still there, but it burned under the weight of betrayal.

Manakel's lips curved, not quite a smirk, but close. Except there was nothing playful or kind about it. He leaned in, so close I could see the faint smudge of Elea's lip color on his mouth, like a brand left there to remind me how naive I'd been.

"Just do as you're told, Amadán," he whispered, the word rolling off his tongue like silk laced with thorns. "And I won't have to hurt you."

I couldn't breathe.

It wasn't *what* he said, but *how* he said it. Like I was beneath him, like everything between us had been a game, and like a fool, I had played right into his hands.

My grip on the dagger slackened, and his eyes flicked towards it. His grip on my wrist tightened, a silent warning.

"Don't fight this," he said, voice barely above a whisper. His eyes, dark and unreadable, pinned me in place. "Trust me. You'll regret it if you do anything reckless now."

I yanked my arm from his grasp. "I *did* trust you." My voice shook. "And I won't be making that mistake again."

His jaw tensed. His eyes narrowed. And just for a moment, just long enough, I saw it. *Guilt.*

I held on to that and hoped maybe it meant not everything had been a lie. That maybe he, too, was being forced into this.

"You don't have much of a choice. Now move," he said, louder now, for the others this time. *For her.*

And with that, the march resumed, leading us toward the dark forest threatening to swallow us whole. And with every step we took, the castle faded from view, taking with it the last trace of hope I'd been clinging to.

The walk toward the line of trees stretched on endlessly, every step dragging me further into the unknown. My feet felt heavy, weighted not just by exhaustion but by the oppressive sense of dread that settled over us like a thick fog.

The cloaked figures surrounded me, their formation tight, a watchful ring leaving no room for escape. I could feel their eyes, quiet and unrelenting, tracking every breath I took. A silent reminder that there was no way out.

When we stopped just before the tree line, I slowed, confused by the abrupt halt. My eyes darted around, trying to piece together why we had paused here.

I scanned the group. Elea and Manakel stood ahead, their heads bent in a sharp, hushed exchange. I couldn't hear the words, but their tension cut through the quiet—stiff shoulders, terse glances, the way Manakel's jaw flexed every time she spoke. It was enough to tell me they weren't in agreement.

Off to the side, Carmenta and Roan hovered, their eyes flicking between the others and me. Low murmurs passed between them, and the way they looked at me sent a chill up my spine.

I shifted slightly, angling my body just enough to study my surroundings. If I were going to run, I'd need to know where we were, or at least be able to identify a landmark. A way back. My father's voice surfaced in my mind, one of his many lessons from my childhood. From when I would wander our village aimlessly for hours.

"Never leave without a way to retrace your steps. Look for something distinct. A sign, a tree, anything you can use to guide you back."

To my left, a massive tree caught my attention. It was thick and gnarled, and etched into its bark was the faded outline of a heart, weathered by time but still visible. The initials K & L rested quietly within a soft bloom of tiny green flowers lining the heart. At first glance, it appeared to be just moss, but now I saw the petals. The cluster of flowers was vivid and alive, despite the lack of sunlight in these parts.

It was more than a carving; it was a promise, preserved by magic. The flowers formed a perfect halo around the heart, a silent declaration of love that had somehow stood the test of time.

I filed it away in my mind. *This is my marker,* I told myself. *If I ever make it out, this is where I'll begin my way back home.*

The group's focus remained fractured, distracted, too caught up in their conversations to notice me. The man behind me, my personal shadow since we began walking, wasn't paying attention to me either. My pulse quickened as I looked between the trees and the small gap between the men. It wasn't much, but it was something.

I inhaled deeply, willing my muscles to stay steady. *Don't overthink. Just run. Now might be your only chance.*

Without another thought, I ran.

The world blurred, wind clawing at my face as my boots pounded the ground. My chest burned, but I didn't stop. *Couldn't* stop. Not when the castle was still in sight, peeking through the trees, not when it was my last hope of reaching the Queen. I heard the shouts in the distance, angry and sharp, but I kept going. Failure wasn't an option, not when survival was the only thing keeping my family alive.

Every ounce of strength I had left surged forward. My lungs burned, and my legs screamed in protest, but I pushed forward. Just a little farther.

I didn't dare look back. And for a moment, I truly believed I might make it. That I'd actually outsmarted and outrun them.

Then something slammed into my back like a thunderbolt from the sky.

The impact knocked the air from my lungs as I hit the earth hard. Pain exploded through my ribs, dirt biting into my palms. I scrambled, gasping, but a crushing weight pinned my legs before I could move.

I twisted, gasping for breath, and my eyes locked onto Manakel.

His face hovered just above mine, shadowed and sharp in the dim light. The cold, calculated look in his eyes froze me in place. The wind caught the edges of his cloak, feathers rustling behind him like a warning.

"Did you *really* think you could outrun me?" he asked, his voice low, biting. "I have wings," he rolled his eyes as his voice dripped with mockery.

His hands pressed into my thighs, anchoring me. I struggled, twisting beneath him, but it was no use. He didn't budge.

My chest heaved as I glared up at him, anger and humiliation burning through me. I wanted to scream, to fight back, to claw my way free. But his grip was unrelenting, and his face held a darkness I hadn't seen before, a cruel edge that sent a shiver down my spine.

This wasn't the Manakel I thought I knew. This wasn't the ally who'd fought beside me, trained me to be prepared, the Sciathain who had seemed so steadfast and protective.

No. This was someone else entirely. Someone who wanted me broken.

I clenched my fists, the cool dirt pressing into my palms. If I couldn't outrun him now, I would find another way. *I had to.*

I could barely breathe as I locked eyes with him, my chest tightening with each second that passed. But no matter how much my stomach churned or my heart hammered, I refused to look away. I wouldn't give him the satisfaction of seeing even a flicker of fear in my eyes. He had once called me reckless and stubborn, and I would show him exactly what those words meant.

"Let me go." My voice barely held together, thin, frayed, but it was all I had.

Manakel's mouth twitched into something too cruel to be called a smile.

He leaned down, his breath brushing my cheek as he whispered, "Just do as you're told, Amadán. And I won't have to hurt you."

My grip tightened in the dirt. My voice was raw when I spat back, "Why would you care if I ran? Looks like you've already got your hands full—*with her.*" I tilted my chin toward Elea. My laugh was brittle. "Besides, I'm just a helpless human not worth your time, remember?"

Manakel's smirk deepened, his brow lifting in that infuriating way that made my blood boil. "Are you jealous, Amadán?"

The sheer audacity of his question made me scoff, and I sucked in a sharp breath, trying to steady my voice. "Not at all, actually. You two look perfect together—dark, brooding, and thinking you're far more powerful than you actually are."

I had no idea where the words were coming from, but they flew out before I could stop them. I braced myself, fully expecting him to explode in anger, but instead, his expression flickered. Just for a split second, something unexpected crossed his face—a crack in his perfect composure.

But I caught it.

I resisted the urge to smile, to let him know I'd seen it. But the crack sealed almost instantly, his expression hardening into something colder, sharper. He leaned closer, his voice dropping low and cutting, each word dripping with disdain. "If only you knew the plans we had for you, then you wouldn't act so brave. Or so *foolish.*"

His voice dripped with mockery, each word cutting deeper. "But I guess it's only right since I've been calling you a fool this entire time… Amadán." He spat out the word like it held all his contempt, his lips twisting with satisfaction at my shock.

The realization stung. Amadán meant *fool.* He'd been calling me a fool all along, a hidden insult wrapped in every interaction we'd shared. Every time he'd said it, every time I'd let it slide because it sounded endearing, it had been a mockery. And he had known, and kept it there, right in front of me, laughing silently at my ignorance.

The cold gleam in his eyes sharpened, and I felt a chill run down my spine. "But now, since you *insist* on being foolish," he continued, his voice cruel and unyielding, "it seems we have to do this the hard way."

I swallowed hard, my throat tightening as I forced myself to meet his stare. "Do what? Where are you taking me?" I demanded, my voice trembling despite my best efforts to steady it. "I'm supposed to see the Queen!"

His laugh was low and humorless, more chilling than any shout could have been. "Oh, you will," he said, his tone mocking. "Just not the Queen you expected to see."

My stomach turned. I shoved against his chest, but he caught my wrist, dragging me upright in a single, effortless pull. Before I could scream, before I could swing, the ground disappeared beneath us, and he launched us into the air.

The earth dropped away beneath me, the wind howling in my ears as rooftops and roads blurred into nothing. We soared higher and faster than I'd ever imagined possible. My stomach plummeted as if I'd left it behind with the cloaked group below. Panic surged, sharp and unyielding, and I instinctively reached out, grasping for anything to steady myself. My fingers closed around him, his grip unrelenting, his presence colder than the icy wind slicing against my skin. The sense of betrayal was suffocating, but his grip didn't waver.

And neither did the weight of what I now knew.

There had never been a choice. The Manakel I thought I knew had never existed, was nothing more than an illusion. A lie crafted to manipulate me. Only this version had been real, the predator in disguise, who smiled as he led me straight into the dark.

I forced my eyes open, desperate to see where he was taking me. But the wind was merciless, slashing at my skin, tearing through my hair, stinging my cheeks until my eyes streamed with tears. Below us, the world was nothing but a blur of green and gray, a shifting smear of forest and stone.

I squinted into the storm, but it was useless. There was no path, no landmark, just motion and cold and sky.

Eventually, I gave up. I let my eyes fall shut and let the numbness spread through me. My head dropped against his shoulder, not out of trust, but because there was nowhere else to go. The sickness curled low in my stomach, hot and sharp. I swallowed it down. There was nothing I could do, no force strong enough to pull me from his grasp.

After what felt like hours, the wind shifted and the momentum slowed. The impact from landing jolted through me, and I staggered as his grip remained firm, holding me upright until I regained my balance. My legs buckled, every muscle in my body ached, a sharp reminder of the relentless flight and the Sciathain who had given me no choice.

Finally regaining my balance, a new wave of unease settled over me. I jerked away from him, stumbling back two steps, gasping like I'd been deprived of air.

My eyes snapped up to his. I searched his expression for something— regret, explanation, anything that would make this make sense. But there was nothing. Just that same cool, composed indifference.

"Where are we?" I rasped, my voice hoarse with windburn and betrayal.

When he didn't answer, I turned and froze.

We stood before an enormous castle, a thing carved from nightmares and grandeur. Thirteen towers loomed above the main structure, each one piercing the heavens. The walls were pale stone, but they gleamed with a strange luster—too perfect, too polished, as if reality had been scrubbed away. Amber-tinted windows caught the faintest glow of the setting sun, the only hint that all of this was real. It was breathtaking, but also terrifying.

A path of silver-gray stone stretched toward the gates, flanked by gardens too immaculate to be real. The hedges were trimmed to sharp perfection. Rows of pale pink peonies bloomed in eerie stillness, their petals unbothered by the breeze.

There was no mistaking this place. It wasn't just any fortress. It was a royal castle. A place built for power, not mercy.

Before I could speak, the massive front doors creaked open.

Elea stepped through them like she'd been waiting, her gown trailing behind her like smoke. Two guards flanked her, tall and expressionless, their armor gleaming under the fading sun.

I frowned, confusion threading through my fear. Elea had been behind us when we'd left the clearing. How could she possibly be here first?

But there she was, smirking as she approached us. Her focus moved to Manakel, and the look she gave him was sharp enough to draw blood. She leaned in, whispered something I couldn't hear, and pressed a kiss to his cheek. Her cold, unblinking eyes never left mine.

It wasn't jealousy that stirred in me; it was disgust.

She turned to face me fully, her sneer twisting into something even more condescending. "I never formally introduced myself," she said, her voice lilting with feigned politeness. "Humans, after all, are rarely worth the effort."

I didn't flinch, but my hands curled into fists at my sides.

She stepped closer, tilting her head as if studying something under glass. "But now that you've completed the rite, you've shed that unfortunate part of you."

The words hit harder than I expected. *I was no longer human.* I kept my mouth shut, jaw locked tight. I wouldn't give her the satisfaction of seeing the confusion or the fear rising in me.

She seemed mildly amused by my silence.

"I'm Elea," she continued, her tone sweet and savage. "Princess of Immorro."

She swept a hand behind her toward the towering citadel.

"And this… is my castle."

I kept my face blank and said nothing, even though the questions I had were multiplying. Because right now, silence was the only weapon I had left. And I needed any advantage I could get.

The truth hit like a bucket of ice water—numbing, sharp, impossible to ignore.

I was in Immorro.

And Elea… was a *princess.*

The realization unraveled every frayed thread of logic I'd been clinging to. If she were royalty, then her mother was none other than Queen Verena. The same Queen Aeron had warned me about, who ruled with a merciless grip and made even the gods seem benevolent in comparison.

But where did Manakel fit into all of this?

If Aeron had cautioned me about the Queen, why hadn't he said anything about Manakel's true motives? Or was he somehow in on it too?

A sharp cough snapped me out of my spinning thoughts.

Manakel stood nearby, his dark eyes fixed on me with thinly veiled irritation. My tendency to retreat into my mind when overwhelmed wasn't exactly helpful here; it only seemed to push their patience closer to the edge.

I forced myself upright, chin lifted in quiet defiance, and faced Elea. "Well, I guess you already know who I am." I said, my voice thin but steady, "Considering all the things Manny must have shared."

I let the faeries' nickname for him slip through, knowing full well how much he hated it. It was a petty jab, but when his jaw twitched, a flicker of satisfaction stirred in my chest at the sight.

Elea's brows lifted slightly, her focus sliding between us with mild amusement. The nickname hadn't gone unnoticed. Whatever silent war had sparked between Manakel and me seemed to intrigue her. She studied me a moment longer, then dismissed her curiosity as quickly as it appeared.

"Yes… Raine, was it?" she drawled. Her voice slithered like smoke, too smooth, too slow, each word laced with condescension. "You're in luck. The Queen isn't quite ready to meet you."

Her smile twisted into something dark, secrets dancing just beneath the surface. The kind of smile that made my stomach churn.

Wait—*the Queen?*

Not *my mother.*

The omission wasn't subtle, and it left me more confused. Was Elea not directly related to her? Or maybe she was, and this was just another carefully curated deception. I couldn't keep up. Every truth I thought I knew dissolved the moment I tried to hold onto it.

"What am I doing *here* instead of Dermaine?" I demanded, my voice steadier this time, though panic clawed at the edges. "Can *she* help with the river?"

Laughter instantly erupted from both Manakel and Elea, sharp and cruel. Elea's eyes gleamed as she composed herself, her amusement cutting like broken glass.

"The river?" she repeated, her tone mocking. "Oh, don't worry. It's drying up exactly as planned."

Her smile widened, fanged with cruelty.

The last fragile thread of hope I'd been holding slipped from my grasp, leaving only a hollow ache in its wake.. My breath caught, chest tightening.

I wasn't here to stop anything because I was already too late.

"You're here for judgment." Elea continued, voice syrupy and smug, "Your fate and your worthiness to stay an immortal will be decided by the Queen, but only when she deems you important enough to meet. Until then, you'll be staying in the castle."

Her tone was casual, dismissive, as if my entire existence, *my fate*, was no more significant than choosing wine with dinner.

I stared up at the massive structure behind her, squinting as the reality of her words sank in. *I was going to stay here.*

In this enormous castle with countless windows, sprawling towers, and more rooms than I could ever imagine filling. But the idea of being trapped here, waiting for someone I didn't trust to decide if I was allowed to exist, sent a cold wave of dread coursing through me.

My hands clenched at my sides, nails digging into my palms, but the panic rose fast and sharp. Faster than I could stop it.

Wasn't my fate supposed to belong to the gods? Manakel had said so. He'd sworn it.

But then again—he'd lied about everything else, so maybe that was a lie, too. Part of his betrayal, and this grand ruse. I still had no idea why I was dragged into this, or why my fate mattered at all. According to Elea, I was just some helpless human, so my fate should be of no significance to her or the Queen.

My mind spun, fragments of information and half-formed questions colliding, refusing to align. I tried to steady my breathing, to ground myself, but it was too much.

I felt the tilt of the world beneath my feet, the sudden weightlessness as my knees gave out and my body crumpled toward the stone. I braced for the impact, for the sharp jolt of pain that would follow hitting the ground. But it never came.

Strong, familiar arms caught me, steadying my limp body.

Manakel.

I wanted to shove him away, scream, curse him for everything he'd taken and everything he'd twisted, tell him I didn't need his help anymore, but I couldn't move. I was too heavy. Too hollow.

His grip was unyielding. Warm and grounding. And all it did was make the betrayal sting worse.

Then the darkness closed in, soft and suffocating, and I let it take me.

I woke with a violent shudder, the chill creeping into my bones as if the stone floor beneath me was alive and feeding on my warmth. My skin prickled as a damp, icy cloth pressed against my forehead, jolting me from the haze of unconsciousness. My breath hitched as awareness rushed back—cold, sharp, and unforgiving.

Blinking against the dim light, I tried to make sense of my surroundings. The air was thick with the sour tang of mold and stone, the kind of musty stench that settled into your lungs and didn't let go. My head throbbed in dull, rhythmic pulses, each one jarring enough to blur the edges of the world before finally snapping into focus.

Reality hit like a hammer.

I was in a dungeon.

And I was chained.

Forcing a shaky breath, I looked around, trying to piece together where I was, or how long I'd been here. But the cell offered no answers. The slick, moisture-covered walls gleamed, the faint orange flicker of dying light slipping through a hairline crack in the stone. No windows. No sky. Just the crack of color hinting that the sun was setting. A steady drip of water echoed in the distance, piercing through the silence like a ticking clock.

My right arm throbbed, the shackle biting into my wrist so tight that bruises were already beginning to bloom. I pulled instinctively, a useless, desperate tug, but the iron didn't give. Pain did. It flared up my arm, hot and immediate, but I barely felt it beneath the suffocating weight of realization.

I was being held captive. Not staying in the castle as a guest, or a visitor, but a prisoner. My stomach twisted as I realized how naive I'd been, clinging to the absurd hope that "staying in the castle" might mean a bedroom. But I should have known better than to assume.

The memories trickled in like poison—slow, burning as they settled.

I was in Immorro, Elea was a princess, and Queen Verena knew about me somehow.

Verena. The name that turned my grandmother pale the moment I uttered it. The same one Aeron had spoken of with that clipped, haunted edge in his voice. She knew who I was, and at some point, I would be brought before her. She knew I'd completed the Imbe Rite, and my future belonged in her merciless hands. She hadn't summoned me yet. But she would.

I closed my eyes, trying to block out the rising tide of despair. I was here because of secrets my grandmother had kept hidden for decades. Because

I thought I could protect my family and my village from immortals. But I was now one of the very things I had fought to keep out to keep my family safe.

I swallowed hard, the dryness in my throat scraping like sandpaper. Bitter laughter bubbled up, uninvited and sharp.

Gods, I'd been so arrogant.

One week of preparation. A handful of lessons. And I thought I could face centuries of power, layered lies, and forgotten truths, like it was some test I could pass by trying hard enough. But there were so many things I still didn't understand.

But I was starting to realize the hard truth. We are all bound—by blood, by secrets, by the lies we tell ourselves and the stories we choose to believe. Some lies just cut deeper than others.

I forced a breath into my lungs, but it came shaky, jagged. My eyes scanned the small cell, barely bigger than my childhood room, yet stripped of everything that had made that space mine. Gone was the warmth of my mother's humming. Gone was the safety I felt with my grandmother nearby, the scent of pine and herbs wafting in from my window. This place was the exact opposite—cold, damp, silent, and suffocating.

The space was sparse. A thin mattress had been tossed into one corner, lumpy and damp, with a single frayed blanket crumpled beside it. My stomach growled, twisting with hunger and dread. There was no food, no water, just time, and the crushing weight that the longer I stayed here, the more it cemented the fact of my failure.

My gaze shifted back to the chain binding me to the wall, and giving it another tug, I saw that the clasp didn't sit quite right. It was as if someone had fastened it hastily, carelessly, or maybe deliberately.

Hope stirred, but I smothered it. I'd learned by now what false hope felt like. It was a warm flame right before the burn.

Still, I tested my legs, bracing myself against the wall as I pushed myself upright. My body protested every movement, pain flaring in my back, shoulders, my thighs, but I gritted my teeth and ignored it.

The chain allowed just enough slack to shuffle toward the mattress.

Each step felt like a marathon, my head pounding in time with the ache in my wrist.

By the time I reached it, my breaths were shallow and fast. I sank onto the edge of it, grimacing as the coarse fabric scratched against my skin. The mattress offered no comfort, only a brief reprieve from the hard, cold floor beneath it.

I leaned back against the wall, staring up at the ceiling. The silence pressed in on me, heavy and oppressive, broken only by the faint drip of water in the distance.

Drip.

Drip.

Drip.

My stomach clenched again, gnawing at itself. My mouth was too dry to speak, each swallow feeling like sandpaper scraping against raw skin. My thoughts were too loud to be quiet, almost mocking in the empty space.

Would they bring me anything for sustenance, or had they left me here to waste away, forgotten and alone in the cold basement of their grand castle? Was this another test I needed to pass? One that would factor into Verena's judgement?

The thoughts wrapped around me like a vice, squeezing until I could barely breathe.

I clenched my fists, digging my nails into my palms, hoping the pain would ground me, but I barely felt it. My mind spun with more questions, all without answers. How long had I been here? Had anyone come to check on me while I was out? Would Aeron even know I was taken? And if he did, would he come to help me?

I didn't know what was worse: the idea that he wouldn't… or the idea that he would and I wouldn't know if he was a part of the betrayal too? That I would have to blindly trust someone who had the potential to ruin me, even more than I already was.

You're not done yet, Raine. This isn't the end.

My mind chanted, but it was getting hard to believe it. Hard to trust my inner voice that had also led me towards Manakel and the woods time and time again, with the promise of success.

I shut my eyes, but I couldn't keep out the creeping dread, the thoughts that slithered into the quiet space left behind.

What if this is it?

What if this cell, this failed test, is how my story ends?

And what if everything I did was for nothing?

45. To Strike Or To Surrender

The cell was quiet, but not silent. Never silent.

Water dripped in the distance, a metronome of madness echoing off stone. Somewhere beyond the walls, wind moaned like a forgotten thing. The torchlight from the corridor outside cast long, flickering shadows through the iron bars, like the flames were trying to crawl inside with me.

That's when I heard it.

Footsteps—soft at first, barely more than a whisper against the stone corridor. Then sharper, crisper, until each one echoed with purpose, drumming louder in the cold silence of the dungeon. I pushed myself upright, spine scraping against the wall, and gritted my teeth as my legs trembled with effort.

I didn't want to appear weak. Not when someone was coming. Not when I didn't know who.

A silhouette emerged beyond the bars, framed in the flickering torch-light, and I forced myself to remain still, not wanting to appear too eager.

The figure drew closer, and my heart stuttered when I recognized her features. It was Carmenta.

She held a tray, and the subtle clink of metal against ceramic carried forward with each step. I told myself not to hope, but hunger is a cruel thing. It doesn't listen. It claws its way forward, shameless and demanding, and as if on cue, my stomach growled loudly with anticipation.

I swallowed hard, eyes dropping to the tray. I scanned for the glint of water, the shape of a plate, anything that might dull the gnawing ache in my gut. Then out of the shadow I saw it—a glass of water, a mug of something warm, and a plate of food perched on top. I wasn't sure what it was, but I didn't care. I nearly sagged with relief, but something else caught my eye and stopped me cold. Slung over Carmenta's shoulder, worn but unmistakable, was my satchel.

I curled my fingers into my palms, resisting the overwhelming urge to lunge for it, to pry it open, desperate to know if any of my belongings had made it here intact. But I forced the impulse down. I couldn't let her see how much it mattered. Couldn't afford to tip my hand—*not yet.*

Carmenta's eyes swept over me cautiously, like she wasn't entirely sure if I'd snarl or beg. I wasn't quite sure why she thought I was capable of that, considering I was here at her mercy. I lifted my chained wrist in mock surrender, letting the metal glint between us and showing I wasn't much of a threat.

Her lips twitched, and a quiet laugh slipped out, one that felt so out of place in this cold, damp prison that I blinked in confusion. It didn't carry malice. It didn't sound like the laughter of someone who meant me harm. It felt warm and oddly familiar. And that, somehow, unsettled me more.

I met her eyes, searching for the catch. The angle, the deception, the reason she was really here. But I couldn't find it. There was something else in her stare, something soft and understanding, a look I didn't understand, and didn't trust.

She unlocked my cell with a jangle of keys and then knelt, placing the tray near the mattress with unexpected care. She glanced at me and gave a slight nod toward the blanket. An unspoken offer, or maybe a command, dressed in civility.

I hesitated, but the pull of hunger and the dull throb in my legs overruled caution. I sank down slowly, limbs trembling, breath shaky, biting back the dizziness that threatened to tip me over. The ache in my legs roared to life as I shifted.

To my surprise, her hand came out to steady me, taking hold of my arm. The warmth of her touch startled me more than the gesture itself. I couldn't remember the last time someone had helped me like that, or touched me with anything but force.

"Thank you," I said quietly, the words raw in my throat. They escaped before I could second-guess them, the genuine gratitude feeling foreign on my tongue.

Carmenta didn't respond right away. She just studied me, her head tilting slightly to the side as if trying to figure something out. Then, finally, a soft smile tugged at her mouth.

I lifted the glass of water first and drank deeply, draining it in just two gulps. The coolness rushed down my throat, and I gasped when I set the cup down, blinking back the rush of dizziness.

"Easy there," she said with a faint smile. "I can bring more. There's no need to act like you haven't had a drink in days."

I didn't respond.

She'd said it lightly, but the reminder stung. For all I knew, I *had* been here for days. Time felt like a shapeless thing in this place, no sun, no markers, just minutes slipping through my fingers too easily.

As if sensing my retreat, Carmenta cleared her throat and motioned to the warm mug.

The scent of something earthy and sharp curled into the air, and my stomach twisted at the sight of the tea. Its surface shimmered faintly like liquid bronze, but it wasn't hunger or thirst that made me hesitate. I didn't trust anything handed to me in this place, not when I'd seen too many smiles mask sharp edges.

"You should drink that," Carmenta said lightly, her voice carrying that melodic cadence that always felt half like kindness and half like a trap. "It'll ease the ache."

My fingers instinctively pressed against my ribs, where a dull throb had settled deep beneath the skin, a souvenir from the Rite and the chaos that followed. I hadn't let myself think about it, not with everything else pressing in, but the truth was every breath scraped like sandpaper, every shift of my body reminded me something inside wasn't right.

"What's in it?" I asked, forcing my voice to stay level even as my throat went dry.

"Just herbs," she replied, too casually. "Yarrow, comfrey, a bit of angelica root. Good for pain and bone healing." Her gaze flicked to my side, uncomfortably perceptive. "You've been guarding your ribs since you arrived."

I hated how easily she saw through me.

Before I could argue, she reached into the folds of her gown and pulled out a length of ivory linen, soft as a whisper. "If you prefer something less… internal, I can bind them. Keep you from making it worse."

For a breath, I said nothing, torn between pride and practicality. Letting her touch me felt like handing over a weapon, but the grinding ache in my ribs didn't leave much room for pride.

"I'll do it myself," I muttered, snatching the cloth from her hand.

Her lips curved into the faintest smile, like I'd just amused her in some secret way, and she nodded. "Suit yourself."

I grimaced at the move, but mumbled my thanks, knowing she had no reason to be kind or care about my well-being, yet had appeared and seemed genuine. Giving her a small smile of appreciation while looking between her and the tray of food still sitting near me, she exhaled.

"I tried to gather some of my favorites from the kitchen without being seen," she said, her voice dipping lower, a faint flush creeping up her cheeks and softening the sharp edges of her face. "I figured you must be starving."

I stared at her, unsure what to make of the embarrassment coloring her words. Why go to the trouble of doing it in secret? Why didn't she want to be seen? Was I not allowed to eat or drink? Was starving me until I was weak part of the Queen's plan to lower my defenses?

My eyes dropped from her face to the tray. Roasted meat, poultry, I guessed, sat beside steamed green beans and a perfectly round crisp-skinned potato. Everything looked too perfect to eat, but what caught my eye wasn't the meal. It was the dessert.

A small cup sat off to the side, thick and pale with a glossy red sauce draped over the top. The smell of strawberries and something tangy drifted faintly toward me, familiar and sweet, an almost indecent contrast to the damp cell. And for the first time in hours, maybe days, something other than fear and exhaustion took hold. It was gratitude.

Carmenta leaned in slightly, lowering her voice like we were sharing a secret as she watched me stare at the dish.

"You can't have a decent meal without dessert. It's strawberry cheese-cake," she whispered, her blush deepening.. "My favorite."

I stared at her, then at the cheesecake. It was such a normal thing to say. So painfully human in a place that had felt nothing but cold and cruel. And I didn't know what to do with that.

She lifted a spoon from the tray, holding it out to me with an awkward smile still hovering on her lips.

"Go on. You can eat dessert first," she murmured. "I do. Sometimes."

I hesitated, eyes locked on hers, searching for any sign of manipulation. But her expression stayed unchanged. Gentle. Quiet.

Slowly, I reached for the spoon and dipped it into the cheesecake. The moment it hit my tongue, my eyes fluttered shut, and a soft sound escaped me. The rich, creamy filling melted against the sweetness of the strawberries, tangy and smooth in perfect balance.

It was indulgent. Comforting. Rich and real. And for a brief, fleeting moment, I forgot everything—the chains, the cold, the questions pressing down on me like stones. I was just a girl tasting strawberries again.

When I opened my eyes, Carmenta was watching me, her expression unreadable and calm. So calm it felt unnatural, as if even breath dared not disturb it.

I lowered the spoon and didn't take another bite. Instead, I met her eyes, the unspoken question hanging heavily between us.

Why are you doing this? Why help me?

She didn't answer. Not aloud. But something in her silence felt close to understanding. Or maybe regret.

The stifling silence felt heavier than before, pressing in like the stone walls themselves were leaning closer. Like, even the air was wary of what might come next.

Carmenta straightened, brushing her palms on her skirts and clearing her throat. "Okay, well, enjoy that," she said gently. "I'll see if I can bring down more water soon."

She turned to leave, and I thought that would be it. That I'd be left alone again since she did her strange duty and brought me food and some conversation.

But she paused.

I watched, confused, as her hand lingered on the strap of my satchel. With careful fingers, she slid it from her shoulder, lowered it, and bent over, slowly, rifling through its contents.

I stiffened, the movement sharpening my stare.

My first instinct was to snap, to demand to know why she was handling my belongings. Or how she even got them in the first place. But something stopped me.

It wasn't just the lingering hunger dulling my reactions or the ache in my head making it hard to think straight. No, there was something about her hands, her expression as she sifted through the bag. Like she wasn't searching for something specific, but looking for answers of her own. Like someone looking for a missing thread in a tapestry they hadn't woven, but were somehow bound to all the same.

I didn't speak. Just watched her with narrowed eyes.

Carmenta's fingers sifted through the contents of my satchel like she had every right to. Her movements were careful, deliberate, but when her hand froze around something near the bottom, a flicker of unease tightened my chest.

She drew it out slowly.

Even in the flickering torchlight, I knew it immediately.

My grandmother's journal.

As if sensing my confusion, Carmenta lingered, shifting awkwardly on her feet as she held the book in her hands.

"Elea and the guards searched you and your bag before bringing you down here," she said after a pause, voice quieter now, almost uncertain. "They took anything they thought might be dangerous—the herbs, your blade…" Her fingers brushed the journal's spine. "But they left some stuff thinking it was useless."

She glanced at me, as if unsure how I'd react. "I thought maybe… maybe you'd want something from home. Something familiar."

Home.

The word struck deeper than I expected. I stared at the journal like it might vanish if I blinked or at least explain itself.

I searched Carmenta's face for any sign that she knew more than she was letting on. But there was nothing, just quiet expectation and a strange softness in her eyes. Like, there was no ulterior motive behind her kindness.

My breath hitched as she held it out to me.

I stared at it—at *her* journal—as if it might vanish if I blinked. It was unmistakable; the brown leather, worn from years of use. The jagged gash across the cover, as familiar to me as the lines on my own palm from all the times I'd traced it as a child, and wondered how it got there. The silver lock, once sturdy and unyielding, now hung uselessly, broken and bent, like someone had pried it open, searching for any secrets it held. It was a violation I felt deep in my chest.

I didn't reach for it right away. My mind was too busy racing, tripping over the same impossible questions.

I hadn't packed this. I was certain of it.

I hadn't even seen it since… since before I left. So how did it end up in my satchel?

And why now, after all these years, had my grandmother given it up? She'd never once let it out of her sight. Even while working in the garden, it was always close enough that her fingers could brush the cover or write any small details she refused to forget. It was the one thing she kept more guarded than the truths she'd held onto for years.

My throat tightened. She must have slipped it in herself. Which meant she'd known I might need it. But for what?

My fingers twitched with the urge to take it, to pry it open and search for answers I wasn't sure I wanted. But I forced myself to stay still, to school my expression into something neutral.

Carmenta held it out further, her hand steady despite the flicker of uncertainty in her eyes.

I reached for it slowly, my hands brushing the leather, almost expecting it to crumble after everything I'd endured to get here—the woods, falling into the pit, the unrelenting cold. And yet it looked untouched. No water damage. No dirt in the stitching. Not even a scuff that hadn't been there before.

The texture sent a wave of memories rushing over me, quiet evenings spent watching my grandmother write in it, her face calm and focused. The stories she would never tell me spilling silently across its pages. I brushed my thumb over the gash, and a faint, unfamiliar warmth bled through the leather, subtle enough that I almost convinced myself I imagined it. But it lingered, just long enough to leave my skin tingling.

This journal was her constant. Her shield. And now it was mine.

But I had no idea what I was supposed to do with it or what any of it even meant.

"Thank you," I said, the words catching in my throat. My voice was quieter than usual as I gestured toward the tray of food and the journal. "I really appreciate it."

I turned the book over in my hands, checking the pages. They were still blank. The same quiet emptiness I remembered. But even that didn't feel the same anymore.

Carmenta's expression shifted into relief, or maybe something close to it. She tucked a loose strand of hair behind her ear, caught off guard by my gratitude. "They tried to open it," she admitted. "But the guards kind of broke it. Thought it might be hiding something of use, but once they saw it was empty, they decided it wasn't important and tossed it aside."

A shadow crossed her face before she added, "I figured… maybe you'd want to write something in it while you're down here. You know, somewhere to jot down your thoughts and feelings. Sometimes it helps. To put things somewhere."

I blinked. That same flicker of confusion burned hotter in my chest. The journal had always been my grandmother's shield, her private ritual. I wasn't sure what unnerved me more: that it was here with me, or that someone else thought I should write in it.

"I didn't pack a pen," I murmured absently, still turning the book in my hands.

Without a word, Carmenta reached into her pocket and pulled out a slender silver pen. She held it out with a small smile like an offering.

"I couldn't find one in your bag," she said quietly. "But you can use this. I have plenty of others."

I stared at it, unsure whether to take it or question her motives. She kept surprising me, and I didn't like the way it made my guard slip. But I took the pen anyway, fingers curling around it with a reluctant kind of gratitude as a strange warmth that bloomed in my chest.

Why was she doing this? What did she want from me?

But instead of asking, I simply said, "Thank you." The words felt heavier this time, and I let out a small, strained laugh, trying to lighten the moment. "I do have a ton of thoughts, so this might help with sorting through them."

Carmenta's lips quirked upward, her smile soft and genuine. "Me too. It's like my mind doesn't know when to quit," she murmured, her cheeks tinged with a faint blush as she stepped back.

"Okay, well, I'll check back in tomorrow," she said, turning toward the door. "And I'll try and bring more water, if I can."

She turned toward the door, and for a moment, I thought she'd leave without another word. But as her hand touched the bars, she paused.

Our eyes met through the gap in the cell door, hers searching, mine still guarded. There was something she wanted to say. I saw it in the way her mouth parted, in the crease between her brows. But whatever it was, she didn't speak it. Instead, she gave a quiet nod and disappeared into the corridor.

The iron door closed behind her with a final, echoing thud, and I heard the clanking sound of a lock shifting into place.

I stared at the journal in my lap.

It shouldn't have been here. And yet… *it was*. Another mystery I didn't have the answers to.

As if wanting to distract me, my stomach rumbled, reminding me of the food I'd left untouched. I forced myself to eat, small bites, slow and mechanical. I needed the strength, even if my mind couldn't stop spinning.

The torchlight danced along the damp stone, casting long, flickering shadows across the floor, and I sat in silence, alone with a book full of empty pages, a pen that didn't belong to me, and more questions than I had the strength to ask.

I ate in silence, each bite a quiet act of defiance against the hunger gnawing at my insides. The spoon felt awkward and clunky, but I managed, grateful for every mouthful. The food was far from perfect, dry in places and under-seasoned in others, but it tasted like survival. Like something real in a place where everything else felt twisted and unfamiliar.

Beside me, the journal sat untouched, its leather cover catching the soft light from the torches. It felt heavier than it should, as if it carried more than just blank pages. It taunted me, its presence a constant whisper in the back of my mind. I tried not to look at it, not to let it pull me into a spiral of questions I couldn't answer. But my thoughts kept circling back.

Why had my grandmother packed it? Why now? And why did she do it in secret?

The guards had pried it open, broken the lock, searched the pages, and found nothing. Just empty parchment, unmarked and untouched. I knew the confusion they must have felt because I'd done the same, once. Back in Laochra, that day in our bedroom. I'd flipped through it, searching for clues or secrets I thought she kept from me. But the pages had been quiet and empty.

Still, she must have slipped it into my bag on purpose. She'd always been so protective of it, her fingers curling around the edges whenever I came too close. Whenever I'd asked about it, she'd only smile, her eyes distant and wistful, and say, *"One day, you'll understand."* It was as much a part of her as her voice, her hands, the steady rhythm of her breath as she wrote things I would never read.

I turned the journal over in my hands for what felt like the hundredth time, tracing the deep gash across the cover as if the leather might give me answers. My grandmother didn't do anything without reason. If she wanted me to have this, it was because she'd decided I needed it, and I knew I wouldn't understand *why* until I was meant to.

I chewed another bite of roasted meat, letting the salt and herbs distract me for a moment. But the distraction didn't last. My mind returned to the journal and the woman it belonged to.

I didn't know how I'd never realized sooner what she was—immortal, or at the very least, gifted with magic. All my life, I'd been enamored by her presence, the quiet confidence that seemed to wrap around her like a second skin. I'd thought it was just who she was, but I suppose centuries of experience will do that to a person.

Her garden was always overflowing, no matter the season or weather. Her tonics and teas could mend in days what would take others weeks to heal. As an elder, she was respected, but I wondered what the village would think if they knew the truth, if they saw the secrets she kept close. And what would my mother say? Or Baren and Wren?

I didn't know much, how long I'd been here, why I'd been brought here in the first place, or what the immortal Queen wanted with me. But I *did* know why I'd started this journey in the first place: to keep my family safe. *That* hadn't changed, even if the path looked far different from what I'd imagined.

But if my grandmother decided I needed her journal, then I didn't have the luxury of questioning the why. All my life, she'd known what I needed before I needed it. And I had to believe this was no different.

I leaned back against the wall, stretching out on the thin mattress. It was barely more than cloth over stone, but after the flight, the fight, and the fall, I welcomed the stillness.

My focus shifted between the journal and the last few bites of cheesecake, the only thing on the tray that still waited for me. I wasn't hungry anymore, not really, but the rich, sweet tang of strawberry and cream was too tempting to ignore. I scooped a bite into my mouth and let it melt on my tongue. It was easily the best thing I'd eaten in days, maybe even weeks. Definitely, since the carrot cake loaf I'd indulged in with my family as we celebrated my early birthday.

And then it hit me.

Today was September 21.

It was still my birthday.

The realization crept in quietly at first, growing louder as it spread warmth and ache through me all at once. I'd spent so much time running, surviving, and trying to out-smart whatever cruel plans the gods had in store for me that I'd forgotten the one day I used to count down to.

Eighteen.

I should feel different. That was the whole point, wasn't it? The whole coming-of-age bit that had been drilled into me since childhood. Putting the Imbe Rite and immortality aside, even in Laochra, turning eighteen was a milestone. An age where one could choose their future path. But instead of experiencing the freedom I once believed would come when midnight struck, I felt more trapped than ever before. Chained to a wall instead of a village I once viewed as being too small to hold me.

I didn't know how twenty-four hours could stretch this long, dragging the day and cementing everything I'd endured since it started.

I'd completed the Rite. I was supposed to be immortal now, waiting on my gift from the gods. My body should have felt lighter, stronger, or something. But sitting here, chained, aching, and hollow, I felt exactly the same.

Mortal.

Tired.

Alone.

I stared down at the cheesecake, a bittersweet smile tugging at my lips.

"Happy 18th birthday, Raine," I whispered, the words barely audible over the crackle of the torches. The sound of my voice in the empty cell felt strange, both comforting and painful, but still mine. One thing they couldn't take from me.

For a moment, I let myself pretend. Pretend I was back home. That the flickering light came from a candle, not a wall of iron sconces. That I wasn't chained in the depths of Immorro Castle, the prisoner of an immortal Queen I hadn't even known existed a week ago. That I wasn't caught in the tangled web of my grandmother's secrets. I let myself pretend I was just a girl eating cheesecake on her birthday.

I scooped another bite, letting the sweet taste linger longer than before.

This wasn't how it was supposed to be.

I'd imagined this day my whole life, a turning point, a chance to leave Laochra behind and step into freedom, independence, and adventure. Instead, I was *here*. Captured, chained, and surrounded by the very monsters I'd grown up fearing. *Becoming* one of them.

A soft, humorless laugh slipped out.

It was almost poetic in a twisted way, turning eighteen, gaining immortality, and getting captured all in one day.

I set the spoon aside and glanced at the journal. It hadn't moved, but it felt… *expectant*. Like it was waiting for me.

The weight in my chest was heavy with everything I'd lost. My home, safety, family, the trust I'd placed in Manakel, and the naive hope that eighteen would be the beginning of something freeing. An adventure that I would embark on.

But I was here instead.

I didn't know what my grandmother expected of me when she told me about the Imbe Rite, when she revealed what we were, or why it had brought me *here*, of all places.

But I knew this much—this wasn't the end. It couldn't be.

Not after everything I'd faced and endured.

Let them try to break me. Let them try to cage me. I'd carve my way out with nothing but my will if I had to. And maybe this journal was the key to showing me how.

I drew it into my lap, my fingers curling against the scarred leather. The familiar texture grounded me, a quiet anchor in the chaos. The ache didn't fade, but beneath it something small flickered, stubborn and alive.

I wasn't done.

I'd made it this far. *Somehow.*

And I wasn't giving up.

Not now. Not ever.

46. Bound By Chains And Hidden Truths

The journal sat heavy in my lap, its leather cover worn and familiar, yet foreign. I turned it over, tracing the spine, half-expecting to find something hidden, a note, a map, a secret I'd somehow overlooked, or a clue that would make sense of everything.

But there was still nothing.

Just untouched pages stretching before me, empty and endless.

Mocking me.

I clenched my jaw, fingers tightening around the worn leather. What was I supposed to do with this? I had no plan, no way out, no answers. And yet... she had left it for me. My grandmother, who always seemed to know what I needed before I did.

The flint. The river stone dust. The tonic. Each had saved me when I needed it most. Maybe this would, too.

Maybe that was why she always kept this journal close, filling its pages with things she never spoke aloud. But why leave me something that, by all accounts, should have been overflowing with her words, yet sat silent in my hands?

None of it made sense. Not the emptiness of these pages when I knew, *knew for a fact,* this was the same book she had written in my entire life. Not the way I had walked straight into a trap because I'd been a fool and trusted the wrong people. Not even the strange pull I felt now, as if some unseen force was urging me to write, to carve my thoughts into the empty space as though it might tether me to something real and waiting.

But who was I to question anything anymore?

Everything I thought I knew was unraveling, breaking apart in ways I never saw coming. From the moment I stepped out of Manakel's grasp to the moment I clutched this journal after Carmenta gave it to me, nothing had gone as expected. And yet, something inside me stirred.

I pressed my palm against the paper. The weight of it grounded me, the scent of leather and ink curling through the cold, damp air. My pulse steadied. Without letting myself think further, I picked up the pen.

I should've known the moment I crossed that line, there was no going back.

But anyone who knows me would tell you I don't back down easily. That if you prepare accordingly, fight hard enough, and ask the right questions, you'll find the answers. That knowledge is power, and with the truth on your side, you can control your own fate.

Turns out, I was wrong.

I paused, the faint scratch of the pen still lingering in the air, but the words wouldn't stop flowing out of me. I didn't know who I was writing for, or if I was even writing for anyone but myself. Maybe I was addressing the journal itself, as if it were capable of understanding the tangled mess of thoughts I couldn't sort through alone.

It was either destiny or sheer stupidity that led me here—trapped in the bowels of a dungeon, swallowed whole by the kind of darkness that seeps beneath your skin and takes root. My back pressed against the cold, unyielding stone, the damp clinging to my clothes like a second skin, heavy with filth and failure. The air thick with rot and something else—something older, more insidious—like the bones of the forgotten whispering their grievances into the void.

The pen hovered for a moment, my grip tightening as I blinked hard, forcing down the lump rising in my throat. The whispers curled around me, the shadows pressing in, shifting just at the edge of my vision like they were waiting—watching.

This wasn't how today was supposed to go. How any of it should have gone. I had always imagined my eighteenth birthday as something monumental—a defining moment, a threshold between who I was and who I was meant to become. The day I would finally step into the world on my own terms, free from the walls of my village and its expectations. And in a way, I did exactly that.

I just never expected it to look like this.

Now, instead of freedom, I was chained in the dungeon of a castle, in a city of immortals, alone, with nothing but the ache in my chest, the cold bite of iron around my wrist, and a suspiciously empty journal as my only company. And yet, for some reason, I kept writing.

I used to believe I knew the difference between right and wrong. Between truth and lies. Between friend and foe. But somewhere along the way, those lines bled into one another, blurred beyond recognition, until I could no longer tell the difference between a lifeline and a snare.

I don't know who to trust.

I don't know what to believe.

And everything I thought I did know was a lie.

This... was definitely not how I pictured spending my eighteenth birthday.

A week ago, I thought I'd be at home, walking the familiar paths of my village, eating my favorite meal, and pretending not to care that my future was a giant question mark. I would've spent the day convincing my parents I was responsible enough to make my own choices. That I was ready for adventure. That I was ready for more outside of the village I'd called home.

Well. I got my wish.

Instead of cake, I got chased through two forests, crossed a river I wasn't supposed to survive, fought ancient creatures that shouldn't exist, and, as a grand finale, ended up in the clutches of a rebel army led by an immortal princess who wants me dead.

Oh, and the cherry on top of all of it? The man I had convinced myself was worth risking it all for—who I maybe, sort of, had started picturing as my first boyfriend—was the one who led me straight into their hands.

Turns out, while I was busy wondering if he'd kiss me again, he was busy setting me up and laughing about how helpless I was behind my back. But at least he gave me a cute nickname I didn't understand, so I wouldn't suspect a thing.

So yeah, so far, eighteen has been anything but boring.

And yet, if I could, I'd go back in an instant. Back to my boring village, my small, predictable life. Back to when immortality was just another story told during bonfire nights—something meant to warn us, not for me to become. But given my current position, I'm not that lucky.

I smirked to myself, the bitterness cutting through my words, sharper than I expected. But the pen didn't stop.

It's funny, really. I always imagined my story beginning with 'Once upon a time,' like the great legends I grew up hearing. That I would embark on some grand adventure, face impossible odds, and live to tell the tale of my hero's journey.

But this?

This feels less like a story and more like a warning.

And I don't know what's worse—the fact that I was captured before I even had the chance to fight, or the nagging suspicion that maybe... maybe I walked straight into it. That the freedom I spent my life craving came with a cost I never stopped to consider.

The cell somehow felt smaller now, as if the words on the page were pressing outward, filling the space with truths I hadn't dared to say aloud. The weight of them seemed to push against the very shadows, forcing them to retreat, if only for a moment. The whispers, once a constant presence in the back of my mind, faded into something quieter, less suffocating.

I paused, letting the welcome silence settle before I wrote the next line.

But I'm getting ahead of myself.

To understand how I ended up here—why this is the exact opposite of the path I was meant to take—we have to start at the beginning.

Just over a week ago, to be exact. When I was still the girl who thought she had it all figured out. When my biggest concern was turning eighteen and disappointing my parents. When I didn't expect to be confronted with a truth so sharp it carved its way through everything I thought I knew, leaving me here sitting on the cold, jagged stone, as if the very foundation of my world had splintered beneath me.

But alas, here I am.

The weight of those words lingered, heavier than the chain binding me to the wall.

I could feel it—this wasn't just a rambling journal entry. It was a record of my truth, maybe the only place it would ever live. And that thought alone had my pen pressing back into the paper, determined to make sure that whoever found this journal, whether in days or decades, would know one thing: *I fought. And I did the best I could.*

I had survived the river, the forest, the beasts. I had faced my own fears, clawed my way through the unknown, and still, somehow, I had made it this far. I just hadn't accounted for the worst threat of all.

Betrayal.

I was at a severe disadvantage, considering the short notice I had to decide to become immortal. My usual strategies, analyzing every possibility and calculating every risk, had been impossible. I didn't have *time* to weigh my options or to second-guess what was right in front of me.

But that didn't excuse my biggest mistake.

Trusting *him.*

I'd trusted my so-called guide to lead me through the dangers ahead, to help me survive what was coming. Instead, he led me straight into a trap. And I walked beside him willingly.

Dramatic? Maybe. But so is the undeniable fact that, whether I like it or not, my fate has already been decided. Even if I have no idea what it looks like. Which, for someone who prides herself on questioning everything, the not-knowing is a humiliating blow to my reputation as a know-it-all.

But hey, if I make it out of this alive, then I'll have plenty to say.

And if not?

Well, I suppose this could double as my memoir.

So, let's rewind. Because somewhere, buried in the wreckage of the last seven days, there was a moment—a single, stupid choice I made—that led me straight into this mess.

I stared at the last line, the blunt edges of each word cutting deep. I didn't know which moment *exactly* had led me here, or if it was a collection of small choices. Decisions I made before fully understanding the implications. And for a long moment, I just sat with that truth, staring at the journal as if expecting it to provide the answers. As if it could somehow point me in the right direction this time.

But it didn't. *Of course not.*

I almost closed it, ready to let exhaustion take over, when something shifted.

The pen slipped from my fingers, my breath catching, trying to understand what I was seeing. Words began curling into existence on the opposite page, the ink blooming stroke by deliberate stroke in a familiar slanted script I knew as well as my own. It was my grandmother's writing. The small swoop and scrawl I'd seen her write a hundred times before.

The ink gleamed faintly in the dim light, a shimmer in the dark like a lighthouse beam through fog, letting me know I wasn't imagining things.

She was writing back.

I froze, my heart beating faster than normal as I yanked the journal closer, gripping it so tight my knuckles ached and the chains dug further into my skin. My eyes devoured every curve of the letters, desperate to drink in every word, afraid, *terrified,* that if I so much as blinked, the ink would fade and I'd wake to find this was nothing but a dream conjured up by my exhaustion. I watched in stunned silence as each letter carefully manifested into existence, one slow stroke at a time, as if she were writing it in real time.

> *Raine, by now I assume you have realized my journal has magic coursing through it—magic that has not only kept my secrets safe but holds every thought, lesson, and truth I have recorded for the past 133 years.*

I read it again. And again. As if repetition could anchor it in reality. The words felt impossibly intimate, stretching across time like she was speaking directly into my ear.

It was magic.

I brushed trembling fingers over the words, half-expecting them to smudge. But they remained solid beneath my touch, more real than the stone at my back.

My throat tightened as I flipped the page, desperate for more, *needing it.* For a heartbeat, nothing happened. Then, as if summoned by sheer will alone, faint lines began to bleed through, delicate as breath, until the words sharpened into clarity.

> *This book is spelled to protect what's inside, locked away until I chose to pass it on. The stories I have chronicled are not just for my memories but for you. To guide you, to help you navigate the path ahead, and to remind you that no matter what happens... you are not alone.*

I could barely breathe as I read, each word wrapping around me like a thread of warmth, a tether pulling me back from the hollow, echoing loneliness of this cell.

Tears blurred my vision, and my fingers instinctively found the rough gash in the leather—the same one I'd traced countless times as a child while watching her write beneath the oak tree in our backyard.

How long had she been preparing for this moment? To give me her words and wisdom?

How had she known this was exactly what I needed?

And how... *how* was this even possible?

A tear slipped down my cheek, and as if she knew I needed more, needed her here with me, more words bloomed at the bottom of the page, their ink soft and fading, like a whisper across time and realms.

> *Not all gifts are weapons. Some are words, ink pressed to paper, waiting for the right hands to turn the page. Waiting to remind you of who you are.*
>
> *Remember everything I have taught you. Remember your curious nature and your wild heart. I know anything you do with this knowledge will change lives and keep Laochra safe. Always trust yourself—you know the way. I love you, and believe in you, my Wildheart.*

A sob broke free before I could stop it. I bent over the journal, clutching it to my chest as though holding it tighter might pull her closer.

This wasn't an empty book.

It was a lifeline.

A thread connecting us and stretching across whatever distance lies between mortal and immortal realms.

This was everything I'd ever wanted from her—everything I'd been too afraid to ask. She had given me her voice, her wisdom, the missing pieces of herself—hidden in these pages, waiting for me to find them. Even though she wasn't physically here, it now felt like she was. And she had left me the tools to survive.

I ran my thumb along the edge of the cover before closing it with care, the echo of her words still pulsing through me, my heart still hammering in my chest.

Carmenta's gift, the tray of food, the water, the journal, they all felt heavier now. More meaningful than I'd realized in the moment. I owed her more thanks than I could express.

But for now, I could only sit in the silence, feeling the weight of my grandmother's words settle into place inside me.

I wasn't alone anymore.

Not truly.

Her words were with me.

Her strength was written in every line, every hidden story, every ink-stained secret she had left behind and entrusted to me. She had believed in me long before I'd known to believe in myself. Had prepared me for this journey long before I even knew what I was preparing for.

And now with her as my guide, I would not fail.

No matter how long it took, I would read every word.

And with her help, I was going to make sure that *this* was just the beginning of my story.

Acknowledgments

To every reader holding this book in your hands—thank you. Thank you for giving this story, and an independent author like me, a chance. Your time, your trust, and your willingness to step into this world mean more than I can ever put into words.

Books have always been my escape. Growing up, they were the place I turned to when I needed comfort, understanding, or just a little bit of magic. Writing this series was my way of giving that back, of creating a world someone else might want to get lost in.

This story has lived in my heart for years. These characters have whispered to me in quiet moments, kept me up at night, and pulled me back to the page even when it felt impossible. They've grown alongside me, teaching me about bravery, sacrifice, and what it truly means to fight for the people you love. My greatest hope is that they've found a place in your heart, too.

The world-building was the most complex and time-consuming part, constantly evolving over years of notes, charts, character sheets, and updating ideas every time a challenge or character appeared in my mind. As the story came to life, the layers of history, power, and secrets unfolded into a story about resilience and choices, and I knew Raine's journey needed a series to fully do it justice.

Like life, the story is full of shifting truths, hard choices, and the weight of what comes after. One of the messages I hope readers take away is that every choice matters—that even when the world feels uncertain, your decisions still hold power.

Raine's journey is about questioning what she's been told, standing up for what feels right, and choosing love and loyalty over fear, again and again.

To Indie Forge Publishing and Samantha Palmer—thank you for believing in this story, these characters, and for reminding me that every story deserves to be told, especially the ones you can't stop thinking about. Your faith in Bound by Blood and Fate gave me the courage to put these pages into the world.

To my husband, Nick, thank you for being my sounding board, my sushi delivery guy, and my teammate. You may never sit and read my books (I've accepted this), but your support never wavers. Whether it's helping me wrestle through two versions of the same sentence or indulging my endless rambling about fictional characters as if they were real people, you make space for my creativity in the most loving ways. I love you and your patience more than words can say.

To Natasha, my fellow fire sign, thank you for being the first to read this story, and for your need to know what happens next (because it gave me the fire to finish book two).

To my besties—you know who you are. You show up for every story, every celebration, and every messy middle. Your early reads, late-night motivation texts, and constant encouragement mean the world to me. I'm endlessly grateful for your love, loyalty, and willingness to share book boyfriends.

This is only the beginning. The river still runs, the shadows still move, and Raine's journey is far from over. Stay tuned for the next book in the series—*Bound by Chains and Hidden Truths*. There's so much more to uncover in Luminara, and I can't wait to share it with you.

Bound by Blood and Fate is the first book in The Wildheart Series.

About the Author

I've been escaping into stories for as long as I can remember—first as a reader, then as a writer. Whether it was scribbling poems, song lyrics, or stories, words have always been my way of communicating. My magic. My connection. My safe place to run to.

Now, as an independent author, I get to spend my time writing and getting lost in the stories I create. Worlds filled with fierce heroines, slow-burn romance, and just enough chaos and intrigue to keep you turning the pages way past your bedtime.

There's a quiet kind of magic in creating characters who feel achingly real, flawed, tender, unforgettable. I've carried them like secrets in my heart, and now they're finding their way onto the page, where they can finally fall in love, break, heal, and live the stories they were always meant to.

As a neurodivergent author, I've poured my heart (and a lot of hyper focus sessions) into creating a world and characters that feel alive and real. My goal is to create characters so compelling, they'll plant themselves firmly in your heart and make you wish you could grab a tea or slay a monster with them.

Writing complex characters and crafting story lines feel like second nature to me, so when I started dreaming up the world of Luminara—

its characters, rich history, and magical chaos—I knew it had to be epic enough to span a whole series. Enter *The Wildheart Series*, a fantasy world filled with intrigue, romance, and all the exciting twists that come with immortals, trials, and magic powers.

When I'm not busy plotting twists or writing epic romances, you'll probably find me:
    - Writing and recording original songs
    - Designing cool things as a freelance graphic designer
    - Cooking/baking the best gluten-free treats you've ever had (yes, I'm that confident)
    - Sipping tea and soaking up the morning sun
    - Indulging in ice cream

Being from Canada, I love taking advantage of the warm weather when it makes an appearance and spending most spring/summer weekends soaking up the sun, going on adventures with my husband, and spoiling our bunny, Willow. When I'm not writing, you'll usually find me buried in a book, listening to an audiobook or a curated playlist, but when the TV *is* on, it's usually reruns of One Tree Hill, Gossip Girl, or cheesy Hallmark movies. (Especially Christmas ones)

So whether you're here for swoony romance, or sword-wielding fantasy and complex magic systems… welcome to the adventure.

Let the stories begin.

My debut New Adult Fantasy Romance novel, **Bound by Blood and Fate**, is the first book in *The Wildheart Series* and is set to release in September 2025. It's packed with everything I love—romance, magic, and a whole lot of heart. I can't wait to share the world of Luminara with you!

You can connect with me on:
 https://gabriellawilderbooks.com
 https://www.instagram.com/gabriellawilder.author